"L. E. Modesitt, Jr., works well with his characters and carefully considers the economics of empire. There's a lot of bridge building, literally, and road building, and [the protagonist] Anna also needs to convince an entire culture that women are not just heir-producers and chattel."
—*San Diego Union-Tribune*

"Among the pleasures of the book are Modesitt's descriptions of the rigors of sorcery, the dilemmas of finding oneself suddenly somewhere else without a wardrobe, and the political ambiguities of her role."
—*San José Mercury News*

"Volume Two, *The Spellsong War*, is a worthy successor to the first book, well written and engaging. You will enjoy it."
—*Sasha Miller*

THE SPELLSONG WAR

BOOK TWO OF *THE SPELLSONG CYCLE*

····································

L. E. MODESITT, JR.

TOR®
fantasy

A TOM DOHERTY ASSOCIATES BOOK
New York

THE SPELLSONG WAR

Edited by David G. Hartwell

A Tor Book
Published by Tom Doherty Associates, Inc.
175 Fifth Avenue
New York, NY 10010

Tor Books on the World Wide Web:
http://www.tor.com

Tor® is a registered trademark of Tom Doherty Associates, Inc.

ISBN: 0-812-54002-6
Library of Congress Card Catalog Number: 97-29837

First edition: January 1998
First mass market edition: January 1999

Printed in the United States of America

0 9 8 7 6 5 4 3 2 1

To
my one and only soprano sorceress

....

CHARACTERS

....

Anna *Regent of Defalk and Lady of Loiseau*
 [Mencha]
Jimbob *Heir to Defalk [Falcor]*
Hanfor *Arms Commander of Defalk*
Dythya *Counselor of Finance*
Essan *Lady and widow of Lord Donjim*
Herene *Younger sister of Lady Gatrune [Pamr]*
Herstat *Saalmeister of Eldheld*
Menares *Counselor*

LORDS OF DEFALK

Jecks *Lord of Elheld [Elhi], Advisor to the Regent*
Arkad *Lord of Synfal [Cheor]*
Birfels *Lord of Abenfel; consort is Fylena*
Clethner *Lord of Nordland*
Dannel *Lord of Mossbach; consort is Resengna*
Dencer *Lord of Stromwer; consort is Wendella*
Fustar *Lord of Issl*
Gatrune *Lady of Pamr*
Geansor *Lord of Sudwei*
Genrica *Lord of Wendel*
Gylaron *Lord of Lerona; consort is Reylan*
Hryding *Lord of Flossbend [Synope]; consort is
 Anientta*
Jearle *Lord of Denguic*
Klestayr *Lord of Aroch*
Mietchel *Lord of Morra*

Nelmor *Lord of Dubaria; eldest son and heir is Tiersen*
Sargol *Lord of Suhl*
Tybel *Lord of Arien*
Vlassa *Lord of Fussen; heirs are twin sons, Ustal and Falar*
Vyarl *Rider of Heinene*

FOSTERLINGS AND PAGES

Alseta *Daughter of Chief Player Liende*
Barat *Page*
Birke *Heir of Lord Birfels [Abenfel]*
Cataryzna *Daughter and heir of Lord Geansor [Sudwei]*
Cens *Page*
Hoede *Youngest son of Lord Dannel [Mossbach]*
Kinor *Son of Chief Player Liende*
Lysara *Daughter of Lord Birfels [Abenfel]*
Resor *Page*
Secca *Daughter of Lord Hryding [Flossbend]*
Skent *Page*
Ytrude *Daughter of Lord Nelmor [Dubaria]*

DEFALKAN ARMSMEN

Alvar *Captain*
Himar *Captain*
Jirsit *Undercaptain*

DEFALKAN PLAYERS

Daffyd *Viola; first Chief Player*
Liende *Woodwind; second Chief Player*
Delvor *Violino*
Duralt *Falk horn*
Hassett *Violino*

Kaseth *Violino*
Pallian *Violino*
Yuarl *Violino*

OTHERS OUTSIDE DEFALK

Ashtaar *Spymistress of Nordwei*
Behlem *Prophet of Music, Lord of Neserea; consort is Cyndyth*
Bertmynn *Lord of Dolov, Ebra*
Ehara *Lord of Dumar; consort is Siobion*
Hadrenn *Lord of Synek, Ebra*
Konsstin *Liedfuhr of Mansuur*
Maitre of Sturinn *Leader of Sturinn; master of the Sea-Priests*
Matriarch *Head of State, Ranuak; consort is Ulgar*
Nubara *Overcaptain of Lancers, Mansuur, stationed in Neserea*
Rabyn *Heir of Behlem, Neserea*
Tybra *Leader, Council of Wei, Nordwei*

I

OUVERTURE

1

WEI, NORDWEI

The heavy gong sounds, and the two women in the uniform of the Council turn and open the lacquered double doors, each bearing the ancient symbol of the Council of Wei. Each wears twin black-lacquered scabbards at her hips, and the scabbards contain the infamous short swords of the Nordan Guard.

Ashtaar moistens her lips and steps through the doors, then down the black carpet toward the dais.

The black-lacquered Council table is also ancient, and behind it sit seven figures. The woman in the center wears a silver-and-black seal on a heavy silver chain. Her dark eyes hold Ashtaar as the spymistress walks down the dark green carpet toward the space below the dais holding the table.

"The mist-world sorceress now holds Defalk. The Council has read your report, and would like to inquire further."

"Yes, Ancient One." Ashtaar bows.

"Please summarize the major events that led to the current state of affairs. Briefly."

"A travel sorceress and a player summoned the lady Anna from the mist worlds. Both are dead now. The sorcerer Brill spirited her away and tutored her in the ways of both Darksong and Clearsong. The Dark Ones tried to kill her and failed. She supported Lord Barjim against the Ebrans at the Sand Pass. Barjim and Brill were killed, and she collapsed, but not before she destroyed two-thirds of the invaders. She somehow found her way south and recovered in Synope, in the lands of Lord Hryding. Lord Behlem of Neserea then marched into Defalk and took

Falcor, but not before Lord Jecks rescued the heir, his grandson Lord Jimbob. Lord Behlem offered his support to the sorceress, and she accepted it and went to Falcor. The Dark Ones gathered another army and marched toward Falcor. The sorceress used water magic and song to destroy the entire Ebran army and all the darksingers in Defalk. The Evult responded by flooding the Fal and destroying half of Falcor. Lord Behlem attempted to remove the lady Anna, and she used her sorcery to kill him and his consort and enlist the support of many of the Neserean troops in Falcor. Then she proclaimed a regency for young Jimbob. Shortly, almost at the dawn of winter, she marched a small force through the Ostfels and used her sorcery to destroy the Evult, the city of Vult, and most of Synek. She almost died, but the lords of Defalk, especially Lord Jecks, rallied behind her. So did the people. She has a reputation for being good and fair, and vindictively just." Ashtaar bows once more.

"The rains now fall on Defalk, do they not?" asks the red-haired woman to the left of the Council leader.

"Yes. The sorceress removed the chains on the clouds when she destroyed the Evult."

"Will the sorceress attempt to rule directly and put young Jimbob out of the way?" asks the dark-haired Council leader.

"That does not appear likely. She can have no children and has, in effect, adopted the boy."

"And Lord Jecks has not objected?"

"He publicly supports the sorceress. As do the lords Birfels, Nelmor, Hryding, Geansor, Clethner, and the lady Gatrune, and the Rider of Heinene. There are doubtless others, and none of the thirty-three have raised voice or hand against her."

"With her powers, I doubt any of sound mind would do so," suggests the Council leader. "Are there any whispers of discontent?"

"Almost none that we have been able to track. She holds but one hostage, and that is Wendella, the consort of Lord Dencer of Stromwer. Dencer is rumored to be less than happy."

"No others?"

"None that we know or can scry."

"What of Ebra?"

"The land has been flattened, mostly by the floods she unleashed down the river Elha, and Vult lies buried under the fire peak the Ebrans are calling Zauberinfeuer. Hadrenn has claimed the ruins of Synek. He is the one of the sons of an ancient lord, and several pretenders are struggling over Elawha. A lord named Bertmynn is raising armsmen in Dolov. He wishes to be lord of all Ebra." Ashtaar waits.

"We have received a scroll from the Liedfuhr. He protests our interference in Defalk. He also informs us that young Rabyn is the Lord of Neserea and under his protection and regency. What beyond that do you know?" The dark-haired Council leader smiles faintly.

"He has dispatched fiftyscore lancers to Neserea. They were delayed by the snows in the Mittpass, but travel the south road through the Great Western Forest."

"Spymistress of Nordwei . . . is it fair to say that a year ago we faced possible threats from the Prophet of Music and the Dark Ones, and both have been destroyed?"

"Yes, Leader Tybra."

"Is it also fair to say that you chose not to remove the soprano sorceress?" asks Tybra.

"I waited to see whether the Dark Ones and the Prophet were successful in their attempts. The Dark Ones failed in four attempts. The Prophet and his consort failed as well. We have been able to trace at least two attempts by Neserea." Ashtaar inclines her head. "I thought it best not to turn the sorceress's wrath against Nordwei."

"So . . . now we have a strong and united Defalk on our southern borders, and this is your doing?"

"We have a united Defalk, ruled by a woman for the first time in recorded history, and a Defalk that will take

a decade or longer to recover from the drought and dep-
redations of the Dark Ones and the Nesereans.''

''That is what you say. For now . . , for now, we shall
see. You may go, but do not hesitate to inform the Council
should this sorceress take any action that could possibly
affect Nordwei.''

''Yes, leader Tybra.'' Ashtaar bows a last time, then
turns. She does not wipe the dampness from her forehead.

2

Through the scarcely cracked high window behind
her, Anna could hear the half-frozen rain clattering
on the stones of the liedburg. The entire keep felt damp,
and even the small fire in her receiving room and de facto
office wasn't enough to remove the dampness. She needed
the slight draft from the window to keep from being suf-
focated from the fireplace, which drew poorly with small
fires.

Sorceress, Regent of Defalk, Protector of the Heir, not
to mention being Lady of Loiseau, and she had to worry
about firewood. She hadn't thought about firewood being
a problem—but nearly a decade of drought had wrought
enormous damage on the once-wide forests of Defalk.

Then, there was so much that she'd never thought she'd
have to consider. She'd been trained to be a professional
opera singer, and fallen back on university teaching with
the demands of Avery's career. Later when he'd left her
and the children for his slim blonde young thing, the
teaching, and several additional part-time jobs, had become necessities. Anna laughed softly to herself. She was
slimmer and younger looking than Paulina now, and
Avery—the self-styled Antonio, king of the comprimarios—

would never know. Neither would Mario and Elizabetta. Irenia . . . Anna's eyes misted. Her oldest daughter's death had been the catalyst that had left Anna open to poor Jenny's and Daffyd's spellsong—that had brought her Liedwahr—and all the rest had followed, like dominoes falling, until she had become regent of a ravaged land. And she'd done little enough, with the press of the Regency, with the lands bestowed on her—Loiseau— because Brill had left no heirs. She'd granted the present tenants the right to remain, but she needed to do something about a more permanent arrangement. That meant traveling to Mencha, and she didn't have ten days to spare, not counting the time she'd need at Loiseau.

Anna sighed. She stood, pushed back the chair from the worktable, and moved toward the center of the room, her eyes shifting toward the high-backed gilt chair on the dais, the chair she avoided using whenever possible. After a moment she turned, stepped away from the side of the dais, and walked to the single window at the back of the receiving room, where the base of the sill was nearly chest-high. Once again, the dimness reminded her that she'd planned to rearrange the liedburg, perhaps put the receiving/conference area somewhere with more ventilation and light.

She sighed—another item low on her long, long list. Before long, she would need to use some of that sorcery to replace the bridge over the Falche, one of the casualties of the war with Ebra when the late Evult had melted all the snow off the northern Ostfels and sent a flood careening down the Fal River and into the Falche with enough force to rip out all the bridges and denude the banks for two hundred and fifty deks. Roughly, a hundred and fifty earth miles, she translated mentally, rubbing her forehead. She still had trouble thinking in rods, furls, deks, and leagues. There weren't any feet, and yards were still basically yards, and the units above were decimal-based, but she'd never been that good in mental arithmetic.

"Lady Anna?" Giellum knocked on the heavy door

even as he peered inside. "Counselor Menares to see you. And your midafternoon repast." The young guard set the platter on the only open space on the table before straightening.

"Send him in." She headed from the window back to the worktable.

The heavyset and gray Menares stopped short of Anna and the table, and bowed, extending the scroll. "This arrived by messenger, Lady Anna."

"From whom?"

"Lord Arkad of Cheor, I believe."

Anna looked at the plate heaped with bread and cheese before her on the round oak table that served as worktime eating place, desk, and conference table, then at the sealed scroll.

She didn't want to eat any more, and she certainly didn't want to read the latest scroll from Lord Arkad—or his scribe. But she had to eat, because of the energy demands of sorcery, or she'd literally wither away into anorexia or the local equivalent. She also had to read the scroll because Arkad was one of the thirty-three lords of Defalk. From what she recalled, he was also one of the handful who still hadn't paid his liedgeld to the Regency, nearly a season past the end of harvest when it was due.

"Sit down, Menares." She took the scroll, then motioned to the chair across from the one where she sat. After a long look at the platter, she took a swallow of water and a mouthful of bread and cheese, and a second, forcing herself to eat, still fighting a lifetime of habit that equated any healthy amount of eating with gluttony.

Menares shifted his weight on the chair, but said nothing.

Anna broke the seal and began to read to herself.

Arkad has always supported the rightful rulers of Defalk, and certainly recognizes the legitimacy of the late and great Lord Barjim, and of his son Jimbob. As we have expressed earlier, while Lord Jecks and other respected lords of Defalk have reluctantly endorsed the expediency of a prolonged Regency, as did we, our initial concerns about the continuity of such an arrangement remain, especially about the use of the liedgeld. As a loyal lord, we are deeply concerned that such funds, which have been sweated from the very soil, be employed in support of Defalk's long and glorious tradition. We ask your assurance and your pledge as regent that such funds be used as traditionally required. We look forward to your response, and to your continued efforts on behalf of Lord Jimbob. . . .

Arkad hadn't signed the missive, but concluded with a sealmark and his name printed beside it.

Anna snorted. Lord Arkad of Cheor was getting to be an even bigger pain, with his missives and not-so-subtle hints that a male Regency or ruler was to be preferred and trusted, not to mention his use of the royal *we*. She had to put an end to such garbage, preferably without putting an end to the writer. She couldn't ensorcel or flame every chauvinistic lord in Defalk—not and have much of a king- dom left for Jimbob to inherit.

She sighed.

"Lord Jecks, Lady Anna," announced Skent, the dark- haired page, from the door.

"You may go, Menares. Lord Arkad has found another excuse to delay paying his liedgeld. You might think of the possible actions open to a disgusted regent."

The white-haired counselor rose and bowed. "As you wish, Lady Anna."

"Have Lord Jecks come in." Anna took another mouthful of bread and cheese, then stood.

"Lady Anna." Jecks inclined his head.

Jecks still reminded her of a young-faced and white- haired Robert Mitchum with the smile of a Sean Connery. Despite his white hair, and a muscular frame somewhat stockier than the movie stars he resembled, his hazel eyes were clear and intelligent. Although he looked older than Anna, she suspected that in actual years, the long-widowed lord was probably even younger than she was. Certainly, the clean-shaven Jecks remained the most attractive man she'd met in the year she'd been in Defalk. He was also one of the few lords respected near-universally by both his peers and the armsmen and workers of Defalk.

Then, part of that was the sorry state of Defalk. Jecks was widely respected by the common people not only for his fairness and honesty, but also for not taking his pleasure with every comely young maid on his lands, and instead providing them with a modest dowry. What a place, where women were usually chattels. *Careful,* Anna reminded herself, *it hasn't been that long since all of earth was that way, and a lot of it still is.*

"Please sit down. I need to eat. Again." After another sip of water previously orderspelled and a mouthful of bread and cheese, she added, "You had something to say. Please go ahead."

Jecks eased into the chair across the table from Anna. "Lord Birfels sent me a message."

"Yes." Anna wanted to scream. Birfels had supported her, but he much preferred to work through Jecks—or any man. "What is his difficulty?"

"Besides his reluctant acceptance of the present situation?" Jecks offered a wry smile. "He noted that the return of the rains offers the first opportunity in many years for the planting of all his fields. He also noted that seed grain is scarce."

Anna nodded, waiting for the shoe, or boot, to fall.

"The only source of such seed grain is the Ranuan factors in Sudwei or Ranwa, and they are hesitant to extend credit to Defalkan lords, especially when the Regency itself has not completed repaying those funds borrowed by the former lord."

"And I suppose Lord Birfels lacks sufficient golds to purchase the seed outright?"

"He did not write of that, but, as you know, the past years have been hard. Were I in his situation, even I would be pressed . . ."

"Except you're more prudent than most and saved the necessary seed grain?" asked Anna, glancing toward the closed door to the receiving room.

"It was not easy, but Herstat and Dythya also insisted." Jecks grinned. "Herstat has been my saalmeister for many years, and when they insist, a lord should listen."

"That's why you let me borrow Dythya to get the liedstadt and liedburg accounts in order?"

"I do not feel quite so outnumbered now—at home. Here . . ." As he smiled, Jecks' eyes went to the closed door of the receiving room, almost as though he were nervous about being alone with the regent.

Nervous? Why was every man in Defalk nervous to be around her? When she had appeared on Erde, and especially after Brill's death spell had turned her permanently young-looking, they'd all been leering, except Jecks, but he'd been interested, just more restrained.

Now . . . once she'd demonstrated some power, and ability to rule, the leering and interest had vanished. *Of course, using spells to burn up a dozen or so assassins and plotters didn't exactly help your sex appeal.*

"I take it that this seed grain would be a problem for most lords in Defalk?" she finally asked, ignoring Jecks' glance past her.

"Many," admitted Jecks. "Especially those in the south. Ranuak is close, and they have relied on the grain dealers there for generations."

"How can I repay the Ranuans when I can't even get the lords of Defalk to pay liedgeld?" She extended the scroll from Arkad to the white-haired lord. "Please read this."

Jecks read slowly, then looked at Anna.

"What am I supposed to do with this Arkad of Cheor? Is it because he has no money?"

"That I would doubt. His lands, many of them, hold the bottomland between the Falche and the Synor. They are among the richest in Defalk, and there is water."

Another penny-pinching, chauvinistic self-centered prig! Or a troublemaker. "Was he like this before, or is he really upset about a female regent?"

"He was a problem to Barjim, I believe."

"He's getting to be more of a problem to me, and that's not going to help Jimbob any."

"If it should come to that, Jimbob will have fewer problems. Arkad's sons died without issue, and he had no daughters, only a niece."

"So . . . the lands will revert to Jimbob?"

Jecks frowned. "No. Should Arkad die without issue, as is now the case, you or Jimbob could bestow the lands to someone . . ."

"More supportive?" asked Anna. "What about the niece—or her consort?"

"She might have a slight claim."

"But the other thirty-two would welcome another man?"

Jecks shrugged. "They will await your action."

This chauvinism . . . can you ever make things better? "In short . . . like everything else around here . . . it's my problem." Anna forced another wedge of cheese and some bread into her mouth and chewed slowly.

"As I told you before," Jecks looked at her thoughtfully, "you have done the impossible, and your people will expect that and more. You are the destroyer of dissonance, the savior of the land, lady and sorceress, great Regent of Defalk. They will not wait for the healing of time."

She nodded, then swallowed. She'd read something like that, once. What had it been? The revolution of rising expectations, where the more a leader did, the more people expected?

"The problem of expectations." After another swallow

of the water she'd orderspelled that morning, she added, "Let me call Dythya."

She lifted the bell and rang it once. A dark-haired page opened the door and peered inside. "Yes, Lady Anna?"

"Skent? Would you see if Dythya's free?"

"Yes, lady."

As the door closed, Jecks asked, "What will you do with that one?"

"Educate him, and marry him to the girl he loves."

"The lady Cataryzna?"

"Lord Geansor could do worse," Anna said dryly, thinking about the crippled Lord of Sudwei and his blonde daughter.

"He could indeed." Jecks laughed softly. "That is why you are dangerous. You look for ways to forge people's dreams into what must be."

That's dangerous? It seemed more like common sense to Anna. "Pardon me, Lord Jecks. Would you like some cheese or bread?"

"No, thank you, lady. Not even a young armsman could eat as you must. But do not mind an old warhorse."

Anna wanted to kick him under the table for the slight tone of self-pity. Then, he probably did think of himself that way. Why did girls always think that young men were so appealing? Then, why did so many men think shallow, pretty girls were so appealing? Like Avery had.

"Lady?"

Anna smoothed her face. "Sorry. Old memories. . . ."

Jecks accepted her explanation with a nod.

Shortly, the dark-haired and graying Dythya appeared. "Lady Anna."

"Please sit."

Dythya took the seat at the table to Anna's right, and to the left of her former lord.

Anna waited until Skent closed the door to the receiving room before beginning. "I understand that, unless we further soothe the Ranuans by paying some or all of the debt incurred by Lord Barjim, a number of our lords may find it difficult to buy seed grain.''

Dythya frowned momentarily.

''And most of those are in the south.'' Lord, how she hated the politics. Of course, they were in the south, and they could threaten to pledge fealty to the Matriarchy or even Dumar, she supposed, on the grounds that the regency was not meeting its obligations to them.

''Where do we stand?''

''I did not bring the accounts.''

''Just in rough terms.''

''We have almost five thousand golds in the treasury. We will need to spend close to eight before harvest. We still have not received the liedgeld from eight lords. That would be about five thousand golds more.''

''The eight we'll have to spend—does that include what we owe the Ranuans?''

''No, Lady Anna.''

Anna winced. Another fifteen hundred golds she—or the liedstadt—didn't have.

''All right. We'll have to make arrangements to send another five hundred golds. But we'll send a message which says that we expect our lords and people to receive normal commercial terms, especially as regards seed grain.'' She looked at Jecks. ''Will that help?''

''Were Lord Barjim still lord . . . I would say not.'' The older-looking lord shrugged. ''With this, you will have made two payments, and defeated the Ebrans. I would think it would be in the interests of the . . . women of Ranuak to accede to your request.''

''Let's hope so.'' Anna turned back to the de facto accountant. ''Can you make the arrangements and have a scroll drafted for me to sign? Have Menares work on the wording.''

''Ah . . .''

''I know,'' Anna said tiredly, realizing that Menares would resent the implication that he was taking orders from Dythya. "Tell Menares that it is my request and not yours and that if he has any questions to come to me."

"Thank you, lady."

"And Dythya? Could you write out a summary, a shortened version of the liedstadt accounts, so that I can have it to refer to? Make sure you list all the lords who are short on their liedgeld—all of them."

Dythya nodded.

"That's after you take care of the payment to the Ran-uan Exchange or whatever it is."

When the door closed again, Anna turned back to Jecks. "What do you hear about Ebra?"

"I am not a sorcerer," he pointed out with a smile.

"Sorceresses have their limits, too," she answered. "According to what I've called up on the glass, the place remains a mess. There's nothing happening in Vult, and there won't be for years. Someone is rebuilding parts of Synek, and most of the wreckage in Elawha has been cleared away. I can't tell who's in charge from the glass."

"The whispers from the peddlers are that Hadrenn holds Synek. He is the youngest son of Jykell, who was the last Lord of Synek before the Dark Monks seized Ebra." Jecks looked at the empty goblet before him.

"Wine or water?" Anna asked.

"Wine, please."

The red wine she poured was slightly better than high-grade vinegar. As she had discovered from experience, trying to improve things like food and wine involved Darksong and was chancy at best. Then, any spell that affected something that was living or had once been living was Darksong—and invited trouble.

Jecks took a hefty swallow. "The Liedfuhr of Mansuur has dispatched a force of lancers, and they are riding to Esaria."

"To support Rabyn?" She paused. "Or an advance force for an attack on us?"

"Young Rabyn still can claim the loyalty of many who supported his sire, and who feel he is the legitimate

Prophet of Music." Jecks set his goblet down gently. "I do not think the Liedfuhr will attack Defalk until matters in Neserea become more clear."

"You mean, until the mighty Liedfuhr Konsstin has Rabyn firmly under his thumb?"

Jecks laughed softly. "One forgets—for a time. You have such strange phrases, Lady Anna."

"Thank you." Anna didn't point out that, for her, Defalk often had very strange turns of phrase, with a language that was far more Teutonic in origin and only *sounded* like English at times.

"My pleasure, lady." Jecks rose. "By your leave? I had arranged for Jimbob to receive blade instruction from Himar."

"You're a better blade," Anna said.

That got a wintry smile. "True. But children oft receive instruction poorly from parents and grandparents."

"Have fun watching, and don't wince too much." Anna returned the smile. She knew Jecks' frustration all too well. None of her children had wanted her as a voice teacher. Still, it was hard to see the handsome Jecks, white hair or not, as the grandparent of a boy as old as Jimbob.

After a time, Anna looked up. She sat alone in the receiving room. Alone, if she didn't count the guards outside the door, or the pages. Skent was there now. Then, weren't rulers always alone?

She stripped off the purple regent's sash, laid it across the gilt chair on the dais and walked to the door.

Blaz and Giellum followed her up the stairs and down the corridor to the door to Lady Essan's rooms, the sharp-voiced but observant consort of the late Lord Donjim, the Lord of Defalk before Barjim.

Anna rapped on the door.

Synondra edged the door open. "Oh, Lady Anna . . . please do come in."

Anna had not so much as stepped inside when Lady Essan spoke. "Synondra, you may take a walk or otherwise amuse yourself."

"Yes, Lady Essan." Synondra bowed to Anna, and added in a low voice, "She is tired."

Who isn't? Anna wanted to say, but didn't. "I won't stay too long, but I do need to talk to her."

Blaz shut the door as Synondra left, stationing himself outside on one side, Giellum on the other.

Lady Essan sat before the fire, her ubiquitous glass of apple brandy half full, a wool shawl around her shoulders. The room felt almost stifling to Anna, and she took the chair farthest from the fire, unfastening the top button of the loose green shirt she wore under the green-and-gold-trimmed tunic. She was glad she'd left the Sash of the Regent in the receiving room.

"You not be cold, girl-woman?"

"Not here."

Essan shook her head. "Times I think you might still be from Erde . . . then . . . cold it must be in the mist worlds."

"It gets much colder than anything I've experienced here." *Especially the winters in Iowa.* Those she didn't miss at all.

"These old bones would not be pleased."

"In those places, these younger bones weren't pleased." Lord, she'd disliked Iowa—even if it had been about the only place she'd managed to land a decent-paying job.

Essan took another sip of the apple brandy and looked at the fire.

"What do you know about Lord Arkad of Cheor?" Anna asked.

"It has been years since I heard that name." Lady Essan took a sip of the brandy. "Fine figure of a man he was then, but only a figure. Donjim said he followed the last words he heard. He had no heirs, then. Has he now?"

"Jecks says there are no direct heirs. I don't know about others," Anna admitted. "Arkad keeps weaseling out of paying the liedgeld. This time he wants assurance

that I'm spending the coins truly for the defense of Defalk.''

"Those lands be prosperous, even now.''

"That's what Jecks said.''

"Rulers and regents cannot brook outright defiance, not
even great sorceresses,'' the white-haired woman offered,
her hand going to the glazed almonds in the small dish.

"It's a problem,'' Anna admitted. "I don't want any
more lords to get the idea they can flout the Regency, but
I don't want them to get the idea that the only solution I
have to every problem is force.''

"Why not? That is the way their minds work. If a ruler
cannot force or coerce them, most lords feel that such a
ruler be not strong enough to hold Defalk.''

Anna held the wince inside, knowing that what Lady
Essan said was doubtless true. But it bothered her. Using
force and sorcery against outside enemies made sense, but
against her own lords?

"That was Barjim's greatest fault. He did not use his
strength enough when times were good. Then, he did not
have enough strength to establish fear and respect when
times worsened. Like it or not, sorceress-woman, men
bend only to force.'' Essan half laughed, half cackled.
"Except in the bedchamber, and even there, it be best for
a woman to be strong.''

"Always strength.''

"Always, and more so here in unsettled times.'' Essan
readjusted the shawl around her shoulders.

"Will you join us for dinner?''

"And leave my fire? That moldy hall be no place for
old bones in winter. Synondra will fetch me a plate, if
you mind not.''

"For your advice, Lady Essan, and your friendship,
Synondra may fetch plates any or every night. But you
are always welcome at the table.'' Anna eased out of the
chair, her forehead damp from the heat of the stuffy room.

"For that I thank you. Too bad I had no daughter like
you. Nor a sister.'' Essan lifted her brandy glass. "I might

even try to linger on and see what you do.'' The older
woman offered another chuckle, followed with a raspy
cough.

"Are you all right?"

"Fine. Right as any old fool can be. Go . . . you need
to be regent and sorceress again. Go on.''

Anna slipped out, and motioned to Synondra, who hov-
ered outside the door. "Please let me know if that cough
gets worse. I don't like . . .''

"I will, Lady Anna, and thank you.''

The sorceress, still followed by her guards, strode down
the corridor to her own chambers, small for a regent or
ruler—just a bedchamber and an adjoining bath and jakes,
but sufficient and easier to ward and guard.

In the dim light cast by the bedside candles, Anna
glanced at the shutters closed over the windows she'd in-
stalled with sorcery, then at the black lines etched into
the stones of the outside wall of her room. The black lines
were her reminder of her inability to use her sorcery to
see earth—and her daughter Elizabetta. That last attempt
had created a small explosion, etched the outline of the
mirror into the stone, and nearly killed Anna.

The most powerful sorceress in Defalk, and she
couldn't even view her daughter for a second, not without
risking explosions and fiery catastrophe.

A second mirror hung on the wall beside the outline of
the vanished first mirror, its frame already singed, its var-
nish bubbling from the heat of sorcerous far-seeing. The
sorceress shook her head. Menares was right in his insistence that she adopt the reflecting pool used by most sorcerers. At least the water wouldn't catch fire.

Anna slipped into the washroom and glanced in the
mirror, catching sight of the blonde hair, the thin face,
and the eyes that had seen far more than her otherwise
youthful countenance showed. Then, her features were
finer than a younger woman's would have been, but the
complexion, hair, and skin tone were those of an eighteen-

year-old—apparent eternal youth—the dream of all the earth media promoters.

"Time for dinner, and all that entails." She finished washing away the grime that still seemed to accumulate, then brushed the blonde hair that was again getting too long, before heading out the door and down the stairs, trailed by Giellum and Blaz.

As her stomach growled, once more reminding her that sorceresses had to eat twice what a healthy armsman needed, Anna glanced at the candle mantels. They needed cleaning again. She hoped she'd remember to have someone tell Virkan, but she wasn't going to disrupt dinner.

Skent waited outside the middle hall. The sound of voices drifted through the door that was slightly ajar. The page bowed. "Mutton stew with potatoes, lady."

"Thank you." Anna wished they had less mutton and goat, but the drought had left those as the most plentiful meat animals in Defalk. Perhaps after a few years of the returned rains, that would change—except there would be some other problem.

"The lady Anna," announced Skent.

The middle hall went silent as Anna stepped in, Skent behind her.

"Go on," she said with a smile, still vaguely amused that the girl born Anna Mayme Thompson in Cumberland, Kentucky, could silence an entire hall of people merely by appearing.

As she settled into the chair at the head of the table, Anna noted that Skent had managed to find a seat near the foot of the table across from Cataryzna, the only heir to Sudwei and attractive as well.

Jecks followed her eyes and nodded. "Good match, if their affection holds." Jecks sat to Anna's right, Hanfor to her left. Hanfor was commander of the liedburg armsmen and of the nucleus of what Anna hoped would be a standing and highly professional national army. Young Jimbob sat below his grandsire, and below Jimbob and Hanfor sat Menares and Dythya.

Anna wanted to smile as she regarded the two would-be lovers at the foot of the table. Beside Cataryzna was her thin-faced and stern aunt Drenchescha, a lady who would certainly ensure that Skent did not become overly friendly too soon.

"I see you did not protest when Lord Geansor requested that his sister accompany Cataryzna on her return," said Jecks, pouring some of the red wine into Anna's goblet.

"I cannot be everywhere, and Drenchescha is most capable of looking after Cataryzna's interests."

"Geansor seemed pleased to return her for your program of fostering and education."

"That's what I thought. Why did you think so?" Anna took a small sip of the wine.

"It's to his advantage. She could be no safer than with you, and anyone who attacked Sudwei could not take the heir. Also, you will find her a husband, and one you favor, and one that she can accept, and that means more support for his lands. How can the man lose? He is capable, but remains a cripple." Jecks filled his own goblet and handed the pitcher to Hanfor, who in turn filled his goblet and passed it to Dythya.

"I hope he sees it that way."

"He will, Lady Anna," said Hanfor.

At Hanfor's words, both Dythya and Menares nodded. A faint look of puzzlement crossed the redheaded Jimbob's face, then vanished.

Anna wondered if she should speak up, and avoid anything vaguely private. Somewhere, sometime, she'd read that sotto voce conversations by rulers in public made people uneasy.

"Have you had any luck in the search for a weapons smith?" Anna asked more loudly, turning to the graying arms commander.

"No, my lady." Hanfor smiled briefly. "Yesterday, a journeyman wheelwright tried to convince me that he could do the job. He couldn't explain the difference between a shortsword and a rapier." He paused as one serving girl set the large bowl of stew before Anna, and another eased a basket of hot bread beside it.

"We need to advertise," the sorceress mused.

A puzzled look crossed Jecks' face, hidden quickly by a pleasant smile. Hanfor merely waited, as did Dythya and Menares.

"Can we send scrolls or messages to Ebra or Ranuak suggesting that the position of weapons smith to the Regency for the Lord of Defalk is open?"

"To whom . . . ?" began Menares.

"Do they have guilds or something?"

"Of course, that would work," added Dythya with a smile. "You could also send scrolls to the portmasters at Encora and Narial."

"And they would pass on such news?" asked Menares skeptically.

"They would contact the mastercrafters," Dythya explained. "If the master smiths had journeymen who needed positions, they would tell them. If positions are few, then they would tell any one who came about the opportunity so that the newcomers would not take from those already smithing there."

"I could see that," mused Hanfor. "I could send scrolls to a few armsmen who might know of weapons smiths."

"We'll talk about that tomorrow." Anna wanted to rub her forehead. Even at dinner the problems kept assaulting her. She used the overlarge serving spoon to ladle out her portion of stew, then eased the huge bowl toward Jecks, and the bread toward Hanfor.

"It smells good," offered Dythya. "Better than the heavy noodles and the fried dumplings."

As her stomach growled again, Anna hoped so. She also hoped she could get some sleep uninterrupted by some nightmare or another.

She took a bite of the stew—spicy, but not burning,

thank heaven, or the harmonies, she mentally corrected herself.

Anna looked to the server. ''Jysel, would you convey my thanks and compliments to Meryn?''

Jysel bowed and flushed. ''Yes, Lady Anna.''

''Thank you.'' Anna needed to work in another visit with the cooks, among everything else, but the personal touch was what made the difference. It definitely did, but it took time, and that was something that was also in short, short supply.

Like everything else in Defalk, she mused, taking another mouthful of stew, nodding to herself as she did, appreciating a meal that was neither bland nor tongue-searing.

3

MANSUUS, MANSUUR·

What have you discovered, Bassil?'' Leaning forward in the silver chair, Konsstin peers across the polished walnut of the desk at the raven-haired officer who has entered the Liedfuhr's private study.

''About Defalk, sire?'' Bassil's words are formal and barely contain the hint of a question in their tone.

''What else? I did not send you out to seek out the price of grain in Encora.'' Konsstin leans back and tugs at his beard, half light brown, half silver, and close-trimmed.

''The seers show that the sorceress has recovered. Lord Jecks and the heir have returned to Falcor, and the liedburg flies Jimbob's ensign with a Regency symbol. They are training more armsmen.''

Konsstin frowns. ''The bitch is serious.''

''So it appears, sire.''

"What about the dissonant northern traders?"

"Nothing. Their seers watch us and the sorceress. The Ranuans have been silent."

"And about Bertmynn?" Konsstin pushes back the heavy chair and stands, clasping large hands behind his back for a moment, pushing back the silver cloak, revealing the close-fitting sky-blue velvet tunic and trousers with the silver piping that nearly matches the silver in his hair and beard.

"As you requested, we sent a hundred golds and two-score blades. You know that another young lordlet has taken Synek?"

"That's Hadrenn. We can't have two of them fighting over a corpse. We'll have to choose before long." Konsstin paces in a small circle for a time, then looks straight at the dark-haired younger man. "Send Hadrenn fifty golds . . . no weapons. Tell him it's a token to help rebuild the devastation caused by his nettlesome neighbor. Use those exact words—'nettlesome neighbor.' I don't want them thinking of her as a danger, just as a troublesome problem."

"Just fifty?".

"In another two weeks—make that three weeks—send off another fifty golds. People remember unasked-for and repeated smaller gifts more than large ones. Besides, our lordlet Hadrenn will use them more wisely if they're small." After a pause, the Liedfuhr adds, "Gifts need to be bigger than pocket change and small enough that the recipient can delude himself into believing he's not being bought."

"I will remember that, ser." Bassil stands, waiting, apparently relaxed, his eyes never leaving Konsstin.

Konsstin's head and eyes turn toward the wide windows to his left. "We need a true Empire of Music, Bassil."

"Yes, ser."

"Don't humor me!" Konsstin's voice rises to a bellow.

"I don't need someone who tiptoes around agreeing with me."

Bassil has stepped back, but his eyes meet those of the Liedfuhr. "You do not like those who agree, nor those who disagree, nor those who question. What would you have me do, ser?"

Konsstin's frown is broken by a hearty laugh. "That's the first honest thing you've said today."

"It can be dangerous to be too honest around those who are powerful."

"Perhaps I am too hard on people . . . but everyone has a scheme, and those who do not scheme flatter in the hopes of position and influence." His hazel eyes harden, then smile. "What do you want, Bassil?"

"Position, influence, and enough coins to be comfortable. I would rather obtain all three through ability than through scheming or flattery."

"Do you have enough ability for that?"

"I think so. You would have to be the judge of that."

"So," laughs Konsstin, "you grant me my due."

"How could I do otherwise? You are the Liedfuhr."

"Careful, that verges on flattery."

Bassil swallows.

"Enough of these games. I know what you want, and you'll have the opportunity to prove that ability . . . or to fail. That's all anyone can ask for." The Liedfuhr's fingers brush his close-trimmed beard. His lips tighten, and his eyes close for a moment before he continues. "I wasn't spouting idle thoughts about an Empire of Music, you know. It will not be long before the ships of Sturinn seek Liedwahr for more than trade. And what will they find? A bunch of ragtag holdings and merchant city-states scrapping with each other?"

"Unless matters change, that is what they will find," points out Bassil. "That is the way the eastern half of Liedwahr has always been."

"The western half was that way, too, until the time of my great-grandsire." Konsstin clasps his hands behind his back once more and paces back and forth in front of the walnut desk. "You know, the Maitre of Sturinn is building warships with three masts, ones tall enough to touch the clouds. The Ostisles have submitted."

"It will be years before—"

"A Liedfuhr has to think years in the future, Bassil. No one else does." Konsstin offers a snort. "Defalk was practically prostrate while that sorceress was recovering. Did anyone think what would happen once she recovered? Did any of those close enough to act do anything?"

"What might they have done?" asks the raven-haired younger man. "Your seers' pools showed that Ebra was ravaged. The Norweians were still rebuilding Wei, and there was no effective ruler in Neserea after the death of the Prophet . . . and his consort. That leaves Ranuak, and the Matriarchy has never used arms except at sea or in defending their own lands."

"And Dumar," adds Konsstin.

"You would have expected Ehara to march his small armies up the Great Chasm in winter?"

"They should have done *something*. Why am I the only ruler in Liedwahr who sees the images in the pool of the future?"

"The sorceress seems to see the future."

"That she does. I must grant her that. But what can she do? Defalk is surrounded on five sides. She has no access to the ocean and thirty-three stiff-necked and feuding lords who are only agreeable when you have their necks under your boots. She can only be in one place at a time, and she has no standing army, and no naval forces, and a land that can barely support its people."

"Yet the people support her."

"For now. They once supported Barjim, and then half fled Falcor at the first whiff of battle." Konsstin unclasps his hands and stretches. "For that matter, what am I supposed to do? I proposed a confederation to that idiot my daughter married. No . . . he had to have his own empire, and now where are they? Charred corpses under a monument that no one will recognize a generation from now."

"Lord Behlem was somewhat headstrong," temporizes Bassil.

"That's like saying . . . Oh, never mind. And now I have to deal with Neserea. My grandson takes after his mother and his grandmother, both vipers, the harmonies soothe their departed spirits, and I'm in the most awkward position of being his regent—from a thousand deks away." Konsstin turns and marches toward the windowed door, which he flings open, and steps out onto the balcony, where the wind blows the silver cloak back over his shoulders.

Bassil follows, standing back from the sculpted limestone balcony railing.

From the western balcony of the blufftop palace, the Liedfuhr surveys the stone walls of the fort below that commands the junction of the Ansul and the Latok Rivers. Then he swivels on one boot heel and studies Bassil. "I've sent the lancers to support that lizard Nubara . . . but it will take a lizard to deal with a viper."

"Should you not take a stronger position?" asked Bassil.

"Are you suggesting that I should?"

"You know your grandson and Neserea far better than I do, ser. But you do not trust him, and you did not trust his father or your daughter, and Neserea flanks Defalk and Nordwei."

"And Dumar. Let us not forget the ever-ambitious Ehara." Konsstin turns back to the balcony and the view of the two rivers that form the Toksul, the great river of Mansuur that flows westward to Wahrsus and the ocean. "So I should cross the Westfels and expand Mansuur . . . because no one else can see the dangers . . . or because I am ambitious . . . or because . . ."

His words die away in the stiff wind that blows uphill to the palace and eastward across the bluff.

Bassil waits for what the Liedfuhr may command.

4

Under gray clouds that appeared to be slowly lifting, Anna looked out over Falcor from the north tower, the one in which she had stayed when she had first come to the liedburg, the one where poor Garreth had sketched that sole image Anna had been able to send across the mists between Erde and earth for Elizabetta. Garreth—tortured by the prophet Behlem's consort Cyndyth, another innocent who had died just because she'd been close to Anna.

Anna shook her head. Now she couldn't use her skills even to *see* her youngest, much less send anything across the gulf between worlds. Her eyes traveled westward over the roofs of Falcor, seeing what appeared an endless stretch of gray and brown and white. The white was the already melting slush from the first snow seen in Defalk in nearly a decade.

Behind her, Giellum and Blaz stood at the top of the tower stairs. Giellum watched the stairs, Blaz the tower and the grounds.

Several plumes of smoke rose from the chimneys surrounding the liedburg, barely standing out against the morning mist that swathed the brown of the winter fields and that rose around the gray of the walls and roofs of Falcor. Half the city's structures were still vacant, Anna suspected, but she hoped that would change as Defalk recovered.

After a last look across the liedburg and Falcor, Anna turned and headed down the steps of the tower and then down to the main-level receiving room. The candle sconces and mantels on the left side of the hall had been

cleaned, but not those on the right. That was some prog-
ress.

Menares was waiting for her outside the door. She nodded for him to follow her inside the receiving room.

"Have we had any response to all those scrolls we
sent? Or from the Matriarchy about Barjim's debts?" She
slipped the purple regency sash over her green tunic and
trousers, wishing she'd thought more about color coordi-
nation earlier, but she was stuck with both colors for differing reasons. She even had a purple-and-gold vest that
someone had made for her.

Menares shrugged his heavy sloping shoulders. "Lady
Anna . . . with the rains, and now the snow, the roads are
muddy swamps. Messengers, wagons, all will be slow for
the winter."

How had people on earth dealt with muddy roads?
Paved them, but asphalt and cement weren't exactly prac-
tical for Defalk. She frowned. Hadn't Brill used sorcery
to create a brick road to the fort at the Sand Pass? And
the ancient Romans had built stone roads that had lasted
centuries.

Lord, she wished she knew more. "Until when?"

"Spring planting, I would say. The roads might dry
sooner. Then they might not. It has been many years since
Defalk has had rainfall, Lady Anna."

In short, no one was prepared for mud, and she hadn't
even thought about what it would do to roads in poor,
backward Defalk.

"Menares . . . go talk to Tirsik. See if he can give the
messengers ideas on where and how to travel through this
mess more quickly. Then let me know."

Menares bowed and departed.

Anna hoped that Tirsik, the stablemaster, could help
Menares out. She looked at the murky water in the pitcher,
then sang her water spell, watching as the swirling subsided into a clear whirl, before filling her goblet and taking a long swallow.

The door creaked ajar.

"Arms Commander Hanfor," announced the stocky and blond Cens, another page from the time of Barjim.

"Come on in," Anna said.

Hanfor's weathered face carried a half ironic, half sour expression as he stepped into the receiving room.

"What problems now?" asked Anna.

"There's nothing new, lady."

"You looked so disgusted."

"I feel like a graybeard with that title," admitted Hanfor.

"You're more than an overcaptain, and you are the arms commander of Defalk," she pointed out. "Is there some other term of office you'd prefer?"

"The others are worse."

"Then you're stuck being arms commander." Anna gestured to the chair across the table from her and waited for Hanfor to seat himself. "Menares told me the weather had slowed our scrolls and messengers."

"Mud is hard on horses and men." Hanfor added, "Especially those who have not experienced it."

"That's anyone from Defalk who's under twenty," suggested Anna. "What do you suggest?"

"There is little I can suggest. The rain the land needs. The roads . . . they could be better, but one cannot build roads in winter and rain." The arms commander shrugged. "Who would build them? You have given me coins to pay armsmen I do not have, and cannot find. Not enough. If we cannot find armsmen, where will we find those to build roads?"

"Or repair bridges or houses or . . ." Anna shook her head. "Even if our message scrolls do get through, when will craftspeople or armsmen arrive? Next summer?"

"Not before spring for most."

Anna paused, then asked, "What did you want? I just hit you with my problems."

"We still have no weapons smith." Hanfor stroked his beard. "Himar received a scroll from his brother who heard that the Ranuans have a ship loaded with blades that were destined for Elawha.''

"How much?''

"I do not know. A good blade fetches a gold, sometimes two.''

"We could spare a hundred golds, perhaps two hundred, but wouldn't we have to send a large guard?''

"We could send twenty or thirty golds, and arrange to take the blades in Sudwei.'' Hanfor laughed. "Now, after the destruction you rained upon Ebra, there cannot be that much of a market for blades there.''

Anna chuckled. "Why not? Work out the details with Dythya and have her see me if she has a problem . . . or a better way.''

"Thank you.''

"Thank you,'' she answered. "If what Himar's brother heard is true, it would give us more time to find a weapons smith. If not, we haven't lost anything. Is there anything else?''

"Not at the moment.''

"But you're worried about those blades?'' Anna smiled.

"Good weapons are hard to come by. As hard as to find those who can use them.''

Especially in Defalk, thought Anna. "We'll try to purchase what we can.''

The arms commander bowed.

Anna managed another swallow of water after Hanfor departed and before the receiving room door opened again.

"The lady Wendella begs your indulgence,'' said Resor.

The last person Anna really wanted to see was Wendella, Lord Dencer's consort, who remained as a hostage because Anna trusted neither Dencer nor Wendella.

"Have Giellum or Blaz escort her in.'' Wendella deserved an armed guard, if as nothing more than a more blatant reminder of her status.

Resor's eyes widened. "Yes, lady."

The brown-haired woman bowed low, carrying the child in her left arm. "Lady Anna."

Blaz stood behind her.

"You asked to see me," Anna said quietly.

Wendella bowed. "I would ask your indulgence. My son has not ever seen his father, nor have I seen my lord in more than half a year. Nor my brother, the lord Mietchel."

"Lord Dencer is always welcome here," Anna said truthfully. *Her brother is a lord? Why didn't I know that?*

"I would like to return to Stromwer and to my lord. Please, my lady Regent?" Wendella went to her knees.

Anna ignored the gesture, distrusting it, knowing that over the fall and early winter Wendella had continued to bad-mouth Anna to whoever in the south tower would listen, until even the stern Drenchescha had told Wendella to cease her complaining, and the pages had been able to repeat Wendella's words from memory.

"She's a bitch from the mist worlds . . ." And that had been one of the phrases that people had dared to repeat.

"Lady Wendella," Anna said, "Lord Barjim didn't trust your lord, and nothing you've done—or said—has given me any reason to reject Lord Barjim's opinion. Lord Dencer has continued to court both the Matriarchy and most lately, Lord Ehara of Dumar. I have found, if anything, that Lord Barjim was extraordinarily trusting for a lord of Defalk."

"You are a bitch! Go ahead, flame me! See where that will get you!" Wendella lurched upright, words and spittle flying from her mouth.

"Blaz—" Anna began. Lord, she wanted to fry the impertinent bitch, but she couldn't. That would have been within her rights, especially in Defalk, but it would have freed Dencer to wed someone else and to cause even more trouble.

Blaz stepped forward, and Wendella backed away from the regent.

"I'm going!"

"No. You're not going. Not for a moment." Anna turned and riffled through the spell folder, until she had the sheet she wanted. Then she stood and took the lutar from its case, quickly checking the tuning.

"No!" Wendella turned, then stopped as she saw Giellum at the door, behind Blaz.

"Just see that she stays here," Anna said tiredly, taking the grease marker and altering the spellsong she'd once used on both Madell and Virkan.

"You can't do anything to me. I'm a daughter of the Thirty-three."

Anna continued to mark the margins of the heavy brown paper.

"No!"

"You want to go home to Stromwer. We'll be happy to make that possible." Anna glanced at the notations and hummed through the melody, once, then again. Then she lifted the lutar and strummed the chords.

Wendella lurched toward Anna, for an instant before Blaz grabbed her.

Anna began to sing.

> "Wendella wrong, Wendella strong,
>   loyal be from this song.
>   Wendella young, Wendella old,
>   faithful be till dead and cold.

> "Consort of lord, mother of son,
>   woman of means, this be done.
>   Treachery prevent to all this land
>   with your cunning and your hand."

"Nooooo . . ." As the notes died away, the dark-haired woman collapsed to her knees on the polished stones of the receiving-room floor. "No . . ." she sobbed, barely hanging on to the infant in her arms.

Anna felt like she'd been shaken momentarily, and for

a few moments, there seemed to be two images of Wendella before her, one *colder* somehow than the other.

Forcing herself to ignore the strange reaction, Anna lifted the bell and rang it, then set the lutar on the chair beside the one she used. Even after the double image faded—something that hadn't happened to her ever before—her head ached. It had the few times before when she had used personal spells, probably because they were technically Darksong, and Darksong didn't always agree with her bodily harmonics—and probably would less and less, from what she understood. The strange double image confirmed that.

Clearsong would have been easier on her, but it didn't work on people.

"Yes, Lady Anna?" This time Skent was the page who peered into the room, his eyes going from the sobbing form on the floor to the regent.

"Would you have a message sent to Lord Dencer that the lady Wendella and his son and heir are free to return to Stromwer at her and his convenience?"

"Yes . . . Lady Anna."

"If she has the coins for an escort, she may leave immediately. But draft a message for me anyway." Anna's eyes went briefly to Wendella. "And I'll need something to eat."

Skent nodded and vanished.

Anna shouldn't have yielded to her temper, but she was so tired of spoiled lords and ladies, some of whom were worse than the most ungrateful students she'd taught, and that was saying a lot. The headache had not subsided. In fact, it was worse.

"Waaa . . ." The child in Wendella's arms began to cry.

"You have killed me. . . ." sobbed Wendella, cradling her son and struggling into a sitting position.

"Why? Because I bound you not to betray me or Defalk? If that's so, Wendella, then you've admitted that my judgment of you and your lord is correct." Anna smiled coldly. "You're going home, and you'd better find a way to keep your lord loyal to the Regency and Jimbob. For your own sake, if not for Defalk's."

"You are cruel . . . so cruel. . . ."

"I don't have time for games and intrigues." Anna nodded to the guards. "And I have even less for the people who attempt them. Good day, lady."

A stone-faced Blaz took the dark-haired lady's arm and helped her to her feet. Giellum opened the door.

Alone momentarily in the receiving room, Anna took a deep breath. Then she set aside the lutar, replacing it in its case, and refiling the spell in the folder.

She massaged her forehead, then poured another goblet of water. Both Blaz and Giellum had been shocked. Had it been because she'd used sorcery? Or because she'd let Wendella live?

She rang the bell again.

Skent peered in.

"Have Blaz and Giellum step in for a moment, please."

The two guards stepped inside the receiving room, and the door clunked shut. Giellum swallowed. Blaz remained stone-faced.

"I'm not upset or angry," Anna said quietly.

Neither guard moved.

"But I do have a question for you. Blaz . . . do you think I was too lenient on the lady Wendella?"

"It be not my place to judge." The guard's voice was hoarse.

"Giellum?"

"I . . . How . . . would . . . ?"

"I know." Anna sighed. "Anything you say would be wrong. That's the problem with being a ruler, even a regent. No one wants to tell you what they think. If they agree, it's flattery. If they don't, it's dangerous." She smiled wryly. "So I'll have to guess."

Giellum swallowed again.

"Giellum . . . you don't have to swallow."

That got another swallow, and Anna wanted to sigh in exasperation. Instead, she continued. "The lady Wendella was extremely rude." She glanced at Blaz. "I think that's something we can all agree on."

The wary look in Giellum's eyes, and the fractional nod from Blaz confirmed that.

"In fact, after I spelled her, she as much as admitted that she and her lord Dencer were disloyal to the Regency. Did either of you wonder why I let her go?"

The lack of reaction confirmed her guess.

"You did, but you don't want to second-guess a regent. Think about this. If I had executed the lady Wendella, several things would have happened. First, Lord Dencer would immediately start telling everyone how I killed his wife and heir, and how I was out to take over all Defalk by replacing all the old lords. Then, he would be free to marry whoever he wants, possibly even some relative of Ehara of Dumar. This way, he has a struggle with his wife. If he kills her, and he may, probably with poison, it will take some time. I can certainly accuse him of proving his disloyalty, and I don't have her blood on the Regency. He might even get the message and become more loyal." She shrugged. "It's a nasty business, but the fewer disloyal lords and ladies I have to execute outright, the stronger Lord Jimbob's position will become."

Blaz gave the slightest of nods. Giellum had turned pale.

"You look shocked, Giellum. Ruling isn't all battles. A lot of it is positioning things so that your enemies look bad and unreasonable. Wendella and Dencer have been trying to make me look like the bitch of Defalk. We'll announce to all the lords that we are pleased to return Lord Dencer's consort and his heir to him and wish them both every happiness. It should confound just about everyone." Anna took a sip from the goblet. "And you can tell anyone you want what happened. I will, and there's no secret about it." *In fact, I hope you do tell just about everyone.*

She studied the two, catching the hint of a smile in Blaz's eyes. Well, one out of two wasn't bad, and maybe the older guard could get it across to Giellum.

"Do you have any questions?"

"No, lady," said Blaz.

"No . . . lady," added Giellum.

No sooner had her guards left than Resor opened the door again. "There is a player here, Lady Anna. He says his name is Delvor."

"I'll see him." No one else could, and at times like this she missed Daffyd. She really needed another player-master, but where would she find one?

Blaz followed the would-be player into the receiving room and stood just inside the door, hand on his blade.

The young man stepped into the receiving room and looked down at the floor. Lank brown hair—too long—spilled across his forehead. His fingers were white where they clutched his violino case.

"You . . . summoned me, sorceress." His thin voice trembled out of a thin face.

"I requested players." Anna waited. Yes, she had requested players, from everywhere and even with the promise of a healthy wage. And this trembling youngster was only the second since harvest—two in half a season, when she needed a good dozen, if not more. The first so-called player had carried a falk horn on which he couldn't play "Come to Jesus" in whole notes. Anna's eyes focused on the youngster. "Are you interested in being a player for the Regency?"

"Yes, lady." He looked down.

"I take it that you are worried about playing for an unknown sorceress, but you need the coin even more than you worry?"

The youngster just shivered.

"What is your name, young player?" Anna hated it when she'd been given a name and didn't remember it, but she'd never been that good with names.

"Delvor, lady."

"Delvor, I don't eat players. I do pay them well, if they can meet my standards. That's a silver a week." She paused.

"A silver . . . ?"

"Take out that violino and play something for me."

Delvor's fingers still trembled as he fumbled out the old and polished instrument. The trembling lessened as he began to tune the violino.

"Anytime you're ready."

Slowly, he raised the instrument and the bow.

After the first unsteady notes, the short melody was clear. Delvor didn't squeak or shriek, and his fingering looked sure.

From where he stood by the door, Blaz gave the faintest of nods. Anna wasn't so certain.

"All right." Anna gestured for the violinist to stop. "How do you learn a new melody? Can you read notation?"

The look at the floor answered that question.

"I take it that you learn by ear?"

"I can play what I've heard," the player answered. He swallowed. "Sometimes, I must hear it more than once."

More than sometimes. Anna nodded, then cleared her throat. "I'll sing a short song—just the notes, not the words. Listen carefully. I'll want you to play it as well as you can."

Delvor lowered the violin and bow and nodded.

"La, la, la . . ." Anna sang the water spell melody. That couldn't cause any trouble, or not much, if it were passed on to others.

Delvor cocked his head, listening.

"Now . . . you try it."

The player picked up the bow. All in all, Anna had to repeat the song more than three times before Delvor could basically replicate it.

She wanted to shake her head. Still . . . he had been able to pick it up. She supposed he would have a use, if only as the equivalent of third or fourth chair, not that sorcerers' players were classified that way.

"Delvor?"

"Yes, lady." The player hung his head.

"There is a great deal you do not know. If you stay here, you will have a lot to learn."

Delvor licked his lips.

"You may stay. You will receive a silver a week, and, until the rest of the players arrive, you will also be required to assist in other areas. Nothing heavy, but I may have you learn new skills or serve as a messenger. Do you understand?"

"Where . . ."

"There are players' quarters in the liedburg. You get quarters and food and the silver. Do you wish to serve the Regency?"

Delvor went to his knees. "Yes, lady."

Anna lifted the bell, and Cens entered.

"Cens, this is Delvor, and he is one of the new players. He can have one of the small rooms in the players' quarters by the stables. I'd appreciate it if you'd get him settled. Then tell Dythya about him."

"Yes, Lady Anna."

When Cens and the player had left, she looked down at the table. There was another reason why poor Daffyd hadn't been able to find many players. Most of them didn't have any spines—except for those who'd already died at the Sand Pass or in the destruction of Vult.

She sighed. Then, what player in his or her right mind would want to serve her when most of those who had were dead? Poor Daffyd—he'd been a good viola player who had helped spell her to Defalk and then served as her chief player, and he was buried under the lava of the volcano she had raised to destroy Vult and the dark Evult who had directed the darksingers of Ebra against Defalk. So were all of the others who had followed her to Vult. She sighed again. *Get back to a problem you can do something about . . . maybe.*

She couldn't get supplies or move troops if the roads turned to mud every time it rained. She couldn't use sorcery to repair the roads without players and stones being carted nearby, and she couldn't have the stones carted except in dry weather. And she couldn't find enough players.

Anna took a deep breath. She still hadn't paid that visit to the kitchens and Meryn. She might as well do that, before she forgot. The liedburg ran on meals as well as coins and arms.

The ubiquitous Blaz followed her down the corridor and out to the section of the liedburg that jutted into the rear courtyard, almost standing alone—probably for fire reasons.

Meryn stood at the far end of the huge hearth, with one of the oven doors open, easing a wooden paddle containing the dough that would be bread into the oven. At the table behind her, Jysel was plucking a just-scalded chicken, and other sodden birds lay beside the first.

Anna waited until Meryn closed the oven door.

"Oh . . . Lady Anna." The head cook's hands fluttered. Behind her, Jysel's mouth opened.

"I don't have any problems," Anna said. "I've enjoyed your cooking, and I really liked the way you spiced the mutton stew the other night. It wasn't bland, and it didn't burn my tongue."

The cook's hands stopped fluttering. "We do as we can, lady. But with so many mouths . . ."

Anna held in a sigh. Like everything else in Defalk, the liedburg kitchen was probably overworked. "You could use another good cook?" She gave a smile.

"I could use three, lady, not that there be three in Falcor I'd want." Meryn shook her head.

"If you find one you would like to help you, let me know." Anna sniffed. "The bread smells good. I don't know how I'd manage without all the bread you've baked for me."

"That be good." Meryn smiled. "Unlike some, you

appreciate good food, and the folk who fix it." She paused. "Molasses for the dark bread, it be getting dear."

Anna half nodded to herself. Everything was getting dear. "Once, a long way away, I fixed a lot of fancy meals." The sorceress offered a laugh. "And not with sorcery. But I had things that made it easier. I wouldn't want to try to cook in that hearth."

"Takes watching, lady, that it does."

"I'm sure it does." She glanced toward Blaz. "I wish I could stay longer, Meryn . . . Jysel . . . but I wanted to tell you again, personally, how much I appreciate all the cooking and the work."

Both women bowed.

Once back in the receiving room, Anna rang the bell even before seating herself at the worktable.

"Find me Menares."

While she waited, she began to make a list—yet another of the endless lists that grew faster on the bottom than she could complete on the top. This list held the key roads from Falcor to the borders. Should she add molasses to the supply list?

"Lady Anna?" Menares bowed. His eyes flicked away from her to the floor, then to the empty gilt receiving chair.

"What did Tirsik say?"

"The stablemaster will talk to the messengers, he and Captain Alvar. They should ride on the edges of the roads, and he will tell them where not to ride."

"Good."

"He also sent his thanks for the coins for the extra straw."

Anna nodded. "I need you to find something else. Find me an artist. One who can do good sketches of bridges and roads and forts. There ought to be someone who can draw somewhere near Falcor. I'll pay him—or her." With the word "her," she thought of poor Garreth, who'd drawn her picture, and who had been killed merely on a

whim by Cyndyth while Anna had been saving the
Prophet's armsmen.

"Yes, Lady Anna." Menares' voice contained a resigned tone, the one that suggested she was being unreasonable or frivolous.

"I'm not crazy," she snapped. "We need better—"
She groped for a suitably impressive word. "—infrastruc-
ture here in Defalk, and that means roads and bridges, and
since we don't have any dissonant builders and no coins,
that means sorcery, and I need images for sorcery. Is that
clear?"

Menares nodded, backing quickly out of the receiving
room.

Once again, she was getting a reputation for being a
temperamental bitch. Why couldn't they see? She wasn't
even a military type, and it was obvious. Defalk was surrounded on all sides by potential enemies.

With Blaz and Giellum following her, she left the receiving room and took the small service hall. Her boots
echoed on the stones of the narrow passage. She opened
the back door to slip inside the large hall that was being
used as the de facto schoolroom for her pages and fosterlings. Trying not to sneeze, she remained behind the long
tapestry and listened.

Dythya was speaking.

"Remember . . . the position of the numeral determines
the amount of its greatness. In the first position, a six is
just a six. In the second position, it is a sixty, or ten times
greater. In the third position . . ."

"Numbers different when they are in different places.
New symbols! You confuse us. Why do we even have to
use new characters for numbers? The old ones were fine,"
said Hoede, almost red-faced.

"Once you learn them, using figures is easier," Dythya
said patiently. "It is easier to check accounts, and to keep
track of what you have spent."

"You haven't told me why we must use different symbols for numbers."

Anna decided to put an end to the discussion. She stepped out from behind the dusty arras depicting Lord Donjim's grandsire.

"Lady Anna . . ."

"Sorceress . . ."

"I beg your pardon, Dythya." Anna nodded to the woman who was the liedstadt accountant, or the closest thing to an accountant.

Dythya merely nodded, a faint smile playing around her lips.

Anna turned to the youngsters seated at the long table, grease markers and rough brown paper before them. Her eyes took in each in turn. Secca, the youngest redhead, glanced up at the sorceress openly. Skent, at the end of the table, did not quite meet her eyes. Nor did Ytrude, the shy and tall blonde. But Anna did get a flashing smile from the redheaded Lysara, the older sister of Birke, who remained with his father at Abenfel. On the other hand, Cataryzna smiled shyly. Cens just looked blank, as did Resor. Hoede swallowed and pursed his lips. Jimbob, at the end of the table, met her eyes for a moment.

"Hoede." Anna fixed the sandy blond with blue eyes that were as cold as the Falche River beyond the liedburg walls. "If you spent as much time learning your digits and how to use them as you do arguing about it, you'd not only be able to improve your sire's accounts, you'd have time left over for more pleasant pastimes."

Hoede's eyes fell.

"Since you want an answer, I'll make it simple. Defalk almost perished under the old ways. Nordwei, Ranuak, Neserea, and even Mansuur have adopted more modern ways of doing things. We either adopt even better methods, or we will be forced to submit."

"But you have sorcery," murmured a voice.

Anna shook her head. "I managed to hold off the Dark Ones, and bring back the rain. Magic does not work on crops, or on accounts, and a sorceress can only be in one place. I cannot be there to tell every lord and holding how and when to plant. I will not live long enough to advise your children. If you don't learn as much as you can, most of you won't hold what you have.'' She smiled. ''I know . . . some of you are not the heirs, and that means knowledge is even more important for you, because what you can do is determined even more by what you can learn.'' She turned back to Hoede. ''You can ask all the questions you want about *why* something works or *how* to calculate or use your knowledge. If you wish to ask questions about the necessity of learning such matters, then come to me. If you persist in wasting the time of those who teach you with such childish inquiries, then I will send you and anyone else home and invite another young person.'' She smiled. ''Is that clear?''

''Yes, Lady Anna.'' The murmured answer was nearly in unison.

''There's an even shorter answer, Hoede,'' Anna continued. ''I saved Defalk when no one else could or would. Since my ways worked, and nothing else did, you'll learn my ways.'' She paused. ''I also might point out that the more powerful lords in Defalk have already adopted these numbers and this system. They say it takes less time and works better. Now . . . Hoede, I've given you three reasons. Do you need any more?''

Hoede looked down, his face as red as the stripe in his tunic.

''Dythya will examine you on how well you learn the new number system, all of you. I expect you all to do well.'' She smiled, then nodded, and left by the front door, where Giellum waited.

She glanced at the young guard. His eyes dropped.

Why did everything she did shock the young? Or some of them? She was supposed to accomplish grand deeds— like figuring out how to keep Defalk from being dismembered by its neighbors when she had next to no armsmen, few coins, and drought-ravaged cropland that would take years to recover even with the return of the rains.

Anna paused outside the receiving room and looked to Barat, the one page not in lessons.

"Yes, lady?"

"I'll need some bread and cheese. And a piece of fruit, if there is any."

Leaving Giellum outside with Blaz, who had hurried back from the large hall, she entered the receiving room, glancing to the rear window, and the hint of sunlight after the days of mixed rain and snow.

With a sigh, she slumped into her chair at the table.

One player, no weapons smith, no messengers getting anywhere fast, and enemies on just about all sides.

She had to do *something*!

First, she shuffled through all the papers she'd reclaimed from Loiseau, Brill's hall in Mencha, until she found those dealing with building. There were no spells of bridges—just for a barn and a fort. For a moment, she studied Brill's spell for the fort, probably the one he had built at the Sand Pass, murmuring the words as she read, trying to get a feel for the rhythm.

> "... replicate the bricks and stones.
> Place them in their proper zones ...
> Set the blocks, and set them square
> set them to their pattern there ..."

The spell melody notes were a cross between chord symbols and medieval tablature—and hard enough to decipher, let alone turn into music.

"Lady?" Barat stood in the door with a platter in hand.

"Thank you." The growling of her stomach reminded her—again—how she couldn't put off eating, especially with what she had in mind for the afternoon.

After she finished everything on the platter, a feat that would have turned her into a butterball once upon a time, she began to scrawl out possible spells on the brown paper.

Then she took out the lutar, tuned it, and tried the words—only in her head—with the chords.

Finally, she lifted the bell and rang it. This time Resor opened the door.

"Resor, would you tell Fhurgen that I am going riding in a bit, and that I'll need two squads of guards, or whatever he and Alvar think is right."

"Yes, Lady Anna." Resor did not close the door, then asked, "What should I tell them if they ask me your destination?"

"Somewhere around Falcor."

"Yes, lady."

Anna replaced the lutar in its case, and picked up both the case and her jacket and hat.

Blaz and Giellum flanked her on the walk from the main building to the stables.

Tirsik met her before she had taken a pace inside. "Lady Anna." The white-haired and wiry stablemaster nodded, glancing at Anna's riding gear and the lutar case. "The roads are foul."

"I'm not going far. Just to the other side of Falcor up by where the bridge was."

"Even the roads in Falcor are slippery."

"Then few will be out."

A wry and wintry smile crossed the white-haired stablemaster's face. "As you wish, and it usually is, my lady."

"I know, Tirsik. I'm being difficult. So is most of Liedwahr at the moment." She added, "I hope I didn't ask too much of you when I sent Menares over to have you instruct some of the riders and messengers on foul-weather traveling."

"It be my pleasure, lady, and glad to put what these gray hairs have learned to service."

"You are a learned rascal."

"Once, lady. No longer."

Anna grinned and headed for Farinelli's stall. The palomino gelding greeted her with a loud *whuff*.

"I know. I'm late, and you want to be groomed on schedule." By the time she had Farinelli brushed and saddled, Fhurgen and her guards had formed up in the liedburg courtyard.

Anna pulled on the leather riding jacket and the floppy-brimmed hat of the type that had seen her through her time in Defalk, then strapped the lutar in the case behind the saddle. She led Farinelli out, mounted and nodded to Fhurgen. "Let's go."

She let Farinelli pick his way across the wet stones of the courtyard and out through the main gate. Fhurgen and the guards followed.

The north breeze was chilly, even for Anna, but the leather jacket kept her comfortable. She could sense the shivers of the guards, and catch a few phrases.

". . . know she comes from the mist worlds . . . day like this . . ."

". . . doesn't even *look* cold . . ."

". . . went through the Ostfels in six feet of snow . . . Tyres said . . ."

Anna wanted to snort. The expedition against the Evult had been in late fall, and there hadn't been any snow to speak of. Some cold rain, but no snow.

As she rode across the flat outside the liedburg and toward the road that led through the part of Falcor north of the keep, Anna studied the buildings. A few more bore signs of life, like smoke from chimneys, or new shutters or even windows. There were still too many empty structures.

Two blocks up, she saw a new sign—a picture board depicting a golden lutar outside a refurbished inn. Anna laughed. The Golden Lutar—clearly an attempt at flattery, since the instrument had been made by Daffyd specially for her and was, so far as she knew, the only one in Liedwahr.

Still, the rebuilt inn was one good signal at a time when there were few enough.

Her smile faded when they reached the north end of

Falcor and the Falche River. Anna reined up and studied the ruined bridge buttresses, the remnants from the flood unleashed by the Evult of Ebra, and the riverbed, through which ran a muddy and winding track.

Originally, the old bridge had consisted of three spans, the ends of each outer span anchored in the rock on each side of the river. The center span had been anchored on the western side to a pier sunk into the rock beneath the riverbed and to a second pier on the eastern side which had rested on a rocky islet in the river. Parts of the two piers remained, and muddy water swirled around the disarrayed stones, covering the lower section of the rude trail that travelers had used after the bridge had been swept away.

Anna finally turned in the saddle and fumbled with the lutar case, easing the instrument out, and then easing Farinelli forward.

"Fhurgen, please move the armsmen back."

"Yes, lady." The dark-bearded squad leader raised his arm. "Back. Back to the pedestal there."

As her guards guided their mounts back toward the pediment that might once have held a statue, Anna ran her fingers over the strings and checked the lutar's tuning. Then she ran through the spell melody once, thinking the words.

She cleared her throat and began the spell, not belting, but using full concert voice.

> ". . . replicate the blocks and stones.
> Place them in their proper zones . . .
> Set them firm, and set them square
> weld them to their pattern there . . .

> "Bring the rock and make it stone . . ."

The stone under the bluff seemed to shift even before she finished the first verse. *Strophic spell,* her thoughts corrected automatically.

A shiver in the harmonies underlying all Liedwahr followed the last chord, except Anna knew only she heard that shiver, she and any other sorcerer or sorceress. The lightning that flashed across the half-clear sky was visible to all, and murmurs swept across the armsmen as the white-and-gray clouds began to darken into black.

Anna, holding the lutar one-handed, used the other on the reins to urge Farinelli away from the edge of a bluff that suddenly felt all too insecure.

The ground rumbled, and dust puffed from beneath the sodden upper soil that overlay the rocks beneath. Another flash of light seared across a sky that had become dark gray.

The edge of the bluff from where Anna had begun the spell shivered, then peeled away in a brown-and-gray cascade, even as a shimmering mist of silver, sheathed in the faintest of rainbows, began to arch across the river.

The sorceress, feeling lightheadedness slashing across her consciousness, struggled to get the lutar back in its case.

How would you replace it now?

The ground shifted again, and Anna struggled to stay balanced in the saddle as Farinelli sidestepped and she tried to close the lutar case.

A line of fire seared across her eyes, and again that gigantic harp that affected only her strummed somewhere she could not see, but only sense.

More dust rose around her with the grinding of rocks below, and the river began to boil, sending steam up to mix with dust and rock powder, until the entire area from one edge of the Falche to the other was cloaked in a gray mist.

Anna's eyes burned, and her head swam, and she grabbed for Farinelli's mane, as the entire world turned black.

5

ESARIA, NESEREA

The dark-haired youth shivers and draws his green cloak more tightly around him. He sits on a green cushion in the gilt throne chair that comprises the official seat of the Lord of Neserea, and the Protector of the Faith of the Eternal Melody.

A cold breeze seeps into the receiving room that adjoins the empty, columned, hilltop chamber used in the summer. Through the single window, the youth who is neither boy nor man can see the fluted marble pillars, and beyond them, the whitecaps of the Bitter Sea.

"Am I not the Prophet of Music, Nubara?"

"Young Lord Rabyn, you are indeed the heir of the Prophet of Music and will rule Neserea—" The officer in the maroon uniform of a lancer of Mansuur breaks off his words as the youth's eyes flash.

"Grandsire's message said I was Lord now."

"He also confirmed me as acting regent for him in your name." Nubara smiles politely.

"But you should serve me." The hint of a pout frames the full red lips.

"I serve the will of the Liedfuhr." Nubara smiles broadly. "Always in your interests, most assuredly."

The music of low strings sifts through the morning stillness from the adjoining Temple of Music, providing a soothing background that neither Lancer nor youth acknowledges.

"What are you doing about that evil woman who killed my mother and my father the Prophet?" Rabyn's eyes narrow as he watches the older man who stands below the low dais.

"The sorceress Anna, Lord Rabyn?" Nubara's smile narrows. "Your grandsire has indicated that he was most displeased, and that he will take such matters into his own hands. Fiftyscore lancers make their way here to Esaria."

"That's not what I asked. What are you doing?"

"Following the orders of the Liedfuhr. I am, after all, a Lancer of Mansuur."

"You are a . . ." Rabyn frowns, then smiles. "I should be thankful to you."

"It is hard to be patient when great wrongs have been done, Lord Rabyn. You must recall that the sorceress subverted fully a third of your sire's forces, and murdered most of those officers who were loyal to him . . . and to you. We are working to rebuild your armsmen."

"All of the Prophet's Guard returned, except for their commander. You could command them."

"I could indeed. Would you have me lead them against the evil sorceress and lose them as well? She has never lost a battle, and those who have opposed her have never lost less than the majority of their forces. There are no armsmen left in all of Ebra." Nubara bows slightly, raising his eyebrows.

"She can be defeated. Anyone can be defeated." The pout on Rabyn's lips grows fuller.

"That is what your grandsire believes. That will take many armies. The sorceress can be in but one place at one time. She must be encircled so that her armies are reduced and destroyed."

"That is why you are seeking more armsmen?"

"Exactly, Lord Rabyn. Exactly." Nubara smiles and bows.

"Thank you, Nubara. You may go." Rabyn's eyes remain on the lancer until the older man leaves the chamber. Then the young Prophet of Music shivers and readjusts the heavy cloak.

6

"You are so good with young voices, Anna dear. I really do not understand why you persist in this sorcery business." Her eyes cold, Dieshr smiled across the too-neat desk at Anna.

Anna wanted to scream, but what was the use? Dieshr was Music Department Chair, and Anna didn't have tenure. And what was this sorcery Dieshr was talking about? Anna certainly didn't believe in witchcraft.

"Besides, you should devote your energies to obtaining a doctorate. That would make you far more marketable in today's academic community."

A doctorate? After all the years when Avery—the great Antonio—had offered reason after reason why it wasn't the right time, or appropriate, or whatever? "The children are too young." "We can't afford it . . . perhaps next year." "You wouldn't take off now, not when I've just gotten this break with the New York City Opera?" "Teenagers really need their mother . . . it's the most sensitive part of their life."

Anna did scream, and Dieshr vanished into gray smoke, and the scream came out of her too-dry mouth more like a groan. The gray smoke turned into gray walls.

Her head ached—throbbed—and her mouth was dry. A blonde face swam into view.

"Lady . . . please drink. You must drink."

She drank what tasted like vinegar, and the gray walls turned black again.

The next time she woke, Cataryzna was still waiting.

"Can you drink, lady?"

Anna nodded and sipped from the cup. Her eyes still

burned, and her head continued to throb, if less violently. She took a small swallow, then another.

The door opened, and a white-haired figure slipped into the chamber, and settled onto the chair beside the bed.

Anna wondered if she looked as terrible as she felt. She could tell she was dehydrated and started to reach for the cup. Cataryzna lifted it to her lips.

From the light, Anna thought it was morning.

"Morning?" she finally asked.

"It is morning, lady," answered Cataryzna. "We were not sure you would see it."

Anna tried to struggle into more of a sitting position, and her blonde fosterling—Lord Geansor's daughter— adjusted the pillows behind her.

"More . . . wine." Anna drank again, and could almost feel the worst of the headache subsiding. Lord, was she that dehydrated? She probably had no blood-sugar level at all, either.

"Some bread might help."

"I will get it." Cataryzna slipped toward the door and out into the second floor corridor, her shoulder-length hair flying out behind her.

"Lady Anna," Jecks said slowly, from the chair beside her bed. "You cannot rebuild Defalk by destroying yourself with sorcery."

For a moment, Anna just took in his words, then sipped more of the vinegary wine. She wished it were water, but in her condition she couldn't orderspell water, and trying to drink unspelled water would invite disaster of another type.

"If you destroy yourself, everything you have preserved will vanish." Jecks swallowed.

"Lord Jecks." She wanted her voice to be hard, but it just sounded tired. "Everyone counsels me to patience. Everyone tells me that we cannot do this. We cannot find players. We cannot find weapons smiths. We cannot travel or whatever because the roads are too muddy."

"You cannot rebuild Defalk in a season." He forced a

smile. "You cannot do that in even two seasons or a year."

"We may not have a year," Anna said. "If you want your grandson even to have a land to rule, we have to find ways to do all those things everyone tells me we can't do. Now . . . do we have a solid bridge over the Falche?"

"Yes, Lady Anna. Hanfor thinks it will outlast Falcor." Jecks smiled. "The channel beneath is also rather deeper. It is almost a gorge."

So that was where the stone had come from. Anna nodded. It would have been easier with players—much easier—but Delvor alone wouldn't be much help. A name popped into her head—Liende, the woodwind player injured in the Sand Pass battle.

"Liende, the player? Isn't she still at Elhi?"

"I believe so."

"Would you have her summoned to Falcor?"

"You may summon anyone you wish."

"Stop humoring me!" Anna hated any hint of condescension, even from Jecks, even if he did resemble her favorite movie star, even if he had actually shown some real concern for her as a person, not as a regent. "I'm not being whimsical. I need players. She knows who many of them are, and if I can't do anything else, I'll build roads. To the west first."

"You cannot—"

"Why not? The first threat will be from the west, won't it?"

"That will not come for years, and you must recover."

Anna doubted she'd have that much time, but she couldn't argue everything. "Good. Then we can build lots of roads and weapons and train an army." Anna took another swallow of the vinegary wine. Her stomach growled. She needed to eat. Another problem—the demands of sorcery drove her metabolism so high that anything that left her unable to eat for very long was practically life-threatening. She wasn't sure she wanted to see how thin her face had become.

The door opened, and Cataryzna scurried back in at almost a run, carrying a platter. Skent followed with a second. The dark-haired page's eyes took in Anna, and she could see the shock there. She'd wondered how bad she looked, and now she knew.

"Can you eat?" asked the blonde.

Anna reached for the bread, and slowly began to chew. She wanted to smile as she saw Skent and Cataryzna standing side by side. Perhaps her weakness—how she hated to be weak!—had had some positive effect.

She tried the white cheese that Skent had brought. She'd need protein and fat. Lord, she needed everything.

In between bites, she turned to Jecks, noting absently that he continued to worry one hand against the other. "I'll be fine. At least with rest and more food, I will be."

"You cannot . . . You must not . . ." Jecks stammered.

"Lord Jecks . . . we have no choice. We must rebuild Defalk as quickly as possible." She swallowed more of the wine.

"I will have Liende sent for," Jecks said. "And I will tell her to bring any players she knows."

"Good." Anna could feel tiredness creeping over her. Not the draining exhaustion that had felled her at the bridge, but a fuller feeling.

"Why are roads so important, lady?" Cataryzna said quietly. "You murmured of roads and of doctors."

Anna sighed, even as she could feel the lassitude creeping back over her. She shouldn't have gotten upset. Anger always tired her, and she was already exhausted—and what she'd done had been Clearsong. "I'm tired. So tired." She forced out the remaining words. "So all the dissonant lords of Defalk don't go on thinking they're independent little countries. So that we or Jimbob can put an army at their gate in two days instead of two weeks. So that . . ." *So many things. . . .*

She shut her eyes.

7

ENCORA, RANUAK

H ave you discovered what caused that vast harmonic
shudder yesterday, Veria?" With a cheerful smile,
the round-faced and gray-haired woman sniffs the steam
from the cup she has lifted level with her double chins.

"Yes, Matriarch." The black-haired woman at the
other long end of the oval ebony table sips her own cup
of scalded cider. "There is no one left but the soprano
sorceress—"

"Best you call her the Regent of Defalk, for that is
what she is and will be for many years," suggests the
silver-haired man who seats himself across the table from
the Matriarch.

"The Regent of Defalk, Father," Veria corrects herself,
slightly readjusting her powder-blue robe. "She used the
harmonies to replace a huge stone bridge across the
Falche. It was one of those destroyed by the Evult's
flood."

"There is a rough balance in that," judges the Matriarch, after taking a sip of steaming cider.

"It will be a while before she balances all the dissonance created by the Evult," suggests Ulgar. He twists
the end of his silvered handlebar mustache before adding
another pinch of cinnamon to his cup. "I wish she had
tortured him more before she destroyed him."

"Father . . ." protests Veria.

"That is vulgar, Ulgar," suggests the Matriarch.

"Honesty, my dear, honesty. All proclaim the need for
honesty, but none allocate so much as a silver for it." He
slurps his cider. "Not so much as a single silver."

Veria glances to her mother.

"That's the Regent's problem," continues Ulgar, reaching for the pot and refilling his cup. "She is honest enough to see what was, what is, and what yet must be done, while all those around her are blinded by the dishonesties of the past."

"You are being obscure—again, dear." The Matriarch pats back a stray iron-gray hair.

"Exactly how are those around the sorc—the regent, blinded by the past?" asks Veria.

Ulgar lifts his cup, then a silvered eyebrow. He sips without speaking, as if the answer were obvious.

"Father . . ."

"Very well, if your mother the Matriarch consents to hearing the views of an old and foolish man."

"Ulgar, mock humility doesn't become you. It's also dishonest, and rather hypocritical when discussing the honesty of others." The Matriarch smiles broadly.

Ulgar returns her smile with one more sheepish. "Very well," he repeats, clearing his throat. "Defalk is bordered by five other lands. Ebra has been devastated, but already conflict between two successors brews in there, fostered by the golds of the Liedfuhr. In Nordwei, the Council of Wei has met to discuss the Regent, and, should she prove successful in strengthening Defalk, will seek her destruction. Ehara of Dumar has already begun to consider sending aid to Lord Dencer, hoping to win him to Dumar and to provide a staging area for Dumaran armsmen. Neserea has become a true protectorate and pawn of the Liedfuhr, with the cunning Nubara moving the stones. Lord Behlem's son Rabyn has his father's lack of intelligence, but not his cunning, and his mother's viciousness, but not her brains."

"You did not mention us," points out Veria.

"We are as bad as the others. Those of the trading faction have declined to extend credit for planting to the southern lords of Defalk, when for the first time in a decade such plantings will succeed."

"The Regent still owes fifteen hundred golds to the Exchange," notes Veria.

"Those were not her debts, yet she has paid five hundred and pledged to pay the remainder. She has kept every promise she has made—for good or for evil." Ulgar smiles blandly. "Is there another leader in Liedwahr who can claim that?" He turns to the Matriarch and raises his cup. "Saving you, of course, dear."

"The Exchange will not be a problem, Ulgar, not for the spring planting," answers the Matriarch. "I have suggested that the Exchange be willing to grant such credit to the lords of Defalk for seed grain and planting necessities if the Regent of Defalk reaffirms her commitment to repay the loan. She has already sent a message doing so, along with a second payment of five hundred golds."

"You knew that, and didn't tell them?" asks Veria.

"I told the Exchange-mistresses no lies. I never tell lies. The harmonies do not permit that." The Matriarch takes another sip of tea, then nods at Ulgar. "I don't believe you ever finished explaining about Defalk, dear."

"Oh . . . well . . . it's simple enough. All of the lands that ring Defalk fear the sorceress-regent, but those lords and advisors around her believe that, because wars were slow in coming in the past, they will be as slow in the seasons ahead. Yet Konsstin has already dispatched fifty-score lancers to Neserea."

"The harmonies yet favor her." The Matriarch smiles, still cherubic. "That the Exchange-mistresses do not understand." The smile vanishes, and her eyes fix on Veria. "Nor do the SouthWomen."

"The SouthWomen?" asks Veria. "What have they to do with this?"

"Everything," answers the Matriarch. "They would have us re-create the Guardians of the South once more in Encora, and thus mimic our enemies. They would have us retreat from financing the trade of those who are not our friends, and thus starve those who are." She shakes her head. "I have said it before, and I will again, and some will not heed. Matters balance; they always do."

Ulgar slurps his tea, and Veria winces.

The Matriarch smiles half fondly at the silver-haired man. As her eyes go to her daughter, the smile turns cherubically perfunctory. She rises from the table. "I must go and reassure those who doubt the force of the harmonies."

"Matriarch," asks Veria carefully, "do you believe that the sorceress-regent will not turn on Ranuak?"

The Matriarch pauses by the door. "Anything can happen under the harmonies, but the Regent of Defalk uses all the harmonies, and distrusting the good will of one in accord with the greatest of the harmonies of Erde can create vast dissonance. I would not will it that Ranuak be on the side of dissonance. Nor should you."

With another smile, the Matriarch nods her head to her consort and to her daughter. Veria turns and watches her mother depart, again readjusting the loose-fitting powder-blue robe.

Behind Veria's back, Ulgar shrugs, then shakes his head.

8

Anna eased herself onto the stool in front of the group gathered in the main hall of the liedburg, the makeshift schoolroom. Her eyes flickered to the door where Jecks and Blaz stood. Jecks was trying to hide a frown.

"Because there have been too many questions, I'm going to tell you all something about sorcery." Anna forced a smile, her eyes surveying the fosterlings and pages.

The silence was the most absolute she'd heard in the entire time she'd observed lessons for them.

"Some of this, you may have heard, but not everyone here knows all of this." That was a safe bet, because she doubted even Brill had known some of what she was about to say. "There are two kinds of sorcery here on Erde. One is Clearsong; the other is Darksong."

"Like the moons . . ." Lysara murmured, nodding at Anna.

"Like the moons," Anna agreed with Lord Birfel's daughter, recalling Erde's two moons—the baleful red point-disc of Darksong and the small white orb that was Clearsong. "Clearsong is what a sorceress uses to deal with things that are not alive and have never been alive. Stones, metal, bricks, if there's not too much straw in them, glass . . ." She struggled for examples.

"What about wood?" asked Jimbob.

"Wood comes from trees, and they were once alive. That takes Darksong." Anna took a deep breath. She was still too weak, but she had to do *something* besides eat and lie in bed or sit behind her table in the receiving room.

"Darksong is used for living things or things that were once alive—like wood or bone. Darksong also takes more skill in singing the spells, and more energy. If you do too much of it, a Darksong spell can kill you." She paused. "So can a Clearsong spell, but it takes a bigger spell."

Anna paused, breathing harder than she would have liked. The room remained silent.

"What is a spell?" she asked. "It is the combination of music, sung words that match the music, and the meaning of the words themselves. They all have to match. You can speak the words of a spell to music, and nothing will happen. You can sing the words of a spell—and unless you are very, very good, nothing will happen. And if it does, without music, it will take most of your energy—and, if you survive it, at least until you're as experienced as I am, you'll feel like someone's lancers ran their mounts over you."

She could see the doubt on a few faces, especially those of Lysara, Cataryzna, and Skent—the ones who'd heard her use spells without accompaniment. "Yes, I have cast spells without anything but my voice." She shook her head. "Do any of you know what sort of training I've had?"

The blank looks—just like the students in her music appreciation classes at Ames—confirmed the ignorance.

"My oldest daughter, were she alive, would have children almost as old as Secca. I've worked on my voice for over thirty years, and most of the time that's meant two to three glasses of solid singing every day, and another three to four glasses studying the music and . . . the spells that accompany it." She shrugged. "You can believe it or not. That's what it took Lord Brill, and that's what it took the Evult. That's what it will take you if you want to be serious about it. If you have a voice and talent."

She cleared her throat.

"There are also rules for sorcery. First, no sorceress, or sorcerer, can cast spells that directly affect her. I can't change my appearance or make myself older or younger, or less tired, or heal my own wounds. I think some of you have seen that. Second, the stronger and better the supporting players, the more effective the spell. Third, sorcery does not create things from thin air. It rearranges what is already in this world. When I used sorcery to make a gown when I first came to Falcor, the spell transformed old cloth into new cloth. When I made the bridge the other day, the stones came from the riverbed. You can see that there is a gorge there that wasn't there. Finally, sorcery is limited by the strength and talent of the sorcerer and sorceress."

Anna felt lightheaded, and knew she should stop. Besides, they all had that dazed expression—like children who had discovered there was no Easter bunny . . . or something.

"Magic, like everything else in this world, takes a lot of skill, a lot of raw talent, a lot of training, and you can only do so much. You all need to think about what I've said." She slipped off the stool and walked slowly past the table to the door in the silence.

Jecks offered his arm, his brows knit in concern.

She took it.

Outside the main hall, once the door had closed behind them, he whispered, "You're not strong enough for this yet."

"They need to know I can't work miracles all the time. Better I tell them than they find out and feel I've deceived them."

"Some will feel that way now."

"They may," she agreed. "And they can leave, and we won't waste any more effort on them." She wanted to scream, but she was too damned tired. Why was everything a double standard? Why was it that people could understand that an armsman could only fight so long, and that he couldn't defeat an entire army single-handedly, but they thought that a sorceress who couldn't sing spells endlessly was weak?

9

STROMWER, DEFALK

Your son and heir, my lord." The dark-haired woman bows deeply, almost prostrating herself on the rich maroon of the time-worn carpet in the private study.

"What bargain did you make with the bitch?" The gangly Lord Dencer, pushing a lock of brown-and-gray hair off his forehead, surveys the woman and the infant she carries, but makes no move toward her.

"I said nothing, and I agreed to nothing, my lord." She straightens, and her son clutches at her shoulder. "I had hoped you would be pleased to see us. We rode as fast as we could."

"So . . . Wendella, my consort, what message do you bring?" Dencer's words are hard, bitter. He puts both hands on the wood of the desk and leans forward, looking improbably like a long-legged heron about to spear a marsh frog. "For you must bring message or bargain."

"I was sent with no messages and no bargains."

"The bitch knows I do not favor her, and she is far brighter than either Barjim or Behlem. She would not have released you without gaining something. Something!" Dencer bobs his head. "What are you hiding?"

Wendella's eyes meet Dencer's. "My lord, the bitch sorceress . . . she sent no message to Stromwer. Yet she delivered one to me in bidding me leave. While it was to me, you should hear it."

"To you?"

Wendella shivers, but clears her throat, and shifts the infant higher on her shoulder, absently patting his back. "When she dismissed me, the bitch said that you had continued to court both the Matriarchy and Lord Ehara of Dumar. Then she said, and I remember this most clearly, 'I don't have time for games and intrigues. And I have even less for the people who attempt them.' " Wendella shook her head. "My lord, you are lord, and you must handle your lands and your affairs as you see fit. But I see great danger in opposing this sorceress without great power behind your cause." The brown-haired woman paused, then added, "I fear that power great enough to break the bitch sorceress will be great enough to destroy us."

"That was your bargain . . . to seek my loyalty to her! You would bind me! No harmony in you, Wendella. Was that why your brother, the honorable Mietchel, was so agreeable to letting you become my consort?"

"I pled, and I groveled, my lord. I told her that your son had not seen you in half a year . . . that I had not seen you in that long."

"And out of kindness, she just released you? I find that as improbable as a spade on a sow."

Wendella flushes.

"As impossible as a beard upon you. Yet you would shave me for your release from Falcor." Dencer straight-

ens, and his eyes glitter. He steps forward, and his hand
lifts.

"Is it wrong to tell you what I saw, my lord? Is it
wrong to tell you that she is most powerful?" Wendella
watches Dencer's eyes, not the hand that strikes her cheek.

"Do not tell me how powerful she is! You do not deceive me, Wendella. Your tongue slithers like that of a
snake. Your words are smeared in filth. You have betrayed me. You have betrayed Stromwer and Morra." His
hand falls, and he looks at it. "I feel unclean."

The dark-haired woman, a welt the shape of an open
hand rising on her cheek, continues to watch Lord Dencer.
She mechanically pats the child who has begun to sob.
"I did not make you unclean. I hate and despise the bitch
regent. I offered you truth, my lord, and you have struck
me for that. I can do nothing. You are lord. Yet I fear for
us both should you oppose the sorceress-regent."

Dencer lifts his hand, then lowers it. "You should fear
me, Wendella. I am lord in Stromwer, and I will be lord."
His voice hisses, and his eyes glitter more darkly.

"You are lord," Wendella acknowledges, but she does
not turn her eyes or her head.

"You will have new quarters, my lady." Dencer lifts
the brass bell, and it clangs off-tone. "Then we will see.
Indeed, we will see."

10

In the dim early-morning light of midwinter, Anna studied her face in the washroom mirror. The hair remained
blonde with a trace of curl, the nose still fine and straight.
No lines or bags circled her eyes, even without makeup,

not that she had any left except half a tube of lip gloss. The chin and neck lines were firm.

The cheeks were another question, deep and sunken, as though she were starving. Her eyes seemed sunken as well, and there was a darkness behind the blue. Was that the darkness of having seen and experienced too much?

The regent and sorceress washed and dressed in the green shirt, overtunic, and trousers that she'd adopted as her official working uniform. In hotter weather, though, the tunic went. Gowns and dresses were for rare formal dinners and state occasions not requiring riding.

A last look in the mirror confirmed that she had to eat more, and that she should refrain from spells as much as possible for a time, except one to get clean water. She just couldn't bear the thought of drinking more vinegar.

With a deep breath, she finally headed out the door, trying to ignore the black rectangle on the stone wall that reminded her too painfully of her last attempt to look across to earth—the mist world—to see her daughter Elizabetta. Before coming to Erde and becoming a sorceress she never would have dreamed that a mirror could explode. Or that her grief over her older daughter's death would have left her open to sorcerous transport to Erde.

The fire-etched stone also reminded her of the need to create or have built a reflecting pool. She couldn't keep destroying mirrors.

Blaz and another guard—Lejun, if she recalled correctly—followed her along the corridor and down the stairs to the receiving room.

"Good morning, Skent, Resor."

"Good morning, Lady Anna." Both pages bowed, and Resor opened the door for Anna.

Dythya stood to the left of the doorway, across from the pages, waiting for Anna.

"Come on in, Dythya." Anna nodded toward the doorway, then led the way into the room, still cold despite the low fire in the hearth.

The Regent cleared her throat, wondering whether to

crack the window to dispel some of the smoke, or to leave it closed and hope the chimney's draw would improve as the receiving room warmed.

Dythya stood, waiting.

Anna looked at the platter on the worktable, with a sliced and already browning apple, hard white and yellow cheese, rock-hard imitations of crackers, and, thankfully, a small loaf of dark bread fresh enough that it still steamed in the chill air. Then she turned to Dythya. "Where do we stand?"

Dythya extended a sheet of brown paper. "This is the reckoning you requested, lady. The top part shows the coin on hand, the recent receipts, and the liedgeld owed. The bottom shows what we have spent since the harvest, what we have received, and what I would guess we will have to spend before the next harvest."

Anna gestured to the seat across from hers. "Please sit while I study this." In turn, she seated herself, and took one of the apple slices and chewed it, then reached for another.

Almost absently, she coughed, trying to get her throat clear, before singing the water spell to ensure the water in the pitcher was pure. Clean water was scarce anywhere in Defalk, as she supposed it was in any medieval-type culture. Even before she finished, she felt dizzy.

Damn! Damn! Damn! One lousy water spell, and she was reeling. Anna forced herself to set down the paper and eat several mouthfuls of the hot bread, and two slices of cheese. After filling her goblet, she followed the cheese with a swallow of water, and then more of the apple slices, and more bread.

Finally, as the worst of the dizziness began to subside, Anna checked the liedgeld owed. Arkad of Cheor hadn't paid. Neither had Gylaron of Lerona. Dencer had paid half. So had Lord Sargol, after sending a complaining scroll. Lord Vlassa of Fussen had died, and his twin sons were still sorting it out, probably with blades, and liedgeld was doubtless low on their priorities. Four other lords had various reasons for not paying.

Then she laughed, ironically. The holding of Mencha had not paid. As the Sorceress and Lady of Loiseau and as Brill's successor, she owed herself, as Regent, liedgeld, and she probably couldn't raise it, although at two hundred golds, it was less than half of what almost all the others owed.

"My lady?"

"Dythya . . . I owe myself liedgeld, and I doubt I can raise it. I've let some of those who wished to remain continue to live there, but there's not even anyone there now to run the lands."

"You owe liedgeld?"

"I ended up as the Lady of Loiseau and holder of Mencha."

Dythya's mouth went into an O. "I am sorry. I should not have put that on the list."

Anna shook her head. "I'm not angry. It's another problem. I probably needed to look into that as well." *Along with everything else. Who can I get to manage the place? Surely a good manager could raise enough for the liedgeld and even some coins for my personal use.*

Who could she have manage Loiseau? What had happened to Gero, Brill's personal assistant? Or Serna and her daughter Florenda? Anna remembered how good Serna's breads had been. Quies, the stablemaster who had thought Farinelli would be a good mount for her—he and his son Albero, who'd taught her the basics of using a knife—they'd been among those who had petitioned her to allow them to return to Loiseau. But some of the others, she'd scarcely thought of, and they were people, too.

She forced her mind to the paper before her. "Have the golds for the Ranuan Exchange left?"

"Three days ago, lady. Even with good roads, it would be another five days to Ranwa, and two on the river. With the ways as they are . . ." The accountant shrugged.

"A month?"

Dythya looked puzzled, and Anna corrected herself. "Two weeks? Or four?" From what Anna could figure, months didn't exist on Erde, just seasons, each twelve weeks long. That made the Erdean year shorter by a month than the year on earth, she figured, since she couldn't tell any real difference in the length of the day. With twenty glasses in a day, a glass was longer than an hour, but how much longer? Who knew?

"It is possible."

"We've done what we can. Now, we need to send a scroll to Lord Birfels, telling him that we have taken steps to ensure that he can obtain seed grain. If he has any more trouble, he should let me know as soon as possible."

"I can have that scroll for you to seal this afternoon, lady."

"Good. I take it you feel that it's important."

Dythya nodded.

"So do I." *Especially since Birfels and Geansor are the only ones I even halfway trust in the south of Defalk.* "And we probably ought to send one to Lord Geansor as well. Is there any other lord who might have that sort of concern? Oh, Lord Hryding," she answered her own question before Dythya could speak. "Sorry."

"Perhaps Lord Sargol of Suhl," suggested Dythya. "There are rumors."

"Can you do that?"

"It will be done, lady." Dythya rose as Anna did.

Once the accountant or bursar or whatever Dythya was—minister of finance?—once she left, Anna turned to the now cooler bread and cheese, forcing herself to eat more than her stomach said it wanted by concentrating on how thin and almost anorexic she'd appeared in the mirror, and how dizzy the simplest spell had left her. By the time she finished the apple slices and four more chunks of cheese, each mouthful was an effort, each swallow leaving her feeling as though she would gag.

"Arms Commander Hanfor and Lord Jecks are here."

Her mouth full, Anna motioned Resor to send the two

in. She stood and swallowed, grateful to put off eating for a few moments more.

"Lady Anna."

"Lady Anna," Jecks said a moment behind Hanfor.

"Please be seated." She gestured and sat without waiting, knowing both men would stand until she took her seat at the table. She looked at Hanfor. "I never did ask you about the Sand Pass fort."

The graying arms commander smiled. "The Ebrans repaired most of the outer walls before they left. Lady Gatrune's levies included some masons . . ."

Anna nodded, recalling the big woman who had been the first landholder, as administrator for her late husband, to recognize Anna's regency.

". . . and Alvar managed to get the rest of the rents in the outer walls patched, and one more quarters' block usable. The Ebrans had restored two. The walls won't hold off more than brigands. . . ."

"But that's an improvement, and we won't have to worry about an attack from there for at least another year."

"Perhaps next fall, Alvar could finish the job," Hanfor said.

"Do you think we should put a small force there?" Anna asked, looking from Hanfor to Jecks.

"We do not have many armsmen here in Falcor," pointed out the white-haired lord.

"I wasn't thinking about the best armsmen," the sorceress said. "Just a few to keep an eye out, and to show that the regent cares about the area."

Jecks and Hanfor exchanged glances.

Then Hanfor nodded. "A squad with a graybeard who has seen enough, perhaps." He paused. "They will need some silvers for supplies."

"Figure out how many and talk to Dythya." Anna didn't shake her head. Everything she thought about cost silvers, but an abandoned outpost on the eastern border wouldn't help impressions at all, not even if Ebra were still prostrate. "Have we heard about those blades in Encora?"

"Not yet, lady. I would not expect a reply for another week at the earliest." Hanfor inclined his head slightly.

Jecks nodded.

"I've been thinking about roads," Anna ventured.

"You have mentioned them." A glint entered the arms commander's eyes.

"After my recent . . . experience with the bridge," Anna spread her hands, "I have been cautioned to be somewhat more . . . careful."

"Far more careful," suggested Jecks mildly.

"I would like your thoughts on something. If we could get large piles of rocks beside the roads, that would make my sorcery much easier. Is there a way to encourage that on the part of the holders and lords?"

Jecks fingered his chin. "I would gladly do that on the roads to market."

"But some of the market roads go through swamps and rivers," Hanfor pointed out. "The roads we need for armsmen and lancers should follow the ridges where possible."

"The high roads," Jecks added. "But the holders will not wish to have their tenants and freeholders work on roads that offer them no benefit, nor will the farmers—"

Anna held up her hand. "Even I can't rebuild a fraction of the roads in Defalk, not in years. Three sorcerers couldn't."

"I did mention that, lady," Jecks said.

Even if he were as handsome as any movie star, Anna wanted to clout him for the condescending tone, but she smiled perfunctorily instead. "Which roads are most important—and which sections of those roads? I'm talking about fords or places that turn into swamps or where we've lost bridges?" She gestured vaguely, wishing she could articulate what she meant more clearly, but she'd been a singer and an opera professor, not a sorceress or an engineer. She needed a Regency engineer, a Regency weapons smith, a Regency schoolmaster and tutor, not to mention an agronomist, along with a chief of players. That didn't count the expertise she needed and didn't know she needed.

"The bridge at Elhi . . ." began Jecks.

"The ford at Sorprat or the road to Denguic—"

"Gentlemen," Anna said with a laugh. "Gentlemen. I think you need to get together with Tirsik and with Himar and Alvar and Lady Essan and Dythya. Then bring me a list, with the most important part of the most important road at the top."

"The lady Essan?" asked Hanfor.

"She was Lord Donjim's consort, and she rode with him on many of his early campaigns. She will know the roads as well as anyone, and she will know which roads used to be important and why they are not." *She's also likely to be far less biased.* The problem was that Hanfor was relatively unbiased, but didn't know Defalk well enough, and Jecks knew Defalk, but would still lean toward benefiting Elhi. She wanted to shake her head. Instead, she smiled once more. "Surely, you can get together and figure that out for me?" She looked at Jecks. "You did say I should be cautious. Would you also think about how we can persuade the lords and others to carry rocks to places beside the important roads?"

Jecks returned the smile, a glint between amusement and anger in his hazel eyes. "Yes, Lady Anna. We should be able to provide such a list."

Anna stood. "Thank you both."

For a moment after the two men had left, Anna looked at the platter and the remaining crackers and cheese. She *couldn't* eat any more, not for a while.

Instead, she took out the grease marker and a sheet of the coarse brown paper. What should a road look like? *If* she recalled correctly from that long-ago ancient history course, the Romans had built their roads on yard-deep stone-and-gravel bases, and surfaced them with long smooth paving blocks nearly a foot thick.

She began to sketch.

How wide? Enough for two wagons abreast? But could she physically sustain that much sorcery?

"You'd better limit it to key bridges and marshes or things like that," she murmured. Defalk wouldn't have the resources to build good roads for a decade without sorcery, but the country might not last a decade without a better internal transport system. She sighed, and set aside the sketches, then lifted the spellsong folder that had come from Brill's workroom in Loiseau. She began to read. Perhaps there was something in his spells that would help. Perhaps.

"The player Liende," announced the dark-haired Skent, sometime later, peering around the door as if afraid that Anna would snap at him.

Anna gestured for Skent to have the player come in.

"You summoned me." Liende bowed as she entered the receiving room.

"I did." Anna gestured to the seat across the worktable from her. "Please be seated."

The player sat on the front edge of the wooden chair, stiffly, as though she had been summoned for her own execution. Anna decided to plunge right in, since no amount of reassurance without substance was likely to relax the horn player.

"Liende . . . although it was not my intent, I stole from you what you wished for most." Anna forced her eyes to meet those of the gray-and-red-haired player. "What Lord Brill had intended for you, I received. When he was dying, I went to his side, and he thought I was you. And he made me young with his death-song."

"I know." The words were scarcely a murmur.

"I did not ask for that, and I tried to call you, but you were hurt . . . and then it was too late. For that, I am sorry. You have every right to be angry with me."

The silence was broken only by the sound of rain against the window and shutters at the back of the receiving room. Anna waited, her eyes on the horn player.

"At first." Liende paused and swallowed. "At first, I was angry. I was most angry, and I watched, and I would hear nothing good of you—"

"You don't have to—"

"Hear me, Lady Anna. Let an old woman have her pride."

Anna swallowed. Liende couldn't have been over forty, and she thought she was old? Then, on Erde, forty was old.

"I would hear nothing good of you. But Lord Jecks almost wept when he described how you stood alone against the Ebrans. And he said how you dealt fairly with him and how you stood against the Ebrans alone a second time. And you restored Jimbob's heritage to him. But still, I avoided you. You came to Elhi, and I thought you were cold and aloof. Then they carried you back, and you wept in your sleep, and a healer walked twenty deks to try to help, and grown men sobbed as though they might lose their consort or their mother." Liende swallowed.

Anna waited, wondering, wondering how the woman could forgive her.

"Lord Jecks sent a scroll. It was the bridge, Lady Anna. No one who cared not for Defalk or Falcor would spend herself on replacing a bridge. You gained nothing from that. I was ashamed." Liende's eyes were damp. "I am here. Do not shame me further."

Anna's throat was thick, and she had to swallow again. "I won't shame you. I never thought of that. I was the one who was ashamed and guilty because you had stood by Lord Brill, asking nothing. You only hoped, and I was the one who dashed those hopes." So often, Anna thought, so often had others dashed her hopes, and she hated being the one who had dashed another's dreams.

"Life does not happen as we hope," Liende said slowly, "and you did not ask for what you received. Nor did I." She smiled wryly. "Thank the harmonies. For without you, all of us would have been lost, and like as not, I would have been used by every Ebran armsman, then tossed aside, if I had even endured. Far better I live, in hope and well-fed, than to have been young for a few days and perished in rape and slaughter."

Anna wanted to protest, but something stopped her. Could she really have done what she did without the strength of her second youth?

"Even now, you doubt, lady?"

"I've come to doubt a lot," the sorceress finally said. "There's not much in life that's as simple as we think."

After a nod, Liende asked simply, "What did you wish of me?"

"I have no right to ask," Anna said, "but I need your help. I cannot save Defalk without it."

"My help? What have I that is so precious that the greatest sorceress on Erde must beg?"

Anna wanted to smile at the involuntary bitterness that Liende still harbored, wanted to hug the woman for being human. Instead, she answered. "Your skill as a player, your knowledge of players. I'd like you to become the leader and teacher of the Regent's Players. You will be honored and safe. I can't risk losing you or your knowledge."

"I play a good woodwind horn. I am not a leader of players." The brown eyes met Anna's.

"You could be."

"A woman lead player?" Liende's eyebrows arched.

"A woman regent?" Anna asked softly in return.

Liende smiled faintly.

"It is not just a favor," Anna added. "I will pay you for finding and organizing the Regent's Players."

"Coin . . . and kindness. Neither can I afford to turn down, lady."

"Two silvers a week to start. Three a week, and two golds bonus, if you can gather enough players for two groups." Anna paused. "And you don't play for battles. What I had in mind is several groups of players, if we can find or train enough. A group that will learn and perform the songs for building, another group for battle songs, perhaps a third for other functions.''

"I know much about building songs,'' Liende said. "Could I not lead such a group?''

"As long as you're not close to battles.''

"Lady . . . the others would think ill—''

"It's not kindness, or favoritism.'' Anna shook her head. "I made a mistake with Daffyd, a terrible mistake. I should not have brought him with me to the battle with the Evult. I can teach singing, in time. I cannot teach players. I cannot make instruments. If anything happens to my lutar . . . who would replace it?''

Liende smiled. "A strange sorceress you are. You hazard yourself, but would save others less valuable. Yet . . . I will not protest. While Kinor is near grown, Alseta is but twelve and young for her years.''

"I did not know. They are welcome here, and you will have quarters large enough. Alseta and Kinor could join those being schooled.''

"To me, lady, that be worth as much as the coins.''

"Then you accept?''

"How could I refuse?'' Liende smiled. "Palian will join me, and I trust Kaseth will. Jaegel will not. He could not play under a woman.'' She shrugged. "You will see. I be no bargain.''

"I can help you with conducting,'' Anna said. "I already have many of the songs, both my own and some from Lord Brill. I can guide you, but I can't be a sorceress and a lead player at the same time.''

"You have led players before?''

"I've studied leading players, and I have led large groups of singers,'' Anna admitted. Her conducting classes were far behind her, but she doubted many in Liedwahr had had even that much training. She paused. "Can you read Lord Brill's notations?''

"No. He kept those to himself. Most sorcerers do, I understand.''

Anna understood, but it was just something else to

make her plans—and life—a little harder. "Oh . . ." She shook her head. "There's one violino player I've found. He's barely adequate, but we don't seem to have much choice. His name is Delvor."

"I do not know of him, but I will hear him."

Anna reached for her belt wallet and extended a gold. "This is to help get you and your family here. Dythya is the accounts mistress, and she'll pay you and your players."

"Dythya I know."

Of course, Anna thought. After the battle of the Sand Pass, Liende had found refuge at Elhi, Lord Jecks' holding.

Anna took out the quill pen, and carefully, most carefully, wrote out a short note to Dythya, explaining Liende's commission, and pay, and that she would need two to three rooms in the players' quarters.

Both the ink and the brown paper ensured that the note would take time to dry. While it did, Anna pointed to the paper and added, "This note—please give it to Dythya— it explains that you are the chief player and requests that she give you all possible assistance." Anna paused. "How soon can you start?"

"Why . . . now, lady. Alseta and Kinor can travel here as they can from Elhi. Lord Jecks often sends a few armsmen and messengers."

Anna nodded. "Then get settled, and talk to Delvor and check his playing. Later this afternoon"—Anna fumbled as she tried to convert hours to local time—"around the eighth glass, please come back with your horn, and we'll go over several of the spellsongs we'll be using. One or two you may know, but I want you to be familiar with the main ones." Anna took a sip from the goblet, then continued. "Can you send for Palian and any others? If you need a scribe, see if Dythya can help."

Liende bowed her head slightly. "You do not lag, my lady."

"We'd better not." Anna said. "We have to be ready."
Exactly what she was readying Defalk for, was another
question, but her intuition told her that it was necessary,
and whenever she'd doubted that intuition, she'd found
trouble and more trouble.

Anna waved the short note a last time in the air, and
seeing that the ink had finally dried, stood and extended
the paper to Liende. "Until the eighth glass."

"Thank you, Lady Anna."

Anna paused, then said, "Liende. I am not being short
with you. I am not displeased. I am gratified that you are
here. I am asking you to pardon me if I seem short, or if
I do not spend more time being courteous and gracious.
In time, I hope I will not feel so rushed. Now there is
much to do, and I know so little." *And I'm still tired,
damned tired.*

A smile played across the thin lips of the player. "Most
rulers would not explain, but I thank you. Alseta will also
be grateful." She bowed again, then slipped out.

Anna still felt embarrassed by the situation, but what
else could she do?

She had yet to deal with a reflecting pool—and where
to put it. The small room across the corridor? No one had
been living there since the Neserean forces had left, and
it was probably better not to guest strangers too close to
her quarters.

Still, that would have to wait, since it would take sorcery, and she dared not try anything significant for a few
days yet.

Why was everything so fucking difficult? She'd replaced one lousy bridge, and she'd been a basket case for
over a week. Why? Why had the bridge been so hard?
Had it been because she'd done Darksong with Wendella
just before?

Anna just sat at the worktable, slowly chewing through
a hard cracker, knowing she was stalling, almost not car-

ing. She finished the cracker, then looked at the papers on the corner of the table.

Her nails clicked together, and she looked down, surprised that her old nervous habit had resurfaced. Were things getting that bad?

11

DUMARIA, DUMAR

The broad-shouldered man in the gold-trimmed red tunic lifts the dagger, momentarily balancing it on his forefinger. "It's not right," he murmurs to himself before half turning to the window and the gray downpour outside. "A gold, and it's not balanced right."

The man in the gray cloak waits on the hard wooden chair.

The red-clad man leaves the window and sets the knife on the dark wooden writing table, beside the flickering oil lamp. He picks up the scroll once more and studies the words before setting it on the desk and letting it rewind itself. "And why will your master not come himself, the honorable soul that he is?"

"The bitch sorceress knows his likeness, Lord Ehara." The man in gray shifts his weight on the hard chair.

"—and she holds his consort and heir. I know. Too bad that he cannot put his consort aside and take another. Heirs are easy enough to come by. The harmonies know, I've got enough of them." Ehara's bass laugh booms off the walls of the small study. "Your master writes that the lords in the south of Defalk would willingly swear to me. Yet he does not say why this should be so. Perhaps you could explain that, Master Slevn." Ehara's voice drops into an almost silky bass as dark as his beard and hair.

"Not a one of the southern lords of Defalk have much

love of the bitch, save perhaps Geansor, and he's a cripple who can't live forever.''

"I had heard Birfels supported her.''

"For lack of a better alternative, Lord Ehara. He has removed his older son from Falcor, you may have heard. His younger remains in Abenfel. Only his daughter is hostage to the sorceress.''

"You say that Birfels is hostile to the sorceress. Why, pray tell, if he did remove his sons, would he leave his daughter?'' Ehara again turns his back to Slevn.

"She must find a consort, I would imagine,'' Slevn says slowly. "None of Birfels' neighboring lords have sons of an age. I do know that Birfels told the sorceress that he had no love of the sorceress's efforts to educate the daughters of lords at Falcor. Nor of allowing the widowed ladies to hold their dead lords' lands. I understand you have no love of such thoughts, either.''

"What of Lord Gylaron?'' asks Ehara abruptly.

"Gylaron has been brooked too often by Lord Geansor, and by those in Falcor who side with the cripple in order to keep the south weak and divided.'' A faint sheen of perspiration coats Slevn's forehead.

"Oh . . . so your lord would be the overlord of the south under me, relying on my armsmen and their blades and blood? Why did he not write me such a proposal?''

"He did not say such, my lord Ehara.''

"Yet he thinks such, or you would not have voiced it.'' Ehara laughs again. "Tell your master that I ask much of my overlords. More, I wager, than he would dream or wish.'' Another laugh follows. "What of Lord Arkad? His lands are the key to the south of Defalk.''

"Lord Arkad is ailing. His seneschal runs his lands. They are rich lands, perhaps the richest in Defalk.'' Slevn blots his forehead with the back of his hand when Ehara half turns toward the window and the continuing rain. "And he has no heirs, not ones close enough to worry about.''

"Your master would tempt me, then? Ha! Defalk once

was rich, and may be again. Now it is but a ruin of a land, governed by a madwoman for an underage boy and lords who do not know that the world must change.'' Ehara touches his black beard, and the blue eyes flash for a moment, although his voice drops into an even tone as he finishes. ''It must change before the ships of Sturinn flood our coasts. One way or another, we cannot ignore the Maitre of Sturinn.''

''Now is the time to take Defalk, then, and you can reap the riches of its rebirth,'' suggested Slevn.

''Poetry now? Riches of its rebirth? Your master is known for his turn of phrase. Did he suggest you use that phrase?''

''No, Lord Ehara.''

''You coined it? Then, coin no more phrases in the hearing of Lord Dencer. He might not take it well.'' Ehara glances from the table to Slevn. ''I must think about what you have suggested. Tell your lord I am strongly considering his proposal and I will inform him shortly after your return to Stromwer. You may go.'' The lord pauses. ''Who knows of this?''

''Only my lord and you, sire.''

''That is for the best.'' Ehara nods, then extends his hand, which bears both a golden coin and a small sealed scroll. ''These may speed your passage.''

''Thank you, Lord Ehara.''

Ehara waits until Slevn has left the study before he beckons to the officer waiting outside.

When the door shuts again, the Lord of Dumar turns to the lancer in the red uniform of Dumar. ''The man in gray will be set upon by brigands or thieves when he reaches the Sudbergs—or if he talks to anyone who seems of import. Then the thieves will slay them both. Is that clear?''

''Yes, sire.''

''Good.''

The red-clad lancer departs, and Lord Ehara beholds the rain and clouds once more.

12

Anna pushed away the plate that contained but one scrap of meat and a crust of bread. She felt totally gorged, and yet she knew she'd be ravenous in another few hours—another few glasses, she mentally corrected herself, still trying to adjust to Erdean terms. Glasses instead of hours, deks instead of miles, except a dek was much closer to a kilometer.

Across the cleared space of the receiving-room worktable, Jecks took a sip of wine from his goblet, then spoke. "Were I to eat half what you do, Lady Anna, in a few weeks they could stuff me and serve me to all Elhi, and there would be leavings for the dogs."

Hanfor, seated beside Jecks, finished a last scrap of cheese, and nodded in agreement with the older man.

"If I ate half what I'm eating, I'd die of starvation in two weeks," Anna said dryly.

"I know. Your cheeks are still too thin."

"I'm still paying for rebuilding that bridge, but it's a good thing I did. The Fal is rising. No one would be able to ford it now, and probably not for the rest of the year, if ever."

Jecks looked to the window and the gray clouds outside, then back to the table. His eyes did not quite meet hers when he spoke. "Lady Anna, much as you wish to help all, you cannot. You did rebuild the bridge, and it has taken half a season for you to recover. As you told the fosterlings, not even the most powerful sorceress in Liedwahr can do everything that needs to be done. Not even you can do all that needs must be done in Defalk or even in Falcor itself."

Then who will? Anna wanted to ask, even as she answered, ''That's the problem.''

''All rulers have that difficulty, lady.'' Jecks laughed, a short but warm sound. ''That is why I grow increasingly glad that I am not a regent or a ruler.''

''Careful, I might just resign in your favor. After all, you are the grandsire of the heir.''

''No one would let you. They trust you more than they do me. They will let you kill yourself on their thoughtless behalf, but that is another kind of sheep.''

That's always the way people treat the willing horse . . . or regent—flog her to death with overwork.

''We're nearing spring, and I'm even more worried about the liedgeld, and especially about this lord Arkad.'' Anna decided to change the subject slightly. ''All the others have either made an effort or faced extraordinary difficulties.'' She laughed. ''The difficulties may or may not be real, but a prudent ruler should move cautiously in those cases, I think.'' She turned to the handsome Jecks. ''What do you think?''

''I doubt both Lord Arkad and Lord Gylaron of Lerona,'' Jecks said slowly, ''and Lord Dencer, as you know. The troubles of the others seem real enough, and all have made some effort except for Lord Vlassa's heirs.'' A wry smile crossed his face. ''A regent should avoid conflicts between heirs unless you mean to kill all but one.''

Anna winced. ''I'm not up for that.'' *Yet.* ''Gylaron's effectively Dencer's northern neighbor, isn't he? I don't care much for that. There seems to be a disproportionate number of southern lords who are reluctant to pay.''

''I had noted that before.''

''Arkad is the closest. Perhaps we should visit him.''

''You wish to remind him personally of his obligations?''

''None of my other reminders have worked, have they?''

Jecks shook his head.

"How many armsmen should I bring?" Her eyes went from Jecks to Hanfor and back again.

"As many as you can spare, I would say," answered Jecks. "I would have your spells and instrument ready as you ride toward his gate."

"I would that we had more archers," added Hanfor.

"You think Arkad is likely to rebel?"

"If he has not paid his liedgeld, he has already rebelled," said Jecks dryly. "Best you put an end to it quickly."

"Do you think the other lords will regard any action against Arkad as too high-handed? Or me as the madwoman of Defalk?" asked Anna.

"Better to be thought headstrong and high-handed than weak." Jecks touched his chin and the hazel eyes twinkled. "And those lords you worry about already say you are headstrong."

In Defalk, having an opinion meant a woman was headstrong.

Anna took a swallow from her goblet. "Another week, if the roads don't get worse?" She glanced to Hanfor.

The veteran nodded.

"Lady . . ." Jecks coughed.

Anna turned toward her local equivalent of a movie star.

"I might suggest that Jimbob be with us." Jecks covered his mouth and coughed.

"To give an impression of friendliness—or to convey that the Regency is acting on his behalf?"

"Both, and to give him a greater understanding of how frail a lord's loyalty can be."

"Is it wise to have us all together?"

Jecks laughed. "It matters not. If you fall, so do we all."

Hanfor nodded. "He must see things as they are, while he is still young enough."

Anna wanted to wince, even as she recognized the truth of the two men's observations, even as she wanted to protest that she was scarcely that important. Except, Lord knew how, she had become just that.

The door creaked ajar, and Cens peered inside. "Counselors Dythya and Menares, as you requested, Lady Anna."

"In a moment," Anna said. "I'll ring."

Cens nodded and closed the door.

"Dythya will never return to Elhi," Jecks said. "Not since you have made her a counselor."

"I needed someone to put Menares in his place, and I couldn't keep ordering him to work with her." Positions and prestige and titles were almost as bad in Defalk as they had been in academia, except in Defalk a lot more was at stake.

"And will you find someone to do that to me?" Jecks' tone was somewhere between idle and playful.

"I already have. When I need her, Lady Essan will do quite nicely."

"Ha! You are a dangerous woman."

Anna doubted that. In order to stay alive, she'd done what had been necessary, and as a result, got stuck doing a very large job that she didn't know nearly enough about. The one saving grace was that no one else alive knew the job, either. The bad part was that those who knew the job had died trying to do it.

The sorceress lifted the bell and rang, and the door opened. She waited until Menares and Dythya had seated themselves around the table.

"You sent word that we had gotten an answer from the Ranuan traders, the Exchange or whatever?"

"Yes, Lady Anna," answered Dythya, half rising from her seat and extending a scroll.

Anna took it. "What does it say?"

"They will extend credit to the southern lords for this crop year, and they hope that the debt can be resolved after harvest."

"That means we have to come up with another thousand golds by next year at this time."

Menares and Dythya nodded. Jecks frowned.

"Has there been any response to our scrolls and messages for artisans and smiths?"

That got two headshakes.

"It is early," Dythya said.

"Very early," Menares added. "Those who might seek another situation would not do so until the roads clear."

Always, it was the roads, the damned roads. Anna shrugged. "Can you two write some messages for my signature to Birfels and the other southern lords noting that I've made the necessary arrangements for them to obtain seed grain on credit?"

"Who might the others be?" asked Menares smoothly.

Anna wanted to grin and smack Menares simultaneously. The former counselor to the late and unlamented Lord Behlem still tended to ensure that Anna spelled out anything that might reflect unfavorably on him later—a great tendency for an academic or a bureaucrat, but not exactly what she wanted. Still . . . it made her think.

"Lord Geansor, out of courtesy, although he probably won't need it. Lord Dencer, Lord Sargol, and Lord Gylaron. Maybe, the other lord down there—Arien . . ."

"Tybel," supplied Dythya.

"Thank you. That should do it." Anna pursed her lips. "And in the scrolls to Sargol, Dencer, and Gylaron, add a few words about how this should help in ensuring that they pay the remainder of the liedgeld they owe."

Jecks smiled. Hanfor grinned.

"Is that all, Lady Anna?" asked Dythya.

"For now," Anna answered. "Thank you."

"By your leave?"

The sorceress and regent nodded.

After the two had left, Jecks spoke. "The reminder to the three lords will be helpful. You are telling them that you've done them a service and suggesting that they've failed in their obligations without quite directly saying so. You would not be disturbed if I sent out a few scrolls to some of those more friendly to the Regency, pointing this out along with some other news?''

''Heavens no.'' Anna wished she'd thought of that.

Hanfor shifted his weight in his chair, and Anna suppressed a smile. The senior armsman still wasn't much for meetings.

''I don't think that there's anything else right now.'' She rose with a bright smile. ''Thank you both.''

''My pleasure,'' said Jecks, warmly enough to have meant it.

''Thank you, lady,'' said Hanfor.

After they left, Anna shook her head. The sparks were there with Jecks, but the situation wasn't exactly wonderful. Not when he was the grandsire of the underage Lord of Defalk for whom she was regent. And, more important to her, there were so many differences between their backgrounds. He wasn't the chauvinist that most of the lords of Defalk were. He actually respected women of talent—or seemed to—but Defalk was still a macho culture.

Before long, once again, the door to the receiving room opened, and Barat gingerly eased his head around the heavy oak. ''There is a messenger with a scroll from Lord Hryding, Lady Anna. He insists he must deliver it personally.''

''I'll see him. Have Giellum and Blaz accompany him in.'' Much as she disliked it, there was no sense in taking unnecessary risks, even with a messenger from Hryding, who had supported her when she had been recovering from her first battle.

A dark-haired young man dressed in leathers and a pale green sash with an empty sheath at his belt entered the receiving room and bowed. ''A scroll from Lord Hryding, lady.''

Blaz and Giellum stood behind him, hands on blade hilts.

''Thank you.'' Anna struggled to remember his name. Why did she have so much trouble with names? She'd ridden all the way from Synope to Falcor with the young man, and the name, on the tip of her tongue, still escaped her.

"How has it gone with you since our ride?" she asked. "And the others?"

"Well enough, thank you, Lady Anna." The young armsman smiled. "Stepan is in charge of the levies, and Markan is over all the armsmen now that Gestatr has returned to Ebra."

"Returned to Ebra?" Anna puzzled through the names, then almost nodded. Fridric had to be the younger armsman before her. Stepan and Markan had been the two others who had escorted her to Falcor when she had pledged her support to the Prophet—before he had turned on her.

"His family served the Lord of Synek before the Dark Ones, and the youngest son has returned. Synek was Gestatr's home," Fridric explained.

"I see." Anna nodded and lifted the scroll slightly. "If you would wait, Fridric, while I read this?"

The young armsman nodded.

Anna broke the seal and began to read silently. "Regent Anna, Lady and Sorceress, and Protector of Defalk . . ."

Anna paused. She definitely didn't like messages that opened with flowery titles. They generally meant bad news of some sort, like memoranda from Dieshr had, with all the flowery praise at the beginning and lousy course assignments or forced moves from a desirable voice studio to a less desirable one.

It is with deep concern that I am writing you at the behest of my consort, the Lord Hryding. He has fallen gravely ill, and beseeches that, should he not recover, you will continue to honor his requests regarding Secca and the preservation of Flossbend and the lands of Synope. . . .

While we all pray and trust in my lord's return to health, in the interim, I am administering the holding in his interests, and request, in deepest ad-

miration, your support in this endeavor. Both Jeron
and I stand ready to do your bidding and that of our
lord.

The seal, on maroon wax, was that of Lord Hryding,
but the signature read, "Anientta, his consort and servant."

Anna let the scroll close and glanced to Fridric. Too
many things, far too many, were making a sense she
didn't like. Markan, while intelligent and honest, was still
young for a lord's senior armsman, and probably those
older had been among the ones who had perished at the
Sand Pass. Fridric had been sent because he knew Anna,
but also because he was loyal to Hryding. She hoped that
Stepan and Markan didn't meet with some form of "illness" or "accident." And Anna had never trusted or liked
Lord Hryding's consort, especially the way Anientta had
spoiled her sons while almost turning out poor Secca in
rags. That had been one reason why Anna had invited the
little redhead to Falcor as a fosterling, at an age far
younger than Anna herself thought generally advisable.

Anna lifted the bell and waited for a page. This time
the sandy-haired Barat peered into the receiving room.

"Barat, would you find the young lady Secca? I believe
she should be at lessons with Tirsik in the stable."

"You wish to see her now?"

"Yes."

Barat bowed and vanished.

"And how has the past year treated you, Fridric?"
Anna looked back to the young armsman.

"It has been quiet, Lady Anna. Most quiet until Lord
Hryding's illness."

"Do you have a consort?" Anna had an idea.

"Oh, no, lady. I am much too young for that."

"And what about Stepan and Markan?"

"They don't, either. Calmut does. He has not forgotten
you, lady." A smile played across Fridric's face.

"I imagine not." Anna had been forced to soak the

sour young armsman with buckets of cold water applied through sorcery in order to get access to Lord Hryding— and now it sounded like Hryding was dying. "What about young Jeron?" Anna watched Fridric's face closely.

"Jeron? He is Lord Hryding's heir."

The tightness of Fridric's face and words told Anna enough. The armsman didn't much care for Jeron.

"Young Secca has been here, you know," Anna added.

"She was a sweet child," Fridric said, his voice even, but without an edge. ·

"She has been sweet here, as well, and she seems very bright."

The door opened, and Barat peered in.

"Fridric? Would you wait outside for a moment?" asked Anna, before turning to Barat and standing. "After the armsmen leave, please have Secca come in."

Fridric nodded and bowed. "Of course, lady."

Anna waited as the armsman stepped out, followed by her guards, and, after a moment, the petite redhead stepped gingerly into the receiving room.

"You sent for me, Lady Anna. Have I displeased you?" Secca looked almost ready to cry, and Anna was reminded that the child was barely ten, and that Secca wouldn't have been at Falcor except for Lord Hryding's plea, and the debt Anna owed him for his early support.

"No, Secca, you haven't displeased me or anyone. You have been very good, and I've enjoyed your being here." Anna paused, wondering how she should break the news. "I've just received a scroll from your mother."

"I saw Fridric. He didn't come for me, did he?" The redhead went to her knees. "Please don't send me home, Lady Anna."

Anna stepped around the table. "You may stay at Falcor so long as you wish. At least while I'm regent," she added. "But that was not the message. Your father is sick. He's very sick."

For a moment, Secca stared at Anna, silently. After a

moment, the girl's eyes misted. Then tears welled up and oozed down her cheeks, and she began to shiver.

"I'm sorry." Anna stepped forward and hugged the child. "I'm sorry, Secca."

"Poor Papa . . . poor Papa . . ." Secca kept repeating the words.

"Poor Papa"? Does she suspect what I suspect? Of her mother? Anna managed to keep from shaking her head. After a time of holding the redhead, she finally asked, "Do you want to go home?"

Secca shivered more violently, shaking her head against Anna's shirt and sash. "Papa . . . he said I should stay with you. I should stay even if times are bad. Will you let me stay?"

Anna wanted to shiver herself, fearing that Secca had confirmed her suspicions of Anientta. Instead, she just hugged Secca again. "You can stay as long as you want." *At least while I'm regent . . . or Lady of Loiseau.* "As long as you want. . . ."

Anna finally sat down, drawing the still-sobbing child into her arms, wondering how she'd ended up with another little redhead.

After the scattering clouds and shifting light from the window had played across the wall for a time, Secca gave a last sob, a cough, and blotted her eyes.

"You really won't send me back to Flossbend?"

"You can stay here so long as you wish. If I'm no longer regent, you may come to Loiseau with me . . . that's if you want to."

"Can we play Vorkoffe soon? Tonight?" Secca asked.

"A short game," Anna conceded with a laugh. The game was similar to the box game Anna had played in college, where whoever got the most boxes completed won, but in Liedwahr the object was to distribute stones by twos, and the complexity made the outcome less certain.

"You must have a lot to do." Secca straightened. "And I want to play tonight." She looked straight at

Anna, and her eyes watered again. "You are good. Papa said you were." She swallowed. "I'd better go."

After Secca had left, Anna took out the smooth brown paper that was so expensive in Liedwahr and the quill, and began to write the response to Lady Anientta, slowly and carefully, to avoid smudging the ink that seemed to take forever to dry. Once she finished, she reread the key parts in a low voice.

> ". . . share your grief at the illness of one with whom you shared so much of your life. . . .
>
> "We also regret deeply that a lord so able and supportive of Defalk and the Regency is unable to fulfill his duties, and trust you will continue in his tradition. . . .
>
> "In accordance with Lord Hryding's wishes, as expressed directly to me, and to Secca, she has asked and will remain in Falcor to complete her fostering and education. . . .
>
> "In this time of grief and turmoil, Secca sends her love to her father, to you and to Jeron and Kurik. . . ."

It wasn't perfect, but it would have to do. She rang the bell.

"Yes, Lady Anna." Skent peered in.

She lifted the scroll. "Skent, would you please make a copy of this, right now, and then return both to me?"

The page's eyes widened.

"Dythya says you're quite capable of copying and that you have a fine hand."

"Yes, Lady Anna." Skent crossed the room and took the scroll.

"Send Fridric in on your way out."

The page inclined his head.

Fridric bowed as he entered. "Lady Anna."

"I will have a scroll for you to return to the Lady

Anientta. At this time, I am adhering to Lord Hryding's wishes that Secca remain in Falcor.''

Fridric bowed.

''You and Stephen and Markan are also welcome here, at any time,'' Anna added, deciding against being too explicit.

''Thank you, Lady Anna.'' Fridric stopped, then swallowed. ''We serve Lord Hryding.''

''Lord Hryding is a good lord,'' Anna answered, ''and I know you will serve him well.''

Fridric looked relieved.

''If you wouldn't mind waiting outside for the scroll. . . .''

''Oh, no, Lady Anna.'' The young armsman practically backed out of the receiving room.

After Skent returned with the two scrolls and she signed and sealed the original and sent Fridric off with it, Anna glanced at the sandglass on the wall stand, nearing the eighth glass of the day. Four o'clock, earth time, she converted mentally, and time to meet with Liende to go over the spell songs.

Her eyes passed across the piles of paper, and she wanted to groan. Was she really doing anything? Or was it all an illusion?

Jecks was right. She had to think about efficiency. She hated the very word. It had been one of Avery's watchwords, and Sandy hadn't been much better.

Clearly, creating things almost from scratch—like the damned bridge over the Falche—took a lot of effort. But what about rearrangements? Would it take less effort to rebuild houses or shops? What if she started fixing up abandoned houses in Falcor? She shook her head. They couldn't be gifts. Gifts never worked, not with children, friends, or enemies. Was that it? Dwellings for artisans and craftspeople—in return for services to the liedstadt and to entice them back to Falcor?

She looked at the sandglass. Time for working out more of the spell arrangements with Liende. She stood and stretched, trying not to think about all the problems she still hadn't resolved, from roads to liedgeld, to dead and possibly dying lords, and hostile countries on almost every border of Defalk.

Followed by Blaz and Lejun, Anna hurried out of the receiving hall and across the courtyard to the players' quarters and the large room that had become Liende's rehearsal hall.

The strains of the building song, played by several violinos and the clarinet-like woodwind of Liende, seeped through the planks of the stained-pine door. Anna paused to listen, with her guards standing behind her.

One of the violinos was slightly off.

Abruptly, the woodwind quit.

"Enough." Liende's voice came through the door. "Delvor, you're not holding the pitch. You have to follow Kaseth. This sorceress is more forbearing than most, but if you do that when she's casting a spell, she's not going to be pleased. I won't be at all happy, because you're endangering the rest of us. You need to practice more. If you don't, I'll tell the regent you can't play well enough."

"Please . . . master player. I'll practice. I'll practice more," promised Delvor.

"You must practice better."

The regent suspected the wavering words belonged to Kaseth, who had been Lord Brill's lead player. Anna still wondered how Liende had persuaded the older man to play under her.

The sorceress knocked on the plank door, then opened it, and stepped into the cool room, lit by only two candles in glass mantels. The flames of both candles wavered with the door's opening.

The three string players rose, Delvor scrambling rather than merely standing.

Anna looked at the youngster. "If Liende doesn't think you've improved enough in two weeks, you will leave. Do you understand?"

Delvor's lower lip trembled. "Yes, Lady Anna."

"Delvor . . . I may not look it, but I've practiced and trained for nearly thirty years." Anna kept her voice cool. "My oldest daughter was almost old enough to be your mother. Music and sorcery aren't things you just play at." She gave a perfunctory smile. "If the rest of you wouldn't mind, I need a few moments with Liende."

The three string players bowed. Kaseth met her eyes briefly, and gave the faintest of nods, as did Palian. Delvor's eyes were on the floor.

Once the door closed, guarded on the outside by Blaz and Lejun, Anna turned to the woodwind player. "I hope you didn't mind, but it's better that I'm the bad person. Then you can seem reasonable."

"I have told him." Liende shook her head. "The young, they do not understand."

"No, they don't," Anna agreed, thinking of all the students she'd taught over the years, and how few ever truly understood the difference between adequacy and perfection. In sorcery, or music spells, competency was barely enough, and a mistake could be dangerous or fatal. "If you think he isn't up to it, then send him away."

"He might practice now," the red-and-white-haired woman said with a short laugh.

"Or he might sulk and think we're unreasonable," Anna said dryly. She'd certainly seen that type before.

Liende waited.

"I'm going to need you for a building spell, the second one. How soon can you have that ready?"

The woodwind player frowned. "We have just started, and it is different with only four players. A week, perhaps?"

"All right." Anna had hoped for a date earlier than that, but Liende seemed reasonable, and Anna hadn't yet learned whether the player was one who was too cautious, or too optimistic, or relatively accurate in judging timing. Another thing she needed to learn.

And . . . .she'd promised Secca a game of Vorkoffe.

Was there ever time for what needed to be done?

13

ESARIA, NESEREA

The brown-haired officer in the maroon uniform of a Lancer of Mansuur drops to one knee, and looks up to Rabyn. "Your grandsire the Liedfuhr has pledged us to your service, Lord Rabyn."

"To my service, Overcaptain Relour?" asks the dark-haired youth, leaning forward slightly, and almost indolently, in the gilt throne chair.

"To the service of the Lord of Neserea, and the Protector of the Faith of the Eternal Melody," answers the overcaptain, standing and turning to his left to face Nubara. "And, of course, following the counsel of the hand of the regent, Counselor and Overcaptain Nubara."

"Of course," echoes Rabyn, smiling broadly. "You are indeed most welcome here in Esaria, and I am certain that Overcaptain Nubara will ensure that you and all of your men are quartered and fed. Then, we must talk, the three of us, about the Liedfuhr's wishes on how we are to defeat the evil sorceress of the east."

"That is one reason why I am here, my lord. We await your pleasure, and that of the hand of the regent." Relour bows, but not deeply. "By your leave?"

"By our leave." Rabyn smiles again, leaning back in the gilt chair. "We are most glad to see you and your lancers, and we look forward to ensuring their use against our enemies."

Relour offers a last head-bow before turning.

The doors to the winter receiving-chamber close behind the lancer commander, leaving Nubara and Rabyn alone.

"You may be lord and prophet in name, Lord Rabyn," Nubara says quietly as he edges up beside Rabyn, "but his lancers are a greater force than any single one you have left in Neserea.''

"Did you know that the Prophet's Guard has seventy-score armsmen?'' asks Rabyn, his tone guileless as he turns and looks at Nubara, his eyes wide. "That's what Captain Gellinot told me yesterday. He is the cousin of the late captain—Zealor, was it?''

"Zealor is his cousin. Or was, until the sorceress killed him,'' Nubara replies.

"Do you think he will make a good captain of the Guard?''

"He is loyal to the throne, and to you.'' Nubara's voice is smooth.

"Do you like him, Nubara?''

The Mansuuran officer laughs, softly. "Lord Rabyn, I have liked men who would have killed me, and disliked those who have given their life for me. Liking does not matter. Trust does. If you cannot trust someone, you must control them. You can like them, but never count on liking when blades are drawn.''

"You are wise.'' Rabyn cocks his head to one side. "Should rulers like anyone?''

"You can like who you wish. Just don't confuse it with trust.''

"Can we trust Overcaptain Relour?''

"He will do as he has been ordered by your grandsire. That you can count upon.'' Nubara shrugs.

"And what are his orders?''

"We know he has been ordered to protect you and the borders of Neserea.''

"But not to support an attack on Defalk and the sorceress?''

"No.'' Nubara smiles widely, but only with his mouth. "Not until your forces are stronger. And that will not be too long. Overcaptain Nitron reports that the Mittfels Foot is at full strength—''

"Why is he still an overcaptain?''

"Because he was the most senior officer who remained

loyal to your father and to you. And he did bring back not only his levies, but the rest of your forces."

"Those who didn't desert," snaps Rabyn. "What about the Prophet's Lancers?"

"Reforming is slower there," admits Nubara. "Most of the senior officers remained in Defalk. Overcaptain Relour might be persuaded to lend an officer or two. . . ."

Rabyn frowns, then nods. "If you would ask him . . ."

"I'm sure he would be most pleased. Most pleased."

"I'm hungry." Rabyn gathers the green cloak around him and slips off the gilt throne.

14

Even with the candles in the wall sconces lit, as well as the lamp on one side of the writing-desk table, Anna's quarters were dim, and the black etched rectangle on the stone outer wall, next to where her replacement scrying mirror hung, seemed to shift with the flickering light.

Anna moistened her lips. How long, how many seasons, or years, before she dared to use the mirror to see Elizabetta? Would a spell even work anymore? The last attempt hadn't, and the heat and explosion had nearly killed her. Would another attempt, after a season or two, be any better? Would the reflecting pool she planned across the hall make it easier? Her eyes dropped to the redheaded child on the other side of the table, a brown woolen shawl wrapped around her narrow shoulders.

Secca looked at the two black stones in her hand, then at the game board with the intertwined lattices, and the grooved slots designed to hold the stones.

Anna glanced from the white stones before her to the

window, and the darkness outside the panes she'd in-
stalled a season earlier. Sorcery had some benefits. Then
her eyes went back to the redheaded fosterling across the
table from her. Secca's hair was the color of Elizabetta's,
but her face was thinner, more intense, and her eyes were
amber, unlike the green of Elizabetta's.

Secca stared intently at the game board, then placed her
stones in adjacent slots in the lattice at the edge of the
board to Anna's far left. "There!" She grinned.

Vorkoffe was similar to NIM or NEM—at least that
was what Anna thought it was called. That was the box
game Anna had played in college, where whoever got the
most boxes completed won, but on earth you'd completed
boxes with a pencil. In Liedwahr the object was to distribute stones by twos. Five stones completed a lattice. If
you surrounded an opponent's lattice, it became yours.

Tonight, Anna was losing, though she'd held her own
recently.

*Is that because your mind's not on the game? Imagine
that.* Winning or losing wasn't that big a deal, no great
gain or loss, but she hated to seem incompetent. Anna put
her two stones on the board and completed the big center
lattice.

"That's wasn't fair, Lady Anna." Secca offered a hint
of a pout.

"You're pouting again." Anna laughed. "Do you
know that when I was your age . . ."

"I know." Secca sighed. "You put your lip out so far
that your mother said she could ride to town on it."

Anna wondered if she were repeating herself too much.
Early Alzheimer's? Or stress? "I don't want you to have
that lip stuck out all the time."

Secca completed a corner lattice. "There! You need be
careful."

"The way you're playing tonight, that's for sure."
Anna juggled the two white stones, looking at the ten-
year-old who munched on a corner of the dark bread.
Secca certainly hadn't wanted to go home to Flossbend—

not at all, even with her father ill, and that tended to confirm Anna's suspicions about Anientta.

Anna started a secondary lattice beside the center one by putting one white stone on each of the open side slots.

Secca shivered again.

Anna looked at her. "You're cold."

"I'll be all right."

Were her lips actually blue? The sorceress stood, and walked over to the hearth, where the wood was stacked, then back to the corner where the lutar lay on the chest. She began to tune the instrument.

"You shouldn't do sorcery, lady."

"Just a little spell." Anna stepped toward the hearth, then began to sing.

> "Fire, fire, burn so bright
>   in this hearth tonight,
>   burn well and warm and light
>   and have the chill within take flight."

The hearth flared into flame, not a roaring blaze, but a warm glowing steady set of flames. Anna smiled to herself.

"Oh . . . you didn't have to do that," Secca said.

"You're cold. I could tell that." Sparkles flashed before Anna's eyes. *One little spell? I can't even do a spell to warm a child?* Wanting to scream in frustration, instead she turned so Secca couldn't see her face and carried the lutar back to the chest, setting it down gently, despite her trembling hands.

"I wish . . ." Secca shook her head.

Anna slipped back to the table, with the game laid out upon it, and eased into her chair, trying not to sit heavily, trying not to show the lightheadedness. Slowly, she reached for the bread and broke off a chunk.

Secca sat up straight in her chair. "Are you all right, Lady Anna?"

"I'll be fine."

The redhead reached for the pitcher and, standing on tiptoe, refilled Anna's goblet.

"Thank you," Anna said after she swallowed the mouthful of bread. She reached for the goblet.

"Would the cheese help?" Secca's voice was small.

Anna had to smile at the concern. "I'll have some in a moment." She took a swallow of the water. "The fire does feel good."

"I like fires when it's cold," answered the little redhead, in a voice that reminded Anna all too much of Elizabetta.

"So do I." Anna put a small chunk of cheese into her mouth, wondering how much she'd have to eat to dispel the lightheadedness.

15

After a last vocalise, the regent and sorceress cleared her throat. She looked down and studied the drawing of the reflecting pool. Then, the sketch in hand, she stepped from her chambers into the corridor. Lejun and Giellum straightened as she appeared. The five waiting players shifted from one foot to the other on the stone floor tiles in the dimness of the corridor, holding their instruments loosely.

Anna walked past the players, her boots nearly silent on the stones, to the open doorway. She glanced through the squared arch to the piles of granite and limestone resting on the floor stones of the empty chamber that had once been used for guests—or relatives of the lords of Defalk.

With a nod, she turned to Liende. "Are you ready? The second building song?"

"We are ready, lady." Liende's voice was firm, if low. Kaseth, as lead string player, stepped back even with the others. Anna recognized Palian and the thin-faced Delvor. The other, a young woman, she did not. All four players lifted their instruments.

Anna hummed, more to herself, took a last look at the sketch to fix the image of what she wanted in her mind, then nodded.

The four violins began, then the woodwind, with the smoothness of practice.

Anna began the spell. *Strophic again,* a small voice in her thoughts reminded her. *But aren't all spells with more than one verse strophic?* She forced her mind to the job at hand, and the words and melody, simultaneously holding the mental image of the reflecting pool.

> "Shape this pool in solid granite stone.
>   Ensure its reflection for me alone.
>   Smooth the base, and let it shine,
>   when the water holds this sorcery's design . . .
>
> "Let the water be; let it see.
>   Keep from others this pool to be . . ."

A small tremor shivered through the liedburg, and a cloud of dust swirled up, obscuring the former guest room.

Anna staggered slightly, feeling some energy leach out of her, but she straightened immediately. Sorcery was definitely easier with players, and when it was Clearsong. She bowed to Liende.

"Thank you, Liende, Kaseth, Palian . . . all of you." She forced a smile, then stepped forward into the room, looking at the circular pool that rose smoothly from the floor to a height not quite waist-high. The stones were smooth and polished, almost black, although they had been more of a reddish brown when rough-stacked on the floor, and there was no sign of any joints between them.

Now she wouldn't have to worry about the heat of far-seeing blistering her mirrors. The water might boil, though, she realized. In time, she might even be able to sneak a look across the worlds at Elizabetta.

Not for a long time. She shook her head and studied the reflecting pool.

The basin, about a yard and a half across, was filled with silvered water that gave a nearly perfect reflection of her as she looked down. Anna frowned, and so did her image. Her face remained too thin, and her eyes, though not sunken, were too dark.

A whispering rose behind her, in the corridor.

". . . where did she go . . ."

". . . stepped inside and vanished . . ."

The sorceress took a deep breath. Once again, whatever she'd done had been more than she had anticipated. Slowly, she turned and left what had become her scrying room.

"See!" Delvor closed his mouth sheepishly as Anna stepped through the doorway. He brushed back the lank brown hair from his forehead.

"I didn't mean to surprise you," Anna said. "It turned out just fine." She smiled. "We'll be doing more spells now. Building spells, mostly, I think. Thank you."

Liende offered a smile in return, mostly of relief, Anna suspected. "May we go?"

"Of course. I'll need to talk to you later, Liende, about some more spells."

Anna still felt slightly lightheaded, but nothing like the way she'd felt after rebuilding the bridge. Then the re-flecting pool had been much smaller, and accomplished with players, and she hadn't done any Darksong lately.

She took her time going downstairs to the receiving hall, and the meal that someone—Skent?—had ensured was waiting for her. The bread and cheese and the water helped the lightheadedness, enough that she felt almost normal by the time Dythya arrived with the accounting charts and papers.

"Again, I must thank you, lady." Dythya bowed, and added, with a twinkle in her gray eyes, "My father was surprised that he had raised a counselor to the Regent of Defalk."

"So was Menares," Anna said, wondering if Dythya's father Herstat had to be faintly envious. "But you work as hard as he does, and I need you both." Actually, Dythya worked harder, but that wasn't something that needed to be said.

"Menares . . . he knows the intrigues. I know the accounts." Dythya spread the brown sheets on the table.

Anna wished she had the equivalent of a finance minister or liedstadt accountant. Then, wasn't that what Dythya had become? Anna still had to make the decisions on how to spend the funds—or how not to—and there was so much that she didn't know.

Anna stood so that she could see the numbers on the charts Dythya had hung from the easels. She forced herself to go over each account slowly, comparing what she had budgeted against current expenditures line by line. Some discrepancies were obvious—such as coins budgeted for the weapons smith the liedstadt still hadn't been able to find.

Then came the revenues. There was no change there. Those who hadn't paid liedgeld the last time, including Lord Arkad of Cheor and Lady Anna of Loiseau, still hadn't paid. Anna hadn't done anything about arranging to have someone manage her lands. Quies and Albero were doubtless trustworthy, but neither had broader experience, and others would resent their being chosen. Gero had some experience as Brill's assistant, but he was barely more than a boy. She took a deep breath. Perhaps Jecks could recommend someone.

The tax levies on the merchants of Falcor, more like a tithe, actually were revenues from Jimbob's holdings. Until Jimbob was of age, Jecks and Anna had agreed that they would be handled as part of the liedstadt accounts, since the Regency was there solely to protect the youth's patrimony—and needed every possible gold to do so. Again, that was something else Anna wasn't totally happy with, but it had been Jecks' suggestion, and she had accepted it, at least until matters improved.

"What isn't in these accounts?" Anna asked warily.

"How many players do you plan to have, Lady Anna?" asked Dythya.

"Players? I'd hoped for at least twelve."

"At what you are paying, that will cost you over a hundred golds a year, and that does not count their food and clothing and any supplies you must provide."

"Two hundred golds we hadn't counted on," Anna admitted.

"I have guessed that a weapons smith will cost fifty golds a year, and another hundred in materials," Dythya added. "I did not guess that you would spend two hundred golds on blades."

"Another two hundred," Anna said wearily. "If we actually get them. We still haven't heard from Ranuak."

"You know about the five hundred for the Ranuan Exchange, and the thousand that must be paid after harvest."

That was almost two thousand golds—and her reserve had been a thousand. Add to that around two thousand golds in liedgeld that had not been paid, and the government of Defalk—the liedstadt—was in big trouble. Unlike the United States, Anna reflected, with currency being solid metal coins, she didn't have the option of printing more money.

She turned to Dythya. "I need two more lists. No, three. One should be a list of all the items we've spent coins on that we didn't budget for. The second is a list of the liedgeld we don't still have, and the third is a list of items where you think we *might* be able to spend less. You should talk to Lord Jecks, Arms Commander Hanfor, Tirsik, and anyone else who spends coins and might have ideas." Anna paused. "They'll all tell you spending less is impossible. You tell them that we won't have the coins by the end of the year, and if they make a decision now, then they get to suggest what would be best. Otherwise, I'll have to choose." Anna smiled. "Try to get across the idea that you're looking out for their interests and giving them some advance word."

"Advance word?" asked Dythya, then nodded.

Anna kept forgetting that some expressions didn't translate.

Dythya was barely out of the receiving room before the door opened again.

"There is another messenger from Synope, my lady," announced Giellum.

"Escort him in." Anna had a feeling about the message and messenger, and seated herself in the official gilt chair on the dais.

The messenger was none other than hatchet-faced Calmut. He bowed and extended a scroll. "Regent Anna, a message from Synope."

"I'm glad to see you in good health, Calmut." Anna nodded to Giellum. Lejun stepped up beside Calmut as the younger guard took the scroll and carried it to the regent.

The sorceress broke the seal and began to read, her eyes catching the important words and phrases. "Regent Anna, Lady and Sorceress, and Protector of Defalk . . ."

Anna pursed her lips—still the same sort of flowery opening that meant that the trouble presaged by Calmut's arrival was bad indeed.

It is with the deepest regret that I must inform you that my lord and consort, Lord Hryding, has passed into the harmonies beyond Liedwahr. His last wish was that I again beseech you to honor his requests regarding Secca and the preservation of Flossbend and the lands of Synope. . . .

Until you have made a decision regarding his lands and holdings, I will continue to administer Flossbend and its lands as temporary custodian for

Jeron. In deepest admiration, I beg of you your support. Both Jeron and I stand ready to do your bidding and await your response.

The wax seal remained that of Lord Hryding, but the
signature was somewhat different from the last scroll,
reading, "Anientta, his consort and administrator for his
heir, Jeron."

While Anna couldn't prove it, she doubted Hryding's
death was from natural causes. The whole business stank,
and it created a real problem. She'd already set the prec-
edent of letting consorts administer for children, and now
she had a consort who could be a disaster, but with no
way to prove it.

"I am indeed sorry to hear of your lord's death," Anna
said to Calmut. "He was a good man and a good lord."

"Yes, Lady Anna. Many regret his death." Calmut's
voice was low, properly respectful, and Anna didn't trust
him in the slightest.

"Lejun, would you have one of the pages make sure
that Calmut is fed and given a place to rest while we
consider Lady Anientta's request?" Anna smiled profes-
sionally. "And Giellum, would you have one of the pages
summon Lord Jecks?"

Her smile faded once the three armsmen left and the
door closed.

She read the scroll again, then set it down and finished
the last of the bread and cheese, and drank almost another
full goblet of water before Jecks arrived. She waited until
he sat across the table.

"Lord Jecks . . . you may have guessed. Lord Hryding
has died." She shook her head. "I probably should have
gone to Synope."

"You could not have reached there on these roads before he died." Jecks gave a sad smile. "You feel not all
was as it was presented, lady?"

"Anientta's a scheming bitch, from what I saw. Her

son Jeron is a living replica of Nero. Actually, both her sons are. Kurik's not any better, and—''

Jecks' brow furrowed.

"Sorry. Sometimes, when I get angry I use names from earth. Nero was a ruler whose mother schemed to get him to be emperor. In gratitude, he poisoned her.''

"You think highly of both of Hryding's heirs, I see.''

"I thought highly of Lord Hryding, and Secca shows promise.'' Anna shook her head. "There's no way she's ever going back to Flossbend.'' Hryding had known—or at least suspected.

"Lady Anna, you cannot solve all problems. Even if you had gone to Flossbend, and you had reached there before Hryding died and saved him—then what would you have done? Could you prove he was poisoned? And if you did not kill Lady Anientta, what would have saved him the next time? If you did kill her, without proof, how many consorts would welcome you to their holdings? How would other lords feel?''

The room darkened as clouds outside covered the late-morning sun. Anna wondered if Falcor would get more rain. From the amount she had seen over the winter, she was beginning to appreciate just how much moisture the Evult's sorcery had withheld from the land—and how long it might take to recover from the years of drought.

"That still gives me a problem. Anientta's scheming against me. That's what I feel, but I don't have any real evidence of that, either.''

"Perhaps you should visit her.''

"That's a possibility. But we need to visit Lord Arkad first.'' Anna thought. If they followed the Synor River, they could go to Synope after Cheor, and then come back along the Chean. If she took the players, they could rebuild the ford at Sorprat, and perhaps repair a few stretches of highway or bridges.

She certainly wasn't accomplishing the rebuilding of Defalk by sitting in the liedburg.

"You have a certain . . . look, Lady Anna,'' Jecks said

warily. "The same one you had when you decided to cross the Ostfels and take on the Evult by yourself."

"That may be." Anna smiled brightly. "You suggest I do nothing except confirm Lady Anientta as regent for her son for the time being?"

"You might suggest that, as in all other cases, you will visit her and discuss her administration periodically." Jecks' forehead crinkled. "I will tell a few other lords that you are not allowing consorts who hold their lords' lands to do so without some oversight."

"That should make them happy."

"Less unhappy," suggested Jecks.

Anna lifted the bell. "First, I have an unpleasant duty."

"Secca?"

Anna nodded as the door opened.

"Resor, would you find the young lady Secca for me? I need to talk to her."

Resor nodded, and the door closed.

Anna turned back to Jecks. "While we wait, I have another question."

"Yes, Lady Anna?" A glint of a smile appeared on both Jecks' lips and in his eyes.

"I find I am the Lady of Loiseau, and I owe liedgeld. As you might have guessed, I have no one to manage the lands, and I haven't the faintest idea of who I could trust to do a good job."

"You need a steward."

"That's pretty clear," she admitted. "Do you have any ideas?"

"Hmmm." Jecks frowned. "You should send a messenger to the tenants, at least. Suggest that they only owe half what they paid last year because of the troubles. See what coins you get. I also do not think that anyone would find it remiss if you excused Loiseau from last harvest's liedgeld because the previous lord had died in defending Defalk and because the succession had not been established." The white-haired warrior gave a crooked smile.

"You may have to do that for Lord Vlassa's heirs in Fussen before it's all over. In both cases, do it quietly."

Anna understood that part. What Jecks said made sense, but she didn't like it. She sighed.

"You do not like not paying your debts—even those you owe yourself."

"No. I don't see an alternative right now. I didn't even know I was the Lady of Loiseau. . . . I mean, I sort of knew, but I didn't understand that accepting the lands meant I owed liedgeld. I'm not exactly from Defalk, you know."

"No one would ever question you on that, Lady Anna."

Again, Anna could feel the sparks smoldering between them. What was she going to do?

This time, she was saved by Secca's arrival.

"You sent for me, Lady Anna?" Secca bowed as she stepped into the receiving room. Her eyes were dark and sunken.

"She did," said Jecks softly, rising. "If you would excuse me, ladies?"

Anna nodded, appreciating Jecks' tact. She stood and stepped around the table, waiting for the receiving room door to close.

"Secca? I've had another message from your mother. . . ."

"Papa's dead! I knew it. . . . I saw Calmut, and I knew it."

"Yes," Anna said quietly.

As the girl sobbed, Anna held her—for a long time.

Once Secca left, Anna requested more to eat. She was worried and emotionally drained. Between the financial worries, her concerns about her attraction to Jecks, and Lord Hryding's death and Secca's grief, she was exhausted—and lightheaded once more.

When she finished with the cold slabs of meat, the bread and hard yellow cheese, she stood. She had to walk around, somewhere, somehow, just so she could digest everything she'd stuffed inside herself.

Followed by Lejun and Blaz, Anna walked down the lower corridor and into the main hall, where her foster-lings and pages sat at the long table, young men at the right end, and young women at the left. Her eyes traversed the familiar faces—Skent, Barat, Cens, Hoede, Jimbob, then Cataryzna, a subdued and blotchy-faced Secca, Ly-sara, and Ytrude. The two new faces were those of Alseta, Liende's strawberry-blonde daughter, and Kinor, Liende's son and a wiry redhead taller than most of the others, except for Skent and Ytrude.

Several sets of eyes went to her, but Menares was fac-ing the map on the easel and continued to lecture.

"Dumaria is divided into two areas, the higher mead-owlands and farms, and the lower and drier grasslands. Dumaria itself is situated almost on that point where these two regions meet and where the Envar River joins the Falche. . . ." Menares' pointer went to a spot on the brown map where two blue lines joined.

"Lady Anna." Menares turned from the map, lowering his pointer.

"I'm sorry to interrupt your lesson." Anna wasn't so sure she was sorry. "Please go ahead."

Menares coughed, then shifted his feet.

". . . Ah . . . there are two major cataracts above Du-maria. The second cataract is the farthest north and marks the end of the Great Chasm. The first is where the higher section of the northern highlands end. . . ."

When Menares got to the geography of Ebra, Anna slipped out of the hall and walked slowly back to the receiving room—the empty, chill, and desolate receiving room. Suddenly, she grabbed her lutar, and marched back out and up the stone stairs to the new scrying room. Lejun and Giellum followed her, stationing themselves outside the door. She stepped inside, closing the door behind her with a thud.

For a time, she looked at the blank waters. Then she

tuned the lutar and hummed through the spell, mentally fixing the words in her mind. Finally, she strummed and sang.

> "Water, water, in this my hall,
>   show me those in power who seek my fall.
>   Show them bright, and show them fast,
>   and make that strong view well last."

Eight images appeared in the pool, each a circlet portrait of the individual. There were eight—five men and three women.

The ones she recognized were Nubara—the Mansuuran lancer who'd been Cyndyth's advisor in Falcor and who was now effectively young Rabyn's regent; Lord Dencer; a dark-haired youngster in an ornate green cloak who resembled his mother too much to be anyone other than Rabyn; and, of course, Anientta, Lord Hryding's widow.

At the sight of Anientta, Anna snorted. The woman was not only a poisoner, but stupid, since Anientta wouldn't have lasted a moment as Regent of Flossbend under a male lord of Defalk—or under any of those who wanted to conquer it.

The ones she didn't recognize were a big black-bearded man dressed in red, another man in sky-blue with mixed brown-and-silver hair, a black-haired and dark-eyed woman in deep green with a heavy chain and seal around her neck, and another heavier dark-haired woman with red lips dressed in a loose-fitting powder-blue robe.

From what she'd heard, she figured that the man in red was probably Lord Ehara of Dumar and the one in blue was probably Konsstin, the Liedfuhr of Mansuur. The two women—they could have been from Ranuak and Wei, but which came from where was another question and what roles or positions either held, she couldn't guess, although she suspected the older woman in green was more likely from Wei.

Anna took a deep breath and studied the likenesses

again, trying to fix the images in her mind. Finally, she sang the release spell.

> "Let this scene of scrying, mirror filled with light,
> vanish like the darkness when the sun is bright."

The pool turned silver, vacant, empty of the images of those who plotted against her. So . . . what else was new? Someone from every country that surrounded Defalk—except Ebra—was plotting her downfall. And her sorcery showed that Anientta was, too. Anna still wanted to scream.

She didn't have enough armsmen, enough golds, enough supplies, or enough strength to do all the sorcery required to rebuild Defalk. She also didn't have enough time, and she hadn't really the faintest idea of where to start, and she couldn't exactly blurt that out to anyone. After all, she was the sorceress and regent, the powerful one, who'd done the impossible.

What made it worse was that nothing looked that bad at the moment. Anna could feel how bad it was going to get, but no one understood feelings, and she didn't have any way to explain why she thought things were going to get a lot worse.

Hanfor? Could she get him to talk? Perhaps he'd offer an insight that she could build on. She replaced the lutar in its case, then decided to leave the instrument in the scrying room.

She found Hanfor in the courtyard, sweating as he practiced with Himar with a rapier—or so it seemed—wrapped in some kind of coarse cloth.

Both officers stopped.

"Lady Anna?"

She forced a bright smile. "Nothing." With a nod, she turned and left, knowing she left both officers with puzzled looks on their faces.

How could she explain?

The walls were still closing around her, and she walked

quickly, too quickly back into the main building and up the stairs. She knew she was behaving like a madwoman, and she wanted to scream. But sorceresses and regents weren't supposed to scream. And she wasn't a man who could beat at someone with a sharp—or blunted—weapon.

Guards still trailing her, Anna walked to the north end of the corridor and rapped on Lady Essan's door.

"Oh . . . come in, Lady Anna." Synondra backed away as she opened the door, trying to bow simultaneously.

"You may go, Synondra," Essan said from her chair before the low fire.

"Yes, ladies." Synondra slipped out between the two guards, and the door shut with a clunk.

"No sorceress I, but these old eyes can see the fires fly from you," said Essan.

Anna settled into the straight-backed chair across from the white-haired widow. Questions swirled through her mind, and she settled on the easiest. "Is there some color that the Ranuans wear?"

"They wear many, just as we do," said Lady Essan. "I'm told the Matriarch often wears bright colors, but the Sisters of the South—I think they're also called the SouthWomen—wear pastels, often blue. I once met Sister Merthe, but that was years back, and she's dead now. The previous Matriarch had most of the Sisters killed after they stormed a ship from Sturinn and slew the crew."

Anna wanted to sigh. One question—just one question—and the answers gave rise to at least two more. Was it always going to be like that? "Sturinn?" she asked. "Why Sturinn?"

"The Sturinnese keep their women in chains. Some chains are little more than jewelry, but many are heavy links. A merchant from Sturinn who lived in Encora whipped two concubines to death, and fled to the ship before a mob. The captain refused to return him to the Sisters. They stormed the ship. Almost all the women were killed, but none of the Sturinnese survived."

And Anna had thought the situation in Defalk had been bad. "Why did the Matriarch have the others killed?"

"Trade. Far Sturinn has hundreds of ships that ply the Western Ocean, and most are heavily armed. Should the Sturinnese choose, they could blockade Ranuak easily, because almost all the trade comes from the port at Encora. The port at Sylwa is distant and small and hard to use in bad weather."

"And Ranuak depends on trade."

Essan nodded.

"Why not the other countries in Liedwahr?"

"Donjim told me it was because Mansuur has many ports, and they do not need much sea trade. Wei has many ports, and almost as many ships as Sturinn."

Anna nodded. In time, she might sort it all out. "Dumar only has one good port, but it doesn't need trade."

"Dumar is famous for its wool." Essan smiled, and lifted the corner of the heavy shawl. "Donjim had this brought from Envaryl for me. The isles of Sturinn are warm, compared to Liedwahr."

The sorceress shook her head.

"You are still upset, sorceress-woman. Would you care to tell me why?" Essan lifted a goblet of her apple brandy and sipped.

Anna swallowed, then began to speak. "We are surrounded. Defalk is, I mean, and everyone except Ebra is plotting how to take us over. The Liedfuhr has sent lancers to Neserea. The Lord of Dumar is up to something, and so are those women in Wei and Ranuak, some of them anyway. We don't have enough coins for the year. . . ." Anna spread her hands. "Our roads are so much of a mess so that we can't move armsmen or messages or goods or anything very well, and I've got a handful of lords who don't even want to pay liedgeld—"

"Defalk has never been much different," said the older woman. "You think being a sorceress would change that?"

"No." Anna almost laughed at Essan's dry tone.

"What bothers me is that everyone says just that . . . as if nothing can be changed. If I can't change things, then Defalk will fall. I'm a sorceress, not a miracle worker."

"Already you've worked miracles." Essan lifted her brandy goblet again, almost as in a toast. "People expect more. Donjim, he put down a peasant uprising, then another. The second one happened because the lords, they thought that they could abuse the peasants and he would bring in his armsmen and back them up." The white-haired woman took a solid swallow of the amber liquid. "Those uprisings killed Senjim and broke Donjim's heart. I rode with them, on the first one, you know. Better they had killed me."

"You're too tough for that," Anna said.

"I was then. Not now. I sit in front of a fire, and look at you. This is a hard land, sorceress who looks like a girl. A hard land with hard lords. Aye, hard lords and selfish ones." She refilled the goblet. "You must be hard, too, Anna, or they will break you and your heart, just as they broke Donjim, and Barjim, and Brill."

"You must be hard." Was that what it took? To be stronger and harder . . . perhaps more cruel? Anna shook her head.

"You say no, sorceress-woman, and that means, should you succeed, you'll end up being harder on yourself than on anyone." Essan laughed softly. "I know about that. I do. So do you, I'd wager."

What am I supposed to do? That was what Anna wanted to ask, but she didn't, because . . . it didn't matter, she realized. She had to do what she could, what she thought best. The only question was where to start. The sorceress took a deep breath.

"Aye, and this weather helps not," Essan continued. "Damp, like once it was, and good for the trees and crops, but not for old bones."

"Not for young ones, either," murmured the regent, sitting back for a few moments to listen to Lady Essan reminisce.

"Years ago, in the times of snow . . . those were truly cold years. . . ."

Later, even after visiting with Lady Essan, perhaps even more so, Anna could feel the walls of the liedburg closing in around her. She had to get out, rain or no rain. The more she tried to do, it seemed, the more isolated she got because efficiency—damned efficiency—meant delegating, and that meant she saw fewer and fewer people.

Back down the stairs to the receiving room she went, ignoring the looks between Lejun and Giellum. Once there, she looked around, glanced to the window. The clouds were scattered, white and gray and puffy. Good!

She rang the bell—too loudly, but she really didn't care.

Skent peered in, keeping the door between him and Anna.

"I'm going riding," she announced. "If Alvar is free . . ." She paused. "Is Alvar training armsmen this afternoon? Could you please find out, Skent, and let me know? I'd like you to come as well."

"Yes, lady." Skent's face brightened.

"Oh, and let Fhurgen know, if you would."

The door closed, and Anna glanced around the receiving room, then departed herself. She reclaimed her floppy brown riding hat from her room, as well as a riding jacket, and the lutar from the scrying room. Her fingers went to the dagger and truncheon she wore at her belt whenever she left the liedburg. Then she headed for the stables.

Within the southwest corner of the outer walls, the stables held the familiar odors of straw, horses, and manure, although the scents were mild, and the packed-clay floors swept clean. Tirsik saw to that.

The wiry stablemaster, who looked far older than Anna and probably wasn't, greeted her. "That great beast has been asking for you."

"Unless I ride him into the ground, he's always complaining."

"Riding's good for the soul, and the harmonies," Tirsik observed. "For horses and rulers."

"I hope so," answered Anna.

"Do young Skent good as well."

"He's already here?"

"Like a bird, he flew out here."

Anna grinned, then headed for the stall.

Whuff!

"Yes, I know. It's winter, and I've been neglecting your riding. Grooming isn't enough for you."

Farinelli stepped sideways as she picked up the brush and entered his stall, then offered a second *whuff*, more subdued than the first. She finished grooming and saddling Farinelli, and the blond gelding fairly pranced as she led him into the courtyard where Fhurgen and a squad of guards rode. Skent sat upon a bay mare and smiled at her.

She smiled back, checking her gear. The lutar was strapped behind her saddle, and she mounted, with an ease she still found surprising.

"Where to, Lady Anna?" asked the dark-bearded armsman who had replaced the unfortunate Spirda as the head of her personal guard.

"Falcor . . . the merchants' shops south of the liedburg." She might not be able to shop, but she could look and listen . . . if anyone would talk.

Hoofs clicked on the damp stones of the liedburg courtyard as the group rode out under the raised portcullis.

Anna nodded to the armsmen at the gate, but neither moved. Hanfor's training—or Alvar's or Himar's, she suspected.

The flat expanse outside the gates that separated the liedburg from the buildings of Falcor was a good hundred yards square. The damp clay was level with the stones of the roadway that led to the gate, but it had taken most of the winter to remove the piles of dirt and debris that the Evult's flood had swirled through the eastern parts of the town.

Anna turned Farinelli south. Once past the open space,

she rode slowly down the street. Various structures, shops on the lower floors and dwellings above them, filled both sides. Even in the chill, small handfuls of people gathered here and there, talking.

"... still the best spices in Falcor ..."

"... hot fowl! Hot fowl on a chill day ..."

"... you sure there's no worms in that flour?"

Anna wanted to smile when she neared the cloth merchant. In the window were the deep-green velvets she remembered from the hot summer day when she'd taken her first ride through Falcor, young and stiff-necked Spirda beside her. She had wanted to stop, but she'd decided that the Erdean equivalent of shopping wasn't a good idea on her first ride. Now, as regent and sorceress, she actually could afford to shop even less.

A thin girl, her brown hair braided into a roll at the back of her neck, looked at the sorceress from the cloth merchant's door.

Anna reined up, then dismounted, and handed Farinelli's reins to Fhurgen. She walked toward the girl, who seemed frozen in place.

Fhurgen handed the reins to another guard, a blond, and vaulted down to stand just behind and beside Anna.

"You know," Anna said conversationally, "I've ridden past here many times and I've always wanted to stop. Is this your family's shop?"

"Yes, lady." The girl's voice quavered.

A squat figure appeared in the door, that of a gray-haired man with drooping mustaches. "How might I help you, lady?"

"Is this your daughter?" Anna asked.

"My niece, my sister's daughter. Sirlina, my sister, she was taken by the fever after the flood last fall." His eyes went to the armsmen and to Skent, all except Fhurgen still mounted in the narrow street, then back to Anna. "Forgive me, my lady. What would you have of us?"

Anna forced a smile as genuine as she could. "I've

often admired your shop, and I just wanted to stop and look. I've never had the time."

"Everything we have is yours." The shopkeeper's forehead was damp, despite the cold.

"No. It's yours. When I need something, I'll buy it, just like any other customer." She smiled. "You work for what you earn, and you pay your levies. I'm not about to make your life harder."

The street darkened as one of the puffy clouds drifted across the sun, and the girl shivered in the slight breeze. Anna found the thin jacket more than warm enough. Winter, even late winter, in Defalk was far warmer than even parts of fall and spring had been in Ames, but not nearly so windy and gray.

The cloth merchant frowned. "Our velvets and woolens are the finest—"

"I can see that." Anna took a deep breath and looked toward Fhurgen, fumbling at her belt wallet. She had some silvers and golds that were hers personally, mostly left from the expenses she'd received from Behlem half a year earlier. "I'd like to look here for a moment."

The black-haired Fhurgen marched past Anna and the merchant, looking around the shop before nodding at Anna.

The regent stepped inside and turned to the girl. "What's your name?"

"Kirla, lady."

"Kirla, can you tell me about the velvets?" Anna gestured toward the bolt of green.

The girl glanced toward her uncle. The shopkeeper offered a thin smile, then said, "Go ahead, Kirla."

"Well . . . lady. The green, that's a cotton velvet, and it's from Sylwa. The cotton is pale green, and they dye the threads first before they go on the looms. The red is from the Ostisles, and Uncle says that it's not as good because they dye the fabric after they cut the pile." She glanced back at her uncle again, who nodded.

"What about the blue?" prompted Anna.

"The blue is like the green, but the blue dyes don't hold as well because the cotton is dun, not green or blue. I mean, with the green, lady . . ." Kirla opened her mouth, then shut it helplessly.

"I think I understand. Because the green is dyed over a natural light green cotton, it holds its color better over time. Is that it?"

The brown-haired girl nodded. "Yes, lady."

"How much is the green?" Anna turned to the shopkeeper. "Normally, that is?"

"Ah . . . last year, last year, before the troubles, the green was five silvers a yard."

Anna managed a nod, even as the cost of the cloth staggered her, momentarily—a yard of velvet more than a half-year's earnings for a peasant. Still, from what history she remembered, before steam looms cloth had been equally expensive on earth.

Anna glanced to Fhurgen, then to the girl. Neither seemed surprised. "But you haven't sold any since then?"

The shopkeeper looked down. "No, lady."

Anna thought. She could use another gown—she only had three, and a regent needed more. Sorcery would turn the cloth into a gown, when she had a moment, and she'd already worked out the spellsong. For what she had in mind, she'd need a good four yards, maybe five.

"Do you have five yards?" she temporized.

"Lady, I have ten," the shopkeeper blurted.

"Ten, I can't use. Two golds for five yards." That would make a serious dent in her personal funds.

The shopkeeper looked stunned. "I would give you a mere five yards."

"No. All I ask is that you pay your levies and . . . be a good person." She'd wanted to ask him to be a good citizen, but that concept didn't really exist in Liedwahr, not in the way she would have meant it. Anna dug out the two golds and extended them. "If you wouldn't mind cutting the fabric and delivering it to the liedburg . . . ?"

"Of course, Lady Anna. Of course." He sounded as though he had finally realized exactly who she happened to be, but Anna had to take his hand and actually put the coins there.

He looked down at the two golds as if he could not believe they were real.

"They're real. No sorcery." Anna looked to the girl. "Thank you, Kirla."

Kirla bowed. "Thank you, lady."

Anna smiled. "I've always wanted to come here. I just never had time." She didn't know what else to say. So she inclined her head slightly, still smiling, and left.

Outside, once she had remounted, Fhurgen leaned toward her.

"They will tell everyone, and that will be good."

Good? That she had paid for what she needed, and not taken it? Anna took a deep breath, thinking again about the high cost of the velvet, then waved to Kirla who stood in the arch of the doorway. The thin-faced girl returned the wave with a deep bow.

Anna managed to smile, even as she thought how much there was to do—in so many ways.

16

WEI, NORDWEI

The dark-haired spymistress glances from the desk-table where she sits in the black high-backed chair toward the single wide window. Through the open window, Ashtaar notes the rebuilt harbor piers that define the well-dredged juncture of the river Nord with the Vereisen Bay and the two-masted Norweian ships loading at those piers.

The door opens, and a woman with close-cropped

golden hair steps inside, walking slowly toward Ashtaar. She bows.

"You may sit, Gretslen."

The seer sits.

"What have you to report?" Ashtaar's fingers slip around the polished black agate oval on the desk.

The blonde seer bows her head slightly, then straightens. "The soprano sorceress has finally created a reflecting pool in the liedburg at Falcor."

"That is worthy of note?"

"She has begun to gather more players." Gretslen clears her throat almost silently. "We cannot see the pool, nor her when she employs it. It is as if she is not there." Gretslen's green eyes flicker downward. "This has not happened before."

"Where this sorceress is involved, a great deal seems to have happened that never occurred before." Ashtaar's fingers caress the black agate in her hand.

"Yes, Ashtaar."

"What else?"

"The sorceress re-created the bridge across the Falche at Falcor, so that the city will not be isolated from the fertile lands east of Falcor. A hundred masons would have taken a year to do what she did in an afternoon. Even her it prostrated, but she has recovered. She plucked the very harmonies in doing that."

Ashtaar's eyes leave Gretslen and go to the unfinished bridge across the Nord, the one being rebuilt to replace what had been destroyed by the Evult's other flood—the one he had loosed on Wei.

Gretslen waits until Ashtaar's eyes refocus, then continues. "The bridge will outlast Falcor."

"An eternal bridge?" Ashtaar turns her hand to look at the black agate oval, caresses it a last time one-handed, and then sets it back on the desk. "More, if you please."

"The Lancers of Mansuur have arrived in Esaria, and the SouthWomen of the Matriarchy are pushing to isolate Ranuak from the rest of Liedwahr."

"Again . . . how droll. The last time that happened in Ranuak most of them died. People never learn. What of Ebra?"

"The lands in the east around Dolov have sworn to Bertmynn. Hadrenn has asked for no pledges, but many around Synek would follow him because of his lineage."

"Do we know how much coin the Liedfuhr Konsstin has sent to Ebra?"

"There have been messengers with heavy purses, going from Mansuur to both Synek and Dolov, but no strong-boxes that Kendr or I have scried."

The spymistress's brows wrinkle for an instant. "You have missed something, Gretslen. I do not know what it may be, but I sense trouble, great trouble, for us." Ashtaar's smile is cold. "I am not a seer, nor have I your talent, nor Kendr's. I only know. Watch the sorceress closely, and Konsstin. They are the great players here."

Gretslen bows her head. "As you wish, Mightiness."

"I wish I were," murmurs Ashtaar, in a voice so low that only she can hear the words, before adding in a louder tone, "You may go, Gretslen."

17

Anna forced herself to finish the last of the heavy dark bread and the white cheese. The look in the mirror that morning had shown her that some little bit of the sunkenness in her cheeks was beginning to vanish. Lord! How much food did it take?

She swallowed and glanced across the worktable to Hanfor. "How many armsmen should go with us to Cheor?" She took a long swallow of water from her goblet, then refilled it from the pitcher she'd orderspelled earlier in the day.

"As many as possible," he answered, running a scarred hand through his gray thatch.

"You said that before," Anna said with a laugh. "How many is that? Fivescore? Six-?"

The arms commander fingered his gray-and-white clipped beard. "If I send Alvar with tenscore to accompany you, that will leave sixscore here. That is, sixscore that are trained, with another threescore that I would not trust anywhere—not yet."

The sorceress and regent wanted to laugh. Her standing army consisted of a few more than three hundred armsmen—not all of them even trained—and Konsstin had just sent a thousand trained lancers to Neserea. "We need more armsmen."

"We need more armsmen, even more recruits," Hanfor admitted. "And more arms. Konsstin has fiftyscore lancers in Esaria, and I would wager that Nubara will move them to Elioch as soon as possible. That doesn't count the two hundred–score armsmen left in the Prophet's forces. We've barely twenty-five–score everywhere in Defalk. More than a few score of those I wouldn't want anywhere near a fight. Not yet."

"We're going to need more than three times that, you said."

"I did." The arms commander fingered his white-and-gray beard. "And I could use fiftyscore—or more. Easily." He laughed harshly. "Except we have no weapons and no weapons smith for that many."

"No word from Ranuak?"

Hanfor shook his head. "The roads . . ."

Damn the roads! "What about the levies?"

"*If* all the lords honor their commitment to the liedstadt, you could marshal two hundred–score in levies. I wouldn't want even to try to use them in one place."

"You could put some under Jecks, and some under

Firis," Anna suggested. "Aren't there other lords who are trustworthy?"

Hanfor raised both eyebrows.

Anna nodded. There might be, but neither of them knew who they might be. Perhaps Jecks did, but right now, they didn't need to know. Yet. "Besides the roads, why can't we get more recruits?"

"You have been too successful, lady."

Anna looked at her arms commander.

"When crops are bad, when trade is poor, then the peasants, the farmers, the younger sons, they will accept the risk of arms for food and shelter and the few coppers paid raw recruits." Hanfor offered a wintry smile. "There is rain again in Defalk. They hope the crops will sprout and all will be well again in Defalk."

Another instance where she was a victim of her own success. Anna wanted to groan. "Don't they see it won't last if we can't protect Defalk?"

"You are the mighty sorceress. You will protect them." Hanfor's tone was sympathetically ironic.

"No. You're right. They don't care. No one's ever cared for them." Anna frowned. Where was there adversity?

"What about Ebra? Could we have Jerat . . . Has that group left for Mencha? The ones to regarrison the Sand Pass fort?" she asked, remembering that detail inadvertently. "Are you counting them?"

"They leave the day after tomorrow. Jerat is pleased; his sister lives there." Hanfor smiled. "He knows enough to start training any recruits he may find, and he has some extra coins to pay them. That's another score, and I didn't reckon them in the numbers I told you because half wouldn't be that much good in a battle. They'll be some help in repairing the Sand Pass fort."

"Do you think Jerat can find some more armsmen or recruits? Across the border in Ebra?"

"There were more than a few who disappeared after the Sand Pass battle. I told him to be very careful of any men who wanted to join who looked experienced. I will suggest that after he obtains those he can in Defalk, to make inquiries in Ebra.'' Hanfor laughed harshly. ''He will be careful, but I'd wager he can round up a score or more easily.'' The veteran shrugged. ''After that, we will see.''

A score? What was that against the hundreds of scores of Defalk's enemies? Anna wanted to shake her head. Instead, she repressed the gesture . . . and found she was clicking her nails again. A wry smile crossed her face. The nail-clicking had driven Sandy crazy, she thought, but he'd never said anything before he'd left. Not like Avery who'd given her a lecture on repressed anger.

She forced her thoughts back to the immediate problem—armsmen. Even if Hanfor could find another fifty-score armsmen or the equivalent of lancers, how would she pay them?

''Every score counts, and it is better to build a force slowly, and train them as you wish,'' pointed out the arms commander. ''You can also call on the levies of the Lady Gatrune and of Lord Jecks. They are almost as good as professional armsmen.''

''That's only another thousand.''

''You are their commander, and that counts for far more,'' Hanfor said. ''Far more.''

Perhaps . . . if everyone doesn't attack at once from every border. ''If I can employ sorcery,'' she answered. ''I'd feel better if we had a force that could stand off one enemy without me.''

''Before the end of the year, we will,'' promised Hanfor.

''I wish I had your confidence, Arms Commander.''

''I have seen what you have done to large forces who opposed you. Men will fight for you who would not have fought for Defalk before.''

''Let's hope so.'' Anna took another swallow of orderspelled water. Even in the chill of winter, she needed more liquids than others. Then, that had been true on earth as well. She'd always been prone to dehydration.

The graying veteran took a sip of wine from the goblet Anna had provided, then looked at his empty plate. "I will groan all the way back to the stables, and you ate twice what I did."

"I wish I didn't have to." Anna smiled. "The stables?"

"I am leading the lancer training this afternoon."

Anna felt guilty for keeping him. Like her, he was trying to handle too many things. Except he didn't complain, and she felt she was always complaining, if only to herself.

"Lady Anna?" Skent stood in the doorway.

Anna nodded for the page to enter, recognizing somehow that he needed a moment with her. Hanfor stood, but Anna raised her hand, gesturing for him to wait a moment.

"There is a woman in the courtyard. She has a babe and a child, and she says she is the sister of the player Daffyd." Skent offered a puzzled look.

Anna's guts churned. Dalila. Daffyd's sister and the woman who had taken her in when no one else would after the Sand Pass battle—and whose consort had tried to rape Anna. Anna shook her head. She'd placed a spell on the man—Madell—and had worried about it ever since.

Then, while she was recovering from the battle with the Evult, Anna had sent some golds and a message about Daffyd's death, but Dalila wouldn't have traveled to Falcor, not unless something was wrong, terribly wrong.

"I'll see her. Now."

"Perhaps I should go," suggested Hanfor.

"Not yet. Something might have happened in Synope."

As Anna recalled, Dalila was brunette and stocky and stood barely above Anna's shoulder. The pertness Anna remembered was gone, replaced by hollow eyes and exhaustion. Her face was smudged with dried mud, and her trousers ragged above shoes barely held together with thongs. Dalila cradled an infant, mechanically rocking the child. The dark-eyed, dark-haired Ruetha clung to her mother's dusty and tattered cloak. Ruetha's cheeks were streaked with dirt, a combination of dust and tears, Anna suspected.

"Dalila," the sorceress began, "what happened?"

"Lady . . ." Dalila sank to the polished stone floor and bent her head, as if unable to speak.

"Dalila," Anna said slowly, "you're welcome here. You welcomed me, when I had nowhere to turn, and you'll always be welcome. I don't know what happened, but you are welcome."

Only the faint shudders betrayed the silent sobs.

After a moment, Anna spoke again. "Is there . . . trouble in Synope? Because of Lord Hryding's death?"

A choked "No," was the only answer, followed by more sobs. Dalila did not look up.

Anna lifted the bell, rang it, and waited for Skent, then addressed the dark-haired page.

"Skent . . . Dalila and her children need food. They'll be staying with us. For the moment, after they eat, put them in one of the larger rooms in the players' quarters for now. And make sure they have some water and some towels to get cleaned up." Anna paused, and added, "Dalila took me in when no one else did. I'd like you to take care of all of this personally."

Skent nodded, his face impassive.

The sorceress stepped forward and reached down, slowly helping Dalila rise.

"Lady . . . I . . . be . . . so . . . No one else . . ."

"Dalila . . . I told you, and I meant it. You are welcome here." Anna squeezed the too-thin shoulder gently. "When you are fed and rested, we'll talk some more. Now you and Ruetha and the child need food and rest."

Dalila began to sob again.

Anna hugged her. "You'll be all right. You'll be safe." What else could she say? "Now, go with Skent. He'll make sure you get fed, and you have a room to rest and recover." Her eyes went to the page, fixing him. "They'll need to eat regularly. Make sure they get fed with the players for now. But they must eat. All right?"

"I understand, Lady Anna." Skent's eyes went to the pair, softening as they rested on Ruetha.

Anna helped Dalila to the door, and Ruetha tottered beside her mother, one hand still holding the tattered cloak.

."And see that they have some clean clothing, too."

Skent nodded again.

When the door closed, Anna found Hanfor smiling.

Anna raised her eyebrows in inquiry.

"You do not forget kindnesses, lady, and you repay your debts. I am glad I decided to remain in Defalk."

"So am I," Anna said. "But I'm not sure I've repaid all the kindnesses I've received."

"You will."

Anna wondered. "Will you make the arrangements for which armsmen will accompany us?" She paused. "Lord Jecks and Jimbob will be going with me."

"Twelvescore, then," Hanfor said firmly. "I held back some to protect the young lord."

"I'll be taking the players. I hope I can do some repairs along the way."

"You are still determined to travel to Synope after Cheor?" Hanfor asked.

"If I don't have too much trouble. I'd thought about stopping at Arien to see Lord Tybel, but Jecks thought that might not be a good idea, not after dealing with Arkad."

"He suspects you will have to use sorcery on Arkad."

"I hope I don't."

"If you really believed that, Regent Anna, you would not have to undertake this journey." A faint smile creased Hanfor's lips as he stood.

Anna grinned sheepishly.

"I will talk to Mies, to make sure you have two good supply wagons." Hanfor inclined his head before he left.

Alone, Anna walked to the window and looked down on the courtyard. Didn't the paving stones ever dry in the winter?

Had Madell driven Dalila out? Why hadn't anyone been willing to help her? Synope had to be three weeks by foot, if not longer with two children. Anna could feel herself seething. Every time she thought she'd come to understand and accept Erde, something like this reminded her how much women were looked down upon and abused.

"It's still that way on earth," she murmured to herself. Some places were worse than Defalk, although she didn't recall anywhere as bad as—where was it?—Sturinn? Where they still chained women? She shivered, hoping that she didn't have to deal with those people anytime soon. That would take more than simple sorcery.

Sorcery . . . that reminded her. She'd need players if she meant to do road and bridge work on the trip to Cheor. She hurried out of the receiving room, this time with Giellum and Lejun following her.

Anna crossed the courtyard, placing her boots carefully on the damp stones. Had she really understood how much rain Defalk had gotten before the Evult's sorcery had created the drought? Defalk in winter seemed more like . . . parts of Oregon, perhaps? Except it had more sunlight. Already the water level of the Falche where the Fal and the Chean met was two-thirds of what the older armsmen said was normal, and, based on the shape of the banks and the traces of old river beaches and the dried-up oxbow lake to the northwest of Falcor, they seemed to be right.

Liende wasn't in the rehearsal room, nor in her own room. Anna finally caught up to her on the top of the north tower.

The player looked out on the grayness that was Falcor in winter, with thin trails of smoke rising from scattered chimneys. Liende turned at Anna's boots—or Lejun's—on the stones.

"Regent . . ."

"I wanted to talk to you." Anna turned to her guard. "Lejun . . . if you would wait at the foot of the top stairs."

Lejun nodded stiffly and eased out of sight.

The sorceress had begun to understand why public figures became recluses, especially those who were more than figureheads. Then, sometimes, when so many things seemed beyond her control, she felt more like a figurehead than a real ruler.

Anna stepped toward the red-and-white-haired player.

"Your wish, Lady Anna?"

At times, especially in dealing with players, Anna wished for a little less deference and a bit more warmth. *You'll have to get used to it,* she told herself, forcing a smile. "We will be traveling to Cheor in several days. I would like you and the players to accompany us."

"I can only vouch for the two building spells right now. We might have the third one ready by then." Liende did not meet Anna's eyes.

"It's harder than you thought," Anna said.

Liende looked down.

"It's hard because I'm asking more than Brill did," Anna said quietly. "I'm asking you to use harmonies, and that makes it a lot harder. It makes stronger spells, but it's not easy."

"You are not saying that to ease my fears?"

The sorceress shook her head. "I mean it. I talked to Brill about harmony, but he wouldn't consider it. He said it was too dangerous, but I think that's because he wasn't trained with harmonies. He didn't understand harmony."

Anna had realized that for most people on Erde, even players, the term *harmony* had a far more general meaning in Liedwahr—something akin to "not creating dissonance" rather than the earthly technical musical meaning of parallel chords or supporting lines of music distinct from the melody line. Then, she supposed a lot of people on earth thought of the word in the same way.

"He did understand much," said Liende. "And he

would use Darksong. Mayhap he had reason to distrust this . . . use of harmony.''

The sorceress had to remind herself that Brill had been Liende's lover, and that Liende would hear little about his shortcomings. She paused, then spoke carefully. ''Any sorcerer can only do so much. Lord Brill could do many spells I have not even tried. I have been trained in some he did not know. All the spells I have used with the lutar are based on chorded harmony.''

Liende nodded slowly. ''You risk more than your players.''

''Can you have your players ready?''

''We will be ready with those spells, lady.''

''That's all I ask.'' That was all she could ask, Anna reflected, and, as usual, it wasn't really as much as she needed. ''Thank you.''

She headed back down the tower stairs.

Instead of remaining in her office in the receiving hall, she stopped there only long enough to reclaim the lutar. She carried it up the main stairs. She felt strong enough to engage in some limited sorcery, although she wanted to be at full physical strength when she began the journey to Cheor.

The smooth waters of the reflecting pool confirmed that she had gained back some weight. Her eyes were no longer sunken, nor her cheeks so hollow.

She took the lutar from its case, fingers caressing the smooth wood. Her eyes burned momentarily as she thought of its maker, poor Daffyd, entombed in lava in the valley of Vult—all because he'd summoned her to revenge his father's death.

With the grease marker, she made the changes to the mirror spell, then hummed through them—without the words. Then she strummed through the chords. Finally, she put it together.

''Water, water, in this my hall,
show me now that Konsstin who seeks my fall.

Show him bright, and show him fast,
and make that strong view well last.''

Konsstin still wore the sky-blue tunic, but no cloak. The Liedfuhr sat behind a dark wooden desk, outlined by the light from windows behind him. A map—what appeared to be Liedwahr—was spread before him. As he studied the map, he frowned, but his lips did not move.

Anna strummed the lutar again, singing the brief couplet to end the view in the pool.

Konsstin apparently remained where he had been, Mansuus, presumably, but was studying a map. In preparation for what? Anna wished she knew.

She checked the lutar—it still had a tendency to slip out of tune—and changed the spell for Dencer.

Dencer was riding, wearing a breastplate and carrying a lance. Anna watched the image in the pool only long enough to see that he was practicing thrusting the lance at a target as he rode by it. He'd been working hard. That was obvious from the red face and the shimmer that indicated sweat.

The sorceress released the image with the couplet and exhaled. One was studying maps and the other improving warlike skills. Not conclusive, but not exactly reassuring. But unless she wanted to spell all her strength all the time following them in the pool, it was about as good an indication as she was likely to get at the moment.

Wasn't anything easy?

For you, of course not. She immediately felt ashamed of the thought. Lots of people had it far harder than she had. Like poor Dalila, exhausted, with nowhere to turn, and ashamed of having to prostrate herself at Anna's feet.

The sorceress pursed her lips. What else had she meant to check? Oh, the question of harmony. She looked at the books on the shelf—the ones she'd moved in right after she'd finished the reflecting pool. The first handful of the leatherbound books were those Brill had let her use in the workroom he'd lent her at Loiseau—*Boke of Liedwahr,*

The Naturale Philosophie, Proverbes of Neserea, Donnermusik.

She pulled out *Donnermusik*, searching for the sections that had alluded to harmony, hoping her memory had been correct, but worried about Liende's dubious looks.

> . . . harmonic variants be most important as a musical consideration, for they must in truthe effect a change of musical resemblement through the constant repetition, with most suitable variants, of the bass pattern . . . through trommel. . . .
>
> . . . the relationship between the thunder, and that needs must be represented by the falk horn, supplemented by a continuous bass provided by a trommel, and the lightning . . . must be joined by a melodic line of the violincello. . . .

She remembered those lines and skipped ahead to another section. Nothing there, except more discourses on storms. Another few pages . . . Where was it?

Anna took a deep breath. *You've got to slow down. You won't find anything just flipping through pages that are half Old English and half bastard German.*

Another breath, and she forced herself to read more deliberately. Ten pages farther on, she found what she thought she'd remembered.

> . . . in truthe the greatest of sorceries shulde result from dissonant clothing played with gewalt equal to that gewalt of the spell melodie. . . . The players of each parte needs must kraft their resemblements. . . . Any endliche resolution . . . must needs embodye harmonic consonance. . . .

Her head aching from puzzling through the archaic language, she slowly closed the book.

Leaving the lutar in the scrying room, she slowly

walked back along the corridor toward Lady Essan's room, trying to ignore the guards that followed her.

"So . . . another venture you be off on," said the white-haired widow, even before Anna settled into the chair across the low table from Essan.

"Why do you say that?" Anna took a handful of the sugared nuts from the dish, then another, realizing that, again, she was hungry.

"Synondra told me that you rush hither and yon, back and forth. That stern arms commander works with Mies to make sure of the finest wagons and teams, and blades clash all the time on the practice quarter. My ears are still sharp, would-be daughter."

Anna laughed. "Just like a mother. You know what I'm about even if I haven't told you."

"And you were saying, sorceress-girl, my daughter you'd be." Essan grinned over the brandy goblet.

"So I did."

"What be on your mind, seeing as much there'd be you would be doing?"

"What do you know about Lord Arkad?" Anna asked.

"He was a problem for Donjim, and he must be one for you, too. You asked about him a time back." Lady Essan sipped her brandy.

"He hasn't paid his liedgeld," Anna admitted.

"If any lord could afford liedgeld, Arkad could. Donjim envied those lands, you know, but Arkad always supported him. He even sent more levies than he had to for the second peasant uprising. I didn't ride with Donjim then. I should have, broken leg or not. Donjim wasn't ever the same after that. He died right after he returned." Essan fussed the embroidered pillow behind her back.

"I'm sorry."

"You had nothing to do with it. Long before your time, sorceress-woman. You were having your own children then, like as not, never dreaming you'd be here."

Anna certainly hadn't ever expected she'd end up on a world she once would have regarded as a total fantasy.

"He couldn't understand it. No, he couldn't, my poor Donjim. Twenty years of peace, prosperity, and the very peasants he'd supported rebelled." Essan snorted. "Some foolishness about land reverting to the lord if a man had no direct heirs. All stirred up by those high and mighty women in Encora, I thought."

"Do you still think so?"

Essan laughed, more a cackle than a true laugh. "I was right, and I was wrong. It was women from Encora, but not the Matriarch, or the traders, but those crazy ones, the Sisters of the South. They were so crazy their own Matriarch had to turn her own guards on them. The Sturinn thing, you know. Did I tell you about that?" Her eyes glazed over momentarily. "That be the problem with growing old. You talk, and you don't remember."

"You said that some group . . . the Sisters of something . . . stormed a ship from Sturinn. . . ."

"Sisters of the South—they were the ones. They sent blades to the women of Stromwer and Sudwei and Lerona. Terrible mess, it was. Now, some say, the crazy women have a new name, the SouthWomen, excepting they're still the same, not even remembering what happened to the last bunch." Essan took a hefty belt to drain the apple brandy in the goblet, then refilled it from the crystal decanter without looking at Anna. "Terrible, it was, back then, and old Wassir's son used those very blades to try to overthrow his father. That was Aaslin, not Geansor. Blood everywhere, Donjim said. Wassir died, and Donjim killed Aaslin himself, and Geansor near died. Might have been better had he. Geansor's other brother, the youngest one, he was killed by raiders, but that came later."

The more Anna heard, the worse it got. If Lady Essan were right, then all her consort had gotten out of twenty years of decent rule was heartbreak and revolt. If she were wrong, then Defalk had been in turmoil for far longer than the past decade. Neither thought was exactly comforting.

18

DUMARIA, DUMAR

Three men enter the audience chamber, led by a tall and rangy man in a heavy brown woolen jacket. Under the open jacket, he wears a short-sleeved white tunic, and white trousers. His face is tanned. The two men who accompany him are also rangy and tanned.

Ehara stands before the gilt chair upholstered in red velvet. "Greetings! Welcome to Dumaria."

"We are pleased to be here." The tall man answers in a heavily accented voice, bowing. "I am Sea-Marshal jerRestin." He gestures to the two who flank him. "Sea-Captain jerKillek and Sea-Captain jerHallin."

"A small token for the warm welcome we have received." The Sea-Marshal lifts the small chest he carries and offers it to Ehara. "From Sturinn to Dumar."

Ehara, looking burly before the rangy Sturinnese, accepts the chest, a wooden box no more than two spans long and one wide that is almost lost in his overlarge hands. The sides of the chest are carved with intertwined serpents rising out of a mother-of-pearl surf, and the top bears the crest of Dumar—the mountain ram on a tor, wrought in rubies and gold. "You are welcome, and my thanks for such an artistic treasure."

"Please open it."

Ehara does, and glances at the unset rubies, diamonds, and pearls in the small container. "A most generous and artistic treasure." He closes the case gently. "And to what do I owe the pleasure of your company and such a *small* token of appreciation?"

"We merely wished to meet the famous Lord Ehara."

"My fame as ruler of the smallest nation in Liedwahr

has carried all the way to the lands and isles of far Sturinn?'' Ehara laughs self-deprecatingly.

"Your fame has carried farther than you would have imagined, Lord Ehara,'' returned jerRestin.

"What have I done that merits such notice?'' Ehara's eyes narrow ever so slightly.

"We understand that you are considering efforts to strengthen your northern border, Lord Ehara,'' suggests the Sea-Marshal, the accent in his voice stronger.

"I've never mentioned such an action to anyone.'' Ehara smiles easily. "Are you Sea-Priests able to read the tides of the future?''

"When the tides run strongly and pluck at the very harmonies of Erde, then anyone who stops to look can see where they will take the unwary.'' The Sea-Marshal offers a bland smile.

"What is this disturbing tide of which you speak?''

"We understand that the Regent of Defalk is also a sorceress, and one who would change all of Liedwahr. Surely, that is a tide you would watch . . . and have watched.''

"I wasn't aware that the Sea-Priests bothered themselves with the petty affairs of poor and distant Liedwahr.''

"We look on Dumar as a bulwark against this riptide of destruction that will change all you—and we—hold dear. That is why we offer a mere token of friendship and appreciation.''

"I see.'' Ehara tilts his head to the side fractionally, still holding the carved chest. "And in return for such generosity . . . what must poor and lowly Dumar provide to mighty Sturinn?''

"Only friendship, Lord Ehara. Only friendship.''

"You value my friendship highly.''

"It is said that those who share enemies must be friends. Our fortune-seers have declared that the Regent of Defalk is our enemy.'' JerRestin shrugged. "Since she is also your enemy, we must be friends and allies.''

"What of the Liedfuhr of Mansuur?" Ehara's voice carries a tone between bemusement and curiosity.

"The Liedfuhr is preoccupied with his own concerns and has expressed little interest in the friendship of Sturinn." The rangy Sea-Marshal shrugs. "We must seek friends among those who would have friends."

"So you must. So must we all." Ehara laughs once more. "And I bid you welcome, welcome as friends and allies." He sets the chest on the red velvet of the chair, then steps off the dais and embraces the Sea-Marshal, who refrains from flinching.

19

After discussing the last of the arrangements for the next day's journey toward Cheor with Hanfor, Alvar, and Jecks, Anna waited until the receiving-room door closed. She stood and stretched, then took a deep swallow of cold water from the goblet, draining it.

As she lifted the pitcher to refill the goblet, her eyes went to the window, and to the gray-and-white clouds she could see. What else did she need to take care of before she left?

It had been two days and she still hadn't seen Daffyd's sister Dalila. That didn't seem like Dalila, but, then again, with all her preoccupations, Anna might not have seemed that approachable.

With a deep breath, she lifted the bell and rang it, standing and gathering herself together.

Her dark-haired page, Skent, appeared.

"Skent, would you take me to the room where Dalila is?"

"She's in the players' quarters, like you told me, Lady

Anna. And I have made sure she and the child have gotten food." Skent's lips pursed.

"You've had to take it to hĕr?" asked the regent.

"Yes, lady. She won't leave the room—except for the jakes." Skent flushed. "I guess . . . I mean . . . I don't know."

Anna laughed wryly. "I understand." She added, "Thank you. I knew I could count on you, and I appreciate it."

Skent flushed. "You . . . you keep your word."

"I try." *You try . . . but how long will you be able to? You said you'd be there for Elizabetta, and . . .* She pursed her lips and forced herself to keep walking. Only Skent, of all her pages, would have trusted her enough to say that, a good harbinger for what she hoped of him.

They crossed the courtyard, the wind whipping the purple sash Anna had forgotten to remove and leave in the receiving room. Behind them followed Giellum and Blaz.

"The second door, lady." Skent gestured.

After marching up the narrow staircase, Anna rapped on the door to the second-level room.

Dalila opened it, falling back. "Lady . . . I am . . ."

Anna shook her head as she stepped inside and closed the door, leaving Skent and the guards in the narrow passageway. "Dalila, you've seen me in your robe and dusty boots doing laundry. Do you think I've changed that much?"

The brunette's eyes remained on the plank floor, and her shoulders slumped in a posture of defeat. Behind her, on the bed, sleeping in a faded gray blanket, lay the baby.

Ruetha looked up from the floor by the single wide pallet. The girl's fingers clutched a rag doll, and she hugged the cloth figure to her, taking her eyes from Anna.

"I said we'd talk, Dalila. I'm sorry . . . things have been busy, but . . . I'm here."

A soft snore came from the bed, and Anna smiled as she glanced at the sleeping infant. The smile faded as her eyes returned to the defeated-looking Dalila.

"I should not . . . I would not have come . . . but where could I turn? If it were just for me . . ."

Anna could hardly imagine walking for weeks on end with two children. She could remember once, when her own mother had taken Anna to visit the back holler where her grandparents lived, how her mother had carried the heavy suitcase along the half-dry creek bed for a hundred feet or so, and then come back and carried Anna those hundred feet, time after time. And that had only been for a few miles!

"You have to think of the children. Mothers always do." *And now you can't.* The image of the black-lined rectangle on the wall of her room slipped into Anna's mind momentarily.

Again, Dalila did not look at the sorceress or speak.

"Tell me what happened." Anna feared she already knew. "When did he leave? What happened?"

The silence lengthened in the late afternoon, but Anna forced herself to wait, forced herself to remain calm despite all the items she needed to deal with before dinner, before riding out to the south in the morning.

After a time, Dalila began to speak, her voice barely audible above the light breeze that whispered past the single shuttered window. "Madell . . . After you left, he scarce would come home. When Anandra—please don't be angry with that—when she was born, he yelled . . . He told me I wasn't even good for sons . . ." The words broke off into sobs.

Anna stepped forward and put her arms around the smaller woman, holding her as she cried. Dalila was scarcely more than skin and bones, and Anna wanted to call down all the harmonies and disharmonies on Madell. Instead, she swallowed and waited. "I'm not angry. I'm sad for you, and flattered that you would do something like that." Would anyone on earth even remember her name? Or would she be remembered as the mother or grandmother or whatever, who just vanished? Anna swallowed.

In time, when Dalila's sobs had subsided into small shivers, Anna stepped back and prompted gently. "And after that?"

"Then . . . I got your scroll about Daffyd—and the golds. You bespelled Madell so he could not touch me. But he took the golds, and he sold the house and his share in the mill to Reuten—"

"Reuten?" Anna asked involuntarily.

"His older brother. Reuten never cared for me. I was not from Synope." Dalila took a deep breath. "Madell took his clothes and left. No one saw him again. Reuten said he went to Dumar. He claimed that I drove him away."

Anna didn't think much of Reuten, either. "And the house?"

"Reuten told me I had to leave. The house was his, and I had no sons."

Sons again! Damn masculine-dominated society! Anna swallowed. "So you left?"

"What else could I do? Lord Hryding was ill, and I was turned away at his gate."

Another mark against Anientta, Anna reflected, and another reason to stop at Flossbend on her return from Cheor. *Assuming things go as planned and nothing else goes wrong.* She swallowed the sigh. Something else would go wrong. She just didn't know what it might be. "Lord Hryding would not have turned you away, but he was so ill that he died."

"They say he was a good lord." Dalila's voice was flat.

"He was, and I'll miss him. But we can't change what's already happened. And you can't change what's happened to you." Anna forced a smile. "There's a place for you and the children here."

"Lady . . . the silvers you gave me for the children, I had to use them." Dalila looked down as though Anna would spell her or strike her.

"To get here?"

"Aye." Dalila's voice was low.

"Then they were well spent."

"You say . . . a place for me . . . me? I am no player like Daffyd." The brunette's eyes darted to the sleeping Anandra, and then dropped to the plank floor. "What can I do? I have the bairns."

"Dalila? Can you write?"

"I know my letters. Da made sure of that. He beat me when I missed." The woman shivered.

"A sorceress can only do so much. Will you help me? I will pay you, like all those who help." Anna forced herself to be patient, recalling that no one had been ex- actly patient when Avery had dumped her. She'd still had to get up and go to work, to teach not only the willing, but the whining students, and there'd been too few of the good ones and too many of those who sat there like lumps and said, in effect, "Teach me. I don't have to learn; it's your job to make me learn."

"How could I help?"

Anna laughed softly. "There is so much to do, and I'm only one person. One of the problems I have is that too few people know their letters, and they learn them too late. They should learn them when they are not much older than Ruetha. I would like you to teach letters to the younger children. For that, you would get your room and food and a half-silver a week."

Dalila sank onto the floor planks. "For teaching the letters to children. You are too generous. I cannot . . . That is too much."

Anna thought, then added, "You can also, if you wish, help in the kitchen. You cook well, and Meryn is always complaining that she doesn't have enough help."

Dalila nodded. "I can cook."

"I'll let Meryn know." Anna paused. "I am leaving tomorrow, and you will have to talk to her yourself. We won't be able to work out your lessons until I return." She lifted her hand. "But you'll be paid starting on one- day."

"You are good, lady."

"No. I am not that good. Had I not come to Synope, you would still have Madell, and your brother. I owe you at least this. You can help me. I wish I could do more, but Defalk's a poor land, and there's only so much that I can do."

Dalila shook her head. "My father sent me away. My consort deserted me, and his brother turned me out. My lord could not help me. You are a stranger, and you have offered more than all of them." She bowed her head. "I am glad I named Anandra after you."

Anna swallowed. "Thank you." What else could she say? What else could she have done after all the damage that followed her?

20

STROMWER, DEFALK

LORD Dencer." The young-looking Dumaran officer in red bows to the taller and slightly older man who stands by the ornately carved desk. "Gortin, captain of lancers for Lord Ehara."

The tall and gangly Dencer nods his head sharply, and a lock of thinning brown hair droops across a too-high forehead, almost screening his left eye. "To what do we owe the courtesy of a visit from a neighbor to the south?" His eyes flicker imperceptibly to the pair of armsmen in tan leathers at the door, and the one who stands by the tall bookcase to his left.

"A sad courtesy, a sad one indeed." Gortin bows again. "We were led to believe that one traveler by the name of Slevn came from Stromwer. He paid a courtesy visit to Lord Ehara, and we had thought he returned to Stromwer."

"You had *thought* this . . . visitor . . . had returned?" Dencer's eyebrows rise, and he brushes the wayward lock of hair back and across his balding pate.

"Until we discovered he had been beset by bandits. He was traveling alone." Gortin shrugs. "Even in a land as ordered as Dumar, when one reaches the Sudbergs, there are places for evildoers to hide." The red-uniformed Dumaran extends a pouch. "We returned his effects to you, as his lord, since we were headed to see you."

"How convenient," Dencer responds mildly, taking the large canvas sack and setting it upon the desk without opening it.

"It was the least we could do. We were already riding this way, and it appeared that this fellow had been heading home." Gortin smiles blandly.

"I am curious. How did you know this . . . person . . . was the one who visited Lord Ehara?"

Gortin bows. "I could not be precisely certain, my lord, but there were certain indications. This Slevn wore a gray cloak and trousers, and so did the unfortunate we found. His purse was gone, but he had tucked a scroll with Lord Ehara's official seal inside the lining of his cloak, and a shiny fresh-minted gold. Lord Ehara sent the scroll with him. It was still sealed, and we didn't open it, seeing as it was addressed to you. It be in the pouch."

"The bandits did not slit or take his cloak?"

"It was covered with blood, Lord Dencer. They were hasty, from the signs."

"Tell me," says Dencer, standing erect by the desk, cranelike, but a predatory crane. "Might anyone in Dumar know why this—what did you say his name was?—this fellow went to see Lord Ehara? Was he a trader or some such?"

Gortin shrugs. "None would know but Lord Ehara. Lord Ehara saw him alone. That is why, when we came across his body, I had thought to inform you when we arrived."

"My thanks for your . . . rectitude, Captain." Dencer

frowns. "Surely, you and your squad did not ride all the way from Dumaria merely to return the effects of an unfortunate traveler."

"No, ser." Gortin bows again, and extends a scroll, trimmed in gilt and sealed with both red wax and a scarlet ribbon. "Lord Ehara sent us to offer his friendship. Lord Ehara understands that all must be neighbors and friends in these unsettled times."

"There is friendship, and there is friendship," Dencer observes.

Gortin turns and takes a velvet pouch from the lancer who stands behind him, then extends that. "A token of the quality and sincerity of Lord Ehara's desire to demonstrate his most earnest desire to establish friendship between his lands and yours of Stromwer."

Dencer lifts the pouch. "He makes a weighty gesture indeed." The pouch goes beside the first on the desk. "Your lord has a way with gestures." He smiles, although the hard glitter does not leave his eyes. "After riding so far with such a generous gesture, you must join us for the evening meal. Your lancers will be fed with my armsmen."

"I would be most pleased. I understand you have a most talented consort."

"Ah, yes, I do." Dencer's smile vanishes, and he looks down at the polished wooden floor. "Alas, she is indisposed, and will not be joining us. At times, I fear for her health. These times have weighed hard upon her. You know that she was held in Falcor, and she has yet to recover from the . . . effects of that . . . stay."

"Oh . . . I had not heard. I am so sorry. . . ." Gortin offers a solicitous smile. "Lord Ehara had said that these times have indeed fallen hard upon some of Defalk."

"We do what we can, and we can but hope that the surroundings here will ensure her full recovery."

"With such a burden, Lord Dencer," says Gortin gravely, "I could not impose upon your hospitality. That would be asking far too much of your charity and good-will.''

''Nonsense, your presence and news will divert me. Surely, you would not gainsay me that in, as you put it, this time of trouble?'' Dencer offers a tentative smile.

''Are you sure of that? We would not add any burden to those you already bear.''

''I would be most pleased to hear of your lord and of how matters fare in Dumar these days. Most pleased.'' Dencer nods, and then brushes back his unruly hair.

II

THEMA

21

Anna stood in the saddle for a moment, trying to stretch her legs. After just two days in the saddle, her legs ached—youth spell or no youth spell.

The fine, cold rain that had begun to sleet around her and the others in the last glass, just before midmorning—when they were nowhere close to any real shelter—didn't help her mood much, or her legs. The warm rains of the previous week had heralded spring, according to Skent and even Ytrude, but the mist that fell around her was anything but warm.

"Spring?" she said, more to herself than anyone.

"It is spring. You can see some shoots in the fields," answered Alvar, riding beside her. "The roads have almost dried." His fingers stroked the leather of his reins, almost absently.

"Let's hope they stay that way. The last thing we need is more muddy roads."

"Indeed, lady." Captain Alvar nodded, then touched his black beard with his left hand.

Anna's eyes went to the Falche River, a muddy swatch of water that filled perhaps a third of the riverbed to her left. The scrub by the river's edge, and the rushes and grasses, remained tannish brown and bent downstream—the legacy of the Evult's flood of the past harvest season. A pair of teals paddled in the backwater formed by a sandbar, apparently indifferent to the chill mist-rain.

Farinelli whuffed and tossed his head, as if to fling dampness out of his eyes . . . or something. Anna didn't pretend to know much about horses, except how to feed, saddle, and groom the big palomino gelding and to pay attention to the signals he sent. She didn't always understand them, but she'd learned that Farinelli had a reason for anything he did. Then, she supposed most horses did, unlike people, who all too often seemed to act against their own best interests, or for no reason at all.

She laughed softly to herself. Were her thoughts getting to be like those of the horsy types who seemed to prefer horses to people? Those people she'd never thought she'd understand.

Alvar looked over from his mount inquiringly.

"I'm beginning to understand why some people prefer horses to people."

"Horses don't talk back unless you mistreat them," the veteran armsman said. "For most mounts, kindness goes farther than with people." He readjusted the oiled leather poncho, and driblets of water skidded off the dark leather toward the rain-darkened clay of the road. So far, the rain hadn't been heavy enough to turn the road to mud—yet.

"How much farther to Cheor?" Jimbob rode behind Anna and, for the past few deks, beside Jecks.

Anna smiled at Jimbob's question to his grandsire. The impatience of the young with journeys hadn't changed between worlds or universes. Of her own children, Mario had been the worst, especially on the long drives from New England back to Cumberland to visit family, the trips that Avery had avoided whenever he could.

Now . . . now she was ruling a kingdom, and she couldn't even use her sorcery to see Mario or Elizabetta. In a season, maybe? Brill had said that he had been able to see the mist worlds—earth mostly—in his reflecting pool if he were sparing in his attempts. The sorceress shrugged her stiffening shoulders.

"Two days, mayhap three. Or four, should the rain fall harder and the roads turn to mud." Jecks' words were clipped, as though the white-haired and hazel-eyed lord's thoughts were elsewhere.

Anna respected Jecks, his honesty, his comparative open-mindedness, and his intelligence. And there was definitely chemistry between them . . . but there was also a huge cultural gap—and the endless problems of the country she'd ended up ruling as regent for his grandson.

Anna glanced up at the indistinct grayness. Was the rain lessening? How could she ask for it not to rain, when Defalk had suffered such dryness for so long? Especially in the case of a gentle rain.

"There might be a way station at Hygris," Jecks offered, easing his mount onto the shoulder of the road and drawing abreast of Anna. He gestured at a group of buildings emerging out of the mist and rain ahead.

"There wouldn't be any real shelter for the lancers, would there?"

"Not likely. The old inn burned three years ago."

"We'll stop for a little rest," Anna said. "But we might as well push on. There's no point in having armsmen sit in the rain and get wet so I can stay dry."

"I thought you might say that." Jecks laughed. "Just like Alasia."

"We're similar, but not exactly alike." Anna wasn't sure she wanted to be thought of as Jecks' daughter. "For one, I'm a little older. And I'm not . . ." She broke off the sentence with a rueful laugh. "Let's leave it at that." She didn't want to state blatantly that she had no intention of being treated as his daughter.

"No, you're not," Jecks answered with a grin. "As your actions often declare."

Alvar struggled to keep a straight face. So did Anna, almost forgetting the rain that misted around her and the column of armsmen and wagons that followed.

22

ENCORA, RANUAK

The two women stand at the edge of the crowd in the wind-swirled square. Behind them rises a canvas banner that flaps in the wind, proclaiming in bright blue lettering, *SouthWomen: For Eternal Harmony!*

"Mother warned you, Veria," says the slender brunette.

"She only said that it was unwise to distrust someone in accord with the greatest of the harmonies. This sorceress is nothing more than another power-hungry woman of the north who will turn on anyone at the first need or opportunity. She also supports a man's claim to rule Defalk. She will not even rule in her own right. There is nothing worse than a woman serving as a stalking goat for men. Better an honest man than a deceitful woman." Veria's words are low, but intense. "Mother or Matriarch, she did not say one word against my joining the SouthWomen."

"Not in so many words, but it was a warning."

"Why are you here, Alya? To act as Mother's spy?"

"Mother didn't send me." Alya coughs twice, then continues. "I'm here because you've always heard what you wanted to hear and seen what you wanted to see."

"She has you spying on me."

Alya laughs. "She knows what you're doing. She needs no spies. She has let us choose our own way. This way is wrong, and in time, you will pay dearly for it."

"Then let me pay in my own coin. Why should you care?"

"You are my sister, and you will suffer."

"You've never cared that much before. Why now?"

"Because Mother and Father care, and when you suffer, they will suffer."

"You really believe that rubbish about the harmonies? That a power-hungry woman from the mist worlds really cares about anything we hold dear? How could you?"

"It's very simple, Veria. Very simple. Simple enough for you to see . . . if you would. Let me ask you this—on the important events, has Mother ever been wrong? Have she and Father ever been wrong about what has happened?"

"They did not foresee the very sorceress they caution against opposing."

"Then see as you will." Alya shakes her head. "Do as you will. Only recall that I have tried to caution you. Those blades you will buy—if you have not already— will cut you more dearly than any of you would wish."

The noise of the crowd rises as a tall woman steps onto the platform below the banner. Alya's eyes flicker toward the speaker as the crowd subsides. When she looks back beside herself, Veria has slipped away.

23

Anna stretched surreptitiously in the saddle, then shifted her weight to ease the continual soreness in her posterior, a posterior far more slender than it had been a year earlier. Her stomach grumbled slightly, reminding her to take another of the hard biscuits from the cloth pouch tied to the front saddle ring.

The road followed the ridge west of the Falche River, and the higher tilled fields between the road and riverbank already showed signs of green. It was barely past dawn, and the lower fields were still clothed in ground fog. The green sprouts in the higher fields, though, she could clearly see, unlike those outside of Falcor pointed out by Hanfor days earlier.

"Not too much farther to go," said Alvar.

"Do you think Arkad knows we're coming?"

"If he has seers, he could see us on the road." The captain straightened his burly frame and turned in the saddle as if to check on whether someone watched.

"But he wouldn't know where we're headed. Not yet."

"Not yet," added Jecks.

Anna peered through the morning mist toward the river, toward the buildings rising out of the white ground-fog beyond the stone bridge that arched over the Falche and into Cheor itself.

Supposedly, Synfal—Arkad's liedburg—lay farther north of Cheor on a low hill that overlooked both the Falche and the Synor Rivers. That meant crossing the river and then riding back north.

"How much farther to Cheor?" Jimbob asked from Anna's right. As it neared the river town, the road had widened enough for Anna's force to ride four abreast—if no one happened to be headed north out of Cheor.

Anna smiled again. Definitely, some things remained constant with human nature, like the impatience of the young, although Anna had to admit that Jimbob hadn't asked that question until after the second day, unlike Mario, who had asked it ten minutes after the car left the house.

Within two deks, the ridge the road had followed began to slope into bottomland, dark rich soil tilled recently and filled with green sprouts. The ground fog began to dissipate with the growing warmth of the spring sun.

Anna gestured toward the fields that seemed to stretch westward from the river for deks and deks, looking at Jecks.

"Corn and maize here—even some sorghum, about the only place in Defalk. We grow more barley. Heartier stuff."

"Barley is better for beer," offered Alvar.

Anna hadn't seen that much beer in Defalk, and she glanced at Jecks. "Do you brew much beer at Elheld?"

"Some. More in recent years. We lost many of the old vines."

Were the vineyards another casualty of the Evult's drought? Along with how many other crops and people you don't even know about?

The road curved over the next dek to head directly toward the river. An arched bridge with three spans and two heavy stone piers in midstream offered the sole access to Cheor from the west—a bridge that had been far enough downstream to survive the Evult's floods of the fall before.

The dark-brown clay road widened even more closer to the bridge, as the riverbanks narrowed and deepened and the muddy water filled the entire streambed. From what Anna could see, when the Falche was full, the river would be nearly ten yards deep. The battered clay levees on both sides testified that the Falche had indeed run deep in the past and that it had not recently, not with the gaps in the banks in places.

As they rode closer to the bridge, Alvar leaned toward Anna. "I would suggest a van."

A van? Anna paused, then finally had to ask, "A van? I'm not a military person, Captain. . . ."

"A forward guard, lady. We do not know exactly how friendly . . ."

"Of course."

"Just a half-score," suggested Jecks.

Alvar nodded.

"And you might have your instrument and a spell ready," added the white-haired lord, turning to Anna.

"First ten from the purple company!" called out Alvar. "Form a van!"

As the armsmen eased their mounts onto the shoulder of the road and around Anna, she twisted in the saddle and extracted the lutar. What spell could she use for defense? A variation on the repulsion spell? She hummed the melody, mentally trying to fit the words into the tune.

A single-horse wagon groaned over the stone paving blocks of the bridge and toward the column. The driver looked up at the line of riders, and immediately drove the cart south along the crude way formed by the levee.

"He didn't like our looks," observed Alvar.

"Would you?" asked Jecks with a laugh. "With near two hundred horse?" He glanced at Jimbob, and added in a lower voice, "Most tradesmen and farmers will flee armsmen. They fear losing their goods and life. Never give them reason to fear. Remember, armsmen grow nothing and create nothing. They only allow you to hold what others grow and create. Farmers and tradesmen are the heart of a land."

Anna nodded, almost to herself, then glanced at Jimbob, who nodded at his grandsire's words, but with a nod that meant he heard the words, not necessarily their meaning.

Jecks glanced at Anna.

She shook her head and offered a faint smile.

He shrugged in return. "We say what we must."

"As often as we have to," she answered.

Alvar nodded slowly, but a vaguely puzzled expression remained on young Jimbob's face.

As Farinelli's hoofs clicked on the stones of the bridge, Anna one-handedly readjusted her felt hat, a copy of the one she'd lost at Vult, comfortable, but scarcely stylish. She doubted she looked stylish even without the hat, not in pale green trousers and tunic, although the green leather riding boots might have offered a hint as to her station.

Station? You're worried about that? She smiled to herself.

From the height of the second arch, Anna could sense that Cheor was an old town, clearly older than Falcor. Less than fifty yards past the stone-paved approachway to the bridge, a hodgepodge of buildings began. The houses were not stone, but mainly of yellow bricks. Some were covered with stucco, once whitewashed, but now dingy and gray. The roofs were made of a dark red tile, and more than a handful of the roofs showed cracked and missing tiles.

The vanguard rode silently off the bridge and down the main thoroughfare, if a street paved with cracked stones, with weeds sprouting intermittently, and open sewers on each side of the pavement, if that constituted a main thoroughfare. The sound of the main force behind on the bridge echoed down the constricted street.

A calico cat sidled up to a damp-sided rain barrel on the right, then vanished into the adjacent alley. On the left side of the narrow street, before a shop that bore a weathered green sign with crude line drawings of a basket and a barrel, stood a dog, straining at a heavy rope tied to a post that supported a sagging porch roof. The dog continued to growl as the riders neared.

From the basketmaker-cooper's porch, a scar-faced woman glared as the column neared. Anna met the woman's eyes, and, after an instant, the woman looked away, her mouth moving, but with words inaudible to the sorceress.

Anna took a slow deep breath as she passed the basketmaker's, and wished she hadn't. The stench reminded her of an ill-tended jakes—or certain public *banos* she'd encountered on her sole South American tour.

Two women bearing large baskets glanced up at the clacking of hoofs, then darted down a side alley.

Farther toward the center of the town, a man with wispy white hair stared from under a tattered gray awning that sheltered three tables as they passed and rode into the open square.

The square of Cheor held a low yellow-brick platform roughly thirty yards square. The platform was empty except for a bearded man covered with a ragged gray blanket and slumped in one corner. His mud-covered feet were bare. A rope ran from his hand to a yellow dog who lay on the bricks, his eyes on the riders.

The street around the platform was cobbled, except for a handful of irregularly spaced potholes, each partly filled with rainwater.

On the far side of the square was another cooper's, with a man-sized barrel over the door, bound with twisted willow rather than with iron hoops. The sound of hammering echoed from the general direction of the cooper's shop. Beside the cooper's was a larger structure, bearing the crossed candles of a chandlery. On the other side of the cooper's was another shop, or something, which had no sign.

On the short side of the square—to Anna's right and beyond the restaurant or cafe under the awning—were four buildings, each two stories high, and narrow. The windows and doors of the last building were boarded closed, and one of the second-floor shutters of the adjoining building hung at an angle, as if held only by a single hinge.

A heavyset red-haired woman peered from the window of the second building, one with a white sign bearing the image of a pair of boots. At the sight of the horses entering the square, her mouth formed an O, soundlessly, and her head vanished.

Alvar eased his mount toward a gangly figure standing by the mounting block before the building Anna would have called a dry goods store. The red-painted shutters were drawn back to reveal an unglassed window, behind which were bolts of cloth displayed on a rack.

Anna reined up, waiting, and behind her the column slowed.

Is this a good idea? We could be sitting ducks . . . or whatever. Her eyes flicked around the square, but she could only see what she would have expected to see—women carrying bundles, a young woman half holding the hand of a toddler, half dragging him toward the cooper's, a youth carting a plank into the cooper's.

"Which way to Lord Arkad's?" asked Alvar.

"Ah . . . I couldn't be saying, ser armsman." The man

swallowed almost convulsively. "His holding's north somewhere, they say. Me . . . I never been there."

"You've never been there?" asked the captain flatly.

"No, ser. No, ser."

Anna recognized the signs. No retainer of Arkad's would reveal anything, fearing the wrath of a local lord far more than that of even armed men who would pass and might never reappear. It also meant Arkad was indeed feared, and that bothered her.

She turned in the saddle, and her fingers ran over the lutar. Then she sang.

> "Tell the truth and tell us true,
> all we've asked of you . . ."

The gangly man's mouth opened, then closed.

"You haven't met the regent, have you?" said Alvar with a smile. "She doesn't care much for those who'd lie to her."

"The . . . north . . . road . . . there, by the coppersmith's."

Anna's eyes blurred, and, again, for a moment, she saw two images of the gangly man. She shook her head, trying to clear her sight. Then she massaged her forehead for a moment.

The double image faded, and Anna's eyes went back to the narrow building in the far left corner of the square, where a copper pot glittered in the early morning sun. In the instant her eyes shifted, she could sense that people were easing out of the square, or back into buildings, anywhere away from her armsmen.

Alvar gestured toward the street by the coppersmith's, and Anna flicked Farinelli's reins, trying not to frown. The truthspell—was it Darksong? Was that why she'd gotten the double image?

Even before she passed the coppersmith's, riding behind a vanguard clearly more alert, the square had emptied.

The echo of hoofs was the only sound as they rode northward and away from the center of the town.

Was it her imagination, or were most of the shutters of Cheor closed as they rode northward through the town? Anna glanced this way, and that, but the street was empty. Even the dogs and cats seemed to have vanished.

"Guilty, they are," said Alvar. "Not a good omen."

"Not at all," agreed Jecks.

"This didn't happen when we rode through Elhi," Anna said.

"I had nothing to fear or hide," pointed out Jecks, with a smile.

"That's true." Anna smiled back momentarily. Jecks' directness remained appealing, as did his smile.

A dek or so north of the square the houses spread more widely, with patches of ground, and gardens around each. The majority of the outlying houses were of unstuccoed yellow brick, and many had thatch or split-reed roofs.

Anna pushed back her felt hat, already getting battered, and wiped her forehead. The sun had burned away the earlier mist and ground fog, and the day, early as it was, was getting warm. She eased off her jacket and thrust it through the saddle loops, then took a deep swallow from her water bottle.

Still wearing his leather jacket, Jimbob glanced from the water bottle to Anna, clad in a pale green linen shirt and a green sleeveless tunic, and then to his grandsire.

"She is from the mist worlds, Jimbob," Jecks said quietly.

"They must be chill indeed." The redhead turned to Anna. "Are you really warm now?"

"I would be if I kept the jacket on."

Jimbob shivered.

Anna almost smiled. Another thing that was hard to believe. On earth, it had seemed that, except in the summer in Iowa, she had been cold more often than not. In Liedwahr it was usually just the opposite.

Outside a small hut, a dark-haired woman, barefooted,

hoed at the dark soil of a garden row, as if to prepare it for planting. With almost every stroke of the hoe, she struggled with a toddler tied to a rope wound around her waist. Several gray geese pecked along the crumbling yellow bricks of the wall of the old house. The woman scarcely looked up at the column of riders.

Anna understood. Mario had been a handful at that age, and there had been times when she wouldn't have cared if a row of tanks had rumbled past the little house outside Williamsburg, if only her son had given her a moment's peace.

She shook her head. *Now what wouldn't you give to have that time back?* Her eyes burned for a moment. *Careful . . . just get it together. You're the sorceress. You can do this.*

As they continued northward and Cheor receded behind them, Anna studied the fields—all rich dark bottomland formed in the area between the two rivers. Had it once been a swamp? It was flat enough. What Papaw wouldn't have given for land like this, rather than the rocky patch around the holler.

There were low hedgerows around many of the fields, but no stands of trees, except in the distance to the east. A single horse pulled a plow guided by a stocky figure in the fields off to the right. The farmer was nearly a mile away—more than a dek and a half, Anna corrected mentally, trying again to keep her references in Liedwahran terms.

To the left were several other figures, carrying baskets and pointed sticks. Planting? Anna wondered.

Ahead, a low yellow-brick wall stretched across the fields, forming the southern side of a rough square that looked to be almost two deks on a side. In the center of the square was a low hill whose base was encircled by a second and higher yellow-brick wall. On the crest of the hill was a sprawling, high-walled complex—also of yellow bricks.

"That's Synfal," Jecks announced. "It's been home to the lords of Cheor since before there was a Defalk."

A skeptical look crossed Jimbob's face, and Anna wanted to say something, but she bit her lip. Now wasn't the time, not in public, especially.

"Big place," offered Alvar, from where he rode slightly ahead of Anna, Jecks, and Jimbob.

"Aye. Only a rich holding could support that."

As they continued toward the nearer wall, Anna looked more closely. The first wall, almost waist-high, was rough-formed, and covered in places with vines, showing a few new leaves. By full summer, it would vanish into the green of the surrounding fields, Anna suspected. There was no gate where the road met the wall, nor any sign of one. The wall just ended in a tumbled pile of bricks on each side of the road.

"Wall from the old days," explained Jecks. "From when this was part of Suhlmorra."

Anna raised her eyebrows—another part of Liedwahr's history no one had bothered to mention. "How long ago was that?"

Even Jimbob turned in the saddle as Jecks answered.

"So long ago even the poets don't count the years. Synfal"—Jecks gestured toward the keep on the hill a good two deks ahead—"was the northern march and the place where the Corian lords and the Morran lords usually met in battle." He grinned. "The Corians usually won."

"I take it your ancestors were Corian," Anna said dryly.

"How did you guess?"

"And that they were proud folks, too."

Jecks flushed.

Anna grinned.

Jecks shook his head.

Beside his grandsire, Jimbob merely looked puzzled, and Anna and Jecks let him remain that way.

As the column neared the second wall, a barrier Anna could see was at least four yards high, she reclaimed the lutar from the left saddlebag. As she tuned the instrument, her eyes went to the walled edifice ahead, a structure nearly twice the size of the keep at Falcor, if with brick walls, rather than more solid stone.

Could they just demand admittance? Jecks had said that was the right of the Lord of Defalk—and thus Anna's, especially with Jimbob beside her. But would Arkad accept that right? Or would she have to use one of her destructive spells to enforce that right?

She really didn't like the idea of tearing up the keeps and holds of lords disloyal to the Regency—or killing their armsmen—not until all the other lords perceived that such action was a necessity. The missing liedgeld was less than two seasons in arrears—not enough to create such a perception on earth. Here, everyone assured her, it was an obligation of honor, and two seasons' default was more than dishonorable enough for Anna to act.

Even for a woman regent. She wanted to snort. Instead, she adjusted a tuning peg and turned in the saddle, leaning toward Jecks, and saying in a low voice, "You know I've hesitated to put Jimbob into trouble, and here I'm putting him forward."

The white-haired and clean-shaven Lord of Elhi shook his head, leaned back toward her. "Best he learn under your protection."

Anna still wasn't sure how much Jimbob was really learning, and how much the redheaded heir was pretending to learn. Mario had been like that, too, playing the game until he was out from under her control—or Avery's.

Her eyes went to the road ahead, and the second wall. The taller wall ended at each side of the road in a set of pillars. On each pillar were rusted iron brackets, four of them, that had once held gates. Of the gates there was no sign.

"No guards here." Alvar cleared his throat and looked toward Anna. "Should we . . . the banner?"

"Yes." She should have thought of it herself, but she

still wasn't fully accustomed to Defalk. Less than a year wasn't time enough to learn all that was necessary, whether she was a sorceress or not.

"The banner! Forward!" ordered the swarthy and wiry captain. "Forward."

Anna watched as the purple banner with the golden crossed spears and the crown, with the *R* beneath, billowed for a moment in the light breeze, then drooped, even as the young armsman she didn't know rode to the head of the column bearing the standard.

"We should stop before we get within bow range, Lady Anna," Alvar offered.

"How much farther is that?" Anna had no concept of bow range. She knew Alvar had brought a half-score of archers and considered himself lucky to have so many in his command. Good archers seemed to be rare. Not so rare as sorcerers, but rarer than any other kind of armsmen.

"By the waste ditch there." The spot where he pointed lay another thirty yards ahead on the road.

A faint odor wafted toward Anna on the light breeze out of the north. "How about stopping right here?" She reined up.

Jecks grinned, but said nothing.

"Column halt!" Alvar reinforced the command with a raised blade.

As Alvar rode back to ensure some form of order, Anna, lutar held ready, ran through a vocalise, while idly looking toward Synfal. The entrance to the keep was by a gate partway up the hillside, perhaps five yards above the flat of the plain.

Alvar rode back and reined up as Anna finished the second vocalise.

"That hill's not natural."

Jecks frowned.

Anna didn't know that much geology, but she did know that it was highly unlikely that one isolated fifty-foot-high hill would rise out of bottomland as flat as a lake. Had some earlier lord built the mound? Or had a series of holds resulted in the hill? Did it matter?

The walls of the keep, unlike the outer and untended walls, were over eight yards high and clearly in good repair, although Anna suspected that the yellow bricks were more susceptible to sorcery or to the cannon she didn't have than stone would have been. The twin gates, doubtless with a portcullis behind, were of heavy oak, ironbound, and closed.

"You must request entrance, lady," Jecks said softly.

"He won't grant it."

"Still . . ."

Anna understood and turned to Alvar. "Do you have someone you can send closer?"

Alvar gestured to the standard bearer, and the young armsman eased his mount up beside the four. "What would you have him say?"

Anna cleared her throat. "His lordship Jimbob, the regent Anna, and the lord Jecks . . . here to see Lord Arkad of Cheor." She looked at Jecks. "What else?"

"You request hospitality on his honor."

Anna nodded. "His lordship Jimbob, the regent Anna, and the lord Jecks . . . here to see Lord Arkad of Cheor. We request his hospitality, on his honor."

The armsman repeated the phrase, then eased his mount forward and past the waste ditch, halting on the gently rising road about fifty yards from the closed gates. He raised his voice and declaimed Anna's words.

For a time, there was silence.

Then a voice replied, words spoken too faintly to be heard.

Anna eased Farinelli forward, but halted short of the wooden planks that served as a bridge over the waste ditch, steeling herself against the pungency that rose from the dark liquid that oozed toward a pond to the right.

The armsman repeated his message.

"How do we know you're who you say?" demanded

a round-jowled man in purple from a parapet over the gates.

"You know the banner. Who are you to deny the regent?" snapped Alvar.

"The servant of Lord Arkad."

"A nameless servant, and you would deny two lords and the regent?" responded Alvar.

Anna nodded.

The round-jowled figure drew himself up. "I am Fauren, head seneschal and counselor."

Anna could see that she needed Arkad and his scribe or counselor in hearing distance before she could cast a spell. She also had another problem, and that was that Liende and her players, farther back in the column, didn't know enough of the spellsongs Anna used to be useful. That meant spells had to be supported only with the lutar, and that meant Anna couldn't afford to waste any.

Still, there was no sense in delaying. Fauren—two syllables—the same as the word "armsman." Anna rode forward another few yards.

Jecks accompanied her, but waved Jimbob to stay back. "Enough," he suggested to Anna.

She glanced toward the walls rising above them, then cleared her throat. She strummed the chords, then sang.

> "Fauren right, Fauren wrong.
> Obey this regent's song.
> Open all gates strong . . .

> "Faithful and obedient be,
> to Anna and the Regency!"

Silence followed the song. A silence Anna welcomed with the faint throbbing that had invaded her skull with the spell—and another double image of the hold before her. She slowly extended her free hand to the water bottle and fumbled it open, drinking slowly.

Beside Anna, Jecks shifted his weight on the dark stallion. The broad-shouldered and black-haired Fhurgen urged his mount forward and before her, as if to act as a human shield. Farinelli sidestepped two steps.

Then a creaking followed, and the dark gates swung open. The iron portcullis lifted.

"Do we ride in?" asked Jimbob, who had slipped forward and reined up behind his grandsire.

"No," said Jecks. "Lord Arkad must come to us. Especially after this." He looked to Anna. "Can you offer another spell?"

"If I have to," she answered, again lifting her water bottle one-handedly.

" 'Have to'?" Jimbob's freckled face reflected puzzlement.

Anna ignored the expression and drank once more, then replaced the bottle. Jecks bent over and extracted the travel biscuits from the bag tied on the left saddle ring, offering her one. She took it and began to eat, trying to swallow all the dry crumbs. Then she took another swallow of water.

Her headache was mild, and the double vision had faded, but she'd need both the energy and the water.

Behind them, horses milled, and the low buzz of conversation sounded like the beehive in Papaw's back field.

Shortly, Fauren limped out and stood in the shadow of the open gates. "My master bids you enter."

"Return with your master, Fauren, and have him bid us welcome and enter. On his honor," snapped Jecks, the first time Anna could recall hearing anger in the white-haired lord's voice.

"I bid you welcome for him." Fauren bowed, almost obsequiously. "He is indisposed and ill."

"Then have him carried here." Jecks' voice was cold.

"Alas . . ." pleaded Fauren.

Anna caught sight of movement on the walls. Was that an archer? She cleared her throat and lifted the lutar, glad she'd thought about the spell earlier.

> "All within this faithless hall
> forever serve in lifelong thrall
> the regent and the lord she serves . . .
> . . . Defalkan order she preserves."

Anna tried not to wince, but the rhyme scheme was the best she'd been able to do.

A horrified look crossed the seneschal's face, and his hands curled toward himself, and his heart, and he staggered. His knees buckled, and then he collapsed, writhing, on the road.

A single figure plummeted over the wall and landed with a sickening thud on the ground beneath the walls.

Anna reeled under an equally sickening thud that seemed to rock her skull. Her eyes watered, and she could see clearly, side by side, two images, as if her brain could not integrate the separate visions from each eye—except that the left image seemed "warmer" and the right one "cooler." Her once mild headache was scarcely mild, and her free hand grasped the front of the saddle to steady her.

"Are you all right, Lady Anna?" asked Jecks in a low voice.

"I will be." *And I have no intention of collapsing before Arkad's gates because of a little spell.*

"Perhaps you should send a squad to see the keep is safe," suggested Jecks, his eyes still on Anna.

"Fine."

"Our job, Regent." Alvar stood in the saddle and turned. "Green company! Forward!"

With Fhurgen's and his men surrounding them, Anna, Jecks, and Jimbob waited as the twoscore lancers rode around the still figure of Fauren and through the open gates. Not an arrow flew. Not a blade flashed, but Anna kept shifting her weight in the saddle.

Finally, she reached for the biscuits again. Her head still ached, and her eyes still saw double. Jecks leaned from his saddle and reclaimed the bag. "Here."

She ate and drank.

Alvar rode out through the gates alone, a wide smile on his face. "Your spell worked. You'll not have any trouble."

Anna finished the last of her water and stowed the bottle back in the loops. "You're sure?"

"Some of the thralls and peasants were smiling. Some of the others . . . you'll see." Alvar turned his mount back toward the keep, raising his blade, and gesturing for the rest of the column to follow.

Anna still glanced at the heavy dark gates apprehensively as they rode through the heavy brick walls and arch and into a courtyard below the main keep. Two more bodies lay in the courtyard, both purple-clad, like Fauren.

As Anna reined up, the two armsmen by the double oak doors to the keep prostrated themselves on the stones.

"Lady Anna . . . Lady Anna."

"Impressive," murmured Jecks.

Jimbob's eyes went from the Synfal armsmen to Anna, then back to the armsmen. "I don't understand." The youth leaned in his saddle toward the sorceress. "You didn't use a slaying spell, but some people died. Can you slay without asking for death?"

"That's why I don't like to use sorcery." Anna took a deep breath. *Just one reason of the many I keep discovering.* "Jimbob . . . some people. They feel strongly. If I cast a spell that compels them to feel something against their nature, some will die rather than change their nature."

"A good thing, too, young Lord Jimbob," rumbled Fhurgen from where he sat on his mount directly behind Anna. "Anyone who's so against you and the regent's better dead."

Once, Anna had wondered about anyone being better dead, but after seeing what had happened to Madell—and Dalila and her children—she wasn't so sure if Madell wouldn't have been better off dead. Certainly, everyone else would have been better off if he were. She absently massaged her forehead. "Now what? I suppose I need to find Lord Arkad—if he's alive."

"We'll find him," Alvar affirmed. "You wait where you can be guarded." He vaulted off his mount, gesturing for several armsmen to follow, and unsheathed his blade.

Anna glanced toward the walls, but while the handful of armsmen watched her, none seemed more than curious. Some had seated themselves in patches of shade afforded by the walls. Anna closed her eyes as she sat on Farinelli. That way, she didn't see double, and the faint sense of nausea and vertigo that went with the double vision disappeared.

In time, Alvar reappeared with the armsmen.

Anna opened her eyes and looked at the captain, pleased that the sick feelings didn't reappear, although the double vision remained.

"Lord Arkad is alive. He sits in his receiving chamber. He be alone." Alvar shook his head.

"Is it safe?" Jecks asked, his voice so slow it almost rumbled.

"We found no armed men, and all the servants wish to please. Your sorcery was most effective, lady."

Anna hoped so. Her head still ached, and seeing two images of everyone was a strain. She almost wanted to take a swig of the medicinal alcohol in her pack, but that wouldn't have been the best idea. Perhaps Lord Arkad had good cellars and a decent wine. That she could use. Definitely.

"We will escort you both," Alvar added.

Jecks nodded. Anna dismounted first, deliberately and carefully, fearing that her balance was not what it should be. The white-haired lord and Jimbob followed her example. After a moment, she decided to bring the lutar.

Jecks held the door as Anna entered the cavernous hall, an echoing chamber that held little but dust, and the odor of mold. They were greeted by a serving girl, thin and nervous, who bowed once, twice. "Lady Anna, Regent

Anna, this way to Lord Arkad's chamber.'' She bowed again.

Behind the hall was a corridor running perpendicular to the hall, and the serving girl turned right. Fhurgen stepped up beside her, blade unsheathed, his head turning from side to side.

Alvar walked on Anna's right, Jecks on her left, both with blades out.

Anna frowned. The entire experience seemed almost surreal. Walking through an ancient castle or hold in dim light, surrounded by armed men, treating her like an ancient queen to be protected. Yet her sorcery had apparently turned the keep's defenders into allies, unwilling or not. *And you can't take a step without wondering if you'll fall over.*

Her fingers tightened around the lutar, her thoughts skittering into the burning spell. She didn't want to flay anyone with fire, but she could if the need appeared. *Correction. You hope you can.*

The serving girl stopped at the foot of the massive yellow brick staircase, turned, and bowed again. ''He's up the main stairs here, in the upper room, Regent Anna.''

Anna nodded, then followed the girl.

Fhurgen, Jecks, and Alvar kept abreast of her, with Jimbob lagging, his eyes darting from side to side. Close to a score of armsmen followed the group, but the only sounds were the echoes of boots on brick.

At the top of the stairs, under a huge portrait of a man in unfamiliar armor on a white horse, they turned right, down another brick-walled corridor for perhaps twenty yards to an open doorway.

The time-stained door was open into a square and high-ceilinged room nearly ten yards on a side. At the right end of the room was a raised wooden dais. On the dais was a carved chair, nothing more. An old, white-haired figure sat on the chair.

Jecks slowed slightly, gesturing for Jimbob to do the same.

Anna, flanked by Fhurgen, stopped short of the dais, squinting in trying to make out Arkad. Her nose itched. Mold? Dust?

"Pay homage to the regent," growled Fhurgen.

Arkad looked up from the carved chair at Fhurgen, then to Anna. "I honor you, Regent. I honor you. I honor you." Tears seeped from the rheumy eyes, disappearing into the food-stained and tangled white beard.

Anna paused. Something didn't feel right. She lifted the lutar slightly, her fingers feeling for the strings.

"I honor you," cackled Arkad, a line of saliva drooling out of the left corner of his mouth. The Lord of Cheor tottered erect and bowed his head. "I honor you."

Anna glanced toward Fhurgen momentarily. Did Arkad seem as . . . mad . . . as she thought?

The ancient figure stumbled down from the dais toward Anna. "Honor you!"

With the flash of silver Anna threw up her right hand and jumped aside, trying to protect the lutar and herself from the blade. A line of fire grazed the side of her hand.

"Bastard!" Fhurgen's bare blade slashed, and the knife clattered on the stones. The guard's second effort threw the tottering figure onto the bricks.

Arkad did not move, and blood began to pool on the stained yellow floor bricks. Then the ancient figure twitched once and was still. Anna knew he was dead.

After a moment, Anna looked at the gash on the side of her palm. "Good thing you brought the alcohol," she murmured to herself.

"I am sorry, Regent." Fhurgen's voice almost broke.

"It wasn't your fault, Fhurgen. I was careless." She shook her head. *Sorcery doesn't protect you if you don't use it . . . or if someone's so twisted and mad that the spell has no effect . . . or if you're seeing double and don't react.*

"There's a bottle wrapped in green cloth in my saddle-bags. Would you send someone for it?" She looked back down on the emaciated white-haired figure in the stained maroon tunic lying in already-drying blood.

Fhurgen nodded to the blond armsman behind him. "You heard the regent, Rickel."

Jecks looked to Anna.

"I'll be all right. It's not much more than a scratch." She shook her head. "What a mess. What a fucking, dissonant mess."

24

DUMARIA, DUMAR

Ehara swings into the saddle of the roan, glancing from the stable back at the white limestone of the palace, then urges his mount toward the parklike preserve that stretches from behind the white stone building to the top of the bluffs overlooking the Falche River three deks to the east and to the north gate little more than a dek away, where the road winds down the steep hill past the mansions of the wealthy traders.

The gray-haired lancer officer spurs his mount to catch up with the Lord of Dumar.

"You're a lancer, Overcaptain Keasil. It took you long enough to catch me." Ehara's voice booms across the turf that leads to the woods.

"You are known as an excellent horseman, sire." Keasil's voice is lower than Ehara's as he settles his mount into a walk beside Ehara. "You asked me to accompany you?"

"Away from the palace and the ever-listening ears. I'm sure you understand." Ehara urges his mount into a trot.

Keasil manages to react quickly, and the two men ride side by side toward the tended woods.

"Keasil . . ." Ehara turns in his saddle and grins.

"Send a token of our appreciation to Lord Sargol in Suhl. You can select something from the chest, a diamond or two, I think, when you come to my study later. Siobion prefers the pearls and rubies. I will have a scroll ready for you shortly after I return to my study. I'll send for you."

"Lord Sargol? Not Lord Dencer?" Keasil's bushy gray eyebrows lift in inquiry.

"Lord Dencer would be our agent. He has made it quite clear how he would be both agent and overlord in southern Defalk." Ehara shakes his head, in mock sadness. "That is why Captain Gortin rode to Stromwer. He looks younger than his years, and that was not by accident. I am not fond of agents. They place their interests above mine."

"That can be so."

"It is so. Remember that."

"Yes, sire." Keasil frowns as he guides his mount clear of the marble walled fountain that sits alone in the grass.

"You look displeased."

"Oh, no, sire. It is just that . . ." He pauses and guides his mount closer to Ehara's. "Your pardon, lord, but if I am to act properly . . ."

"Yes?"

"Would it not be wise if I had a general idea of what message I am to convey?"

"A scroll to Lord Sargol." Ehara reins up short of the first line of trees.

The officer inclines his head to Ehara. "I will do my best, ser."

"I will *probably* convey my felicitations. A good word, felicitations. My felicitations about the situation in which he has been placed. I might suggest I sympathize with his uncertain condition, mentioning in passing a sorceress unfamiliar with his particular situation as a regent for a boy whose forebears were scarcely distinguished. That might be viewed as unsettling, even without having neighboring lords with loyalties regarded as close to rebellious by such a regent. And I will offer him friendship.''

"That is all?"

"That is what you need to know, Keasil." Ehara smiles. "The scroll will be spelled. Don't try to read it."

"Yes, ser. No, ser, I won't, I mean."

"I know what you meant." Ehara smiles. "No more talk of scrolls and messages. Let us ride."

25

After Fhurgen walked through the chamber, blade out, Anna glanced around the guest quarters—a large room with an adjoining bath chamber. Like everything else in the hall, they smelled, as if the bath chamber had never been used, but they smelled less than either Fauren's quarters or those of the late Lord Arkad.

The walls were yellow brick, covered with plaster that had once been whitewashed and now looked more like dirty yellow, either from the brick showing through or from an accumulation of dirt, smoke, and grease. The light from the two narrow windows was further darkened by heavy brown drapes that drooped from wrought-iron brackets set above the casement and by inside shutters. Two wooden armchairs were pushed against the outer wall.

A double-width bed, with a dirty brown quilt and two lumpy pillows, a bedside table with a candle and smudged glass mantel, and a writing table with a wooden straight-backed chair completed the bedchamber furnishings.

The regent's boots scraped, as though on sand, as she crossed the brick floor to the nearest window and pulled back the drapes and opened the shutters.

"*Khhhchew!*"

Anna rubbed her nose, then sneezed twice more, before opening the shutters of the second window. "Damned dust . . . bed's probably worse."

Fhurgen had retreated to the half-open door, watching as Anna studied the room, one hand touching the full black beard momentarily.

She turned as another set of boots echoed down the corridor.

Jecks stepped into the room, followed by the redheaded Jimbob. "We have inspected the strong room and the lower levels."

Had it taken her that long to disinfect the wound and inspect the top floor of the keep?

"How be the hand?"

"It hurts." Anna shrugged, her eyes going to the dressings. "Other than that . . . Other than being stupid . . ." She shook her head. "This place stinks."

"No worse than many," Jecks said.

"I'll have to have it cleaned up to sleep here." She eased herself into a straight-backed chair.

Jecks nodded. "There is much to be done here."

Anna had the feeling Jecks wasn't talking about cleaning. "Does Alvar have the hold under control?"

"Your spell did that. Your armsmen hold the gates and the ramparts, but the servants are obeying willingly. So are the few crafters."

"Good." Anna started to rub her forehead, to massage away the headache, but doing it left-handed felt subtly awkward.

"Lady Anna?" Jimbob's voice was uneven.

"Yes, Jimbob."

"Might I ask . . . ?"

"How Lord Arkad managed to lift a knife against me?"

"Yes, lady."

"It's simple and it's complicated," Anna said tiredly. "Spells like the one I cast on the holding only work on a mind that's healthy. Lord Arkad was not well. I don't know if he was spelled or old or insane, but he didn't know that what he did was against the spell." *And you didn't cast it to make an attack physically impossible.*

"Everyone talks about how your spells stop people or kill them." The youthful face screwed up in puzzlement.

Jecks started to open his mouth, and Anna shook her head, then took a deep breath, trying to gather her thoughts. She really needed something to eat. "Jimbob . . . someday you will command an army. It might happen that a lord will refuse to pay liedgeld. I hope not, but these things can happen. He has an army—many armsmen, and many other people behind his walls. What will happen if you use all your armsmen—or sorcery—to kill that lord and all his armsmen and people?"

"They'll die."

"And who will harvest the crops? Who will ever wish to surrender to you, if they know they'll die? How many of your armsmen will die? How will you replace them?"

"I'll use the golds from the rebel's strongbox."

Jecks nodded. "And then more lords will rebel. Will you destroy them? And if you do, who will stand behind you?"

Jimbob's eyes went from Jecks to Anna to Jecks, as if he could not believe that his grandfather was supporting Anna.

"Jimbob . . ." Jecks said softly. "Armsmen and sorcery do not create crops or golds. They can sometimes seize it, but such seizures must be seldom, and every man must think that you were right to use armsmen and sorcery."

"But Lord Arkad was evil," protested Jimbob.

"You're right," Anna said, "but I'm a stranger in Defalk, and I didn't know he was evil. Do you think most of the other lords thought he was evil?"

"They will now."

"Some will," Jecks said. "Some will yet protest the regent's efforts to secure your future. All would have been

angered if the regent had brought the hall down around
Lord Arkad and his seneschal.''

"All of them?''

"All of them,'' Jecks repeated. "Now . . . off with you.
The regent and I need to talk.'' The white-haired lord of
Elhi glanced toward Fhurgen. "Can you ensure him a
guard?''

"Yes, sire.'' Fhurgen grinned.

"And find us some wine and something to eat?''

"Yes, Lady Anna.'' Fhurgen was still smiling as the
door closed.

Once they were alone, Anna shifted her weight in the
chair.

"It is good he is away from Galen,'' Jecks said.

"I wondered when I met . . . his tutor.''

"We do what we can. I should have spent more time
with Jimbob when he was at Elheld, but I trusted Galen.
Now . . .'' Jecks shrugged, then seated himself on the
brick window ledge closest to the writing table, ignoring
the chairs.

"You suggested we needed to deal with more than a
few things.'' Her nose still wrinkled at the smell as a gust
of wind swirled from the windows through the chamber.
"There's who gets the holding.'' To whom could she en-
trust the custody of Lord Arkad's lands? Arkad had no
heir, not according to Jecks. None of her would-be pro-
tégés were old enough nor experienced enough. "And
what else?''

."You should settle that soon,'' Jecks said. "I also
question whether we should continue to Synope.''

"We have a day or two to consider that. First, we have
to deal with this mess. We can't just leave Synfal without
someone in charge,'' she mused. "What do you suggest?''

"You could rightfully administer it,'' Jecks answered.
"You could have someone act as saalmeister or seneschal.''

His emphasis on "rightfully'' did not escape her and

confirmed what she had in mind. "No. It has to be some-one clearly perceived as being of Defalk. Right now, it has to be a man."

"You were considering a woman?"

"There will be ladies in the future, but I doubt Defalk is ready for such a shock for the first lord I replace. Besides, I can't even find someone to run my own estate." She lifted her right hand to set it on the table, and managed not to wince. She didn't think any muscles or tendons had been cut, but it still hurt. "I was thinking that we'll need both an heir and an administrator."

"Both?" Jecks lifted his white eyebrows.

Anna smiled. "What about Jimbob as the heir?"

"What?"

"Make Herstat the saalmeister and administrator in Jimbob's absence."

"My Herstat?" Jecks laughed. "You will take every talent I possess."

"Not every one." She made a gesture that she cut short as the combination of double vision and pain reminded her of her wounds—seen and unseen. "These are rich lands, and they will give him income and a greater impression of independence. . . ."

"He is young. . . ."

"They're his upon his maturity. Have Herstat present a yearly report to me and to any lords interested enough to come to Falcor to hear it. Any changes or improvements Jimbob wants to make will have to be approved by you and Herstat."

"Not you?"

"Definitely not me, and everyone should know that."

"Again, Lady Anna, you surprise me."

"Why? One of Donjim's and Barjim's problems was that they didn't have enough income and were too beholden to the Thirty-three."

"When others discover your intentions . . ."

"It will only confirm what they want to believe," Anna said wearily. "Besides—tell them that Jimbob benefits, not me.'' She cleared her throat. Something in the air was affecting her allergies. Brill's youth spell hadn't taken care of that problem. "I don't think we should announce it for a time, maybe not until we return to Falcor. I should be considering who will be the heir."

"Some would find that indecisive."

"Let them. If I announce Jimbob right now, everyone will say that it's all a pretext for me to take over lands of the old guard and use Jimbob as a puppet. That's another reason why you'll need to get Herstat here quickly, before I announce the new heir." She rubbed her nose, hoping she wouldn't sneeze. "Did you find out who was Fauren's second in charge, or whatever?"

"His name is Halde," Jecks ventured, his voice thoughtful. "He waits in the corridor."

"You sound puzzled."

"Best you speak to him first."

Anna nodded. Jecks wanted her to form her own view.

Halde was dark-haired, with a trimmed beard that concealed his comparative youth. He couldn't have been much past his early twenties. "Lady Anna, Lord Jecks." He bowed, deferentially, but not obsequiously.

"What was your position here in Cheor?" Anna asked.

"I was an assistant to Fauren, the saalmeister, lady." Halde's light gray eyes met Anna's. "I did as he asked."

"What sort of duties?"

Halde glanced warily from Anna to Jecks. "Whatever Fauren asked. I was in charge of the account books, and the strongbox room. And of all the supplies for Synfal. Irkiik, he was the one who inspected the fields and collected the tariffs. He also could use the scrying glass a little. Onnbor maintained the armory and trained the guards."

"Did you agree with Lord Arkad's decision not to pay liedgeld to the Regency?"

"I was not in a position to question the lord, lady. Fauren would caution us that even the saalmeister dared only so much."

"Where is your family?" asked Anna.

"My mother lives with my uncle in Cheor. He is a cooper. I have no consort." Halde offered a quick and wry smile. "Fauren did not leave us much time for dalliance."

"What do you think should happen to Cheor?"

"You must decide that, lady. I would hope that those who served will not be punished severely."

Anna nodded to herself. Whether they knew it or not, all those in Synfal had indeed been punished. Her spell would hold for all but the mad, at least as long as she lived. "I hold Cheor until a new lord is appointed. For now, Halde, you will act as . . . saalmeister." Anna struggled for the word. "Someone must ensure Cheor continues to prosper. If it does, and you perform well, I will find some suitable reward."

"You are most charitable, lady."

"No. Despite Fauren's faults, it is clear that Cheor was well run. People know their business and seem happy. Generally, that means a good . . . saalmeister. I will let the hold know."

"Thank you, my lady." Halde turned to Jecks. "Grace to you, Lord Jecks."

"What do you think?" Anna asked after the door closed behind Halde.

"It is the best choice for now."

"Once Herstat takes over, and learns all he needs to know, we'll have to replace Halde, I think."

"You would punish him?"

Anna shook her head. "Find a job for him in Falcor or somewhere. I just think that the top people here should be loyal first to Jimbob, and then to Synfal."

Jecks rubbed his chin. "That will take time."

"Which we don't have," Anna admitted. She hoped things with Halde would work out, but something had to be done, and she just had to trust her instincts . . . again.

"What other thoughts have you?" Jecks smiled. "Besides taking every good servant I have?"

Anna frowned. "If there is a large surplus in Arkad's strongboxes—or his late seneschal's—I think half should go to the liedstadt to fund our efforts . . . this expedition. There's no reason the liedstadt has to pay for rebuilding Defalk."

"Two-thirds," suggested Jecks. "Leaving a third will make you seem generous. By rights, you could claim everything of a rebel lord. You could take up to half personally."

Anna smiled crookedly. "Could I claim a few hundred golds half-personally, to pay my liedgeld? Or would that upset the Thirty-three?"

"I am certain that no one would object to the regent using a small part of the spoils to pay yet more coins to the depleted treasury of the liedstadt. Especially not after rebuilding the major bridge at Falcor."

"All right." Anna hated the maneuvering. "We'll pay me three hundred golds for sorcerous construction, and that comes from Arkad's treasury, and two hundred goes back to the liedstadt for Loiseau's liedgeld."

"Take a thousand," Jecks said. "The servant who handles Arkad's accounts said there are more than six thousand golds in the chests. Your crops and levies may not be that great this year."

"A thousand?" Anna sighed. He was probably right about that. If she didn't start building some of her own funds, she'd be in the same position Barjim had been and the one she was trying to get Jimbob out of. But it bothered her, and she wasn't sure why. "Let me think about it."

Jecks smiled. "You may think as you wish. It is a decision only you can make."

Like everything anymore. Anna wanted to groan, but regents and sorceresses didn't groan. They smiled, like singers. So she did, still trying to ignore the disconcerting double vision.

26

Three ships from Sturinn are docked at Narial, and a group of the Sea-Priests traveled to Dumaria to meet with Lord Ehara.'' Bassil inclines his head.

''I told you, Bassil! Doesn't anyone see tomorrow's sunrise?'' Konsstin turns toward the windowed door that leads to the study's balcony. ''They refuse to treat with me, or with the northern traders, and here they are sneaking into Dumar. They'll establish a regular trade route. Then they'll undercut the shipping tariffs charged by the traders and provide grain cheaper than the bitches of Ranuak . . . or than our farmers and the traders of Cealor. That's for now.''

''How do you know that? All your seers know is that Ehara met with the Sea-Priests.'' Bassil's voice is resonant, but neutral, and he continues to stand before the desk even though Konsstin has walked toward the balcony door.

''A sea-tiger doesn't turn into a cow because it says it does. Sea-tigers don't change their stripes just because they're in Liedwahr and not Sturinn.'' Konsstin purses his lips, puts his hand on the door lever, then lifts it without opening the balcony door, and turns.

''What will we do?''

''What would you suggest, Bassil?'' asks the Liedfuhr. ''We cannot match the Sea-Priests upon the ocean.''

The raven-haired aide frowns, then scratches behind his left ear. ''Yet if you attack Dumar, after sending fiftyscore lancers to support your grandson . . .''

''No one will even pay any attention to what I say

about Sturinn. They might even send assistance to Ehara and the dissonant sorceress of Defalk.'' Konsstin offers a sound between a laugh and a snort.

''Do you have any choice? You must attack and take Defalk before the Sea-Priests can turn Dumar into their first conquest in Liedwahr.''

''Your words make the task appear so easy, Bassil.'' The Liedfuhr snorts. ''The Evult squandered five hundred–score in armsmen, and Vult is buried under molten rock. I have no desire to follow that example. Do you?''

''You would rather attack Dumar?''

''It would be much easier.''

''But the sorceress . . . ?''

Konsstin fingers the trimmed silver and brown beard. ''We appeal to her sense of survival—and her instincts as a woman. For now.''

Bassil shakes his head, his eyes narrowing as a shaft of light from the setting sun momentarily blazes through the western windows.

''The Sturinnese keep their women in chains. Much of that is ceremonial pigswill, but it is clear that this lady Anna dislikes men who try to subdue women.''

''How do you know that?'' The black-haired aide blinks against the glare.

''It is obvious, for those who have eyes to see. Even without reflecting pools.'' Konsstin raises his eyebrows, then continues. ''We will have Nubara shift the lancers to the south, on the other side of the Sudbergs from Envaryl, and we move some of our own forces to the west. More than a few. We send a message to the Regent of Defalk explaining our concerns with the incursion of the Sea-Priests.'' Konsstin pauses. ''It won't hurt to send scrolls like that to the Council of Wei and the bitches of the south. In the one to this lady Anna, we also say that our intention all along was to move the lancers south, but a gesture was needed to affirm Rabyn's reign over Neserea.''

''She won't believe that,'' points out Bassil.

''No. But she's likely to believe that we're trying not to give offense, and that we feel that the Sea-Priests are a far greater danger to Mansuur and Liedwahr than she is. We also point out that she should be concerned about the possible customs of the Sturinnese being implemented in Dumar.''

''What customs? The chains?''

''We don't say what customs. If she has to inquire, then it makes our point stronger.''

The room dims as the western clouds again shade the dropping sun.

''You want me to draft these scrolls?'' Bassil adds quickly, ''How soon?''

''Draft them immediately, but do not date them. Yet.''

''As you command, sire.''

''There's no point in hurrying. The Sturinnese will strike at the sorceress first. Let us wait until she is under attack. Then any gesture we make will seem more reasonable.''

Bassil waits.

''If . . . if she is successful against Ehara and her own southern lords, then we will see. I'd wager there are others besides Dencer and Gylaron, perhaps Sargol of Suhl, quiet as he is. Some of them will throw in with Ehara, I'd also wager. If she is successful, then Defalk will be further impoverished, and perhaps she will even be wounded or killed. If she is unsuccessful, Ehara and the Sturinnese will be weakened. In either case, we wait. Until the time is ripe.'' Konsstin pauses. ''You can start arranging for supplies and wagons. That way we can move immediately when we must.''

''Yes, sire.''

''Well . . . Bassil . . . get on with it.''

The dark-haired young officer bows, then turns and leaves the Liedwahr's study.

Konsstin smiles, then turns to look at the rose-colored clouds that frame the blaze of twilight. He nods to himself.

27

I need a tour of Synfal.'' That was what she'd said, and now Anna was descending worn yellow-brick steps, lit only by intermittent candles, into the depths of the oldest section of the hold. The scooped-out edges of the steps indicated that the hold's age was considerable.

Anna found herself using her left hand to steady herself from the disruptive impact of the double vision, while still trying to ignore the disability she hoped was temporary.

At the base of the stairs, Alvar stopped and gestured to a stooped and gray-haired man with a wispy goatee, dressed in a clean but faded gray tunic and trousers. ''This is Vierk, Lady Anna. He does the accounts for the liedburg.''

''Were you with Lord Arkad long?'' Anna asked.

''We were boys together, lady. I did what I could, but . . . in the recent years, he listened but to Fauren.'' Vierk's eyes dropped to the brick floor.

Was everything in Synfal brick?

Anna glanced down, realizing that she still had blood across the cuff of her shirt. In the press to take charge of Synfal, she'd forgotten that. *You're worried about that, now?* ''Did he talk with you?''

''Not often, lady. And he talked about the past, and how Fauren and he would make Synfal great again, as in the days of Suhlmorra. Then he laughed.'' Vierk shivered.

''What about Halde? What did he do?''

''He did the ledgers in the strongbox room, and he checked my accounts. Fauren was most firm that two must check all accounts.''

''Let's see the strongbox room.'' Did everyone everywhere romanticize the past? She hoped she didn't . . . but would she ever know?

The strongbox room met the conditions of its name. Two iron gates, one on the outside of the archway that pierced the three-foot-thick wall, and one on the inside, stood open, guarded by four Defalkan lancers, besides Fhurgen and the other lancer who followed her.

Five small chests and ten large ones stood on four sturdy and ancient oak tables. All were iron-bound. Before each of the large chests was a leatherbound book.

Anna glanced at Alvar, then Vierk. "How much is there?"

"The first nine large chests contain a thousand golds each. I would have to check the book for the last. The small chests, those are for trade. Each has fifty golds, but they can hold three hundred."

Anna figured—nearly ten thousand golds stashed away, with the winter already gone, and the rents for the next harvest yet to come. And Arkad, or Fauren, hadn't paid liedgeld—a mere nine hundred golds.

Anna stepped forward toward the table and the nearest large chest. She opened the cover of the well-thumbed book, turning the pages until she reached the last one with entries on it.

". . . ten silvers . . . rents from Gerhing, farmer in the north quarter of Ashfaal, for ten morgens of good land."

Anna frowned. Morgen meant morning in German, but the farmer wasn't renting mornings. Another term she didn't understand. "Lord Jecks, how much land is a morgen?"

Jecks frowned momentarily. "It is the amount of land a farmer could plow in a morning. I would say a square sixty yards on a side."

That didn't seem all that much for a morning's work, until she thought about Papaw and how long it had taken him in the holler with old Barney. Anna nodded. "Are these rents high?"

Jecks glanced over her shoulder at the entries. "A silver

a morgen? That is a gold a year for this peasant. My farmers could not raise that. This land must be rich indeed.'' He began to look through the ledger before the adjoining chest.

Anna frowned. Doing math, even approximations, in her head required concentration. Defalk was roughly seventy leagues from east border to west, and eighty leagues from north to south—say four hundred miles by five hundred—twenty thousand square miles. A morgen was smaller than an acre, something around two-thirds, she'd guess, and a square mile had six hundred forty acres—she remembered that from somewhere. So . . . nine hundred morgens to a square mile . . . something like eighteen million morgens in the country . . . and if only ten percent were farmed by tenants, that still totaled close to two million silvers in rents at the rate charged by Arkad or Fauren. And she had trouble collecting eight thousand golds—equivalent to eighty thousand silvers.

''You look displeased, Lady Anna.''

Anna glanced at Alvar. ''If you would escort Vierk up the stairs, Alvar?''

''Yes, Lady Anna.''

Anna waited until she heard boots and sandals on the bricks. ''If only ten percent of Defalk brings in rents, and every lord charged like Arkad, each of the lords of Defalk would each get something like . . . five or six thousand golds a year.''

Jecks nodded. ''But that is not the case. I would say that more like two-thirds of Lord Arkad's lands are rented, from what these books show.'' He coughed almost apologetically. ''Elhi . . . I am fortunate, and Herstat says that one in five morgens brings in rent, but only five coppers a morgen.''

''So your rents are around ten thousand golds a year,'' she said quietly.

''Lady Anna . . . you are dangerous.''

''Dangerous? It's only taken me a year to understand

what a good accountant would have figured out in a week.''

Jecks offered a puzzled look at the word "accountant," but answered, "I doubt Barjim ever understood."

"I'd bet your daughter did." *Better than I do.* Anna wanted to shake her head. She'd paid close to thirty percent in taxes, between social security and income taxes, and these high-living lords were complaining about a tax of what . . . less than ten percent?

"You look angry."

"I am. I'm beginning to understand, and I'm going to get very upset if I get any more excuses from people like Arkad. Or his seneschal.'' She also felt a lot less unhappy about claiming a thousand golds for her own efforts.

Jecks glanced back to the iron gates where Fhurgen and the two lancers stood, almost as if he wished he had gone with Alvar.

Unhappy? Anna had to wonder. Jecks had told her the strongbox room held six thousand golds, and Vierk had pretty clearly indicated the total was closer to ten. Had Jecks been mistaken, or had Vierk underestimated originally, or was something else going on?

She took a long slow breath. What was it that Herod Agrippa had said in *I, Claudius*? "Trust no one." *Does it come to that?* She hoped not, but she'd hoped for a lot of things that hadn't turned out as she hoped.

She closed the ledger or whatever the book was called. "I'd like to see the stables and the kitchens next." Anna glanced to Jecks and turned. "Fhurgen? Can you make sure this is well-guarded, and that it all remains here? I'd hate to have to use sorcery." She kept her voice sweet, but the last phrase was for the guards, and she hoped both Jecks and Fhurgen understood.

"Yes, Lady Anna." Fhurgen suppressed a smile.

Anna began the climb up the three long flights of brick steps, Jecks and Fhurgen and two guards behind her.

The stables were to the left of the main building, left

as one entered the hold, built as in Falcor against the outer wall.

Anna sniffed as she neared the brick arches where two more armsmen stood with a thin young man in brown trousers and a sleeveless leather vest. The area smelled clean, and that was a good sign.

"This is the ostler, Lady Anna."

"You're young for the head ostler," Anna observed, noting that the man didn't seem as old as Mario, and she wouldn't have trusted her son with the horses of an entire liedburg. Then, people grew up faster in Liedwahr.

"My da was stablemaster till the fever took him last year."

"Lady," suggested Fhurgen.

"Lady," the man added with a glare.

"What's your name?" Anna asked.

"Bielttro . . . lady."

"Will you show me your stables, Bielttro? I've only seen where Farinelli's stalled, and I wasn't really paying attention. I need to groom him."

"The big gelding—he's yours, lady? You groom him?" The surliness vanished from Bielttro's voice.

"He makes sure I do. He doesn't let many others near him," Anna said dryly, reflecting that Farinelli was a better diplomat than she was these days. "He deserves it. He's saved my life a few times. If he wants me to do the grooming, that's a fair trade. More than fair," she added.

"You are the lady Anna?"

"She is," Alvar said.

Bielttro shook his head as Anna eased into the stall beside Farinelli. She loosened the girths and slipped off the saddle, awkwardly because her hand hurt, but managed to get it over the rack on the stall wall, sloppily because the double vision didn't do much for depth perception.

Bielttro glanced from the saddle to the dressing on her hand.

"Lord Arkad tried to slice me up. I wasn't expecting it. It makes lifting heavy things awkward."

"You always saddle and unsaddle . . . him?"

"Sometimes, others have unsaddled him," Anna admitted.

"When?" asked Alvar from beside the ostler. "The last time I recall was after you destroyed the dark army. I got his saddle off, and he almost killed me. He'd eat and drink, but that was about all."

"I wasn't in the best of shape," Anna grunted. "Easy, there." She slipped off the bridle and scratched Farinelli's forehead.

Whuuuff . . .

"I know, fellow. You're hungry." She looked over the shoulder-high wall, brick, of course. "Do you have any grain, oats, that sort of thing?"

"I will get some."

Alvar shook his head after the stablemaster left. "Horses—stablemasters judge people by their mounts."

"It's not a bad way," reflected Anna, struggling slightly with the curry brush in her left hand.

Whufff!

"Sorry. I'm not as good with this hand." The gelding turned his head slightly as if to offer assent.

"Thank you," Anna said. "I'm so happy you agree."

"This should help." Bielttro reappeared with a wooden bucket, which he poured into the manger while leaning over the stall wall. Farinelli just watched.

"He likes you," Anna observed.

"He doesn't dislike me," the stablemaster corrected. "You really are the sorceress?" He studied Anna frankly.

Anna sighed. "Bielttro, it's hard explaining, but please believe me when I tell you I have a son your age. He's the youngest of my children."

The dark-haired man glanced at Alvar and Jecks. Both nodded.

"I saw her soon after she came to Liedwahr," Jecks

said. "She was beautiful then, but one could see that she had experienced much."

"All say you never lie, Lord Jecks." Bielttro met the older man's eyes for a moment. "Still . . . it is hard to believe."

"Watch and listen for a time. Then you will believe," suggested Alvar.

Fhurgen, standing farther back, nodded, and Anna felt like a third party being discussed. She set aside the brush and stepped out of the stall. "If you would show me the rest of the stables . . . ?"

"I would indeed." Bielttro smiled and started down the line of stalls. "The big mounts, they go in the front stalls, and the workhorses. The roof is higher." He pointed to a shaggy beast that was a good four hands taller than Farinelli. "That is Hoofa. That is what I call him. He is the lead for the big wagon team."

Hoofa lifted his head and regarded the stablemaster placidly.

"And there is Olaaf . . . he is younger and works best beside Hoofa."

Olaaf's coat was lighter than the deep reddish brown of Hoofa's, and his big head turned toward Anna and Bielttro more quickly.

". . . next are the stalls for the favorites of Lord Arkad . . . he rode until the year before the last . . ."

Anna just nodded as the young stablemaster walked her through the entire complex, nearly twice the size of those at Falcor, but every bit as well-organized and clean, if clearly older. All the straw seemed fresh, and both stable boys she saw smiled, rather than cringed.

"Thank you, Bielttro," she said as they neared the front archways to the stables. "It's very impressive." She smiled.

Bielttro glanced at the bricks.

Anna understood, and wanted to kick herself. He was young, and he was afraid he'd be replaced.

"Bielttro . . ." she said softly. "I am not the one who will hold Synfal, but I will put in a good word for you."

That got a shy smile. "Thank you, lady."

"If you keep working the way you have, I don't imagine you'll have too much trouble in convincing the new lord of your worth." She paused. "I may end up grooming Farinelli at odd hours—glasses, I mean. My schedule is not always what I would like."

"I will make sure he has grain."

"Thank you."

"He is young," Jecks observed as the group walked back across the courtyard, followed by Fhurgen and another armsman.

"He'll kill himself for those he respects, and you can't buy his respect," Anna said. "Jimbob will need to know that. If it doesn't work out, I'll find him a place."

Jecks raised his eyebrows.

"I do have a holding, remember."

Jecks chuckled. Behind the older lord's shoulder, Alvar smiled.

Anna reflected on the stables, trying to cross-check her feelings against her observations. As in Loiseau, and at Falcor, the stalls were all swept and filled with clean straw. The mounts appeared well-fed and without whip-marks or signs of abuse. After his initial coldness, Bielttro had been positively voluble, and clearly the young man loved horses.

She shook her head. Synfal remained a puzzle.

A group stood in the late-afternoon shadows in the courtyard—the players.

Anna walked forward. "Liende . . . do you all have quarters?"

"Lady Anna." Liende wrinkled her nose.

"They smell?" asked Anna.

"The rooms are large enough, but not pleasant."

"I'll have some work for your players. I'd like to have you gather them in my quarters with their instruments in another glass."

"As you wish, lady."

"Thank you." Anna wondered if Liende would ever be more than cordial, or was it Anna? Everything pushed her toward being pushy and bitchy. She'd tried not to level Synfal, and nearly been killed by a madman, and was still fighting impaired vision. She'd been lenient with Madell, and the result had been disaster for Dalila. She wanted to shake her head. Instead, she added, "I'm sorry. I'm not being clear." Anna paused. "I'd like to use a spell to clean out my quarters and then your rooms. That way, we'll all sleep better. But . . . I have to think about it. . . . I haven't done cleaning spells."

That got a faint smile.

"Liende . . ." Anna added. "Please bear with a regent who's trying to do too much too quickly. I'll see you all in a glass."

Liende offered another smile, less tentative. "We will be there."

"Now, the kitchens," Anna said quietly to Alvar.

Jecks merely nodded.

The kitchens were at one end of the main holding building, and five women stood in the middle of the recently-swept floor. All bowed as Anna entered.

"Regent Anna."

"Thank you." Anna took a long and slow look around the main room of the kitchen area—two large hearths, and two small ones, and what appeared to be a third hearth containing several iron doors. Bread ovens?

One of the hearths contained a number of iron brackets for spits or something similar.

"Do you roast a lot of things?" she asked.

"We used to, Lady Anna. Lately, it's been bullocks for the guardsmen. Lord Arkad, all he could eat was boiled fowl, not even game birds." The heavyset and gray-haired cook half nodded as she finished her statement.

"Did his illness change things beyond the kitchens?" she asked.

A puzzled look passed over several faces.

Finally, the heavyset cook spoke. "Not so as we'd notice. Excepting that he would have none in the main hall save the cooks. No maids, none."

That answered—partly—one question. Anna nodded. "How many can you feed at once?"

"One time we fed twentyscore and we'd not have strained to feed twice that." The cook pointed to the narrow hallway to the right. "There—down that . . . I be showing you, lady. Not meats . . . those come from the animals and fowls in the old side bailey—that's the sunny one with the grass. Had a hard time making that clerk Fauren understand the need for grass." She snorted.

Anna followed as the cook escorted her down the hallway, opening doors.

"Beans—the black ones, more than a hundred scheffels here. White beans here . . . lentils . . . Fifty's more than enough."

The sorceress tried to keep an amused smile from her face as the head cook continued to point out all the dry supplies.

"Dried and shelled maize here, then the flour in the next one, next to the barrels of the hard wheat, and then the next ones are the soft cake flour. . . ."

They came to a staircase.

"Down here be all the roots." The cook took a candle from the holder, and with a deft motion of the striker hanging beneath it, lit the taper.

Anna, Jecks, Alvar, and the armsmen followed her down the narrow brick staircase.

"Potatoes, I used to keep two hundred, but right less than half that now. . . ."

"Beets—one of the few roots the lord wouldn't eat. Could have fifty scheffels, but just ten or twelve, for the soup for the holding folk. . . .

"Onions . . . three bins here, white, purple, and yellow. White keep best. Yellow turn mushy . . . have to watch them closer. . . ."

Anna grinned in the dimness.

When they emerged into the fuller light of the storage corridor, the sorceress was convinced that not only could the cook feed a small army, but that she had provisions for years.

"You are . . . ?" Anna finally asked. "I mean, your name."

"Me? I'm Hilde. Always been Hilde, lady. Always will be."

Of that, Anna had no doubts. "Thank you, Hilde. You have been very helpful."

"You know yet who our new lord will be?"

"That hasn't been decided yet," Anna said. "But there won't be many changes in the people who work here. Not unless they don't feel comfortable with the new lord."

"So long as he lets us run the kitchen, don't matter too much."

Anna nodded. "I'll let whoever it is know that."

"Be a fool to change us."

The sorceress agreed, if not for quite the reasons Hilde probably had in mind. One thing Anna had noted. There were no locked cupboards or closets. No guarded storerooms. She frowned. Again, she was missing something.

"Are there any official chambers?" she asked Jecks as they took the door that led along a narrow back corridor to the main entry hall.

"I did not look." He shrugged.

"There is a large dining salon," Alvar said, "and some larger rooms. They are very dusty."

What might have once been a state dining room held a long table and matching benches, although Anna had to lift the blanket-like coverings to look at both. The ornately carved wood was dark, but Anna had no way of knowing if that darkness were because of age or stain or natural coloring. An odor of mildew clung to the coverings.

"*Khhchew!*" She stepped back and rubbed her nose.

The hall adjoining the large dining area was empty, except for several twice-life-sized paintings of men in armor, several faded tapestries, one of which appeared to be a rendition of Synfal itself. The floor, unlike the others in the holding, which were either polished stone or brick, was wooden.

"Odd," she murmured.

Jecks was frowning. "Abomination. . . ."

"What?"

"I had heard, but one never believes all one hears."

Alvar nodded, but both Fhurgen and the armsman acting as guard looked as puzzled as Anna felt.

"I may be regent," Anna finally said, "but I don't know what you're talking about, and I have the feeling that I should."

"Dancing," Jecks said. "This is a . . . place for dancing. I knew the Suhlmorrans were decadent, but . . ."

Anna managed to keep her jaw in place. Her talents didn't lie in that direction, and she certainly wasn't the world's best dancer, but why would anyone call dancing decadent?

"It's a misuse of the harmonies," Alvar added.

The sorceress wanted to shake her head. Dancing, a misuse of the harmonies? How could movement in time to music be a sacrilege? Just when she thought she might understand Liedwahr, something like this popped up. How many more surprises were there?

Too many. "Are there places on Erde where dancing still goes on?" She finally asked, not wanting to say anything directly about dancing.

"They say that the Sea-Priests use it in some of their ceremonies," Alvar said.

Jecks was still shaking his head as he turned and surveyed the room. "They didn't even hide it."

"They obviously didn't think it was evil," Anna ventured.

"I am glad Arkad died without heirs." Jecks' voice was cold.

Anna wanted to shiver. Just as she'd thought he was approachable . . . "We can't do much now," she said quickly. "Jimbob or Herstat could turn this into something more . . . appropriate."

"They must—before Synfal is acceptable for guesting."

Anna moved toward the arched double doorways. After a moment, Jecks and Alvar followed.

The next hall was smaller, and contained a dais, with a covered chair or throne upon it, and a series of straight-backed chairs lined up around the wainscotted walls. Bronze sconces on all the walls held age-discolored candles behind relatively clean glass mantels. The receiving room would have held two of the largest halls at Falcor.

"Another remnant of the Suhlmorrans?" Anna wondered if agreeing to give the holding to Jimbob was wise, or whether he would get delusions of grandeur. She and Jecks definitely had some educating to do.

"It would seem so."

There were other smaller chambers, including an intimate dining room almost off the kitchens and a library that held more empty shelves than volumes—or so it seemed to Anna. But there were no more surprises, just rooms, all of them dusty.

By the time they finished the inspection and returned to the second floor, the players were gathering outside the guest quarters Anna had adopted for her use.

"I'll be a moment," she told Liende. "Why don't you tune while I check out the spell I'll need?"

"I will wait outside," Jecks said.

Anna nodded, aware she was getting distant again, but fighting fatigue and discomfort took some toll. Once inside the smelly guest quarters, she rummaged through the folder she carried in the lutar case. Where was the basic spell?

She wondered if part of the room's smell weren't coming from one sorceress, dirty from days on the road. It probably was, but the place was so dirty that she couldn't be sure.

After using her knife to sharpen the grease marker, left-handed and awkwardly, she sat down on the chair and pulled it up to the small table, making sure the chair didn't touch the bed she was certain was vermin-ridden. How could she adapt one of the spells the players already knew?

It has to be short. That meant the shorter building spell.

After studying the spell for a time, she shifted the marker to her right hand. She finally closed one eye, trying to see the paper well enough to read as she wrote.

Abruptly, she stopped.

"Idiot! Why do you have a headache and double vision?" *Because the damned spell you used on the keep was Darksong....* "And what are you doing now?" *Drafting a spell that will do the same thing.*

She rubbed her forehead again. All she wanted to do was rest and sleep, and she wouldn't get either in the pigpen that Synfal's main hall had become. And she didn't want to ride elsewhere. She took a deep breath and closed her eyes, trying to think.

She'd killed thousands, without the impact on her that the truthspell or the loyalty spell had created. So a spell that created death wasn't necessarily Darksong. Manipulation of living things—or once-living things?

"Wait a moment." Anna considered the structure of her battle hymn. After a moment, she smiled . . . if grimly. It was simple, and it was clear, and it was insane. Her battle spells had only *moved* inanimate objects against animate objects. Even her household spells had impacted inanimate objects.

So you can kill . . . Don't even think about it! Just figure out a quick way to clean this pigpen with Clearsong . . . and only Clearsong.

Anna managed to ignore the stabs of pain in her hand as she wrote slowly, and with one eye closed. Writing was one thing she couldn't do well left-handed.

Finally, she rose. The words weren't wonderful, but they fit, and she'd just have to visualize strongly.

Anna turned to Fhurgen as she opened the door. "After

we leave here to clean some of the other rooms, could you get someone to fill that tub in the washroom?'' She paused and smiled. ''Not your armsmen. Someone here should have that duty. I'm sorry, but . . .''

Fhurgen nodded, not grimly.

Jecks stepped forward, almost beside Anna, concern in his hazel eyes, saying in a low voice, ''Should you . . . ?''

''I think I can. . . . Don't want to sleep in filth, and from what the cook said, there's no one to clean up.'' Anna gestured toward the players. ''If you'd play right outside the door. I'm going to try to extend the spell to cover some of the rooms on this end of the hall.''

She waited until they rearranged themselves. ''The first building spell, the short one.''

Liende gestured, and the melody rose. Anna sang.

''Clean, clean, the bricks and wood and lesser things,
    And take the dirt until all shines and spotless
        sings . . .
    The very air and song . . . ensure all filth and vermin
        gone.''

The impact was as though a silent whirlwind had rushed through the spaces, and every surface glistened.

Anna staggered, and Jecks slipped his arm under her left to steady her. She took a deep breath. It definitely smelled better, and her head didn't ache any more than it already had. Nor was her double vision any worse. She wanted to smile. She'd managed it without doing Darksong . . . so far.

She smiled directly at Liende. ''Now . . . the players' quarters. Go ahead.''

As the players headed for the stairs, Jecks turned to Anna. ''Is this wise?''

''I can manage one more spell.''

''Are you certain?''

She nodded and began to walk toward the steps. She did let Jecks steady her.

Jecks paused to look in his spaces as they passed. He smiled at Anna and shook his head. "That is much cleaner."

"I'm glad. I'd rather not use sorcery for cleaning, but there are times when it's almost easier."

The quarters Alvar had found for the players were up on the third level, smaller, dustier, and with an even less appetizing aroma. Anna shook her head as she stopped. "This definitely needs sorcery."

Even Kaseth smiled.

Beside her, Jecks did not.

"Let's do it." At the bewildered look, she added, "The spell."

There was more enthusiasm in the playing on the third level. *Amazing how much better it gets when it helps you.*

Her head ached after the spell, but her vision remained unchanged—still double, but no worse. She turned to Jecks, still helping her unobtrusively. "I would like to wash up. Then maybe we could find something to eat." She paused. "Can the kitchens feed all our armsmen and players? They need to eat, too."

"I have already made those arrangements, Regent Anna, as you requested," Jecks added.

She hadn't requested that, but she appreciated Jecks' covering for her.

"They will eat at the tenth glass." Jecks nodded to Alvar and Liende.

"Thank you, again, all of you," Anna said to the players.

She got a scattering of smiles before they dispersed.

Liende slipped up to Anna. "I thank you."

"I'm glad I could do it."

"You will have more playing for us?"

"I'd planned on it. Not here, but I'm told that the bridge on the other side of Cheor is ready to fall."

"We will be ready." With a brief smile and a bow, Liende stepped away.

"I'm ready for a bath," Anna said. "What about

you?'' She blushed, realizing that she hadn't quite said what she'd meant.

A twinkle flashed in Jecks' eyes, but his voice was evenly modulated as he answered. "I look forward to washing up."

They walked down to the second level, where Jecks bowed after he had escorted her to her own door. Then he turned and entered his quarters.

Anna closed her door behind her, glad in a way that there were guards outside her door. The more she'd seen of Synfal, the more puzzled she'd gotten, because of the conflicting impressions she'd received.

Was it because of her own preconceptions?

She sat on the chair in front of the writing desk for a moment, pouring herself a goblet of water, and drinking.

In some ways, Liedwahr was so like her image of a medieval culture that she'd assumed it was one. *Bad assumption.* She glanced down at her hand. Luckily the cut had been shallow and relatively clean, and her alcohol had seemingly been effective in disinfecting the wound. Not painless, but better than the alternatives.

Finally, she stood and walked to the bathchamber and the tub filled with murky cold water. She winced as she thought about the necessary spells, but walked back to the main room and retrieved the lutar.

Her head and her hand were throbbing before she had the water clean and steaming and the lutar replaced in its case, and the wound had oozed more blood on the dressing.

More alcohol. She needed more alcohol for internal, not external, purposes. But she had a deep swallow of orderspelled water instead.

Finally, thank God, she could ease into the tub. *Thank God?* From nowhere, seemingly, came another thought. There were no churches in Liedwahr. She hadn't seen one, anyway. Why not? In every culture on earth there was a worship of some form of supreme being. Why not on Erde?

Yet Jecks had been truly appalled at the idea of a ballroom and dancing, and Alvar had been upset as well, more in a disgusted sort of way, as though dancing were obscene, rather than evil.

She washed slowly, hoping the hot water would loosen the stiffness in her shoulders. The heat helped, but not enough, by the time the water was cooling, and she pulled out the plug. She still found it amusing that the few tubs for the well-off all had drains, but were filled by buckets. It made sense, in an offbeat way.

She forced herself into a clean set of riding clothes. Laundry of the old set could wait, would have to wait.

At least she'd been able to get her room clean and disinfected, even if it had taken all her players, and the spells involved had given her a splitting headache. *But no more Darksong side effects.*

Finally dressed, and with her wound resterilized and rebandaged, she poured another goblet of orderspelled water and took a long swallow, then another, and refilled the goblet. After that, she ate one of the hard biscuits left over from her travel provisions. She could almost feel the worst of the headache subside.

Food and more food—you're always eating.

Was the room dimmer? She laughed. Of course it was. It was twilight, twilight of one of the lengthiest days she'd spent in a long time. Finally, she sang the candle spell, and the wall candles lit. Her head only twinged.

At the *thrap* on the door, she stood. "Yes?"

"Lord Jecks to see you, Lady Anna," Fhurgen announced.

"Oh . . . please come in."

"My lady." Jecks wore a clean blue tunic, and had washed up. He looked more handsome than ever.

"Lord Jecks." Anna wished she were more in the mood to appreciate him. "Please sit down."

Instead of sitting on the window seat, he pulled one of the wooden chairs over to the side of the writing desk opposite her.

"Jecks?" she ventured. "Will you humor me and answer some questions?"

"I would well humor you after all you have done for Jimbob."

She wished he hadn't put it quite that way. "Even after my railing on about the greediness of the lords of Defalk?"

"You did not rail. You frowned." Jecks laughed. "That was enough." He paused. "Vierk said that there were six thousand golds. I told him you were the sorceress. Then he said there were ten, and that some of the rents had not arrived." Jecks shrugged. "I have never seen ten thousand at once, not in the whole time I have held Elhi. Some farmers, they can offer no coins, and I have accepted fowl and beeves, even. Such help feeds the hold."

"I have another question. It doesn't have anything to do with golds."

"You have many questions. That is why you are regent." The white-haired lord's voice was wary.

"Do people believe in a god here?"

"A god?"

"A supreme being . . . a supernatural . . . entity . . . in charge of the world?"

"An almighty Lord of Harmony, do you mean?"

"Something like that."

"There are some." Despite her concerns, his slightly crooked smile warmed Anna as Jecks shifted his weight on the plain wooden chair. "The . . . women of Ranuak believe that harmony is governed by the earth mother. The Sea-Priests, they believe that harmony and disharmony flow with the tides of the great oceans. The Pelarans, who might know? The Evult thought he was the Lord of Harmony, until you appeared." Jecks offered a wider smile, somehow tentative. "Some are saying you are the Lady of Harmony."

"Me?" asked Anna involuntarily.

"So they say."

"Not me." A growling from her stomach reminded Anna of other necessities, and rescued her. "I need to eat."

Jecks stood immediately. "If I might join you? Alvar ate with Jimbob already. Jimbob sleeps now. He still is young."

"Of course." Anna offered a smile, hoping her concerns didn't show through too much. "I had thought you would. Earlier, I mean. And I understand about Jimbob. Sometimes you forget he's only twelve."

The Lord of Elheld nodded, then stood as she did, and they walked silently down the wide main brick stairs.

They sat at a corner of the large table in the intimate dining salon beside the kitchen. The three lit wall sconces gave a dim but adequate light. Two platters rested on the table, one of a roasted fowl, uncut, evenly roasted brown, and oozing golden drippings, and a second of sliced meat over thick noodles, covered with a white sauce.

Anna could smell the duck. Was it as greasy as it looked? And smelled? Then, she'd never cared that much for either goose or duck. She helped herself to the noodles, her mouth watering. She'd really eaten far too little over the course of the day.

She'd almost finished her first helping before she spoke. "You saw the kitchens."

"Yes?" mumbled Jecks.

"And the stables?" Anna paused. "They were well kept, better kept, and cleaner in many ways than the rooms people lived in here."

"I do not think anyone has lived here for some years, except for Lord Arkad. Alvar said Fauren's quarters were with the armsmen." Jecks took a hefty swallow of wine from his goblet, then reached for the pitcher to refill his goblet. "Those are clean."

"I wonder." Anna carefully lifted the goblet and took a small swallow of wine, since she hadn't felt like order-spelling any water besides that in her quarters. The pewterlike goblet was heavy, and she wasn't used to using her left hand. "I had the impression that Fauren was the evil plotter behind a weak and crazy old lord. I suppose it doesn't matter now. Except it does." She pursed her lips.

"Lord Arkad had some greater plan, you think?"

"I don't know. He kept the ballroom—the dancing room—and the old throne room. He was gathering huge amounts of golds, and outside of the main part of the hall, everything is clean and in good condition."

"Our weapons difficulties may be slighter, now," Jecks said after taking another mouthful of the duck that had proved too greasy for Anna.

"There was an armory somewhere?"

"Over two hundred good blades, and close to a hundred lances. A number of bows. Those I did not count."

"Won't that leave the liedburg's armsmen without weapons?" she asked.

"Those were racked below. The armsmen have their blades."

Anna nodded to herself. One way or another, the blades needed to go to Falcor. "That will help Hanfor. And if we can get the ones from Ranuak . . ."

"A blade in the hand is worth two in the forge."

Anna yawned. "I'm sorry. I didn't realize I was so tired." She shook her head.

"You amaze me. You have ridden nearly two leagues, cast numerous spells, been wounded, and taken over a strange hold, and you are astonished that you are fatigued." Jecks' eyes twinkled as he stood and offered his arm.

Anna took it. "It makes sense that way."

Not much else does, but that does. She stifled another yawn and took the first step toward the stairs, glad for his stability in an unstable world.

28

WEI, NORDWEI

Ashtaar glances at the black agate oval, then at Gretslen, who sits in the chair before the flat desk. "Send
a message scroll to Menares."

"He has not acknowledged any previous instructions
and messages, and he fears the soprano sorceress so
greatly that he will not admit to receiving anything from
Wei." The blonde seer's voice is matter-of-fact.

"His fear of her is exactly what I am counting on."
The spymistress smiles. "Ehara is being courted by the
Sea-Priests. What can we do about it?"

"There is little we can do, not with the Bitter Sea yet
frozen, not until the spring gathering."

"We can ensure that she knows."

Gretslen frowns.

"Do we want the Sea-Priests to get a foothold in Dumar, and then in Ranuak?" Ashtaar sighs. "I should not
explain, but I will. Ehara reckons to use the Sea-Priests'
coin to take over the south of Defalk. He sends arms and
golds to Lord Dencer. What the ambitious—or desperate—
Lord Ehara does not know is that the Sea-Priests will cast
him aside as they can, and Dumar will become where their
ships port in Liedwahr. First will come their control of
the wool trade, and then of the grain."

"You think the sorceress can do aught about this?"

"If she knows that Lord Dencer is receiving golds from
Ehara, she must act. Provided she knows this is happening—"

"Menares will not tell her."

"Oh, but he must. Should she ever discover that he
knew of the threat and did not inform her, what would

his life be worth? No, she would not kill him. She would do worse. She would send him back to Neserea, or to Wei.'' Ashtaar picks up the stone that is deeper and blacker than night. ''Draft the scroll. I would see it by evening.''

''As you wish, mightiness.'' Gretslen's voice remains neutral.

''You doubt my desire to warn her? Even the Council would not. With a known danger in Dencer and Ehara, she will not move north. Nor can she consider taking territory in Ebra. She is strong enough to bring down Ehara, one way or another, and that will bring her into conflict with both Konsstin and the Sea-Priests.''

''And you feel that she will use her sorcery against them?''

''She will not have any choice,'' predicts Ashtaar, glancing down at the black agate oval she holds. ''She never has had that choice. Nor do we.''

''Why can she not see what we see? She is a greater sorceress than any of us . . .''

''How many seers do you have in the tower, Gretslen?''

''Five, besides myself,'' admits the blonde.

Ashtaar smiles. ''There is but one of the sorceress, and she needs must hold her strength for the mighty works required of her. Also, strength is not skill. There is much she does not know, much she cannot yet know.''

Gretslen frowns momentarily, smoothing the expression away before Ashtaar looks up.

''Draft the scroll.''

29

I n the bright midmorning spring sunshine, Anna eased Farinelli to a halt on the rutted and packed clay of the road that led to the bridge across the Synor River. She smiled, glad that she could see again, undoubled, unimpaired. Two days of rest had helped. *Can you count on days of rest after every major bit of sorcery?* She pushed the thought away.

On her right rode Liende, as her chief player. On the left rode Jecks, and immediately behind them, Alvar and Jimbob. A faint line of clouds rose on the southern horizon, but the skies overhead were clear, and a light and pleasant breeze gusted out of the south.

"There is the bridge," Jecks announced.

"It looks as rickety as Halde and everyone said," the blonde and youthful-looking regent acknowledged.

"It has served for many years," Jecks said.

"It won't serve us that many more. Not unless the river goes dry," Anna answered. She glanced at the road and the bridge again, then toward Alvar. "Let's keep everyone back from the bridge until I'm done. Send a squad across the bridge to the other side. When they get there, have them set up a post . . ."

"A picket line?"

"A picket line a good hundred yards from the bridge." Anna cleared her throat, hoping the spring tree pollen wasn't going to trigger her allergies. Brill's youth sorcery hadn't done anything for that. "The last thing we need is someone trying to cross a bridge while I'm trying to replace it."

"Yes, Lady Anna." The swarthy captain nodded and

turned his mount away, riding back toward the lancers who had halted perhaps five yards behind the players, in turn five yards behind Anna and Liende.

Jimbob eased his mare up beside his grandsire.

"Liende?" asked Anna. "Would you have the players wait here for a moment? I need to see where I want you all to play. It may take me a little bit to get ready, but I hope it won't be too long."

"We stand ready." Liende nodded.

Anna flicked the reins gently, and let Farinelli carry her off the road and closer to the edge of the slight bank overlooking the lowland and the river itself. When she reined up, to her right was the low timber structure that had served as the main crossing of the Synor for more than fifty deks. The last scattered houses of the eastern-most part of Cheor lay a good two deks westward, along the road she had just traveled from Synfal.

While the Falche—to the west of Cheor—was wider than at Falcor, and much wider to the southwest after it was joined by the Synor, the Synor itself was a narrow river. The water flowing under the old bridge wasn't much more than twenty yards wide, with grasses and rushes extending a few yards beyond. As Jecks had pointed out, though, for the forty deks upstream of Cheor the Synor ran deep enough that it was well over the head of even a mounted rider, with several yards to spare.

Despite the flatness of the land, she had noted that there were scattered boulders, some sizable, along the river, probably either from beneath the delta or carried down-stream over time. She was counting on there being enough for her sorcery. Otherwise . . . she shook her head. *You do what you can.*

Anna continued to survey the river and the bridge, pon-dering how the old timber bridge had lasted. She thought she could see it waver even as her lancers crossed it and then set up a picket line to keep the road and bridge clear.

Farinelli *whuffed* and sidestepped as Jecks eased his

mount up beside Anna. Jimbob halted his mare slightly farther back.

"Are you sure this is wise?" Jecks frowned.

"We don't have any battles to fight. I have a set of players, and that means I'm not doing it all myself. And that bridge is the key to all the lands in the south of Defalk, isn't it?"

"Except for Morra, that is true. Still, your bridge will also let an enemy march north to Falcor."

Anna smiled grimly. "If an enemy gets that far, we won't be around to worry."

"A regent who does not retreat." Jecks gave a short laugh.

Alvar and Fhurgen had reined up slightly behind Jecks and Anna, but neither spoke as the sorceress continued to study the river and the bridge.

"When we fight on their lands, our people don't suffer as much." Anna wondered where she'd thought of that, even as she said it.

An expression flicked across Jecks' face, too fast for Anna to identify it. Was it surprise? Or dismay? She wasn't sure she liked either. She turned in the saddle, absently patting Farinelli on the neck. "Alvar, I think the lancers should keep everyone on this side back, say, as far as that path that joins the road there. That should provide enough of a margin of safety." *You hope.*

"Yes, Regent Anna." The captain turned and rode back toward the lancers, and the cart and wagon they had detained. "All squads back. Back behind the cross-path there."

Anna dismounted and extracted the two sheets of paper she had prepared earlier—the spell and the sketch of the bridge. Then she looked at the still-mounted Lord Jecks, then at Fhurgen. "If you would not mind hanging on to Farinelli, Fhurgen?"

"He has not troubled me before. Let us hope he does not today."

"I hope not." She turned to Jecks.

"Have you a task for me?" The white-haired lord smiled, a faint twinkle back in his eyes.

"No. This time, you and Jimbob can just watch."

"You ... I ... we will watch."

Anna wondered what Jecks had been about to say, or why he hadn't. Offer a compliment? Was she that formidable? "Thank you." She tried to make her words warm, and she smiled.

Jimbob smiled back, almost with a puzzled cross between a smile and a frown, and Jecks returned the warmth.

Then Anna walked to the top of the low rise where she could see both river and bridge. On the far side, her armsmen were stretched out. Two had stopped a cart drawn by a pony, and a woman leading two sheep.

She hummed the spell tune, then started through a vocalise. "Holly, lolly, polly ... pop ..." She coughed up mucus. It was going to be one of those days. Thank goodness, or the harmonies, it wasn't a battle or some other disaster.

The youth spell hadn't really returned her to youth, not her own youth. She'd never had bad allergies when she'd been young. Brill's dying effort had rejuvenated her current body, given it strength and a youthful form, but she was still struggling with allergies and intermittent mild asthma.

Clearing her throat, she tried another vocalise. Her voice didn't feel clear until she'd run through four vocalises, and she tried to ignore the impatience she felt was building around her.

Across the river the lancers had stopped another wagon, and on her side, Alvar had halted a cart and a shepherd with a dozen sheep.

Finally, Anna turned and motioned to Liende, and waited until the red-and-white-haired woodwind player rode forward. "I think about here would be right." The sorceress added, "We'll use the long building spell. Warm up and run through it a few times while I finish getting ready."

"Players to position," said Liende, with a gesture to the others to dismount and circle around her.

Anna walked forward a few steps, looking at the sketch of the bridge and trying to visualize it over the waters and the still-brown rushes of the Synor.

While the strings and horns began to tune behind her, she began to sing the notes of the spell, using "la" instead of real words, and visualized the stone arch she wanted to replace the rickety wooden span that had seemed to sway and sag even under a single wagon earlier.

After one run-through, Anna concentrated on just the drawing of the bridge the spell was supposed to create, ignoring the cacophony of tuning, and the creaking of yet another wagon nearing the river.

Then, as the players waited, she finished a last vocalise and mentally went over the spell melody and the words. Finally, she nodded to Liende. "The long building spell-song."

Once the melody rose, Anna sang, not belting, but with full voice.

> ". . . replicate the blocks and stones.
>   Place them in their proper zones . . .
>   Set them firm, and set them square
>   weld them to their pattern there . . .
>
> "Bring the rock and make it stone . . ."

The ground around the river shuddered, but Anna held her mind on the image of the new bridge and the stone approachway to it, keeping her voice open and clear.

The shiver in Erde's underlying harmonies seemed less pronounced. Was that because the players were stronger? Still, there was a flicker of lightning across the half-clear sky—again visible to but her, she suspected. The few puffy clouds did darken into a heavy gray.

Anna swayed on her feet, feeling dizzy, lightheaded, but she caught herself.

Damn it all! More rest before we get out of here. All
she ever did, it seemed, was cast spells and get weak and
recover in time to cast more spells. Her eyes narrowed.
The new bridge seemed solid, although the stones shimmered as if they had been glazed.

"Lady Anna?" Jecks stood beside her, offering her
both her water bottle and a biscuit bigger than his fist.

"Thank you." She took a swallow from the bottle and
then a bite of the crumbly biscuit, and another . . . and
another. After a moment, she realized she'd eaten the entire biscuit. She was still lightheaded, but didn't feel as
though she'd fall over any moment, and she had no problem with double images.

With a smile, Jecks offered another biscuit.

"Thank you," she said again, taking it, and chewing
off a crumbling corner.

Alvar eased his mount toward her. "My lady? The
bridge? Can it be used?"

"They can use it," she confirmed.

"Another bridge that will outlive us both," Jecks said,
with a shake of his head.

"Better bridges than battles," she mumbled as she finished the second biscuit and lifted the water bottle.

30

ESARIA, NESEREA

I won't. I can't." The girl sits up in the bed, and swings
her legs over the edge, letting the sheer green cotton
fall away from small and well-formed breasts that shimmer in the faint light that comes through the door from
the outer room.

"You're sure?" Rabyn's voice is concerned, warm.

"I can't . . ." She shakes her head. "That . . . that's awful."

"I'd hoped you'd be sweet to me."

"The other . . ." She shakes her head. "Not that. . . ."

The dark-haired youth sits up beside her, offers her a goblet of wine. "Here. It's all right. I didn't realize it would upset you."

"You're so young. You're not old enough to think like that. How . . ." She takes a swallow, and her mouth puckers slightly. "Sweet. Too sweet." Another smaller swallow follows.

"Honey. I like my wine sweet. I like girls sweet, too, Dylla." Rabyn offers a smile.

"Sickening . . . sweet." She wipes her lips with the back of her hand, and her mouth puckers again.

"I like things sweet. That's why you should have done what I asked," he adds slowly, taking the goblet from her, as her hands begin to tremble.

"You . . ." Her mouth opens spasmodically, and she begins to choke. Her hands reach for him, but the trembling increases, and Rabyn steps out of her grasp easily.

"You should have been sweet to me," he repeats as he stands and steps away from the bed, carrying the goblet.

Dylla slumps, then topples forward, and her nude form, lying half across the green braided rug and half across the cold tiles, twitches and shudders for a time. She also moans softly, softly only because she cannot make a greater effort.

Before long, twitches and moans cease.

Then Rabyn pulls on his tunic and trousers, and a pair of gold threaded sandals, and walks into the antechamber where he rings the crystal bell and waits by the single flickering candle.

"Yes, sire?" answers the page as he opens the door.

"I would like to see Nubara. Now. Here."

"Now?" The servant glances toward the dark window, then at Rabyn. "Yes, sire."

The door closes.

Rabyn goes back to the bedchamber and amuses himself for a time, waiting for Nubara.

When he arrives, the hand of the regent does not have himself announced, but throws open the door and marches through and into the bedchamber.

Rabyn smiles. "She wasn't nice to me, Nubara. I don't like people who aren't sweet to me."

Nubara looks at the naked body on the floor. "Was that necessary, Rabyn?"

"Lord Rabyn," corrects the dark-haired youth. "She wouldn't do what I wanted. She didn't make me feel good." Rabyn smiles. "You said she was only a peasant."

"I beg your pardon, Lord Rabyn." Nubara's voice is cold. "She still had family, and they will not be happy. Neither will their friends."

"Tell them she died of the flux. It does happen. Offer them a few golds as consolation. Every peasant loves golds." Rabyn's lips curl. "They see few enough of them."

"Would you be so kind as to help me dress the body? It might be easier to explain."

"I'm the Prophet, Nubara. I'm sure grandsire wouldn't wish anything to happen to me. You know that, don't you?" Rabyn pauses. "Her clothes are on the chair there."

Nubara compresses his lips, then walks to the chair and picks up the silken trousers. His eyes go to the still form. "What a waste," he murmurs to himself.

"She should have done what I wanted," Rabyn repeats. "You will, won't you, Nubara?"

Nubara forces a smile. "Of course, Lord Rabyn, of course."

31

Anna looked out the guest-chamber window at the low clouds and the driving rain, then walked back to the table and picked up a flaky roll—better than a biscuit—and began to eat slowly as she sat down.

She finished the roll with a sigh, and topped off roll and sigh with a long swallow of water. Her eyes flicked toward the window and the rain outside.

"You still wish to travel to Synope?" Jecks asked from the other side of the writing table.

"After the rain lifts, assuming it does lift, yes, I do. I worry about Anientta, and I don't like the idea of her controlling Flossbend."

"That is a hard ride of eight to nine days," Jecks pointed out. "You know that there is little you can do about this consort of Lord Hryding's right now. If you are worried about repairing the ford at Soprat, you could turn north at the wide bend in the Synor and travel straight north. That would save almost five days' travel in returning to Falcor."

"Why are you so worried about time? You and Hanfor practically insisted nothing was going to happen for months—seasons, I mean."

"You have spent more time in Synfal than you had planned."

"There has been more to do than I expected." Anna took another sip of water. "You want me to get back to Falcor to announce that Jimbob will inherit Synfal?" She grinned. "I thought we'd agreed that should wait a bit."

Jecks looked at the time-dulled oak of the table, then

gave an embarrassed smile. "Menares sent a message scroll to you through me."

Anna frowned. Again . . . it had to be bad news. No one wanted to tell her that sort of thing directly.

"What's the trouble?" she said, reaching for another roll.

"There are two troubles." Jecks coughed. "You had best read it yourself." He handed Anna a scroll.

She began to read, skipping over the flowery salutations.

> . . . I have not made any contact with the ladies of Wei. This you must know and convey to the lady Anna. Yet they have taken it upon themselves to impart information, and I have enclosed their very message scroll as proof. The lady Anna must know this, and yet I fear that she will not believe I have acted in good faith.
>
> Still if what they have sent is true, and they have not lied about what has happened elsewhere in former scrolls, you both should know the contents. . . .
>
> My humble best to you and to the great and glorious regent, whose fairness has become legendary. . . .

Anna laughed. "He knew you'd give this to me, the scoundrel."

"His last words are sung in your direction," Jecks said. "They are true, but they are a plea."

True? What's true is that no man around here would plead to a woman. Damned few, anyway. "He addressed his plea through you."

"Most men would."

"It would be better if they didn't." Anna managed to keep the words polite—barely—reminding herself that Jecks wasn't the problem. He'd dealt with her directly from the beginning. Was that because he'd had a strong daughter? Had his consort been like Alasia? She pushed that thought away.

"I would not wager against that." Jecks smiled broadly.

Anna smiled back, momentarily. "Let's see what the ladies of Wei have to say." She unrolled the second scroll.

Menares, honorable counselor to the Regent of Defalk,

We think it advisable that you inform the lady Anna, sorceress though she be, of a matter of grave import of which she may not be aware. The Sea-Priests of Sturinn have sent an envoy to Lord Ehara of Dumar, with a chest of precious stones and gold. Lord Ehara has already sent officers of his guard to Lord Dencer of Stromwer and Lord Sargol of Suhl. These officers bore coins and tokens of friendship.

If Lord Ehara be acting on his own or at the behest of the Sea-Priests, that we know not. Neither is to the interest of Defalk, Nordwei, or Liedwahr. We trust you will follow your own good judgment and convey this information to your regent and sorceress.

A sealmark without lettering—just a four-pointed star with an *N* above the topmost point—was set in black wax below the carefully scripted letters.

"That is the seal of Nordwei," Jecks said.

Anna clicked her fingernails together. They were getting ragged again. Thank heavens she'd had a nail clipper in her purse, now in the large green leather pouch-wallet attached to her belt. She hoped she never had to use a knife the way she'd seen Jecks trim his nails. "Why would they send me that kind of message?"

"It is in their interest that you fight for them." Jecks shrugged. "If the Sturinnese can gain a foothold in Liedwahr, and one with a good port, such as Narial is supposed to have—''

"Narial—that's the one south of Dumaria?'' Anna was trying to recall her too-recently-acquired Erdean geography.

"That is the main seaport. The Falche is wide and deep and slow enough that smaller seagoing vessels can sail all the way up to Dumaria. I would doubt that the larger vessels of Sturinn could.''

"The traders up in Wei want me to stop Ehara and the Sturinnese? Why would they think I'd want to get involved in a war there? Defalk is still a mess. Muddy roads, lords who don't want a woman as regent, debts . . .''

"They may feel you have no choice, and they would warn you.''

No choice?

Her face betrayed her thoughts.

"If Lord Ehara uses the coin of the Sturinnese to buy rebellion in Defalk, you must fight—either in Defalk or Dumar.''

"What do the Sturinnese have against Defalk? We don't have a port. We haven't offended them.'' Anna frowned.

Jecks shifted his weight in the chair, like a boy with a secret. He even looked boyish for a moment, and Anna wanted to smile. Except he was uncomfortable, and that bothered her. She found herself clicking her nails again, and she clinched her fingernails into her palms for a moment, then forced a long slow breath before she spoke. "You're worried about telling me how I've offended the Sturinnese. What is it?''

"It is not the Sturinnese. It is their Sea-Priests.'' Jecks shifted his weight in the chair again. "Some seafarers, they have great concern about having women on board their ships.''

"I doubt somehow that the Ranuans and the traders of Wei have those concerns.''

"No, lady, they do not. The Sturinnese do."

"There's more than that."

"They feel women are the agents of dissonance, and they chain them."

"They do what?" Anna wasn't sure she'd heard Jecks. "They chain some of their women?" Something ... something . *. someone else had told her about chains.

"All of them, Lady Anna, from what I have heard. Some wear chains that are little more than adornment, but most wear heavy links."

"Chains as adornment. Adornment." Rather than speak more, Anna stood and walked to the window. Lady Essan had mentioned that, and she'd hoped not to have to deal with the Sturinnese. Why? Why did she always have to deal with what she'd rather not? The perversity of the universe? Mercury in retrograde, except there wasn't any Mercury in the skies of Erde. Darksong in ascendence? Was that the local equivalent? The red moon of darkness?

As the thoughts cascaded through her mind, the rain still fell, and the gray clouds seemed to touch the dark and recently tilled fields.

Had any place on earth chained *all* its women? She shivered. No wonder the traders of Nordwei were confident she would try to stop Ehara, if not the Sturinnese. Then, how much did the traders of the north know of her? Too much, it seemed.

She turned back to Jecks. "You must know how I feel about women in chains."

"I cannot see you favoring the Sea-Priests." Jecks' tone was wry. "Or Lord Ehara, if he is bound to do their bidding."

"I thought things were bad enough with Konsstin threatening to take over Neserea." She paused. "How do we know that this isn't a ploy to get us tied up down here?"

"That, we do not know, save that the Norweians have not sent their armies into any other land in memory."

"That means they aren't likely to invade. That's if

things don't change. They could still want us to fight a war to weaken us, or keep us from invading them.''

"The Council of Wei has been known for such.'' Jecks' voice remained wary, but Anna wasn't certain the wariness was from deliberation or concern that she might still explode over the customs of the Sea-Priests.

"Lord Sargol still owes half his liedgeld,'' mused Anna. "So does Dencer.'' She half flushed as her stomach growled.

"Lord Gylaron has paid none, is that not so?'' asked Jecks, politely ignoring her audible signs of continual hunger.

"There's more behind your question. Doesn't he hold the lands between Stromwer and Suhl?''

"You mark my meaning.'' Jeck laughed.

"I'm not sure I do. I'm missing something. The two lords north and south of Gylaron have paid half their liedgeld, but Gylaron's paid none. Dencer would like to see me dead, but he's paid half. I don't know anything about Sargol, but Ehara's courting both of them.''

"I doubt Gylaron is our friend.''

"Nor Dencer. Nor Sargol.'' She shrugged. "Let's see what the glass will tell us.''

Jecks rose.

"No. I'd like you to watch. You may see something I don't.''

"You are not wary of revealing—''

Anna laughed. "You've heard me sing enough spells. Those were far more deadly than mirror spells. You've probably heard your share of spells, anyway.''

Jecks nodded, his eyes twinkling momentarily. "A few.''

"So why don't you sing any?''

"Spellcasting is untrustworthy for the untrained.''

"Like handling a blade?''

"It is more dangerous, from what I have seen.'' Jecks leaned back slightly in the straight-backed chair and steepled his fingers together. "Once, I'd not have said that. Now . . ." he shrugged.

"Now?"

"Barjim's forces fell to sorcery, and so did those of the Evult's." Jecks' brow furrowed. "What do you plan?"

"To see what the mirror will show me. I have an idea."

Jecks nodded and sat back, as if to wait.

Anna took a deep breath, then ran through one vocalise, then another. Her voice wasn't as clear as it should have been. Allergies from the rain and the mold that had to infest the ancient pile of bricks that was Synfal?

She cleared her throat and tried again. Finally, she picked up the lutar, then stopped at the quizzical expression on Jecks' face. "You don't see this in public, all the time it takes sometimes to be able to sing."

"I have seen you cast spells . . ."

"Without all the preparation?" Anna nodded. "Half the time I'm afraid they won't work when that happens. Sometimes they don't. That's how I ended up defending myself with a knife." She shivered as she recalled how she'd gutted the poor young armsman whose only real fault had been following the orders of the wrong person.

Jecks offered a half-nod, turning in the chair to be able to see the mirror.

Anna turned to the dark wood framed mirror on the yellowed plaster of the wall. Her cleaning spell had not been enough to return the plaster to any semblance of white, assuming it had ever been white.

> "Mirror, mirror on the wall,
>   show me now Lord Dencer's hall.
>   Within its gates, Wendella show me fast
>   and make that spell well last . . ."

In the silvered oblong on the wall was an image of a brown-haired woman. She sat, alone, almost slumped at a table in what appeared to be a tower room. Her hair was braided, but she turned and appeared to look at Anna and Jecks. The red eyes were sunken in dark circles. Those, and the barred window, told Anna enough.

After a moment, the sorceress released the image with a quick couplet, almost a chant. A moment of dizziness followed, but the lightheadedness vanished almost as swiftly as it had struck.

"You asked to see her, not Dencer."

"I had a feeling." What Anna had felt was that Wendella's situation would reveal more than seeing Dencer. Had it? She wasn't sure.

"Better that she had remained in Falcor," said Jecks, leaning forward in the chair. "Dencer fears you have suborned her."

"That's not likely. She hates me."

"He fears your sorcery."

"He fears any woman who will stand up to him." Anna took another swallow of water and forced herself to eat the last roll. "Why do so many men fear women here?"

Jecks cleared his throat.

Anna waited.

"There have always been more sorcerers than sorceresses." The white-haired lord coughed.

Anna let the silence continue.

"The sorceresses have always been more powerful. The Evult . . . he was perhaps the greatest sorcerer ever—and you destroyed him." Jecks forced his eyes to meet Anna's. "All know you have yet to claim fully the power that is yours."

"I've almost been killed twice, and nearly killed myself more than that," Anna pointed out.

"No one else would have survived the smallest portion of your travail." Jecks gave a strained smile. "Do you wonder that Dencer, or the Sea-Priests, or Konsstin, all fear you?"

"I've never been out to build an empire. All I've tried to do is to preserve Defalk."

"When folk hate, they do not think," mused Jecks.

"That is why a thinking warrior, if he can survive the first few moments against a madman, will triumph."

"If there are enough madmen," suggested Anna, "like the dark ones . . ."

"Then there is no time to think."

"Great." Anna set down the lutar, realizing that it felt heavy, too heavy. "I need to eat—again. So do you." She looked at Jecks.

After a moment, he returned the smile, boyishly, despite his white hair, and Anna almost wanted to hug him. For that instant, the warrior lord was a cross between a teddy bear and a movie star.

"I could use some food," he admitted gruffly. "Not so much as a certain sorceress."

Anna walked to the door and opened it.

Fhurgen stood there, waiting.

"If you would, Fhurgen, could you have Captain Alvar join us here? And see if you can get someone to put together a platter with enough food for the three of us." She didn't want to try another spell without eating. "Don't you do it, either. Have the kitchen handle it." She flashed a smile, trying to convey warmth.

"We can manage that, Lady Anna." Fhurgen's dark eyes twinkled for a moment.

"Thank you." Anna closed the door and walked to the window to join Jecks. They both watched the rain, falling less forcefully, and more like a cold mist. She could sense just how close he was, and she started to reach out. *No . . . you can't muddy things. Play like the virgin queen.* But she was all too conscious that she didn't want to be a virgin queen or regent—not in the slightest.

She stepped back and sideways to look at the mirror on the wall. The finish of the ebony wood around the glass showed bubbles and discoloration.

Then she recovered the lutar. "I'll try one more while we're waiting for Alvar and food."

Jecks turned so that he could watch the mirror.

Anna retuned before she sang the mirror spell.

"Mirror, mirror, on the wall,
    show me now Lord Sargol's hall.
    Within its gates, show Lord Sargol fast
    and make that spell well last . . ."

The mirror swirled white, then blanked.

Anna frowned, then she shook her head. The way she'd composed the spell wouldn't allow showing Sargol if he weren't in his hall.

She lowered the lutar. How could she change it? It took several attempts with the grease marker before she had something. After humming through the tune to fix the new words, she looked at Jecks.

"It's not as easy as it looks to outsiders." Then she lifted the lutar.

"Mirror, mirror, in your frame,
    show me Lord Sargol in his fame.
    Where'er he may ride or be,
    show him now to me . . ."

The second image centered on a gray-haired and slender man, with a trimmed gray beard and a regular tanned face. A darkly handsome figure, Anna decided. Lord Sargol rode a gray mount, with a gray cloak half open.

Behind him rode armsmen. How many, Anna could not tell from the image presented in the wall mirror. Nor could she tell where he rode. She wanted to stamp a foot, childish as it felt. She needed better spells—more precise ones . . . or something.

Her eyes went to Jecks. "Have you seen enough?"

"Yes, Lady Anna."

Anna released the spell. This time, the dizziness didn't pass immediately, and she walked slowly back to her chair, setting the lutar on the bed behind it.

She sat and took a long swallow of water, hoping it wouldn't be that long before Alvar and supper, or whatever a late-afternoon meal might be called, arrived.

"You need to eat more," suggested Jecks, mildly, not quite meeting her eyes.

"I know. I know." She closed her eyes for a moment, but that only got her white sparkles against the red-tinged darkness, and she opened them nearly immediately. "Do you know what it's like to have to eat all the time? To worry that you'll die if you can't eat?"

"Once . . . many years ago, I had to eat much more." Jecks laughed, half humorously. "Now, I wish I could. Always, we wish for what we have yet to reach or what we have left behind."

That was true enough. With a gust of damp air, Anna looked toward the window. The rain had picked up again, and she could hear it splatting against the outer walls of Synfal.

It wasn't that long before a *thrap* on the door.

Jecks rose, and Anna let him.

Alvar followed the two serving girls and the heaped platters into the room. He glanced around, then slipped out, only to return with another chair from somewhere even before the girls left.

On one platter was a variety of white and yellow cheeses, as well as slabs of cold meat. The second platter held noodles of some sort, covered with a steaming brown sauce. There was a large basket with a long dark loaf of bread, and a smaller basket with three apples.

Anna felt her mouth watering. She tried some of everything, and found herself wolfing down the mint-spicy noodles, not caring that much that her eyes were watering.

Again, she ate twice what either man did, and then had some more of the white cheese and the dark bread. After that, she sliced up the tart apple and ate that, and more cheese.

"Good food, and I thank you, Lady Anna," Alvar said as he finished.

"I, too," said Jecks, adding, "Sorcery is wearying work. More wearying than wielding a blade from what I see."

"I never would have thought it," Anna admitted, reaching for the last crust of the hot dark bread.

Finally, with her headache and dizziness gone, she picked up the lutar again. "Let's see what other sorcerers are following me."

Alvar swallowed as she began to sing.

> "Of those with power of the song
> seek those who'd do me wrong
> and show them in this silver cast
> and make that vision well last."

This time the images in the glass were fewer, far fewer. There was the blond seer from Nordwei whom she'd seen from the beginning, a hawk-faced man in white who had to be one of the Sea-Priests, and a young black-bearded man with intense eyes that burned.

She turned to Jecks and Alvar.

Jecks shook his head.

As she could smell the heat of the mirror's wooden frame, Anna released the images.

The looks of hatred on the faces of both the Sea-Priest and the unknown young man bothered her. She couldn't prove it, but she felt those looks were directed at her, and she'd learned the hard way what happened when she didn't take into account her feelings.

At the same time, she had to wonder. Were there that few with power who would do her wrong?

"The woman's from Nordwei. She's been following me ever since I got here, I think. Is the man in white one of the Sea-Priests?"

"I do not know, lady," answered Alvar.

"I would say so, from his garments," said Jecks.

"What about the young man?"

"He looks like a dark monk or a commoner," answered Jecks.

Why would a commoner hate her? Should she investigate more? She frowned. She couldn't sing spells for everyone who opposed her—not all at the same time. Still carrying the lutar, Anna walked over to the table and finished the last of the water. She'd need to orderspell more. That could wait.

What else should she scry? Dencer? She took a deep breath. How could she craft a better spell?

> "Lord Dencer, show me then and now,
> what he does 'gainst me and how.
> Show the scenes both far and near
> and show us what one should fear."

The mirror obligingly split into three scenes. In the one in the upper left third of the glass, Dencer sat on a low ridge watching what appeared to be lancers practicing something. From what Anna could see, there were hundreds of lancers, far more than she had. In the left-hand side of the glass, Dencer stood beside a desk, holding a velvet pouch. Across the desk was an officer in a crimson uniform. The lower scene showed an aerial view of the land. Anna didn't see anything familiar. There was a road, flanked by several hilltops, and fields and perhaps a keep or holding in the distance.

After several moments, she turned to Alvar. The captain lifted his shoulders. "Lady Anna, I do not understand."

"It is a vision from the heavens," Jecks explained. "That could be anywhere in southern Defalk. I do not see anything I recognize, but the land is softer and greener than in the north."

As heat radiated from the wooden mirror frame and it threatened to burst into flames, Anna released the spell. As she looked at Jecks, a *crack* broke the silence. Black lines split the mirror into three sections, still held by the frame.

"I think I need another mirror."

"You are hard on glasses." Jecks glanced at the window as rain splattered into the room. "Perhaps the shutters?"

Anna nodded.

Alvar used a striker to light the candles, while Jecks stood and went to the window to close the double shutters.

"The armsman in red—you think he was from Dumar?" she asked in the flickering light from the candles.

"Ehara's lancers are said to wear red." Jecks sipped the amber wine.

Anna thought she might have some . . . later. "Ehara's sending golds to Dencer, like the Norweians warned me."

Alvar gave a single sharp nod.

"And he's training a lot of lancers." Anna thought. Maybe she should go straight back to Falcor. Or follow Jecks' advice and just repair the ford at Soprat. If the southern lords were preparing revolt, she might need quick access to and from the east. Anientta would have to wait—like a lot of things. "You may be right, Lord Jecks. This is not the time to visit Synope." She paused. "Do you have any idea where that last scene might be?"

"No, Lady Anna. I do not. It has to be south of here, because there were red quince trees on the hillside, and they do not grow north of the Synor."

"I hope Hanfor's had some luck in finding armsmen and blades for them to bear." She shook her head. "We'd better make plans to leave as soon as possible."

"I feel that is wise, lady." Jecks cleared his throat. "I would also feel happier if you would wear a breastplate."

Alvar nodded.

"Armor?"

Jecks looked down. "If . . . Arkad had been younger . . . If you are caught unaware . . . you can recover from injuries to limbs, if anyone can."

"I suppose I should learn to wear a helmet, too?" She softened her tone and added, "I'm sorry. I'll give it a try."

"You are Defalk, Lady Anna," Alvar said slowly.

Now she had to worry about armor? And another fight? She didn't want to use sorcery against Dencer, but would she have any choice? He didn't seem likely to listen to reason, and she certainly didn't have a large enough army to avoid using it. In any case, she needed to be in Falcor . . . or somewhere not so out of touch as Cheor.

She took a deep breath, then reached for the pitcher of wine. She needed it. She hoped she wouldn't need it too much in the days ahead.

32

STROMWER, DEFALK

Dencer opens the iron-bound door and steps into the narrow, stone-walled room.

Wendella looks up from the table, then stands, and inclines her head. "My lord, what wish you?"

"What wish I? What wish I? What sort of fool do you take me for? What wish I?" He lifts the leather quirt in his hand. "Do you see this? See you this?"

"Yes, my lord." Wendella's eyes meet Dencer's.

"The sole good you have done, the sole good is my son! Better I had your tongue ripped out."

"My lord?"

"You said you made no bargains with the bitch!"

"I said I made none, and I made none."

"You lie. You lie as rushes on a peasant's floor." Dencer reaches out with his left hand and rips off the thin shift that Wendella wears. She stands erect, motionless as his second motion rips away her smallclothes, leaving a red scratch across her hip.

"I told you no lies, my lord. I suffered captivity for you. Never did I agree to anything."

Smack! Dencer's hand rocks the brown-haired woman's head back.

"Will you never stop lying to me?"

"I . . . did . . . not . . . lie." Her words are evenly spaced.

"You lie as rushes lie." He slashes the quirt-whip across Wendella's bare buttocks, leaving a line of red. "You made a bad bargain with the bitch sorceress. Tell me you did!"

"I made no bargains."

"Then why does Lord Ehara send an overcaptain to proffer friendship to that gray pig Sargol? Why does he spurn me with a stripling captain and a handful of golds? What bargain did you strike with the bitch?"

"My lord, I offered nothing." Wendella's jaw remains firm, though tears seep from the corners of her eyes.

"Liar!"

Wendella does not speak.

"Liar!" *Thwipp! Thwipp!* The quirt strikes again, and again . . . and continues until she lies on the stone tiles.

Then the door shuts.

33

With the midafternoon sun streaming down, Anna took off the floppy felt hat and blotted her forehead. Although Jecks and the others still wore riding coats, she had doffed her jacket. That still left the breastplate and a feltlike pad and a light green shirt. All of that made her feel hotter. She hoped she could get used to wearing the breastplate. Or was this the first step in getting her used to a lot of armor? Did Jecks see her as an overage Maid of Orléans? Despite the heat, she shivered. She didn't fancy following that example. She just wished she could stuff the armorplate into her saddlebags, along with the discarded jacket.

She glanced ahead. The road clay remained mostly damp from the heavy rains, but two days of steady sunlight had dried patches to the point where hoofs raised some dust.

Two days . . . and we're still less than halfway to Soprat. Destroying the Evult's army under Eladdrin had been the only way to stop the invasion of the Ebrans, but the spells necessary had also ripped out the ford, and Anna was definitely beginning to regret the destruction of the only decent crossing point on the Chean River west of Pamr. *Some things don't change. You make a mess, and you're the one who gets stuck cleaning it up. Why do some people never have to pay for their mistakes? And why do you feel you always pay double?*

She shook her head. She doubted that she'd ever be able to answer that question. Once . . . just once in her life she'd offered a really thoughtless plea. *Anywhere but Ames, Iowa!* The harmonies or gods or fates had laughed and granted that wish, and poor dead Jenny's spell had hurled her from earth to Liedwahr. How many years would she pay for that? With fights and angry men, and children she'd never hold again?

She tried to push those thoughts away, at least for a time, and forced her eyes to the sprouts of green in the fields to the right of the road.

While Alvar rode beside her, immediately behind rode Jecks and Jimbob.

"Who will inherit the lands of Synfal, grandsire?" Jimbob's voice was still a boyish tenor, but the redhead had started to grow, and Anna knew his voice would deepen before long.

"That's for the regent to decide, Jimbob. You watch how she handles it, for you may have to do the same one day."

"Why didn't she just announce whoever she wanted?"

"How would you feel if a ruler killed a lord and before the body was cold declared a new lord?"

After a moment of silence, there was an, "Oh. I'd think she'd planned it all out."

"Do you think she did?" Jecks asked.

"No. Even I know she doesn't like killing. That's why her hand got cut up."

For someone who doesn't like it, you've certainly done your share, Anna thought. After brushing away a persistent fly, she looked to the north, at the line of trees less than a hundred yards north, across the rushes and marshy ground that bordered the river proper.

That the road ran south of the Synor River, on the northern border of Lord Sargol's desmaine, bothered her somewhat, but the marshes and swamps appeared even larger on the northern side.

"It is dangerous to be too bloodthirsty," said Alvar quietly, his voice barely audible above the sound of hoofs and conversations, "but even more dangerous to be too merciful."

"Have I been too merciful, Alvar?" Anna asked.

"No, lady. You have not sought blood that did not need to be spilled, either." The swarthy captain lifted his shoulders in a shrug. "I worry. Some of the lords in this land see wisdom as mercy."

"You mean, they see failure to slaughter all of a rebellious lord's armsmen as weakness?" Anna used a tattered green cloth square to wipe her forehead, then gave Farinelli a pat on the neck. "Hope you're not as hot as I am, fellow."

"Even Lord Behlem was not that stupid," Alvar said. "Dead armsmen cannot fight for you, and most armsmen will fight for whoever can give them silver."

"I hope you're not sticking with me for my vast supplies of nonexistent silver," Anna said with a laugh.

"You do not waste armsmen. That is worth more than coin." Alvar frowned, and his eyes narrowed.

"What's the matter?"

"The tracks in the road. They came from that path there." Alvar gestured back at the narrow lane they had passed, which emerged from a woods several deks to the south and crossed the tilled fields to join the main road.

"Horses, and a cart, heading the same way we are," added Jecks, easing his mount up to Anna's left.

Even Anna could see the clear outlines in the damp clay, once she looked down.

"A big cart, sire?" asked Jimbob from where he trailed them, his voice serious.

Anna wanted to smile at the politeness Jimbob demonstrated when he knew his words were heard by her, but she refrained.

Jecks shook his head. "Their mounts are well-shod. Not traders."

Anna studied the tracks in the road. The wheels seemed to have created a fairly deep rut. "Is that a heavy cart?"

"Heavier than most," opined Alvar.

"The wheels are too narrow," added Jecks. "A wider rim is better for a working wagon on these roads."

"For supply wagons, too," said Alvar.

That made sense to Anna, although she'd never thought about how wide wagon wheels should be.

"Too wide or too narrow is hard on the horses," Jecks continued, half turning to Jimbob. "That's why a lord needs good wagonmasters and wheelwrights."

Anna smiled, her eyes drifting along the road as it turned south and away from the river, presumably because of another marsh or soggy ground. Less than a dek ahead on the south side of the road rose a low hill, half covered with fresh-leaved trees in lines, an orchard of some sort. She peered ahead. A line of hills, each slightly higher than the one before, lay along the south side of the road. Most appeared to have orchards.

"The peaches of the south," confirmed Jecks.

"How did you know that was what I was wondering?"

"You near fell from the saddle straining to make them out." The white-haired lord smiled. "Tybel is said to make a fine brandy from them."

Tybel? Anna strained to put the name with the lands.

"He's the Lord of Arien. We sent him a scroll about the seed grain. I don't think we ever heard from him."

"Better that than hear as from Lord Dencer."

"I still don't understand. Not really." Anna reached for her water bottle and took a long and deep swallow. Even the minimal armor made her normal dehydration problems worse.

"Lords only talk to rulers and regents when times are bad or when they want something." Jecks laughed. "Best not to hear from them."

Except for close friends, isn't it that way with most people? In Liedwahr, people are like people everywhere. "When you put it that way . . ."

"They want something," Jecks continued, with a look at Jimbob, to make sure the youth was still listening, "and if you deny them, they get angry. You grant it, and every other lord wants something, or gets angry because you granted something to the first."

"You make ruling sound hopeless," Anna ventured.

"Unless one has great power that inspires fear, ruling often has proved hopeless," Jecks said mildly.

They were back to fear and power again. What was it that Machiavelli had said? Better to be both loved and feared, but feared rather than loved? Some things didn't change from place to place, even universe to universe. Somehow that depressed her. She could understand it, but she didn't have to like it.

"Is that why the Liedfuhr has so many armsmen, grandsire?" asked Jimbob.

"Yes. And why the Sea-Priests have so many ships, and the . . . Ranuans so many golds piled up."

Anna took another swallow from the water bottle and then replaced it in the holder, giving Farinelli another pat on the neck. She got the smallest of snorts in return, as if the big gelding were suggesting that he deserved more than affection for his efforts. "You do," she said quietly.

"Halt!" Jecks raised his arm, and his voice boomed out.

Anna reined up and followed Jecks' eyes to the right. Behind them harnesses jangled, and horses whuffed. Had one whinnied, complaining about another's jostling?

Anna rubbed her nose as dust rose around them in the still and warm air.

On the bare ground above the orchard on the next hill— the one less than a dek away—were a handful of figures. Some bore items—violins, horns? Anna squinted. Were some of them players?

Her stomach twisted at the thought of sorcerers preparing that sort of unwelcome welcome for her.

Something was anchored—or attached—to a squat pole set in the ground, and two men struggled with a lever or crank. As they did, the sounds of a faint melody drifted downhill.

Anna watched as a figure turned the triangular shape toward them, her mind spinning. What was the gadget, and why was she so fearful? She should know or recognize what was happening. Why couldn't she think quickly?

Farinelli sidestepped, *whuff*ing.

"Some sort of crossbow. Too far to be accurate, but we'd better hold up." Jecks turned. "Alvar! Send a troop after them." Then his eyes went to Anna. "Best we ride back."

"Green company! Forward!"

As the lancers trotted past them, Anna could sense Fhurgen easing his squad around her and Jecks and Jimbob. One of the newer guards—Rickel—stood slightly in the saddle, looking toward the mound. His thick bowl-cut hair resembled a strawberry-blond helmet.

Fhurgen stood in his stirrups for a moment. "Don't like this none, Lady Anna," rumbled the black-bearded chief of her guard.

Anna glanced back, but she couldn't move Farinelli, not with her guards so close around her.

The strains of the distant music crescendoed, almost drowned out by the sound of the lancers' mounts.

Through the dust, Anna could see the two men fall away from the crossbow.

Her stomach twisted, and her right hand darted for the blade at her waist yanking it out and up.

A knife against an arrow? Anna wanted to laugh but didn't have time or breath. She only *knew* she had to get the knife out and up, and there wasn't time to think about it.

Her right hand jolted. Fire slashed along her arm, and a hammer smashed into the light breastplate Jecks had insisted she wear. As in a dream, she felt herself being lifted from the saddle by the power of that hammer.

What . . . ? How could an arrow . . . ?

She could sense Farinelli's scream, and her back bouncing against another mount, and then the compacted clay of the road.

For a time, she lay on her back, feeling pressure on her chest. Pressure and fire welling out from her wounds.

Jecks was beside her, kneeling.

"Alcohol . . . elixir . . . bathe the wounds . . ." she gasped.

"Frigging quarrel."

"Get it out," Anna said slowly, forcing each word. "Use the alcohol."

She could sense his puzzlement, but each word was an effort. "Get Liende. Pour . . . the alcohol over the wounds. . . . Clean it . . ."

She was getting dizzier. *Lord, why . . . why . . .*

"Went partway through the metal. Shouldn't have done that." Jecks fumbled with the breast plate. "Went across . . ."

"Get it out." Anna clamped her mouth shut as Jecks worked the black shaft free. Her eyes were having trouble focusing.

"There."

"Alcohol. In my saddlebags."

The splash of the liquid burned worse than the arrow had.

"Arm . . . too."

The second line of fire was too much, even as Anna fought the combination of dizziness and blackness.

34

PAMR, DEFALK

"Good morning." The dark-haired young man in brown nods to the two older and full-bearded men who enter the chandlery.

"Good morning, Farsenn. Rastr said we ought to stop by. . . . Something about wanting . . . You know, I don't remember." The taller and ginger-bearded man who has led the way into the building bobs his head.

"I think I know," Farsenn says quietly. "It's in the back room. Let me check." He smiles politely, and steps through the doorway out of the dimly lit main room.

The ginger-bearded man picks up one of the leather saddlebags on the table. "Better stuff than old Forse. He was more interested in what woman he could get out back. Farsenn looks after the stock more than his father did."

"He liked the women, Forse did, all kinds," answers the other brown-haired farmer. "Till that sorceress turned him into a bonfire."

"Bitch . . . Don't like uppity women like that. Next thing you know, Mostan, she and that Lady Gatrune be telling us how to wear our trousers." A raucous laugh follows.

The sound of a low drum rumbles from the back room, getting louder as Farsenn returns, leaving the door open.

"Deurn, Mostan . . . I'd like to show you what Rastr was talking about."

As the three enter the small windowless room and Farsenn closes the door, the young drummer in the corner beats his drum slowly . . . *thurummm . . . thurumm . . . thurummm . . . thurumm . . .*

On the pedestal is a life-sized statue of a slender blonde woman, breathtakingly beautiful and so lifelike that the spun golden hair seems to move in the faint movement of air caused by the door's closing, and the open blue eyes seem to follow the men. The statue—or the woman—totally naked, does not move.

"Real pretty, Farsenn."

". . . like it better were she real. . . . Ha!"

"That's the way sorceresses should be." Farsenn's voice remains warm and friendly. "Now . . . if you'd listen for a moment . . ."

"Sure. . . . Let me look. . . ."

Farsenn begins to sing, his bass voice weaving around the rhythm of the drum.

"Men of Pamr, heed no woman's song,
    for Farsenn will make you proud and strong
    so put your trust and all your heart
    behind the chandler and his part . . ."

When he finishes, Farsenn smiles slightly. "You see? We men need to stand together these days, don't we?"

"Sure do. Whatever you say."

"Like your statue, young feller."

As the drumbeat dies away, Farsenn blinks rapidly and shakes his head, as if to clear it, then offers a conspiratorial grin. "Just don't tell any of the women . . . you know what I mean?"

Both visitors grin.

"It was good of you to come to see me." He makes a vague gesture toward the door, and both men turn as though commanded. The chandler follows them back into the main room of the chandlery.

"Got to tell Enslam about this," remarks the ginger-bearded Mostan.

"You can tell your friends," says Farsenn conversationally. "It would be better if you didn't mention it to any of Lady Gatrune's armsmen. They might not take it well." He shrugs. "No sense in stirring up trouble."

"Makes sense." Deurn picks up the worn leather saddlebag. "How much?"

"Silver and a half. Might let it go to you for a silver. . . ."

35

Anna opened her eyes gingerly, glancing around the too-familiar guest quarters in Synfal. She could feel a comfortably warm breeze, coming through the open shutters. The sun lit a rectangle of yellow-brick floor.

Yuarl—a young string player Anna didn't know beyond her name and expertise—sat at the writing table. She stiffened as she realized Anna was awake. "Can I get you anything, my lady?"

"Something more to drink . . . and eat," Anna rasped. Her voice was hoarse, her chords clearly swollen.

The trip back to Cheor had been a nightmare. That was the way Anna had felt, neither awake nor asleep, filled with chills one moment, and fired with fever the next. She recalled talking, but not what she had said.

The wounds in her arm and chest had burned continually, and they still did, if not quite so greatly.

She vaguely recalled insisting on eating and arguing

with someone—Jecks—about whether she should be eating. She even remembered seeing Synfal from the fields.

Her next memory was that of waking in the dark, with only a lone candle flickering, and trying to drink wine laced with something, and wondering why she had so much trouble staying awake and concentrating. For the next day, or days—she wasn't exactly sure—she had drifted in and out of consciousness.

Anna straightened herself against the lumpy pillows, resigned that all pillows in Defalk were lumpy. She took a sip, then a swallow, of the sweetish wine that Yuarl had offered, then another swallow. Sweet or not, it calmed her throat.

"Might . . . might I summon the chief player?"

"And Lord Jecks." The words were enough to bring up some mucus, and Anna coughed once, and then again. The two coughs sent a searing pain through her chest, and she pressed her arms against her rib cage. "Shit . . . shit . . ." The words dribbled out, both from the pain in her chest and from the lesser ache in her bound right arm.

Yuarl, her eyes still on Anna, went to the door, opened it, and spoke to one of the guards outside.

Anna tried to look down at her wound, but even under the loose shift could only see a bulky dressing and radiating bruise lines that appeared to be turning yellow.

Despite the pain that had finally begun to subside, she had to wonder about her wounds. The arrow she'd taken outside Loiseau almost a year earlier had been far more serious, and she'd barely made it, despite Brill's sorcery. So why was she having so much trouble with a slash on her arm and a relatively superficial chest wound? All the bruises wouldn't account for her dizziness and fevers.

Poison? Anna shivered.

"Are you all right, lady? Can I do anything?"

"Just thinking." Anna managed to suppress another cough. She knew she probably needed to cough the garbage out of her throat and lungs—but it would hurt—a lot. She tried clearing her throat. That didn't help much.

A gentle half-cough helped, but she almost choked on the mucus.

Damned asthma! Damn . . . She felt like screaming and crying simultaneously. Neither would help her or her image as regent and sorceress. At that thought, she wanted to damn her image as well. Instead, she tried to clear out whatever was in her nose, throat, and lungs.

Yuarl watched, almost wide-eyed.

Before either Jecks or Liende arrived, a young strawberry-blond armsman lurched through the door. Rickel bore a tray which Yuarl intercepted and then carried over to Anna. The sorceress studied the platters—slightly wizened apples, hard white cheese, something that looked like an egg custard, and two bran muffins. She sniffed the custard and decided that whatever had been done to the eggs wouldn't set all that well. Slowly, she picked up one of the muffins and nibbled a corner. Her mouth watered at the hot and moist nutty taste, and she slowly ate the entire muffin.

Then she had more of the wine. As Anna forced herself to eat the second heavy bran muffin, the door opened, and Liende slipped inside. "Good day, Lady Anna."

Her mouth full, Anna nodded as the player with the white-streaked red hair pulled up one of the chairs and sat beside her bed. Liende waited without speaking.

With a quick look at the two women, Yuarl slipped out the door, and shut it behind her without a sound.

"How many days?" Anna finally asked into the stillness.

"You rode in the gate the day before yesterday," Liende answered.

Yesterday? It felt like she'd been out of commission a lot longer than three days. "Just yesterday?"

"You are stronger than most warriors."

Anna doubted that. "It looks like I owe you again. Thank you for helping save me. Again." She started to shake her head, then decided against it. She certainly owed Jecks for insisting that she wear the plastron or breastplate or whatever it had been. And Fhurgen . . . and . . . Alvar and all the armsmen.

"You owe yourself." Liende smiled. "The elixir . . . it helped much in cleaning the wound." The smile vanished. "The quarrel had been smeared in foul matter. Most do not survive those wounds."

Anna wanted to wince. "Could there have been something else there?" From what she recalled, bacteria wouldn't have been able to act fast enough to give her a fever within moments, and she'd have to watch the wounds for any signs of sepsis or infection. That would really be a joy.

"You suspect poison?"

"Yes."

"The quarrel was smeared with a tar. It could have been mixed with any substance." Liende gave a half-smile. "Your elixir, and your own strength, surmounted whatever was upon the quarrel."

"I don't feel like I've surmounted much."

"More than most," Liende answered.

"Are the players still here?"

"Where else would we be?" asked the player gently.

"Sorry. I'm still not thinking that well." Anna gave a small headshake, a very small headshake. "Can you start them working on the next two spellsongs?"

"We have started."

"Good." Anna glanced around the room. "In a day or two, I'll hear them. There's room enough to practice here."

"We will not be soon returning to Falcor?"

"I have not decided," Anna temporized. She wasn't about to decide anything until she found out from Jecks exactly what the situation was.

Liende nodded, then stood as the door to Anna's quarters opened.

Jecks stepped into the room, his eyes going to Anna. Since he didn't look shocked, he must have looked in on her a few times. That, or Anna was beginning to look human. She suspected Jecks' lack of surprise wasn't because of her improved appearance.

Liende moved away from Anna with a nod. "By your leave, Lady Anna?"

"Until later, Liende."

Jecks inclined his head to Liende. "My thanks to you, chief player."

"We did as we could, but she is strong, and her elixir is powerful," Liende acknowledged before easing out the door.

"Lady Anna." Jecks stepped toward the bed.

"Lord Jecks." What could she say that wouldn't sound stupid or helpless or hopeless? Anna glanced at the white-haired Lord of Elheld. There had been times when she had wished him in her bedroom, but the present didn't qualify, even if she did need to talk to him.

"I am pleased to see you are awake. Are you still fevered?"

"Sometimes, but it seems to be getting better." She frowned. Without antibiotics, a fever should have worsened. She gestured toward the chair with her left hand.

He nodded. "Good." Then he sat down.

Anna still hadn't figured out exactly how the damned arrow had gotten her, especially since Jecks and Alvar had said that they'd all been beyond range. She was also less than pleased about being a target for the second time in less than a year. "That arrow . . ."

"The arrow was ensorcelled," Jecks said.

"Spelled somehow?"

"Aye. It curved. That I saw."

Anna wanted to beat her own head—again. Not having been born on Erde left her blind to the simplest matters. She'd been required to use huge spells, and ones that took all her ability and strength, so often that she'd totally overlooked the simpler—and still potentially deadly use of spells. *You aren't devious enough, either. You're not used to poisons and other local nasties.*

"You are troubled," offered Jecks.

"Troubled and angry," Anna said. "I didn't think about spelling arrows or poisoning them. Even when I saw those players, it didn't really dawn on me." *Stupid!*

"The quarrel was tainted?"

"It had to be poison. I wouldn't have gotten a fever or chills from . . . filth that fast."

"You are fortunate—or enchanted."

You're a damned fool, Anna. She shook her head slowly and far from vigorously. "I still don't know enough. I've been incredibly lucky."

"You were prepared. You had the elixir."

"And that breastplate." She met his hazel eyes. "How did you know about the breastplate? That I'd need it?" Anna forced herself to take another slice of the white cheese. At least it was hard and cold, rather than soft, moldy, and mushy, like so much of the white cheese Brill had favored.

Jecks glanced at the yellow brick floor. "I was fortunate. We were fortunate."

"There's something you're not telling me, my lord Jecks," Anna said wryly. "Why not?"

The white-haired lord shrugged, but did not speak. Finally, Jecks answered. "At times . . . I feel as though I know things. Sometimes I am wrong. Most times, I was right to fear. I have feared this journey from the day you first spoke of it." His eyes did not meet hers.

"What else do you fear?" she queried.

"I have no feelings of danger now." He smiled his movie-star smile.

Anna wanted to smile back. She didn't, though she hoped he was right. "That's good."

"I still worry." The smile vanished with a frown.

"So do I." She coughed gently, trying not to wince.

Jecks' frown deepened.

"I'll be all right." *You hope.*

"You should not strain yourself."

Anna tried not to bridle at the male condescension in his tone. "Was it Lord Sargol?"

"We do not know with certainty. I did not feel we should spare armsmen to chase those on the hilltop. Your safety was more important." Jecks shrugged. "Once well . . . I thought you would be able to find out."

"If I got well, then I'd be able to find out. If I didn't, you and Jimbob had bigger problems." Anna forced a smile.

"You surprise me, even when I expect it."

She did not answer immediately, but sipped more of the wine, wishing she were strong enough to orderspell just plain water. Could she have someone boil some? How would she know if it had been boiled enough, or put into something that was clean enough not to be contaminated? "I suppose we'll have to do something about Sargol now."

"There is no hurry," Jecks said.

"You mean, there's no hurry beyond the time when I'm strong enough to bring his whole holding down around him?"

"You cannot bring down every holding in southern Defalk."

Anna understood that. She wasn't sure she could, but even if she could have, razing them all except for Geansor's keep wouldn't help in welding Defalk together. She had the glimmer of another idea.

The damned arrow had actually given her an answer— use sorcery to influence what was—like arrows. That approach would take far less energy. It took as much skill, but skill wasn't her problem. Energy was. She pursed her lips. There might be a problem with finding archers, lots of them, but she didn't need marksmen, just people who could put a lot of arrows into the air at the same time.

She'd also need to craft some defensive skills. *Why does everything keep getting more complicated? . . . Because it always does, no matter what,* she answered herself.

Before she could actually implement her ideas, she

needed to get well, and get stronger. While she was healing, though, she could work out the spells.

She glanced worriedly at Jecks. "The lutar?"

"I put it in the chest there." He inclined his head toward the carved chest at the foot of the bed. "It was not damaged."

Anna released her breath slowly, but it still hurt.

Damn! If she had anything to say about it, one Lord Sargol and one Lord Dencer, and their allies, were going to pay dearly for their shenanigans. Except their actions were far worse than shenanigans.

She could see Jecks stiffen as he watched her. Would it always be that way? Would men always back away when she looked determined? Why didn't they understand that she had no choice? Even as they didn't think they had to understand women, they always wanted women to understand.

She snorted . . . softly.

36

Outside the keep of Synfal, rain sleeted from the gray clouds down onto the thirsty fields and the wet brick walls, a warm rain that turned into mist where it struck yellow brick. The shutters to Anna's quarters were half closed—held that way by a casement bar, a compromise that allowed some fresh air without too much water splashing inside and onto the polished brick floor.

At the writing table, Anna finally pushed away the pile of accounts that Dythya had sent with the scrolls that had begun to appear with a semblance of regularity.

Of course, Gylaron hadn't paid his liedgeld, nor Dencer and Sargol the remainder of theirs. Lord Vlassa's heirs continued to quibble, and she'd heard nothing from Lord Birfels about whether Birke would return to Falcor for more education. She and Jecks had sent for Herstat, but even the message to Elheld summoning Jecks' saalmeister-accountant would take days to get there.

Time slipped by while she recovered. About the only physical things she could manage at first were an awkward one-handed grooming of Farinelli and short walks around the corridors, chafing at the time it took her wounds to heal. She knew that the Sea-Priests of Sturinn were probably weaseling their way into Dumar, while Lord Ehara continued his mischief in trying to subvert Defalk's southern lords. Konsstin was up to something, massing more troops in Neserea, or worse. And who knew what the traders of Wei were trying?

And you can't afford more than an occasional mirror spell that's shown nothing new. Or one for clean water. What a place—it takes magic even to get clean cool water.

She recalled Shakespearean England had been like that, too. After a small shudder, she pushed the accounting paperwork to the corner of the table and reclaimed her spell folder. She concentrated on the crude brown paper, trying to work out the spell, murmuring the first words.

> "All the arrows we have shot into the air,
>   have them strike . . ."

She pursed her lips. Trying to create the spells without writing them made it too hard to remember all the parts. Finally, she lifted the grease marker and crossed out several words, humming the tune again.

> "Those arrows shot into the air,
>   oh, make each strike one armsman there . . ."

The first lines would do, if she could find another couplet that would define which armsmen were to be struck.

After a long slow exhalation, she sipped the too-sweet wine, then swallowed.

Then she froze. Arrows? What were arrows?

"Shit!"

The damned arrows were metal arrowheads fitted onto wooden shafts and fletched with once-living feathers. She cradled her head in a left hand propped on the writing table. She couldn't even direct arrows without getting into Darksong. But how had they ensorcelled the arrow? . . . She wanted to shake her head. It had been a crossbow quarrel and all metal.

She looked at the crude brown paper. Back to the drawing board—literally.

Her right arm ached only slightly, if somewhat more at the end of the day. After more than a week, the gash on her chest, thankfully above her breasts—lower would have been a real mess—was beginning to heal, and all the bruises had turned faded green-and-purple.

Sometimes, she felt as though all she did was either get wounded and recover, or kill someone and recover, and most of the time was spent trying to deal with some administrative mess or another.

She had the gist of an idea—maybe—when someone *thrapp*ed on the door.

"Yes?" She tried to conceal the irritation in her voice.

"Lady Anna?" Fhurgen peered in. "Halde would request a moment with you."

Anna understood Fhurgen's body posture. Her chief guard didn't trust totally anyone of Synfal. "Escort him in."

She straightened in the chair.

"Lady Anna," Halde began almost before he stopped opposite the writing table. "In the past several years, Fauren and Lord Arkad left the higher fields fallow. Those were the ones where the ditches from the rivers did not reach. We have had much rain this past season." The acting saalmeister of Synfal glanced down at the yellow-brick floor.

"You're thinking of planting them, but it will take coins and seed and time, and the crops will be later, and you should have thought of it earlier." Anna waited.

The dark-haired acting saalmeister flushed and said nothing.

"Halde," Anna said gently, but firmly, "I do not punish questions or honest mistakes, provided they aren't repeated. I do get angry at people who do not speak what they mean and people who try to deceive me." She paused. "What would you plant, and why? What would it cost? How late would the crops be?"

The flush faded. "Lady . . . I would not plant maize. It drinks too much water, even in the wettest year. Wheat corn, I think, and some barley. The hard wheat can weather periods of drought."

Corn? Anna remembered from somewhere else that corn meant grains like wheat and barley and something else. The Corn Laws of England had been to protect British agriculture. She nodded after a moment. "Go on."

"We have enough seed corn, but it would draw down our stocks."

"Go ahead," Anna decided, then added, "Heavy rains won't hurt early in the year, will they?"

Halde shook his head. "Rains at harvest, yes, they could destroy the crop. And a rain right after planting could wash away everything."

"We'll take that risk. We'll need the grain."

"Thank you, lady." Halde stood silently.

"What else?" Anna tried to keep from grinning. Halde had his way of conveying that he wanted more.

"Some of the tenant women have asked that they be allowed to plant the silt marsh flats with melons."

"Is that a good idea?" Anna countered.

"Lord Arkad's sire allowed it, according to the record books, if they would provide one in five of the melons to the keep."

"But Fauren didn't?"

"No, lady."

"Why not?"

"He told Vierk and he told me that we would spend more time arguing over melons than we would receive."

Anna laughed. "He was probably right. We won't argue."

Halde looked at her quizzically.

"Tell them they can plant, on the old terms. We'll trust them. If I find that trust is misplaced, they won't plant again." She smiled. "You don't have time to count melons. Oh . . . and tell the armsmen and a few others that half the melons that the keep gets will go to them one way or another. You can figure out how, later."

The skeptical look on Halde's face at Anna's last words made her want to sigh. "Halde, I don't know that you'll stay as saalmeister. I won't lie to you. I do know that I can't afford to waste talent and loyalty. My arms commander, the head of my personal guard, and Captain Alvar, all served Lord Behlem. My chief player served Lord Brill. You do a good job, and you'll have a good position. Talk to any of my people, if you doubt me. Make up your own mind." She took a slow breath. "Is there anything else?"

"No, lady. Thank you." Halde bowed and turned, followed by the silent Fhurgen.

Before the door closed, she could hear Fhurgen's voice. "Saalmeister, best you listen . . ."

Anna smiled faintly, wondering what Fhurgen might say, and whether Halde would listen. Then she went back to the arrow spell. What about spelling the arrowheads? Would a spell that dragged the once-living matter of the shafts and the fletching be Darksong? She frowned. She didn't know why, but she thought that might work. She could test it, at least.

She had another version of the second couplet almost worked out when there was another knock on the door.

Jecks stepped into Anna's room, followed by Hanfor.

"Hanfor?" Anna looked up from the table, but did not stand. "What are you doing here?"

The gray-haired arms commander bowed. "Lord Jecks suggested I bring those armsmen I could spare, and I thought that might be wise. We can return with greater speed and reach Falcor before any others can reach it—though I doubt any will try."

Anna gestured to the chairs on the other side of the writing table. "I'm glad to see you, but that means trouble."

Jecks' eyes twinkled momentarily as he seated himself. "You see, she is almost recovered."

"That's the story of my life. Get wounded so I can recover and survive." Her eyes went to Hanfor. "Which problem do you want to start with?"

"There is another difficulty," Hanfor said slowly. "It is not so great a problem as I feared. Now that you hold Synfal and Cheor."

She held Synfal? That was a laugh. Synfal held her. For the first few days, she'd even had trouble holding a mug or a knife to cut meat for any length of time. "Oh?" she offered cautiously.

"The armory here has many good blades," Hanfor added. "Enough to spare for our armsmen."

For now, thought Anna. "Still no weapons smith and no blades?"

"No smiths have answered our scrolls." The veteran paused, then added, "You recall the blades in Encora? All were sold before our offer was received. Or so we were told."

Anna frowned. "I don't like that. How many?"

"Over three hundred."

Anyone who wanted and could afford three hundred blades was definitely serious about something. Not that many people—or even lords—had five hundred to a thousand golds to spare. Anna certainly knew that. "Did our man find out who bought the blades?"

"A trader in Encora. A Ranuan trader."

That bothered Anna, but it was a feeling she couldn't attribute to anything logical. "What else?"

"There are rumors that the Liedfuhr is sending more armsmen to Neserea."

"Just rumors?" She glanced at Jecks.

He nodded.

"What else?" she asked tiredly.

"Bertmynn has attacked an outpost held by Hadrenn's forces."

Anna frowned, trying to remember who was who. "Hadrenn's the one who holds the west part of Ebra?" She pursed her lips, remembering Hryding's messenger Fridric. "The one Gestatr went to serve, that's right."

Hanfor inclined his head, waiting.

"So we have troops massing on our western borders, an uprising in our own south, and a civil war starting to our east." She forced a wry grin. "Have I missed anything?" Then she added, "Besides the fact that someone in Ranuak is buying lots of blades, and our neighbor to the southwest is being supported by an enemy that wants to see every woman in Defalk in chains?"

"I think you have stated the situation clearly," stated Jecks.

Anna's eyes hardened, even as she forced her voice into an unnatural sweetness. "You might recall that I suggested this would happen."

Hanfor and Jecks exchanged glances.

She shrugged, glad that there was but a twinge in her chest. "It doesn't matter. We'll do what we have to. Hanfor . . . can you round up several hundred men who can shoot arrows? They don't have to be accurate, just strong enough to get the arrows released with force in the right direction all at the same time."

"Most of our armsmen could do that now," admitted the arms commander with a rueful laugh. "They just cannot hit anything." He frowned. "I do not know about bows and arrows."

"Round up as many as you can."

Hanfor's eyebrows rose.

"If Sargol can spell one crossbow quarrel, there's no

reason why I can't spell several hundred arrows in return." *You hope.*

Hanfor swallowed.

So did Jecks.

"Gentlemen." Anna smiled. "I've learned that fighting here is a nasty business, involving poisoned arrows, assassinations, sorcery, and economic coercion. Surely, you do not think I should limit my efforts out of a sense of misplaced chivalry?"

"But the armsmen . . . They are not . . ."

Anna looked at Hanfor. "I know some didn't have much choice, but they did choose. And if we don't end this rebellion quickly, we won't have a land left to protect." She turned to Jecks. "You've led me to believe that destroying keeps and everyone in them is unwise. Is that still true?"

The white-haired lord fingered his chin before answering.

A stronger gust of wind hurled rain past the half-open shutters and onto the yellow-brick floor.

Finally, Jecks answered. "If you were to destroy many keeps with sorcery, some of the lords of the north would feel you would turn on them. I cannot say how many."

"Would they turn if I were a man?"

"Some would."

"Just not so many." *Double-standard—again.*

Anna glanced back at Hanfor. "We either kill armsmen or lose support."

"Always the armsmen pay," murmured the arms commander.

It had been that way back on earth, too, Anna recalled. "It's true on all worlds. That's because people are people."

After another silence, Hanfor asked, "Have you other duties?"

"No." Anna softened her voice. "I am glad you came, and I do value your skill and advice. It's just that we don't seem to have many choices."

"That be not your fault, lady. I will do as we must."

Anna could hear the unspoken words—*"but I do not have to like it."*

Hanfor rose. "By your leave."

"I'll try to spare those I can," Anna said.

"You do, and they may fight for you."

Anna had thought about that, too.

After Hanfor bowed and departed, Jecks said quietly, "It will get worse, first, I fear."

"All the lords are afraid that they'll lose their privileges and power."

"In this uncertain world," answered Jecks with a short laugh, "does not every man fear loss?"

"Armsmen and peasants and women lose their lives every day. Lords worry about golds and power." Anna sighed. "I suppose that if any of the others had power and golds, they'd fear losing them, too."

"You have seen the hard life, have you not?"

Anna hesitated. "Yes and no. Earth is different. I've had to work hard, but I've never been poor the way people are here." *Then, Uncle Garven and Papaw had been close to it.*

"You have seen enough. And you have seen to know that change may be good." Jecks shook his head. "In Defalk, for many years, change has always heralded trouble. Can you blame them?"

Yes, but it won't do any good. "They'll have to learn."

"I wager you will see to that." Jecks handed Anna a scroll, still sealed. "This should cheer you."

The sorceress glanced at it warily.

"It's from young Secca."

Anna broke the seal, noting the carefully impressed *S* on the blue wax, and the thin strip of blue ribbon.

My dear Lady Anna,

I must write this quickly. Please forgive the poor letters. You must get well. All of us feel you must. Now you are all I have. Please take care and eat

a lot. I love you. I hope we can play Vorkoffe when
you come home.

Anna's eyes blurred, and she set down the scroll on the
writing table, shivering.

"I thought you would be pleased." Jecks' voice was
puzzled.

She did shake her head, not able to see him through
the tears. She'd lost her own little redhead—Elizabetta.
And Irenia, and Mario. Now, she had another redhead,
one she'd practically ridden off and abandoned. Was she
going to lose her, too?

She shuddered, unable to stop the sobs that burst forth.

37

A hot and damp breeze slipped through the open window of Anna's quarters. A gust of wind rattled the
large replacement mirror on the wall. Even though she
was the Regent of Defalk, she still didn't feel comfortable
in the "throne room" used by Arkad, and probably never
would. Besides, for dealing with her small traveling staff,
her quarters were fine.

Anna glanced across the writing table at Jecks, then at
Hanfor. "I think it's time to name the heir to Synfal. I've
decided. Lord Jecks had nothing to do with this."

Hanfor raised his bushy gray eyebrows.

"No . . . I'm not giving Synfal to him. I am giving it
to Lord Jimbob, under the same terms as the Regency,
except Herstat and Jecks will administer Synfal, but Jimbob will have some small say to begin with."

Surprisingly, Hanfor nodded. "That is most sensible.

A lord must have coins enough to support his realm in times of trouble, and the lands adjoin each other.''

"I've also made Lord Jecks agree to part with Herstat as part of the bargain, to be saalmeister here. Halde will stay on to assist him, but only for a time, until Herstat is comfortable.'' Anna turned to Jecks. "What have you discovered about Halde?''

"He is honest, according to all. He works hard. He does not appear to listen, but he does.'' The white-haired lord shrugged. "A courtier he is not. That is why he would have remained an assistant, I would judge.''

"The armsmen of Synfal speak of him in a like fashion,'' added the Arms Commander. "They respect him. They do not like him, but they do not dislike him.''

"Well . . . let's get this over.'' Anna raised the iron bell and rang it, wincing at the off-key clang.

Fhurgen opened the door.

"If you would ask Halde to come in . . .''

The dark-bearded acting saalmeister entered the chamber, closing the door gently but firmly, and bowed. "Lady Anna, lords.''

"Halde,'' Anna said, wondering how she was going to handle telling Halde he was about to be replaced.

"Yes, Lady Anna?'' The black-haired young man bowed again.

"I will be naming the heir to Synfal shortly.''

"That is your right as regent.''

"The heir will have his own saalmeister.''

"That is his right.''

"Halde,'' Anna repeated, adding slowly. "Everyone in Synfal believes you are hardworking, good at the work of your job, and honest. Most find you cold and difficult to talk to. I promised you a good position if you worked hard and well, and I will honor that promise.''

"All say you honor your word.'' Halde bowed his head.

"Halde . . . I have a request.''

"Your word is my command.''

Anna wanted to stamp her boots or slap the young saal-meister. Instead, she forced a smile. "Herstat will be arriving to become saalmeister. He will need your assistance to learn all he needs to know about Synfal quickly. He would learn it in any case, but your assistance would make matters easier." Anna waited.

"I will offer all assistance I can," promised Halde, his light gray eyes meeting Anna's.

"My request is that you also learn from him. Watch how Herstat talks to people, how he makes them feel good without giving away what he must not." Anna's eyes focused on Halde, and she emphasized the next words slightly. "If you will learn from Herstat, if you work at knowing people as you know the keep, then I will indeed reward you."

For the first time, Halde appeared uncertain, and his hand went to the neatly trimmed dark beard. "Lady . . ."

"You have talent, Halde, and I need talent. But I need someone who does not make people feel like tools. People need to feel like people. That is not weakness; that is another skill." Anna cleared her throat. She wasn't good at this sort of lecture, but she was desperately short of people who were good at what they did. "Do you understand?"

Halde nodded, then swallowed. "Might I ask . . . of the heir?"

"I'd ask you to say nothing until I make the announcement." Halde nodded. "The heir will be Lord Jimbob. The past lords of Defalk have been weakened because they didn't have enough coin or lands. That left them unable to protect their people. After the heir is named, I will not have any part in the day-to-day running of Synfal. That will be up to you and Herstat. Now, and when Lord Jimbob visits in the future, as he will more frequently as he gets older, he will learn all he can."

Halde inclined his head. "In these times, few could fault your decision. Some lords may rage behind their walls, but few will say so where any can hear."

"What of those in Synfal?" asked Jecks.

"Already, it is clear that the regent is fair and just. That is rare as well, and most call themselves fortunate."

"Most?" asked Anna.

Halde smiled ironically. "I have not found anyplace where all agree, even in my father's house."

"Do you have any questions?"

"Do you know, lady, when I might expect this . . . Herstat?"

"Within the next two weeks, Halde. And no," she anticipated the question, "I do not know how long he will need your assistance. I do know that he is just and fair, and as kind as he can afford to be."

"Thank you, lady." Halde bowed again.

"You may go, Halde. Thank you for all your help and hard work. I do appreciate it."

After the door closed, Hanfor shook his head. "He listened. I did not think he would. You are a wonder, Lady Anna."

Anna just felt tired.

"What have you in mind?" asked Jecks.

"I need a saalmeister for Loiseau, and I need someone who can put it back together so that it works without sorcery." She reached for her goblet and took a long swallow of water. "I hope he can learn. I'm asking a lot."

"He has skill," Hanfor added.

"But can he learn about people?" Anna turned to Jecks. "Was I right about Herstat? I only have met him once."

Jecks smiled broadly and shook his head. "One would never have guessed that. You described him well. At times, my lady, you indeed astound me."

"Then, let's hope he can teach young Halde." Anna coughed. Her chest still hurt when she did, but it was far more of an ache than the stabbing pain it had been. "We'll need to draft a proclamation or whatever's necessary to grant the lands to Jimbob. . . ."

Jecks nodded.

"We'd better talk to Jimbob, first, too, before he hears something."

"I will get him." The white-haired lord walked swiftly from the quarters.

Hanfor looked at her once the older lord had left.

"Am I risking disaster, Hanfor? Probably. Except that the alternatives are worse. These lands are too old and too traditional to give to you or someone else who isn't from an old family in Defalk. If I hold them, it will make more lords rebellious, and if I grant them to Jecks, it will be seen as a scheme of some sort." She shrugged.

"When you speak that way, it does ring true." The veteran coughed. "Will the power not affect the boy?"

"I'm going to try to stop that."

Hanfor nodded. His face went blank as Jecks returned with Jimbob.

"Lady Anna?" The redhead bowed. "Grandsire said you needed to speak to me."

"I do." Anna waited until the door closed. "You had asked the other day who would inherit Synfal. Your grandsire said I could not make an announcement immediately. Do you remember that?"

"Yes, lady."

"I'm going to inform the heir," she continued with a smile, "and I thought you should know."

Hanfor's eyes twinkled as Jimbob's face took on a puzzled expression.

"Once you have the age and experience, these lands of Synfal will be yours, along with those of Falcor, and eventually, I would guess, those of Elheld."

Jimbob's mouth almost opened. He swallowed.

"I would ask you *not* to speak of it. I will make the announcements within the next few days."

"Yes, lady."

Anna turned to face Jimbob, and her eyes fixed his. "I want to make some things clear, Jimbob. First, while you will be the lord of Synfal, the lands will be administered for you by Herstat while you learn about them and everything else you need to know. Second, your word, unless it is supported by your grandsire or Herstat, is not yet law. Do you understand that?''

Jimbob frowned. ''Then why, Lady Anna, are you naming me now?''

''To settle things as quickly as possible. And as smoothly. So the people have a chance to get accustomed to you, and so that you can learn what you need to know.''

The red-haired boy nodded, as if he were unsure.

Anna looked from Jecks to Jimbob. ''There are a couple of rules I will insist on. Until you are of age, you will never contradict Herstat or question his actions or judgments in any public place. Nor will you question me or your grandsire in public about what we have done. I expect you to ask questions—that's one way of learning—but in private chambers, never where you will be overheard.'' Her eyes went to the youth. ''Is that clear?''

''Yes, lady.''

''Second, if you strongly disagree with an action Herstat has taken, you will talk first with your grandsire. If he feels it is necessary, he will come to me. Third, you will keep in mind that most people will do what's necessary if you make it clear what needs to be done and that you respect them. They also must respect you.'' Anna's eyes focused directly on Jimbob. ''Your sire and mother were respected, your mother especially, because they knew what had to be done and how to do it. Authority and power—or birthright—will never inspire true respect. Knowledge, skill, understanding, and strength will. You need to learn more of these. Herstat will help you learn that, and to keep you from making too many mistakes.''

''Yes, Lady Anna.''

''I would only add one thing to what the Lady Anna has said,'' Jecks remarked. ''By granting you Synfal, she has given you the chance your sire never had. She has also given you even greater power to destroy yourself.'' He grinned at his grandson. ''But if you look like you're going to try that, I am still not too old to knock you back into your britches.''

Jimbob swallowed. "I will do my best, grandsire . . . Lady Anna . . ."

"You will do better than that, lad," said Jecks, the smile vanishing. "You will do better than you think you can."

Jimbob glanced from Jecks to Hanfor to Anna, then back to Jecks. Then he straightened his shoulders. "Yes, grandsire. Yes, sire."

Anna suppressed a smile. "You may go, Jimbob. We'll talk more about this once Herstat arrives."

"In the meantime," added Jecks, "not one word."

"No, sire."

Not more than a few moments after Jimbob left, after a heavy thump on the door, Fhurgen peered inside. "A scroll for you, lady, relayed by messenger from Falcor."

Hanfor slipped out of his chair and claimed the scroll from Fhurgen, tendering it to Anna as the guard closed the door.

Anna glanced at the words. "Hadrenn?" she murmured. The name was familiar, but he wasn't one of the Thirty-three of Defalk. Then she wanted to shake her head at her stupidity. He was one of the two fighting it out in Ebra. She opened the scroll and began to read. After reading through it silently, she repeated the key phrases to Jecks and Hanfor.

". . . times have changed, and we of Ebra must change with them or perish. . . . I would propose an arrangement of mutual benefit, pledging the lands of Synek, my ancestral lands, in fealty to the regent and Regency of Defalk. In turn, if the Regency could see fit to recognize me as one of the Thirty-three when that would be appropriate . . .

". . . maintaining such fealty will initially be most difficult . . . particularly given the recent coins

and arms provided by the Liedfuhr of Mansuur to
the usurper Bertmynn. . . .

". . . Ebra can no longer stand against the rest of
Liedwahr, nor should it. . . . Synek, and in time, all
of Ebra, would be most benefited to share arms with
Defalk. . . ."

"He is begging for any sort of aid you are willing to
provide," said Hanfor. "We have little to provide."

"There have always been thirty-three lords," Jecks said
deliberately. "Changing that might be difficult, especially
in these days."

"We don't change it," Anna said. "Cheor belongs to
Jimbob, right? Now, doesn't he count as the Lord of Falcor, and the Overlord of Defalk?"

A smile crossed Hanfor's face, quickly vanishing, as he
raised a hand to cover a mock cough.

Jecks nodded, his lips crinkling into a smile as Anna
continued.

"We actually lack at least one lord now. Also, if we
grant lordship to this Hadrenn, that might make it more
difficult for anyone else to claim lordship over Cheor."

"In theory, Lady Anna."

"Do we want to fight in three lands?" asked Hanfor.

"Why can't we get Hadrenn to fight there for us?"
responded Anna. "We can spare a little coin. We'll tell
him that most of the Thirty-three have paid between eight
hundred and a thousand golds a year in liedgeld, once
their times of trouble have passed. We'll promise help as
we can, knowing that we must swim together or sink sep-
arately." She wondered where she'd come up with the
last phrase. She didn't even like swimming.

A quizzical look passed across Jecks' face.

"Coins? How do we know he won't turn on us?" asked
Hanfor. "You buried part of his land in fire and molten
rock, and devastated the rivers. Yet now he would turn to
you, and you would send him coin?"

"Right now, we don't know if he will be trustworthy.

Remember . . . I didn't oppose him, but his enemy the Evult. And besides, he has nowhere else to turn, does he?'' Anna shook her head. ''If he's asking us for coin, I'd bet that this Bertmynn is getting golds and weapons from some of our other friends—like Konsstin and maybe the Sturinnese. Why else would Hadrenn turn to us? He can't have anywhere else to turn.''

''Can a mountain cat so cornered be trusted?'' Hanfor touched his trimmed but graying beard.

''It's a risk, but I'd think it's worth it. He's not going to invade Defalk, not with Bertmynn knocking at his door to the east.''

''I do not know,'' mused Jecks. ''We know nothing of him.''

Anna could see that nothing she said would make much difference at the moment. Instead, she stood, walked to the chest where the lutar rested, and began tuning the instrument. Then she stepped over to the mirror and lifted the lutar and began to sing.

> ''Those in Stromwer strong,
>   those who'd do me wrong
>   now show them in this silver cast
>   and make that vision well last . . .''

Even before the notes died away, an image filled the glass. From what Anna could tell, well over two hundred large tents clustered below the walls of Stromwer—or whatever Dencer called his keep. A banner with a gold big-horned sheep or something similar poised on a peak, backed in crimson, flew from a pole amid the tents in what had to be a stiff breeze.

''Dumar—Ehara's banner,'' said Jecks. ''Outside the walls. Dencer does not fully trust so many armsmen.''

Anna glanced at Hanfor, who stood and stepped forward, peering at the image. After a time, he nodded, and she released the spell.

''How many armsmen are there?'' she asked.

"A hundredscore at least."

"Most are from Dumar?"

"It would seem so."

Anna raised the lutar again, and did the second spell-song.

> "Those in Suhl so strong,
> those who'd do me wrong . . ."

The next image in the glass showed a second keep, of stone and red brick. Below the keep's outer wall, nearly a dek from the wall, hundreds of men labored at an earthwork—or a mound. Beyond them milled several hundred lancers.

Anna snorted. She suspected another outsized crossbow would be mounted there, or something similar, with the lancers for distraction or cover.

"And here," she asked after releasing the spell.

"Twentyscore," suggested Hanfor.

Anna tried a third rendition, one for Lord Gylaron.

The image was equally clear—a gray stone keep with what appeared to be catapults mounted on the walls, and with armsmen on every wall.

Fighting lightheadedness, Anna set aside the lutar and reseated herself, taking a swallow of water and crunching through two already stale biscuits before she felt more steady. She still wasn't back to normal, and the world didn't seem to want to let her recover before rushing in on her.

At the same time, Anna wanted to smile. She was one small woman who could do sorcery, a regent with perhaps three hundred armsmen, and the three southern lords acted as though she were the scourge of the earth—or Erde.

"Do you still want to turn down potential allies?" she asked. "One that could not hurt us unless we were beyond help?"

"What do we gain?" asked Jecks.

Anna could see, once again, she was running against tradition. Defalk had always been the thirty-three lords within their mountain walls, and Jecks consciously or unconsciously was resisting any change.

"In time, we eliminate forever an enemy to the east." That seemed simple enough. If she could co-opt Ebra in time . . . and do something about Dumar to stop the Sea-Priests. She shook her head. What was she thinking? Just about trying to take over large chunks of Liedwahr when they were practically under siege from every side.

Hanfor nodded. "We have little to lose."

"If you think best," Jecks finally grudged.

"I'll write something, and then let you read it," Anna said. "You would know better what phrases would work best." She offered a smile, and got a faint one in return. *Lord, politics again, even with Jecks.*

The white-haired lord nodded politely.

"We'll have to work out something to deal with Suhl," she said.

"That would be wisest," Jecks offered. "Something that will not endanger you."

"I had figured on that." Anna coughed again. "Let's think about that. I need to take care of some things. How about in another glass or so?"

After they left, she looked at the closed door, wondering once more how she'd ever gotten into the mess, or how everything she did seemed to hurt the best people.

Life wasn't ever fair. By all rights, Daffyd, who'd been loyal, supportive, and talented, should have been in charge of her players. He and the players who had supported her early on were all dead. Jecks' daughter Alasia should have been planning the campaign that lay ahead, but she was dead. Lord Hryding should still have held Flossbend, and Anna didn't dare take the time even to investigate that mess.

In the meantime, at least, she could send a scroll to Flossbend, reserving her right to name another administrator in place of the bitchy Anientta for her spoiled son Jeron. That would keep Anientta from causing too much trouble, for now, anyway. She sighed, reaching for the parchment. At least, she could do that.

38

MANSUUS, MANSUUR

I have scrolls from both Nubara and from Rabyn,'' Konsstin says wearily, his large right hand pushing a lock of brown-and-silver hair off his forehead. ''Would that Kestrin were older.''

Bassil nods.

''I found Jyrllar too late, after Kandeth, and so my heir is younger than Rabyn. Would that he will be more perceptive and less vicious.''

The younger man nods once more.

''What do you think they say?'' Konsstin leans back in the heavy silver chair, his eyes flicking toward the window to his right, and the gray clouds that seem to hover not far beyond the balcony.

''Neither is happy with the other?'' suggests the raven-haired officer in the lancer's maroon uniform.

''Brilliant! Absolutely brilliant.'' The Liedfuhr stands and lifts a scroll from the slightly smeared polish of the walnut surface. ''The snake and the lizard, and they do not like each other.''

''You feared this,'' Bassil says quietly.

''I feared it, and what we fear too often comes to pass. Is that because we fear it, and that fear becomes embodied in our lives?''

''That I could not say, sire.''

''You repeat my words and refuse to offer judgment.

How judicious of you. Are you, too, becoming a courtier?"

"I would hope not, sire."

"You would hope not?" Konsstin laughs harshly. "What would you advise, my dear advisor Bassil?" asks the Liedfuhr. "My own sworn agent, the good Nubara, advises me, most delicately, that my grandson is indeed the viper that his mother was, except worse. My loving grandson informs me, most properly, that his guardian is intent on assuming full rule in his own name in Neserea, and that Nubara is a scaly lizard who oozes oily charm to disguise his claws."

Bassil swallows.

"So what should I do?" Konsstin's voice is level. "What do you advise, oh, forthright Bassil who would not hope to be a courtier?"

After a long moment, the officer answers. "Let the two of them make enough of a stew that the Neserean people will welcome your presence."

"You would advise me to let the situation worsen?" Konsstin sets down the scroll, and it rerolls itself and skitters off the desk. The Liedfuhr ignores it, and his eyes burn down at the lancer officer. "To let a poor situation worsen?"

A faint sheen coats Bassil's forehead, and he swallows. "Yes, sire. If you take sides now, you are seen as interfering, and the Neserean people will oppose you, as will either Nubara or Rabyn, depending upon whom you back and how."

"So . . . I should do nothing for now?"

"Send each scrolls telling them that you believe that they should work together to ensure the continuity of the line and the stability of Neserea. Suggest that the growing presence of the Sea-Priests means they should cooperate."

"You are more devious than Rabyn, Bassil," says Konsstin almost lazily, glancing toward the drizzle outside for a moment. "And what of Dumar in this dissonant mess?"

Bassil swallows again. "Ah . . . I would let the sorceress deal with that."

"She lies wounded, and you would have her be our shield against the Sea-Priests?"

"If you order the lancers south now, will they go? If they are loyal to Rabyn, he would not wish that. Nor would Nubara, if they are loyal to him. I have no better answer, sire."

"Nor I, Bassil." Konsstin smiles wickedly. "We will have to move quickly, and before long. Convey my order to the third and fifth lancers to be ready to leave Mansuus within the next three weeks. Send a scroll to the eighth and tenth in Deleator requesting that they stand ready."

"And the scrolls to the sorceress, the Council of Wei, and the Matriarchy?"

"We will wait a little longer. Timing is everything, Bassil. Everything." The Liedfuhr nods.

Bassil bows and departs.

In the growing dimness of his study, Konsstin turns back to view the darkening storm.

39

Anna wanted to wipe her forehead in the heat of the shuttered quarters at Synfal. With the shutters closed, she got a brighter image in the wall mirror, but she wished she had a reflecting pool.

Stop wishing for what you don't have, and keep your thoughts on the spell.

She and Jecks studied the image in the wall mirror. Hanfor held a grease marker over a large section of heavy brown paper on the table. The arms commander sketched rapidly, his eyes darting from the mirror to the paper and back again.

"There is the mound where they would use their evil weapon," the white-haired lord pointed out.

"We're not going to get that close again." Anna's chest still throbbed at times.

"What if we marched down this side road?" Jecks asked. "We could come up on the flat here. The ground rises here, it looks like."

"We would do well to stay farther north. I would not want to have the horse too close to the ditches and the creek there," Hanfor pointed with his left hand momentarily, before he continued sketching. Despite the heavy tunic, he looked cool and composed.

Anna envied him. She felt overheated, sweaty, and bedraggled, and it was barely midmorning.

"Then we could move across the lower side of the field," Jecks suggested, as he glanced toward Hanfor.

The gray-haired veteran armsman nodded. "There would be room to wheel, even if we were surprised."

"We'd better not be surprised," Anna interjected.

"It can happen," Jecks cautioned.

Anna supposed it could, but the idea behind using the mirror as an aerial observer was to avoid such unpleasant surprises. She held out a hand, feeling the heat building in the dense wooden frame. "That's enough for now." She released the spell after she spoke.

"I have much, but I have not all of it," Hanfor said.

"Later," she promised, opening the shutters, and standing in front of the light breeze, then turning to let the air dry the sweat-soaked back of her shirt.

"I am glad you thought of showing such an image on the glass," Hanfor said. "Is it possible to do that in the field? Can you do that without straining too much?"

"I would think so," Anna said, "if I don't have to hold the image long. I'd be closer to what the mirror displays."

"She must use such skills far enough from the traitors that she can regain her full strength before . . . confronting them.'' Jecks coughed once, then turned to study what Hanfor had drawn.

Anna frowned as she realized that none of them had even mentioned negotiating with Sargol, Gylaron, or Dencer. Her eyes dropped to her linen shirt and the thin dressing beneath. She didn't feel like negotiating or being charitable. She'd been charitable to begin with, and it had gotten her nowhere with the rebels.

She laughed, thinking that she sounded like one of the Vietnam warhawks that Avery had been so opposed to back in their student days. Somehow, your perspective changed when you were the target.

Jecks lifted his eyebrows, but Anna didn't enlighten him. She didn't want to try to explain hawks or doves or Vietnam, even in general terms. How could she explain a war where the generals weren't allowed to be generals, where the side that won lost almost all the battles, and how people Jecks would have regarded as peasants forced an end to the fighting.

''How long before Herstat arrives?'' she asked.

''Another few days. He will hasten.''

Anna hoped so. There were too many things still left undone. ''Jimbob can remain here with Herstat and a small detachment.''

Jecks frowned, then rubbed his chin. The hazel eyes grew distant, almost glazed over as they did when he disapproved of something but would not voice his disagreement.

''I did spell the entire hold for loyalty to the Regency,'' she pointed out. ''And it's farther from Neserea and Nordwei.''

''It is closer to Sargol.''

''None of them have armsmen beyond their own lands.'' Anna shrugged. ''If I fail, you can get to him sooner. If we both fail, distance won't save him.''

Hanfor continued to sketch from memory, not looking at the lord and the regent.

After a silence, the hazel eyes refocused on Anna. "That is true."

Anna refrained from telling him that was what she'd said to begin with. Why antagonize him? Besides, he was doing better than most in accepting her as a person of intelligence in a culture that automatically devalued women. She frowned momentarily. Actually, over time, she hadn't done that badly with those lords she'd been able to meet with, although she had her doubts about Birfels and Nelmor. Then, that was always the problem with prejudice. It was based on stereotypes, and women were certainly stereotyped in Defalk, and kept out of decision-making. Stereotyping was always easier when you didn't work with people. Most of the people she'd had trouble with in academia were those who'd never come to her recitals or seen her direct her operas.

"How are we doing for bows and arrows?" Anna directed the question at Hanfor.

"If we strip the armory here at Synfal, we can raise fivescore uncertain bows," said Hanfor. "Very uncertain bows."

"Just so they can get the arrows into the air strongly on command. I hope that will be enough for Sargol. We'll need more for Dencer." Anna stretched slightly, trying to lift the damp cloth away from her skin.

"I would that we had a source for more blades." Hanfor paused, as if he wished to ask a question.

"Yes?"

"I did wonder. You built a bridge . . ."

"Whether I could create blades through spells?" Anna frowned. "I don't know. I hadn't thought about that. I was worried more about Dencer."

"Dencer?" Jecks frowned.

"We have to find a way to take Stromwer quickly," Anna answered. "There's no point in waiting. Dumar can pour more than ten times the armsmen we can raise into Defalk," Anna pointed out. "They're less likely to do that if we hold the rebel keeps and lands."

"And others will think twice about revolting," said Hanfor.

"That is true," Jecks mused. "Still . . ."

"I know. It's foolhardy," Anna answered. "Everything I do is foolhardy. Attacking the Evult was foolish. It's just that everything else would have been more foolish." Even as she said the words, she wondered. *Are you right about that, really? There's so much you still don't know. So much. . . .* As events kept proving. She shrugged, trying to shift the slow-drying linen-cotton shirt away from her skin, away from her shoulders and back. The breeze helped, although it was moister than in Falcor or Mencha.

"About the blades?" Hanfor suggested.

"I'll see what I might be able to do." That was all Anna could promise. Theoretically, she could see no problem—but no one else was creating blades through sorcery, that she knew of, or that there was any record of, and when people didn't do things that seemed obvious, there was usually a reason. *Unless it's something no one thought of . . . or thought possible.* But she didn't know.

Anna moistened her lips. Another thing to add to her endless lists—try to create swords.

Hanfor stood and carefully rolled up his de facto map, then bowed. "Have you any other need for me at the moment, Lady Anna, Lord Jecks?"

"Not right now," Anna said.

Jecks shook his head.

With a last nod, Hanfor closed the heavy door behind him.

"Are you worried about this?" Anna gestured toward the blank mirror that showed only a reflection of her quarters at Synfal—the writing table, the chairs, the bed she'd rid of vermin with sorcery. "Sargol, I mean?"

"I do not worry about Sargol. Nor even about Gylaron or Dencer. Lord Ehara and the Sea-Priests, they concern me." Jecks scratched the back of his head momentarily.

"What about them?" Anna pursued.

"Your former lords, they do not understand your

power. They deceive themselves. Even so, they do not wish to destroy Defalk. Or Liedwahr." Jecks' lips turned into a crooked smile. "The Sea-Priests would see as much destruction and death as possible."

"I doubt they want to spend too many golds," Anna suggested.

"That does stand between us and all their ships and armsmen," Jecks admitted.

"I understood that they worry about Mansuur and Nordwei."

"Not about Mansuur. They could not conquer the Lied-fuhr, but he has few ships and less trade. The traders of the north have all too many ships, and their council is mostly of women."

"So . . . the Sea-Priests can't afford to spend too many ships on poor Dumar and Defalk?" questioned Anna.

"I do not know. I would think not. Have you any spell that would show such?"

"No." Anna shook her head. "Getting a spell to show something is still partly a matter of luck. I'm just trying to get a better feel for things." Feel was about all she had sometimes.

"If you do not need me . . ."

"Not right now. I need to think."

For a time after Jecks left, Anna sat at the writing table, looking vacantly first at the empty sheets of brown writing paper and then at the window, and the shutters. The shutters reminded her of the house in Richmond, the one that had been perfect—for all of three months—until Avery had decided they needed to move so that he could be closer to New York. He'd only gotten one role with the New York City Opera, not even the Met, but that meant that the whole family had to move, and that had meant she'd left the job with Eastern, one of the few places that had treated her well.

Irenia had been eight then. Lord, had it been that long ago? Now . . . she was dead; Mario was in Texas, and Elizabetta at school in Atlanta. At least, she hoped her littlest redhead had gone back to Emory—as her only letter across the worlds had indicated.

Anna's eyes burned, and through the tears she saw the black-edged rectangle on the stone wall of her quarters at Falcor, the rectangle that proclaimed that even the most powerful sorceress in Defalk couldn't see her daughter. Not even as an image in a mirror or reflecting pool.

Maybe later . . . Brill said. . . . But Brill was dead, too.

"Enough." She shook her head, and blotted her eyes. "I can do this. I can."

She looked at the paper and lifted the grease marker.

Almost a glass later—and with one new spell roughed out—there was a *thrap* on the door.

"The player Liende," announced Rickel, inclining his head. The heavy strawberry-blond thatch did not move.

Anna inclined her head and rose, waiting by the writing table.

The chief player stepped into the quarters and walked toward Anna, then stopped and bowed. "Lady Anna."

"Liende." Anna smiled. "Thank you again. I'm almost fully healed, and there won't be that much of a scar."

"You healed yourself."

"I know who helped." Anna shook her head. "Again."

"Alvar says that you ride again to battle. We would ride with you." Liende's voice was firm, if soft. "You are proud, lady. Often too proud to ask."

That came of her French and Indian forebears, Anna suspected, although her Irish ancestors hadn't been known for their humility. "I told you I wouldn't ask that of you. Alseta—"

"Without you, Alseta will have no future. Nor will I." The player smiled apologetically. "If you fail, she will wear chains, or her daughters will."

"Chains?" Anna murmured.

"All Liedwahr must know by now that Lord Ehara

backs the insurgent lords, and the golds of the Sea-Priests are behind Ehara.''

"And what does all Liedwahr know about Lord Ehara?'' Anna asked, adding quickly, "Remember I'm not from Liedwahr, and people always think I know more than I do about things.''

"Lady Siobion is his third consort, and his favorite for now. Lady Gestorn he joined for her coins, and she perished of the flux.'' Liende snorted softly. "Lady Eligne— she had two daughters. She drowned in a boating accident. Lady Siobion bore him five sons in twice that many years, and all are healthy.''

How healthy is Lady Siobion? "He sounds charming.''

"By all accounts he is handsome and charming.''

Anna nodded. "His image gives that impression.''

"He is strong, and he would have Dumar be more than it has been.''

Another conqueror, another male ruler who thought that more force would make things better. "There seem to be a lot of lords like him in Liedwahr.''

"There have been many.'' Liende's lips quirked momentarily. "But few rulers like you willing to stop such. What would you have of your players?''

Anna forced a smile in return. "I'd have nothing, if it were my choice. It isn't. I'm going to try some things less catastrophic than in the past. Some songs against spelled weapons and some spells to make ours more effective. The tunes are simpler than the building spells.''

"That is good.''

Anna wasn't sure. She'd have liked more harmony—it was stronger, but she was no composer, and tunes that she had to create from scratch were simpler, much simpler than those she had been able to adapt. "Are you sure, Liende?''

"I would not see Alseta in chains, even gilded ones.''

Anna could not argue that.

40

The morning sun was already hot, and Anna could feel the sweat oozing down her back as she glanced to the players, arrayed well back from the wall across the middle of the fields to the south of Synfal, to the straw figure on the wall a good hundred yards away, and then to the archer standing beside Hanfor.

"Liende?"

"We stand ready, Regent."

She gestured to Hanfor. "When I drop my arm..."

"Yes, Lady Anna."

She could sense Jecks standing perhaps a yard behind her, waiting to see what the results of her demonstration might be. Beside him stood Jimbob, shifting his weight from one foot to the other.

"Go ahead." Anna looked to Liende.

The sound of strings, woodwinds, and the falk horn rose over the fields, joined by Anna's voice.

> "Arrowhead once in the air,
> turn and strike the target there—"

Anna dropped her hand, and the bowstring sang.

> "—Strike the target on the wall,
> strike and make the target fall..."

With the last of her words, she watched the wall, having lost sight of the arrow that she'd directed be aimed slightly away from the target to ensure that the spell would indeed change the arrow's course.

Abruptly, the straw figure toppled off the wall, transfixed with the heavy shaft.

Anna smiled inadvertently. The spell worked; she could direct arrowheads, and the shafts followed. More important, Anna had neither headache nor double vision. So . . . she could use spells directed only at inanimate objects, even if they affected animate objects.

You're rationalizing like a lawyer. . . . She didn't want to think too much about that, though she knew she would, sooner or later. She always did.

Jimbob closed his mouth as Anna turned.

"I'm just working out what was used on me," she said, suddenly conscious that the wound on her chest still ached slightly, probably from tension.

"You have that reckoned," said Jecks with a slight laugh.

"Now, for the second test." Anna looked at Jecks.

"The forging one?"

"I'd like to know exactly what we can count on—or can't." She turned toward where Fhurgen held Farinelli's reins. The gelding *whuff*ed as she neared, as if to tell her that he'd be just as happy to get out of the sun. His tail flicked at a fly that buzzed past Anna.

"Do you think one test is enough?" Jecks inclined his head toward the wall where an armsman reclaimed the target.

"For that, yes." She nodded as she climbed onto Farinelli, waiting for Jimbob and Jecks to mount.

The three rode slowly back to Synfal, trailed by Fhurgen and Rickel, and a squad of armsmen.

Bielttro, the thin-faced ostler, was waiting outside the stable when they reined up inside the keep. "How was he, lady?"

"He was fine. I should have ridden farther, but that will come."

"He seems disappointed when you do not ride."

"He's been disappointed a lot lately." Anna laughed gently.

"You may take care of our mounts, Jimbob," Jecks said quietly to the red-haired boy.

"Yes, ser."

Anna dismounted and led the gelding to his stall. There she handed the lutar to Jecks, who set it aside. The muscles across her upper chest and shoulder definitely twinged as she reached for the saddle.

"My lady . . . you are not that recovered." Jecks stepped past her and lifted the saddle, moving gracefully and quickly to rack it.

Farinelli turned his head, but did not protest.

Anna did give her mount a quick brushing before leaving the stable and heading for the armory and the adjoining practice yard. Jecks carried the lutar, and Anna didn't protest.

Hanfor was waiting in the shade of the eaves before the armory door, an unsheathed blade in hand.

Anna took it, and almost dropped it, so much heavier was it than it looked. "Is this a good blade?" She looked to Hanfor.

"It is a good blade for the average armsman."

Anna felt the weapon for a time, studied it, and finally returned it. Then she reclaimed the lutar and began to tune it.

"It would be good if we could obtain blades," said Hanfor. "Yet I know of no sorcerer who has created blades."

"There are many things she has created not seen before in Liedwahr." Jecks smiled ironically.

Hanfor laughed.

"I'm ready. Can you lean the blade against the wall there?"

The arms commander carefully propped the blade against a niche in the bricks and stepped back.

Anna strummed the lutar, since she hadn't been able to create a spell that went with the songs that the players already knew.

"With iron, carbon, and heat be met,
    metal heat and steel be set;
    forge this steel into a blade,
    as good as the finest ever made . . ."

Even before she finished the spell, a gray haze appeared beside the first blade, a haze that solidified into a second blade, one appearing nearly identical to the one Anna had modeled it from, except that the hilt was metal, rather than leather wrapped over a tang.

Hanfor lifted the new blade, hefted it. He frowned. "It doesn't feel quite right. I cannot say why that might be." The arms commander turned to Jecks. "Perhaps we could spar—just the blades against each other."

"That might be best." Jecks lifted the original blade, leaving his own in his scabbard at his waist.

Anna watched. While she couldn't tell the moves, she could listen, and Jecks' big blade rang almost in its own true key, while the one she had spellforged sounded somehow flat.

Abruptly, the new blade shattered, and chunks of metal rained across the practice yard, and Hanfor staggered back, a line of red across his cheek.

Jecks lowered his blade, brow furrowed, and stepped forward.

"Hanfor!" Anna ran toward him.

"It's just a scratch." The gray-bearded arms commander held up the hilt with a smile. "I fear, Lady Anna, that your other spells are more effective."

"It looks that way."

Theoretically, there was no reason why her spells couldn't forge a blade. Maybe she didn't know enough about sword construction or smithing to visualize the blade correctly. Or metallurgy . . . or any one of a thousand things.

But why could she build bridges? Because stone was more forgiving? Or because she'd seen enough bridges? Or because of her design classes?

Again . . . background knowledge seemed to play an important role in the effectiveness of visualization . . . and spells. And, again, she really didn't know enough, not by a long shot.

41

Jecks stepped into the room, followed by Hanfor.

"Lady Anna, Herstat has arrived. He will be here in a few moments." Jecks bowed, his eyes twinkling, as though to ask if she felt ready to continue her internal revolution in Defalk, the revolution that would be fueled by her efforts to grant young Jimbob greater wealth and power than his predecessors.

Great . . . you're undertaking internal revolution while you've got to put down an obvious revolt and threats of invasion. And you still don't really know what you're doing—except it's already taking a lot of sorcery, and you've barely started. It seemed so strange. She was trying to give a ruler more power when she came from a place where dictators and absolute rulers were considered evil. *Except feudal chaos is worse than a strong ruler.*

She offered a pleasant smile. "Would you have Jimbob join us?"

"I would be most pleased." Jecks bowed slightly and left.

Anna wondered, if she used Synfal as a headquarters for much longer, whether she should consider refurbishing the old throne room. She shook her head.

Jimbob, Jecks, and Herstat arrived almost all together.

Herstat, an older, grayer, and stooped male version of his daughter Dythya, bowed. "Lady Anna."

"Herstat, it's good to see you again." The regent offered a smile. "I apologize for hijacking you from Lord Jecks and upsetting your life."

"Both Lord Jecks and my daughter your counselor have persuaded me that such minor upsets are to be far preferred over the alternatives." Herstat offered a rueful smile.

"That may be," Anna admitted. "I'll be honest," she continued. "I have two jobs for you here. One is long-term. One is much shorter. The long-term job is to ensure that Synfal is well-run and that Lord Jimbob understands every aspect of how it is run. I will ensure he spends time here with you. At times, you may have to come to Falcor. If you feel you have trouble with him, then I expect you to let me know. If you cannot reach me, let Lord Jecks know."

"Might I ask a question, Lady Anna?" asked Herstat.

"Please do."

"Much of this could be accomplished at Elheld." Herstat waited.

"You mean . . ." Anna shook her head. "I'm sorry. I'm afraid I didn't explain this well. Lord Jecks is the lord of Elheld; Jimbob will someday hold Elheld, but right now, he is the legal Lord of Synfal. The people have to get used to him, and he has to understand what is involved. You manage people well, and that is something that he must learn. . . ."

"You think too highly of me," Herstat protested.

"I know what people say, and what I feel." Anna looked at Jimbob and then at Herstat. "There are a couple of rules I will insist on. First, as I told you earlier, Jimbob, until you are of age, you will never contradict Herstat or question his actions or judgments in any public place. You can certainly ask questions—that's how you learn—but only in private chambers, never where you will be overheard." Her eyes went to the youth. "Is that clear?"

"Yes, lady." Jimbob nodded, the nod conveying that he understood also that Anna wanted all parties to know the rules.

"Second, if you strongly disagree with an action Herstat has taken, you will talk first with your grandsire. If he feels it is necessary, he will come to me." Anna turned to Herstat. "You may and should suggest actions to Lord Jimbob. If he fails to learn skills or acts in a way that would hurt the holding, you, or himself, you are to let Lord Jecks know immediately. If you feel that Lord Jecks is unable to deal with the situation, you will come to me. Is that clear?"

Herstat nodded. "Yes, lady."

Anna frowned. She really didn't want to tell Herstat how to manage anything. He'd clearly done well enough. "The real point of this arrangement is for you, Herstat, to help Jimbob learn all the aspects of being a lord and landholder." She turned to the redhead. "And to keep you from making too many mistakes."

"Yes, Lady Anna."

"Finally, I don't expect you two to come to Lord Jecks or me often." Anna offered a wry smile.

Herstat nodded. "I am at your wishes, lady."

"Yes, Lady Anna," said Jimbob earnestly.

"There's one last thing," Anna said. "No . . . no more sermons. It's the acting saalmeister—Halde." Her eyes went to Herstat. "He knows how the holding runs as well as anyone could. I've directed him to give you every assistance, and when we're done here, I'll formally introduce you. His problem is that he thinks everyone is like he is. That is, he understands and does what is necessary. I'm sure he gets impatient when people don't understand, or don't want to do their jobs, and I suspect his first thought is to punish. I've asked him to watch you, and learn, and I'm going to ask you to offer quiet suggestions. I'd like to use him elsewhere, but he needs to learn more about people."

Herstat half smiled. "You do not offer easy tasks, lady."

"No. None of our tasks are easy." She grinned at Jim-

bob. "Last set of old people's sayings. Some people will
try to flatter you, to tell you how important you are." She
paused, trying to come up with the right words. "How
important am I?"

"You . . . ? You are very important."

Anna waited.

"The most important person in Defalk, lady?"

She shrugged. "I don't know about that." She opened
the green shirt enough to show the still-purpled bruise and
scar. "People have tried to kill me, and they almost succeeded several times. Do you know why they didn't,
young Jimbob?"

"You're too strong."

She shook her head. "I would have died three times,
at least, if people hadn't made a lot of effort to save me.
I'm not perfect." *Is that an understatement!* "But I was
able to treat enough people well enough that they cared.
No one . . . no one," she repeated, "is strong enough to
survive without the help of others. You have to learn how
to make others want to help you. It's not something you
can order them to do. And even if you could," she finished, "how could they help you if you're too wounded
or tired or far away to give them orders?" She didn't
know how much, if any of it, Jimbob would retain, but
she'd had to try.

After another short silence, she said, "Time to introduce Herstat to Halde." *And then to work out the last
details of the violence ahead.*

She smiled, instead of taking the long deep sigh she
felt like taking. "I hope your trip wasn't too tiring, Herstat."

"No, Lady Anna. We missed the rains, or most of
them."

"You were lucky," said Jimbob. "We got a whole sky
full of rain . . . for days."

Anna and Jecks locked eyes, and Jecks nodded almost
imperceptibly.

So far . . . so good. Until we have to meet Sargol, and Gylaron . . . and Dencer.

One problem perhaps solved, and three more to go. Just about the way her entire life had gone.

42

After looking back at the solid bridge over the Synor, Anna gave Farinelli a hearty thump on the neck. "We did a good job there, fellow."

The gelding *whuffed*, as much of a mutter as anything else.

"I know. Bridges aren't your thing." She just hoped she'd be as successful in dealing with the rebellious southern lords as she had been in rebuilding bridges.

On the flat and dusty road eastward, empty once they were more than a dek from the bridge, Anna shifted her weight in the saddle. She hadn't been riding recently, and she was going to be stiff again. She couldn't keep up with being in practice for much of anything, it seemed. That aspect of her life hadn't changed. It had been like that when she'd been teaching, and it was worse in Liedwahr.

The road was wide enough for three riders, and Hanfor rode on her left, silent, thoughts hidden behind blank eyes.

"A solid piece of work, Lady Anna," agreed Jecks from the chestnut he rode beside her.

"I wish I could do more. Too many of the roads and bridges . . ." She shook her head. She could only do what she could do, and that wasn't near enough.

"You will have time," Jecks promised.

Anna nodded, not convinced. She should have been able to make blades, but the second and third trials had produced no better results than the first. Maybe she just didn't have the right feel for blades.

Her eyes flicked to the road ahead, the same road she'd ridden weeks earlier, right into an ensorcelled crossbow bolt. This time, she was better prepared, but so probably was Sargol—and Gylaron and Dencer.

"Good hearty day," observed Jecks, half turning in the saddle and then turning back, as though he'd belatedly realized that Jimbob was not with them. "Not all that hot yet."

Anna blotted her forehead. She could hardly wait for weather Jecks would call hot. Even with the Evult's drought clearly broken, full summer was on its way, and it promised to be hot—again. Even for Jecks.

Was there some connection between hot weather and war? Good dry roads? Lack of illness and hunger?

A puff of dust appeared on the road ahead. As they rode on eastward, Anna could make out the figures of a horse and cart.

"A peasant heading to market in Cheor, no doubt," suggested Hanfor.

"There is no one behind him," Jecks said.

The column neared the distance until Anna could make out the dusty figure of a man seated on the cart seat.

Abruptly, with a fearful glance toward the armed riders that Anna led, the driver turned his single horse cart down a side lane that was little more than a rutted path between fields filled with green shoots. Anna didn't know the plants, but thought they might be beans of some sort.

Dust puffed from under the waist-high wheels and from the hoofs of the bony gray horse as the cart bounced southward down the uneven lane and away from Anna's force.

"Sargol has spread the word," said Hanfor dourly. "We are here to destroy and pillage." His eyes followed the dust raised by the farmer and his cart.

"Best we disappoint their expectations," growled Jecks. "Save for Sargol himself."

"No pillaging," Anna said. "Destruction will be bad enough."

Hanfor nodded.

They rode eastward, not speaking, to the sound of hoofs on the dusty clay.

43

ENCORA, RANUAK

The Matriarch descends the wide polished limestone steps to the floor of the Grain Exchange. Men and women standing around the raised platform in the center watch the tally poles, as the prices are changed periodically. Several glance toward the round-faced and gray-haired woman in pale blue on the stairs, their eyes alternating between the tally changes and the Matriarch.

A tall thin woman in a sea-blue tunic and trousers steps to the front of the platform, and a gong reverberates through the high-ceilinged space, the tone echoing off the stone walls and columns.

"Trading is temporarily suspended," she announces, "for this visit of the Matriarch." She extends a hand in a vague gesture toward the older woman. "We would not wish any to be distracted or to lose coins by another's distraction."

"You are most kind, Abslim," answers the Matriarch as she nears the head of the Exchange.

"What brings you to our humble Exchange?"

"Me? The harmonies, I suppose. I had heard rumors that the Exchange was considering a surcharge on handling grain and transactions that involved Defalk. I thought I would come to see for myself."

A series of murmurs whisper across the polished white floor.

"The surcharge was begun yesterday. There is much unrest in Defalk."

The Matriarch nods as she proceeds through and around the traders and toward the trading platform at the south end of the hall. "Are you imposing a surcharge on Ebra? Or Dumar? Or Neserea?"

There is a moment of stillness.

"Not at the moment."

"Ebra has a civil war brewing and no central government. Neserea has a struggle between an outside regent and an underage lord. Dumar has accepted the presence of a Sturinnese fleet. Do not those merit consideration?"

"We will consider such."

"Ah . . . Abslim . . . why does the Exchange deal so harshly with Defalk?"

Abslim squares her shoulders. Finally, she speaks. "Is it not true that the sorceress continues the old ways in Defalk? She has announced that the new heir to Synfal will be young Lord Jimbob. She has not allowed any of the consorts to dead lords to become full noble holders in their own rights, but only administrators for male heirs." The tall and thin woman in sea-blue tunic and trousers smiles coldly across the floor of the Exchange. "This lady Anna may be a woman, but she has done little or nothing for women."

"That may be, although I would suspect you have not stated all that has occurred. Still," muses the Matriarch theatrically, as she steps from the trading floor to the platform, "what has the sorceress to do with the cost of transactions involving Defalk?"

"It raises their costs," answers Abslim. "Because you are the Matriarch, we have acceded to your request to allow normal credit to the lords of southern Defalk. Now we find that they are in revolt against the very regent who has guaranteed that such loans would be repaid."

"She never guaranteed more than repayment of past debts," answers the round-faced Matriarch quietly, yet her voice carries, and the whispers die. "She has repaid half of a debt she did not incur. How does that make her responsible for guaranteeing the debts of those who rise against her?''

''She is the Regent of Defalk.''

''There is no authority in Ebra, but you have no surcharge there,'' points out the Matriarch. ''You have oft said that the price itself knows the problems of trade. Why have you changed that?''

There is no answer.

''Abslim, what do you desire?''

''I desire that the Matriarch use her power and the harmonies to improve the lot of women throughout Defalk, not to impose her wishes through the Exchange.''

''You are imposing your wishes through the Exchange. Banning further loans to Defalk reflected your wishes. Or those of the SouthWomen.'' The Matriarch smiles.

''The marketplace is always right,'' says Abslim.

The Matriarch shakes her head. ''The prices set by the market are right, in the end, but that does not mean you or the traders are right.'' A gentle smile follows. ''You know that, and so do the harmonies.'' She turns. ''I have said what I will say.''

The whispers on the trading floor remain low until the round-faced Matriarch has climbed the stairs and vanished.

Abslim's face remains as cold as the limestone columns, long after trading resumes.

44

The dusty road wound around yet another orchard-covered hill, with a narrow strip of bean fields separating road and orchard. The fields appeared to have been recently tended, but nothing moved in the still morning air, warm already, with the sun barely above the trees and low hills.

The road was empty as well. It had been all the way from Cheor, expect for an occasional dog, one or two farm carts that vanished upon seeing the riders, and a handful of older women in the fields, most of whom slipped out of sight behind trees or hedgerows once the riders appeared.

Anna sipped the last drops from her second water bottle, then replaced it in the holder. She readjusted the uncomfortable breastplate, hoping she wouldn't need it, but knowing that she should get used to wearing it. Under the light armor that rested too heavily on her, the scar from the crossbow bolt still itched, and the itching was worse because the plate made her sweat more. The slash on her arm itched as well.

"Glories of warfare, Liedwahr style," she murmured, half wondering, far from the first time, how a singer who'd hated fantasy had ended up in a world with two small moons, music magic, and medieval warfare. "God, or the harmonies, have a nasty sense of humor."

"Pardon, Lady Anna?" asked Jecks.

"Nothing, Lord Jecks. I was just muttering to myself." *As you find you're doing more and more.*

Jecks nodded, but did not pursue the conversation.

Riding beside Jecks, Hanfor studied his map, and occasionally spoke to the riders who shuttled messages to and from the scouts.

The sorceress slowed Farinelli as they neared a brick marker—a roadstone that read, "Osuyl—2 d." She peered eastward, but could see nothing except those scouts who rode almost a dek ahead and the fields which slanted gradually upward and ended in a rise about a dek away. Osuyl had to be beyond the low hill.

When the column halted, so did some of the scouts, while a single rider eased over the rise and out of sight along the road toward Osuyl.

"How far to Suhl?" asked Jecks.

"Four deks beyond Osuyl, from what we figured, and more to the south," said Hanfor.

"Time for the mirror," Anna said. The intelligence would be valuable, and she wanted time to eat and recover after using it. She reined up and waited until she was sure Hanfor had signaled Alvar and gotten the armsmen to halt in reasonable order.

Then she dismounted and extracted the mirror from its padded leather case atop her saddlebags. Next came the lutar.

A good thing you don't travel heavy, she reflected as she tuned the instrument.

Finally, she glanced at Jecks, then Hanfor. "Ready?"

They both nodded, Jecks first.

Her fingers touched the strings, and she began the spell-song.

"Those in Suhl so strong,
    those who'd do me wrong . . ."

The image in the mirror on the roadside grass was clear. On the mound she had discovered weeks earlier was a huge crossbow, unattended and attached to a log frame set into the ground. Below the vacant summit in the meadow between the keep and the mound were more than a score of tents. Several strings of mounts were lined up, as though on some form of tieline, to the north of the tents.

Anna frowned. Weren't they keeping tabs on her? Sargol's forces seemed almost relaxed. What did that mean? She glanced at Hanfor and Jecks. Jecks smiled faintly, but did not speak.

"They have something else planned, I would say, Lady Anna," Hanfor suggested.

Anna released the spell, then set down the lutar and took a long swallow of water from one of the remaining bottles.

"They do not have many armsmen on guard," mused Hanfor. "I do not like that."

Neither did Anna, even if it happened to be early in the day. Setting aside the water bottle, she tried the second spell, ignoring the line of hot and dusty armsmen who lined the road, waiting on equally hot and dusty mounts under a sun getting hotter each moment.

"Danger from Suhl, danger near,
    show me that danger bright and clear . . ."

The next image in the glass was that of fields and a road similar to the one that stretched before them to Os-uyl. Orchards crowned the low hills to either side of the road. Anna squinted, trying to discover . . . something.

"There," murmured Jecks. "The soil is different."

Anna followed his finger, as did Hanfor.

"Pits . . . stakes."

"Blinds there, I'd wager. Archers." Jecks shook his head. "Signs of mounts there."

"Is it just my imagination," Anna asked, "or are there traps all along the direct route to Suhl?"

"That is what your glass shows," Hanfor pointed out. "They will have scouts on all the main roads."

"Main roads?" Anna had already noted the lack of the wider roads throughout Defalk. "Is there another one?"

"There is but one," conceded Hanfor. "They will have scouts on the larger lanes as well."

With his patient tone, Anna felt small. "I'm sorry. I'm feeling bitchy." *Who wouldn't riding for days after a lord who's tried to kill you and who's probably got ambushes everywhere?*

A quick frown passed across Jecks' face, and Hanfor showed no expression at all, both indications that regents weren't supposed to admit bitchiness in public.

Feeling the heat from the glass, and seeing the grass next to the frame begin to brown, Anna released the spell, then blotted her forehead, and searched for the water bottle.

After drinking, Anna decided to try again.

> "Show me now and show me clear
>   the way to avoid this danger near . . .
>   Like a vision, like a map or plot . . ."

The mirror remained blank. Anna frowned. Jecks and Hanfor exchanged glances.

The mirror couldn't advise? It could only display. What about showing a lane without armsmen? Would it do that?

"Let's try something else." Anna tried to get the words in her mind. *Of course, there's no simple way to do it.*

She could sense the impatience of the riders waiting in the hot sun, yet she had to find a way to keep them out of an ambush.

> "Show me now and show me clear
>   a lane to Suhl without armsmen near.
>   Like a vision, like a map or plot . . ."

This time the glass showed an image—of a lane leading from a group of buildings—Osuyl?—down a lane that branched to the north of the main clay road. The lane swung around one hill and then swung south uphill through a few small hovels and then down another lane and through an older and neglected orchard. Beyond the orchard was an open field just to the northeast of the mound containing the enchanted crossbow.

"There are some hovels along this route, but there are no signs of armsmen," noted Jecks. "Not now."

"They will find us soon enough." Hanfor had out the greasemarker and was sketching the route rapidly on his map.

Anna broke the spell, and the image faded. She walked back to Farinelli. She was faintly light-headed, and that bothered her. Three biscuits and several chunks of cheese later, she looked at Jecks and Hanfor. "If we find that lane, can we get to the field and get set up before they charge us?" she asked Jecks and Hanfor.

"We will find it," averred Hanfor. "It is not far ahead." He turned his mount to the armsman beside him. "Tell the scouts to look for a lane to the left of the road. It will be shortly past the hill crest. We will take that if they find no signs of mounted armsmen."

"A lane to the left past the hill crest. Yes, ser." The armsman spurred his mount into an easy canter.

Hanfor shook his head. "I hope your glass is true, and none lurk in the orchards beside the lane."

"So do I," Anna said. "It's been right so far. How much time will we have?"

"They will not charge at first," said Jecks. "They will want you to attack. Even from the field below that orchard you will be too far from that infernal device. If they do charge, it will take a half glass for them to assemble."

Anna wasn't so sure that Lord Sargol would be that slow, and it wasn't something she intended to leave to chance. She nodded to the two and walked back past her personal guards until she reached Liende and the players.

"Lady Anna."

"We're getting close. I'd guess about a glass. We may not have much time to prepare." Anna shrugged. "Jecks thinks we will. I don't know. I'd like to start with the long flame spell."

"The long flame spell—the one against their weapons?" Liende leaned forward in her saddle, then had to brush a lock of white hair back off her forehead.

Anna nodded, wondering if Liende were graying so quickly because of the magic, if all players and sorcerers—except her—died young in Liedwahr. She certainly hadn't run across any old sorcerers. She wanted to laugh. Liedwahr was a violent and primitive place, and she hadn't run across many old people of any occupation, except for a handful of lords and ladies.

"What will be the second spell?" asked the head player.

"The first arrow song . . . I think." Anna didn't shrug, though she wanted to. How would matters go after the first spell? She had no idea.

"Players!" Liende's voice rose over the murmurs of the armsmen.

"Green company!" called Hanfor.

"Purple company!"

"Gray company!"

Anna coughed as she walked back to Farinelli and remounted in the dust that sifted around her as the light wind shifted. Once in the saddle, she groped for the third water bottle. Four bottles—they probably wouldn't be enough, and Jecks thought the weather was pleasant!

After riding a hundred yards, she was out of the worst of the dust and had managed to clear her throat. Dusty horseback travel didn't always agree with spellsinging, but at times not much did.

With scouts moving over the rise and out of sight, they rode slowly eastward along the road that sloped gently upward. The tops of trees with pale green leaves appeared to the south, their trunks hidden by the crest of the hill that held another bean field.

"The first lane should be about five hundred yards ahead," suggested Hanfor, "on the left just over the rise and beyond the orchard."

Anna peered from the saddle, absently patting Farinelli.

Hanfor was right. A narrow lane, barely wide enough for two mounts, ran through the bean fields across from the orchard. Two of the scouts waited. The others had started down the lane, distant dark blots between the fields and scattered hedgerows.

"To the left. Down the lane. Take the shoulders. Four abreast!" ordered the arms commander. As the orders were repeated by Alvar and the subofficers, he leaned toward Anna. "We don't want to be too strung out." He shrugged. "Some of the fields may suffer."

"Better the fields than us," Jecks concurred.

Anna merely nodded, her eyes on the dusty lane, her thoughts on the spells she would have to use, and the notes that held them.

For another dek or more, they followed the lane over and around the low hills, moving more and more southward. Though she strained, Anna could see nothing except fields, the few scattered orchards, the lane itself, and dust.

"That looks like the next turning point," Anna said, pointing down the lane past the end of the fields. Four hovels or small houses stood at varying distances from where the two lanes crossed. Around the houses were gardens, and pens made of rough-trimmed branches. The pens were empty.

A scout waited at the crossroads; the others had taken each of the roads.

"We should head due south again at that crossroads," said Hanfor, glancing from his rough map, then nodding at the messenger riding beside him.

"Tell them to scout the south road, ser?"

Hanfor nodded.

"Yes, ser." The messenger rode ahead of the column toward the tiny hamlet and the single waiting scout.

"Over the next rise is an orchard," Anna recalled, "and then a higher field that overlooks that mound."

"Ready arms," ordered Hanfor, and Alvar echoed him. The muted orders passed back along the column.

"No one around," said Jecks as they neared the crossroads and the small houses.

Anna could feel and see that.

The thatched roof on the first house on the left sagged so much that one side held a small pool of rain water. A dusty black dog scurried down the side lane, to the north, as if the canine knew the riders were headed south. The rear door to the cottage swung in the hot breeze. On the woodpile by the door, in the narrow band of shade cast by the overhanging eaves, crouched a black and white cat.

"Boots in the dust," said Hanfor. "Less than a glass old. Work boots. No mounts."

"They were warned," said Jecks.

Anna didn't mind the people being warned. She did mind the stories that had caused people to flee their homes in fright, even terror.

At the small crossroads, if where two lanes intersected were indeed a crossroads, the column turned south.

Anna stood in the saddle and turned. "Liende . . . it won't be that long. Tell the players to get ready. We won't have much time when we get to where we can see Suhl."

"Yes, Lady Anna," said the head player, nodding her head as she did before turning to those who rode behind her. "Make ready. The long flame song will be the first spell."

Once the column passed the houses, Fhurgen eased his mount up behind and closer to Anna. "Lady Anna?" The black-bearded armsman's voice rose above the clamor. "Should we not lead?"

Anna supposed—no, she knew—that at least some of her guards should precede her. "A few, Fhurgen, but I have to be able to see."

"Then I will lead, and Rickel will flank you." Fhurgen was counting on Jecks to cover her right. The guard swung his mount around and quicktrotted to the fore.

The strawberry-blond and broad-shouldered Rickel eased his sorrel up beside Anna. Jecks slipped his blade from its scabbard, examining it as they rode southward.

"Lord Jecks?" asked Anna.

Jecks nodded.

"Is there any reason why some keeps have their own names, and some have the name of the town?"

The white-haired lord cocked his head for a moment, then smiled ruefully. "I do not know . . . save that Elheld was a keep long after Elhi was a town."

"So . . . you think that the older holdings have the town name because they grew together?"

"Mayhap . . . but Synfal was a keep before Cheor was much beyond mud hovels." He grinned.

Anna had to grin back. Some things you couldn't explain. Her grin faded as she glanced back and saw the column of dust. Surely, someone from Suhl had seen them.

Anna cleared her throat and tried a vocalise. "Hollylolly, polly-pop . . ." Less than a half-dozen notes into the exercise, she half coughed, half choked on mucus. After clearing her throat, finding the water bottle, and taking a small swallow, she started again.

Lord . . . is it going to be one of those times?

One of those times it was. Her voice kept cracking, and she couldn't seem to clear her cords. Anna rode and kept doing vocalises, half aware that they were passing through bean fields and fields with sprouts too low for her to identify. Every so often, she had to moisten her mouth and get rid of the dust.

After a half-glass—or longer—she felt better, well enough to handle the spells she had planned.

Another orchard appeared ahead, and the lane split the trees. On the right of the road, the trees sprawled to the west for a dek or more. On the left were only scattered handfuls of the old and gnarled apple trees. The ground beneath the orchard's trees bore the trace of tattered white apple blossoms, and the faintest scent of the fallen flowers. The leaves were already cloaking the old and twisted branches.

"Suhl's beyond this," Anna said.

Hanfor nodded. "The scouts have seen it. No one is coming this way."

"Not yet."

The high field Anna had first seen in the glass spread out below the rise where she reined up, the main bulk of the orchard to her right, a few trees and mainly fields to her left. The wide meadow in the valley held a man-made mound that commanded the main road that split the val-

ley. That main road ran perpendicular to the lane that
Anna and her forces had taken.

"No armsmen on the hills to either side, ser," panted
another messenger, drawing up beside Hanfor. "There's
a galloping lot of them coming up on the other side of
the valley, where this lane would lead, if'n we'd taken it
farther. They look to be a dek back, almost like they're
a'waitin', ser. They've got a different banner."

"Another joins Sargol's cause," opined Jecks. "Gylaron, I would wager. He is shrewd."

"Fighting on someone else's land?"

Jecks nodded, checking his blade again.

Beyond the mound, on the rise across the low valley,
hulked Suhl, a thick-walled and square keep of dull red
brick and gray stone. Below the keep was a welter of
tents, and mounts tethered in long lines.

A horn sounded, and dust began to rise as riders scrambled for their mounts.

"They didn't expect us to come this way," said Jecks.

Why not? Anna wondered. Or were back roads too dangerous, because they were narrow and forces could be
trapped? She shook her head. She was too slow. Talking
was wasting time. "Players!"

"Yes, Lady Anna?" called Liende.

"A quick warm-up, and then the long flame song."

"Way for the players! Way for the players!" shouted
Fhurgen.

"Green company to the fore!"

The players spilled off their mounts and onto the
ground, arrayed facing the valley and the mound.

Anna dismounted, clearing her throat, and going
through a last vocalise as the players straggled through a
warm-up.

"Together. We must play together, else we die sepa-
rately."

Why does that sentiment come up so many places?
Anna wondered absently even as she looked to Liende.
"Ready?"

"We stand ready." Liende gestured, and the warm-up stopped. "The flame song. On my mark."

"Go!" Anna tried to ignore the sound of horses, of both her forces and those of Sargol and of Hanfor's terse orders, concentrating instead on the notes and the spell she would sing.

"Mark now!" called Liende.

Anna waited for a moment, then began.

"Fill with fire, fill with flame
  those weapons spelled against my name.
  Turn to ash all tools spelled against my face
  and those who seek by force the regency to replace.

"Fill with fire, fill with flame . . ."

The line of fire exploding across the south, across the valley, even across the walls of Suhl, seemed almost endless.

Anna just stood, light-headed, dizzy, nauseated, as her words and the music ended.

Even the mounts, Farinelli included, remained still as though stunned, but only for a moment.

Fhurgen pressed her water bottle on her. "You must drink, Lady Anna."

She drank, mechanically, her eyes blurring, not sure she wanted to look out across the valley, where she could already hear cries and screams and moans.

"Sargol has yet hundreds of armsmen. His captains are rallying them," Hanfor noted, easing his mount up beside the sorceress.

"Where are our archers?"

"Our *bowmen* are ready, as ready as necessary. So is the trumpet."

Anna frowned. "Will the arrows carry to the tents or the keep?"

"We can take the hill the scoundrel raised. You have

cleared the path to, it, if we hasten,'' Jecks said. "Will that help?"

Anna nodded, then said, "Yes." The height would help carry her voice and the players' support. "Can we put the bowmen there, too?"

"We can manage that. Only a handful of their armsmen remain there." Hanfor turned. "Alvar! The Green Company—take the mound."

"Ser! Green Company . . . Green Company . . ."

Anna turned to Liende. "We'll have to remount, and ride to the mound."

"Mount and ride. Follow the regent." Liende had already slipped her horn into its case. "Now. We must remount and play again."

Another ragged trumpet sounded. From across the valley to the west came the sound of riders, hoofs, harnesses.

"Those are not Sargol's," Jecks said. "Leronese lancers."

"From Gylaron?" Anna struggled into the saddle and urged Farinelli downhill. Rickel eased his mount beside her, and Fhurgen led the way, following the three companies that swept down the low hill.

Anna shrugged to herself. She'd thought all along that they'd have to defeat all three lords. She coughed and spat out more mucus, hoping her asthma wouldn't act up too badly.

A faint smell of burning flesh drifted with the dust into her nostrils, and she pushed aside the sensation. Beyond the mound were dark lumps across the low green grass, hundreds of dark lumps. Some moved. Most did not.

Anna swallowed, and put the thoughts out of her mind. Sympathy, concern, those would have to wait. She concentrated on riding, on staying close to her charging armsmen, although it seemed less than a handful of mounted figures even remained of those that had been riding toward her forces. That handful turned back toward the tents.

Reaching the mound took little time, and Anna reined

up, finding she was panting slightly. Holding her breath? That wasn't good. She forced herself to breathe easily and deeply, but not too deeply.

"Dismount!" ordered Liende as the players rode up behind Anna. "Your pleasure, Lady Anna?"

Anna frowned. What spell? What did she need? Then she looked west, at the oncoming lancers.

"The arrow spell." That shouldn't take that much effort, and she needed to husband her strength, shaky as she was after the first spell.

"Arrow spell. Warm-up."

Again, horns and strings tumbled out of cases, and Fhurgen's men grabbed reins and gathered players' mounts.

Anna eased out of the saddle and toward the players, who stood in the middle of the mound. To the south of the mound where she stood were a handful of foot levies, forming up beside the tents below the keep of Suhl, and a scattering of Suhlan mounted armsmen. To the west, drawing up in ragged order, were the lines of Leronese lancers. They had also taken a less direct route to the battlefield, or that might have been the shortest way from Lerona. Joining them were another group of lancers, nearly two score under a crimson banner.

Anna shook her head. Again, someone else was paying for the games of the damned chauvinistic lords—but Sargol was nowhere in sight, not surprisingly.

"Which forces, lady?" asked Hanfor.

"The Leronese, I guess." She looked at the arms commander. "What do you think?"

"The Leronese are the threat. And the red lancers. They must be from Dumar. You have felled most of Sargol's lancers in the valley. His levies gathered by the keep could not reach here soon. He may have others in the keep, but they are not a threat."

Not yet. "When I signal—I'll drop my hand—can you have our archers loose their arrows toward the Leronese?"

"That. That we can do." Hanfor turned in the saddle. "Bowmen! To the west, to the lancers. Nock your arrows."

Anna cleared her throat, then gestured to Liende. "Once through—the first arrow song."

As the music rose, in tune, she began to sing.

"These arrows shot into the air,
  the head of each must strike one armsman there
  with force and speed to kill them all,
  all those who stand against our call!"

Anna dropped her hand, aware that a humming or thrumming sound vibrated somewhere before her.

"These arrows shot into the air . . ."

As the music and her words ended, she half smiled, pleased that she wasn't dizzy or light-headed, then looked at Hanfor, consciously avoiding a glance toward the lancers.

"If you could do another," he suggested, his eyes flicking toward the west.

Anna could hear hoofbeats. She glanced toward her chief player. "Liende? Can you and the players manage the arrow spell again?"

"We can, Regent." Liende turned. "Players! The arrow spell again. At my mark."

Anna nodded.

"Mark."

With the second release of arrows, and the end of the spell, Anna felt a brief light-headedness. She glanced toward Hanfor.

He smiled grimly. "A handful remain, and they have turned back to the west, on their way back to Gylaron."

That's what we hope, anyway. Anna slouched toward Farinelli, absently patting him before extracting the water bottle and drinking deeply.

"Do not forget to eat, lady," suggested Fhurgen.

To eat—a good idea. She fumbled out another stale biscuit and slowly chewed, moistening her mouth. Then she glanced southward. The gates of Suhl stood ajar, and men and horses straggled through them, leaving tents on the flat empty.

Dozens of mounts walked riderless across the flat. Some grazed amid the dark lumps of death. Anna looked, blankly, and ate. After a time, she turned and looked at the squat timber framework that held a burned and broken crossbow, wondering who had broken it. Hanfor? Fhurgen? Someone else? Did it matter? She ate another biscuit, sipped more water.

Jecks eased his mount nearer, stopping next to where Fhurgen sat mounted, holding Farinelli's reins. He looked down at the dusty sorceress. "They retreat behind their walls."

The sorceress glanced south.

A lone individual hobbled toward the keep, behind the others, squeezing inside before the iron-banded timbered gates swung closed.

For a moment, Anna closed her eyes. Then she turned. Liende sat on the dirt, limp. Most of the other players slumped in similar positions. Kaseth lay stretched out, eyes closed, his white head on a folded blanket, his breathing ragged. Delvor looked whiter than snow, and seemed to sway as he looked at Anna, then glanced hurriedly away. Even Liende's eyes were glazed.

Her players were more spent than she was. Then, after a fashion, she'd trained harder than they had. Still, she hadn't even considered what all the playing of spellsongs would do to them. She just hadn't worked with players for extended spells under stress, and her inexperience showed through. Again.

"Fhurgen! They need food, water."

Anna wondered. This was the first time her players looked as exhausted as she felt. She snorted, almost to herself. They'd never played so many spells so long and so close—nor ridden across a valley in between sets.

As her guards went to work, Anna turned back to survey the keep. After a time, she turned to Jecks. "Can we ask Sargol to surrender?"

"You cannot pardon him," Jecks said. "He tried to kill you, and he has raised his banner against you. If you offer him a pardon, what will you do to Gylaron or Dencer?"

"And we just can't sit here and beseige him, right?" She already knew the answer to that one. She had no siege engines, no wealth of supplies, and only a few hundred armsmen that she couldn't afford to tie up all summer waiting around Sargol's keep.

"I do not see how."

"What if we offer mercy to his family and retainers?"

"That would not hurt." Jecks' smile was cold. "He will refuse, because he does not know your strength. Nor will any man of Defalk surrender to a sorceress."

Not to a mere woman . . . is that it? "Send someone to offer mercy to his family and retainers and the armsmen who remain—but not to Sargol."

Jecks turned his mount toward Alvar and Hanfor. "We can but try."

Anna watched as the three talked. Alvar gestured and Hanfor beckoned. Two armsmen, one bearing a battle trumpet, joined the three, then rode toward the silent walls of Suhl.

The trumpeter sounded a call, wavering across the afternoon. After a time, it was repeated.

Anna didn't see anyone appear on the wall, but the armsman with the trumpeter called out a message. Anna caught enough of the words.

" ' . . . offer mercy to all but Lord Sargol . . .' "

Even Anna didn't miss the scattered arrows that were the response, or the hurried retreat of the de facto herald.

Jecks rode back to Anna.

She looked up. "I saw."

"He does not believe that you can touch him within his walls." Jecks paused. "You have not torched the fields or orchards. He would think that weakness."

Weakness? Why would I set fire to— "Oh . . ."

Jecks sat astride the warhorse, waiting.

Again, Anna had the feeling of being in a totally alien culture. Without cannon, without siege engines, a lord could remain within walls for weeks—or seasons. The only damage an invader could do would be to the crops and the followers outside the walls. What was common sense to Anna became weakness to a rebel lord.

Anna nodded slowly. "I need to think." She patted Farinelli absently.

Jecks turned his mount back toward Hanfor, and Anna studied the walls of Suhl once more, her thoughts spinning.

She didn't have the manpower or the time to put Suhl under siege—not with Dencer and Gylaron left to deal with—and Sargol knew that. She didn't want to use the standard tactic of burning the fields and murdering all the productive peasants or serfs. Defalk had suffered enough, and her goal was to build—not to destroy. *Not to destroy the common people, you mean. You wouldn't mind taking down a few chauvinistic lords.*

What else could she do? She hated relying on sorcery so heavily, but she didn't have thousands of armsmen, nor cannon, nor siege engines, nor . . . What she didn't have was far more than what she had.

A glass later, the gates of Suhl remained closed, iron-banded and dark, without word or signal. Anna glanced toward Liende and the players. They looked tired, but all appeared well.

"What will you?" asked Jecks. "Sargol lies behind the walls, and he has refused your offer."

The sorceress just looked at the older lord. Jecks had been right, but it didn't make matters any better.

Jecks looked away, and for the moment, Anna didn't

care. She might later, and then again, she might not. For some reason, she recalled his reaction to the ballroom in Cheor. Dancing, so innocent, even with the harmonies of Liedwahr, yet Jecks had found it blasphemous, or dissonant. So had Alvar, though the younger officer had been more temperate in his words.

Her eyes went to Hanfor. ''Can we leave Suhl behind us?''

''After this?'' he asked ironically, gesturing down the mound at the heaps of dead armsmen and mounts, and the handfuls of still-wandering mounts.

Anna understood. In for a copper, in for a silver, or some such. Better to get it over with, better to do it before she thought, before she felt. With a long and slow deep breath, she began to walk toward Liende.

''I'm going to try to reach Lord Sargol with an arrow spell. Would you get the players ready?''

''We will ready ourselves.''

Next, she needed Hanfor, but he was already riding toward her, as if he had guessed something from seeing her talk to Liende.

''Yes, Regent?''

''I'll need a score of bowmen, ones who can loft arrows over the keep walls.''

''I will gather them.'' He turned his mount.

She walked toward Farinelli, slowly. As if he sensed her thoughts, the gelding sidestepped.

''Even you're worried, old fellow.''

The regent and sorceress took her time readying herself.

Finally, she finished a last vocalise, then cleared her throat, and looked at Jecks and Hanfor, then at Liende. ''We'll need to get closer. How close to the walls could I safely go?''

''No farther than the tents,'' offered Hanfor.

''If that,'' added Jecks.

''My lady? Must you?'' growled Fhurgen.

''Yes. Unhappily.'' She swung herself into the saddle

and urged Farinelli down the slope and toward the tents, toward the closed keep.

Rickel rode on her left, Jecks on her right, Fhurgen and two other guards before her, and the players, and a good two score armsmen around and behind them.

Anna stopped short of the tents, empty canvas that had once held men, men who had died or fled or both. She forced her thoughts to the spell in her mind, the last one for now. *The last one,* she reminded herself, as she climbed from the saddle, her boots hitting the dusty ground heavily. For a moment, she just held to the saddle before swallowing and stepping away from Farinelli.

She glanced back at the players, dismounted and tuning, and she waited. After what seemed an interminable time, Liende called, "We stand ready, Regent."

"Then start the spellsong."

Anna timed the music and lifted her voice toward the silent keep.

"These arrows shot into the air,
    the head of each must strike Lord Sargol there—"

Anna dropped her hand, and sensed the release of the arrows.

"—with force and speed to kill him dead,
    for all the treachery he's done and led."

Slightly light-headed, she watched as perhaps two dozen arrows flew over the walls of Suhl. Had she heard a slight clatter?

The walls remained as silent as before.

Anna turned toward Farinelli, and laboriously got out the lutar and the mirror. After tuning the instrument, she cleared her throat.

"Show me now and show me near
    Lord Sargol bright and clear . . ."

The glass was explicit enough. Sargol was clad in gray inside a stone-walled room, one with iron shutters—iron doubtless because he thought it proof against sorcery or some such. And it had been proof against the arrows. Sargol's eyes glittered, but he was very much alive.

Anna took a deep breath, feeling Jecks beside her, also studying the glass before she cleared the image. *Now what?*

Her eyes flashed toward the hulking brick and stone keep of Suhl, its gates barred, its lord raging. She shook her head and turned to Jecks.

"Now what do I do?"

"I do not know."

Why? Why . . . because it's the perversity of the universe. She turned and walked back to Liende.

The chief player watched as the regent approached.

"Liende, I'll need the flame spell—again."

"Lord Sargol still lives?" The chief player looked down.

"Unfortunately."

Anna waited as the players reorganized. Neither Jecks nor Hanfor said a word, though they exchanged glances—and kept exchanging them.

Finally, in the late afternoon silence, with the brick and stone keep brazed in golden flat light of a sun that hung over the low hills to the west, Anna gestured to Liende and the players, then let her voice rise.

> "Those who will not be
>   loyal to the regency,
>   let them die, let them lie,
>   struck by fire, struck by flame . . ."

This time, the chords of Harmony did shiver the sky, and the ground trembled. Then came a wailing that should have been a counterpointed chord, except that nothing matched, not intervals, not key or scale or *anything*—the closest sound Anna had ever heard to pure dissonance, again a sound that no one else seemed to hear.

Her teeth and jaw ached, and her eyes watered, first from the sounds, and then from the lines of fire that arrowed from the impossibly azure blue of the sky, endless line of fire after endless line of fire.

Anna shuddered as she could sense a few of the fire arrows slash into her own armsmen. *Bad spell. . . . How do you know all your own forces are loyal in their hearts?*

Sweat burst out on her forehead, a sweat of fear. Was she *that* loyal, even to herself?

Even before the last chord, darkness had begun to gather around her, swelling, vibrating, alternating with light. Anna fought to hold on to consciousness, fought, and the darkness receded, ever so slightly, hanging at the corners of her eyes.

Someone held a water bottle, and she drank before realizing that Jecks stood beside her and held it. Then she ate, heavy brown bread, dry like sawdust in her mouth.

After that she sat down in the dust, unmindful of the sneezes that racked her, the fires in her eyes, and the knives that twisted in her stomach. Her eyes open in the late afternoon, she saw nothing. Her ears clear, she heard nothing. *Too damned close to Darksong . . . far too close.* Maybe it had been part Darksong?

It couldn't have been—no double vision. But that raised more troubling thoughts. She could destroy people—if the spell were worded correctly—but not change them? Walls could stop arrows, but not fire?

In time, Hanfor returned to where she still sat in the dust. "Lady . . . Suhl lies open to you." The arms commander bowed deeply. "None of those who survive gainsay your regency, nor that of Lord Jimbob. Even the two detachments of Dumaran lancers fell to the last man."

Anna shivered at his tone, at the blankness of face and expression, at the ill-concealed fear. "Thank . . . you." After a moment, she added, "I didn't want it to be this way. I offered terms. . . . I did." *The only ones I could. . . .*

Hanfor nodded, but she could sense his feelings that the choice had been hers, and it had been. Hers alone. She couldn't blame Dieshr, the music department chair at Ames, or Avery, or Sandy, or the kids, or the economic pressures. She'd chosen the spells and used them.

She tottered to her feet and looked at Suhl, looked at the open gates, sensed the horror she had created. The bodies—sprawling from the walls, seemingly lying everywhere—were the worst, with red-and-purple burns and blackened skin, with clothing scorched and seared.

The stench of burned meat was everywhere, carried by the light and hot breeze.

Anna forced the bitter bile back down her throat, with every breath. She slowly turned to a pale Jecks, who stood beside his mount.

"Well . . . Lord Jecks," Anna croaked. "Was it worth it? To save the delicate sensibilities of the northern lords?"

Jecks' face, white as that of a marble statue, paled even more, whiter than his hair.

With invisible starbursts flashing before her eyes, Anna could barely see, let alone stand. She let herself slump back to the ground and sat there.

"Lady Anna . . . here is a blanket." Rickel's voice was soft.

Mechanically, Anna shifted herself onto the blanket, then closed her eyes. The starbursts still cascaded across her now-dark field of vision, and she opened her eyes.

Fhurgen handed her a chunk of bread. She took a small bite. Then she twisted and retched across the dust, adding yet another stench to those of fire and death.

Fuck Defalkan conventions! I'm not doing this again. . . . Despite the violence of her thought, Anna wondered. In Liedwahr, with its emphasis on force, could she totally avoid the use of greater force? And how?

How . . . in the name of God or the harmonies . . . or whatever?

45

A nna stood on the worn stones of the battlement of the front corner tower of Suhl, looking blankly over the valley. The surface of the mound Sargol had raised was bare, with no sign of the infernal crossbow. The tents had been struck, brushed clean, and stored in one of the keep's storerooms.

Three deep holes gaped in the ground—mass graves. Four wagons were scattered across the grass, each heaped with bodies. Under the watchful eyes of subofficers, armsmen stripped each corpse of weapons and valuables before lifting it onto the wagons.

Caaaw. . . . A large crow flapped its wings in settling onto the other corner tower. Nearly a dozen of the scavengers circled over the meadow, under the wispy thin clouds scattered across the morning sky.

Absently, Anna's hand strayed to the wound on her arm. It was still red and itched, if less than before. Behind her, by the steps up from the lower wall, stood Rickel, his broad-shouldered form casting an even broader shadow. Another guard was at the base of the stairs.

Boots scuffed on the tower steps, and Anna turned as Jecks emerged into the hazy sunlight.

"Lady Anna, how do you feel?"

"Close to human, until I look out there."

"You did what had to be done." Jecks crossed the stones of the tower, then stopped next to the stone wall, perhaps two yards to her right. "Sargol would not have surrendered. He tried to kill you twice." He paused. "And he would rather have stopped his ears against your spells of obedience."

"I suppose so." She frowned. Obedience or loyalty spells were clearly Darksong, and her body and the harmonies were telling her their use was most definitely limited—if she wanted to survive. Yet . . . was the alternative slaughtering thousands? Did that make her any better than Sargol? Wanting to survive?

She looked down at the bricks of the rampart walk underfoot.

"You did what needed to be done. You showed mercy at Synfal, and that was first. You have shown what will happen to those who resist."

"What's left of Suhl? Besides mass graves filled with loyal armsmen?" asked Anna abruptly. "A handful of shattered souls? Serfs and women too frightened to think. Three idiots, and a dozen infants, a handful of children. Three of them were Sargol's." She laughed, bitterly. "At least, he had heirs. At least, I don't have to worry about finding someone else to make a lord of the Thirty-three. At least, they'll be southern lords without delicate sensibilities."

Jecks' face went stony again, and Anna didn't care, or almost didn't care. Her eyes focused on the wagons and the armsmen dumping bodies into the pits in the meadow. The light wind carried the faint odor of death.

"You asked me how those lords would feel, lady. I told you." His voice was hard.

"You did, and you were probably right," Anna said quietly. "I don't have to like a situation where I must choose between letting Defalk disintegrate, slaughtering thousands, or dying trying to use Darksong."

Jecks did not answer, but stood by the battlement, turned so he faced neither toward her nor away from her.

"My lord," she prompted quietly, but firmly.

"What would you have me say?" The words sounded dragged from his lips. "That I did not know how terrible your sorcery would be? From me, who has seen battles for all his life? I did not know?"

Anna remained silent, and the methodical clank of

spades and the dull sounds of teams moving wagons drifted across the tower. The wagons carried far too many bodies.

"You saw the Sand Pass."

"Those were dark ones, not Defalkans."

Anna felt less sympathetic to Jecks. "They were people, Lord Jecks. Just as those poor armsmen I slaughtered the day before yesterday were people. They loved; they hoped; and they died."

"Lady Anna. Think of your flame spells. Did you not direct them at those who rebelled. Only those who rebelled?" Jecks asked softly.

"Yes," she admitted.

"Yet but a handful survived. What would you have? An entire hold seething in rage? This is not Synfal, where Arkad did not incite revolt, where no one raged against you. Arkad did not like the regency, but in his own way, he honored Defalk."

Anna forced herself not to answer, to consider his words first. After a time, she spoke, slowly. "Are you saying that so many died here because they violently opposed the Regency and Jimbob?"

"That is what I believe."

The regent and sorceress leaned on the warm worn stone, resting her head on her arms. *Lord, Lord . . .*

"Their ties are to these lands, to their lord, not to Defalk. They still think of themselves as Suhlmorrans."

"You said the Suhlmorrans had not ruled here for centuries . . . for hundreds of years."

Jecks shrugged, almost sadly. "Still, they call themselves Suhlmorrans."

"How can we ever . . ."

"You already have."

"No. Enough lived that they'll hate Jimbob and the Regency more."

"Not if you direct the heirs."

"Where will I get another administrator?" Anna asked.

"Who will hold the keep? We can't garrison it, not with Gylaron and Dencer left to deal with."

"You need not leave more than a handful of arms-men—the wounded among them. No one will dare attack here. There would be no advantage, either. You will declare that his infant son will be the heir, will you not?"

"Have I any choice, realistically?"

"No," Jecks admitted.

"Have someone draft up the statement, but don't make it too specific, only that his heirs will hold the land. Don't name names. I'll sign it, and have a messenger take it to Synfal and let Herstat have it copied. He can send them to all of the thirty-three who haven't risen—and to Hadrenn." She hoped whatever reached her didn't need too many changes, but she was still too tired to think as clearly as she'd like. The harmonies help her if she ever had to handle large battles on two days running.

After another silence, punctuated with the clank of spades from the graves, Jecks asked quietly, "What will you with the golds in the storeroom?"

"The same as always." Anna laughed harshly. "The Regency gets some. I get a little. You get a little, and most of it stays here for Sargol's administrator and heirs."

"What of your armsmen?"

"You think they should get a bonus?"

Jecks frowned at the word.

"Something extra?" Anna corrected. "A silver each? Two? What would be customary?"

"Two silvers would be most generous, and appreciated."

Anna tried to calculate. Roughly two hundred lancers, and the players should get more. That worked out to . . . what? Forty golds? She wanted to shake her head. If that were expected with every battle, she'd be paying several hundred golds, maybe a thousand before the whole mess was resolved.

For some reason, the thought that she'd paid two golds for five yards of velvet crossed her mind—and an armsman who risked his life got a pair of silvers. Yet a bonus of a single gold—several times during the campaign ahead, and there would be a campaign, that was clear—that bonus would bankrupt Defalk. *Cloth was always overly expensive in pre-technology societies.* She frowned. Another excuse, no matter how true?

Jecks waited silently.

"That sounds reasonable, but let's talk to Hanfor. He has to lead the men." She paused. "Any ideas on who could run this place?"

"It would not take great experience," Jecks offered. "Not at first. What about the sister and ward of Lady Gatrune?"

Anna tried to remember the young woman's name. Anna had met her at Lady Gatrune's holding in Pamr, when Lord Hryding's armsmen had been escorting Anna to Falcor to offer her services to Behlem after the Lord of Neserea had conquered Defalk. "Herene?" Tall and blonde, like Gatrune, but thinner than her older sister. Anna nodded to herself. "Herene."

"A woman here would be good," Jecks said. "With a solid armsman and officer at her hand before long."

"So that the other lords would understand it wasn't a power grab?" Anna also understood another element of Jecks' logic. A male caretaker or administrator meant takeover—such as with Jimbob and Herstat at Synfal—while a woman meant continuity of the male heirs. She took a deep breath. *You can't change everything all at once.*

"They would be less threatened."

"I can see that." Anna wanted to threaten them all, but she only said, "In this case, that makes sense. If something like this occurs again . . . we'll have to see."

"That will be your decision, as always." Jecks bowed slightly, his voice formal.

"Let's find Hanfor." Anna turned from the battlement, blotting her damp forehead, and started down the steps, followed by Rickel. Two other guards swung behind her at the base of the tower. The sorceress had begun to feel that, no matter where she went, she was leading a parade.

Hanfor stood on a mounting block in the courtyard, directing officers and armsmen. When he saw the two, he stepped down, shaking his head. "Sargol was not organized."

Anna had suspected that from the beginning of the fight two days earlier. "We won't keep you, Hanfor, but Lord Jecks and I have been thinking. Would an extra payment of two silvers an armsmen be an appropriate reward for their efforts?"

Hanfor's face crinkled into a smile. "So long as you tell them now, and let them know that they will receive it when we return to Falcor. Otherwise, too many will find local spirits."

"Should I announce it, or should you?"

"Normally, I would announce that." The arms commander grinned. "But if you would prefer . . ."

"I'd prefer the normal," Anna said. "Two silvers when they return to Falcor."

"To be received when they are not on duty," Hanfor added.

Jecks smiled.

"Of course," Anna agreed. "You set the terms."

"You see, Lord Jecks, why so many of us prefer her reign?"

"So do many of the lords. Would that all understood." Jecks' voice was dry, barely rising above the clop of hoofs, and the clamor of voices of the armsmen crossing the courtyard, and the wagons returning through the gates.

"They will," Hanfor affirmed. He glanced over his shoulder.

"We'll talk later," Anna said, "about what we do next. After dinner?"

"I will be there." Hanfor bowed, and then turned to where Alvar stood, waiting.

"The wagons?" asked the swarthy officer. "Can we use two of them to gather provisions?"

Anna stepped back, letting Rickel, Jecks and her guards follow. "I need to talk to Liende, Lord Jecks. If you would excuse me?"

"As you wish, lady." The white-haired lord inclined his head.

"Thank you." Anna forced a smile. "At dinner?"

"At dinner, my lady." Jecks offered a pleasant smile in return.

It took three inquiries to find the wing where the players were quartered, and Anna had tried two doors before she rapped a third time on the ancient oak.

"Yes?" Liende opened the door, sleepy-eyed, hair rumpled. "Oh . . . Lady Anna. Oh . . . I was so tired."

"Don't worry about it." The sorceress stepped into the small room, shutting the door, and leaving Rickel and the guards in the brick-walled corridor. "I feel that way still."

Liende glanced around the room, her eyes touching on the single chair and the pallet bed. Anna pulled out the chair and sat. The player perched on the edge of the bed.

"Your pleasure, lady."

"I've been thinking, Liende, and I wanted to talk to you. I don't want to repeat what happened here at Suhl," Anna said. "Perhaps Sargol and his armsmen deserved it for their treachery earlier . . ."

"It was treacherous to attack you unprovoked."

"I don't understand why." Anna shrugged. "I wasn't even heading toward Suhl."

"He was fearing that you were."

The sorceress nodded.

"And he claimed the lineage of Suhlmorra."

"He wanted to re-create the kingdom of Suhlmorra?" asked Anna.

"So it is said." Liende offered a tight smile.

The regent shook her head. The last thing Defalk needed was fragmentation into more small countries. "Anyway . . . I hadn't wanted to use such terrible spells. . . ."

"Even with Lord Brill. . . ." Liende looked down.

"No. Lord Brill was too gentle." Anna laughed, then cut off the laugh before it turned hysterical. The thought of her as a ruthless and bloody butcher was insane. It was also true. "Too gentle."

"Yes," agreed Liende. "But Defalk needs you."

Defalk needs a woman butcher? What does that say about Defalk? Or you? "I will try to do what we need with less violence."

"That may not be possible, Lady Anna." Liende offered a sardonic smile.

"I know. We'll try, though. I'll be giving you two more songs, short ones, that I hope will help."

"No one can play before the morrow. Kaseth . . . he may not play for another day, yet. His fingers shake."

"We won't leave Suhl until all of you are ready to play."

"Thank you, lady."

Anna wanted to scream. Thank her for what? For butchery or common sense or both? She just stood. "You're welcome. Take care, and let me know if any of you need anything."

"We are well quartered and fed." Liende rose, slowly, as though she were stiff.

Anna nodded again, then slipped out into the corridor.

46

Anna's boots clumped heavily on the worn stone floor tiles of the dim corridor. Her nose itched, and she rubbed it. Like everything else in Suhl, the corridor held the faint odor of mold and must. Even five years of drought hadn't been enough to destroy that—or the recent rains had revived the spores quickly. She rubbed her nose again, trying not to sneeze.

"The family quarters and the nursery are just ahead, lady," said Fhurgen. "We've removed . . ."

"They need an honorable burial," she said tiredly. "And stone markers or whatever's customary." Her head still throbbed; her legs ached; and sharp pains stabbed through the balls of her feet with each step.

"Honorable?" asked Hanfor. ";After his treachery?"

"He and his consort paid for it, didn't they? There's no point in disgracing the dead." Anna stopped and looked at the hollow-eyed Jecks. "Is there?"

"An honorable burial in the lords' plot would serve many purposes."

And mollify the sensibilities of my squeamish northern lords. "Fine. Let's set that up." There was so much to set up with only a few handfuls of retainers remaining. Yet Anna couldn't afford to have Suhl go down in ruins, not when her goal was to rebuild Defalk, not destroy it. *Great start you're making.*

"The nursery." Hanfor gestured to the open door.

Anna stepped into the long narrow room, with its narrow embrasured windows and weathered inside shutters. Only Jecks accompanied her. She glanced at the three children—the dark-haired girl and the two brown-haired boys—then at the short and stocky woman who stood behind them protectively.

"I'm not about to hurt them," the sorceress said, even as she could sense the nursemaid's doubt. Still, the woman had survived, and that meant she wasn't disloyal. Or that her first loyalties were to the children. "They weren't the ones who tried to kill me."

"Lady, Lord Sargol was a good man." The nursemaid's voice quavered.

Anna respected the opinion, and the courage it took to voice it. "He was good to his people, I'm sure. He wasn't good for Defalk or those who lived around him. And totally good lords don't refuse to pay their liedgeld and attempt to kill regents who aren't even threatening them. Nor would he have died if he hadn't been planning treachery. You weren't, and you're alive.''

The maid's eyes widened slightly, as though she had not thought about that.

"Tell me the children's names."

"Keithen is the older boy. He's five. Resthor is his brother. He's two, almost three, at eight-week of summer. Dinfan, she be the daughter. She's eight, I think.''

Anna turned to the girl. "Dinfan, do you know who I am?''

"Da, he said you were a harpy of discord.''

That's one for honesty. "Some people have said that. It's not true. I'm the Regent of Defalk.''

"He said you were bad.'' The girl's voice was unsteady, but she held her chin firmly, almost defying Anna, much as her own Irenia had. Irenia, the accident, the funeral—they all seemed so far away, so distant.

Anna swallowed, trying to keep her composure before she spoke. "I have done bad things. So has your father. So do most people. So, child, will you. That doesn't make us bad people.'' Anna waited, still measuring the girl.

"Will you kill us, too?''

"No. You, if you learn enough, will hold Suhl. If you don't, one of your brothers will.''

"Women aren't lords.'' Again, that defiant echo of Irenia.

Anna forced a smile. "Lady Gatrune holds Pamr. Lady Anientta holds Flossbend. I am Regent of Defalk.''

For the first time, Dinfan's eyes dropped.

"You are your father's daughter. You must learn all you can. Perhaps, when you are older, you will come to Falcor to learn. Then you will know more when you are old enough to hold Suhl.''

There was no answer. Behind her, the nursemaid's eyes widened. "Do ye play with the child, lady?''

"No. I don't play games. Lord Sargol didn't understand that. Some of the other southern lords still don't. Suhl is

Dinfan's so long as she is responsible and loyal to Lord Jimbob and the Regency. I hope you will make that clear." Anna paused. "I will ensure she, and her brothers, have a tutor until they are old enough to come to Falcor. You will ensure they are loved. You will not tell them tales. You may tell them that their father rebelled and tried to kill me, and for that I slew him." Her eyes fixed on the nurse. "Do you understand?"

The nurse shivered. "Your will is law, Regent."

"Take care of them well. Their people will need them." Anna nodded.

The nurse bowed.

"Good-bye, Dinfan."

"Good-bye."

Anna gave a last smile and stepped back into the corridor, back to her entourage.

"I don't have the faintest idea where to get a good tutor, but we need to find one." Anna looked at Jecks.

"You will not foster them at Falcor?"

"They're too young right now." *And I'm not even there, and Lord knows when I will be.* "In a year or two for the girl, or three if she's young for her age."

"I will have Herstat and Dythya inquire after tutors."

"Good."

She walked slowly back to the small hall she had appropriated for her receiving and work space. Somehow, no matter where she went, there were messages and paperwork and people to see . . . and scrolls that seemed to follow her across the countryside.

The hall, like most in Defalk, had but high windows in the rear. Hanfor stood waiting, just inside the door, bowing momentarily.

Anna inclined her head.

The lit candles in the four wall sconces added minimal illumination to what little of the gray day's light seeped through the windows. The table was square, old, battered, and could seat six people. Four armless chairs were drawn around it. Anna slumped into one, glad to get off her feet. "Please sit down."

She poured a goblet of wine better than what she got at either Loiseau or Falcor, or even at Synfal, then took a long sip. Jecks followed her example.

Hanfor sat and pursed his lips.

Dinfan seemed bright enough. She might be another possible match for Jimbob. She shook her head—thinking like the rest of the thirty-three lords of Defalk, or Machiavelli. What else could she do?

"She's only four years younger than Jimbob," she ventured.

"I thought you had young Secca in mind."

Anna blushed. "I did. I do . . . but I guess . . . I'd like there to be some choices. I don't want to have consorts who can't stand each other."

"Alasia liked you," Jecks mused. "Don't know as I understand it all. . . ."

"We don't have to decide that now," Anna said quickly. "There could be others." She turned to Hanfor. "You look concerned."

"You were most effective, Regent Anna." Hanfor paused. "We lost but ten men, and another ten are injured."

"That's still a score," Anna said. "Is that what you're trying to say? That we can't afford even little losses like that for many battles?"

Hanfor shrugged. "I do not like that, but it has taken all winter to find five-score additional armsmen."

"If you rout Lords Gylaron and Dencer, blades will flock to your banner," Jecks said.

"People always support you after the dirty work's done." Anna took another sip of the wine. It felt good to be off her aching feet and legs. She hadn't walked that much, but they'd always hurt when she'd gotten tired, and she was still tired, damned tired. Or, should she say, dissonantly tired? "Now what? How are we going to get enough people here to keep this place going?"

"The tenants will farm as always," Jecks said.

"It must take a staff of fifty to keep this pile of brick and stone operating, even on a minimal basis, and that doesn't count armsmen. We've maybe got a score of retainers left."

"There are many at Synfal," mused Jecks. "Not that all were well-used."

Anna considered that. They certainly hadn't cleaned the main hall. Then, maybe Arkad had gotten to be like Howard Hughes, a recluse who let things close to him fall apart. "We'll have to send a message to Herstat to arrange for some of them to come here, the younger ones mostly, with some whose children are grown. We'll have to see what skills are missing, first." Another inventory, and she and Jecks would probably have to do that. She sighed. "Have the scouts found out anything about Gylaron's lancers?"

"There are no signs. Those who survived rode south."

"In a day or so, when I'm feeling better, I'll try the glass."

"That might be best," offered Jecks.

"I have scouts on the roads and the hilltops," Hanfor added. "They have seen no one."

"Let's hope they don't." Anna took another swallow of wine. Lord, she missed really good wine, and hot baths where she didn't have to spell the water herself. And . . . She shook her head. *Don't get into that.*

Thrap.

The three heads turned to the door.

"You have some messengers here, of a sort," announced Fhurgen, with a grin.

Anna frowned. "Messengers?"

"You should see them, Lady Anna." Fhurgen kept grinning.

"All right. Send them in."

The short black-haired armsman stepped into the chamber, followed by a taller brown-haired figure. Both wore somewhat faded greens.

"Fridric . . . Markan?" Anna paused. "What brings you here?"

"We bring a message from Lady Anientta." Markan extended a sealed scroll. "And a score of armsmen who seek your service."

"My service?" Anna rose from her chair to accept the scroll, then glanced at Jecks, who smiled openly, then at Hanfor.

Markan shook his head, then pushed back a lock of brown hair. "Things are not as they were at Flossbend. Stepan has left to join Gestatr in Synek."

"Does Gestatr serve Lord Hadrenn?" Anna reseated herself.

"How did you know, lady?" asked the brown-haired armsman.

"I didn't, but some things are beginning to make sense."

Jecks' eyebrows lifted.

"Are you sure you all wish to serve the Regency?" Anna asked.

"We would not be here, otherwise."

Anna nodded, then broke the sealed scroll and began to read. "Regent Anna, Lady and Sorceress, and Protector of Defalk . . ."

Anna wanted to groan. Still the flowery openings that Anientta seemed so fond of and that meant to Anna that more trouble lay ahead.

> We were pleased to have your most gracious confirmation of our status as protector and administrator for Jeron. . . . We will do our utmost to fulfill your trust in us. . . . In this regard, you should be pleased to know that my sire, Lord Tybel, has graciously provided some considerable assistance. . . . Onfel, second officer of his guard, and one of his clerks . . .
>
> Secca has been most courteous in sending an occasional scroll and is pleased to be in Falcor, and

for this we are all most thankful for your generosity. . . .

. . . as always, both Jeron and I stand ready to do your bidding in any endeavor in which we may be of assistance. . . .

The wax seal remained that of Lord Hryding, and the signature read, "Anientta, administrator of Flossbend, for the heir, Jeron."

Anna nodded and turned to Markan. "I accept your service. I take it that Onfel was not to your liking?"

Markan smiled so faintly the expression was not a smile. "Say, Lady Anna, that we were not exactly to his liking."

"A picked guard of Lord Tybel?"

"Who could say? We felt that our . . . services might be better used elsewhere."

Anna smiled. "We can use your services. Markan, this is Arms Commander Hanfor. I should have introduced you sooner, but I'm tired, and I'm not thinking very well."

Both Markan and Fridric bowed.

"Honored, ser. We have heard much of note of you."

"Honored," murmured Fridric.

Hanfor shook his head. "Good men we can use."

Anna looked at Fhurgen, still standing in the doorway. "Why don't you have someone get them settled?" She glanced to Markan. "Then Hanfor will talk with you and we'll see exactly how you can be best used."

"Thank you, Lady Anna." Markan smiled more widely.

After a moment, so did Fridric.

When the door had shut behind them, Jecks laughed. "You have not put down all the rebellious lords, and already they flock to you. A score—will not that help, Hanfor?"

"That will help."

Jecks frowned. "Who is Gestatr?"

"Gestatr was Lord Hryding's chief armsman. Fridric told me more than a season ago that he'd gone back to his home in Synek."

"And Hadrenn holds Synek?" Jecks finished. "You think that is why you received that scroll from young Hadrenn?"

"Exactly."

"You had a glint in your eye," observed Jecks, "when you looked upon the older of those two."

Jealousy? wondered Anna. "I do. Markan is responsible and trustworthy. I was thinking about leaving him and Fridric here to run things."

"You know this?"

"Markan was my escort from Lord Hryding's to Falcor after the Sand Pass battle. He was the lead armsman at Flossbend after Gestatr left."

Jecks nodded. "That is a horse of another color. One can place a lead armsman from one hold in another, and none will object, young as he may be."

"Young . . . he may be effective longer," Anna pointed out, "and he understands guarding a lord's household."

"There is that," agreed Jecks. "And he will favor you and Jimbob."

"Exactly." Anna rose and went to the door. "Fhurgen? Will you summon Markan and Fridric back? Or have someone do it, please?"

The black-bearded guard smiled. "You have a task for them?"

Anna nodded, her lips in a wry smile.

The head of her personal guard laughed softly. "I will get them."

"While they're summoning those two," Anna told Jecks, "I'll draft a scroll to Herene, and I suppose to Lady Gatrune, too, explaining why I need Herene."

Jecks nodded, and Anna wondered what else she'd forgotten.

47

The woman in the mirror wore faded green trousers and tunic, and had a smudge on her left cheek. The blonde hair was cut short, shorter than a bob. The fine features were those of an older woman, but the lightly tanned and flawless skin, the trim and muscular figure, and the clear eyes belonged to an eighteen-year-old—except for the darkness behind them. Three days not on the road and regular nightly sleep had erased the worst of the dark circles.

Anna grimaced. So did her reflection in the near-full-length wall mirror. The wooden mirror frame's wood was age-darkened so much that it resembled oiled ebony, and the shallow carved vines were nearly invisible.

The sorceress readjusted the lutar, ran her fingers across the strings, and then twisted one of the tuning pegs ever so slightly. She cleared her throat and began the spell.

Behind her, Jecks and Hanfor stood, uneasily watching the cloudy silver surface of the antique mirror as the notes echoed slightly in the cavernous bedroom Anna was using for her scrying.

> "Mirror, mirror, in your frame,
>   show me Gylaron in his
>   fame,
>   where'er he may ride or be,
>   show him now to me."

The mirror displayed Gylaron—swarthy, solid, but not quite stocky, with a trimmed and pointed black beard. He stood in a surprisingly small wood-paneled bedchamber talking to a heavyset black-haired woman with a heart-shaped face and dark eyes.

"She does not appear pleased," offered Hanfor.

"No." Anna studied the images, first of Gylaron, who shrugged and signed dramatically as she watched, and then of the woman, apparently his consort, from the dark red velvet she wore. Tears rolled down the consort's cheeks, but her hands remained folded in her lap.

Anna released the spell and took a deep breath.

"He looked worried," said Jecks.

"A man about to attempt a desperate venture," suggested Hanfor.

Anna swallowed, then checked the lutar's tuning, even as she mentally rearranged the spell she'd used earlier to scry danger.

> "Show from the south, danger to fear,
>   Gylaron's threats to me bright and clear . . ."

The words were cramped to that melody, but she hoped it wouldn't matter too much.

The mirror remained blank, then swirled into a feature-less silver, and finally showed an image not of Lerona, but of a mountain hold.

"That be Stromwer," Jecks said.

Anna frowned. Had her spell failed? Or did Lerona truly pose no dangers? With a sigh, she set aside the lutar and went to the spell folder on the table. With the grease marker, she drafted another version of the spell.

Once she had it in mind, she lifted the lutar and offered it.

> "Show me bright and show me clear,
>   threats from Gylaron for us to fear . . ."

The silver swirling repeated, this time remaining fea-tureless.

A *snap* filled the silence, and Hanfor looked down disgustedly at the broken marker in his hand.

Anna shook her head.

"Maybe there's something going on with Dencer." She distrusted Dencer more than she had Gylaron, or Sargol, even if she couldn't have explained precisely why.

Jecks shrugged.

"We still haven't seen Gylaron's keep," she said disgustedly. Sometimes, even scrying was dissonantly imprecise. *Sometimes?* What about most of the time? *You're exaggerating.* Still, she'd overkilled bandits, gotten images she hadn't really wanted, killed singing dark monks instead of armsmen, and nearly killed herself a half-dozen times.

She'd just have to use a direct mirror spell. She strummed the lutar and readjusted the peg for the top string. Then she cleared her throat. She really needed something to drink.

Hanfor held up a hand. "A moment, Lady Anna?"

"When you're ready." Anna couldn't help grinning as the Arms Commander used his belt knife to sharpen the grease marker he used for sketching. Setting down the lutar, she took a sip of the wine from the pitcher on the table, although she really wanted water.

Then she walked to the window and pulled the shutters wide. The fresh air, warm as it was, helped. The fresh earth over the mass graves reminded her of wounds... or scars. Would it always be like that?

Hanfor coughed. "Lady Anna."

"Oh." She turned and crossed the stone floor to reclaim the lutar.

> "Show me now, bright and fair,
>   Gylaron's keep as it stands there..."

Gylaron's liedburg rose out of the town of Lerona itself, on a small hillock to the north of the center of the town.

The walls were low, no more than five to six yards high, and the gates were wide open.

"No defenses," murmured Jecks.

Hanfor shook his head. "Some form of treachery?"

Anna released the spell and set aside the lutar. "I don't think so. The mirror showed us Sargol's treachery. I just didn't understand what it meant. Three different spells, and we get nothing. That means that Gylaron isn't trying anything."

"Or there is a greater wizard?" asked Jecks.

Anna took a deep breath and went back to the table and spell folder. After a time, she scrawled out another variation of the mirror spell.

Again, she faced the mirror and sang.

"Spells and wizards show me bright
those who aid Gylaron's fight."

What filled the antique mirror was a silvery mist, seemingly mixing with a faint steam from the mirror frame. Hurriedly, Anna released the spell. Then she took a hefty swallow of the red wine, followed by another. She sank onto the hard chair, glancing around for something to eat. There was only the pitcher of wine and three pewter goblets.

"Satisfied?" she asked, still holding the goblet, debating whether she should have more wine so early in the day.

Jecks looked down at the sharpness of her voice.

Anna felt both ashamed of her pettiness and angry. *Don't they understand this is work? Why would they? No one on earth understood that an hour and a half recital was work. No one understood the energy it took to teach lessons hour after hour. Why would things be different on Erde?*

If she destroyed something . . . that was work. She forced her jaw to unclench and sipped some wine—very slowly, very deliberately.

"Would you like something to eat?" Jecks asked, walking toward the door.

"Yes, please."

Jecks slipped out of the room.

Anna sat quietly, drawn into herself, knowing her blood sugar was nonexistent, knowing that she'd regret anything she said, waiting.

Hanfor sat on one of the chests against the stone wall, sketching something, a rough map, perhaps.

Shortly, the door opened again.

"Mayhap, this will help, lady." Jecks set the basket with the still-warm loaf of dark bread on the table before her.

"Thank you." She forced a smile, then broke off the end and slowly began to eat.

No one said a word until Anna had eaten for a time. One shutter creaked and swung partly across the window with a brief gust of warm air.

"Gylaron has not paid liedgeld . . . yet he makes no plans," mused Jecks.

"That be not quite so," suggested Hanfor. "The glass shows that any plans he makes present no danger. We must still approach Lerona with care."

Anna nodded, chewing on another chunk of the moist and dark bread, before speaking. "We need to see what Dencer plans."

"Especially after your glass has shown Stromwer," agreed Hanfor.

After she had finished most of the loaf, Anna stood and lifted the lutar.

> "Lord Dencer, show me then and now,
>   what he does 'gainst me and how,
>   show the scenes both far and near
>   and show us what one should fear."

Four scenes appeared, two side by side on the top of the mirror, the other two below. In the top right-hand vision, Dencer stood in his private study, his angular frame looking down upon a younger officer in the crimson uniform of a lancer of Dumar. In the top left side was an image of a group of men digging a large pit. Sharpened stakes were stacked at the side of the excavation.

The third image held no people, just a view of a small circular fort containing a large iron caldron. Below one side of the caldron was a circular stone basin from which ran a polished stone trough. The trough ended in a circular opening in the wall of the small fortress overlooking a narrow gorge.

The last scene, the one on the bottom right of the ancient glass, showed men working to fill nets with rocks. The thick hemp nets were braced with huge round timbers—rough-smoothed treetrunks—and extended over a rocky escarpment overlooking a road. Several sets of the netted rocks were visible. Hanfor sketched and jotted furiously. Jecks' eyes flicked from image to image. Anna just studied the last three images in turn, until the mirror frame began to smoke and steam. Then she released the image, set the lutar on the chest by the wall beside the mirror, and took a deep breath, finally walking to the window and stepping up to the open air, pushing back a shutter that had swung halfway closed in the light breeze.

The morning air was less fresh, and warmer. After several breaths, she stepped back toward the other two. "Dencer understands sorcery and its limits."

"All of those defenses are the kind that have an effect from afar, like Sargol's giant crossbow," added Hanfor.

"Isn't there a way to get around those?"

"From what I remember," mused Jecks, "the town is in a mountain valley, and the keep guards the roads to the valley. The main roads east and west enter the town right under the keep's walls."

"It all makes sense," Anna said. "He could swear allegiance to either Dumar or Ranuak."

"Not Ranuak," said the white-haired lord. "They

wouldn't have him. Ehara would. That was a Dumaran lancer Dencer was talking to.''

"So Ehara tries to gain Dencer's allegiance, and Sturinn supports Dumar." She shook her head and sat at the table, picking up the last of the bread. Had she eaten an entire loaf? She snorted, thinking that she probably should have eaten more.

"The Sea-Priests would add all Liedwahr to Sturinn's rule," said Jecks.

Hanfor nodded.

Not if I can help it. "The big pot?" Anna asked after swallowing a mouthful of the bread.

"To boil oil, and the stone pipes spray it out over the road that leads to the keep," said Jecks. "Stromwer is at the foot of the Sudbergs."

"We'll have to find a way around those defenses," Anna offered, "but that will wait until we deal with Gylaron."

"Will other sorcerers help him?" asked Hanfor.

In for a copper, in for a gold. Anna stood and retuned the lutar.

"Again?" asked Jecks.

"I'd like to see what other sorcerers are working on." Anna took a deep breath and strummed the strings, then tightened the bottom tuning peg, and restrummed.

> "Of those with power of the song
> seek those who'd do me wrong
> and show them in this silver cast
> and make that vision well last."

She studied the images in the glass. They were the same as the last time she'd used the spell—the blond seer from Nordwei, the hawk-faced Sea-Priest, and the young black-bearded man.

The Sea-Priest—if he were the same one—sat across a table from Ehara, his eyes bright even through the silver of the glass. The hatred that burned on the faces of both the Sea-Priest and the unknown young man still disturbed her. Were the Sea-Priests that fanatically against women in power?

The intense young man—he wore nondescript brown clothing, not the colors of a sorcerer and not the livery of any of the neighbors or enemies of Defalk. He stood in what seemed to be some type of storeroom. Yet her sorcery indicated that he had power and was an enemy. But who was he?

"Do you recognize the younger man?" She released the spell and replaced the lutar in its case.

"No."

"He wears a tradesman's browns," said Jecks.

She'd have to keep tabs on the unknown young man, but she was tired, and her spells indicated that he wasn't associated with any immediate danger. Still . . . she'd have to remember. Nonimmediate dangers left untended usually became immediate at the worst possible time.

"The Sea-Priest schemes with Ehara."

"Everyone schemes," Anna snorted.

Jecks cleared his throat, and Anna turned.

"Perhaps it will do no good, but would you not consider sending scrolls to Gylaron and Dencer suggesting that their defiance of the Regency is unwelcome and requesting their allegiance?"

"And their liedgeld?" Anna asked ironically. "It can't hurt, and I suppose it would set better with the other lords if at least I asked."

"That it would."

"You don't think they'll agree?"

"I would think not," said Jecks. "Yet, they had not heard of what befell Suhl." He shrugged. "There is a chance."

"Would you draft what you think we should say?"

"That . . . that I can do."

"Thank you. I should have thought of it." Anna turned to Hanfor. "How soon will your scouts have their reports on the roads?"

"By nightfall."

"Can we march on Gylaron by two days after tomorrow?"

"We could march the day after tomorrow, but two days would be better."

"Let's plan on it. Unless we get a total downpour." She paused. "Or Gylaron decides to return to the fold."

That got another blank expression from Jecks.

"Rejoin the Regency." Anna stood. "I'm going to check a few things around the keep."

Both men rose.

When she left the chamber, Fhurgen and Rickel stepped from their post at the door. Both marched behind her down the dim corridor.

She eased open the nursery door and stepped inside alone, as quietly as she could. Dinfan sat at a table with her back to the door, and the nurse sat on a stool looking at the girl.

". . . your ma, she was from Fussen. That be where your cousins struggle to see who will be lord." The nurse looked up, her eyes widening.

Anna shook her head, and motioned for the woman to continue.

"Ah . . . she be . . . the elder. . . ."

Dinfan turned, holding a chunk of bread. Her wide eyes fixed on Anna, those eyes so alike, and so unlike Irenia's. "Did you know my mother?"

"No, Lady Dinfan. I did not."

The nurse stood and bowed. "Regent."

"She called me lady, Bregha. She called me lady."

"You are the lady of Suhl," Anna said gravely.

"Indeed you be," added Bregha.

"Ma, she was lady of Suhl."

"She was, but she did not hold Suhl. If you study and learn, you will." Anna smiled faintly, turning to the nurse. "Does she know her letters?"

"Some."

"We will find someone to help with that. The Lady

Herene will be her guardian, and she can help her with her letters. It may be several weeks.''

The nurse bowed.

"Take care, Dinfan.'' Anna smiled.

Dinfan offered a faint smile in return.

As she left, Anna shook her head, ignoring Fhurgen's frown as he fell in behind her. Would every child always remind her of her own, blocked as she was from even using sorcery to see their images?

"Do you know where Liende might be, Fhurgen?''

"In her quarters on the second level, lady. Beyond the back stairs.''

Anna could hear the woodwind player's practice from well down the corridor. She rapped on the door, and the notes stopped.

The chief player opened the door, horn in hand.

"Lady Anna.'' Liende looked rested, more rested than Anna felt.

"Liende, you look more rested.''

"Several days' sleep has helped.'' A wry grimace crossed the older woman's face.

"That's good. Unfortunately, I have some work for you. I'd like you to keep the players working on those songs. I may have one more for you in a day or so.''

"Kaseth cannot play yet.''

"I understand. He collapsed. But you and the others can start, can't you?''

Liende nodded. "Kaseth, he has more experience, and he can learn more quickly.''

"There will be a gold bonus for each of the players for this past battle. Two for you. That's when we get back to Falcor.'' While they had found somewhere over fifteen hundred golds in Sargol's storeroom, the amount left after deducting the past due liedgeld would be less than a thousand, and most of that had to be left in Markan's care to run the holding. *Another reason why Sargol hadn't paid? Then why hadn't he asked for relief? Male pride? Damn male pride!* Anna swallowed, trying to get her thoughts back in line, and added, "We aren't carrying lots of golds with us."

"Your word is more than good, lady." Liende smiled. "All the players know that, and it will be better to have their golds safe."

"Good." Anna hoped they all felt that way, and still would after their ever-extended journey was over—if it ever ended. "We'll be leaving for Lerona three days from now. I don't know what we'll need. We may not have to fight . . . and we may."

"We know you will do what is necessary, and no more."

"Thank you." Anna smiled. "I'm glad you're here. I know it's hard on you to be away from Kinor and Alseta, but I appreciate it."

"I can return to them." Liende smiled sadly. "You have lost yours, and . . . I wish it were otherwise."

"So do I." Anna swallowed. "Thank you." After a moment, she turned and started toward the stables. She still had Farinelli to groom.

Anna had hoped not to have to use Liende in battle. That hadn't worked. She'd hoped not to have to kill off so many Defalkan armsmen. That hadn't worked. She'd hoped not to have to continually rely on sorcery . . . but pitched battles took armsmen and equipment she lacked . . . and so the list went.

48

That's her. . . ." hissed a young voice from the darkness beyond the stall where Anna saddled Farinelli. "The regent."

"Looks too pretty to be a regent."

"That's 'cause she uses sorcery. Bet without it, she'd be ugly."

Anna smiled, then called back toward the two unseen stable boys. "I look the way I am, boys."

Scurrying feet and the rustle of straw were the only answer.

Anna led Farinelli out of the stables, hoping that Markan could find a good stablemaster. She'd ended up mucking Farinelli's stall at Suhl because the big gelding hadn't let anyone else near, not that there had been many souls left in the keep after her magic.

Fhurgen waited outside, already mounted, his dark eyes flicking from side to side. Rickel stood guard on his mount a dozen yards across the courtyard, his eyes more toward the open gate.

Anna checked her four water bottles, the lutar case, and the leather pack that contained her spell glass, then swung easily into the saddle.

Farinelli whuffed once, and she patted his neck, glancing toward the stables as Jecks led out his mount. The white-haired lord was still muscular, if slightly stocky, and still handsome.

If only . . . If only what?

"Lady Anna?"

The sorceress turned toward the armsman approaching on foot. "Markan."

"Lady Anna . . . you know we would ride with you," Markan offered, his eyes momentarily traveling past Anna to the players and the armsmen mounted up along the length of the courtyard. Behind him, Fridric nodded.

"I know. But many can ride with me. I'm asking more of you, Markan. Much more. I'm entrusting you with the heir of Suhl, and with the lady Herene, once she arrives. You must keep them safe, and you must ensure that all here respect *and* love the Regency and the reign of Lord Jimbob to come. That's not easy." *Building things is much harder than destroying them.* That was becoming all too clear.

"I will do my best."

"I know. You need to find a lot of people . . . including a good stablemaster." Anna shook her head.

"I will take that on, lady," volunteered Fridric. "Until we find one. My father ran the stable in Aroch."

"Thank you." Anna smiled.

The smaller armsman flushed.

Hanfor rode back from the lower section of the courtyard. "Lady, all are ready."

"I'll be right there." She nodded to the arms commander, then turned to Markan. "I've told you what needs to be done. You have those lists. Don't hesitate to send a scroll to Herstat at Synfal or Dythya in Falcor if you need something."

"Yes, Lady Anna."

"Good." She turned Farinelli toward the gate, and Jecks eased his mount beside hers.

"He will find out how hard are those tasks you have laid for him," Jecks prophesied as they rode down the causeway in the hazy morning light to join Hanfor at the head of the column.

"We all find that out."

"A good armsman we could use, and the half-score you left with him and the wounded," murmured Rickel from behind Anna.

"We could," Anna admitted, leaning forward in the saddle and giving Farinelli a solid pat on the neck. "Taking Suhl, we lost a score, one way or another. Would you like to lose that many again? Or hundreds, without sorcery, if Suhl rebels again?"

Fhurgen, to the left of Anna, guffawed. "Winning battles, my friend Rickel, that is just the start. That's why we're armsmen. Be glad you are."

"The battles you don't have to fight, Rickel," Jecks added, "those are the ones that could save your life."

Anna could sense the young blond armsman's embarrassment, and she turned her head to him. "Rickel . . . it takes time. Even I thought about just winning battles, just getting through them." She laughed ruefully. "Sometimes I still do."

For how long?

She had no answer to that question. So she smiled as she rode to join Hanfor, Jecks beside her, and her guards flanking and trailing them. Hanfor raised a hand in salute, and she returned the gesture, trying not to sneeze as the dust tickled her nose.

Across the valley, past the raw earth of the mass graves that held most of those who had served Sargol, lay the road to Lerona.

49

STROMWER, DEFALK

The bitch avoided Sargol's traps—all of them. And her archers—they turned his armsmen into targets." Dencer shakes his head, and the brown-and-gray hair flops onto his too-high forehead.

"One attacks a sorceress most safely from afar." The officer in crimson, standing before the wide table, bows his head slightly. "As you have prepared to do, Lord Dencer."

"Oh, spare me the compliments, Captain Gortin." The lanky lord bobs his head. "Your master sent two companies of lancers to aid Lord Sargol, and she destroyed them with a few words of song and then turned his keep into a flaming abattoir."

"Yes, she did that." Gortin's words are neutral.

"Well . . . Captain Gortin? What will you do? She is riding south to Gylaron's keep." Dencer pushes back the chair and stands, like a predatory heron, jaw forward, beady eyes on the lancer.

"Let Gylaron face her. She lost some-score men at

Suhl. She will lose more at Lerona." Gortin smiles easily. "Then we will see."

"Will you send for more lancers?" Dencer lurches around the writing table and steps to the bookcase, where he extracts a small leather volume.

"They could not reach Stromwer before the sorceress," says Gortin.

"So they could not. And what am I to do? Throw myself on her mercy? Die so that my ungrateful consort shall hold my patrimony?" Dencer smiles bitterly. "Where is Dumar's friendship now?"

"I am here, Lord Dencer. So are my lancers. We stand with you."

"Stand with me. . . . Ah, that sounds so reassuring." The tall lord lifts the leatherbound volume. "Here. Tactics against sorcery. From Pelletara. 'Do not allow a sorcerer close to your men. If possible, fight any battles in rain or snow, preferably in a heavy thunderstorm.' " Dencer looks at Gortin. "Perhaps your master can bring us a thunderstorm."

"Thunderstorms are possible here in the Sudbergs." Gortin shrugs. "I question whether the sorceress would choose to attack in one. Or whether we could find one at the right glass to cover any movement we might make."

"For a representative of a mighty power, you offer little comfort."

"I am here to fight, Lord Dencer."

"Fight you will." Dencer closes the book with a snap. "You may go."

"Thank you, Lord Dencer." Gortin nods and turns.

50

S couts report a wagon ahead, sir,'' the messenger puffed to Hanfor, turning his mount to ride beside the arms commander.

"A wagon?" The veteran's eyebrows lifted.

"Just a wagon. Three people in it. Two horses. Nice matched grays, sir. It be a fancy wagon, with brass trim."

Anna and Jecks listened. Anna blotted her forehead with a gray cloth that was reddish brown with road dust turned to mud by continual sweat under the hot late-spring sun. A line of puffy clouds dotted the southern horizon, but seemed no closer than they had at daybreak.

"And, ser, there be some armsmen, three, four deks south of the wagon. They are not riding anywhere."

Hanfor turned to Anna. "Your wish, lady?"

"Let me see what I can see."

As Hanfor called out orders, and the column slowed to a halt, and dust boiled around her, Anna dismounted, handing Farinelli's reins to Rickel. She unstrapped the mirror pack and then the lutar. She walked away from the column, forward along the road shoulder until she was out of the dust. The mirror went on the scraggly grass, uncovered, and she took the lutar from its battered brown case and began to tune it.

Rickel and Fhurgen followed, mounted, with Farinelli. The gelding *whuff*ed and sidestepped as the two guards reined up.

Jecks and Hanfor arrived, walking their mounts and standing back from Anna and the mirror.

It took three vocalises to get her cords clear. By then

Farinelli had settled down, and a dull muted buzz—the murmurs of waiting armsmen—filled the midday heat.

Anna cleared her throat a last time, then sang.

> "Show from the south, danger to fear,
>   all the threats to me bright and clear . . ."

The glass showed Dencer's keep, nothing more.

She tried again, using Gylaron's name, and the mirror remained silver.

"The harmonies say Gylaron offers no danger?" hazarded Jecks. "Even with armsmen?"

"That would be my guess," Anna answered. "There's nothing close here. Nothing from Gylaron, either." She replaced the lutar in its case, then wrapped the mirror and strapped both in place on Farinelli. Then she remounted.

"Let us approach carefully, with arms ready," suggested Hanfor. "Your guards before you."

Anna nodded, and Fhurgen and Rickel rode to the fore. She coughed at the dust, and wiped more of the muddy film from her forehead. Then she had a long swallow from her second water bottle, almost empty.

They rode another dek.

Ahead, in the middle of the road, in a flat section deks from woods or hills, with just bean plants nearby, there stood a wagon. A solid man in maroon velvet, with a leather belt bearing an empty scabbard, sat on the wagon seat, open hands resting on his knees, palms up. His swarthy face was slightly sunburned. With him were a boy and a girl, neither older than ten, Anna judged.

On the wagon bed were two chests. Each was open, and from each glimmered gold coins.

On a low hill to the south were dark spots, mounts and armsmen, as the scout had said, a good three deks away. Anna tried to see more detail, but could only catch an occasional glint of sun on metal.

"All that gold, and no guards?" murmured Rickel from behind Anna.

"Who needs guards? There's us here, and the Leronese at the hilltop. You want to try to make off with any of it?" asked Fhurgen.

Beside Anna, Jecks grinned.

The sorceress again looked past the wagon. The hill in the distance, and the armsmen on it, seemed the same. Gylaron's armsmen, they had to be.

Rickel and Fhurgen moved directly before her, their blades drawn. All stopped a good thirty yards from the wagon.

"Lady Anna?" called the man on the wagon seat.

"Yes," answered Anna cautiously.

"I am Gylaron. These are my two oldest. In the chests is all the coin that I have. All the golds of Lerona."

Anna shivered inside, fearing what might come, and not knowing exactly why.

"I have received your scroll, but know you that I had made the decision to come to you before it arrived." Gylaron coughed and continued. "Do what you will with me. Do what you will to my heirs. Hand over my lands to another. All I ask is that you not visit the fires of dissonance upon my people." Gylaron's eyes were bleak, but his voice was firm. "Do not do to Lerona what you did to the keep of Sargol."

"Why should I trust you?" Anna asked, even as she fumbled to extract the lutar from its case. "You have all your armsmen on the hill there."

"They are there to keep anyone from stealing the golds, no more."

Anna believed him, believed the bleakness and desperation in his voice. "Will you swear allegiance to the Regency and to Lord Jimbob?"

"I will swear aught to save my people and my consort."

Anna fumbled with the tuning pegs, then managed to clear her throat. Her voice cracked with phlegm on the first note. She broke off, coughed it clear, and began again.

"Gylaron wrong, Gylaron strong,
  loyal be from this song.
  Gylaron now, Gylaron old,
  faithful be till dead and cold.'

"Your heirs of lord, daughter and son,
  holders of lands, this be done.
  Treachery prevent to all Defalkan lands
  with your cunning and your hands."

All three figures on the wagon seemed shrouded in silver for a brief flash. All shivered.

Anna shuddered herself as a knife slashed through her skull, leaving a dull and throbbing ache—and double images. *Shit! One little loyalty spell and you can't see or think very well. You can destroy a whole keep and you can't ask for loyalty?*

"Lady Anna?" Jecks' voice was low, concerned.

"I'll be all right." She forced herself erect in the saddle, then nodded to Fhurgen. The guard let Farinelli carry her closer to the wagon. Both guards flanked her, their blades out, as she rode toward Gylaron. Jecks rode on the right of Fhurgen, and his blade was also bare.

"Lord Gylaron."

"Lady Anna, I swear allegiance, by the harmonies, and upon the heads—"

"No!" snapped Anna. "Not upon your children. Upon anything else, but not upon them." She found herself, shaking, wondering about her reaction, wondering how she'd known what his words would have been. Her headache throbbed more momentarily, and she blinked, but the double image remained.

Gylaron's eyes widened. So did those of the children.

"I . . . swear allegiance, by the harmonies, by my sire's honor and spirit, to you, the regent, the Regency of Defalk, and to Lord Jimbob, heir of the realm." Gylaron swallowed.

"Thank you." Anna took a slow breath, forced her

voice to be firm. "I'm . . . sorry, Lord Gylaron. I can't explain, but your children must declare their allegiance, and I don't want your loyalty on their heads." She turned her gaze to the boy, who seemed older. "You are?"

"I'm Gylan. I'm nine."

"Will you swear to be loyal to the Regency, Lord Jimbob, and the Realm of Defalk?"

"Yes, Lady Anna. I swear . . . allegiance." Gylan's voice stumbled over the last word. "You won't kill us?"

"I have no intention of killing anyone who is loyal. There's been too much killing." Her eyes went to the child's father. "I will not hesitate to kill those who are disloyal." Then she looked at the girl, whose black hair was so dark that it nearly shimmered blue-black in the sun. "What's your name?"

"I'm Reylana. I'll be eight at the season-turn."

"Will you swear allegiance? That you will be loyal to me and to Lord Jimbob?"

"Da says I'm to do as you say."

Anna swallowed. "Promise me that you will be good and that you will be loyal."

"I always try to be good. I'll be loyal." Reylana paused. "Can we go home? I'm hot."

"I think that might be a good idea. In a moment," Anna said, stifling a smile, before turning her eyes back to Gylaron and the chests. "You will send this year's liedgeld and last year's to Falcor to Counselor Dythya. Save the rest for your needs and your people."

Gylaron went to his knees, if casting a wary look at all the armsmen.

"No, my lord. That is not all," Anna forced her voice to be hard. "You will assemble all your armsmen, all those on the hill to the south, and all those in your keep. You assemble them without arms, and they also will swear loyalty to me and to Lord Jimbob. If *one* lifts his hand, all will suffer, and you will die. If they swear, then I will leave Lerona in peace, except for your obligations for levies and liedgeld, and those other duties of a lord of the Thirty-three.'' She hoped she'd included everything, and her eyes flicked to Jecks.

The white-haired lord nodded almost imperceptibly.

"You would leave us in peace, after what . . . after Suhl . . . ?'' Gylaron's tone was openly disbelieving.

"Lord Gylaron,'' Anna snapped. "If you learn nothing else, learn that I keep my word, for better or worse. Sargol tried to kill me when I was on my way to Synope, not even on the road to Suhl. He refused to pay his liedgeld, and he laid traps along every road to his keep. What would you have done?''

Gylaron lowered his eyes.

Anna had another thought. "I may ask for the use of a fewscore of your armsmen . . . in service of the Regency. I will pay them.''

Despite the double vision, she could see Hanfor nod.

"Anything you wish, lady and regent.''

Anna nodded.

51

"You'll let him go ahead of us?'' Jecks had asked.

"The children will stay with us,'' Anna had answered. "With the loyalty spell and them, I'm sure Gylaron will arrange matters just as I requested.'' She hadn't been totally sure, but nothing was absolute. She'd learned that a long time before.

They had reached the keep without incident, and Hanfor and Alvar had ensured a clear and safe route to the wall overlooking the keep's courtyard. Anna knew she didn't look all that prepossessing, not in faded green shirt and riding trousers and a battered brown hat. She had donned the spare purple tunic with gold trim.

Gylaron bowed as Anna's group, surrounded by Fhurgen and the other guards, their blades out, crossed the open space toward the inner battlement. Behind came Liende and the players, their instruments still in cases. Yuarl studied the old walls in wonder. Palian shook her head slowly. The young violinist Delvor just shuffled along. Duralt, the cocky-appearing falk-hornist, strutted behind Liende. Below, packed in the courtyard, stood the armsmen and servants and staff and everyone else, it seemed.

"I told them that you had a message for us, and that we had reached an agreement that would not require a battle, and that I had agreed to swear allegiance to the Regency." Gylaron's swarthy mouth crinkled. "I did not reveal any more details. That was not difficult, since you provided none." He inclined his head to the woman beside him, the one with the heart-shaped face Anna had seen in the glass. "Lady Anna, might I present my consort Reylan?"

"You are as beautiful as your image," Anna said. "I'm glad to meet you."

"Why did you spare us?" asked Reylan. Her olive skin, flawless complexion, red lips, and black hair made her a beauty. "What trickery do you plan?"

Flanking Anna, Fhurgen shifted his weight, easing toward the woman.

"I plan none, except to ensure the loyalty of Lerona. A regent deserves that."

"Why? What business is this of yours?"

Anna wanted to shake her head. Instead she took a deep breath. "Why is it so hard to understand? Defalk is threatened on all sides—"

"Defalk has always been threatened on all sides."

"The Sea-Priests of Sturinn have cast their lot with Dumar," Jecks interjected, "and Konsstin will be moving his lancers into Neserea."

"They are all gathered, lady," announced Hanfor. "Best you not wait."

"We'll talk more later." Anna gestured to Lord Gylaron. "Join me." Anna's steps were deliberate, trying to compensate for the double vision that remained from the loyalty spell, as she stepped toward the wall overlooking the courtyard.

Gylaron paused, then stepped with Anna to the edge of the inner battlement. Beside her stood Fhurgen and Rickel, each bearing a mid-sized shield, gathered from somewhere, each scanning the crowd in the courtyard below.

Gylaron's appearance, more than Anna's, quieted the murmurs.

Anna began to speak, trying to concentrate, to ignore the continuing double vision. "You have a wise and thoughtful lord. He has pledged support to the Regency, and to Lord Jimbob. Lord Sargol and his armsmen rebelled. They are all dead. Lord Arkad rebelled, but his people did not. Lord Arkad is dead, and his people live." Anna turned to Gylaron. "The Regency supports and confirms you, Lord Gylaron."

With the last words, Anna stepped back, leaving Gylaron standing alone. A sighing crossed the courtyard, and Anna could hear a few scattered voices.

"The regent has been fair—and more generous than any could expect. Honor her." Gylaron turned and gestured to Anna.

Fhurgen released an audible sigh.

Anna stepped forward.

If the cries of "Honor the regent!" and "Long live the regent!" were not overwhelming, they were at least suitable, and Anna stepped back before they died away. So did Gylaron.

Rickel sheathed the blade he had held ready behind Gylaron.

"I am relieved you did not have to use that." The swarthy lord took a long breath, then looked at Anna. "It is better this way."

"I'd hoped so," Anna answered. "It's better than a battle, isn't it?"

Rickel nodded solemnly.

"That it is."

"What else have you concealed?" asked Reylan.

"Not nearly as much as you think," Anna responded politely. "I don't work that way."

Gylaron glared at Reylan and extended an arm. "Might we offer you the hospitality of Lerona?"

Anna glanced toward Hanfor.

"And you, also, Arms Commander."

"There is much to do, yet," demurred Hanfor. "I would that I could join you, but you will do well indeed with Lady Anna and Lord Jecks. I am but a poor armsman."

"Scarcely." Anna grinned. "He has made it possible for Defalk to survive, yet he would take no credit."

"Nor will I," answered Hanfor. "Not until all Defalk is strong and united. Then, I will praise you for changing the world, and I will take my leave for a quiet hill retreat." A wry smile followed. "By then, I will be old enough to enjoy it."

"If you finish your duties, Arms Commander, please join us."

"Thank you." Hanfor nodded, then turned.

"My players will need refreshment," Anna said.

"Your arms commander had said such," Gylaron answered. "They will eat in the hall next to us, if that is agreeable."

"That's fine." Anna nodded and stepped back to Liende. "If you follow us, they've set up a meal for all of you in the hall next to us." Her voice lowered slightly. "The atmosphere might be more cordial there."

"You risk much," Liende said.

"I hope not." Anna shrugged. "I'm doing the best I can."

The regent followed Gylaron and his consort to the stairs, her own guards seemingly everywhere. Jecks, hand on the hilt of his blade, walked beside her. The small dining hall was down a single flight of brick stairs and fifty yards along a vaulted corridor, lit by intermittently spaced candles set in wall sconces and protected by smudged glass mantels.

The players, led by a page or fosterling of some sort in faded maroon, followed, Kaseth almost beside Liende.

Rickel stationed himself and two others at the door to the small dining hall. Fhurgen followed Anna inside. The rectangular table was set for five, one place at the head, and two on each side. The linens were maroon, and the goblets crystal.

Gylaron gestured toward the head of the table. "Regent Anna."

"Thank you. We appreciate the effort and the hospitality."

"Would I be too blunt if I said that we appreciate your forbearance and our lives?" Gylaron's tone was light, but the dark eyes were somber.

"Honest, I'd say," Anna said as she sat. Fhurgen slipped behind her and stood before the arras at the wall to her back.

"Our lady the regent is very direct," Jecks added. "Sometimes, distressingly so. She is not from Liedwahr, and views matters with a different eye, almost always for the best." He laughed. "It has not always seemed that way at first."

"Ah . . . yes . . ." murmured Gylaron, with a sideways glance at Reylan.

After a moment of silence that seemed endless, Anna glanced at the pitcher before her. "Is that wine?"

"It is. It is our best, but poor compared to those from the hills of Sudwei and Stromwer." Gylaron smiled apologetically.

"I suspect it is far better than what comes from my lands."

"I thought . . ." Gylaron's eyebrows rose. Then he closed his mouth.

Anna shook her head. "With the death of Lord Brill, I

inherited the lands of Mencha, dry and to the east near the Sand Pass. I am also, I have discovered, the Lady of Loiseau, and like you, Lord Gylaron, I find I must pay liedgeld to the Regency.'' She smiled wryly. "The domains of Falcor and Cheor belong to Lord Jimbob. I was referring to the vinegar from Mencha, not anything from anywhere else.'' Anna smiled inside. At least, she'd gotten that part right.

"Lord Brill had no heirs?'' asked Reylan.

"No. And no consort.'' Anna poured some of the wine and passed the pitcher to Reylan.

"And you?'' The dark-haired woman poured wine for herself and for Jecks.

"My children remain on earth—the mist world.'' Anna had to struggle not to squint against the continuing double vision, although the headache had subsided to a dull and muted throbbing.

Gylaron and Reylan exchanged glances.

"Haven't you heard?'' Anna asked. "I thought everyone knew. I have children nearly as old as you, Lady Reylan. . . .'' She quickly ran through the story of how she had come to Erde and ended up as regent. "So . . . I have no heirs, and Loiseau will probably go to the next good sorcerer who supports Defalk.'' She laughed softly. "It almost seems fated that way.''

"The harmonies,'' mused Gylaron.

"So it has seemed,'' added Jecks.

A serving girl brought in a large maroon platter, setting it before Anna. Another brought two baskets of still-steaming bread. Anna glanced at the meat and the sauce. Poison? Everyone was eating the same thing. All she had to do was wait for the others. Besides, the glass hadn't shown treachery, and it had been far more accurate than anything else. *Is this what it will always be like? Wondering? Becoming more and more paranoid?* She forced a smile and took a healthy serving of the meat and the white sauce, then passed the platter to Reylan. The dark bread looked and smelled good, and she broke off a chunk.

Everyone looked at her. Hoping she wasn't too paranoid, she took a bite of the bread, then a sniff, and a sip of the wine—easily the best she had tasted in Liedwahr. "This is the best I've tasted in Defalk."

Gylaron smiled at the enthusiasm in her voice. Even Reylan did, momentarily.

"Nuural will be pleased."

"Not as pleased as I am," Anna answered, taking another sip.

For a time, the four ate, quietly. Anna was amazed, again, at how hungry she was, and how much she ate. *You should be getting used to this.* But would she ever?

"You seem reasonable," ventured Reylan. "Why . . . why . . . Sargol?"

Anna frowned. "Sargol sent his armsmen to ambush me when I was traveling to Synope. I wasn't even going to Suhl. He didn't pay his liedgeld, and he brought in two companies of Dumaran lancers—or they came for some reason."

"Lady Anna suffered two severe wounds from crossbow quarrels," Jecks said quietly. "The scars are there still, I would imagine." He inclined his head to her.

Anna pushed back the sleeve of the green linen shirt. A jagged red scar ran along her forearm. "The other is . . . less . . . accessible." Anna flushed.

"The bolt was enchanted and went through her breastplate," Jecks explained.

"When someone goes out of his way to attack you, and doesn't pay liedgeld, and brings in foreign armsmen . . ." The sorceress shrugged. "Then he locked himself in his keep and wouldn't even talk. I offered terms." *Not exactly the best terms,* she reminded herself.

Once again, Gylaron and Reylan exchanged glances.

"Talk to her armsmen, any of them," Jecks said mildly, breaking off a chunk of bread.

"Ah . . . I could not," Gylaron demurred. His eyes

went to Fhurgen, then to the doorway where the blond and broad-shouldered Rickel stood. Then the Lord of Lerona looked at his wine again.

"Perhaps later," Jecks suggested. "At your leisure."

"You would change Defalk," Gylaron continued, abruptly as if to change the subject. "Or so Sargol said. Yet you affirm Lord Jimbob."

"Defalk will change, even if I died today," Anna pointed out. "The only question is whether the people of Defalk benefit or suffer with change."

"You did not mention the lords."

"No. I didn't. Those lords who understand that times must change and help with that will benefit. The others . . ."

"Will suffer?"

Anna nodded, then added, "Because Defalk must change to survive."

Gylaron nodded thoughtfully.

"Might I ask what will become of Lord Sargol's lands?" asked Reylan, a tremor in her voice.

"I have confirmed that his oldest child is the heir. The former chief armsman of Flossbend is running the lands for her for now until she is older. The lady Herene—she is the sister of Lord Nelmor and Lady Gatrune of Pamr—she is coming to serve as guardian for the children." *I hope.*

"His daughter is the oldest?"

"Yes. She's the oldest."

Reylan smiled. "Some lords will not approve."

"I'm sure they won't, but Defalk can't afford to waste its women." Anna took another sip of wine.

"You stood before my people. Were you not afraid someone would attack?" asked Gylaron.

"I worried about it," Anna admitted, squinting and trying to decide which image before her was the real one of Gylaron. *Damned double vision. . . .*

"I would not have stood as a stranger before such," offered Reylan.

"She has stood before the Dark Monks, before assassins, before the Prophet of Music, before Sargol's archers . . . before many," said Jecks.

Gylaron shook his head. "You look young, but your words are not. Nor your actions. Sargol was right to fear you." He smiled sadly. "What would you have with me?"

"I told you. Do your duty to the regency and meet your obligations as a lord of the Thirty-three." *Is that so hard to understand?*

"I fear I do not understand." Gylaron pulled at his chin. "Surely . . . no lord of reason would dispute such a call . . . and yet many—or some . . ."

Anna felt like exploding. *Here we go again . . . "There must be some mistake, Lady Anna . . . you must have done something wrong . . . Why, no reasonable man would ever rebel if you had been logical and reasonable. . . ."*

She slowly unclenched her jaw. "Lord Gylaron, there has never been anything hard about what I asked. I haven't asked anything special of you or other lords. I haven't asked anything that other lords haven't demanded before I ever came to Defalk."

Gylaron looked down, with that blank male look of incomprehension, combined with fear—fear that she was an unreasonable and illogical woman who would explode on the spot.

And she felt like exploding, which would do no good whatsoever. She swallowed another sip of wine, then stood. "I am sorry. For some reason, I feel rather . . . unsettled. I beg your leave." She forced a bright smile, one she scarcely felt. "If you will excuse me. . . . Perhaps Lord Jecks can answer your questions better than I can right now."

Fhurgen followed her out.

"You were kind," the guard said once they were in the corridor.

"I can't afford to lose my temper at every pigheaded lord in Defalk," Anna said bleakly, taking careful steps to ensure her balance against the inaccuracies of double sight and the distraction of her pounding headache. "There aren't enough people who know anything as it is."

For a moment, she stood in the dim corridor. Now what?

A page bowed. "Lady Anna, regent and sorceress? Would you like to go to the guest quarters?"

"Yes, thank you." *Why not? Maybe Jecks can smooth things over.*

52

Sitting on a straight-backed chair before the writing table in the guest chamber and leaning forward, Anna massaged her forehead. Her eyes were closed, shutting out the strange double images—hot and cold. *The harmonious and disharmonious sides of life?* She should have eaten more, and held her temper better. But she was *so* tired of men who either didn't understand or pretended not to understand. Or, when confronted, immediately suggested that the misunderstanding had to have been her fault. Was she oversensitive? Probably.

She looked up at the knock on the door to the guest chamber.

"Lady Anna," announced Fhurgen, "Lord Gylaron to see you."

Anna stood warily, trying not to blink as the dark-skinned lord stepped into the room. Fhurgen followed, his blade unsheathed.

"I offer my apologies, Lady Anna." Gylaron bowed, deeply. "I fear there have been many false tales traveling Defalk."

"I don't doubt that." Anna paused. Jecks had clearly smoothed things over. What could she say? "Sometimes . . . truth is harder to swallow than false tales, and my strangeness . . . the fact that I don't know Defalk as well as you do . . . that can lead to misunderstandings."

"Lord Jecks explained. I did not know how many arrows you have taken for Defalk and those you lead." The swarthy lord shook his head. "You are not as you look."

"Lord Gylaron, I am much older. I didn't look for what happened to me." She paused, gauging his expression. "I have no heirs here on Erde. I never will."

"He told me that as well. That clears another fog." His face wrinkled. "Yet . . . why would you not add my domains to Lord Jimbob's?"

"Lord Jimbob will need more than Falcor to raise the coins a leader of Defalk must have. He shouldn't ever have more than that, but especially not as young as he is. Too much power corrupts."

"You would judge that?"

"Is there anyone else who can?" Anna asked bluntly. "I can't pass anything on. I have no ties to anyone. I could be wrong, but I saw how Lord Barjim couldn't raise the coins or armsmen necessary to save Defalk. I also saw how Lord Behlem squandered golds. I think a ruler should be somewhere between." She smiled. "What do you think?"

"I think . . . Lady Anna, that I am fortunate to retain my head and my lands. I will not trouble you more."

"Lord Gylaron . . ." Anna tilted her head slightly, wondering if that would be too flirtatious even as she did. "I will always be here to answer honest questions. I will do my best to preserve Defalk. I make mistakes. Even sorceresses do. If you have a question, if you have a concern, I will answer. I may not always agree, but I will answer."

"Lord Jecks told me how you spent golds to gain seed corn for the south. I would that I had known."

That, and Gylaron's opening words, were all the apology she would ever get, but they were enough. "When you have pressing needs, let me know."

"I thank you, lady. And Reylan would thank you as well, were she here." Gylaron smiled. "We would see you at the evening meal."

"I will be there," Anna promised.

After Gylaron had left, Anna walked to the window. She didn't wait long before Jecks arrived.

"How did you manage that?" Anna asked warily.

"I did what Rickel suggested. I had him put on arms-man's greens. Rickel took him around. He talked to arms-men. Anyone and anywhere he wanted. Then he came back and we talked some more." Jecks smiled, and his eyes twinkled.

"So he doesn't believe I'm the bitch from dissonance any longer?" Anna walked toward Jecks, seeing the lines around the eyes, the fatigue.

"He has . . . a healthy . . . respect for you," Jecks answered.

"Like Birfels? He respects me, but can't stand what I'm doing."

"Gylaron is distressed that his world will be changed. I did persuade him, as did his consort, that his situation is far better than it would have been under anyone else, including Lord Ehara or the Liedfuhr of Mansuur. Or the Evult."

"I'm so flattered." Anna snorted.

"Lady Anna . . . nothing had changed in Defalk for generations. Then came the drought, and the Evult. Every-one expected that, once the rains returned, so would the good days of the past."

"They weren't that good," muttered Anna.

"That matters not. For the lords, they think those days were good."

"So they're upset now?"

"Not all. Some see beyond their noses and fields." Jecks smiled. "Those like Clethner who live with their backs to Nordwei, or Nelmor, who sees the sun set over Neserea.''

"I don't know. I'm not a very good politician. The older I get, the harder it gets to smile and pretend to be a good little girl. To pretend that it's all my fault that they don't understand. To pretend that I didn't make it perfectly clear when I spelled it out in words a five-year-old should understand.'' Anna walked back to the window and looked down at the courtyard, where several score of her armsmen stood or sat under the shade of overhanging battlements. "I never was that good.''

"Give them time. Like Gylaron, they will see that all you bode for Defalk is good.''

"Do I? Really? I wonder.'' She turned again. "You're tired, and what I did didn't help. Can you get some rest before supper, or dinner, or whatever?''

"Supper, here in the south,'' Jecks said.

"Will you get some rest?'' she asked again.

"I will have some food sent to you,'' Jecks said. "You did not eat.''

"I couldn't.'' She met his eyes. "Please take care of yourself and get some rest.''

"As my lady commands.''

"I don't command you,'' Anna said with a smile. "I doubt anyone's ever commanded you.''

"Not until now, lady.'' Jecks bowed.

"You're impossible.''

"Just ancient.''

"You're not that, either. Now go get some rest, and let a poor sorceress think about how she can avoid swallowing her boots again.''

Jecks bowed once more, and Anna shook her head, ruefully, as Jecks departed, graceful, muscular, and far more understanding than most of his peers. *Most? How about all of them?*

53

MANSUUS, MANSUUR

Rain rattles against the shutters of the large study, and a warm mist seeps in from the darkness outside and around the louvers. Konsstin paces back and forth in front of the wide desk table piled with scrolls, lit with a five-branched candelabra.

Thrap. The knock on the door is diffident, almost timid. "Yes?"

The door opens, and Bassil peers in. "You sent for me, sire?"

Konsstin gestures broadly, his arm passing so close to the candelabra that the flames flicker, twisting the vague shadows that fall on the paneled walls and the bookcases.

The door closes, and Bassil enters, straightens his maroon tunic, and pushes his dark hair back.

"So I woke you?"

"No, sire. I was reading over the dispatches . . ."

"What reports from Defalk?" asks Konsstin cheerily.

"Your seers are overworked." Bassil bows, briefly. "The sorceress has subdued all but Stromwer."

"I suppose she turned them all into abattoirs, or ash heaps." Konsstin forces a laugh.

"One abattoir, sire. That was Suhl. She did save the heirs and established some arrangement for them to keep the holding."

"Clever. They can exert no power for years, and by then it won't matter. Darkness, the woman's devious. Worse than Cyndyth or Kandeth."

"Worse, sire, perhaps. She is not devious. All the seers and all the dispatches report she is most direct. To date, she has always kept her word.'' Bassil licks his lips in the dimness.

"Direct? That is even more devious. She keeps her word, but when will she break it? She does what she says, no matter how difficult. That makes it even easier, for who will oppose her, knowing she is a powerful sorceress and will not be turned? Dissonance, Bassil! If that's not devious, I don't know the meaning of the word.''

"Do you wish me to ready those scrolls I prepared for you weeks ago?''

"Not yet. Not yet. Stromwer is a fortified mountain hold. Let us see how she does against the devious Dencer, with all his aid from Ehara.''

"You hope she wins there?''

"I must hope that, dissonance take them all.'' Konsstin waves an arm generally westward, beyond the closed shutters and night-darkened balcony. "I have no love of the Sea-Priests. I'd hope they all go down—or up—in discord.''

"Do you believe this sorceress will defeat them all?''

"She will take Dencer. None but a fool would gainsay that. Whether she will turn his hold into an ashpit or find some way to preserve it is the sole doubt.'' His fingers touch the silvering brown beard. "She is clever. Too clever by far, and should she gain another hold—''

"Gain another hold?'' blurts Bassil. "She has gained none. Synfal went to the heir. . . .'' He shuts his mouth as Konsstin turns.

. "Bassil. At times you think. Tonight, you are tired. You must be tired. Do you not understand? Lady Gatrune holds her consort's lands; so does Lady Anientta. Administrators or saalmeisters of the sorceress's choosing hold Synfal and Suhl. She has bound Gylaron in some sorcerous fashion, and she will do some-such similar to Dencer. Lord Jecks will do as she wishes, as will Geansor and Birfels, for she holds their heirs, and those heirs of several other holdings as well. The lords Clethner and Vyarl are beholden to Jecks, and Lord Tybel will not cross the sorceress so long as his daughter Anientta administers the lands of Synope. Then, the sorceress holds Loiseau in her own name. Dissonance! Do you not see? How many holds is that?''

Bassil's brow lifts as he calculates. ''Just thirteen or fourteen. Out of thirty-three.''

''Bassil,'' Konsstin says gently. ''Bassil . . . Lord Barjim could count on five holds, at best. Lord Donjim controlled ten. This . . . usurper . . . she has a greater rein on Defalk than any ruler in generations. And she is a sorceress.''

Bassil swallows. ''I am tired.''

''Not too tired, I hope, to understand what I have told you?''

''No, sire. I had not thought of it in quite that fashion.''

''Best we always think of power in that fashion.'' The Liedfuhr gestures toward the door. ''Get some sleep. We will talk tomorrow.''

Bassil bows.

Outside, the warm rain splats against the shutters. Inside, the candles flicker as the Liedfuhr paces.

54

Aware of the sweat beading on her forehead, Anna ignored it and studied the image in the glass again. At her shoulder, Hanfor continued to sketch. Jecks stood to Anna's left, also surveying the view in the hazy silvered glass.

Dencer's keep—a square assembly of gray stones—stood on a rise at the middle of a narrow valley that resembled a T. Behind and to the south of the keep was a small town. Mountains terminating their lower slopes in high cliffs flanked the keep on the east and west, cliffs less than a dek from the keep's side walls.

Dencer or some previous Lord of Stromwer had cut away the slope both in front and in back of the keep, replacing it with two polished stone walls that glistened like shining water even through the glass. On top of those stone-tiled earthworks were walls, easily four yards high, so that the total smooth face was easily fifty yards in height from the cut base of the hill on both north and south to the top of the wall that stretched from cliff to keep and then from the far side of the keep to the other cliff.

A single stone road ran the length of the valley—from the north southward and up an inclined ramp through the hill cut to a fortified gate at the crest of the modified hill and then around the walls of the keep itself on the east side and then through another gate, and down the second stone tiled berm and to the town. The space on the rise on either side of the keep had been kept cleared and in pasture, and the buildings of the town did not begin until almost a half-dek to the south of the keep, well south of the southern stone berm.

On the southernmost end of the valley was the east-west road, running along a stream that seemed to flow downhill from the west. Anna frowned. She would have thought the keep would have been at the south end of the valley to protect the town.

"The road to the west winds up into the Sudbergs and travels to Dumar," noted Jecks.

"And I suppose the one of the west goes to Ranuak?" Anna rubbed her eyes, glad that the double-imaging from her last foray into Darksong had finally disappeared.

"To the port of Sylwa."

Farther to the north the valley constricted into a gorge, the same narrow defile that Anna's earlier scrying had revealed as the site of Dencer's other precautions—netted rocks and boiling oil.

The mirror frame began to smoke, and Anna released

the image with one of the release couplets she'd developed.

"Let this scene of scrying, mirror filled with light,
   vanish like the darkness when the sun is bright . . ."

Her eyes flicked away from the burned square on the wall beside the mirror that represented the firing of the first mirror in the chamber when she hadn't released the spell quickly enough.

After a moment she walked to the narrow window of the guest chamber and let the warm wind blow around her, cooling the perspiration that long scrying efforts seemed to bring.

"The keep has three layers of defense," observed Hanfor. "None of the others in Defalk have such."

"Once it was needed," said Jecks. "The Suhlmorrans wanted Stromwer. So did the ancient Matriarchs, and so did Lord Ehara's ancestors."

"And none of them got it, I assume?" asked Anna.

"No. Uhlan the elder lost an entire army trying to annex it to Suhlmorra."

"Why?" She turned from the window, her eyes on the rosewood antique high bed that had given her a headache to spell for vermin.

"Now, with the fast ships, it makes less difference. Still, Stromwer stands on the shortest land routes between Dumaria and Sylwa and Encora, and between all of southern Defalk and Dumar."

"What about Sudwei?" Anna pursued. "I thought Geansor held the access to the South Pass."

"He does, and that is an easier route from the east and middle of Defalk, but the easiest way to transport goods to Dumar was to use the Falche down to north of Abenfel, and then take the roads through Stromwer."

Anna tried to summon up her mental map of Liedwahr, concentrating. Finally, she nodded. Her eyes went to Hanfor. "Any ideas of how we can get close to the keep?"

"The road is the only entrance to the keep," Hanfor said tiredly. "Unless one travels through Ranuak or Dumar."

"We cannot approach within deks of the walls," added Jecks. "Not unless we wish to be bathed in oil and buried under boulders."

Both men looked at Anna, as if she were supposed to find a solution.

I'm not the military type. I'm a singer, for heaven's sake. Anna stepped past the low chest at the end of the bed, where the lutar rested, and looked down at the table, at the map Hanfor had sketched from session after session with the glass.

"I don't want to turn Stromwer into another flaming mass." *Why not? You did that to Vult, and Suhl wasn't much better.* "That's why," she muttered to herself. As she saw the puzzled expressions on the faces of Jecks and Hanfor, she added hurriedly. "Talking to myself. . . ."

Her throat was dry, and she refilled the goblet with orderspelled water, taking a long swallow. "Would you like some?"

"No, thank you."

Jecks shook his head.

Anna glanced at the map on the table and then away. Two days of scrying, and sketching, and talking, and they still couldn't figure out how to get close enough to the keep to use sorcery to affect those within. She could bring the walls and town down, but she couldn't find a way to take Stromwer without massive force. The way the valley and keep were set up, any force massive enough to destroy Dencer's outer defenses would flatten town and keep. At least, any force she knew how to use.

"We haven't heard any response to our request that he put down his arms, have we?"

"I doubt that we will," Hanfor answered. "The scroll was delivered. We know that."

The lack of response from Dencer brought the question

back to force. *Is there any other way in Defalk?* She cast in her mind for another approach, then frowned.

"I don't understand how Barjim managed to get Wendella as a hostage." Anna turned to Jecks. "He certainly couldn't have taken her by force."

"Alasia captured her on her way from her brother's."

Her brother? Anna tightened her lips. Remembering all the names was still hard for her. Mietchel! That was it; he was the Lord of Morra. The sorceress grinned. "Did she put on finery to do it?"

Jecks' brows knit in momentary puzzlement. Then he laughed. "I wager she did, though she talked little of it. She said it needed to be done. Barjim was not wholly pleased."

Anna bet he hadn't been.

The moment of humor didn't solve the problem.

In her mind, she almost saw two images, but not Darksong images—that of the near-impregnable Stromwer, surrounded on three sides by step cliffs and canyons and the heavily fortified entrance and that of the ripped and sundered hills of Appalachia in her childhood, the results of strip and deep mining.

Why the two images? Was her subconscious trying to tell her something?

Mining? What did that have to do with it? Ditches, holes, tunnels . . . "Tunnels! That's it."

Now all she had to do was find somewhere that a short tunnel would reach a cliff or flat spot overlooking Stromwer. Or where she could create one. *All . . . ? Are you sure you want to do this?*

She inhaled slowly, then let her breath out, as she realized both Jecks and Hanfor stood waiting for her to explain.

55

Anna coughed, then spat clear the mucus and inhaled dust. Farinelli *whuff*ed, with the slightest hint of a head toss, as he carried her along the back trail that headed west away from the main road. Eventually the trail would circle back along the heights of the low mountains on the west side of Dencer's keep. Eventually.

Farinelli *whuff*ed again.

"I know. It's hot and dusty. There's a stream somewhere ahead." She felt guilty as she took a drink from her water bottle.

"How far?" asked Jecks.

"According to the glass, two or three deks, if I remember right."

"Horses could use the water, lady," Fhurgen said from behind her.

"I know," she repeated. "But I can't bring the water closer."

Despite the rains she had brought to Defalk, there hadn't been any moisture in nearly a week. Several hundred horses were enough to churn up dust, especially with slow riding up steep and narrow roads. The light wind out of the north was just strong enough to carry the dust of the main body up and around Anna and those in the van.

The first two days out of Lerona hadn't been bad. An almost straight road south, flat, and they'd made good time through the bean fields and meadows. Then they'd reached the low hills that signified the beginning of Dencer's holding.

Of course, she'd received no reply to her scroll—one way or the other. *He can't even conceive of dealing with a woman regent . . . or those lancers from Dumar aren't letting him . . . or . . . ?* She didn't know. All that was certain was that she had a rebel lord on her hands who, for whatever reason, seemed inclined to respond only to force. *So what else is new?*

She also had a score of Gylaron's armsmen. She hadn't thought she would need any, but Jecks had pointed out that taking some armsmen would ease matters with Gylaron. *His pride, mainly.* And she could always call for a fewscore more if she needed them.

Anna brushed more dust off her sleeves. The main road had gotten narrower, and even dustier. The trees had gotten shorter, with more low evergreens and less broadleafs, and consequently less shade.

". . . wish she'd find a better way . . ."

". . . we took three keeps now . . . lost maybe a score . . . wager 'gainst that if you want . . . eat dust all summer. . . ."

". . . can't breathe . . ."

Red dust, and more sandy red dust, swirled up from the main body. Anna pushed back the battered brown felt hat and blotted her sweating forehead. The gray square of cloth was once again a muddy red.

Beside her, Jecks rode silently, his silver hair marked with blotches of red where sweat and dust had combined.

"A penny . . . a copper," she corrected, "for your thoughts." She shifted her weight in a saddle that had gotten progressively harder and less comfortable.

"You would have us travel a long way to avoid killing Dencer. Yet you dislike the man." Jecks' words were slow, thoughtful.

"I don't have any problem with killing Dencer, necessarily," she answered. "I don't want to turn another keep into something like Suhl." Anna shrugged. "We can't get close enough to Stromwer to use sorcery—the kind that won't kill everyone—unless we do this."

Jecks nodded, the kind of nod that told Anna he wasn't quite sure he believed her.

Did she believe herself—or was she overreacting to the disaster at Suhl? *How much force is necessary in a place like Defalk? Is Jecks right? Would I be better off doing it the simpler way? Can I at least cast one more loyalty spell . . . to spare Defalk.*

The sorceress took a deep breath. *Or is this to ease your conscience?* She winced at the thought.

As Farinelli carried Anna to the top of a low ridge, momentarily out of the dust, she could see the winding strip of green in the narrow valley ahead, green that showed the promised stream. On the other side of the stream, the trail wound back eastward, toward Stromwer.

Toward another set of gambles with spells, another effort to resolve violent feelings with as few deaths as possible. *And for what? So you can ensure a marginally-grateful twelve-year-old will inherit what his father wasn't strong enough to keep? So that you can't move without guards following every motion? So that everything you do is questioned?*

Anna pushed away the thoughts and leaned forward to give Farinelli a solid thump on the neck. "We're getting there, fellow. It won't be long."

56

Anna packed away the glass and strapped the leather bundle to the saddlebags once again. Then she remounted Farinelli, swaying slightly as she swung into the saddle.

"You must eat." Jecks eased his mount beside hers and extended a chunk of bread.

"Thank you." Anna nodded, took a bite of the bread, and chewed. "Another dek, I'd guess." She pointed.

"About halfway up that next section. By the clump of pines there."

"Junipers," Jecks corrected.

"Junipers, whatever." She chewed another mouthful. Why didn't he understand that she *hated* being corrected over little things. What difference did it make whether it was a pine or a juniper? She'd just pointed out a clump of trees as a reference point.

Were men everywhere like that? Avery had been worse, she had to admit, correcting *everything*. Then, he'd been king of the comprimarios, able to get any secondary role anywhere, but never the big roles.

Anna laughed to herself. She had the biggest role ever—sorceress and regent—and, fortunately and unfortunately, it was for real. She unstoppered the water bottle, her third for the day, and took another long swallow.

The dust puffed from under the horses' hoofs. The wind raised it around them and coated them all with fine red powder. Anna took another swallow of water and finished the bread. Without speaking, Jecks extended another chunk.

"Thank you." Anna took it. She was being bitchy, in a way, but he wasn't the one who had to stand out there and wonder if the spell would be right, if fire would turn and kill them all or whatever. Or if she would fail. Sorcerers did fail. She'd seen Brill die from failing, and she'd overmastered the Evult. Who was to say that another sorcerer wouldn't show up with greater power?

Like the Sea-Priest or the young man in brown with hate in his eyes. She'd tried to find out more from the glass, but all she could see was that he lived in a small town and worked in some sort of store, a chandlery, it looked like in the silver-mist visions.

Without thinking, Anna discovered she had eaten all the bread.

"You were hungry," Jecks observed, as if that explained everything.

"Thank you. I was." Anna let him think that she had

only been hungry. She wasn't in the mood for explaining, and now wasn't the time. Instead, she studied the steep hillside to her left as Farinelli carried her closer to the pines—the junipers, she reminded herself—on the downhill side of the trail. Beyond the dry gorge to her right, the hills climbed into even higher peaks, with barren but not snow-covered summits, mountains almost like plateaus tilted slightly sideways.

Opposite the junipers, Anna reined up, then dismounted and handed Farinelli's reins to Rickel. She took out the glass, and unwrapped it again. Then she took out the lutar and retuned it, not that it needed much work in traveling less than a dek.

Words drifted uphill as she touched a tuning peg.

". . . hope we're wherever we're going. . . ."

"Don't hope too much. You might have to fight, then."

". . . avoids fights when she can . . ."

". . . lucky we are, there . . . not like Barjim or Donjim. . . ."

Then, reflected Anna, clearing her throat for a vocalise, Barjim and Donjim hadn't been able to call on sorcery. Would her voice last? She pushed that thought back as well. *Not the time for that. . . .*

Finally, her fingers touched the strings.

> "Show me now and show me clear,
> where I stand to make a tunnel near . . ."

In the glass, Anna stood perhaps a yard uphill of where the glass lay on the dust of the trail. The image in the mirror was crystal-clear, and the spell took nearly no energy at all, a confirmation of her closeness.

After quickly clearing the image from the mirror, the sorceress glanced at Hanfor and Jecks. "This is the place." She almost laughed, thinking of someone else's words in another canyon a world away and years past. *Careful . . . don't get punchy. You haven't even started. Worry? Fear?*

She turned and looked for Liende. "Chief player?"

"We are coming, Regent."

As the players gathered and began to tune, Hanfor called orders in the background.

"Alvar, take the purple company up to the crest. Jirsit, the greens back to the last hilltop there. Scouts. . . ."

"The building spell?" asked Liende.

"The second one," Anna confirmed.

"After that? Do. you know?"

"The loyalty spell . . . if it goes well. If not," Anna winced, "the flame spell."

"Let us pray to harmony it goes well," Liende murmured.

It won't . . . Anna pushed that thought back as well and cleared her throat, bending to retrieve the mirror. First, she packed away the lutar. Then came the traveling mirror. The sorceress noted that the frame was so black it was almost polished like hard coal. How long would this one last? Like singing, sorcery was hard on everyone and everything involved.

Jecks had dismounted and stepped closer to Anna, leading his horse. "So far . . . there's no sign of Dencer's folk."

"That's fine with me." Anna glanced at the wall of red-and-gray rock layers. Red and gray? That seemed odd to her, but it had been twenty years since freshman geology.

She looked up. Above and before her, the rocks climbed several yards more. To either side they towered even farther. The mountains had been Stromwer's protection for years.

"I like it not, not seeing your enemy." Jecks chuckled. "Like as not, we'll see them soon as your tunnel appears west of the keep."

"It won't be over the keep. It's still almost a dek from the overlook I'm trying to create to the keep walls. That's as close as we can get."

"Is that close enough?"

"It will have to be." Anna offered a cold smile. "If it's not . . . well, I can always resort to turning everything into molten rock." She bit off the next words, the ones like, . . . *and what would that do for the sensibilities of your northern lords?* "I hope I don't have to do that."

"Nor I."

Anna stepped away and started a vocalise . . . softly. She didn't want to strain her cords. She had no idea how many spells she might need on the other side of the tunnel—assuming she could create a tunnel, assuming it didn't collapse, assuming . . . The sorceress forced her mind onto the vocalise, onto the exercise itself, shutting out everything.

A second vocalise followed the first.

"Lady Anna?" Liende's voice broke through the sudden comparative quiet, where the only sounds were those of horses and the murmurs of the one company Hanfor had pulled back from where Anna and Jecks and the players stood. Even Fhurgen and Rickel had moved their mounts back, and Anna's and Jecks' as well. "Lady Anna, we are ready when you are."

The sorceress and regent nodded.

"The second building song!" Liende gestured.

Anna took a deep breath. *Are you crazy? Trying to use sorcery to drill a tunnel through a mountain? But it's not a mountain, just a short chunk of rock, and that's not as bad as calling up lava from underground. . . .* She cut off the mental dialogue and hummed, trying to get her pitch. Then she began the spell.

> ". . . remove all boulders, clay and stones.
>   Fix the braces in their proper zones . . .
>   Drill the tunnel straight and true and square;
>   form this hill to my pattern there . . .
>
> "Smooth the rock and make it hard . . ."

The problem with spells wasn't just the words in rhyme but making sure that the word matched the note values as well, and sometimes—too many times, it seemed—she was shading notes or note values or words, or all three. *Just so long as it's musical. . . .*

The ground shivered. The unseen chime, or chimes, or chords that no one seemed to sense but Anna, rang across the skies, for a moment, turning the entire heaven bright blue, before the scattered and puffy clouds reappeared.

Dust, and a gout of hot air geysered from the rock in front of Anna, and she backed up, squinting, then closing her eyes. There was the patter of rain, except it was tiny fragments of rock.

As the haze settled, Anna opened her eyes back to a squint, peering through the semicircle that arrowed into the improbable gray-and-red rock. At the other end was a semicircle of light, light that seemed to cascade and flare around her.

She staggered and sat down.

Jecks knelt beside her, offering bread and hard yellow cheese. "You need to eat."

"Have to hurry. . . ." she muttered.

"You cannot move until you eat."

"Drink?" she asked.

He also had her water bottle, and she took a long swallow, then a mouthful of bread, then one of cheese, and then more water. The pulsating glare receded.

"Not too bad." Anna looked at the tunnel. "I still worry."

"Keep eating," said Jecks. "If your spell is as you planned, what can Dencer do? If it isn't, you'll have to be strong."

She drank more of the water, and then finished the bread, before she looked back. Behind her the players sat on the rocks and the trail itself and followed her example.

When she had finished, Anna slowly stood and stretched.

Liende walked slowly toward the sorceress. "How many more spells?"

"I hope one—the loyalty spell. Otherwise, the long

flame spell. I'm going to see." Anna started toward the tunnel.

Jecks took two quick steps to join her. Both Fhurgen and Rickel hurriedly dismounted, handing off their equine charges to other guards, and scurried after Anna, shields on their arms.

Anna took one step after another, the way getting dimmer as she walked. The floor felt warm, almost uncomfortably so, but a breeze blew from the eastern end. Anna kept walking, but the semicircle of light at the other end grew but slowly.

Her nose began to itch, and she sneezed, abruptly, three times in a row. Sweat dripped down the back of her shirt.

"Hot as dissonance here," murmured someone—Rickel or one of the guards who trailed them.

At last, she peered out of the tunnel onto the ledge—and the sunlight. Her eyes watered. At the end was a low wall, waist-high. *Did I put that in?* She almost wanted to laugh. She hadn't remembered visualizing a safety wall, but her fear of heights had definitely kicked in.

With a swallow, Anna stepped in the sunlight.

"A moment, lady," said Fhurgen.

Fhurgen and Rickel, bearing the shields they used to protect her, stepped out onto the ledge.

Anna followed them, with Jecks beside her, out to the wall. She forced herself to look down at the valley beyond. The tunnel and ledge were more than a hundred yards above the valley floor. With another swallow, she surveyed Stromwer.

Less than a hundred yards to the east, and a hundred yards below, lines of archers were forming up, still ragged, but the bows were obvious—both for the larger group in tan and the smaller group in crimson. So were the four crossbowmen to their left. Behind them, were over twoscore mounted figures, most in crimson—the Dumarans. Behind the archers was an angular figure waving a blade and shouting commands.

"Best you hurry," Jecks suggested. "Their shafts could reach the ledge."

"They can lift arrows that far?"

As if to answer her question, an arrow arched over the wall and clattered on the stone.

Rickel and Fhurgen lifted the shields, and Anna turned and called down the tunnel. "Players!"

"Players!" Jecks' heavier voice boomed against the stones.

Anna dropped to her knees, letting the wall shield her, and took another look at the armsmen below. Two blocks of archers—one in tan, one in crimson—were loosing shafts rapidly. Was the tall figure on horseback beside the archers in tan Dencer himself? The Lord of Stromwer had to have had some warning, some scrying ability, to have gotten his men formed up so quickly. Anna could see Dencer had sheathed his blade and was drawing a bow from horseback. She ducked behind the shield.

Another arrow clattered against the smoothed rock that reinforced the tunnel mouth, then dropped onto the stone of the ledge.

"Players!" Jecks boomed again, his fingers tightening on the hilt of a blade all too useless from where he viewed the valley.

A figure paused at the tunnel mouth.

"Stay there!" Anna didn't need to lose another chief player. "Line up everyone right there inside the tunnel. They've got dozens of archers. I'll need the flame song for them."

Liende paled.

"Just for the archers and the horsemen," Anna emphasized. "Then we'll have time for the loyalty spell."

She tried not to wince . . . but she didn't trust Dencer, even under a loyalty spell, and Dencer didn't deserve mercy. *You're the avenging angel now?* She pushed away the thought, and cleared her throat, going through the simple "polly-lolly-pop" vocalise on her knees. It didn't feel right. She had to cough and clear out her throat. "I need to stand up."

Fhurgen and Rickel locked shields.

"When I tell you, you'll have to step to the side," Anna said.

"Yes, lady." Fhurgen grinned grimly. "But not until then."

Another arrow clattered, this time against the safety wall.

Behind her, a ragged warm-up tune followed as she struggled to clear her cords.

Three more arrows bounced from various angles onto the ledge. A heavier *clank* announced a crossbow bolt that skidded almost to Anna's feet.

"Now!" snapped Anna. The arrows would only get more accurate.

"The flame song. On my mark. Mark!"

The tune was ragged, but not too bad, Anna hoped as she launched into the spell.

"Turn to fire, turn to flame
   those below who reject my name.
   Turn to ash all tools spelled against my face
   and those who seek by force the Regency to
       replace . . ."

Another volley of arrows arched over the wall, one sticking into the shield Fhurgen held, several others clattering against the stone of the cliff above and around the arch of the tunnel entrance.

"Turn to fire, turn to flame . . ."

Fiery spikes of flame seared out of the sky, more like lances of flame than arrows, and the harmonic chord that only Anna seemed to hear strummed deeply, once, twice.

Anna winced as the screams rose from below, as another volley of arrows clattered on the stone, and as more lances of fire slashed from sky to valley.

57

Stromwer, Defalk

The angular Dencer peers down at the clouded image in the glass—an image that shows a woman standing on a road and singing at a rock face. Behind her are the even more shadowy figures of players.

"Where is she?" demands the Lord of Stromwer. "I know she works sorcery. She always works sorcery. But where works she this sorcery?"

"We will try, ser." The sweaty-faced man in tan linens gestures to the three players and begins to sing.

> "Now show in the shining light of song
> where the sorceress may be found . . ."

The singer coughs and the images shiver back into silver mists.

"Show me! Now!" snaps Dencer.

The seer coughs again, then repeats the refrain, the violinos matching his thin voice.

This time the cloudy image shows horsemen along a narrow trail.

"Not much better. Thank the harmonies I know my lands." Dencer glances at the seer. "Cannot you do better than that?"

"Ser . . . she is powerful."

"What use are you all? Worthless! Why have I only the weak and worthless?" The lank-haired lord knocks aside the seer with his gauntleted left arm and strides from the room. "Gortin! Zerban! Form up the archers! Now!"

Dencer still yells commands as he rides from the stables and closes with the waiting Dumaran captain. "Are your men ready?" The Lord of Stromwer gestures toward the gate to the south. "Zerban! We ride!"

"I have followed your orders, Lord Dencer, but I see no sorceress."

"Had we waited until we saw her, too late would it have been. Are all you Dumarans so stupid?" Dencer urges his mount toward the gate. "Archers! Ride to the west! After me!" The gates groan open, and the armsmen in tan leathers flank Dencer as he rides out through the gates and along the berm road to the west.

Gortin gestures to his own lancers and smaller number of mounted archers, then follows the gawky-looking Lord of Stromwer through the gates and across the flat grass of the high berm toward the cliffs to the west of the keep.

"Why here?" asks the Dumaran officer when he finally draws his mount alongside that of Dencer, more than half-way to the base of the cliff.

"The bitch uses sorcery, and if she succeeds, she will make her way through that low point in the cliffs." Dencer draws his blade and gestures. "There. See you not the rock steaming?"

Gortin half ducks as the weapon swirls by him, then looks to the cliffs ahead and overhead. As Dencer has said, steam or mist—something boils off the rock nearly a hundred yards up from the base of the cliff.

"She will level that mountain, if it takes that, to get to us. She is already calling on dissonance to support her attack." The tall lord reins up and half turns his mount. He stands in the saddle easily, despite his awkward appearance, and gestures with the long blade. "Form up the archers! Here! Now! Right before me!"

Gortin gestures, and the Dumaran archers begin to form to the south of the tan-clad forces of Stromwer. Dencer watches as the archers tumble off of mounts and form on the long grass before him.

Above them and to the west, a dull rumbling fills the midday air, and gray clouds of dust spurt from the cliff's side.

"A tunnel. . . . The bitch has created a tunnel. . . . Proves she's not all-powerful." Dencer gestures with the long blade again—toward the gray-and-red layers of the cliff that lies less than a hundred yards from where his archers prepare.

The gray mist swirls away in the light breeze, revealing a rock-walled balcony jutting out of the cliff. Gortin's jaw drops momentarily, but he closes his mouth quickly and glances toward Dencer.

"Your lord—did he not realize the danger this sorceress poses?" Dencer's voice oozes with irony. "The great Lord Ehara . . . he did not realize?"

"I . . . think not, Lord Dencer."

Two shields appear above the wall on the cliff, and then a figure in greens—apparently blonde—peers over one of the shields.

"The bitch! She's there already," mutters Dencer. His voice rises as he sheaths the blade. "Zerban! Archers! Blanket that place with shafts! Now! Every shaft you have!"

To his left, Gortin echoes similar commands, and the half-score of crimson-clad Dumarans begin to loft shafts over the short expanse of wall. Some arrows bounce off the rock.

"More shafts!" insists Dencer, stringing his own great bow, and then loosing one shaft, then another.

The sounds of horns, then of strings, waft out over the valley—followed by a strong voice, a clear voice, a voice that makes that of Dencer's seer seem as nothing.

The Lord of Stromwer glares, nocks another shaft, and releases it. "Bitch! Bitch! Get you if I can . . ." His voice is low and ragged.

The puffy white clouds to the south and west darken into gray, and the ground seems to rumble.

Dencer looses another shaft.

A lance of fire appears from somewhere in the sky and sizzles into the archers before Dencer.

"Ooooh . . ." The muted moan of the dying man mixes with the odor of burning flesh.

"Aeeeiiii . . . aeeiii . . ."

Fire lances begin to fall as fast as raindrops in a thunderstorm, and the screams of the dying rise with the flames that engulf them.

Dencer nocks yet another shaft and lofts it toward the stone wall above him. "Bitch! No sorceress . . . No woman . . . Bitch!"

He struggles to reach one more shaft as the fires enfold him, tries to lift it to the burning bow, while he clamps his lips shut. Then he raises one fist . . . slowly . . . before his charred figure is thrown from the back of the mount that rears to escape the flame, rears . . . and collapses under the rain of fire that appears to be everywhere there are armsmen.

58

As Anna finished the spell, she took a deep breath, then began to cough. Rickel and Fhurgen raised the shields around her.

"Oh . . ." Behind her was a muted cry, and a sound of someone falling.

She turned, still coughing, as the arrows continued to rain down on the rock-walled platform, even as the few clouds began to darken, the ground seemingly to rumble. Fiery spikes flared from the skies, bright enough to dazzle her eyes, and with the spikes came cries . . . and screams from below. Screams that Anna ignored as she saw the body.

On the ledge sprawled one of the more newly recruited players. A crossbow bolt had gone straight through his neck. Even as she scurried toward the figure, with blood that had welled up everywhere, Anna could tell it was too late, probably a slashed carotid artery. The odds against something like that were tremendous, but somehow, warfare didn't always take odds into account.

Shit . . . damn . . .

Anna looked over at Liende, trying to recall the young violist's name. Hasset—he'd been one of the cheerful ones. Blond, curly-haired, laughing, and he was dead. Like that. *How many? How many more?*

As she questioned, both the fire lances and the screams died away, and only the odor of burning grass and burned flesh drifted upward from the valley. *Only?* Anna swallowed, trying not to cough again, afraid she'd end up retching if she did.

After a moment, she turned her eyes to Liende. "I'm sorry. I tried."

"I know." Liende sighed. "It is war."

War—was that what she was good at?

Several of the players swallowed as they looked down. "We're not done." Anna caught their eyes. "You need to get ready for the next spell . . . or what we've done won't mean anything." Her eyes went to Liende. "Out by the wall. It's safe there now."

"Places," coughed Liende. "By the wall."

Anna walked slowly back to the overlook. Both Fhurgen and Rickel had lowered their shields. Jecks stood by them.

Below, streaks of black seared the earth. Small patchy fires burned in several places. Man-sized heaps of charcoal dotted the green meadow. Three horses galloped free. The others had been less fortunate, sharing the fate of their riders.

Poor damned horses . . . but you can't keep coming up with spells for everything . . . . Except that the problem was that spells had to be relatively short, and that meant that people—and horses—suffered. Then, that was true of blades, arrows, and nuclear weapons.

Anna cleared her throat.

The remaining nine players straggled out onto the walled ledge. Kaseth, almost tottering, still clutched his violino. Delvor marched out almost defiantly, followed by Yuarl and Duralt, still half strutting.

Typical brass player . . . Anna forced her mind back to the keep below. "The new spell . . . the loyalty spell. On my mark." With the players behind it, rather than just her lutar, she hoped that the effect wouldn't be as draining on her and more effective on Stromwer.

"Mark!" Liende gestured and began to play herself.

Anna went into the song, without words, without preamble.

> "Folk of Stromwer, weak or strong,
> loyal be from this song.
> Be you young or be you old,
> faithful be till dead and cold.

> "Your heirs of all, daughters and sons,
> workers of lands, while time runs.
> Treachery prevent to all Defalkan lands
> with your cunning and your hands."

The slash of pain was so intense, the pounding through her skull like so many jackhammers, the flares in her eyes so hot, that she could feel her knees fold like an instantly-struck set.

And the darkness was not cold or distant, but hot, prickling.

She could feel herself twitching, moaning, and unable to move, before the hot blackness swept over her and swallowed her.

59

ENCORA, RANUAK

The dark-haired woman strides past the guard outside the door and into the sunlit study. Her eyes fix the gray-haired Matriarch, ignoring the older man in the straight-backed chair across from the writing desk.

"Veria, I had asked not to be interrupted. I presume you have information of great import." The Matriarch's words are level.

"Matriarch, you said that this sorceress used only Clearsong. You said that she was with the harmonies." Veria's cold eyes fix on the cherubic face of her mother. "All Liedwahr felt the dissonance of this . . . abomination."

"I have no doubts that the sorceress meant well, daughter." The Matriarch's face clouds.

" 'Meant well.' You will find an excuse for everything that she does. Did not the Prophet of Music mean well? Did not the Evult mean well?"

"You take on too much, daughter," says Ulgar quietly, rising from the chair.

Veria's eyes flash. "You would see nothing but perfection in every word—"

"What happened to the sorceress?" asks the older woman. "If you will . . ."

"She lies prostrate. The seers say she may not live. Nor should she, with that force of Darksong!"

"And if she does? Do you think she will attempt it again?" The Matriarch turns in the padded desk chair.

"If she can. The woman has no ideals. She is not a woman for us."

"Oh? Was she raised as you to understand Darksong

and Clearsong? Did she have someone tutor her in the finer points . . .''

''Matriarch . . .''

''I think you should leave, Veria.'' Ulgar steps forward, and his eyes are hard. ''We do not know what happened, not well enough to judge, and you wish to judge.''

''I have every right to judge Darksong—and I will.'' Veria bows. ''Good day, Matriarch.''

As the door closes, the Matriarch glances to her consort. ''You should have let her speak.''

''No. She is only looking for ways to hurt you.'' Ulgar's eyes go to the door.

''I cannot explain it, Ulgar.'' The Matriarch sighs softly. ''I *know* that whatever the sorceress did was to avoid more bloodshed. She does not like to shed blood. She is still young at heart, and she would use her skills to change souls to save bodies. As we know—and as Veria will not see—you cannot use the harmonies in such a fashion.''

''You think she used Darksong to avoid bloodshed?''

''That is my surmise. The glasses that pass will tell.'' The Matriarch shakes her head. ''Harmony rests on what is, not on good or evil. What is, the whole basis of Clearsong, does not allow easy decisions. It was ever so for sorcerers and sorceresses, and that is why those few who survive become great. Only the great survive. It is a hard, hard lesson for the young to learn, or for those who have come from elsewhere.''

Ulgar glances toward the window and the street below, where a dark-haired woman hurries toward the harbor. ''It is hard for all of us.''

60

H ot . . . Anna was hot all over. Except she was freez-
ing.

"Cold . . . hot . . ."

Her eyes felt as though they had been replaced with a
mixture of hot coals and ice, and she had no idea whether
it was morning or midday or deep night.

She shivered violently.

Out of the darkness words rumbled, and more words.

"Drink," someone said, and she drank, and kept drinking until she felt wetness running down her cheeks.

"Enough, lady . . . enough . . ."

The words trailed off, and she found herself back in
the darkness where she burned and froze, sweated and
shivered.

Some time later, her eyes opened slowly . . . as if she
had terribly violent allergies or they were swollen so
much that they could barely open.

Two figures leaned over her—one a warm, kindly,
white-haired figure, the other a cool, sneering, gaunt and
bitter man, also with white hair. Yet both were the same,
and both were Jecks.

Each held a mug, and she felt one mug held wine, the
other poison.

"You must drink more. The wine holds honey."

Which mug? Or were they one and the same? She tried
to close one eye, but still two images of Jecks remained.

Finally, she grasped for the mug and swallowed the
contents in a series of convulsive gulps.

Jecks—the two Jecks—took the mug. One smiled
sadly, and the other smiled evilly. "You must rest."

Rest? Or rest forever? Oh . . . Elizabetta . . . will I . . .
"Rest . . . you must rest. . . ."

The words sounded kindly, and then like a promise of death. Anna tried to move, but her arms, her body seemed encased in ice, but ice that burned with every attempt to move.

Is this what it's like to be mad? Mad, mad, mad. . . .

Her tears burned and froze her cheeks as they flowed, before her eyes closed on fire and ice, ice and fire.

61

Anna lay propped up on the cot in her tent—the tent she hated to use because it meant her armsmen were sleeping on the ground.

Under the light of the single hanging lamp, Jecks sat on the stool across from her, deep circles ringing his eyes, his white hair ragged and disarranged. He held a platter of hard cheese and bread, from which she ate . . . slowly.

"The players? Besides Hasset, I mean."

"He was the violino player who took the arrow?" Jecks paused. "All fell as you did, but they were eating yesterday, some the night before. Except the older man."

"Kaseth? How is he?"

Jecks glanced at the earthen floor of the tent.

"He died?"

"Yes, my lady."

Anna took a deep breath. She knew that sorcery took a toll on the players, usually a far lesser toll than on her, but somehow, she hadn't expected . . .

"He was old, your chief player said."

Old, and Anna had brought him to Stromwer to die.

Her record with players left a great deal to be desired. "Are the others all right?"

"Far better than you." He extended the platter. "You must eat more."

"Tell me what else has happened." Anna reached for another chunk of cheese.

". . . We have had to forage some," the lord continued, "but we have taken only what we need, and only from Dencer's personal lands. At least, so far as we could tell."

Anna couldn't argue with that. She slowly ate another small chunk of hard cheese, closing her eyes for a moment to shut out the twin images of Jecks. At least, one image was no longer appearing as an evil twin, though the right one still felt much "cooler" than the left.

"Lady?"

"I'm still awake. Sometimes . . . the two images."

"You see double still? There were no bruises on your skull."

"It's Darksong." She opened her eyes. "If I do Darksong anymore, I see two images." She reached for the mug and swallowed. "I thought I knew what it was—Darksong, I mean—but it's not that simple."

"None of sorcery is simple." Jecks took the mug back from her and extended the platter, probably the only one in her entire camp. "Nor is it easy."

"Brill told me that the difference between Clearsong and Darksong was that one dealt with nonliving things and the other with living things." Anna frowned. "But I didn't get any reaction at first for some things that were probably Darksong."

Jecks was the one to frown. "You were using Darksong before?"

"I didn't think about some of it. I made a gown."

Jecks' face relaxed, and he nodded. "A gown."

"But cotton and wool are from living things, and that means the spell was Darksong." Anna stopped and forced herself to eat another morsel of cheese.

"Surely, such a small spell . . . ?"

"I couldn't do it now—I'm sure of it. It's like an allergy." At the look of incomprehension on Jecks' face, she added. "It's like a poison where a little bit doesn't hurt, but if you keep adding a little bit here and a little bit there . . ."

He nodded slowly. "Then, the spell over Dencer's keep?"

"I knew it was Darksong," Anna admitted. "I thought I could avoid killing all of Dencer's armsmen. I didn't want any more killing. I wanted to end this campaign without killing people. I didn't think the backlash would be so bad."

"You near died. I had to force wine into you."

Anna looked at his face. Were those scratches? "I fought you?"

"You have fought me and all the forces of harmony and dissonance."

"I'm sorry. I really am." Anna swallowed. Her throat was sore, somewhat swollen, and she didn't want to consider the state of her cords. "You had to nurse me, didn't you?"

"There was no one else."

Liende and the female players had been floored as she had been. So who else had there been? "Thank you."

Jecks smiled. "After the beginning, it was not so difficult. I did wrap you in blankets for a time."

"Did it even work? The spell?"

"That we do not know. No armsmen have left the keep, according to Hanfor's scouts. Your first spell killed Dencer." Jecks offered another smile, more crooked. "The keep is yours—if we can reach it."

"Oh . . . the armsmen in the gorge."

"They may fight." Jecks' twin images shrugged. "They may not."

Anna finished the last of the wine in the mug and let it rest on her stomach. "I'm feeling better. We could leave tomorrow. . . ."

"The day after. Tomorrow . . . you walk around the

camp. You assure all you are recovered. That, too, you must do.'' Jecks stood. ''I need sleep. So do you.''

''Thank you . . .'' Anna said quietly.

''You are my lady.'' Jecks nodded and slipped out of the tent and into the late twilight.

For a long time, Anna lay there, eyes seeing faint double images, double shadows from the lamp, her head aching, thinking.

Thinking . . . about Kaseth, and Jecks, and even Dencer . . . and Darksong, and Clearsong.

I can't use a loyalty spell, but I can kill an entire keep? It wasn't fair.

Is life ever fair?

She closed her eyes, but the questions didn't vanish.

62

Anna patted Farinelli, then shifted her weight in the saddle and, with her left hand, reached up and re-adjusted her damp shirt off her sweaty back. Lord, she wanted a bath—as much to get rid of the itching from the fine red dust as anything. The damping effect of light rain of the night before had barely lasted until midmorning, and it had taken them that long to retrace their way back from the camp Jecks and Hanfor had established to the main road to Stromwer. By then, the sun, clear skies, heat, and hoofs had combined to raise the red dust once more.

She still wore the breastplate, and sweat collected under that, mixing with dust. The chest scar from the crossbow, though healed, itched even more than her arm. They'd ended up waiting another day more than she had hoped for, but that had brought the end to her double vision—

most of the time. Sometimes, her vision would still split, almost as if to warn her that she skirted on the edge.

Great! You can use your spells to kill—if they're worded right—but you can't use them to persuade. Her lips tightened, and she forced herself to relax. "You can't change what is," she mumbled to herself. "You can't . . ."

A thought crossed her mind—and she wanted to laugh bitterly. Whatever god or deity had set up Erde had wanted to protect men's and women's souls from being manipulated, but hadn't seemed to care about their physical well-being. Just like the priests of the Inquisition, who had tortured people to preserve their souls.

She pushed that useless thought aside and studied the land. The fields beside the road were already knee-high with bean plants and cotton, Anna thought. Cotton, harvesting that would be a chore. Too bad she didn't know how a cotton gin was built, but she was a singer, not an engineer.

Ahead of the column, the dust of a pair of mounts filled the road that led south to Stromwer.

"Halt!" Hanfor's command echoed down the column as the two scouts reined up.

Rather, one scout reined up two mounts, and Anna saw the figure of the other scout, dead, slumped across his mount's neck. "Ser . . . they still got archers up there."

After Anna reined Farinelli in, she glanced from Jecks to the road before them. Ahead, perhaps five hundred yards ahead on the right, was the point where the northern part of the valley narrowed into the defile that led to Stromwer. The first set of the nets Anna had found in her scrying glass bulged from the escarpment, the lowest part of the boulder-filled hemp nearly fifty yards above the road.

With the halt of the column, three archers stood above the nets and lofted arrows toward the advancing column. Clearly, Anna's loyalty commands hadn't reached the armsmen on the heights, and neither had orders from Stromwer. Or orders to resist had.

Anna sighed and, dismounting, unstrapped the lutar. Then she walked forward in front of Hanfor and the others, almost as though they were not there. Mechanically, she tuned the instrument, then followed with a vocalise, then another. She cleared her throat, and did a last warm-up before her fingers went back to the lutar.

> "Archers high, archers strong,
>   turn to flame with this song."

Her thoughts focused on just those she saw. Still, when her eyes cleared, she saw at least four flaming figures fall into the defile. She lowered the lutar and turned, walking back to Farinelli, her steps careful as she had to tread her way through renewed double images.

"You think like a warrior, lady," Jecks said quietly as Anna slowly replaced the lutar in its case.

"Me?"

"What spell did you choose?"

"Oh . . ." She understood. She had chosen the simplest spell to kill the archers—one that didn't cost armsmen, archers, or even arrows. *Simple and direct—and bloody. What does that make me?*

"You are a warrior regent." He answered her unspoken question. His head inclined toward where Hanfor surveyed the road and the gorge. "Your arms commander knows that. So do your armsmen. That is why they follow you."

Anna fastened the lutar in place before taking the reins from Fhurgen. Then, she shook her head. They still needed to deal with the boulders and the nets. *What were you thinking, woman?*

She gestured toward Liende. "We'll ride closer. That will make it easier."

Then she remounted. As they started toward the gorge,

Hanfor called out orders to the armsmen, and Rickel and Fhurgen moved up to flank Anna and Jecks.

This time, Anna reined up somewhere between one hundred and two hundred yards from the high-walled opening to the gorge.

Jecks studied the rocks above intently. "I see nothing."

"Nor I," added Hanfor.

"Players!" called Liende.

Anna took several swallows from her water bottle while the players ran through their warm-up, then dismounted and walked down the road until she stood several yards before the group.

"We stand ready, Lady Anna."

Anna cleared her throat, then nodded.

"The short flame song. On my mark. Mark!" Liende's voice echoed hoarsely through the canyon.

There was no hurry, not for the moment, and Anna tried to make the words easy, without strain.

> "Nets break and fray,
> boulders to dust away . . ."

With a roar, the nets fragmented, and a cascade of reddish dust plummeted down the cliff, welling up in a cloud that drifted southward into the narrow confines of the defile.

"One down," she murmured, turning back to the big gelding, where she took out the portable scrying glass and set it on the shoulder of the road. She unpacked the lutar again, checked the tuning.

Jecks dismounted and eased close to her, to a spot where he could see the mirror. Hanfor eased his mount closer.

Anna waited for them to stop, then sang the spell seeking dangers.

> "Show from the south, danger to fear,
> all the threats to me bright and clear . . ."

The mirror silvered, then split into images. Anna blinked. There were four—no, five—sets of nets with archers above them, and the circular oil-caldron fort.

"Six more times?" She shook her head.

"They won't have any reinforcements," Jecks said.

"I don't have any, either," she answered. *Lord, six more sets of spells!* With that, she packed up the mirror, and then the lutar, and walked past Farinelli to find Liende.

The chief player stood by her mount, packing her horn case.

"I may need some help," Anna said slowly. "There are six more sets of nets, and I'll probably have to use the mirror to find some of them."

"We are yours to command."

"I know," Anna said tiredly. "This isn't what anyone signed up for. But there aren't that many players . . ."

"And there is but one sorceress to save Defalk," Liende finished. "You ask more of yourself than of us. What spells will you need?"

"The flame spell. For the archers and men that guard these rock nets. I don't like it, but if they haven't surrendered with all the time that has passed, they won't." *And I can't do it with the lutar.* She shouldn't have tried the first spell.

Liende shook her head. "No sorcerer I know could sing it once and have it succeed without players."

"Thank you."

"We thank you."

Anna smiled faintly and turned, walking slowly back to Farinelli. Six more times? She squinted as she remounted.

"Why could she not cast a spell against all evils?" asked Delvor as he packed away his violino.

Anna wished she could just sing a blanket spell that would protect them against everything, but she'd found nothing was that easy. After a moment, she answered. "First, because spells only work against a specific evil, and I have to be able to visualize—see in my mind—who or what that is. Second, the spell has to name the evil and provide a means to stop it. Third, it can't be too big a spell, or it would kill both you and me.''

"Even so, without the first spells, we would have been buried in arrows and boulders,'' answered Jecks. "All the armsmen from the keep could have gone up there and shot down.''

He didn't mention that they'd still lost the one scout before Anna had called fire on the handful of guards who had been out of range of the loyalty spell of—Had it been a week before?

Anna glanced back along the column, to the wagon that carried the body, but it was lost in the dust.

"How many more?'' She hadn't realized she'd spoken aloud until Jecks answered.

"None, if we are lucky. One cannot count on luck in warfare.'' He smiled grimly. "You still wear the breast-plate?''

"Yes. It itches.'' She blotted her forehead, then her neck. Her back itched as well, right between her shoulders where it was impossible to reach. She squirmed slightly.

"Better that than another arrow. Twice have you escaped death . . .''

"I know. The third time might not be as fortunate.''

Hanfor coughed. "Lady Anna?''

"Yes, Hanfor?''

"We must proceed with care. . . .''

"The next danger won't be until the next set of rocks. We'll have to go slowly. The mirror doesn't show detail that well.''

"Then your guards—'' Hanfor broke off.

"They'll ride before me,'' Anna conceded.

"With shields?''

"With shields.''

At times, she felt like a pampered poodle—guards, shields, warning glasses. She understood, but it didn't make her feel better.

"Long day," she murmured.

"Not so long as last week," Jecks answered.

Somehow, that didn't console her much, not when she recalled the lines of fire and the dead archers . . . and the dead Hassett and Kaseth. She fumbled for the water bottle and had another drink as she rode slowly into the gorge that led to Stromwer.

63

Esaria, Nesarea

Rabyn and a small blonde woman sit at the small white marble table in the corner of the Pavilion of the Prophet. Between them is a tray of candied nuts, honeyed dried figs, and glazed apple slices and a basket of lemon bread. Rabyn fills both goblets from the pitcher of dark wine. "This is from Ferantha. It is quite good." A boyish grin fills his face. "Nubara doesn't think I know the best wines come from the valley."

"They always talk about the wines of the south Mittfels." A delicate *cling*ing tinkles through the pavilion as a gentle puff of a breeze off the Bitter Sea fluffs the young woman's fine blonde hair.

"Ferantha is where they make the wines they don't sell. The ones they keep for us and for the great houses," Rabyn continues. "Did you know that, Krienn?"

The young woman glances toward the harbor, where a ray of sun flashes through the mixed cumulus clouds to strike and whiten the sail of a Norweian trader. Her dark brown eyes flick back to Rabyn, and she smiles quickly. "No, I didn't know that."

He lifts his goblet, as if to drink, but then sets it on the table, and instead, takes one of the honeyed figs. "I am young, but I listen, and I know much more than Nubara would ever guess. Or you." He follows his words with a wide-eyed smile.

"You are the Prophet," she answers with a smile, also nibbling on one of the figs. The fingers of her left hand lightly clasp the base of the goblet of wine she has not touched. "I imagine there is much you know."

"I learned most of it from my mother. She was . . . exceptional, you know. She made sure I knew everything." Rabyn smiles. "Everything." His fingers brush the candied nuts and then delicately extract one of the glazed apple slices.

"It is said she was remarkable." Krienn takes an apple slice and chews it quickly—after Rabyn has swallowed his.

The young prophet lifts his goblet and sips before speaking. "She was. She didn't explain. She showed me."

The blonde woman waits until Rabyn has taken several sips of the wine before taking the smallest sip of her own.

"And . . . someday, I will have revenge on that sorceress." The youth picks up one of the candied nuts, holds it up to the late-afternoon light. "I have already persuaded Nubara to send a company of the Mansuuran lancers to Elioch, and to raise another company of Neserean lancers, armsmen under my cousin Bertl."

"Is he a good leader?" Krienn asks.

"Bertl? He's not as good as Relour. That's why I wanted Relour in Elioch. I threatened to behave badly, in public. And I whined a little, and asked why sending one company of lancers to give the sorceress something to think about was so bad." Rabyn smiles brightly, then pauses. "She is blonde, you know? The sorceress, I mean."

"Ah . . . she is?" Krienn reaches almost absently for a nut, eats it quickly, then takes another sip of wine.

"She is." The dark-haired prophet nods, sets the nut he had not eaten on his green-and-cream napkin, and takes another small sip of wine, so small he barely wets his lips. "She is a demon from the mist worlds." He smiles warmly. "But your eyes are brown, not blue. You are from Nesalia, and that is far from the mist worlds." He lifts the goblet and sips again. "You are small and pretty, not tall and angular."

"Thank you, Prophet of Music." Krienn tilts her head slightly. She takes another nut, distracted, and chews quietly. The tip of her tongue barely touches her upper lip, then vanishes.

"I would like you to see my collection of Ranuan silks," he offers.

"You do know a great deal more than your years," Krienn answers. "Ranuan silks? On your bed?"

"They are beautiful. They offer great pleasure," he says smoothly.

"I am sure that they do." Krienn's eyes go to the archway, then to the closed door that leads to the main part of the palace, a door barred from inside. "You would know more than I."

"Trust me." Again comes the boyish smile.

As they rise, Rabyn steps back and gestures toward the archway. His eyes flicker to the candied nuts, the nuts which he has not sampled, and he smiles, coldly.

He steps up beside her, smiling, his hand on her bare shoulder, as they step through the archway.

64

The road through the gorge was no more than ten deks in length, and yet, with six stops and a dozen spells, the sun had touched the western walls of the valley, turning the dark clouds purplish, before Anna and her armsmen rode through the open gates of Stromwer, after Alvar and a score of armsmen had inspected the keep—at Hanfor's insistence.

"Stromwer lies open and loyal to you," Alvar had announced.

Anna hoped a bath, a good hot bath, also lay open—except she had unfinished business. Business she hoped she could complete, half-dazed and double-visioned as she was, although she had used no Darksong on the emplacements in the gorge. *Just the good solid brute force of Clearsong ... bloody Clearsong.* She was punchy and found herself holding back hysterical laughter at the idea that Clearsong magic could be so much more bloody than Darksong.

The dark clouds offered a faint drizzle by the time Anna reined up outside the keep's stable, in a courtyard ringed with her armsmen.

"All are loyal," Hanfor announced.

Score one for my last effort at Darksong. "I'm going to groom Farinelli." She glanced at Alvar. "Have the saalmeister or seneschal or whoever ready to meet me in the hall."

"I can do that." Alvar smiled.

Jecks and Hanfor both frowned.

"Lady Wendella ... if she's still alive." Anna dismounted and led Farinelli into the stables behind Rickel, who carried his blade bared. She forced her steps to be deliberate.

"We are your servants!" called a thin-faced man in gray leathers from his knees on the straw.

"I accept your allegiance," Anna said. "I also remember that you pledged the same to Lord Dencer."

"Lady ..."

"Serve Defalk, and no one will suffer," Anna said more softly.

Their eyes wide, two stable boys looked at the big gelding as Anna led Farinelli past. By the time Anna had groomed Farinelli and ensured he had grain and some water—not too much—a full-fledged downpour greeted her at the stable door where Fhurgen and Jecks waited.

"The saalmeister is in the corridor there," Fhurgen announced, pointing through the rain to the arched doorway that stood fifteen yards away, across the rain-slicked cobblestones and the scattered puddles. "Alvar is with him."

Anna glanced across the rain-pelted courtyard, then at Rickel and Fhurgen. "Better dust than mud on the road, I guess."

"Far better, lady."

Anna walked through the rain, fearing she might fall if she ran, ignoring the roll of thunder and a single flash of lightning.

Four figures waited in the corridor—Hanfor, Alvar, Jecks, and the saalmeister. Anna wiped the water from her hair and face, knowing she scarcely looked like a regent, but more like a damp and shaggy dog, a thin-faced, dark-eyed, and haggard shaggy dog. She didn't even want to think about how she smelled.

Unlike the stablemaster, the saalmeister was heavyset. Dark circles ringed his eyes, a sign, Anna felt, that he had suffered from the conflicts of the loyalty spell.

"Darflan, this is the Lady Anna," Alvar announced.

Darflan went to his knees. "We serve you and the Regency."

"You can stand," Anna said, trying to keep the exasperation from her voice. "Where is the lady Wendella?"

"The . . . lady . . . Wendella?"

"I'm sure you've heard of the lady."

"Ah . . . where Lord Dencer left her. We did not know. It was said . . ."

"Enough. Take us there, and bring the keys."

Jecks glanced at Hanfor. Alvar shrugged.

"Two loyalty spells are enough for anyone," Anna said. "Oh, where is the heir, her son?"

"In his nursery, lady."

"Get his nurse and bring him here."

That got another exchange of glances between Jecks and Hanfor.

"She is his mother." Anna didn't feel like explaining.

"Now . . . lady?"

"Now." Anna's voice chilled. She was damp, sweaty, tired, and wasn't much interested in explanations.

Darflan nodded and waddled quickly down the corridor.

"Alvar," Hanfor said. "If you would make arrangements with the cooks for feeding our armsmen? I had not gotten to that."

"Yes, ser." Alvar turned and headed back down the steps.

"I'm sorry," Anna said.

"That is my job, not yours," the veteran said quietly.

The nurse, in faded brown, a squirming child in her arms, bustled toward Anna and her entourage, with Darflan at her side.

Anna glared. The nurse's bustling confidence transformed into a bow. "Regent . . . lady . . . you wished to see young Condell?"

"I did." Anna looked at the child, already sporting a dark thatch of curly hair. "Please follow us."

The nurse glanced to the saalmeister. The saalmeister nodded.

Don't look to him, Anna wanted to snap. "Let's go."

"Yes, Regent."

The saalmeister led them down the main corridor to the end, then up two flights of steps and back along a narrow corridor. His blade out, Rickel flanked Darflan while Fhurgen trailed. Jecks kept a hand on the hilt of his own blade. The nurse followed most of them, just ahead of Fhurgen.

Darflan paused at another narrow staircase.

"Go on," Anna said.

The steps up to the tower were narrow, even narrower than those in the north tower of Falcor where Anna had stayed. Darflan stopped at the second landing.

"Unlock it," Anna ordered.

When the iron-barred door was open, Anna took the key ring from Darflan and stepped inside.

A hollow-eyed Wendella looked up from the pallet. The sunken eyes were ringed in lines. "Have you come to gloat?"

"No. I've come to set you free." Anna motioned to the wet nurse, who stepped forward. "Your son, and heir to Stromwer."

"For how long, sorceress?"

Anna looked at the pale and emaciated figure. "We need to get you healthy."

"Do not try to tempt me."

"I'm not tempting anyone," Anna said quietly. "Dencer is dead. I hold the keep. Your son is heir. He will inherit his father's lands when he is old enough."

"Why do you play with me?" Wendella's eyes remained on the cold stones of the floor.

"I am not Dencer," Anna snapped. "You should know me well enough to know I don't play games. You don't have to like me. You don't have to like your situation. You're bound to be loyal to Defalk and the Regency, and you're smart and tough. I'd rather have you running Stromwer than some lord's pampered second son."

Wendella's eyes widened slightly. "For how long? Until you hold all Liedwahr?"

"That's not my intention." Anna smiled. "But if it were, I'd need you even more." She nodded to the wet nurse. "Let her hold him."

The nurse eased the child into Wendella's arms.

Anna tried to ignore the tears that oozed from the brown-haired mother's eyes. *At least she can hold him, see him. Stop feeling sorry for yourself. No one whipped and tortured you—not physically, anyway.*

"Your rooms are ready for you," Anna said. She stepped back. "They are, aren't they, saalmeister?"

"They will be, Regent."

"Immediately."

Darflan bowed.

Anna turned to the nurse. "Lady Wendella's wish is your command. In anything."

"Yes, Regent."

Anna turned back to Darflan. "Leave the door open and escort Lady Wendella to her quarters when she is ready. Offer any assistance she wishes. In anything, and make sure she gets a good meal immediately. And hot water for a bath when she wishes."

Wendella looked at Anna, shaking her head. "I cannot pretend I like you, sorceress. You cannot buy my loyalty."

"I have your loyalty," Anna said. "I respect you, but I don't like you, and I never will. But you will run Stromwer far better than Dencer. If you don't, I'll find someone who will until your son can."

"I will run Stromwer, and I will run it well." Wendella lowered her eyes. "I will not, I cannot, speak ill of you. But I will not speak of you, save as I must."

"That's fine. Now . . . get some food and whatever you need." Anna nodded and stepped back out onto the landing, and started down the steps, her boots echoing in the stone stairwell.

At the bottom, in the main corridor, Jecks glanced at Anna.

"You wonder why? She's been tortured, and she's still sane. She has to be loyal, and backing the Regency is the only way her son can hold his lands, because I'm the only one who will back her. She's smart enough to see that."

The white-haired lord shook his head.

Was she crazy? She didn't think so. Wendella had been a bitch, but there was a difference now. She'd never be more than civil to Anna, but that wasn't the point. Preserving Defalk was. "Jecks? Have I taken Stromwer from its heir? Have I imposed an outside lord?"

The hazel eyes met hers. "You, lady, are more deadly than either Ehara or Konsstin. You will not let personal hatred move you from what you know is best. Even the harmonies could not preserve them now."

Anna was the one to shake her head. "Me? The woman who's nearly gotten herself killed a half-dozen times? The woman who has to return a child to his mother before anything?"

"She will come to respect you," Hanfor said slowly. "If she has not already. So will her armsmen."

"Those that survive," Anna said.

"That is most of them," Hanfor answered. "And they appreciate that you limited your spells to those who attacked you." He laughed. "The common armsman is more glad for his life. It is all he has."

Anna shivered. "I think I need some dry clothes and some food. It's been a long day." *How many more to come?* "And a hot bath."

"Now you hold all Defalk," Jecks said. "You can rest."

Anna wanted to laugh. With Ehara and the Sea-Priests plotting something? With Mansuuran forces in Neserea? With a civil war in Ebra, and one side being backed probably by both Sturinn and Dumar?

She took a breath. Jecks was right. She could rest— briefly. And a bath would feel good.

65

DUMARIA, DUMAR

Lord Ehara lifts the crystal decanter, lets the light from the window illuminate the amber liquid, then sets the decanter on the writing desk. He walks to the shorter bookcase and extracts a volume. *The Art of War.* He replaces the leather-bound book. "They never call it 'the profession of war' or 'the faith of war' or some such. It's always an art."

The rangy man in the white of a Sea-Marshal nods from

the wooden chair across from the writing desk. "War is conflict, like the conflict of harmony and dissonance. In conflict, nothing is certain. So warfare is an art. It is not like smithing a blade or plowing a furrow."

"Sturinn has been good at war."

"We deal always with the uncertain. The sea is our home, and it is never sure."

Ehara extracts another book, scans it, and replaces it on the shelf. "Why are you here? Why a fleet of forty ships? Why not just replace me? I could not stand against Sturinn."

"You are perceptive," jerRestin says. "We prefer perceptive allies and friends."

"You talk of friendship, Sea-Marshal jerRestin," says Ehara easily. "I have taken your tokens of friendship and your advice. Now, I have lost hundreds of golds, five companies of lancers, and the confidence of many of my officers. Southern Defalk lies in the bloody hands of that butchering sorceress." Ehara lifts a goblet of wine from the desk in a mock toast, then replaces it, untouched.

"You have taken our advice and our coins when it suits you," answers the rangy man with the tanned face. "And a few gems."

"That may be," Ehara laughs. "Rulers have that habit. What suggest you now?"

"Wait for her to come to you."

"Now you suggest this?"

"Had you not meddled in Defalk, she would have no reason to enter Dumar."

"Oh." Ehara lifts the goblet again in another toast. "A toast to mighty Sturinn. You have encouraged me to enrage my neighbor, knowing my efforts would fail—"

"You began those efforts before we came to offer friendship."

"I stand corrected, mighty Sea-Marshal." Ehara takes a deep swallow of the amber wine. "You encouraged me to increase my efforts. That will encourage the sorceress of the north to invade poor Dumar. Because mighty Sturinn is my friend, Sturinn can then bring all her troops and ships to my aid, crushing the cruel and sorcerous invader. Then Sturinn will bring us trade, and more ships, and new customs. And before long, Dumar will join the Ostisles under the Maitre of Sturinn. Do I have that right?''

"Almost," admits jerRestin. "Except that Lord Ehara will be viceroy for Dumar and Defalk, high above all in Liedwahr.''

"That is so you Sea-Priests can claim you have come but to help your friend and ally.''

"Would you rather stand against the sorceress and the Liedfuhr of Mansuur alone? Who now knows of the Lord of Bultok or the Marque of Cealur? All those lords have vanished into the maw of Mansuur.''

"A sad choice I face.''

"A better choice than without Sturinn," points out jerRestin.

Ehara laughs and lifts his goblet. "Here's to waiting. May it not prove too costly.''

The Sea-Marshal frowns momentarily.

III

....

THEMA
UND
VARIANTE

66

The main guest chamber at Stromwer had two narrow stone windows, opposite each other in one corner, with a hot breeze, a bed, and a small bathchamber built into one corner of the narrow and deep room. Rickel had located a small writing desk and had the servants move it into the room, along with three chairs.

Anna supposed she could have used the late Dencer's study, but she didn't feel comfortable with that. That sort of thing seemed too presumptive, even if she had effectively conquered Stromwer. She massaged her forehead. The double vision had vanished after the last two days of rest, but she still had a slight headache.

With the *thrap* on the door, she turned her head. "Come in."

"My lady." Jecks wore a clean blue tunic, and had washed up. He looked more handsome than ever as he stepped into the guest chamber. Behind him stood a messenger bearing leather bags of some sort.

Anna had to make an effort not to smile insanely. She was glad to see Jecks . . . and his smile and twinkling eyes. She needed something positive in her life. "Lord Jecks."

"My lady. You have some . . . dispatches . . . from Falcor."

"Dispatches?" Anna offered a smile, hoping her smile wasn't too inviting, too forward. *Idiot! You worry about being too distant, and you worry about being too forward.* "I suppose it had to happen." She kept smiling, not exactly sure why. *Hormones? Do I have any left?*

"Put them there." Jecks gestured to the braided brown-and-white rug beside the wide bed.

"Yes, sire, Lady Anna."

As the messenger departed, the regent looked at the three bags of scrolls Jecks had escorted in.

The white-haired lord smiled broadly and lifted the largest bag. "Those are from Dythya." He stacked the scrolls on the foot of the bed behind the small writing desk.

Anna groaned.

Jecks held another bag and began to extract a second set of scrolls. "These are from Menares." A third and smaller bag followed. "These are from Himar."

"Wonderful."

"You are the regent, and some things about the business of Defalk must be handled by the regent."

"Scrolls are better than battles," she conceded.

"They offer less hazard to health."

Anna wasn't sure that administration, especially by horse-carried messages, wasn't hazardous to health and sanity. She took a deep breath and started with the scrolls from Dythya, opening and scanning them and putting them in piles on the bed—those where there seemed to be something she needed to do; those that were information she probably needed to go over; and those complaining about Menares. When she was done, over a glass later, the first pile held a half-dozen scrolls; the second a dozen; and the third, five.

She took a swallow of wine, dark purple and not nearly so good as that of Lerona, and picked up one of the to-do scrolls. "This one says that she and Himar have located a farm smith who's done knives and stuff. They think he could do blades . . . maybe."

Jecks nodded. "How much?"

"A gold a season, plus a silver a finished blade. We purchase all the materials and the equipment." Anna shrugged. "We might as well try. Give him a season trial?"

"We have no other smiths," Jecks pointed out. "If you supply the hammers and anvils and wrought iron, blades will cost you half what you would purchase them for."

"We were talking a gold a blade. . . ."

"Your own smith might cost the Liedstat as little as three or four silvers a blade."

Nodding, Anna pulled out some of the crude paper she'd taken from Dencer's study, and began to write on the small table, carefully, so carefully because the combination of quill and local ink meant everything took forever to dry. Then she laid the sheet on the bed to dry and picked up the second scroll.

"Lord Nelmor has sent his son Tiersen to Falcor for fostering." Anna snorted. "She's enclosed Nelmor's scroll as well. Of course, it's because his sister Ytrude is so pleased. Right! It's because another company of Neserean lancers has been quartered in Elioch. Listen to this.

" ' . . . once you have dealt with the problems in the south, we look forward to your return to Falcor. We remain your obedient servant in all matters. . . .' "

Anna snorted. "All that matters is the danger closest to his lands. Maybe I should ensure there are dangers on all borders."

"Some rulers have done so. For a few years, it has worked. Then people disregarded the danger and the ruler, and so did those who threatened," offered Jecks dryly.

"Well . . ." Anna licked her lips. "I'll send Nelmor a scroll that says how I'm glad to hear that Tiersen has gone to Falcor. I'll reassure him that all holdings in Defalk are dear to me, especially his, given the deep and early friendship offered by his family." Anna paused and glanced at Jecks.

"You are a wicked woman. He will burn at that hint that you hold his sister so highly."

"Good. She was there, when all the male lords—except you—were still twiddling their thumbs. I'm still committing to saving his neck.'' Anna reached for another sheet of paper.

The third scroll was about taxes or tariffs. The merchants of Falcor had requested that the lord's tariff be reduced to one copper on twenty, instead of the one on ten. Anna handed the scroll to Jecks, and looked at the next one.

''Lady Anna?''

She looked up from reading the next scroll—about the need to find golds to repair the street sewers in Falcor that had been clogged by the Evult's flood. ''Yes?''

''Have you reduced the liedgeld for the lords?''

''No. I've let some pay late.''

''Then should you allow the merchants to pay less?''

Jecks had a point. The liedgeld came from the peasants and holding workers, in effect. Why should one group get relief? Or, if she gave the merchants relief, how soon before every lord was at her door?

She sighed. ''Can we suggest that we will review the tariff, but that, given the needs of Defalk, it must stand. Say that we will be looking into fairness for all those who pay tariffs in all forms?''

Jecks grinned. ''You are indeed wicked.''

Anna was just afraid she'd brought American politics to Defalk. She reached for another sheet of paper.

After drafting her political reply she went back to the sewer business, directing Dythya to spend another hundred golds to repair the sewers—and to enforce the rules requiring them to be flushed periodically. It might help reduce disease, but she wasn't sure by how much.

Then came the next scroll.

''We have another message from our friend Hadrenn. Like everyone else he has a problem.'' Anna read selected passages to Jecks.

''As last I wrote, we of Ebra must change with changing times, and we were most pleased with your recognition of Synek as a domain of Falcor, and with the aid you provided most graciously. I was most honored by your later elevation of the domain of Synek to the Thirty-three of Defalk. . . .

". . . Bertmynn has received coins from the Liedfuhr of Mansuur, and blades for his armsmen as well. Now Gestatr has discovered that a ship from the Maitre of Sturinn has arrived in Elawha, claimed unjustly by Bertmynn when it should be a separate domain. From the vessel have come lances, blades, and golds . . .

". . . we of Synek, while not yet hard-pressed, must fear the worst. . . .

"In short," Anna concluded, " 'we're loyal; we're in trouble; and please send coins.' "

Jecks laughed.

"All I do is spend money." Anna glanced at the two piles of scrolls she still hadn't even sorted. "More coins than we really have."

"What will you take from Stromwer's treasury?"

"Some. What Wendella can afford, by *my* reckoning. More than enough to pay for this mess, if it's there."

"More than you reckon," Jecks suggested. "When all is totaled, you will have missed things."

He was probably right about that, too.

"How long before you think to return to Falcor?" asked the older man cautiously.

"I'm not sure we're finished here," Anna said slowly. "I don't want to stay in Stromwer, but Ehara's not exactly disappearing."

"You hold Defalk," Jecks said. "He cannot bring that many troops against you. He lost close to a hundred lancers who supported Sargol and Dencer."

"He has a few more to lose than we do. I don't like the Sea-Priests, either." Anna pursed her lips, thinking about women in dangling chains. "Ehara and his friends the Sea-Priests are still a threat. A big one." Anna gestured toward the wall mirror, and the ashes against the wall under it. *Will everyone remember you as the sorceress-regent who destroyed every mirror in every chamber she slept in?*

"You have perhaps twelvescore armsmen," Jecks pointed out. "The season is early summer, and still we have no proven weapons smiths, and few enough blades for the additional armsmen we need and do not have. You have more golds, but not enough."

Anna thought of the veiled plea for coins from Hadrenn, her newest vassal or lord or whatever, pressed by Bertmynn, who was getting coins from both Konsstin and Sturinn, from what she could tell. That was designed to make life difficult for her and Defalk, nothing more. "We should send a few hundred golds to Hadrenn."

Jecks nodded. "That is cheaper than armsmen, but you will have fewer golds."

"I always end up with fewer golds." Anna rubbed her forehead, then took another swallow of wine. "Would you like some wine?" She filled the other goblet before Jecks could answer.

Ehara of Dumar bothered her. The Sea-Priests, if she could believe Hadrenn's scroll, were pouring coins and arms into Ebra, and they were doing the same in Dumar, and Dumar, unlike Ebra, was neither prostrate nor divided. But what could she do about Ehara?

"How do you think Ehara would react if we sent a scroll to him, requesting his pledge, on his honor, not to interfere with Defalk?"

Jecks laughed. "Why . . . he would send a scroll pledging the very same, almost on the glass, and nothing would change."

Anna felt stupid. She wasn't thinking as clearly as she should, perhaps because of the residual headache—or because ruling wasn't yet a habit with her. "What if we asked for five hundred golds in recompense for the damage he caused, and his pledge never to send coins or armsmen into Defalk?"

"You might get his pledge, but never his golds."

"Then, we'll draft a scroll which basically demands his pledge and the golds, and which states, given his past behavior, that a pledge without golds is without meaning or honor."

"He will not take such well."

"No . . . he may not, but I don't see much point in ignoring him. We've seen his lancers everywhere, and he ought to pay. If he won't, he ought to be put on notice."

"You would fight Dumar?"

"We've already been fighting Dumar. Ehara had no real cause to support the rebels, unless he was already planning a war, or to make trouble for us. Either way, it has to stop."

"Then, you should send such a scroll."

Anna could tell Jecks was less than pleased, but she *knew* that she had to do something to deal with the Lord of Dumar.

By the time she had given Jecks the second draft of the scroll to read, from outside, a golden red poured through the narrow windows.

"Lord, I didn't realize it was that late." Anna glanced at the piles of scrolls in dismay.

"There is always tomorrow."

"And tomorrow, creeping on its petty pace, until the last syllable of recorded time," Anna misquoted.

Jecks paused in lifting his goblet, then drank.

Thrap!

"Yes?" answered Jecks.

Rickel peered inside the room. "The lady Wendella, to see Lady Anna and Lord Jecks."

Almost makes you sound like a couple. Anna coughed, trying to push away *that* thought. "Have her come in."

Wearing a natural cotton gown that left her looking too washed-out, Wendella carried Condell into Anna's chamber. "Lady and regent." She bowed, her face composed.

"Lady Wendella."

"I have come to offer my apologies and to beg of you pardon." Wendella's eyes remained downcast.

"You do not have to answer me, but could I ask why?" Anna inquired.

"I do not like you, Lady Anna. It may be that never I will. You have been fair, for what your duties require. You have not been petty nor spiteful." Wendella coughed. "I have found that your first act, on entering Stromwer, was to restore my son and my station. You have not taken my rooms, nor the study, and the treasury has not been touched."

"I will require some of that," Anna said. "Enough to pay for my armsmen. I will leave what you need to run Stromwer and for the liedgeld. I wish I could do otherwise . . . but the past has left Falcor with little."

"It is said that you, as Lady of Mencha, have paid liedgeld. Is that true?" The words were direct.

"Yes."

Wendella nodded. "I do not like you. I freely grant you my respect and my thanks for my son and my station. And I will write Lord Mietchel telling him so."

"That would be good for us all," Anna said. "I will be equally frank. I respect you for what you have endured. I respect your strength, and I am sorry for your suffering. I suspect we will never be close friends." *And that's an understatement.* "I will help, as I can, to ensure that Stromwer is strong and respected."

Wendella bowed. "I . . . can . . . say no more." Her eyes went to the sleeping Condell.

"You don't have to," Anna said gently. "I am glad you came. I hope you will rest and recover, and take care of Stromwer and your son." She stood, as did Jecks.

The two waited until the door closed behind Wendella.

"I said that she would respect you."

Anna still wondered how much was compelled by her spells. Still, it was better than slaughtering an entire keep. *You've done that, too.* She reached for the wine and took another swallow. Then came the last scroll in Dythya's to-do pile.

She groaned. "The rivermen are asking that we forgo

the tariffs on cargos down the Falche, since this is the first year in the last four that the river has been high enough for their boats. They need every copper to survive.''

"So do you," answered Jecks. "So does Defalk."

Anna hated taxes, and she hated being the local equivalent of both government and the IRS. But how could she keep the country together without revenues to pay armsmen and smiths and everything else?

After a sigh, she took another sip of wine, then reached for more paper.

Thrap!

"A young fellow to see you." This time it was Fhurgen who peered inside the chamber with a wide grin.

"A young fellow?"

"From Abenfel."

"Birke?"

The dark-bearded guard just offered a wider grin.

"Have him come in." Birke? The red-haired son of Lord Birfels who'd been her first page when she had come to Falcor? Who'd effectively been a hostage both of Barjim and then of Behlem?

Wearing a green tunic piped in gray, the red-haired youth stepped into the chamber and bowed deeply. "Lady Anna, at your service." A cheerful smile followed the words.

"Birke! It's good to see you." Anna paused. "Why are you here?"

"We had heard that you were not too far away, and my sire has asked that I offer an invitation of our hospitality to you and your forces." Birke smiled. "We rode from Abenfel in less than four days."

"Your offer of hospitality is much appreciated," said Anna. "I honestly hadn't thought about what we'll be doing after we settle Stromwer."

"We would be pleased to offer a place of rest on your return to Falcor. The river road is not longer than the way through Suhl."

"It is good to see you. And your offer is tempting."

She smiled. "I will think about it." She glanced at the piles of scrolls. "We'll talk at supper." She gestured. "I have a few duties as regent."

"You have always been the regent, and Defalk is fortunate indeed." Birke spoiled the formal words with another wide grin.

"You . . ." She shook her head. "At dinner."

"With pleasure." He bowed again.

Anna refilled her goblet after Birke had left. Was she drinking too much? She'd scarcely had anything to drink until the damned scrolls had arrived. That showed how much she liked administration.

"He's grown," Anna said. "I still wish he'd stayed in Falcor."

"He may have stayed there long enough that it matters not," suggested Jecks. "You have a way of changing people quickly, my lady."

"Me?"

"You, my lady."

Anna shook her head, then glanced at the scrolls. "Changing people or not, we still have too many scrolls to go through."

"At your service, my lady."

Anna mock-glared at Jecks.

67

Anna glanced back at the walls of Stromwer, reddish in the dawn light, rising out of dark red-and-gray cliffs. She stifled a yawn. For someone who wasn't a morning person, the regent business was a tough gig. *And getting tougher, no matter what Jecks thinks.* Absently, she patted Farinelli, who almost pranced northward down the road.

"Riding in the morning is so much better," burbled Birke from Anna's left. "It's cooler, and the air is cleaner. There's less dust, and it's quieter. . . ."

Unless you're riding next to a cheerful morning person, Anna thought, yawning again. All the damned scrolls and paperwork had taken *forever.* She glanced at Jecks, almost as bright-eyed as Birke, and wanted to shake her head. On mornings such as these, she definitely missed coffee, but there didn't seem to be any coffee in Liedwahr and no substitute closer than hot cider. Hot cider was no help, even when it was available, which it wasn't in early summer in Stromwer.

She coughed gently. Something, some pollen, was irritating both nose and throat.

". . . A morning hunt in the higher hills, that is good, too," Birke continued.

"Unless you're the deer," Anna finally said dryly.

Birke flushed.

"Don't mind me, Birke."

"You do not like hunting?"

"Let's say that I know it's necessary." Anna forced a polite smile. "Just as some battles are necessary."

Birke frowned.

"I'm sorry," Anna said quietly. "Could we talk about something besides hunts and battles? I'm a little tired of killing." *You should be, with all you've done.*

After a moment, Birke spoke again. "Did you know that you can see the Falche from the southwest guard tower at Abenfel? It hasn't had that much water in years. If it keeps rising, even the oldest farm trenches to the north will be able to carry water to the fields."

"You're that close to the river?" Anna asked.

"Only a little more than a dek and a half. The keep has its own springs, and that means it didn't have to be close enough to be flooded."

"You must be higher, then?"

"A good two hundred yards. The upper part of the Chasm begins by the keep."

"The Chasm?" Anna hadn't heard about the Chasm, except in a brief mention during one of Menares' geography lectures to the fosterlings and as a label on a map.

"That's the deep canyon that carries the Falche into Dumar and the cataracts. My sire, he's talked about the cataracts. I've never seen them. But the walls of the canyon, some places, they're hundreds of yards tall, and there's one place—it's a ride of several glasses—where you can almost throw a stone . . . well, shoot an arrow anyway, from the cliffs on one side to the other. Another place, there's this beach . . . the sand is so soft . . ."

Birke flushed.

"I can imagine what you might have been doing there," Hanfor said with a gentle laugh.

"You thought of it, you veteran lecher," Anna countered, to relieve Birke's growing embarrassment.

"So I did." Hanfor laughed good-naturedly. "It's been a long spring."

Several of the guards behind Anna laughed as well.

She shifted her weight, conscious that she was beginning to sweat again under the breastplate. She had to get used to the damned armor, she supposed, but would she? Really?

"One of the big pines fell into the river . . ." Birke continued.

"You're not planning on going back to Falcor yet," Jecks said in a low voice, easing his mount closer to Farinelli.

"Not yet. We couldn't stay in Stromwer, and it won't hurt to visit Birfels."

"No, it will not." Jecks smiled. "You worry about Ehara? Do you regret sending the scroll?"

"The scroll? No. I worry about the Sea-Priests. They're using Dumar as a wedge. They won't attack Mansuur or Nordwei. From what you've said, the harbor at Elawha in

Ebra isn't very good. So that leaves Ranuak or Dumar, and if I were a Sea-Priest, I'd certainly try Dumar first.''

''They have sought out Ehara,'' conceded Jecks.

"I don't like going back to Falcor and leaving them to create more trouble,'' Anna said quietly.

"Even with you, Lady Anna, we could not attack Dumar,'' offered Hanfor.

"I understand that,'' Anna said tiredly. "What are we supposed to do? Wait until Ehara and his newfound allies attack us?''

"Have we any choice?''

Anna looked at the dusty red road where it entered the gorge, at the long shadows of morning. "I don't know. I keep hoping.'' *As always, as ever, but things don't change that way.* She took a deep breath. *And you'd better think of something . . . some way to force the Sea-Priests out of Dumar. . . .*

68

Anna lay quietly in the dark, on a cot under the thin silk tent that she rated. Both tent and cot were improvements on her first campaign, if she could call the battle of the Sand Pass and the subsequent flight from the Dark Monks of Ebra a campaign.

The silk overhead fluttered ever so slightly, and Anna opened her eyes, then closed them. Outside, leather creaked as one of her guards shifted his position.

Her arm still twinged at times, the one that had taken the crossbow bolt first, and it twinged now. She turned onto her side, carefully, so that she didn't tip the light-weight cot.

The silk of the tent sidewall fluttered.

She couldn't attack Dumar. Yet Dumar would attack Defalk. Or the Sea-Priests would. Or Bertmynn would use the aid of Sturinn to defeat Hadrenn, and then she'd face the Sea-Priests and their allies on two fronts, with the Liedfuhr on a third.

But she hadn't the resources for an attack, even with sorcery. How could she convince Ehara to throw out the Sea-Priests? What kind of show of force would it take?

You . . . thinking like a hawk . . . or a warmonger . . .

Finally, she sat up and pulled on her boots before she stepped out into the darkness.

"Lady?" whispered the guard, Kerhor, from his voice.

"I just needed some air, Kerhor."

"Yes, lady." Kerhor straightened and followed her the dozen steps she took to a low rise.

On the eastern horizon was the tiny red disc that was Darksong, while high over ahead was the bright white disc of Clearsong. Two moons, music magic . . . sometimes she felt it had to be a dream—until she got shot by an arrow or floored by the backlash of her own magic.

Anna missed the big bright moon of earth. She missed a lot, still. Elizabetta, not that much older than Birke, her little redhead who wasn't little, but all too far away, beyond even the scope of Anna's glasses and reflecting pools.

Was her daughter in love under a bright moon? How long would she really miss Anna? Did Anna want her to grieve too long? Would she even grieve, knowing Anna was alive, somewhere? Should she?

The sorceress and regent shook her head slowly, taking a last look at the red moon on the horizon, then the white disc near its zenith, before slipping back into her tent, hoping she could sleep. Praying that she could.

69

There it is," announced Birke, gesturing ahead as the van rode to the crest of the low hill.

Anna half stood in the stirrups to get a better view of Birke's home. Like Synfal and Stromwer, Abenfel clearly dated from a more warlike period. The tall gray walls were without embrasures, and the gate towers were twice the size of those at Falcor. Despite the height of the walls, they seemed almost squat from their thickness, and each of the four walls stretched nearly a dek.

"It be a big place," murmured Rickel to Lejun—the two guards riding immediately behind Anna and Jecks.

"More than half the rooms are empty. They have been for years, I guess," Birke said. "We always had great fun at steal-away-and-find. I once found a funny set of drums, all attached in a frame, and all different sizes."

"What happened to them?"

"My sire burned them." Birke shrugged. "He said they were ancient magic that no decent folk should use. I think there was a ballroom once on the third level. I saw it in the old drawings, but that was a long time ago, and now that space is where the library is."

Jecks nodded at that.

Anna managed not to frown. Brill hadn't been happy when she'd mentioned the use of multiple drums, but he'd never really explained, despite all her questions. And then he'd died before Anna could follow up. Jecks had clearly been unhappy with the ballroom at Synfal and had already told Herstat to do something about it—without telling Anna. Herstat had asked Anna—quietly. Anna had told him to go ahead. If it upset Jecks that much, it would certainly have upset others. What she still didn't understand was why they all went crazy about dancing. As if it were so immoral. Anna sighed quietly. She wouldn't change that. And drums? What kind of sorcery went with drums? The books she'd gotten from Brill had alluded to their use, but she'd never had the time to pore through them all, not with the struggle of reading a language that was a cross between Old English and German.

As Farinelli carried her steadily along the dusty gray clay road, she studied the approach to the keep instead. Abenfel stood on a low hill, the gates to the north. Directly to the east and the south were higher grassy hills. To the west, the ground sloped gently for more than a dek to a line of trees, which marked, from what Anna could see, a bluff, possibly overlooking the Falche. Because of the haze, she could not make out the far side of the river, but she gained the impression that even the upper part of the Great Chasm was considerable. Was it like the Grand Canyon, or narrower and deeper like the Black Canyon of the Gunnison?

Her eyes went back to Abenfel.

A permanent bridge, of later construction from the darker stone, spanned a dry moat almost a hundred yards wide and ten deep and led to the open gates, roughly three yards high, and bound with dark iron.

One of the riders with Birke unfurled a green-and-gray pennant.

Hanfor nodded and murmured something to one of the scouts, who unfurled the Regency banner. Without speaking, both standard bearers rode to the front of the column.

High thin clouds were turning orange and pink as the sun dropped behind the lower peaks to the west, leaving only the tips of the higher mountains to the south in light, and but briefly.

No one spoke as the column rode across the bridge and causeway.

Anna had barely reined up in the courtyard of Abenfel before Lord Birfels crossed the worn but still well-set gray paving stones. Birfels' red hair was more than half white, and his ruddy complexion was blotched from too many years in the sun. "Regent Anna."

"Lord Birfels." Anna swung out of the saddle.

"You dress and ride like a lancer, as slim as many, if more deadly." The faded brown eyes held a hint of a smile, and Anna could see the similarity between Birfels and his offspring—both Birke and his older sister Lysara, who had replaced Birke as a fosterling at Falcor.

Anna shrugged. "I've had to learn to ride, but a blade is beyond my skill."

"Not a dagger, I understand."

Anna tried not to flush. She'd never live down the time she'd gutted a Neserean lancer who'd tried to ambush her in Falcor's stable. "I was fortunate."

Birfels waited as a slender and white-haired woman neared. Despite the silvery-white hair, her face and figure conveyed that she was a good decade younger than the lord.

"Lady Anna, this is Fylena, my consort."

"Lady Anna," Fylena smiled warmly. "Birke has told us so much about you."

"I am pleased to be here, Lady Fylena. I do hope Birke hasn't revealed too many of my weaknesses."

"From his tales, we were not aware that you had any." Birfels offered another hearty laugh.

The southern lord was certainly more voluble than he had been in the past, and Anna had to wonder why. She patted Farinelli absently. The gelding *whuff*ed. "I have more than my share. I try not to reveal them too blatantly."

"You have been most successful," said Fylena gently.

"I would be honored to place all of Abenfel at your disposal," offered Birfels. "I have even repaired and filled the reflecting pool once used by the lady Peuletar."

"Your hospitality is most generous," Anna responded.

"And most self-serving," added Birfels, self-deprecatingly. "You are the first ruler of Defalk in generations to put down the Suhlmorran lords, something long overdue.''

"You must excuse my ignorance," Anna said. "As you know, I have had to learn the history of Defalk. I presume you do not come from that line.''

"Hardly. That we can discuss at supper." Birfels turned to Jecks, who had dismounted with so little fuss that Anna had almost forgotten he was there. "Jecks, you are always welcome.''

"You would be welcome at Elheld, Birfels, if your bones could stand the chill.''

From behind and to the side of Fylena, Birke grinned.

"It is chill enough here for me, come winter and the snows. The cold I would not mind, only that wind out of the north, and you may keep it there.''

"Lord Birfels, I must confess I am relatively new to this business." Anna gestured to Hanfor, who had remained mounted. "This is the Regency's arms commander, Hanfor. We have somewhere over twelvescore lancers and others with us.''

"Arms Commander, you are most welcome. Syliern will be here momentarily, and he can offer you a choice of quarters for all your men." Birfels offered an ironic grin. "Abenfel was once the southern keep of Defalk during the insurgencies. We have some considerable space.''

"And for our mounts?''

"There are close to five hundred stalls in the rear stable. I believe we might have a hundred mounts.''

Hanfor bowed his head slightly. "We will take care, then.''

"Knowing this lady," Birfels said with a nod toward Anna, "I would wager that you would scarce do aught other.''

Jecks grinned briefly. "Your fame is spreading, Regent Anna.''

Anna replied with a smile, feeling that any verbal answer would come out wrong, tired as she was. Then, she wanted to shake her ahead. She'd almost forgotten the players again. She made another gesture, this one to beckon Liende forward. "Lord Birfels, Liende, my chief of players."

"I see we share some of the same heritage, chief player," bantered the lord, touching his grayed red hair. "Are you from the south?"

"Only from Arien, lord," answered Liende.

"South enough for me. Be welcome. We have quarters for players, too. And replacement strings, as I recall."

"Thank you." Liende bowed her head.

Birfels turned to the regent. "Could I show you your quarters, Lady Anna?"

"In a moment, if you would, Lord Birfels. I will need to groom and settle Farinelli, and it might be best to get that done."

A frown crossed Birfels' face.

"My sire," interjected Birke quickly. "You might recall this is the raider beast that only the lady can curry. He maimed one groom at Falcor."

"Ah . . . I had forgotten. There are so many tales about you, lady." Birfels shook his head.

"It could wait," Anna said. "But I'll have to groom him sometime."

"Best now, and all will be settled. We will be here when you finish."

After ensuring Farinelli was brushed and fed, and watered, Anna, carrying only her lutar, with Jecks beside her, followed Birfels across the wide courtyard toward the center building of the keep—almost one hundred yards, she figured, by the time they entered the arching front entryway.

The entry foyer was nearly three stories high, with twin quarter-circular marble staircases, rising over an arch that fronted a long corridor.

"That leads to the dining halls and the library," Birfels explained as he pointed to the arch. "The guest chambers are up on the second level."

"It's very impressive," Anna said.

"One of my ancestors had hoped to be Lord of Defalk. The Suhlmorrans ensured otherwise." Birfels gave a crooked grin.

"I'd wager all this stone is chill in the winter," added Jecks.

"Not so cold as one might think."

As she followed Birfels up the polished marble steps, old enough that the centers of the stone risers were slightly hollowed, Anna wondered how many other lords of Defalk had similar thwarted ambitions in their background.

The second-level corridor was equally opulent, with pale green marble floor tiles cut in diamond shapes, and matching green marble sheets set as wainscoting. Fhurgen's and Lejun's boots echoed on the stone as the guards followed with Anna's saddlebags and traveling mirror.

Above the marble wainscoting, the walls were painted pale green, and hung intermittently with life-sized portraits—all men, Anna noted. "Your ancestors?"

"The lords of Abenfel." Birfels smiled briefly. "One presumes so, but life is never so certain as we believe. Neither are bloodlines, for all the fighting over such."

"Nothing's as sure as we'd like," Anna agreed.

Jecks merely nodded.

Beside each portrait were sconces with polished mantels and green candles. None were yet lit, although the fading twilight left the hall dim and gloomy.

Birfels stopped and threw open the carved double doors. "These are the sorceress's guest chambers. We haven't had a sorceress stay in them since my father was a lad." He shook his head. "Hard to believe."

Anna stepped inside. On the polished redstone floor was a deep green braided rug. Apparently, braided rugs were the thing in southern Defalk. The guest chambers were truly a suite, with a bedchamber, a second chamber on one side that contained the reflecting pool and a table with chairs, and a bathchamber on the other side of the bedchamber.

Fhurgen and Lejun set Anna's bags on the low chest at the foot of the high bed with the carved headboard that depicted a woman in a flowing gown and an arm raised to a star over a garden of some sort. Anna set the lutar beside her bags.

"The headboard—that's a depiction of the first Lady Peuletar. There were several, all cousins, descendants of sisters, of course."

"Of course," Anna agreed, knowing that by custom and perhaps by Erde itself, sorceresses had no offspring.

Birfels picked up a striker and lit the candle on the small writing table. "Lady Anna, Fylena and I took the liberty of having warm water placed in the bath. Supper will be in a glass, if that would be satisfactory. . . ."

"That would be fine," Anna said. "Thank you for everything."

"It is more than our pleasure." Birfels bowed and turned to the white-haired lord. "Your chamber is on the other side, Lord Jecks."

"I can stand this sort of place," Anna said to herself after the door closed and she was alone.

The writing desk even had a stack of paper and a recently filled inkwell. Anna shook her head, wondering exactly what Birfels wanted—or was it merely to offer amends now that it had become obvious that she was indeed a powerful sorceress. She fingered the golden-green brocade coverlet on the high bed—fine needlework, but somewhat frayed around the edges.

Anna walked back to the sorceress's room, clearly a working arrangement with a polished, if old, conference table on one side and the reflecting pool almost against the inner wall. A heavy black drape was drawn back from the narrow window.

She glanced at the pool, its waters silvery even without sorcery. Sometime, when she was rested, she'd have to use a pool to see if she could view Elizabetta—when more time had passed.

Then she went to the bathchamber, where a soft white

dressing robe and a large green towel were draped across a wooden and bronze stand. The sorceress dipped a finger into the bathwater—tepid, almost cold. With a sigh she went back to the bedchamber and reclaimed and tuned the lutar, then returned to the bathchamber.

> "Water, water, in the bath below,
> both hot and soothing flow . . ."

Once Anna had the water nearly steaming, she replaced the lutar, undressed, and slipped into the tub, trying to let sore muscles loosen, trying not to think at all.

Later, probably too much later, she dressed slowly, easing into the single gown she had carried, glad for the time to relax without anyone around. A timid knock interrupted her woolgathering.

"Ah . . . yes?"

"Lady Anna?"

"Yes?" Anna repeated, padding across the cool floor barefooted.

Lejun announced, "A young lady with a message."

"I'll take it."

A dark-haired girl—vaguely familiar, although Anna knew she had never seen her before—peered in. "Lady Anna, my sire would welcome you to supper."

Anna motioned the girl into the chamber and plopped herself onto one of the chairs. "You seem familiar."

"I am Clayre, Lady Anna. We have not met, but I wanted to see you. So I asked if I could announce supper."

"Are you Lysara's sister?" Anna could see the facial resemblance between the two, although Lysara had red hair.

"Yes. She is two years the elder."

At the regretful tone, Anna shook her head. "Look at it the other way. You're always going to be younger. For most of your life, it's going to be more fun to be younger than your sister."

The hazel green eyes twinkled momentarily. "I had not thought of that."

Anna reached for the green slipper shoes, glad she didn't have to wear boots.

"Lysara said you were beautiful."

"She's kind. I don't feel beautiful." *I just feel tired.* Her feet were somewhat swollen, and the shoes barely fit, even as soft as the leather was.

"You look tired. Was it a long ride?"

"Five days in the saddle is long anytime. I think I've spent half a season riding since the beginning of spring." Anna stood. "I'm ready."

As she stepped out of her quarters, this time, Lejun slipped from his post to follow them. The black-haired Kerhor remained guarding her door.

"We're going to eat in the family hall," Clayre announced. "It's much nicer than the main hall."

The long marble corridor remained dim, with but one candle in every third or fourth wall sconce being lit. A single large taper in a bronze stand lit the foyer.

Rickel waited outside the ancient redstone archway to the family dining hall, nodding as Anna approached. "Good evening, Regent."

"Good evening, Rickel. I hope you've gotten something to eat."

"I ate earlier, Lady Anna."

A group of people, including Jecks and Hanfor, already waited inside. Everyone paused, and the conversation died as Anna and Clayre entered. Birfels bowed and stepped forward. "Lady Anna, you truly grace us."

"I'm pleased to be here, and happy not to be riding." Anna smiled. "I appreciate your kind hospitality and the chance to see Abenfel. It's truly a grand keep."

Birfels gestured to the head of the table. "If you would?"

"Thank you." Anna stepped toward the table, while the others arranged themselves behind places.

Birfels nodded toward his consort. "You and Fylena

have met, and you know Birke." He inclined his head toward the end of the table. "That is Wasle, and then Clayre." A younger redheaded youth sat farther down the table, but above Clayre.

Anna tried not to bristle at the position of the dark-haired young woman below her younger brother. "Clayre came to tell me about supper. I have not met Wasle." She paused, then asked Hanfor, "Arms Commander Hanfor, how are you finding things?"

The gray-haired and green-eyed veteran nodded. "We appreciate the hospitality, the men especially. You have good barracks here, Lord Birfels."

"Old, but good. They date back over three hundred years to the last Suhlmorran uprising, when Lord—"

"My lord," suggested Fylena mildly, "we could sit and eat and then talk. In greater comfort."

Birfels laughed. "That we should."

Anna took the chair at the head of the long table, as indicated, with Jecks at her right and Birfels at her left. Fylena sat beside Jecks, and Hanfor beside Birfels.

Three serving girls appeared. One bore a silver-rimmed porcelain platter bearing slices of meat smothered in a creamlike sauce and garnished with sprigs of narrow green leaves. Another carried two baskets of bread, and the third, a dish of something white and steaming.

The main dish came straight to Anna, who served herself, but waited for the others, taking some bread, and then some of the spiced and steamed apples.

"Will you be heading straight back to Falcor?" asked Fylena, after taking a small portion of the meat and sauce.

"I don't know yet." Anna smiled politely. "I thought I might wait a few days, if your lordship doesn't mind." Her head inclined toward Birfels. "I'd like to see what Lord Ehara's reaction is."

"Lord Ehara?" Birfel's eyebrows knitted up.

"Oh . . ." Anna shook her head. "You live with these things, and sometimes you don't realize that others haven't any idea what you're talking about. Lord Ehara sent something like four companies of Dumaran lancers to support Lord Sargol and Lord Dencer."

"What did you do to them, Lady Anna?" Birke asked brashly.

"They will not threaten Defalk again," Jecks said firmly, his eyes fixing on the redhead.

"Yes, sire." Birke's tone was abashed.

At the end of the table, Anna could see Clayre toying with her shoulder-length dark and wavy brown hair, twirling it around a finger as the girl-woman waited for the large platter of meat and sauce to make its way down to her.

"That is for the best," Birfels said. "Yet . . . lancers of Dumar in Defalk. How did that come to be?"

"Lord Dencer sought aid from Dumar, or was receptive to it," Anna said. "Sargol followed his example."

"Mayhap the other way," added Jecks. "Since both are dead, and the lancers—"

"All of them?"

"All of them," Jecks confirmed.

Wasle and Clayre exchanged glances.

Anna took a small mouthful of meat and sauce, finding it comparatively mild for Defalkan dishes. The knife and spoon at her place were heavy sterling, ornately designed with a nut-and-leaf pattern. The weight and the minute scratches testified to the cutlery's considerable age and quality.

"This is beautiful silver," she said. "A family heirloom?"

His mouth full, Birfels nodded, finally swallowing and answering. "From before my great-great-grandsire."

"How fares Lysara?" asked Fylena.

"You may have heard from her since I saw her," Anna said. "We left Falcor at the . . . turn of spring. She seemed to enjoy her studies."

"She said as much when she came home in the fall." Birfels broke off another hunk of bread.

"Once Lysara is betrothed . . . perhaps you would consider Clayre as a fosterling?" asked Fylena.

Betrothed? Anna took a small mouthful of bread and chewed, rather than risk speaking immediately. Falcor wasn't a finishing and mating school! "Ah . . . Lysara hadn't mentioned becoming a consort."

"She is getting to be that age," answered Fylena.

"Do you have anyone in mind?" Anna lifted the goblet and sipped the pale red vintage. "This is good wine."

"Thank you," acknowledged Birfels.

"I have exchanged scrolls with Lady Resengna." Seeing Anna's unspoken question, Fylena added, "She is the consort of Lord Dannel of Mossbach. Their youngest— Hoede, is he not in Falcor?"

Anna managed to swallow the wine without choking. Hoede, of the thick skull and overbearing manner? "He is one of the fosterlings. He has not expressed any interest in Lysara."

"Ah . . . one cannot expect much of young people at that age. They will see it is for the best."

"I can see that it would be an excellent match for Hoede," Anna said politely.

"Well . . . she must find someone from the Thirty-three, Lady Anna," answered Fylena sweetly. "Perhaps you might find a better match for her. She does respect you so."

Sucker! You fell right into that one. . . . Anna smiled. "I had not thought about it, but I certainly will."

Fylena nodded. "Lysara would be most pleased, and so would we."

"Birke was telling me that you left Dencer's consort to rule his lands for his heir, and that you have a force safeguarding Sargol's young sons as well." The red-headed lord raised his goblet and sipped the wine, then reached for the platter of meat.

"His daughter and his young sons." Anna glanced down. Had she eaten everything?

"Lady Wendella had proved difficult at Falcor, had she not?" asked Birfels.

"She will not prove difficult in that way again," Anna said.

Wasle and Clayre exchanged quick looks again.

"You have managed to settle Defalk in less than a year." Birfels flashed a smile. "No new ruler has managed that in centuries, much less a regent." He laughed. "You know what they used to say about Defalk? Don't worry too much about the lord. If he's to be worried about, he won't last."

"Then perhaps it's better to have a lady," parried Anna.

From beside Hanfor, Birke grinned. Farther down the table, Clayre nudged Wasle and whispered something.

"You have already proven that on the field, my lady," Jecks said mildly. "And in just about every other place. Alasia said you might." He took the smaller basket of bread and extracted the largish heel, turning his head and giving Anna the quickest of winks.

"Ah . . . yes. I see we need some more bread," said Fylena quickly. "Diella!"

A serving girl appeared and scurried off with the empty basket.

"How came you to serve the regent?" asked Birfels, looking at Hanfor.

The veteran smiled pleasantly. "I was serving as one of the Prophet's overcaptains . . ."

Anna took another helping of the sauce and meat and another ladle of the spiced steamed apples, letting Hanfor weave his tale. The less she said the better . . . definitely the better.

70

Dumaria, Dumar

"I would have you read this." Ehara's bass voice emphasizes the last word as he hands the scroll to the Sea-Marshal in white. He continues to sit upright in the chair behind the writing desk, ignoring the small pieces of green wax that litter the polished wood.

"She is angry," jerRestin says. "So much the better."

"*She* is angry? I cannot believe that she would demand a thousand golds and my pledge." Ehara's eyes fix on the Sturinnese officer. "Never have I been so insulted."

"She wishes you to be insulted, to be angry." JerRestin laughs. "And she has succeeded."

"A thousand golds?"

"Lord Ehara, why do you not request two thousand from her? Tell her that the unrest created by her inability to govern has cost you dearly. Suggest that she is in a poor position to demand anything of Dumar."

"I would not give her the satisfaction. . . ."

"What does it cost you to ask of her what is *your* due—both in terms of golds and of honor?"

"I should lower myself . . ." Ehara shakes his head.

"She is a woman and an outsider. She cannot be expected to understand such. The Maitre understands that different standards must be applied to women—lower standards." JerRestin extends the scroll. "You must do what you must do."

"You make it sound as though I must respond to her . . . her presumptions." Ehara stands and takes back the scroll, looking down at the Sturinnese.

"She is like a willful child. She may be powerful, but

she knows nothing of how the world works. If someone does not educate her . . .''

''*I* should educate her?''

''You would not wish the Maitre to speak for Dumar, would you? Or the Liedfuhr of Mansuur?''

Ehara shakes his head. ''You twist words as well as the slippery women of the south.''

JerRestin's eyes glitter, but he remains silent.

''Since I must, I will respond, but for my pains, she must pay three thousand golds.'' The Lord of Dumar sets the scroll on the writing desk.

71

Anna looked out the window from the bedchamber through the gray early-morning mist—wondering why she had awakened so early. She'd never been a true early bird, no matter how many early-morning classes she'd had to teach over the years.

To the west, she could see the trees on the bluff that overlooked the effective beginning of the great Chasm, although, from what she'd seen, the river had cut out a valley that extended another ten deks back to the northeast from Abenfel. She'd meant to take a ride to see the Chasm, but somehow, various things kept intruding, including the continual arrival of scrolls from Falcor and Synor. Herstat, Dythya, and Menares were well-organized . . . but their organization and unwillingness to act unless they had clear directions from her was taking more time than ever she would have believed.

That wasn't why she'd awakened early.

Was it Ehara? There had been no answer from the Lord of Dumar, but Anna already half suspected that she'd either get no response—or one that was impossible. While she worried about what she could—or should—do, whatever had wakened her didn't feel like that.

She turned and studied the bedchamber again. The door bolt was firmly shut. While she could hear noises through the window, they seemed like normal keep noises.

What else could it be? Were even more sorcerers looking for her? How would she know?

That . . . that she could determine.

She took out the lutar and walked into the chamber with the reflecting pool, and softly ran through one vocalise, then another, coughing and crackling, and slowly clearing her throat. Lord, she hated trying to sing in the morning. But she probably wouldn't get that much time later.

Finally, she stood before the pool, as the gray light outside began to turn faint gold.

> "Of those with power of the song
>   seek those who'd do me wrong
>   and show them in this silver
>   cast
>   and make that vision well last."

Anna took more time to study the three images in the glass—the blonde woman seer from Nordwei, the hawk-faced Sea-Priest, and the young black-bearded man.

In the light of dawn, the Sea-Priest stood under a spreading green tree, before a wide, parklike expanse of lawn. Beside him stood another man in the white of Sturinn. The other man gestured vaguely in a direction Anna couldn't discern from the scene. The younger man—not the sorcerer—looked hurriedly toward a building in the background. The Sea-Priest smiled indulgently.

The black-bearded young sorcerer stood in a darkened room where only his face and that of another young man were fully clear. The other man seemed to be standing before what Anna thought was a drum set—a drum set in Liedwahr? But no details appeared.

Anna released the spell and stepped over to the table, seating herself and taking out paper and greasemarker. Before long, she tried again.

> "Silver water 'tween the stone,
>   show me, and me alone,
>   that sorcerer in black and brown
>   and in what land he may be found . . ."

The glass showed something from the air. Anna squinted at the image. Three rivers converging into one? The Fal, the Chean, and the Synor all turned into the Falche—another sorcerer in Defalk?

After a moment, she released the spell and worried her lower lip. Then she returned to the table. It took longer the third time.

> "Silver water 'tween the stone,
>   show me, and me alone,
>   that sorcerer in black and brown
>   and in what town he may be found . . ."

The pool obediently showed another aerial image that could have been one of a dozen towns—or more. Two main roads, buildings in the center, becoming farther apart away from the center of the silver-shrouded image, but with nothing that Anna could recognize as a distinguishing feature.

"Shit . . ." she murmured, releasing the image once more, setting the lutar aside, and reseating herself with paper and greasemarker.

She tried seeking the sorcerer for a fourth time.

> "Silver water 'tween the stone,
>   show me, and me alone,
>   that sorcerer in black and brown,
>   and the river near where he is found . . ."

That brought a close-up of a river, but Anna couldn't really tell the scale, nor could she see anything that would tell her whether the river she saw was the Chean, the Fal, or the Synor. Half the problem was that she wasn't that good with spells when she didn't know a name, and the other half was that she wasn't that familiar with Defalk or Liedwahr.

One thing had become very clear. Names—the right names—were very important in certain aspects of sorcery. The problem was that she didn't have the right names— at least that was the problem in locating the obscure sorcerer.

Finally, she went back to the desk and began to draft a scroll to Menares, to tell him that there was a good possibility that another sorcerer had appeared in Defalk and requesting that he discover what he could quietly. The old schemer was good at intrigue. Perhaps he could come up with some clue that would help her spellcasting.

As she finished the first scroll, she nodded to herself. Best also to send a scroll to Dythya and one to Herstat. They were solid, and would certainly let her know if anything came up.

72

Anna eased into the chair at the head of the table, then smiled at Jecks.

"You look rested." The Lord of Elheld smiled. The dark circles and haggard cheeks that he had brought to Abenfel had also vanished.

"So do you." Even as she said that, it occurred to her that the days at Abenfel had provided her with more of rest than perhaps any time since she had been spirited to

Liedwahr by Daffyd's spell. And that was even with the scrolls from Menares and Dythya that had found their way to Abenfel.

"You needed the days . . ." Jecks' voice dropped off.

"I am so glad you decided to remain longer," interjected Fylena. "Birke has been so pleased. All of us have been." The silver-haired consort of Birfels offered a broad smile.

"You have been most hospitable." Anna glanced toward the foot of the table, where the young red-haired Wasle sat above his older sister Clayre. The dark-haired Clayre was playing with her hair again, absently, as she listened to those around her. Was she bored? Waiting for something to happen in her life? To go to Falcor?

Anna wondered when she'd get back to Falcor. Should she just leave? And then have to turn around when Ehara acted?

". . . have been able to open some of the higher ditches for the first time in nearly ten years. . . ." The words drifted from where Birke talked with Hanfor.

Anna wondered. Everyone was so happy that the rivers were rising, happy that the rain fell, but did they really understand the cost? Or care? Water was vital, especially to countries like Defalk, where everything depended on the rivers or the rains . . . yet somehow people expected the rains to fall and the rivers to flow.

"Yet . . . you look somewhat . . . absent. . . ." suggested Birfels.

"I'm sorry," Anna answered, her fingers curling around the goblet that Jecks had filled. "I was . . . distracted." She smiled. "Your hospitality has been wonderful, and I have enjoyed Abenfel greatly."

"Yet you are regent, and must think of other matters. I understand."

Anna wondered. Did anyone else see what she did? Or was the prevailing modus operandi to wait and react? But wasn't that exactly what she was doing—waiting for Ehara's reaction? But then what? What could she do?

73

ENCORA, RANUAK

"I am so glad you finally deigned to join us for dinner, dear," says the Matriarch as Veria enters the smaller dining room.

"You could make her welcome," suggests Ulgar.

"Why?" asks Veria. "That would be hypocritical, and we both know that. Really, Father." She slips into the seat across from him.

Alya shakes her head infinitesimally, but lifts the long carved wooden bread platter and hands it to her sister.

"Thank you, Alya. You do bake wonderful bread."

"One of the few things you approve of, Veria," responds Alya. "Since we are committed to honesty this evening, and not manners or tact."

"Honesty has much to recommend it," answers Veria easily. "Especially when dealing with a sorceress prone to Darksong."

"So long as it is not selective honesty, which is often worse than falsehood," says the Matriarch, her gray eyes fixing on her dark-haired daughter.

Ulgar swallows silently, and gives a quick shake of his head as Alya starts to open her mouth.

"It was very foolish of the SouthWomen to buy that cargo of blades—even through two trading fronts," observes the Matriarch. "It was even more foolish to send them to the freewomen of Elawha."

"When the Maitre of Sturinn is openly supporting that toad Bertmynn?" asks Veria. "What are we supposed to do? Cheer when the women of Elawha are forced into the chains of Sturinn?"

"Your mother has always opposed Sturinn," interjects Ulgar quickly. "You might remember that."

"She has opposed Sturinn with words," adds Veria, ripping off a second chunk of the flaky-crusted bread with a quick and violent twist. "The Matriarchs have buckled under when it appeared Sturinn might be mightily displeased. Or have we already forgotten the massacre of the Sisters of the South? When our own Matriarch murdered our compatriots to appease the Sturinnese?"

"Two women who chose to consort with a Sturinnese merchant, against the advice of their families and the Matriarch, were whipped and died. Your storied Sisters of the South killed the entire crew of a merchant ship that had nothing to do with the crime, except that they refused to surrender the merchant to a mob." The Matriarch sniffed. "That is hardly the stuff of noble legend."

"Your predecessor once removed executed those women who survived."

"As she should have. As would I—even were one of them my own daughter, dear Veria." The Matriarch's words are even, polite, and like ice.

"I see." Veria sets down the bread on her plate. "So . . . Matriarch and Mother, what would you have had us do with the blades?"

"Let the sorceress have bought them, or given them to the Ebran Hadrenn." The Matriarch smiles pleasantly, although her eyes remain cool. "We have talked about the sorceress, and there you know my reasoning."

"I know you would support a sorceress who uses Darksong to keep men in power."

"We do not agree on that," the Matriarch answers calmly, "but if you had sent them to Hadrenn, he would have the men to use them against Bertmynn."

"You do not think the freewomen will not fight?"

"They will fight, and they will die. The Sturinnese will lose armsmen, and take vengeance on the city. Bertmynn will rightly blame the SouthWomen, and wrongly blame Ranuak, and we will both suffer. Hadrenn will lose more armsmen than he would need to lose. Eventually, the sorceress will be forced to act, and even more Ebrans, many of them women, will die.''

"You know everything and do nothing.''

"I persuaded the Exchange to grant credit to the lords of Defalk. Most supported the sorceress, and the three rebels fell quickly. She will feel compelled to act against Sturinn, and that will strengthen us.'' The Matriarch smiles coldly. "And women will not die, or few indeed, unlike the city's worth your rashness will kill.''

Alya winces, then smooths her face.

"You have an answer for everything.'' Veria rises. "I should not have come.''

"No, daughter, I am relieved you did come.''

"You don't sound relieved.'' Veria steps back from the table.

"I am relieved,'' continues the Matriarch inexorably, "because, if you continue this foolishness, you will do so knowing I will not hesitate to treat you as any other.''

"Matriarch and Mother, that I knew already. Good evening.''

The three at the table wait until the door closes. Even after that, not a voice is heard.

74

Anna pulled on her single simple green gown. Her stomach growled, reminding her that after an afternoon of riding along the Great Chasm, a canyon that certainly deserved its name, she was more than ready to eat. The Falche almost reminded her of the Colorado, winding through steep cliffs, except that the rocks were more like the granite of the Black Canyon. And all that water flowed into Dumar. There ought to be something . . .

Thrap!

"Yes?"

"A message for you, lady."

Anna frowned—more scrolls from Falcor? Her eyes went to the scrolls on the writing desk as she walked barefooted to the door of the bedchamber. "Rickel?"

"Yes, Lady Anna?"

"A message?"

"A message from Dumar, Lady Anna."

Anna opened the door.

Rickel stood there, flanked by Blaz and Lejun. "The messenger arrived here less than a tenth of a glass ago. Alvar took the message and sent it with me. The messenger insisted that someone write a scroll that the message had been delivered to the regent. Lord Jecks is writing such now." Rickel extended a scroll wrapped in gold-and-red ribbon.

"Please have someone find Hanfor and Lord Jecks— once he's finished with writing that scroll for the messenger. I'll need to see them both." Anna took the scroll.

"Yes, Lady Anna." The blond guard bowed.

Anna closed the door and walked into the "work chamber," sitting down at the conference table used so many years earlier by other sorceresses. She broke the ornate red-wax seal and unrolled the missive. At the bottom was another crimson seal over crimson-and-gold ribbons.

While she waited for Jecks and Hanfor, she began to read the scroll, slowly.

To the Regent of Defalk,

  With felicitations and wishes for a fruitful and peaceful year in our neighbor to the north . . .

Anna skipped through the dozen lines of meaningless flattery and well-wishing.

. . . Insomuch as you have neither accorded Dumar nor the Lord of Dumar the honor due both . . . Insomuch as you have failed to satisfy the lords of your own land and to keep the peace . . . Insomuch as many of these lords appealed to Dumar for aid in restoring time-honored ways and customs and order to their lands . . . Dumar will stand ready to assist you, to offer counsel and advice, and to ensure that Defalk's borders remain in accord with the ancient traditions . . . but in view of the great and grievous harms done to Dumar, and to the honor of Dumar . . . such assistance cannot occur unless the Regency of Defalk were to indemnify Dumar for such harms. . . . Three thousand golds would be little enough, a bare pittance given the affront Dumar has suffered, however inadvertent such affronts may have been . . . for surely, as the Regent of Defalk may take liedgeld and honor from the lords of the Thirty-three, so also must the Regency bear the costs of the actions of its lords upon others, as well as the costs incurred by the acts of the regent. . . .

Anna set down the scroll . . . waiting. Her eyes went to the window. She had her confirmation, but what could she do next?

Someone rapped on the door in the adjoining chamber.

"Come in," she called loudly.

After a moment, Jecks appeared, Hanfor somewhat behind his shoulder. "Lady Anna."

"Sit down." She handed the scroll to Jecks. "You were right. He's not about to admit wrong, and he certainly isn't about to pay for the damage he's created."

"Most lords would not."

Especially not to a female regent. "Go ahead and read it. You, too, Hanfor."

Anna waited, still wondering how she could deal with Ehara. She couldn't keep shuttling between the south of Defalk and Falcor. She didn't have enough of an army—

yet—to leave at Stromwer or Abenfel. And she couldn't wage a conventional war—not conventional for Liedwahr, anyway—against Ehara. She didn't even have a way to wage guerrilla warfare against Dumar, and that was if she even knew how—which she didn't.

"He is most offended." Jecks passed the scroll to Hanfor.

"Let me understand this," Anna said quietly, trying to keep from boiling over. "He sent golds and companies of lancers into Defalk to support an uprising, and he's upset that I called him on it? He's cost Defalk thousands of golds, and he's upset that I suggested he repay some of it? He's behaved dishonorably by trying to subvert the legitimate heir of Defalk, and he thinks I've dishonored him by having the nerve to say so?"

Jecks cleared his throat and looked at the polished wood of the table.

Anna waited.

"He does not believe that anything he has done is dishonorable."

"A lord like Ehara," added Hanfor, "believes that all he does is honorable, and that all anyone else does is not."

Anna couldn't see that much difference between Ehara and half the lords of Thirty-three in Defalk. "So how do we convince him? Or make sure that he stops meddling?"

"I know of no way, save defeating him in battle." Jecks frowned. "You have not enough armsmen, even were you to call up levies, to carry the fight to him. This he knows."

"Some other show of force?" Anna wasn't sure what that might be, except the idea of affecting the river came back to her.

"Ehara may respond to no other force." The muscular lord shrugged fluidly.

"Do you wish to use sorcery?" asked Hanfor.

"The only kind of sorcery that I can think of that would

be effective is the kind that kills people,'' Anna said. *Are you sure?*

Jecks shrugged.

''In other words, I have to find a way to slaughter most of the able-bodied armsmen in Dumar, or risk having this tradition-bound idiot continually stirring up trouble in southern Defalk.''

''I know of no other way. Even had you the golds he demands, to pay them would only encourage him to demand more.''

Anna repressed a glare at Jecks. She'd already figured that out. She stood. ''I need a few moments to think before dinner.'' *And to cool off . . . if you can.*

''As you wish, my lady. I would that it were otherwise,'' said Jecks, rising and bowing.

Hanfor just bowed. ''Lady Anna.''

She waited until the door closed.

Why? Why did it come down to how many people she could kill?

There had to be another way . . . there just had to be— some way to show Ehara that she was powerful and was withholding that power. Some way that didn't involve mass slaughter.

She started to look for her green slipper shoes, her thoughts skittering every which way, but always coming back to the issue of force.

As she slipped on the second shoe and straightened, her eyes went toward the Great Chasm. She frowned. The Chasm was big; it had rock walls that looked sturdy, and it could hold a lot of water, maybe even as much as Lake Mead or Lake Powell, and they'd taken years to fill.

How would Dumar do without water?

She smiled. *It's only an idea . . . but . . .*

With a brisk nod to herself, she headed toward the door and dinner.

75

A nna glanced toward the window and the bright morning light—much brighter than she felt as she glanced over Lord Ehara's scroll again. Hanfor glanced at Jecks, and the older lord glanced back. Both watched Anna.

"Before I do anything, I'd like to see how Lord Birfels reacts. That's why I summoned you. He should be here any moment."

"Yes, Regent." Hanfor nodded.

"He knew a messenger arrived yesterday," Jecks pointed out. "He may be unhappy he was not told sooner."

"He'll be the first to know, besides you two. That will have to do."

Both men fell silent, either deciding to see what happened or because of the chill in Anna's voice.

"Lord Birfels," announced Rickel.

"Have him join us."

"You had asked to see me, Lady Anna?" Birfels bowed as he entered the sorceress's work chamber, first to Anna, and then to Jecks and Hanfor. Hanfor and Jecks stood as he entered.

"Please sit down." Anna remained seated at the table, waiting until the ruddy-faced lord slipped into the chair opposite her.

"Thank you."

"You are a lord of the Thirty-three, Lord Birfels." Anna smiled. "How do you feel about Lord Ehara of Dumar?"

"Lord Ehara?" Birfels frowned. "You have told how

he sent lancers into Defalk. Before that . . . none scarce heard of him.''

''Would you say that most lords of the Thirty-three would feel that way?'' Anna's tone was almost idle.

''We have heard little of Dumar nor had to worry little in previous years.'' Birfels shrugged.

''Lord Ehara is beginning to give you good reason to worry.'' Anna extended the scroll with the crimson-and-gold ribbons across the table. ''If you would read this.''

Birfels began to read. By the time his eyes were half-way down the sheet, his normally mobile face was set in stone. Finally, he lowered the scroll. ''He is most offended.''

''Yes, he is.'' Anna forced a smile. ''I'm a little confused. As I pointed out earlier to Lord Jecks, Lord Ehara has sent golds to support rebel lords in Defalk. He has sent lancers directly against the Regency, and against Defalk. I suggested to him that such was neither honorable nor proper and requested that he redeem his honor in gold. This was his response.''

''It does appear . . . unusual.'' Birfels paused. ''Many have seen the Dumaran lancers? The ones in Defalk?''

''Those in Dencer's keep and Gylaron's.'' Hanfor's mouth twisted into a crooked smile. ''Those who were close to them at Suhl . . . perished with them.''

Anna forced herself to remain calm, even as she could sense Birfels trying to rationalize how any lord of Dumar could be dishonorable.

''Ah . . . yes.'' Birfels glanced at the scroll again. ''You did not mention this last night.''

''I wanted to think about it.'' *So the most honorable Lord Birfels was watching the messenger, too.* ''Outside of Lord Jecks . . . and myself''—Anna couldn't resist the reference to her own status as one of the Thirty-three of Defalk—''you are the first of the Thirty-three to see it.''

''He may have been offended that you suggested his honor was not enough to back any pledge of . . . friendship.'' Birfels glanced to Jecks, as if looking for support.

"He may have been," Anna said mildly. "His actions have not been exactly friendly. He does not mention the Sturinnese officers who have apparently pledged great friendship to him and to Dumar."

"Sturinn is far across the ocean to the west." Birfels smiled. "Dumar has ports and trade. Defalk does not."

"That's true." Anna nodded slowly, trying to keep from visibly seething. "Yet a Dumar under Sturinn would not be good for Defalk."

"Sturinn ruling Dumar. That is like worrying about sour cider before the apples have fruited, much less fallen from the trees." Birfels smiled.

"Perhaps." Anna nodded, turning to Hanfor. "Do you know how the Prophet of Music felt about Sturinn?"

Hanfor touched his gray beard, pursed his lips for a moment. "He spoke of the need to put Liedwahr under one ruler before Sturinn turned its ships eastward."

"Aye, and he wanted to be that ruler," said Birfels. "Much good his efforts gained him."

Anna cleared her throat. She'd heard enough. "You can see, Lord Birfels. This places Defalk in a difficult position. Lord Ehara is denying any responsibility for the damages he has already caused. He's actually asking for blackmail—tribute," Anna added at the look of incomprehension on Birfels' face, "before he will assure Defalk he will not cause further trouble."

"That is true," conceded the red-haired lord of Abenfel. "Yet you cannot match his forces, not armsman to armsman, or anywhere close." He frowned. "You are not proposing a levy of sorts on the Thirty-three, or an increase in liedgeld?"

"I hadn't thought of that." Anna kept her tone sweet. "I'm looking into applying some form of sorcery to Lord Ehara—something that would remind him that armsmen are not the only form of force."

"Would that . . ." Birfels broke off, almost embarrassed-looking.

"Be honorable?" Anna finished. "I'd say sorcery is as

honorable as slaughter, and more honorable than lying.''
She smiled sweetly. ''Wouldn't you, Lord Birfels?''

''Lord Ehara would doubtless not see it that way.'' Birfels laughed abruptly. ''I wish you well in whatever you plan. I can spare you perhaps two score armsmen, should you need them, and guesting here for so long as needful.''

''Thank you. I may well need them. If I do, I will pay them. That would be the least I could do.'' Anna rose. ''Thank you for being so forthcoming, Lord Birfels.''

''I am glad I have supported you, Lady Anna.'' Birfels shook his head as he rose from the conference table. ''And I will continue to do so.'' He bowed. ''If I may be of any other service . . .''

''You have been most kind, and most hospitable.'' Anna smiled again.

Once the door closed, Jecks turned to Anna. ''You are dangerous, Lady Anna.''

''Thank you.'' *Not bad for almost losing it.*

''You have a sorcerous plan in mind. Birfels feels you do.''

''I have an idea. I'd like to see what's going on in Dumar first, but I definitely have an idea.'' *Like shutting off their water . . . just like the Evult shut off Defalk's?* ''Isn't Dumar very dependent on the water in the Falche? All the cities are on the river, aren't they?''

''No sorcery could hold that river . . .'' Jecks shook his head. ''. . . not even yours.''

''Not sorcery itself, but a product of sorcery.'' *Maybe.* She stood and headed to pick up the lutar. ''We might as well see what we're really up against.'' *And whether your thoughts about somehow damming the river make any sense—or would do anything at all.*

After tuning the lutar, and spending more time scrawling out adaptations of mirror spells, Anna reclaimed the lutar, glanced in the reflecting pool, then began the spell.

> ''Show in Dumar, high and true,
> what the Sea-Priests do.

Show me now, and show me all,
where their ships and forces fall . . .''

The sorceress lowered the lutar. The silver-shaded waters misted, then glowed before two images filled the pool.
More than twenty three-masted ships lay in the harbor—
Narial—while the split image showed another score anchored in a wide river below a bluff—Dumaria?

Hanfor and Jecks, each flanking Anna, studied the waters.

"Twoscore ships," mused Hanfor. "I'd wager two
hundred lancers or armsmen a hull."

Four thousand trained troops, Anna thought. *That's
what the Sea-Priests can spare. We've got all of four hundred armsmen, plus levies, and that's everything.*

Hanfor jotted down some notes for a moment; Jecks
surveyed the images, nodding every so often.

Steam began to curl off the water, and Anna could feel
the beginning of a headache when she chanted the release
spell. While the image would fade sooner or later, the
spell cut it off—and the drain on her.

"Those ships would say that the Sea-Priests wish to
add Dumar and, in time, all of Liedwahr, to their domains." Jecks fingered his smooth chin.

Anna wondered how he managed to be so clean-shaven
when hot water and safety razors weren't available. He
never seemed to cut himself, either.

"Now that they have consolidated their hold on the
Ostisles . . ." murmured Hanfor.

Anna nodded, thinking. The ships were the key. What
could she do? "What would happen if they lost their
ships?"

"They would not wish to send others, not soon," offered Hanfor. "Armsmen, lancers, they have often lost
such. Ships are prized."

Anna nodded and stepped away from the pool and to
the table where she had laid out her skimpy references.
As they watched, Anna took out the leather folder and

began to page through Brill's notes and papers—the ones she'd retrieved from Loiseau. Some of them made little sense, but she knew that fussy old Brill had to have written something on how he'd created the artificial lake and water gates at the Sand Pass.

She didn't have thousands of soldiers. She didn't have handfuls of sorcerers. She didn't have hundreds of storerooms of grains and strongbox rooms filled with gold. What golds she had already belonged to others, or might as well.

Then, abruptly, she closed the folder. Seeking out water spells could wait—but only until she had time to work one out in quiet.

"You are silent, Lady Anna," ventured Jecks.

"I'm considering more disastrous sorcery to deal with Lord Ehara and the Sea-Priests. I'm going to have to think some, though."

"You should take advantage of Lord Birfels' hospitality while you can," suggested Jecks. "Do not bury yourself here in your rooms."

"I won't." *Not too much, anyway.* "I could use a ride." She smiled. "I'd like to see the Falche, and Lord Birfels certainly might feel happier if I were out of the keep for a bit." She stood. "I'll be down at the stables in a bit. Would you like to join me?"

Hanfor bowed. "I appreciate your kindness."

"But professional armsmen ride too much, and there are duties pressing?" She smiled gently.

"You understand, I see, lady."

Anna laughed gently. "Go do whatever. I'm not upset."

Jecks frowned. "I think I will go with you, lady." He grinned suddenly. "You do little without a purpose."

"I'm taking advantage of Lord Birfels' hospitality," the sorceress pointed out.

"I shall also." The white-haired lord bowed.

When she had closed the door behind the two, Anna walked back to the reflecting pool and picked up the lutar from the chest against the wall, then stepped up to the shimmering water.

> "Show me now so clear to see
> where the Falche's cliffs most narrow be,
> that site so near . . ."

The pool showed an image of a narrow gorge with high gray cliffs. The Falche seemed far below, a narrow ribbon of silver. Anna shook her head. What else could she rely on? And what other options did she have?

> "Let this scene of scrying, mirror filled with light,
> vanish like the darkness when the sun is bright . . ."

She replaced the lutar in its case, closed the leather folder, and walked back to the bedchamber.

"Now . . . for a ride. Let's see what that gorge really looks like. . . . if it's like I remember . . ."

She frowned. Could she dam the river? Well . . . Brill and everyone else had said spells either worked or they didn't. She hoped she could find the right location . . . and the right spell. A dam was a lot bigger than a bridge. *But not as big as turning a valley into a volcano. . . .*

Somehow that didn't comfort her a lot. She paused.

What could happen? The Falche could just grow behind the dam she wasn't sure she could create and fill up all the low canyons feeding into the Chasm behind the dam, maybe flood a few of the lowest fields in a year or two. Some day, it would flow over the spillway, and return to being the water source for Dumar. In the meantime, the Sturinnese might take over Dumar, and she and Jecks would have to decide whether a war in Dumar was worth it.

On the other hand, after a few weeks of dryness, Ehara *might* reconsider.

She shook her head. If Ehara were like all the other lords she'd run across . . . Yet . . . what else could she do?

If she invaded Dumar and blasted everyone with sorcery, without trying other alternatives, then her own lords, and lords or rulers elsewhere, would all be laying for her. They would anyway, but she had to make it harder on them . . . and give the innocents in Dumar a chance, long shot though it might be.

In the end, she reminded herself, she still might have to rely on force and emotion to devastate Dumar and prevent a worse mess later, or be reasonable and wait for an invasion or worse in a year or two, when Ehara was in the midst of a worse civil war and Konsstin was bringing sorcerers and armies into Neserea.

Wonderful options . . . but she knew she had to try the dam. A long shot . . . yes . . . but she had to live with herself as well as with the lords of the Thirty-three.

76

Farinelli's hoofs raised puffs of dust from the gray dirt of the trail. Anna glanced to her right, downhill through a gap in the mixed broadleaf trees and evergreens. The gap had been created, it appeared, when a section of the granite-like rock had peeled away and carried the trees at the edge with it. Beyond the gap was the gorge or the Great Chasm, and she could make out the steep gray cliffs of the far side for a moment. They seemed as solid as she recalled.

Ahead rode Birke and Rickel, while Birfels rode beside Anna to her right, with Jecks and Fhurgen behind. A full squad of armsmen trailed, back twenty yards or so, there at Hanfor's insistence.

The lutar was strapped over near-empty saddlebags, also at Hanfor's suggestion. Anna couldn't really fault her arms commander's caution, not after the ambush by Sargol and the earlier attempt by the Dark Monks.

"Here!" Birke reined up his chestnut on a raised hillock that slanted downward to the west, one where the trees and brush had been cut back to afford a view. The clearing had not been recent, since there were waist-high saplings and bushy evergreens.

Farinelli *whuff*ed as Anna reined the gelding in beside Birke—well short of the overlook's drop-off.

"This is the place where the Chasm is the narrowest," Birke announced. "To the south, the cliffs are higher, but the Chasm is much wider, always over a dek, sometimes as much as five."

"At least several," murmured Birfels.

Anna smiled. Mario had been like Birke, always overstating in his enthusiasm. She pushed away the thoughts of her son, knowing she couldn't afford to dwell on them. Hoping as always that Mario was well, she turned in the saddle to take in the view.

The scene resembled the one that the reflecting pool had revealed, if from a lower vantage point. The river was constrained by gray cliffs which rose at least two hundred yards from the floor of the gorge. Unlike the comparatively narrow stream that flowed past Falcor, between the rains and the drainage from the Synor and tributary streams, the Falche was on its way to becoming a mighty river. Below the cliffs, the river was fifty yards wide, but still filled less than half the riverbed.

Anna half nodded to herself. It would take years to fill a dam even halfway up those cliffs, considering how many deks to the north the valley stretched.

"That is the most water we have seen in many years," offered Birfels. "Once when I was young Birke's age, the water filled the gorge from side to side, so deep there was not even a ripple."

Anna could sense Birke's doubt, but the young man kept a pleasant smile on his face.

"In time," suggested Jecks, "that will again happen. The rains have returned."

"And not a season too early," answered Birfels.

Birke nodded, but his eyes rested speculatively on Anna.

Anna glanced northward, upstream. They had ridden for more than two glasses, a good six to eight deks, almost due south from Abenfel, and the river had flowed through cliffs the entire distance, though the cliffs west of Abenfel had been lower, perhaps only fifty yards high.

The gorge had enough space so that, if she dammed the Falche, there would be a deep lake, not inundated farmland. That was important. Of course, once the water reached the top of the dam, or the spillway, the river would flow again, but that would be several years away, and at least part of the Sea-Priests' fleet would be grounded in the meantime, and Ehara and the Sea-Priests might just get the message to leave Defalk alone—without Anna having to slaughter innocents.

Her eyes went back to the cliffs. They *looked* solid. Her sorcery had indicated that there was no better site. Still . . . would such a spell work? Could it work?

She couldn't know that until or unless she tried. She nodded to herself once more.

77

DUMARIA, DUMAR

She has withdrawn her forces from Stromwer to Abenfel. That is where the messenger found her," Ehara announces, setting aside the scroll and leaning back in the chair behind his writing desk. "So much for your plans to have her attack."

"She must be the one to attack," says the Sea-Marshal.

"You say that," answers Ehara. "Yet those who have attacked her have perished. So have those who have waited for her attack. So, if you would be so kind, can you tell me how to ensure that she attacks where we would prefer and without turning our forces into cinders?"

"Can you send messages into Defalk?" jerRestin asks. "Scrolls, rumors . . ."

"What will rumors and speculations do?" Ehara sits up, and his sudden motion causes the flames from the five-branched candelabra on his writing table to flicker.

"Incite her to anger. Anger precludes true thought and planning."

"For her? She is from the mist worlds. She has ice in her veins." Ehara offers a sardonic short laugh.

"Even ice boils if heated long and fiercely enough."

"What rumors do you wish planted?"

"That you have decided to adopt the Sturinnese custom of decorative chains for consorts." JerRestin pauses. "Or that you have pledged full allegiance to the Maitre. Or that Sturinn has pledged to send as many ships and armsmen as necessary to bring the sorceress down. . . ."

"I prefer the latter," says Ehara. "My own folk would drown me in the Falche if I pledged to any lord outside Dumar, and the chains business . . . well, I see why you find it expedient, and why it would incite her. . . . Perhaps we could add something that said I had rejected that . . . for now . . . unless the Matriarchy becomes too restive." The Lord of Dumar laughs. "The bitches to the east won't act on rumors; they never have, and they never will. It could help provoke the sorceress. . . ." His fingers touch the full black beard. "Now, my friend Sea-Priest, would you kindly explain—before I extend my neck further—just how you expect to defeat the sorceress."

"By devious enchantment." Sea-Marshal jerRestin smiles. "She is not the sole sorcerer in Liedwahr. She is perchance the most powerful, but she is new to Erde. We lure her into a situation where she does not expect and cannot defend herself against sorcery. Without her, Defalk is powerless. Now.''

''Correct me, if I am mistaken, but was that not what Lord Sargol attempted?''

''Bah! He set his trap so that a female child could see it. The sorceress cannot defend what she does not see.''

''And how can she not see it? She scrys everything, you have said.''

''Simply put—if there is no enchantment until the moment before the trap is sprung.'' The Sea-Marshal smiles more widely. ''She cannot detect a trap that does not exist—until it does, and then it will be too late.''

78

Outside the unshuttered window, a bird twittered, one that Anna had not heard before in Erde, something like a finch. A puff of warm air brushed over her as she sat at the conference table in the room once used by another sorceress.

Anna pushed away the pile of spell-noted papers and put her head in her hands. She just couldn't use Brill's spells. The tunes were essentially monophonic, and even if she varied the melody she sang, there just wouldn't be enough harmony and varied textures to support the heavy sorcery she had in mind. She didn't have the theory background to compose a polyphonic spell, not one where the separate melodies meshed strongly enough.

She shook her head. Her eyes burned from trying to force her way through the awkward phrases and spellings Brill had used—awkward to her, but probably normal for Erde, she reminded herself.

The finch twittered again.

Is it right to do this? Is it right not to? Do you want to risk the chance that the Sea-Priests will put the women of an entire country in chains . . . and then all of Liedwahr? . . . But they might not. . . . And who will stop them?

The arguments and counterarguments battled back and forth across her mind until she wanted to scream.

Shaking her head again, she pulled out the crude orchestration she'd done for Daffyd based on "The Battle Hymn of the Republic." If she had to fight another pitched battle, the players could use it. In the meantime, could she write another set of words? One designed to build a dam?

With a long sigh, she reached for the marker and a fresh sheet of the rough brown paper. After a time, she wrote. Then she rewrote. Then she rewrote that. Finally, she murmured the first lines aloud.

"My words must start the damming of the river here below,
   with a building of the strongest stones from where the waters flow . . .
   Let the base be solid as the granite with no single flaw . . ."

Anna scratched out the next words, and glanced to the window, rubbing her forehead. She was no poet, no composer, and words didn't come that easily. What rhymed with "flaw" that would fit the note values?

After a time of staring at the paper and then at the window, she reached for the goblet of orderspelled water.

Could she use the modified chorus? After slowly, carefully dipping the quill in the inkwell, she wrote out the lines.

"Glory, glory, halleluia; glory, glory, halleluia;
   glory, glory, halleluia, these stones will last and last!"

The middle lines were too rough, and she needed a second verse. *Still using strophic spells.* "What else can you do? You're not a composer."

One finch twittered, then another, as if in argument—like the damned lords of the Thirty-three.

Anna stood. Time to find Liende, now that she knew it could be done . . . somehow. She still probably needed to refine her sketch of the dam as well, to ensure supports went well into the cliff walls and well below the sand and mud of the canyon floor.

As she walked toward the door to the corridor, carrying the music, she glanced at the smaller writing desk in the bedchamber where another pile of scrolls lay. Earlier she'd read through close to a dozen. She heard from Lady Gatrune of Pamr that her sister Herene was on her way to Suhl to take on the guardianship and tutoring of Dinfan and her brothers, and that was one piece of good news. The rivermen had petitioned again, and that wasn't. Lord Tybel had requested that, since Hryding had died and since Anientta was Tybel's daughter and since Arien and Synope adjoined, that the two domains be temporarily joined under his oversight. Tybel had also requested that Anna keep that request in confidence, which meant that he probably hadn't. So she had another problem on her hands, another lord who either couldn't stand a woman running the lands, or worse in this case, a woman in Anientta who couldn't run the lands.

She took a deep breath before opening the door.

"Lady Anna," offered Lejun.

"Lady Anna." Jecks stood in the hallway, where he had been talking to Rickel, the broad-shouldered blond guard, and one of the two on duty outside Anna's door.

"I'm going to find Liende."

"The players' quarters are up a level and at the end of the long narrow hall." Jecks gestured toward the staircase at the front of the keep.

"How are their quarters?" Anna asked, feeling guilty that she didn't know personally.

"They are good. I looked."

"Thank you. Sometimes . . . I just feel like I can't keep track of everything."

"Barjim and Alasia felt that way, and there were two of them," Jecks said reasonably.

"I could get the chief player," offered Lejun.

"Thank you." Anna hadn't really felt like running after Liende, but she also hadn't wanted to ask someone directly. She found she had to ask too much as it was, and she'd never liked asking or ordering people around. *And now you're in a position where you have to. . . . How God or the harmonies have a sense of humor. . . .*

"I'll remain," said Jecks with a smile, "so that she has two guards."

Anna doubted she needed even one guard at Abenfel, but she hadn't thought she'd needed any riding the grounds at Loiseau, and that had almost killed her when the Dark Monks had spitted her with a war arrow.

"What have you been doing?"

"Thinking. That is hard for an old warhorse like me." Jecks laughed. "It is much easier to run one's lands or fight battles. Even to discipline a grandchild."

"Old?" Anna shook her head. "You're not that much older than I am."

Jecks studied her, blatantly, for a moment before touching the silver-gray hair behind his temple theatrically and grinning. "It would not appear so."

"You are an impossible and lecherous warhorse, not an old one."

"I defer to your judgment, lady, regent, and sorceress." Jecks bowed. "My bones, in their wisdom, would beg to differ."

At the sound of steps, both Anna and Jecks turned as Lejun returned with Liende.

"Thank you, Lejun. I appreciate it." Anna faced the red-haired player. "I hope you don't mind."

"Lady Anna, we are your players." Liende smiled.

"Liende, Lord Jecks . . ." Anna gestured toward the door to her chambers.

Once the three were seated around the conference table adjoining the reflecting pool, Anna handed Liende the sheets that bore her notated versions of the "Battle Hymn." Old Professor Thomson would have cringed, but the crude orchestration had worked for Daffyd, and Liende had more experience than Daffyd had had.

"I'd like you all to work on this."

Liende glanced across the notation.

Anna repressed a sigh. "Let me hum it for you. Then I'll do it like a vocalise." Sometimes it was a pain, not ever being able to match words and music except when casting an actual spell.

All in all, Anna went through the melody almost four times, and the cobbled-together bass twice before Liende nodded.

"I have it." The player pursed her lips. "This is more difficult."

"It will have to be. Is it possible to get this together in the next three or four days? I'll come to the rehearsals— just let me know when." Anna smiled.

"Everyone is here, Lady Anna." Liende glanced at the notes again. "We could begin in a glass."

"I'll be there." Anna paused. "There must be a space somewhere."

"There is a large storeroom that Hanfor obtained for us, up on the fourth level. We have been working on the other spells."

Anna rose. "Thank you."

"In a glass, lady."

After she had escorted Liende out, Anna returned to the conference table. Jecks displayed a bemused half-smile.

"You look amused."

"This spell will take mighty sorcery. . . ." Jecks ventured.

"Oh?" Anna didn't feel like admitting much. Besides, after humming and vocalising the "Battle Hymn" six times, she had a headache, and there wasn't any equivalent of aspirin or ibuprofen, unless she wanted to chew willow bark, and that cure was probably worse than her headache.

"You have given your chief player music that will have all of them looking darkly and grumbling, once you are not around. There are stacks of paper all about you, and you have requested more. You have ink on your fingers, and your eyes are worried."

"I'm not a composer. I'm not even an arranger. No one around here has dealt with harmony in a couple of centuries, and the whole concept of homophony seems beyond everyone."

Jecks' eyes glazed over, and he shook his head. "I would think that I might understand. Then you speak, and the words mean nothing."

"I'm sorry." *There you go, apologizing again. You are the regent . . . but a year doesn't change a lifetime of apologizing.* "I need spell music that is more complex than anything Brill developed. I was not trained in writing that kind of music. That's composing. I did all right in theory, but composing's way beyond that."

Jecks smiled almost grimly. "For what do you need such music, music so . . . so . . . intricate . . . or mighty . . . that mere words cannot explain?"

"Lord Jecks," Anna said slowly, "there are more than forty ships from Sturinn in Dumar. Half the time I use the glass to see Ehara, there's that Sea-Priest sorcerer with him."

"He is a sorcerer?"

"That's what the glass says." Anna didn't mention the other sorcerers, the blonde Norweian woman and the young man in brown. Her spell efforts hadn't shown much about him, except he was in a small town of some sort, in Defalk, which bothered her. Her efforts to refine a spell to find out exactly who and where he was hadn't come to much, and neither had her inquiries to Menares and Dythya, not that she knew yet.

"A sorcerer from Sturinn serving Ehara. Hmmmm. . . .
Even dense as I be, that is not good."

"I have to do *something*," Anna added. "That's the
way it feels." *Your big problem is figuring out* how *to
make that something happen.* "I'm going to try to block
the Falche, and then suggest to Lord Ehara that his reaction wasn't wise or in the best interests of Dumar."

"Your spells will do this?"

"I think so."

"I do not know. Lord Ehara is proud. He will not suffer, but his people will, and they will blame you."

"That could be," Anna admitted. "But I'd rather try
it than try to march into Dumar and fry every armsman
sent against us until they're either slaughtered or I am."

"You do not have to fight Dumar," said Jecks slowly.

"No. I have to fight Sturinn. The only choice I have is
when." Anna moistened her lips. "If I dry up the river,
that would ground their ships, some of them, anyway, and
it wouldn't kill lots of people."

"The Sea-Priests would not like that. No, they would
not."

"I could suggest to Ehara that the Sea-Priests should
leave Dumar and Liedwahr."

"A show of force." Jecks shrugged. "With some . . .
it might work. Ehara, I do not know."

"I think it's better than waiting for the Sturinnese to
turn Dumar into their puppet."

"If the Sea-Priests overthrew Ehara now," agreed
Jecks, "even the Liedfuhr might join you in an attack."

"If something like that happened," Anna mused, "then
would the Thirty-three be so upset if I used sorcery?"

"They would not be displeased if you used sorcery
before that—so long as it did not affect them."

Anna laughed. "How could any sorcery not affect
them, one way or another?" She reached for the pitcher
and filled two goblets. "I have to think about how to do
this more." *Do you ever!*

"Thinking will not halt the need to act," Jecks said dryly.

"I know that, too." She offered a crooked smile. "Have some wine. It's pretty good."

He lifted the goblet. So did she.

79

Anna waited until the group struggled through the "Battle Hymn" spell again. "No . . . it's too slow. The tempo has to be . . ." She sang the melody like a vocalise. "Da DAH da . . ."

Delvor shook his head slowly, limp brown hair flopping.

"Three separate melody lines at once, and one not exactly a melody line . . . playing such a spellsong is hard," offered Liende.

Anna repressed a sigh, not bothering to explain that the accompaniment was not three separate lines. That would have been polyphony, and what she'd written was scarcely that. "Hard makes better spells, unhappily," she finally said.

"You have proven that, lady," admitted Liende. "We will work harder."

"Thank you." The sorceress nodded. "I'll check back first thing in the morning."

She ignored the whispered "Tomorrow morning?" as she stepped out of the converted storeroom and onto the landing where Lejun and Rickel waited. Then, she walked slowly back from the storeroom and down the narrow steps, half conscious of Rickel's boots on the steps above her.

Would her damming of the Falche really motivate

Ehara to push out the Sturinnese? Or just force them to conquer Dumar? Or something else? *What can you do? You just can't march into another country and turn their armies into ashes. And you can't wait until they've got enough ships and men and sorcerers to take over all of Defalk.*

"Did Napoleon and Hitler think that way?" she murmured. But so many more people got killed when rulers and governments did nothing—like six million Jews and millions of others, a million or so Armenians, five million Cambodians, who knew how many Kurds, Bosnians, Africans . . .

Face it. No matter what you do, it will be wrong.

Shaking her head still, she entered the chambers Birfels had set aside for her and went straight to the writing desk beside the reflecting pool. Before she sharpened the quill, she poured a small goblet of wine and took one sip.

She sat and began to draft the scroll. Lord, she hated writing things. It took *forever*! After a good two glasses, and as the sun began to lower over western Sudbergs, she finally had something. She read over the phrases slowly.

. . . I encountered two companies of Dumaran lancers in putting down the rebellion at Suhl. Another two companies opposed our efforts at Stromwer. One would hope that you, as a lord of a land, would recognize the authority of a ruler or regent to address rebellion without outside interference . . . yet you have responded to my inquiries with defiance and arrogance . . . and a demand for tribute. . . .

In addition, it has come to our attention that over twoscore Sturinnese war vessels are anchored in Dumar.

These events lead to the almost inescapable conclusion that Dumar is attempting to meddle in Defalk. At worse, one could conclude that Dumar and Sturinn plan a war of conquest in Liedwahr.

Such a war would be to the detriment of all, particularly of Dumar. To reinforce this point, without resorting to force of arms, I have stopped the flow of the Falche River. This gesture on the part of the Regency is offered in good faith short of war, and in response to your use of lancers in Defalk and the presence of a large foreign fleet in Dumar, the fleet of a land that has been unfriendly in the past to all Liedwahr.

We would urge you to reaffirm bonds of friendship with Defalk and to take the necessary steps to ensure that the only ships from Sturinn anchored in Dumaran waters are those few necessary for mutual trade.... We also await the payment of those golds required for the rebuilding of Defalk necessitated by your actions....

The next part wouldn't do. She scratched out the line, and laboriously rewrote it, forcing herself to take care with quill and inkwell.

In time, she stood and went to the door, peering out. Fhurgen, Rickel, and Lejun were all there.

"Yes, Lady Anna?"

"Ah . . . could someone find Lord Jecks for me?"

Fhurgen looked at Rickel. Rickel looked at Lejun. Lejun shrugged and grinned.

"He was sparring with Lord Birfels earlier, but he may be in the library now," offered Fhurgen.

"I shall go," said Lejun.

"Thank you," Anna said quietly.

She went back to the smaller writing desk in the bedchamber and began to read the latest scrolls. Menares, Dythya, Himar, and Herstat somehow managed to get messengers to the right place.

The first message was another from Lady Gatrune, thanking Anna for trusting Herene with a position of responsibility. The second was from Anientta, disavowing her father's request to combine the administration and control of Arien and Flossbend.

Anna frowned. She'd already denied Tybel's request, but those messages to both Anientta and Tybel probably had crossed with Anientta's to Anna. Sooner or later, she needed to visit Synope—or send Jecks or someone—to resolve that mess.

She picked up the third scroll and broke the seal.

Thrap!

"Lord Jecks, Lady Anna."

"Come on in."

They walked back to the conference table where Anna handed her rough-drafted message to the white-haired lord. "Would you read this?"

"I would be pleased. You have a fine hand, and a way with words."

"Thank you." Anna forced herself to accept the compliment, even while rejecting the idea.

After he finished, Jecks glanced up. "You are determined to use such sorcery?"

"Unless someone comes up with a better idea. Doing nothing will only make things worse." Anna took the last sip of wine in the goblet and lifted the pitcher. It was empty, and she set it down. "Right now, we have young Hadrenn holding off Bertmynn and the Sturinnese and maybe the Liedfuhr in Ebra. According to Menares, and who knows how he found out, both the Liedfuhr and the Sturinnese are funding Bertmynn. Things still aren't sorted out in Neserea, and we've at least got credit with the Ranuan Exchange for our people. Dumar's the only problem. What happens a year from now when there are twice as many Sturinnese ships and armsmen in Dumar, when the Liedfuhr uses that as an excuse to take over—just for the duration—Neserea—"

" 'For the duration'?" asked Jecks.

"Sorry. That's a sarcastic expression where I come from. It means he'll say his action is temporary because of the emergency conditions, but he never will leave. Neserea will become part of Mansuur, and then we'll have problems on two borders, with Bertmynn using coins from everyone to finish off Hadrenn in Ebra. . . ."

"Matters might not turn so ill."

Anna raised her eyebrows and fixed Jecks with cold blue eyes.

Jecks' lips curled into a sardonic smile. "That is why I am glad you are regent, Lady Anna. You expect the worst of serpents and plan for it. Planning for the worst, season after season, is not to my liking."

"I take it you don't have a better idea?"

"I have those which are more pleasant." He laughed harshly, once. "Yet against what you say, my ideas are like mist. No, I fear you are right. I do not have to like your reason, but I must respect it."

Jecks, an optimist? Anna nodded. He'd have to have been, to have survived. *And what does that say about you?* She pushed that question away.

"I'll have this ready to go." She gestured to the message. "It needs to leave by messenger the moment the dam is completed."

"Why tell me such?"

"Because I'm liable to be exhausted or asleep or not thinking well, and you won't be." She forced a grin.

"As you say, Lady Anna."

"Am I wrong?" she demanded, her eyes meeting his warm hazel ones.

"I think not." He paused. "You are not as other women. You will not tell yourself that matters are other than they are. Defalk is fortunate in that, but I would not say that of you, lady."

"Damned—cursed—to be a realist?"

He shrugged sadly.

"The message will be here, tied in green ribbon." Anna glanced at the empty goblet, then at the clouds through the narrow window, growing more golden by the moment. She could have used more wine. Before long, being regent would turn her into a full-blown alcoholic.

"There's a banquet tonight," Jecks offered.

Anna groaned. "I'm supposed to be entertained, and entertaining?"

"I believe that is what Lady Fylena said."

"Then you don't get to leave before I do." Anna offered a smile.

"Your wish in that is my command."

"You are still most careful, Lord Jecks."

"With sorceresses, and regents, that is wise." He kept a blank expression, but the hazel eyes twinkled, and Anna wished for a moment that she were neither regent nor sorceress.

80

WEI, NORDWEI

Ashtaar turns in her chair to view the harbor through the open window. In the late twilight, the sound of insects hums upward from the trees below the Council building. To the north, points of yellowed orange flicker into being as the larger lamps on the harbor piers are lit. The darkness undotted by lamps denotes the river Nord and Vereisen Bay beyond.

At the knock on the door, the spymistress turns, returning her thoughts to the room illuminated softly by the wall-hung brass luminaries. Behind the spotless crystal mantels, the lamp flames scarcely flicker, but they are bright enough that her dark hair glistens in their light. "Yes?"

"You requested my presence, honored Ashtaar?" Gretslen bows as she steps inside and closes the dark-stained wooden door behind her. The lamplight turns her blonde hair into a faint cloud in the dim room.

"I did." The darker woman gestures to the chair before

her desk. "You have reported that the sorceress now holds all of Defalk?"

Gretslen brushes a lock of short blonde hair off her forehead. "She has subdued all the rebels without destroying their keeps or all heirs, except in the case of Synfal. That she turned over to the heir to Defalk itself, Lord Jimbob."

"She did not raze Stromwer?"

"No."

Ashtaar purses her lips, and her fingers slip around the black agate oval, blacker even than her hair. "She has the loyalty of all Defalk, and yet she neither presses into Dumar nor returns to Falcor."

"She guests with Lord Birfels of Abenfel. She and her forces are his invited guests," Gretslen confirms.

"And the Sea-Priests remain in Dumar? Can you determine why?"

"No, honored Ashtaar, save that their Sea-Marshal spends much time with Lord Ehara, who does not seem overly pleased."

"Would you be pleased?" Ashtaar laughs. "He has the Liedfuhr to the west, the sorceress to the north, and the Sturinnese fleet in his harbor. He has been providing aid to the rebel lords of Defalk, and the sorceress knows that. Would you be in his seat?"

Gretslen shakes her head.

"The worst is yet to come," predicts the spymistress. "Ehara is trapped between the Sturinnese, who will do anything to gain a foothold in Liedwahr and to destroy a powerful female ruler, and the sorceress. She will destroy them—and much of Liedwahr—if she must in order to keep the gilded chains of Sturinn from enslaving the women of Dumar and Defalk." Ashtaar offers a cruel smile. "She does not know that, but she will."

"And what of us?" asks Gretslen.

"We are worse, dear seer. We told her about the chains, and we will let her use her full powers, come what may." Ashtaar's fingers tighten around the black agate before she forces them to relax.

81

Anna glanced to her right at the mist rising out of the gorge and above the trees and brush that blocked her direct view of the canyon and the river. Her eyes went to the damp clay of the trail that led to the narrows where she would try to create her dam. In the leather folder behind her saddle were her drawings, based on everything she could remember, and the elaborate three-stanza spell. *Elaborate strophic, homophonic spell . . .*

She hoped she wouldn't need it, and that she could concentrate on the drawing and the concept of the dam, but the words and melody notations were there if necessary. She felt tired, and she hadn't even done any spellcasting. Then, most of the fatigue was probably from mental conflict. She didn't like what she was planning, but she had to do *something*, besides waiting, and anything else she or Jecks or anyone else had thought up was worse—except doing nothing. And within a short time, *that* would result in even more dire consequences.

The lutar that accompanied her everywhere away from whatever keep she inhabited was also fastened behind the saddle. Jecks rode silently to her right, drawn into himself, and probably fighting the same internal conflicts. Anna snorted. He was probably wondering how they'd ended up saddled with a temperamental sorceress who didn't want a return to the good old days. Women thinking? Openly questioning men? Or running holdings? What had Erde come to?

As she pursed her lips, moistening them, she leaned forward and patted Farinelli, getting the faintest of *whuffs* from the gelding. Ahead of her rode Rickel and Fhurgen, and behind Anna, Hanfor and Lord Birfels. After the veteran and the lord rode Lejun and then the regent's players, followed by the Purple Company.

The players were silent, even Delvor, the struggling violinist, and Duralt, the cocky falk-horn player who was too often full of himself. Anna missed Daffyd. For all of his puppy-dog hurt looks, for all that his misconstrued spell had dragged Anna to Defalk, he'd been a good player and leader and had stood up for what he believed in—and for Anna—and he'd died at Vult doing it.

"Lady Anna . . . ?" Birke's voice almost broke—the problems of adolescent growth—as he edged his mount nearer to hers.

She turned her head, eastward, left, and let the rising sun warm her full face. "Yes, Birke."

"What . . . what will happen . . . after . . ."

"After the sorcery?" *That is a damned good question.* "There will be a dam, and a large lake behind it. When the water reaches the spillway—that's a lower place in the dam—it will flow over the dam, and then the river will continue."

"But . . . why . . . do such sorcery?"

"To let the Dumarans and the Sturinnese know I could halt the river forever. To persuade the Sturinnese to leave Liedwahr." *You hope. . . .*

"They might not," Birke said. "My sire says they are like ants in a granary. You have to remove everything and kill them all before they will leave." He paused. "Would you do that?"

"Birke," Anna said slowly, "one day you will inherit your sire's lands. You'll be responsible for all of the holding. You know what the Sturinnese have done. They've conquered the Ostisles and now they have a fleet in Dumar. Would you like to see Lysara and Clayre in gilded chains? Or your own consort when you have one? What would you do?"

"They have often taken many years . . . and you are powerful. They cannot defeat you."

Anna wanted to shake her head. She'd seen it in academia on earth, and in Erde among the lords . . . and everyone else. If the problem wasn't immediate, ignore it and hope it will go away. "Birke . . . your faith in my ability is touching, but how long will I live? I'm older than your father, possibly older than Jecks. And I can be killed. It's almost happened twice." *More like half a dozen times if you count the backlash of sorcery.* "Then what?"

The youth's forehead furrowed. After a time, he answered. "Lady Anna, when you talk, nothing is quite the same. But it is hard. I remember when you bespelled Virkan. At first, I thought you were fearsome, and then Skent said something strange. He talks more like you, you know. He said that you had only spelled Virkan to do what a good person would not need a spell for." Birke glanced at the winding trail ahead, then looked back at the sorceress. "He said that you seldom spelled except to make things better for everyone." The redhead laughed nervously. "And he looked at me, and he told me that what was better for lords wasn't always better for everyone else. I would have struck him except . . . he's bigger, and he seemed so calm."

Anna glanced over her shoulder. Birfels was talking quietly to Hanfor. "Birke . . . Skent was right. What is good for one lord is not good for all lords, and what is good for all lords may not be good for all people. You remember Secca?"

"The little redheaded fosterling. Lysara wrote me about her, but . . ."

"You had already returned to Abenfel. She has two brothers, one older and one younger. She is brighter than either. She is fairer and more determined than either. Would it be better for her to hold the lands or her brothers?"

Birke looked at the mane of the roan he rode. "The sons. . . . They have always been heirs. . . ."

"Exactly. It's hard, isn't it? If you admit that Secca might be a better landholder, then wouldn't you have to admit that Clayre or Lysara might have that skill, too?" Anna laughed. "I'm not changing the succession laws, except in cases where the sons are incompetent or there aren't any sons." She paused. "Isn't it better that Cataryzna hold her father's lands than some outsider?"

Birke nodded. "That . . . that is better."

"Well . . . that's the sort of thing I am changing. Nothing more." *Not for a long time, anyway. That's enough to turn some of the older lords purple as it is.*

Birke screwed up his face. "But you did not . . . I mean . . . Dumar . . . and the Sea-Priests . . ."

"I didn't, did I?" The sorceress wiped her forehead. Despite the early-morning coolness in the hills, she was starting to perspire. Nerves? "I'm hoping that if I cut off the river to Dumar for a time, that will persuade Ehara to get the Sea-Priests to leave."

"But . . ."

"If they don't?" Anna shrugged. "We'll have to see. At least this way, I'm not using sorcery to kill scores or hundreds or thousands of people." *If it works. . . .* She repressed a shiver. "Isn't that the narrows there?"

Birke stood in the stirrups. "Yes. There goes a buck! If I had my bow out, we'd have venison."

Anna watched as the big white-tailed red deer—was there such an animal?—bounded from the cleared area into the trees that climbed the hills to the east of the trail. She was glad Birke hadn't had his bow out and strung. She turned in the saddle. "Liende, I'd like the players to set up on that grassy spot on the ridge there, right below those bushes."

"Players!" Liende ordered.

Anna eased her water bottle from its holder and took a long slow swallow before replacing it. By then, Farinelli had carried her to the partly cleared ridge that overlooked the narrower section of the gorge.

Most of the mist had cleared from above the river, save for a few wispy strands drifting out of the shadows she couldn't see below her on the eastern side.

"Purple company!" called Hanfor. "Squads one and two back along the trail, up to the crest by that pine. Squads three and four, ride down to where those two bushes sit by that fallen trunk."

As the armsmen followed the arms commander's orders and dust swirled across the high meadow, Anna dismounted, handing Farinelli's reins to Lejun and then unpacking the folder with the spell and the drawings of the dam. Folder in hand, she stretched, then lifted her shoulders, walking in circles to get the stiffness out of her legs. Her steps took her down to the overlook, and she studied the gorge once more.

The Falche seemed wider than even the few days earlier, the silver ribbon twisting in the shade hundreds of yards below. As she watched the play of light and mist and shadow, she cleared her throat, then began her vocalises.

"Holly-lolly-polly-pop . . . Damn!" She coughed, trying to clear out her throat, then began again. It was going to take a long time to get clear. It did—four separate vocalises and a lot of mucus.

Only the faintest of mist streamers were left by the time she turned from her warm-up and view of the Falche. Jecks was waiting for her by Farinelli, water bottle in hand, after she walked back up the gentle slope through the knee-high brush.

"You're worried, aren't you?" she asked.

"I should not be." He shrugged. "I worry every time you attempt the impossible." A small laugh followed. "You have made the impossible possible, time and again, but still I worry."

"This time even more?"

He nodded.

"You may be right. This is a *very* ambitious spell."

"Sometimes, my lady, you try too hard to avoid shedding blood."

"You all wanted me as regent. That's who I am." Anna laughed brittlely and shook her head. "No . . . you didn't want me. You wanted someone to preserve Defalk, and you got me. That's different, isn't it?"

"In these times, Defalk could not have a better ruler."

"You're so careful, Jecks, but I understand. Thank you." She took the water bottle and drank, then handed it back.

The players stood on the cleared part of the ridge, stretching, coughing, clearing throats. The sounds of strings and the clarinet-like woodwind and the deeper falk-horn intertwined as the group finished its warm-up tunes.

"Your players stand ready, Lady Anna," Liende said.

"Thank you, Liende. I'm almost ready." Anna walked to where Hanfor waited, still mounted. "I don't know what will happen, but it could spook the mounts."

"I have told the men that. They understand."

"Good." She paused. "Thank you."

Hanfor touched his brow in an informal salute. "May the harmonies be with you, Lady Anna."

Anna glanced from Hanfor to Jecks, getting a brief smile from the white-haired lord. She took a last swallow and coughed gently to make sure her throat was clear. Finally, she nodded to Liende.

"The battle tune. On my mark. . . . Mark!" The head player gestured, and lifted her clarinet-like horn, turning to join in the melody she had started.

Anna tried to stay focused and relaxed, letting her body and cords carry the music, her mind on trying to hold the image of the dam, her eyes on the drawings, attempting to project them in place in the narrow gorge below.

"My words must start the damming of the river here
  below . . ."

Even from the first words, the sky seemed to silver, and to freeze—a silver-blue hemisphere frozen in time. From the players' separate parts—each note rang like a tiny bell, even the sweet singing of the strings, and the deeper bass of the falk horn.

Anna forced her thoughts back to the image of the dam and to the song. . . .

"With a building of the strongest stones from where the
    waters flow . . ."

The melody from the players welled up around her, and the sorceress half smiled. Never had they sounded so good, so solid.

". . . setting every block into the place that it must
    hold . . ."

The phrasing flowed, just as she had planned.

Just before the last chorus, Anna could sense an enormous pressure behind even the silver-blue sky, and she could feel her knees trembling. Even with all the help of the players, Anna had this feeling she wasn't going to make it. Lights seemed to flash around her, and the ground groaned and rumbled.

She hung on, concentrating on the last words and the notes.

"Glory, glory, halleluia; glory, glory, halleluia;
    glory, glory, halleluia, these stones will last and last!"

She slumped, panting. *Never . . . so . . . hard. . . . Such a short song. . . .*
THRUMMMMM!!!
The entire heavens pulsated with a series of chords, the chords seemingly unheard by any but Anna, and silver clouds that were mist and yet not mist, filled the gorge. Underneath the ground trembled, and shook.

Farinelli half *whuff*ed, half screamed, then half reared, dragging Lejun and his mount uphill and away from the river.

". . . dissonance!"

For a moment, utter silence, a blanket of silence that muffled absolutely all attempt at sound, descended.

THRUMMMM!!!

With the second chord, sound resumed, and the silver mists over the river rose and boiled away. The haze lifted, showing a picture-perfect arching dam of glistening gray stone. The spillway was even there.

Anna could sense tears welling up in her eyes. She tried to take a deep breath—and couldn't. *Damned asthma. . . .*

The world turned red, and then black and swirled around her.

82

DUMARIA, DUMAR

The two lords, one of Dumar, one of Sturinn, sit on opposite sides of the low table which bears a large carafe of wine, a bowl of honeyed nuts, and one of dried fruit. Ehara lowers the scroll and looks at Sea-Marshal jerRestin. "And how far upstream is the Falche dry?"

"Not a drop of water flows over the first cataract or the second. Your sorceress has stopped the entire Falche. Even I would not have thought it possible."

"She's hardly *my* sorceress, Sea-Marshal," Ehara says with a ragged laugh. "It was done, Sea-Priest. Don't tell me how you would not have believed it possible. Half your fleet sits grounded in the mud below Dumaria. The waters of the Envaryl lap around their hulls. What of the other half?"

"They remain at Narial. The bay is tidal." JerRestin reaches for a handful of honeyed nuts. He eats them deliberately.

Ehara lifts the scroll he has been reading. "The sorceress has sent this. She has suggested that it might be better for me and my people if the Sturinnese fleet returned to Sturinn." He extends the scroll to jerRestin.

The Sea-Marshal reads slowly. "Behind the polite words, she is ordering you to dismiss us . . . and to pay her thousands of golds."

"It does not sound like such a bad idea, at least until the river is returned to us."

"You do not wish to pay all those golds. Nor do we wish that, either. The sorceress cannot hold back such a mighty river forever. It will not hurt to wait." The Sea-Marshal smiles. "In any case, the ships at Dumaria cannot sail anywhere."

"What if I requested you to leave?" asks Ehara.

"I would take your request, and then I would send it to the Maitre. It is on his orders that I am here."

"I see."

"I think you do, Lord Ehara. Shall we have some of that wine while we wait for the sorceress to act? It may be some time. You know she is prostrate. The scroll might not even be her work. She reached beyond herself, and she may not recover. Often those who do such great works do not recover." JerRestin smiles. "Some wine?" he repeats.

"Ah . . . of course."

83

Anna opened burning and blurred eyes, slowly, painfully.

Jecks looked solemnly at her, propped up as she was by lumpy pillows in the high-backed bed. She met his glance for a moment, then closed her eyes against the pounding headache and the miniature starbursts that flashed before her.

When she opened them again, the white-haired lord sat in the chair by her bed.

"My lady . . . Lady Anna . . . you cannot continue like this." Jecks extended a goblet. "It is wine, honeyed. You must drink."

Anna drank. Then she closed her eyes for a moment.

"You must eat and drink more before you sleep."

Obediently, she forced her eyes back open and took another sip of the wine, far too sweet for her preference. She tried to get her eyes to focus on the white-haired lord, but one moment he seemed clear, and the next a silvered fuzzy image.

"Another," he urged inexorably.

She took a small sip. A thought struggled somewhere, and finally she asked, "The . . . message?"

"As you ordered, I did send it, under the blue flag of messages and harmony. Lord Ehara doubtless did not feel such harmony when he received your words."

"Received?" Anna rasped.

"You have lain like one enchanted or dead for nearly a week. The message has surely been delivered, but there has been no time for a reply. We have forced water into you, but you are thin unto death." He extended a small fragment of bread. "You must eat."

Anna slowly chewed the bread, hard as it was with a dry mouth, then let Jecks hold the goblet again as she drank. "The dam . . . ?"

"You have wrought a mighty sorcery," he admitted, offering another small fragment of bread. "The river has filled the gorge for three deks and slowed its flow for another five. . . . And it has yet to creep halfway, nay not even a fourth part of the way, up those stones your sorcery laid."

"Is any . . . water going . . . past . . . ?"

"Beyond the dam are only sands and drying rocks. And more sand and dry rock. Before long, Lord Birfels worries that the waters will flood the fields near Emor."

Emor? Anna hadn't even heard of Emor.

"That is a small hamlet fifteen deks upstream of Abenfel." Jecks pressed another square of dark bread upon her.

"Be . . . awhile," mumbled Anna as she struggled with the bread. "Years. It's a deep gorge."

"Not as deep as before. The waters have covered the sands and the shores, and it is a lake of blue." He offered more bread.

Chewing the bread took effort, and her jaws moved as though they were made of lead. She swallowed and took another sip of wine.

Her eyes felt heavy, far too heavy, and she could no longer keep them open.

84

PAMR, DEFALK

I can't believe what Deurn said you had back here," says the thin and wispy-bearded youth. "I just had to see."

"You'll see, Elcean," promises the young chandler. "It is rather remarkable." He closes the door to the small room, and the slow and rhythmic drumming enfolds them—*thurummm . . . thurumm . . . thurummm . . . thurumm . . .*

"Oh . . ."

On the pedestal is an almost life-sized statue of a voluptuous brunette, with an impossibly slender waist and dark hair that falls against creamy skin like a gossamer cloak, just barely covering her breasts. The hair shimmers and shifts ever so slightly in the still air, yet the naked woman—or statue—does not move.

"Oh . . . Farsenn . . . can I touch her?"

"That might not be a good idea," says the chandler. "At least, not until you listen to me. She won't go anywhere."

"I can look . . ."

Farsenn slips into song, bass voice intertwining with the rhythm of the drum.

"Men of Pamr, heed no woman's song,
    for Farsenn will make you proud and strong . . ."

When the spell ends, Farsenn blinks, then squints before he resumes smiling. "You see? We men need to stand together these days, don't we?"

" 'Course . . . like you say." Elcean continues to stare at the brunette. "Sure is pretty."

The drumbeat dies, and Farsenn smiles conspiratorially. "Just don't tell any of the women. . . . You know what I mean?"

Elcean flushes.

"It was good of you to come to see me." Farsenn makes a vague gesture toward the door. Elcean follows the gesture, and the chandler follows him.

Once the door closes, the drummer rises and glances

at the rough clay figure that stands on the crude wooden pedestal, a figure no more than a yard and a half tall. Then he wipes his steaming forehead, then massages it. He also blinks as though he has difficulty seeing clearly.

85

Anna looked at the empty tray on the writing table before her. Had she eaten all that? Every time she pushed her sorcery, she paid, and paid more, it seemed. That was another reason why she wanted to see if she could get Ehara to push the Sturinnese out.

"It won't happen. . . ." she murmured to herself. All that would happen was that the Falche would fill up over the next few years, the Dumaran people would suffer, and she'd take the blame. The Sturinnese would stay put, and she and Jecks would have to decide whether a war in Dumar was worth it. And she would either have to rely on brute-force sorcery to devastate Dumar and prevent a worse mess later, or she could be reasonable, according to conventional lordly wisdom, and wait for a Sturinnese-backed invasion or worse in a year or two. By then, Ebra would be in the middle of a civil war, or the war would be over and she'd have another growing enemy to the east while Konsstin would be bringing sorcerers and armies into Neserea to the west.

Yet . . . how could she live with herself if she didn't try something else? Even if it happened to be a long shot?

She snorted. Of course she could forget Dumar for a time. But then she would have to use force in Ebra to secure Defalk's eastern borders, and that would probably encourage the Sturinnese to attack southern Defalk from

Dumar when she was weeks away in Ebra and could do nothing.

Outside was gray. That she could tell, but it wasn't raining, just hot and gray. Even in the thin shift that wasn't hers, she felt hot, and sweaty, and smelly. She wanted a bath, not a sponge bath, and not a bath in the lukewarm water Defalkans called hot. She wanted a hot and steaming bath, and she wasn't going to get it anytime soon. Not when even boiling water cooled on the long trip up from the kitchens and the mere thought of sorcery sent a screaming pain across her temples.

Still, she was better. She wasn't quite so gaunt, and she could eat, and take short walks, and Jecks didn't look at her as though she were about to die. Yet it seemed her recovery was taking longer than after other similar large spells.

Outside the window the finches twittered, and Anna smiled at the calls that were half song, half argument.

Her eyes flicked to the mirror on the wall—a mirror she could use just as a mirror, thanks to the reflecting pool. She wasn't sure she wanted to see her reflection, not yet, anyway.

Thrap!

"Yes?" she said warily.

Jecks peered in. "Lady Anna?"

"Come on in." After he entered, she gestured to the chair across the writing desk from her.

"You look better," Jecks offered as he seated himself.

"Not as though I'd die on the spot?" Anna reseated herself.

"You are surely in better health," he said with a smile.

"Because I'm back to my old snippy self?" She even felt like smiling in return.

"All were worried."

"You were upset because you don't see what this sorcery will accomplish besides flooding fields?"

"And killing Defalk's sole hope of prevailing against the Liedfuhr." He smiled. "I mean you, my lady."

"You don't worry about Sturinn?"

"We have no ports and need little of what is traded across the Western Sea."

"Forty ships in Dumar doesn't bother you?"

"The Liedfuhr has fifty thousand lancers, it is said." Jecks shrugged. "Forty ships carried a tenth of that number."

Anna forced a smile. Jecks was being logical, and she couldn't fight logic with logic. Her intuition told her he was wrong, that Sturinn posed a far greater danger than Mansuur. But how could she convince him? She took a slow breath.

"You fear Sturinn more than Mansuur." His words were even, not quite a question.

"Yes. I can't explain why or how, but Sturinn is a greater danger." Anna took a sip of the wine, a drier red that was far better than the honeyed stuff she'd swallowed when first recovering. Her legs felt stiff, and she pushed back the straight-backed chair and stood.

Why did she feel like an arthritic old woman? In the mirror, she looked like a worn-out twenty-year-old, but that wasn't the way she felt at the moment.

She needed to get stronger. That she felt, but it had been almost two weeks since the dam had been completed, and she was still slow and tired. Each day she tried to walk farther, get more exercise, but she continued to feel drained.

Her feet took her to the window, and to the gray clouds piling in from the east.

"Sturinn may be a greater danger," ventured Jecks, "but Mansuur is closer."

Anna nodded. She couldn't argue with that, either. "We'll have to do something about Dumar or Ebra."

"None will gainsay your right to back one side in the conflict there," Jecks pointed out.

More damned politics. "I suppose not. We don't piss off either the Sea-Priests or Konsstin, not openly." She shook her head. *Or worry the beloved lords of the Thirty-three. . . . Lord!*

"You could go by way of Synope," Jecks offered placatingly.

"I could." Why did she feel so damned tired? She yawned. "I still think Dumar is the bigger problem."

"You still are tired."

"Yes," she admitted, reluctantly. Her eyes felt heavy. Just how long would it take for her to feel normal again?

He stood. "I must go."

Anna walked toward the high bed. Her eyes were closed within moments of the *clunk* of the door.

86

ESARIA, NESEREA

The heavy, gilt-framed mirror in the hallway to the bedchamber swings away from the wall. A single low candle lights the corridor behind the barred door. On the other side of the door are two Mansuuran lancers.

After several moments, a cloaked figure slips from the opening made by the swiveled mirror and toward the archway leading to the bedchamber. In the bed a man lies, sleeping on his side, his closed eyes facing the archway. He does not move as the intruder enters the room.

The figure in deep brown, far less visible at night than black, steps up to the table by the bed, deftly takes the stoppered wine pitcher from the tray and replaces it with another.

As silently as he has come, the intruder eases his way back behind the mirror. The mirror swings back into place, and without even a *click*, seats itself so that it again appears built into the wall.

As he steps down the stairs to the narrow passage set

partly below floor level, Rabyn murmurs, "You will notice nothing, taste nothing, good Nubara. Not for a long, long time."

He passes several other niches in the wall, each behind a mirror. He also must duck upon occasion when the passageway's ceiling lowers to accommodate windows in those rooms it borders. He turns two more corners and comes to the place where he entered.

There, at the top of the three narrow steps, he presses a lever, and another mirror swings out from the wall. Once he is inside his own rooms, he closes the mirror and carefully checks the boss on the left side, wiping it carefully with the fabric of the brown cloak.

With a smile, he walks to his dressing room, stopping in front of the three-yard-wide polished-wood wardrobe, and drawing wide the double doors. After he opens the hidden compartment at the back of the wardrobe and replaces the enveloping brown cloak, his eyes go to the miniature portrait on the long dressing table.

The dark-haired woman seems to smile at him, and he smiles back.

"Yes, you taught me well. As that lizard Nubara will discover."

87

The sound of heavy raindrops on the walls of Abenfel echoed into the dim study in the late afternoon.

"How long is this rain going to last?" Anna asked, her eyes going to the closed shutters of the study. She felt almost trapped inside the dark-paneled room. The faint odor of wax and burned candlewicks made her nose twitch, even as she stifled another yawn. Would she ever stop feeling tired?

Birfels shrugged, a faint smile breaking across his ruddy face. "Lady, I cannot say. When the winds come out of the east in the spring and early summer, it may rain for a week or more. The Sudbergs hold the clouds and the rain melts the snow on the high peaks . . ."

Anna got the picture, or thought she did.

In the chair in the corner, Birke smiled, but remained silent, as though he feared any statement would call attention to him and result in his dismissal from the de facto meeting of his elders.

Anna wanted to grin, but didn't.

"Ehara, will he cross the Sudbergs in the rain, do you think?" asked Birfels. "Will the Sturinnese not prompt him to attack now that part of their fleet is beached in the empty Falche?"

"There's some water there," Anna said. "We looked in the reflecting pool this afternoon." Absently, she rubbed her forehead, although the headache from scrying had disappeared quickly, and she'd been fine when she'd groomed Farinelli. She still wondered what was upsetting Farinelli. Ever since her creation of the dam, the big gelding had been edgy. Did he sense her continuing exhaustion, a tiredness that had persisted for all too long? The gelding hadn't been that way at such times before, though. She pursed her lips momentarily. There wasn't much she could do.

"From the Envaryl," Jecks said. "Enough to wade in."

"Ehara and the Sea-Priests will not attack Defalk now," said Hanfor. "They will wait until trouble draws Lady Anna elsewhere." The veteran lifted his shoulders and spread his heads, offering an apologetic smile. "Only when she is committed in Ebra or against raiders from the High Grasslands of Neserea, only then will they attack."

"You cannot remain in Abenfel forever," Birfels said.

"No," Anna admitted. "If I attack Dumar, then Ehara

can ask for more aid from Sturinn. I wouldn't be surprised if he asked for aid from Mansuur. He's got enough gall. If I don't attack now, or sometime soon, then he'll attack when we can't stop him, like Hanfor said.''

"You do not depict a happy setting." The Lord of Abenfel frowned. "You must neglect the rest of Defalk to stop attacks on the south, or you must abandon us. . . .''

"Not yet," Anna corrected. "Dumar will not attack, even with the Sea-Priests' help, for at least a year. They will bring more and more armsmen, until Dumar is more like a part of Sturinn."

"Unless matters change," added Hanfor.

And they always do, Anna thought, *we just don't know how.* She stifled a yawn. She was better, but still tired, although she had ridden Farinelli several times in the past week before the downpour had started the day before.

"What will you do, then?" Birfels asked.

"If I had more armsmen, I'd attack Dumar," Anna said bluntly. "I don't. We'll wait another week, if you don't mind, to see what develops."

"And then?"

"We'll see."

Birfels stroked his chin. "Ebra?"

"I can't afford to have Konsstin or the Sea-Priests on three borders. So . . . we need to help out Lord Hadrenn. He's pledged to Defalk." *That doesn't mean I'm going there . . . not soon.*

"Ah . . ." Birfels nodded. "You would secure the east, then."

"At some time," Hanfor said.

"Hopefully," Anna corrected. *And that's a faint hope, indeed, but all I've got.*

She wished that her dam had persuaded Ehara or the Sturinnese to leave, but apparently that hadn't been a great-enough show of force. She repressed a snort. *Not enough blood and gore and destruction.*

"We will see," said Jecks.

"Indeed," added Birfels politely, lifting the wine pitcher. "Would you care for the good red?"

"Yes," said Anna, hoping the politics of Regency weren't driving her to alcoholism, even as she lifted the goblet.

IV

ENDE

88

The stallion reared back, silhouetted by the frequent bolts of lightning against the night stormclouds, yanking the rope. The heavy and rough hemp burned Anna's palms raw, sliding somehow around her hands, ripping, slicing the skin, even though she had wound the rope tightly so that she could keep her grip.

The black beast screamed and turned, heading westward. Despite the fire across her hands and the knives stabbing into her head, Anna dug in her heels and stiffened her body.

Still, she felt herself being dragged toward the river, toward the white water that surged only yards from the wild stallion that dragged her toward it, toward the whitecaps that roared more loudly than surf. She couldn't let go of the rope. She couldn't . . .

THRRUMMM!

Anna woke with a jolt, jarred almost bolt upright in the high bed, as if her entire body had been shocked by the force of the lightning strike that had seemed to shake the entire keep of Abenfel.

She blinked, dazed, glancing around the dark room. Nothing moved in her bedchamber. Had it been just a dream? Or some kind of earthquake? Outside, the rain kept splatting against the stones of the keep. What had happened? It couldn't have been just a nightmare, could it?

In slow motion, or so it seemed, she swung out of the bed, and padded to the shutters, easing them open. Outside, the rain fell in sheets, so thickly that she could see nothing but rain.

She watched for a time, but there were no other flashes
or bolts of lightning, only a rumble of thunder that seemed
distant, and receding. Then, although she listened for a
long time, the only sounds were those of the rain splatting
on stone and puddle, on roof and battlement, in big and
endless drops. Even in Iowa it hadn't rained so hard for
so long.

Finally, she closed the shutters, and yawned, tired as
she had been for what seemed weeks on weeks.

She slipped back to her bed, listening for a time as the
rain continued to pour down in a soothing waterfall, as it
had for the past four days. After what seemed a glass or
longer, she drifted back into an uneasy sleep.

Despite nightmares of rivers and stallions, when she
woke, she felt refreshed, more alive, more awake than in
days. She padded to the window and opened one shutter.
Although the rain had stopped, the gray clouds, while
thinning, blocked any direct sunlight. She nodded and
headed for the bath chamber.

Barely had she gotten out of the hot bath and dressed
than there was a furious rapping on the door. Anna pulled
on her second boot and stood.

"Yes?"

"Lady Anna?"

She recognized Birke's voice and opened the door.

"The dam . . . the sorcery . . ." Birke burst out. "It
has . . . You must see."

Even as she swallowed, Anna felt herself nodding.
Somehow, she'd been pouring energy into the damned
dam. That had been why she'd been so tired! The storm—
or the harmonies—had broken that tie, and the dam.

"You . . . look pleased?"

"No. I know what happened." Anna coughed, clearing
her throat. "We can't do much now. I'll need to eat."

"There is . . . bread and cheese and things in the small
hall," the redhead said. "The others were gathering for
breakfast."

"I'll be down in a moment." Anna closed the door,
then searched for her belt wallet and threaded the green

leather belt through it and the knife scabbard, the same battered but stiff leather one that Albero had given her in Loiseau soon after she'd landed in Erde. Less than two years earlier, and yet so long ago in so many ways.

She picked up the lutar and the leather case with the traveling scrying mirror before she stepped out into the hall.

"I could carry the mirror, Lady Anna," offered Rickel.

Anna surrendered the mirror easily. Her guards knew she seldom gave up the lutar.

Hanfor, Jecks, Birke, and Birfels were standing and waiting in the front of the small hall. In the rear were Fylena, Wasle, and Clayre. The dark-haired girl flashed a quick smile.

"You shouldn't have waited for me," Anna said. "Let's just eat." She sat on one end of the bench, ignoring the empty seat at the head of the table, and reached for the bread.

Birfels finally took his own seat, the one that he'd relinquished to Anna at every dinner, or supper, Anna corrected herself.

After several mouthfuls, Anna paused and glanced at Birke. "How did you know about the dam?"

"At first, I didn't, but Riksar—he's the wagonmaster, and he has a cot to the west—he told me that the water in the gorge had dropped by more than half." Birke shrugged. "So I rode down to see. There is still a lake, but water is pouring over what remains of the stones."

Her mouth full of bread and cheese, Anna nodded.

"It falls over . . . and it roars and the spray is like mist."

The sorceress frowned. It didn't sound as though the dam had actually smashed apart, but she'd have to see.

Rather than talk, Anna ate until she finally felt full. She should have been, after inhaling an entire loaf of steaming dark bread, a large wedge of cheese, and several handfuls of dried apples. She stood.

So did everyone else.

"If you're not done, please finish eating," the sorceress said. "I need to groom Farinelli first." With a nod at the group, she picked up the lutar and slipped out and into the corridor.

Rickel and Lejun followed her to the stable, Rickel still bearing the mirror.

Farinelli tossed his head as Anna stepped into the stall, yet he seemed more at ease than he had in previous days, not sidestepping or flicking his tail at nonexistent flies.

Although she didn't hurry with her grooming, she found herself astride Farinelli in the courtyard, while others scrambled to catch up—except for Jecks and Hanfor, who were also ready.

"I fear what we will see," said Jecks quietly.

"I don't worry about what we'll see here," Anna said. "There can't be that much damage in the gorge."

"Downstream, below the Great Chasm, there will be ruin if your dam failed." Hanfor turned in the saddle as Alvar rode up.

"We are ready, Arms Commander."

Anna glanced toward the stable, where Birke led out his mount, followed by Birfels. "In a moment, once they're mounted."

Alvar nodded.

Farinelli *whuff*ed once, and Anna leaned forward and patted him on the neck, getting another, lower *whuff* in return.

Because the trail was muddy, with pools of water in the low spots, the group rode at a slow walk. Still, Anna had mud splattered across the legs of her trousers.

The slow ride took closer to three glasses than the two it had in drier weather, and the sun—trying to break through thinning gray clouds—was nearly overhead by the time they neared the partly cleared vista of the gorge that overlooked the dam—or what was left of it.

"You see?" called Birke as he stood in the stirrups and gestured downhill.

From where she'd reined up, Anna couldn't see much

of anything. She couldn't miss the roar of falling water, or the spray that drifted above the gorge and trees.

She dismounted, handed Farinelli's reins to Fhurgen, and walked with Hanfor and Jecks down to where she could view the damage. Birfels and Birke joined the three as Anna studied the river and the gorge.

From what she could see, the entire structure had . . . sunk, and tilted forward at a thirty-degree angle.

Some few rivulets spurted out from the chasm walls, as if in those places where the chasm or rocks had weakened, but the dam itself was still intact—just repositioned so that the lake behind it was lower, a third of what it had been. The Falche poured over the repositioned dam, a cascade of water.

"You have created a new cataract, the third great cataract," Birfels said.

Anna had to wonder what had happened in Dumar when that wall of water had swept down the Falche. Whatever had happened, it wouldn't have been good.

She took a deep breath. She had a lot of scrying, and thinking, to do.

89

ENCORA, RANUAK

Veria knocks on the pale oak wooden door a second time.

The door to the Matriarch's private quarters opens.

"You wasted no time, sister," says Alya. "Mother said you would be here." She draws the door full open and steps aside. "Father has brewed the fine green-gray tea."

"Thank you, sister." Veria's voice is stiff.

"Thank the Matriarch." Alya's smile remains formal,

her eyes cold, as the two walk through the circular foyer and into the tea room.

"Veria. Please join us," invites the gray-haired Matriarch with a pleasant smile upon her round face.

"You expected me." Veria slips into one of the two vacant chairs.

"Of course. What has happened will affect the SouthWomen greatly." The Matriarch sips her tea. "Greatly. Your presence will allow them to understand what has happened."

"The sorceress tried to build a great dam with sorcery," Veria begins, "and it failed—"

"It took a mighty regenflut, and the dam did not fail; the ground around the dam failed." The Matriarch corrects her dark-haired daughter with a smile. "Even now the dam holds together, and it will do so for longer than any of us will endure."

"Moth—Matriarch, does that not show her weaknesses still?" Veria's fingers tighten around the pale blue cup.

"Veria, if you will permit your aging father," Ulgar says with a smile as he steps up to the table with a green-and-golden ceramic pot in his hand, "I will refill your cup."

"Thank you." Veria's fingers loosen their grip on the fluted cup that matches the pot, and she inclines her head. "Thank you, Father."

"The sorceress has weaknesses, as you say, Veria," answers the Matriarch. "As do we all. The weakness was not in her sorcery, but in her failure to understand that the rock to which she anchored her sorcery was not so strong as either she or her spell. And the spell was pure Clearsong."

"Clearsong or no, it was a failure," points out Veria.

"Sister . . . that failure destroyed the entire fleet of the Sea-Priests," says Alya. "Not a ship of those in Narial remains."

"Even her failures are successes," says Veria. "This cannot continue. The harmonies will not permit it."

"The harmonies permit what they will," suggests the Matriarch. "I feel that this failure was not the success you suggest. She will pay for it; she has paid for everything, and the harmonies do not permit us to escape. With the forces she has wielded, even less will they permit her to evade fate."

"Yet you support her?" asks Veria.

Alya looks at Veria, but the dark-haired woman refuses to meet Alya's eyes.

"I support the harmonies." The Matriarch smiles. "So does she, as she understands them. So should the SouthWomen."

"You said this would affect the SouthWomen," Veria suggests.

"It will. Lord Ehara and the Sturinnese cannot accept such a devastation. All their resources will go to Dumar. They will not treat with the freewomen of Elawha, and they will kill them immediately and as quickly as possible."

"You had said that such would occur because Sturinn was backing Bertmynn. Now you say that it will happen because the Sea-Priests are not backing Bertmynn." Veria snorts—loudly.

"They will no longer suggest. They will send more coins and fewer armsmen, and the price of those coins will be higher, and paid with the blood of the freewomen and any who oppose Bertmynn and the plans of the Sea-Priests."

"You merely seek another way to forecast failure for those women who wish to be free."

"The women of Ebra will be free, in spite of your plots and blades, Veria. They will be free because of the prices that the sorceress will pay, and you will suffer."

"Are you threatening me?" Veria sets down the green fluted cup.

"No, my daughter." The Matriarch shakes her head sadly. "I know what the harmonies demand. They demand much, and they demand more of those who supply blades for others to fight their battles than of those who lift them for their own ends.''

Ulgar slurps his tea noisily. As the others look at him, he adds, ''That is why the sorceress will prevail. She does what she must, and then asks others.''

The Matriarch nods, but her eyes are sad, and fixed upon Veria.

90

The sorceress glanced at the reflecting pool, then cleared her throat, beginning another vocalise. After three, her voice was firm, cords clear, and she lifted the lutar and sang.

> ''Show in Dumar, high and true,
>   what the raging flow did do. . . .
> Show me now, and show me all,
>   of how it struck and what did fall . . .''

Anna forced herself to lower the lutar gently, even as her eyes were drawn into the scenes in the reflecting pool, even as she heard the indrawn breaths of Hanfor and Jecks.

A muddy sea tossed objects on an equally mud-drenched beach—spars, sections of rope, limp, doll-like figures in muddy white uniforms. Farther along the beach were the remnants of a ship, timbers shattered, jagged ends protruding from the waters like spears.

''The Maitre of Sturinn will not be pleased,'' said Jecks.

That's an understatement, and then some. Anna did not speak, letting her eyes take in the scenes that followed each other, so many that they could not all show in the pool at once.

Another scene displayed brown waters swirling around piles of timbers smashed against riverbank, a bank where grasses and trees had been pressed flat or swept away, where long patches of red earth had crumbled into the waters. Carcasses of animals, scattered human bodies, tree limbs, and debris littered the riverbanks.

Another vista showed rows upon rows of roofless and collapsed houses below a bluff. Behind the collapsed houses was a heap of wet earth, from the edge of which protruded walls and timbers. The wet earth had peeled away from the bluff.

"Dumaria, I think," murmured Jecks. "The lower part is on the river."

River water piled up behind and flowed through and over and around a long heap of stone blocks that had once been a bridge.

The pool showed another town, a small one, where nothing remained but foundation walls and a sea of mud, and figures toiling through the mud, searching for bodies or belongings or both.

Anna's eyes burned and her stomach twisted. She'd wanted to avoid that kind of destruction, and even her attempts at that had created a disaster, another kind, but a disaster, possibly even a greater disaster than killing thousands of armsmen. *Which you will now have to do . . . anyway. . . .*

Another score of scenes followed before she choked out the release spell. She had to sing it twice, because she couldn't hold the words the first time.

"I never . . . planned . . . for that," she finally said after lowering the lutar and setting it on the writing table.

"We know," Jecks answered, "but Lord Ehara and the Sea-Priests do not."

"Surely, Lord Ehara will request the Sturinnese leave," murmured Hanfor.

"Never," said Jecks flatly. "Now . . . now he cannot

give in. His own people will destroy him unless he attacks us. Within days, he will march on Defalk.''

"He will march after such destruction?"

"You speak as an arms commander. You speak as one who sees the power a sorceress wields." Jecks shook his head. "The people and the holders of Dumar will not care. They have suffered great injury, and, unless Lord Ehara redresses that injury, they will turn on him. He has no choice."

"He is a fool."

"Perhaps," Jecks admitted, "but he will be a live fool. At worst, he will live long enough to attack."

Anna winced. "Hanfor, you'd better get the men ready to ride. We'll try to reach the road below Stromwer before Ehara's lancers do."

"He will not hurry that quickly," Jecks said with a bitter smile. "He will have to re-form his armsmen, and find a way across the Falche. You left no bridges and no fords, I wager, Lady Anna."

Anna wasn't about to take that bet. She nodded. "I need to think."

"Of course." Jecks bowed.

So did Hanfor.

After the two had left, Anna lifted the lutar again. The first spellsong was to seek her enemies of power, and she got the same images as always—the young man in brown with the hatred-filled eyes, the blonde seer of Nordwei, and the tall Sea-Priest. Still . . . neither Menares nor Dythya had discovered who or where the young sorcerer might be, and her spells had revealed nothing more.

As for the Sea-Priest, this time he was with Ehara, and the two were on horseback, apparently leading a column of armsmen.

Anna shook her head and released the spell. She re-drafted the danger spell and sang it. The reflecting pool gave her the image of the Sea-Priest with Ehara. Another spell, and she was able to determine that they were somewhere between Narial and Dumaria—at least they were beside the Falche, and she would have guessed they were south of Dumaria.

"Good. . . ." If so, that gave her some time. Not a lot, but some.

She walked to the window, and wiped her sweating forehead.

91

Anna turned and glanced back along the road to the north. Under the hot late-morning sun, the column of armsmen seemed to stretch a dek behind her, with the wagons and their mounted escort out of sight behind the low rolling hills. The threescore armsmen from Birfels and yet another two score from Gylaron had boosted her force to over four hundred. That had meant the need for more supplies—and wagons, and spare mounts.

The sorceress looked ahead at the Sudbergs rising behind the steeper southern hills ahead. Already, the green bean fields of Lerona were giving way to meadows and woodlots and an occasional vineyard, and the soil was turning back into a redder clay. Peasants and farmers toiled in the fields, not approaching the armsmen, but not bolting for cover, either. That was an improvement from the last ride to Stromwer.

She blotted her forehead before she took out the third water bottle and drank. After four days on the road, they still had another two before they reached the rugged cliffs of Stromwer.

She had begun to understand why so many of the English kings had always seemed to be somewhere other than London—and she didn't like how she was finding it out. There was always some problem that no one else could handle, and it took *forever* to get anywhere by horse, even on comparatively dry roads.

Slowly, she replaced the water bottle, looking to her right as Jecks cleared his throat.

"Have you decided on the tariffs for the rivermen?" he asked.

"I can't give them relief without opening the door to everyone who has problems, and then there won't be any money left to defend Defalk." She wanted to shake her head. *Everybody* wanted something. The rivermen wanted relief. Lord Tybel wanted to take over his grandchildren's lands, and wanted Anna's approval for the stunt. The Rider of Heinene wanted coins to buy arms and more horses to defend the grasslands against the raiders from the High Grasslands across the border in Neserea. Hanfor and Himar wanted more coins to hire and train more armsmen. Hadrenn needed coins to hold off Bertmynn . . . and so it went.

"Lady Anna?" Jecks' voice was so deferential that she knew he was going to ask something even more disturbing.

"Yes." She turned in the saddle.

"You said that the Sea-Priest is a wizard, Lady Anna?"

"The one who's always with Lord Ehara is."

"He could enchant arrows and crossbow bolts, then?"

"I'm sure he could."

"You can sense danger only in the mirror?" Jecks was definitely being delicate.

"You're afraid he'll come up with some magical surprise when I'm preoccupied?"

"Could that not happen?"

Jecks was right, but it was one of the last things Anna wanted to think about. She was hot and sweaty, and mud had spattered everything she wore. At least there wasn't any dust but the riding was slower, and the wagons had lagged behind the main body more than a glass or two every day. Finding halfway dry areas to camp had been a problem as well, especially the first two nights. The third night had been at Lerona, where Gylaron had been pleased to see them, and even more pleased, Anna suspected, to see them leave. He had been gracious enough to send an additional two score of his own armsmen, to be paid by the Regency, although Anna had not made it clear she was not officially requesting levies. She would need those later, if she had to face both Konsstin and Bertmynn at the same time.

"I suppose it could," she admitted.

Jecks waited for her to draw the inevitable conclusion.

"And you think I should come up with some sorcerous answer?" Anna finally asked.

"I am not a sorcerer. We have no others here," Jecks answered with a smile.

"What *kind* of sorcery did you have in mind, my good Lord Jecks?" asked Anna with exaggerated politeness.

"Something which would protect you whether you were immediately aware of it or not."

"I don't think pure enchantment would work. I could perhaps strengthen this breastplate."

"That would only protect your chest."

Anna nodded. "So now I should carry a shield? How could I use the lutar?"

Jecks frowned. "That would be difficult."

"Extremely."

He smiled. "Perhaps you should not carry it at all."

"A shield I didn't carry? What use would that be?"

"A small round shield. It could rest like an Ebran shield—forward of your knee, in a holder with an open top. You could enchant it so that it would fly up if anything threatened you."

"That would take some spell," Anna said with a laugh. "You are a mighty sorceress."

"Look where that's gotten me—on a muddy road on the way to a battle I wanted to avoid."

"As you wish, lady."

Anna wanted to sigh. Jecks might be white-haired, but sometimes he was worse than a little boy. Then, sometimes all men were. *And women aren't like little girls at times?* She shook her head. "Let me think about it. Maybe . . . maybe, I can think up something."

"That is all I ask."

She wanted to sigh again, but she forced a smile. "I hope the road dries more as we get toward Stromwer."

"It will be damp until the other side of the crests of the Sudbergs," predicted Jecks.

Great. Mud and a semi-patronizing yet concerned lord. Anna patted Farinelli.

92

NORTHEAST OF DUMARIA, DUMAR

The shadow of a puffy white cloud passes over the road, and sunlight pours down on the long column once more. In the middle of the vanguard ride Ehara and jerRestin. The white uniform of the Sea-Priest appears grayish from the road dust.

"You say we need to reach the Vale of Cuetayl a day before she does." Ehara glances toward the hills that, more than a dozen deks ahead, rise out of the flat plains. Behind the hills are the spired peaks of the Sudbergs, hazy in the distance and heat.

"At least a day. Two days would be better," answers jerRestin, shifting his weight in the saddle once more. "We need some time to set up the attack. The terrain there will be suitable."

"Have you been there?" Ehara touches the dark black beard and frowns. "How do you know?"

"Maps," says jerRestin with a laugh. "Sailors need good maps, and we are quite good at making them for any sea or land that interests us."

"And Dumar interests you?"

"All of Liedwahr interests the Maitre," replies jer-Restin offhandedly. "Surely, you know that by now, would-be Viceroy of Dumar and Defalk."

"I vaguely remember something about that." Ehara forces a smile. "Especially the viceroy part."

"I thought you might." JerRestin shifts his weight in the saddle again. "I prefer ships to horses, but one does what is needed." A hard smile goes toward Ehara.

The Lord of Dumar ignores the smile. "How will you ensure that the bitch dies?"

"If she has no warning and cannot see what flies toward her, then she will die," answers jerRestin. "That is why where we set our attack is important, and why each company must be separated from the others and under rock overhangs where possible. The streams should help as well."

"You think running water will stop her, after what she did to the Falche?"

"Hamper, not stop," corrects jerRestin amiably.

Behind the two leaders, the armsmen in pale brown, lancers with crimson sashes, ride stolidly and silently. Behind them are the two thousand lancers from Sturinn who survived the flood. Their faces are simultaneously blank and grim.

Even the hum of insects and the calls of the plains sparrows and dusky finches is low in the midday heat. Another cloud blocks the sun, and a shadow drifts across the road, then scuds eastward.

93

As the lead scouts of the column emerged from the last of the redstone walls of the canyon, Anna glanced ahead, southward to the ramparts of Stromwer, and toward the sloped, glass-smooth wall of stone before the keep that blocked the southern end of the valley.

The low, rolling hills were mostly green, and Anna could see scattered figures, and sheep, in places. The low hum of insects, the heat, and the sweat soaking into the band of her hat affirmed that summer had indeed arrived in southern Defalk.

Hanfor's scouts had already returned—confirming that Lady Wendella expected and welcomed them. Not that Wendella had any choice, Anna reflected. The sorceress's trousers were encrusted with reddish mud, although the rain had not fallen quite so heavily farther south—or the sun had been hotter and dried the road more.

"A good thing that you did not have to assault Stromwer," Jecks voiced.

"A very good thing, for everyone," added Hanfor.

"You mean because we'll be stronger to fight Ehara?"

The two did not answer immediately because a scout appeared on the road ahead, coming over a low rise and riding a slow canter toward them.

"Now what?" murmured the sorceress to herself. She licked her dry lips and readjusted the floppy brown hat.

"Another rider, a messenger," the scout said tersely, beginning to speak even before he swung his mount alongside Hanfor. "He wears crimson and rides alone."

Anna wanted to sigh. She didn't have any illusions

about the contents of whatever message Ehara had dispatched.

"It is not a good message," observed Jecks.

"A declaration of war?" suggested Anna. "Or a demand for our surrender?"

"From what you have laid on Dumar, it could be nothing else," said Hanfor.

Anna still wanted to sigh. No matter what she did, it seemed to lead to some form of fight or skirmish. If she obliterated someone, that was force. If she didn't, that was weakness, and weakness meant that she had to use force later. If she used indirect force, such as damming a river, that was an insult or created the idea that the ruler involved was weak, and that meant he had to fight. Even the direct force of a flood—however unplanned—didn't seem to get the point across—only blood and slaughter seemed to do that. *Idiots! Idiots . . . everywhere.*

The messenger's mount trotted along the damp red clay of the road toward the head of the column. The bareheaded rider reined up a good fifty yards south, and extended his hands—empty—and then lowered them and waited. His lanceholder held the staff of the pale blue pennant of harmony, the sign of traveling under truce, though the pennant itself hung limply in the still summer air.

Fhurgen eased his mount forward of Anna, as did Rickel. Both raised the protective shields slightly, and both had drawn their blades. Beside Anna, Jecks also bore an unsheathed blade.

"Halt here," said Hanfor quietly.

The column stopped more than twenty yards north of the waiting messenger in crimson, who leaned forward slightly in the saddle, the mounted equivalent of a bow. "I offer this from Lord Ehara to the lady Anna, Regent of Defalk."

Fhurgen eased his mount forward, letting his blade rest across his thighs as he reached for the scroll. Even as she

wondered how he could balance the bare steel that well,
Anna let Fhurgen take the scroll.

"The regent will read it," promised the guard.

"I must know that it reaches her hand." The messenger's voice quavered.

"I'll take it," Anna said quietly.

Fhurgen eased his mount sideways, never taking his
eyes off the messenger, keeping the shield up, until he
handed the scroll to Anna and slipped his fingers back
around the hilt of his blade. "You may tell Lord Ehara
his message reached the lady Anna."

The messenger touched his brow and turned his horse,
leaving at a fast trot, as if to put as much distance between
him and the Defalkan forces as possible.

Anna looked at the rolled scroll, and at the travel-worn
crimson ribbon and the wax seal that resembled a splotch
of congealed blood. Finally, she looked around for a place
to put it, before thrusting it through her belt, unopened.

"You would not read it?" asked Jecks.

"Why? I'd only get madder. What else could I do right
now? We know Ehara's moving every armsman he's got
toward Defalk. He's not asking for peace, not with one
messenger and no escort. Even I can figure that out. That
messenger felt he was expendable. He expected to get
killed." Anna shrugged, then flicked Farinelli's reins. "I
want to get to Stromwer, get some food, and a bath. Then,
we'll see what Ehara has in mind." *As if you don't know
already. . . .*

"I doubt we will learn aught more than we already
know," suggested Hanfor dryly.

"No," Anna agreed, letting Farinelli move out at a
quick walk, "but he's being a good boy, telling us how
bad we are and why he has to go to war and get all sorts
of people killed so that the lords or holders of Dumar can
feel justified." She could feel Jecks stiffen in his saddle,
but she didn't care—almost.

"Not all lords are like that," said Hanfor.

"No—just most of them." Anna thought, and added

quickly, "The good ones keep getting killed, except for Jecks here, and he can't make a difference by himself."

Hanfor offered a laugh. "That was how Lord Behlem gained his power. He removed the good lords and elevated those who wanted all to worship their names."

"It's how a lot of rulers get power." Anna glanced to the left of the road, beyond a low stone fence where three young men and a girl stared, almost openmouthed, at her. She forced a smile, then offered a wave.

The dark-haired girl with the hoe turned to the youth next to her, but Anna did not hear the words. The sorceress's eyes went to the road ahead, but her thoughts remained on lords and people with power who always seemed more interested in making themselves seem more important and powerful than in doing much constructive.

After a time, Jecks cleared his throat, rode nearer to Anna, and asked, "About the Sea-Priest, the sorcerer . . . have you thought . . . ?"

"About a spell to protect me?" asked Anna. "Some."

Jecks waited, and Anna let the silence draw out slightly, knowing she was being petty, bitchy, or worse. But she was tired, and everyone kept asking things, little things, big things—tariffs, arms, smiths, blades, the list seemed endless.

Jecks waited, a patient half-smile on his face.

Anna glanced at the keep, still another two or three deks ahead, gray-and-red stones rising out of the center of the south end of the long valley. Finally, she spoke. "I think I could enchant your very small shield . . . maybe. I have some ideas, and I will try to work them out when we stop at Stromwer."

"Thank you, Lady Anna. I would feel much better, would you try that."

"I'll try," she promised—after a bath, after some decent food.

Again, they rode in silence, Anna occasionally blotting away sweat, trying not to think about how she felt and smelled as the force neared the end of the valley and the walls and ramparts of the keep.

"Out with the standard!" ordered Hanfor.

One of the scouts broke out the banner with the crossed spears over the golden crown with the *R* beneath. The standard-bearer rode to the front of the van as the hoofs of the mounts struck the stone slabs of the causeway leading up to the gates of Stromwer.

The sharp *clopp*ing of hoofs on stone echoed around Anna and back down the valley. Heads popped up from the battlements of Stromwer, heads that just watched as the regent entered the gates.

The brown-haired Wendella stood on the front steps of the main keep building within the walls. "Greetings, sorceress and regent."

"Greetings, Lady Wendella," Anna reining up Farinelli, but making no move to dismount. "We're only stopping for the night."

Jecks reined up beside Anna, while Rickel and Fhurgen stopped farther back into the courtyard. Hanfor and Alvar continued toward the wider section of the stone-paved yard before the stable.

"For the night only?" Wendella looked up with a crooked smile. "And I had wondered if you returned to take my hold from me."

Anna shook her head, forcing a smile. "Your hold is yours unless you fail to keep it well. You should know . . ." The sorceress didn't bother finishing the sentence, realizing that Wendella was baiting her, almost as if to say that as Lady of Stromwer she was loyal, but didn't have to like it.

"Have you heard of what happens in Dumar?" asked the brown-haired lady, cradling Condell in her left arm.

"We have heard little," Anna said. "I know that Ehara is marching all of his armsmen toward Stromwer. What have you heard?"

Wendella offered the same crooked smile. "There are tales that Lord Ehara is so angry at Defalk that he has turned his back on all of Liedwahr and ordered the women into chains, as in Sturinn. . . .''

Jecks glanced at Anna.

''. . . And that Sturinn has pledged its entire fleet to bring down the . . . Sorceress of Defalk. . . .'' Wendella swallowed.

''I assume that was 'the bitch-sorceress of Defalk'?'' asked Anna. ''Or words like that.''

''Yes, Lady Anna.''

''We will discuss that.'' Anna paused, then added, ''You should join us, Lady Wendella. After I stable and groom Farinelli.''

Jecks raised his eyebrows.

Wendella glanced from Anna to Jecks to Anna, then nodded. ''As you wish, Lady Anna. I would suggest the private study.''

''Thank you. That would be good. I won't be long.'' Anna inclined her head and flicked the reins gently. Farinelli followed her guidance and carried her to the area before the stable where Hanfor, with the stablemaster standing by the arms commander's mount, directed the armsmen.

''Purple Company—that's the rear section to the right. . . .'' Hanfor nodded to Anna, then continued. ''. . . subofficers check all blades before supper.''

The sorceress swung out of the saddle. For a moment, her knees felt like jelly as she stood on the stone. Then she headed into the stable.

The dark-haired stable boy bowed as Anna led Farinelli through the open sliding door. ''Regent and lady, the front corner stall . . . it is ready.''

''Thank you.'' Anna smiled.

Farinelli *whuff*ed once as Anna stepped into the stall, swept and filled with fresh straw. A bucket of oats also awaited the big horse.

''Grain, too.''

''They all respect their regent here,'' said Jecks with a laugh from the adjoining stall.

"If it weren't required by spells, I'd be happier." Anna loosened the girths, then racked the saddle and hung the saddle blanket next to the saddle. She groomed the big gelding without speaking.

When she was finished, she carried the lutar and scroll across the courtyard and up the steps to the private study, accompanied by Hanfor and Jecks, and trailed as always by a pair of guards, this time Lejun and Rickel. One of the younger guards followed with the leather-cased traveling mirror and her saddlebags. All three halted and stationed themselves in the dim stone-walled corridor while Jecks and Anna entered the study where Wendella waited.

Anna set the lutar on a chest. Jecks surveyed the study, then nodded at Hanfor who closed the heavy door gently, but firmly.

"You wished my presence, Lady Anna?" asked Wendella, still holding a sleeping Condell.

"I did. I thought you might like to hear what our neighbor Lord Ehara has to say to us."

"Your lands are the closest," Jecks added as a reminder.

The Lady of Stromwer inclined her head.

Anna broke the dark red sealing wax and rolled open the scroll. Her eyes scanned the dark letters and the words quickly, and she nodded as she read, her lips quirked as she discovered that Jecks had indeed understood Ehara.

After she finished, she glanced at Wendella, Jecks, and then Hanfor. "Here's what he says, the most important parts anyway.

"... Once I might have considered peace, but never can there be accord with a nation that turns the rivers of Liedwahr against her people. Never can there be harmony with a ruler who will not fight in honor and who usurps the very nature of the earth. ...

"... I will put every woman in Dumar, every

woman in Liedwahr in adorning chains, before I will treat with you . . .

"We march on Dumar, and all the way through it." Anna's voice sounded tired, even to her.

"Narial is gone, and the lower sections of Dumaria are ruins," said Jecks, a quizzical note in his voice. "You must defeat Ehara, but why would you proceed?"

Anna lifted the scroll and read aloud, "Never can there be harmony . . ."

"We still have nowhere near the forces Lord Ehara can muster," observed Hanfor, his voice mild.

"I don't intend to fight honorably," snapped Anna. "I intend to win. I intend to gain the pledge of every armsman in Dumar or wipe out every one who will not be loyal to Defalk, and I intend to destroy every Sea-Priest left in Liedwahr."

Wendella smiled tightly.

Jecks stepped back at the venom in Anna's voice.

The faintest of nods came from Hanfor.

"Are you surprised, Lord Jecks? I won't live forever. You've told me that. Am I supposed to wait until Dumar is strong again and so that I can kill twice as many innocents? I tried reason and scrolls to get a meaningful agreement from Lord Ehara. That was refused—with scorn. Then I tried sorcery to avoid this senseless war, and what happened? More people died. Because they died, Lord Ehara has to kill me or die trying."

Anna paused, finding she was breathing hard. "I'm tired of this sort of thing. Fine . . . we're going to stop it all—if I possibly can. Sturinn can't get reinforcements here fast enough, and by then I'll hold Dumar—or be dead. One way or another, no one will have to worry."

They think you're crazy.

Only Hanfor nodded, once more, and for that Anna was grateful. He seemed to understand. Jecks was having trouble in reconciling what he had seen with too many years of tradition—that was what Anna felt.

"I'm going to take a bath, and then we'll eat. After that, we'll discuss exactly how we'll take Dumar." Anna knew she was sounding imperious, hated herself for it, and hated herself for not saying anything. *But they all want it handled like I happen to be the tooth fairy, like there's no cost to anything. . . .*

"Yes, Regent." Jecks bowed.

Hanfor bowed, half-smile upon his lips.

Wendella bowed. "Supper will be ready as you wish, Lady Anna. The guest quarters are ready, and there is water in the tub."

"Thank you." Anna turned and walked toward the study door.

94

Thrap . . . *thrap.*

The sorceress readjusted her single, spell-cleaned gown and glanced at the closed door to the guest chamber. "Yes?"

"Lord Jecks for you," announced Rickel.

"He can come in."

The door eased open.

"Lady Anna." The white-haired and muscular lord bowed, then smiled. His warm hazel eyes twinkled.

He can be devastating and charming. "Lord Jecks." *Until we start discussing the foibles of the Thirty-three and others of privilege . . . or dancing.*

From behind his back, Jecks lifted a circular object, not much more than two full handspans across. "This is a very small shield." He smiled again.

Anna looked at the small circlet of bronze and iron.

"You said it had to be small, yet heavy enough to stop anything. And I could not use one with leather."

Anna frowned, then nodded. Still, she tended to forget the limits of Clearsong and Darksong.

Jecks shrugged. "No shield I know can be light and effective."

"All I can do is try," answered Anna. "It was your idea." She added quickly, "I wish I'd thought of it earlier." She gestured toward one of the straight-backed chairs, then sat behind the small writing desk and opened the folder, searching for a blank sheet of paper.

After a time, she dipped the quill into the inkwell and began to write, slowly, almost laboriously, to keep from smudging the local ink that took *forever* to dry.

Abruptly, she looked up. "Lord Jecks . . . I think it would be a good idea for Alvar and Liende to join us for meals from now on—even if other lords are guesting us."

Jecks nodded.

"Would you tell them and Lady Wendella while I work on this?" She smiled. "Please? I'm not trying to make you an errand boy. I should have thought of it sooner."

"An errand such as this I would be more than happy to accomplish." Another smile followed the words as he stood, stepping forward and laying the small shield on the corner of the writing desk. "If you should need this for your spell . . ."

"Thank you."

As the door closed, Anna tried to concentrate on the words. For a moment, nothing came, and the fingers of her left hand touched the cool metal rim of the circular shield. The shield did not move as her fingers pressed on the metal. She lifted it, left-handed, surprised at the weight, and lowered it quickly.

"Heavy. . . ." No wonder shields weren't exactly in vogue. She'd hate to have to carry one and a blade. She wondered how Rickel and Fhurgen managed with the bigger shields they used to protect her.

With a slow breath, she picked up the pen once more, adding a few more words to those on the paper.

A finch, or something, chirped outside the window.

Anna set aside the quill and studied the crude spell written on the brown paper.

"Against enchanted weapons be my shield
   save me from all arms those against me wield . . ."

Perhaps a variation on the flame spell. . . . She stood and took a deep breath, then extracted the lutar from its case and began to tune it. She strummed the flame song, humming the notes as she did and concentrating on the words.

The sorceress shook her head. Not even close, and the note values were stretched too far. She tried several other variations.

"If I untie . . ." She nodded, and jotted down the tune variation she had in mind, then played it on the lutar once more. That didn't work, either. She went back to the paper and jotted down another variation, then lifted the lutar once more, using nonsense syllables to sing the patterns.

With a relieved smile as she realized that note values and words matched, she replaced the lutar in its case, and the case on the chest set against the outside wall. As she straightened, at the knock on the door, the sorceress looked up. "Yes?"

"Lord Jecks, my lady."

Lately, Jecks had been using the "my lady" phrase. Did he want her to be his lady? Anna frowned. More important, did she want to be? "Come on in."

Jecks was still smiling. "Your chief player was pleased. Alvar was worried. I took the liberty of informing Hanfor before Alvar."

"Thank you. I should have thought of that." Much as she was sometimes frustrated by various protocols and customs, Jecks was good at warning her, or, in this case, in simply avoiding the problem. "Hanfor didn't object?"

"No. He said Alvar needed the experience if he were to command larger forces."

Anna laughed. "In short, I should have done it sooner, but Hanfor's too polite to insist." She crossed the room to the writing desk where she glanced from the small shield to the brown paper before her. "I think I have something. We'll have to see once we're headed into Dumar."

"You won't enchant it now?" asked Jecks.

"Not until we leave Stromwer," Anna said, looking down at the shield again. "I'm pretty sure a spell like this drains energy from me."

Jecks raised his eyebrows.

"That was what happened with the dam. That was part of the reason I was so tired, and it took so long for me to recover." *That's what you feel.* . . . "That's what I feel, anyway."

"If you feel that, my lady, then that is what must have been."

"Right now," Anna said, "I feel hungry. Shall we go?"

"I could eat," Jecks admitted.

They left the guest chamber, and the guards fell in behind them. Anna wondered, yet again, if she'd ever get used to guards escorting her everywhere.

On the main level, the others were already waiting. Liende wore a dark green gown, slightly wrinkled and probably borrowed, and Alvar his uniform, brushed. Both bowed as Anna and Jecks approached the hall. Hanfor, who had been standing beside Alvar and talking to the captain, also offered Anna a bow.

"You requested my presence?" asked Liende, stepping up to Anna and bowing again.

"I should have requested it far sooner. I'm sorry. Some things I'm just not thinking about."

A puzzled look crossed the chief player's face.

"I need your thoughts, and your advice, but you can't very well give it if you don't see what I see," Anna explained. "Or if the only real time you see me is when we're riding."

Liende nodded. "You honor me."

"Not enough," Anna said quietly. "Not soon enough, either." She raised her voice. "Let's go in and eat."

Wendella stood by the long and dark table that appeared almost as ancient as the aged wooden paneling that covered the stone walls. She gestured to the place at the head. "Regent and sorceress."

"Thank you." Anna gestured to the table. "Please sit."

There were only the six at table—Anna, Wendella, Jecks, Hanfor, Liende, and Alvar. The swarthy Alvar looked down at his plate, as if asking how he had ended up with the arms commander and the local nobility.

"Because you need to be here," Anna said sweetly to the uncomfortable captain.

"As my lady wishes."

"Enjoy the food," Anna suggested.

"We can all do that," Jecks said dryly, "especially after all the riding."

"I had Waerya prepare something special," Wendella said. "An apple-spiced lamb."

The serving girl carried in a large platter. While Anna had feared seeing a whole lamb splayed across the traylike serving dish, the dish contained more than a dozen cylinders of rolled meat covered with a thick brown sauce.

"The lamb is wrapped around the stuffing," Wendella added, "and the sauce is a family specialty—from the days of Suhlmorra." A faint smile crossed her lips as she glanced at Jecks.

"I don't mind food from Suhlmorra," he rumbled, "just those who still want to bring back another realm."

"Even my dear brother would be too wise to attempt that," Wendella answered. "Mietchel will always be loyal to the Lord of Falcor, or any Regency that supports that lord."

Since the serving platter was tendered to Anna, she stabbed one of the lamb rolls and transferred it to her plate, then a second, and a third. The serving girl's brown eyes flickered from Anna to the platter and back to Anna.

"Thank you," the sorceress murmured to the girl.

"Your brother would be wise to remain so," Jecks suggested to Wendella, before stabbing a smothered lamb roll.

"And what if Defalk is ruled by a lady? Say, if Jimbob has only daughters?" asked Anna.

"That would distress him, were he to live so long," answered Wendella.

"How does he feel about lady holders in the Thirty-three?" Anna pursued, almost idly, breaking off a chunk of dark bread. In a way, being Wendella's guest was almost liberating. The Lady of Stromwer didn't like Anna, and yet had to be loyal. So Anna could be more forthright.

"I had thought that there were few. Am I not the only woman holding lands in Defalk? Besides Lady Gatrune," Wendella added quickly.

"Lady Anientta holds the lands for her heirs," Jecks answered for Anna. "And Lady Anna holds Falcor for Jimbob."

"Lady Herene is acting as guardian for Dinfan at Suhl," Anna added.

"You named the daughter as heir?" Wendella asked.

"She is the oldest," Anna answered after swallowing a mouthful of the lamb, dry despite the spices and gummy sauce-gravy. Her own stuffed pork chops or apple crown roast were far better, but whether she could have done so well over an open kitchen fire was another question.

"And," murmured Hanfor, "Lady Anna holds Loiseau and Mencha in her own right."

Wendella laughed softly. "That is almost a fifth of the Thirty-three, and in but a year. No marvel that my late lord feared you, Lady Anna. Or that the Sea-Priests would give a kingdom for your death."

"You know that from what source?" Jecks held a chunk of bread, suspended in a large hand, as his eyes fixed on Wendella.

"None, save my own feelings." Wendella offered a nervous laugh. "Yet I'd wager that feeling against all others."

"So would I," added Liende quietly in the momentary silence.

Alvar swallowed loudly enough to punctuate the chief player's words.

"That will change," Anna said. "The business about women, that is."

"It changes already," Jecks pointed out.

"True enough," Anna interposed quickly. "But that's enough about it." Her eyes went to Wendella. "Lady Wendella, could you tell us, or me, since I know too little about Defalk, where you grew up and how you came to Stromwer?"

After a moment, Wendella began. "I am the youngest child, and the third daughter, of Lord Mietch. The oldest was Mietchel, and he now holds Morra. My eldest sister—that was Haerl—she was consorted to Arkad, but she died with child, and so did the child."

"Was she his second consort?" asked Anna.

"His third." Wendella paused. "When I was young, Morra was a happy place, with the rose trees always in bloom against the garden walls. My sire said the walls dated back to the days when Suhlmorra was great, when Defalk was a poor land but a sliver of its present demesne. . . ."

Anna leaned back slightly in the chair and listened as Wendella detailed her background.

". . . And then I came to Stromwer to be Dencer's consort when his first betrothed died of a fever in the year that the Falche flooded all the lowlands. You know the rest." The dark-haired lady shrugged.

"Thank you. I wish we could enjoy this longer," Anna said after a moment of silence. "I need all of you to join me and look at something."

"All of us?" asked Wendella.

"Why not? It concerns all of you." Anna rose, and the

others followed her out of the hall and down the corridor to the stone steps. Hanfor ducked away briefly and rejoined the group carrying brown paper and the flat board upon which he sketched battle plans and maps.

Anna nodded to herself. Hanfor and Jecks knew what was coming.

Up in the guest chambers, the five watched, standing in a half-circle around Anna and the wall mirror, as she took out the lutar and retuned it.

Outside the half-opened shutter, there was the *ter-whit* of a bird that rose momentarily over the hum of insects.

Anna smiled at the lone bird call, cleared her throat, and then sang the spell.

> "Mirror, mirror, show all to see
>   where Ehara and his forces be . . ."

The silvered glass of the wall mirror displayed a line of mounted armsmen heading toward a rocky defile, a long line of armsmen, behind the crimson banners of Dumar. Behind the horsemen were wagons and spare mounts. The road appeared to slope upward.

Wendella nodded. "That looks like the road to Dumar, though it cannot be far."

"How might you know that?" inquired Jecks.

"I once rode with my late lord to Finduma—that is the first trading town inside Dumar. If my memory serves me, that part of the road leads to the Vale of Cuetayl." She shrugged. "That was when first I came to Stromwer, though I think the road has changed little."

Anna was grateful for Wendella's knowledge. "It is clear that Ehara plans to attack."

Yet the spell left so much undetermined. What could she do? In the silence, she launched into an improvised second spell immediately.

> "Danger near the Vale, soon so near,
>   show me that land bright and clear . . ."

The glass shimmered, then slowly rippled silver before fading into a map-picture, displaying a small hamlet and a river that seemed to run east-northeast—at least that was the way Anna interpreted it—toward a larger valley. The valley was divided into three sections by low Y-shaped hills.

"Those hills. . . . Cuetayl was a trading stop in the old days," said Wendella, her voice shaky. "There was a town there, but Uhlan the elder razed it when he could not take Stromwer, and it was never rebuilt."

Anna studied the maplike image in the large wall mirror, wondering where on the map might be Ehara's forces. There was no sign of them. She looked more closely at the Vale of Cuetayl. The hills formed a Y that split the lower ground, mostly fields and meadows, into three distinct sections.

"The hills inside the valley control the road to Dumar," observed Jecks, turning to Wendella. "Is there another road?"

"There may be tracks, but no roads that any have talked of."

Hanfor kept sketching, his grease marker flying across the wide sheet of brown paper. "You can see where the road from Encora and from Stromwer enters the valley or the vale from the east here." Hanfor's marker ticked off a point on the right hand side of his sketch. "The hills are upthrust sandstone. They overlook the road."

"If Ehara and the Sea-Priest get there," mused Jecks, "they could use the rocks for cover and blanket the road with arrows."

"You could not see where they might place archers," Hanfor said.

Anna nodded. Even she could see that the terrain would severely limit the use of sorcery—unless she wanted to destroy the whole valley—if she even could. There had been volcanic activity around Vult, already harnessed by the Evult. By comparison, to her amateur eye, the Sudbergs looked old and decidedly unvolcanic.

Abruptly, she strummed the lutar, trying another variation.

> "Mirror, mirror on the wall,
>   show us where Ehara's attack will fall . . ."

The mirror remained blank.

Anna set aside the lutar and reached for the grease-marker and some paper. Improvising wasn't making matters much clearer. After a time, she looked at the next spell, then picked up the lutar.

> "Show us in great outline this day,
>   where Dumaran forces ride their way."

The mirror obligingly displayed a close-up of riders in crimson, looking forward over a rider in white and one in red toward the same defile that the first image had displayed.

"That . . . that is the west entrance to the Vale," said Wendella.

Anna sang the release couplet. As the image faded, she set down the lutar on the chest by the wall. "I need some wine." She poured the dark red wine from the pitcher into the goblet on the writing table, then sat, sipping slowly in the growing twilight. No matter what she tried, there were clearly limits to what the mirror would show— or what she could get it to show. Ehara was headed to the Vale of Cuetayl, and it *looked* like he wanted to set up an ambush there.

"We'll have to find a way to avoid whatever trap they have in mind, and then make them vulnerable."

"How might that be, Lady Anna?" asked Hanfor.

I wish I knew. "That's something I'll have to think about. I can try another spell. After I rest for a moment." She took another sip of wine, conscious that the others had remained standing, except for Hanfor who sat on the floor cross-legged, continuing to sketch something on the brown paper.

Wendella glanced from Anna's drawn face to Jecks, then to Hanfor.

"Yes, Lady Wendella," Jecks said. "Sorcery can be as tiring as battle. It can be more tiring. We have seen that."

Wendella nodded, almost to herself.

No one spoke.

When Anna finally rose and took up the lutar, all eyes were on the mirror as the sorceress sang.

> "Show me now and show me clear
> a road or trail to avoid this danger near . . .
> Like a vision, like a map or plot . . ."

Light strobed from the mirror, so brightly that Liende covered her eyes. Anna felt her own eyes watering as she saw vision after vision flash across the glass so quickly she could not even comprehend one of those images.

Crack! Glass showered out of the mirror frame, and the wood of the frame steamed.

Anna stepped back involuntarily.

"Oh . . ." murmured Liende.

"Are you all right, lady?" asked Jecks.

Anna looked down. Although silvered glass lay almost to her feet, none had apparently touched her. "I'm fine. Except I've ruined another mirror."

Hanfor nodded, his face somber.

Wendella kept looking from the darkened and empty mirror frame to Anna and back to the wall.

"I'm sorry about the mirror," Anna told Wendella.

"A mirror is nothing, Lady Anna."

"I'm sorry," Anna repeated. "I have this problem with mirrors." She cleared her throat. "There seem to be many possible roads," she continued, after a moment, trying to inject a dry tone into her voice. "That's one good thing."

"Many . . . ?" Alvar's voice was shaking.

"That was the problem. The mirror was trying to show

us all the trails we could use to avoid that danger." Anna
was glad to explain and felt her voice strengthening as
she talked, even if she were uncertain of her explanation.
"There were just too many things possible, and they
flashed too quickly to see what any of them might be."

Alvar's face retained a puzzled expression.

"We'll see what happens as we near Dumar," Anna
said. "That's all we can do." She just hoped she happened to be right.

95

VALE OF CUETAYL, DUMAR

The Sea-Priest surveys the hills to the left and to the
right, all crested with sloping red sandstone. He
coughs and then wipes his forehead. Below him, to the
south and overlooking the road, the white-and-green-clad
archers set the reddish net blinds that will conceal them.
JerRestin nods as the last of the nets are tied into place,
and the archers seem to vanish, then shifts his weight in
the hard saddle.

"Not so comfortable as on your fine ships, is it,
friend?" asks Ehara with a laugh.

"Our ships are never this hot." The Sea-Marshal continues dryly, "But I would take this heat to the cold of
the frozen lands below Pelara. There, in winter, when one
throws wine into the wind, it freezes before it can strike
the ice."

"You jest, of course." Ehara's eyes look northward
from the ridge overlook where his own archers take their
position behind the exposed sandstone. The flatiron-
shaped stones crest the hills that control the flat on the
north side of the valley.

"Sea-Priests never jest."

"Your pardon, I beg. My deepest apologies for doubting your veracity."

The Sea-Marshal turns in the saddle, and his cold eyes fix upon the Lord of Dumar as though he were but a junior captain of lancers. "Lord Ehara, listen carefully. The sorceress may call down her wizardry on my lancers or upon yours. I have insisted on the separation so that she must use great powers. My sea-captains know what to do if the wizardry falls upon you. If it falls upon my lancers, you must wait only until the sorcery ceases. Then you must attack immediately, before she can regain her strength."

Ehara frowns. "You speak as though you will not be with your lancers or with me."

"No. I will be concealed near the entrance to the Vale. Even the sorceress will not discern me. If I am successful, she will not have the chance to work any wizardry. If not, you must know what to do."

"What if she does not come? Or arrives by another route?" asks Ehara.

"There are no other routes," states jerRestin.

"There are always other ways." Ehara laughs easily. "She could take a game trail and have her armsmen strung out like an unraveled net, where they could be picked off at every turn by archers." The Sea-Marshal shrugs. "She would still have to attack our armsmen from below, and her wizardry is limited to two or three mighty spells. That is why our forces are on separate hills."

"She has used mighty sorcery before," points out Ehara.

"And every time she has been laid low for weeks, if not longer. She will attempt to avoid such sorcery because she wishes to conquer Dumar, not destroy it."

"You seem to know a great deal about her." Ehara chuckles. "Does she appeal to you? You know of what I speak."

JerRestin shakes his head, with a slight body shudder. "The woman appalls me. She is an unnatural creature from the mist worlds. I would not have her in chains or in any other fashion. She must be defeated, destroyed if that is possible.''

"I might like her in chains," muses Ehara.

"Only with her mouth gagged," responds jerRestin. "She turned Lord Behlem into ashes with but her voice."

"That was no great loss." Ehara scans the hills to the north side of the Vale again, then nods. His archers have seemingly vanished into the red boulders, and his lancers are well sheltered under the natural overhangs and out of sight of the road.

"Except to Neserea." A grim smile plays over jer-Restin's lips. "I must go to instruct my officers on how to put an end to the sorceress."

"The harmonies be with you."

"And with you, friend and ally."

The two horsemen separate, one heading down the ridge to the east, the other to the north.

96

The gelding *whuffed* once, and then, a dozen paces later, once more.

"We'll be stopping for water before long." Anna glanced ahead along the curving road that descended into another narrow valley and toward a line of trees. A stream? She hoped so as she leaned forward in the saddle and patted Farinelli. "Just hold on, fellow."

Her light green shirt was plastered against her shoulders with sweat raised by the summer sun beating down from behind, and the back of her neck was going to be even more sunburned. Even with the return of the rains, Anna reflected, Defalk was just plain hot, hotter than Iowa in summer, more like Georgia or Alabama or south Florida away from the water—except hotter.

Riding beside her, Jecks looked over, but did not speak.

She knew his unspoken question, and she still had no clear answer in her mind, except that they couldn't take the main road into the valley where Ehara was sure to set up an ambush. She hoped that, once they were closer to the Vale of Cuetayl, her sorcery would provide a clearer view of the options open to her.

The sorceress and regent looked toward the arms commander. "Hanfor?"

"Yes, Lady Anna?"

"Will we be stopping to water the mounts at that stream?" Anna brushed aside a pesky horsefly, once, twice.

Farinelli's tail swished as the horsefly buzzed around the gelding's hindquarters.

"The scouts have said that the road toward Dumar remains clear for the next five deks," answered Hanfor. "I had thought we would water our mounts and let the men stand down. Have you a problem?"

"Oh, no. I was going to try the mirror again."

"The players could use a rest also, Lady Anna," Liende added.

Anna laughed. "Everyone gets a break." *Except you. You have to do sorcery.* She stood in the stirrups for a moment, ignoring the tightening muscles in her thighs, then eased back into a saddle that was getting harder by the dek for the ride down to the stream.

"Does the shield spell draw too much from you?" Jecks asked quietly.

"No. I can feel it, like a spiderweb or the faintest brush of something against my skin . . . but so far . . ." Anna shrugged, looking down at the shield in the case by her knee.

"Good." Jecks nodded.

The trees by the narrow river were some form of willows growing so thickly that the vanguard had to ride two-

thirds of the length of the short valley to find a clear
approach to the water.

"Purple Company . . . take your mounts downstream
from where water bottles are filled. Down by the gray
rock."

"Green Company! Wait for Purple . . . I said, wait,
Mykli! You want to fill every water bottle in the company . . ."

". . . don't push, Distek . . ."

". . . enough water for everyone . . ."

Anna let Farinelli drink, then guided him back to a
grove a dozen yards north of the stream, where she dismounted and tied him to a sapling. By the time she had
the mirror unpacked and the lutar tuned, she had been
joined by Hanfor, Jecks, and Liende.

They waited quietly as she ran through her vocalises.
To the southwest, the watering and muted clamor continued. The sorceress pushed away the thought that watering
the mounts of a full-sized army would have been impossible and concentrated on the words and chords of the
spell.

"Danger in the Vale, danger near,
    show Dumar's armed danger bright and clear . . ."

Anna lowered the lutar and took a deep breath.

The glass turned to a map-picture of the Vale of Cuetayl and the Y-shaped hills, centered on the spot where
the road from Stromwer entered the west end of the valley. A small hill flanked the road, and then dropped away
to a flat. The Y-shaped hills were farther back.

"That hill—if there is an attack against you, it will
come from there," said Jecks.

"Me?"

"You remain the force of Defalk," the lord pointed
out. "I know little, except there are books that say the
Sea-Priests have enchanted javelins—much as the enchanted crossbow bolt of Sargol's. The javelins are

barbed. Sometimes they smear the barbs with the poisons of fish.''

''Lovely,'' said Anna. The more she heard about the Sturinnese, the worse it got, and no one seemed to think that much about it—except her. Was she overreacting? Again? Avery had always claimed she overreacted to everything. ''Let's see if the mirror can show us another route into the Vale.''

From behind Jecks' shoulder, Liende nodded. Hanfor held his portable sketching gear, his face blank. Jecks watched Anna, concern in his hazel eyes.

Anna took out the spell folder and rechecked the words, the small changes she'd made in the spell, hoping to avoid a repeat of the mirror-smashing in Stromwer. Before, the mirror had flickered through images so rapidly that none of them had been able to see anything—except that there were clearly many possible solutions, so many that they couldn't be sorted out, even by sorcery.

At the time, Anna had wanted to scream. She hadn't been able to think of one decent solution, and she still couldn't, except in the general sense that she needed a way to flank the armsmen waiting in the Vale.

She cleared her throat, then lifted the lutar once more, and sang.

> ''Show me best and show me clear
> the route to avoid this danger near.
> Like a vision, like a map or plot . . .''

This time the glass came up blank.

Shit! . . . So now what? Anna frowned. ''This is going to take a bit.''

Trying to compose another spell in her head took what seemed forever. Finally, she lifted the lutar once more.

> ''Show the route, where it will start
> to take us to the Vale's very heart,

> away from that road that all do take,
> above the lines our foes do make . . ."

A lousy spell . . . truly lousy . . . .

Weak spell or not, the glass presented another map-picture, showing a depression in the road where a trail wound off to the left. Anna could see what looked to be the narrow gorge that held the road and stream leading down into the Vale of Cuetayl.

"How far from the entry gorge?" she asked.

"Two deks, mayhap." Hanfor sketched rapidly.

Anna thought and waited, thinking. She needed a better map or idea.

When Hanfor nodded, she had another spell ready, one probably equally shaky. Nonetheless, she tried it.

> "Show us now and from the air,
> the southern trail to Vale,
> and how it winds its way to there . . ."

Anna looked at the image in the glass, and there was an image, much to her surprise. The so-called trail looked more like a goat track winding along a series of switchbacks, but eventually coming out on a plateau overlooking the middle of the Vale.

"The destination . . . that is good. But the trail, that is dangerous." Jecks fingered his clean-shaven chin.

As the steam began to rise from the mirror frame, Hanfor sketched even more rapidly, speaking as he did. "We won't reach that trail until late today, I would hazard. The stream is still close to the road. We could stop there."

Anna said nothing, just nodded and studied the image as Hanfor continued to sketch out what he needed.

Finally, he nodded in turn, and Anna released the image with a couplet, and then a deep breath. She lowered the lutar and walked slowly to Farinelli to get her water bottle.

After drinking, she packed the mirror, and then the lutar.

"That's a narrow trail for mounts," mused Jecks. "Even if blessed by sorcery."

"Do you have a better idea?" Anna asked.

Jecks flushed.

"I'm sorry," she apologized. "We have to get rid of Ehara."

"We do what we must," he said stiffly.

Anna pursed her lips. She'd apologized once, and once was enough. She was getting tired of apologizing. Even for a lord who looked like a movie star.

97

VALE OF CUETAYL, DUMAR

The Sea-Priest chants over the silvered water glass in a thin falsetto. Sweat beads on his forehead, mixing with dust to form rivulets of mud down his cheeks while he struggles with the melody and the tempo.

As he finishes, a small and wavering image fills the center of the glass, an image that shows a long line of horses on a narrow trail, a trail clearly not the main road into the Vale.

"The bitch . . . the unpredictable sow. . . ."

The image shatters into silver globules that chase each other for several moments. JerRestin sits down on a boulder, breathing heavily and ignoring the heat that seeps through his dust-smeared white trousers.

After a time, he chants again, using a voice more tenor than falsetto.

When an image forms, it shows a figure in green atop a flat hill. Behind the slender woman in the brown hat, a line of players forms. Behind them are dusty armsmen, still mounted. Flanking the sorceress are two mounted guards bearing heavy shields.

The Sea-Priest chants quickly, and the image dissolves into silver globules once more. He seats himself for a time, breathing heavily, before he climbs wearily from the shelter of the oblong rock overlooking the road and slowly scans the valley, a valley all too still for the life it encompasses.

He can sense the hidden archers and lancers to the west, but the sun has fallen on the side of the sorceress, not on her face.

The sounds of strings and horns echo faintly in the distance, so faintly he can barely hear them—but they come from the south. He scrambles down the scree of the slope toward his mount.

"... bitch ... the bitch. ..."

His mumbled words are lost in the clatter of the small stones dislodged by his boots.

98

The midmorning sun beat down as fiercely as at midday in Falcor, and Anna's shirt was again plastered to her back with perspiration as she shifted her weight in the saddle—carefully, given the steepness of the slope to her left. The trail was less than that, barely wide enough for a single mount, as it wound upward, back and forth on the southern side of the flat-topped mesa. According to Anna's scrying, the mesa overlooked the south side of the Vale of Cuetayl and the central hills where Ehara's forces and the Sturinnese waited to ambush the Defalkan contingent.

Jecks glanced ahead, at the scouts posted on each switchback, and then at Hanfor.

"No one has seen us," the arms commander confirmed. "They do not know about this trail, or"—he smiled— "do not believe that a sorceress would stoop to such trickery."

"Archers could inflict much damage here," Jecks said.

"They have to be here to do such," pointed out Hanfor, as he gestured upwards at the barren side of the mesa where little grew except for waist-high scrubby junipers at wide intervals, and intermittent patches of grass already browning. "And there is as little cover for them as for us. They would be seen from deks."

Jecks nodded.

Anna said nothing, just used the kerchief, once gray and now reddish brown from sweat and dust, to wipe more moisture off the back of her neck. The air was drier than it had been at Abenfel or Stromwer and smelled faintly of some form of evergreen—juniper?

She'd stopped once to use the mirror, but it had shown no armsmen on the trail or near it. She just hoped the spell had been accurate enough.

"Still," continued the graying veteran, "I will be happier when we can re-form all the armsmen."

Anna eased out her second water bottle and drank, nearly draining the bottle. There were two more bottles, fastened behind her saddle. Sometimes, she felt she loaded Farinelli like a pack animal, with the extra water, the mirror and the lutar. But the lutar was light, and she wasn't exactly heavy, not anymore. Sometimes, it was hard to believe she'd ever fought weight, now that she had to struggle to keep every pound.

The sun beat down, and on the slope above the narrow valley to the south of the Vale, not a blade of the sparse grass stirred. Not an insect hummed, and the only sounds were those of men and horses climbing the narrow trail.

Wheeeeee . . . eee . . .

Anna glanced back—just in time to see an armsman

and mount seemingly rolling down the steeper slope below one of the switchbacks, then a second as the mount following took a similar misstep . . . or lost footing on part of the trail weakened by the first mishap. She took a deep breath as the figures bounced, and slid out of sight. *Shit . . .*

The line of riders slowed.

"Better that than hundreds of arrows," suggested Hanfor from ahead.

Anna knew it to be true, but she still felt for the men and their mounts. Then she checked the path ahead.

Near the top of the mesa, the trail entered a depression slightly wider than the path had been on the lower slopes, a U-shaped gulch scooped out by infrequent rain runoff over the years. The sides came nearly to Farinelli's shoulders. The end of the gulch flattened, broadened into a fan-shaped jumble of shallow and dry rivulets opening onto the flat of the mesa.

Just before leaving the gulched part of the trail at the top of the mesa, Anna glanced back. The line of mounts still stretched a third of the way down the slope like a snake running from switchback to switchback. Her eyes turned northward. The generally flat plain of the mesa stretched ahead for nearly a dek, dotted with the same scattered junipers and clumps of grass as the slope Farinelli had carried her up.

In the distance, the sorceress could see the more jagged rocky peaks on the north side of the valley. Was the valley a juncture between geologic plates? Anna pushed the vagrant thought away. She needed to know where the Dumaran and Sturinnese armsmen and archers were.

Liende and the players had reined up to Anna's left, west of where Hanfor, Jecks, and Anna remained mounted. The guards had fanned out in front of the sorceress, watching as the rest of the armsmen appeared, mount by mount, riding up out of the low gulch.

"Best we form up here, and wait until the others are here," suggested Hanfor.

"I'll try the mirror to see where Ehara and his forces are now," Anna said.

Hanfor nodded, his eyes still on the armsmen as they rode onto the mesa.

The sorceress rode Farinelli another fifty yards westward to a space clear of the scrubby junipers and even lower creosote bushes, but sheltered by the higher boulders that cast enough shade for the mirror. Jecks and the guards followed.

She reined up and dismounted, handing Farinelli's reins to Lejun, since Fhurgen and Rickel still bore the heavy shields. The white-haired lord dismounted as quickly as she did, and took the leather-wrapped traveling mirror while she uncased the lutar and began to tune it.

Jecks laid the mirror on the leather wrapping in the shade while Anna ran through a vocalise.

She had to cough her throat clear of dust and mucus. A second vocalise helped. At the sound of hoofs she looked up to see Hanfor and Liende nearing.

"Alvar is forming the companies. I should see where our enemies are drawn up," said the weathered armsman.

"I should have thought of that." There were still so many things she should have thought of, but she hadn't been trained to be a sorceress or a regent or a ruler. Like everything else, she seemed to have to learn what she was supposed to be doing on the job.

Liende dismounted in a businesslike fashion, and Anna motioned for her to join the group. *You've got to make more of an effort to keep Liende included. Don't treat her like furniture. . . .* Lord, Anna hated that when Dieshr and Avery had acted as though she were Queen Victoria's chair—just expected to be there.

Hanfor smiled as he dismounted and walked toward the shadowed space under the largest sandstone boulder. "A regent and sorceress cannot remember everything all the time."

For his words, she was grateful. She cleared her throat,

and stood over the mirror, humming softly to try to get the pitch right.

> "Show me now and oh so clear
> where our enemies now appear;
> whether hidden or in sight,
> show their places in your light."

An overhead view of the vale appeared in the oblong mirror, bordered by a thin band of silver mist. Anna studied the mirror, with Jecks, Alvar, and Hanfor practically at her shoulder. Liende stood farther back.

Anna couldn't see anything.

"There . . . you see they have the archers in the center, where they can blanket the road. Those are nets . . . darker than the rocks." Hanfor spoke softly, but clearly. "The white and green. . . . the man by the overhang right there— he's gone now—lancers—those are the ones from Sturinn—they are on the south hills."

"The ones from Dumar are on the north?" Anna wasn't sure she'd seen anything.

Jecks nodded.

She studied the image again before singing the release couplet. "That valley is wide, and the hills in the middle are high enough to block my voice, even from here. I don't know if any spell will reach the north side—not unless it's strong enough to destroy the whole valley."

"The Sturinnese are more dangerous," Hanfor said. "They are better trained. The Sea-Priest put them closest to the road."

Anna took a deep breath. "We'd better get ready." She turned to Liende. "The first spell will be the flame spell. After that . . . we'll see."

"The flame spell," Liende repeated with a nod.

"I don't think that the arrow spell will carry far enough." Anna doubted that the arrows would carry, even boosted by her spells.

"You rely heavily on sorcery," offered Jecks.

"I know. But what else do I have?"

"I will have the archers form up near the north edge of the overlook. That is the closest to the Sturinnese armsmen." Hanfor remounted and rode back toward where the last of the armsmen were emerging onto the mesa.

Jecks wrapped the mirror, while Anna replaced the lutar in its case. Liende mounted and rode back toward the waiting players.

"They have not moved from their positions," Jecks said quietly. "I worry that the Sea-Priest may have yet another surprise. Is your shield yet enchanted?"

"It feels that way." The faintest sense of an unseen spiderweb tugging at Anna remained.

"Good."

Anna remounted and guided Farinelli toward the section of the mesa that formed an overlook, reining up a good ten yards back from the edge, marked by fissured white limestone, partly covered with the red dirt. The hills in the center of the Vale, dotted with green spots that were junipers and greenish blue splotches that were creosote bushes, seemed almost close enough to touch in the hot clear air.

After studying the Y-shaped line of hills below for a moment, the sorceress dismounted and handed Farinelli's reins to Lejun. Fhurgen and Rickel dismounted quickly and stepped forward of Anna with their shields, one in front of each shoulder, so that they could close quickly to block any arrows or quarrels.

"Archers on the flanks!" Alvar ordered, and the armsmen who doubled as archers dismounted and formed a double row on either side of Anna and Jecks and the players who stood behind Anna and continued to tune their instruments.

"The warm-up song," said Liende.

Anna edged closer to the edge of the overlook, and her guards moved forward with her.

The wind rose from the valley, carrying cooler air from

somewhere, air with the faintest scent of ... something. Horses?

Without the mirror, the sorceress could see nothing but dirt and junipers, red rock and shadows—and the track of the road that traversed the seemingly empty Vale below.

After exhaling slowly, and trying to relax her shoulders, Anna turned to Liende. "The flame spell first." She'd tried to craft the spell to cover the widest range, and it should work. *"Should" doesn't mean it will.* Anna forced back the vagrant thought and concentrated on the vocalise. When she finished, feeling her cords firm, her throat clear, she nodded to the chief player. "Ready."

"On my mark ... mark!" Liende gestured, and then the notes of the clarinet-like woodwind joined with those of the other players.

Anna sang.

> "Archers strong, armsmen strong,
>   enemies bathed in flame from this song,
>   against Defalk and you will burn ..."

Anna shivered, suddenly tired from the short and full-voiced effort. Her eyes scanned the valley, but for what seemed an eternity, all remained as before, silent, except for the insects and the occasional unknown birdcall.

The points of fire flared across the closest range of hills ... then faint cries followed ... and more cries.

Anna looked away, her stomach turning, trying to rationalize it all. *You offered terms ... warned them. ... Would they be any less dead with an arrow through their chests ... ?*

The space around Anna, except for the breathing of horses, remained silent.

Jecks handed her a water bottle, and she drank, deeply. Then he offered her a chunk of bread and a small wedge of cheese. She ate both, and then took another deep swig of the lukewarm water.

As she finished, he gestured toward the Vale of Cuetayl, where a single horseman in white galloped along the road, dust rising behind his mount.

"Archers!" called Alvar.

A rain of arrows arched out over the road, somewhat more than a half dek north and a good three hundred yards lower.

"The arrows curved," snapped Jecks. "Shields!"

The rider turned from the road and continued to ride up the lower slope of the base of the mesa, aimed directly toward the overlook. Abruptly, he halted and pulled a spear from his lanceholder.

Anna couldn't see what happened next because Rickel and Fhurgen stepped in front of Anna, blocking her from the charging wizard.

Still . . . she could feel a tingling—like a smaller version of the great chords she had called over Vult.

A second tingling seemed to fly from her momentarily, though she had done nothing, spelled nothing at that moment. Then a dark streak flew from Farinelli, crashing into something else perhaps three yards in front of Anna, before falling onto the red soil. A barbed javelin seemed to vibrate in the small spelled shield that had hurled itself from the open case attached to Anna's saddle.

Both javelin and shield, bound together, inched across the bare reddish ground toward Anna. The sorceress retreated toward Farinelli and the lutar, trying to recall what spell she could use to stop the magic in the javelin.

Jecks flung himself from his saddle and ran toward the edge of the mesa.

Anna pulled the lutar from its case.

Moments later, Jecks straightened, lunging back toward Anna, and the still-vibrating javelin and the shield, but carrying a flat stone more than a yard long, struggling with the weight.

Fhurgen handed his shield to the guard mounted beside him. "Lejun, cover her!" The black-bearded guard followed Jecks' example, sprinting for the rocks at the edge of the plateau, while Lejun held the shield, edge to edge with Rickel.

Jecks almost eased his stone onto the still-vibrating javelin, then straightened slowly as Fhurgen added another stone. Two other guards added more stones, but the pile vibrated and inched toward the sorceress.

Anna fumbled with the lutar, her mind struggling for something she could adapt.

Fhurgen added yet another stone to the pile, but the stones shifted again as the javelin continued to vibrate toward Anna.

What frigging spell . . . Think! Think. . . . Her mind seemed blank for ages, but it couldn't have been that long before she swallowed. *The flame spell!*

She began to strum the lutar.

> "Javelin magic, javelin strong,
>   turn to flame with this song!"

The stones erupted in a cascade of flame. Liende and the players stepped back from the heat, as did Anna and Jecks and the guards. Hanfor mounted and rode closer to the overlook, surveying the Vale below with only a glance at the burning weapons.

By the time the flames died away, too quickly, it seemed to Anna, even the red stones were dust, and nothing remained of javelin or shield but rust and ashes.

She glanced at the road below, but only a line of dust remained, and the Sea-Priest had ridden somewhere out of sight.

"I'm glad I brought a few other shields," Jecks said.

So was Anna. "I'm glad you insisted my spelling the shield."

"I worried about something such as that." His head inclined toward the ashes. "The Sea-Priests are well-known for their attacks on strong leaders. It is said that was how they brought down the Ostisles—with treachery such as that under a parley banner."

"The burning . . . it is terrible. . . ." Yuarl, violino still in one hand, stood near the dropoff, pointing out across the Vale with her bow.

Anna edged forward, behind the shields carried by Lejun and Rickel. She could see thin columns of smoke rising across the nearer hilltops below. *Of course. . . . Fires just don't vanish. . . .*

Anna wanted to shake her head. How could there ever be peace with a land such as Sturinn where the Sea-Priests would try anything rather than admit that women were people? Where any trickery was acceptable for them, but where an honest attempt not to fight was condemned?

Anna continued to look for the Sea-Priest who had flung the javelin, but even the dust had settled.

"Why not the wizard?" murmured one of the players. "How did he escape?"

Anna knew, but didn't explain. Her spell had been directed at archers and armsmen, not wizards. She'd gotten what she'd spelled, not exactly what she'd meant, and that had resulted in an angry wizard getting free.

"The Dumaran armsmen are retreating." Jecks pointed to the northwest, at the puffs of dust.

"We cannot do much from here," said Hanfor.

"We had best leave before they catch us on that trail," suggested the white-haired lord.

"They could not reach us quickly, but I would agree with Lord Jecks, Lady Anna," added Hanfor.

Anna nodded. "We'll return to where we camped, and then we'll see how we'll enter Dumar." Her vision was blurring, and sparks flashed before her eyes. She needed to eat, and rest.

Jecks exchanged glances with Hanfor, but neither spoke.

Anna could feel herself starting to seethe at the unspoken male questions, but she clamped her lips shut.

99

The dew had barely lifted from the grass along the shoulder of the road, a road churned the day before with the hoofprints of the retreating Dumaran forces, hoofprints since blurred by heavy dew or light rain.

"They retreat now, but Ehara must face you once more before he returns to Dumaria," Jecks said.

"Politics?" asked Anna.

At the puzzled expression on the white-haired lord's face that appeared and vanished as fleetingly as it had come, Anna added, "He won't be able to face his lords or holders unless he does?"

"I would not think so."

"Do we have any idea where?"

"I would guess that he would attempt to hold the Dumaran hills northeast of where the rivers join." Jecks shrugged. "There he could make us attack uphill. Or he could make a normal host attack so."

"That is another three days' ride, four if not pressed," pointed out Hanfor, riding to Anna's left.

"Five—or six," Anna corrected. "We aren't leaving hostile towns behind us. Not large ones."

Jecks and Hanfor's eyes crossed.

"We need some loyalty here." Anna slowed Farinelli as the Defalkan column neared the gray stone oblong by the side of the road. The dek-stone was clear enough: Finduma—3 d.

"Are you contemplating more sorcery?" ventured Jecks.

Anna surveyed the terrain. A small hill rose less than a half a dek north of the road and perhaps two deks ahead, apparently overlooking the town itself. The hilltop had been grazed bare, or logged, or something, and grayish dots that were sheep grazed on the intermittent grass and vegetation.

"I can't use a loyalty spell . . ."

"You did so at Stromwer," pointed out Jecks.

"I almost didn't live through that, and the next time would be worse. The backlash is . . . exponential."

Jecks frowned again, briefly, and Anna was left with the feeling of strangeness . . . of being in a culture where certain terms and ideas just didn't exist.

"The mirror shows no dangers, neither Sturinnese nor Dumaran armsmen," said Jecks. "What have you in mind?"

"I don't want Dumar to ever again present a threat to Defalk or Jimbob," Anna said. *"Ever" or "never" are dangerous words.* "Not for a while, anyway."

"I would have your armsmen take the town and request provisions. Then we should ride on," suggested Jecks.

Hanfor reined his mount up. "The scouts say there are no armsmen. The town is shuttered."

"Jecks thinks we should provision here, and leave them alone otherwise."

"I would do the same. One never knows when provisions will be short, and country folk love best those leaders they see the least of."

Anna smiled at Hanfor's words. While she didn't like the idea of leaving a potentially hostile town behind her, again, the alternatives were worse, and Finduma was small.

She turned in the saddle and gestured to Liende, riding at the head of the players and behind Anna's guards. "Chief player?"

Liende urged her mount onto the shoulder of the road and around the guards. "Yes, Lady Anna?"

"Lord Jecks has suggested that we request provisions in Finduma, and then ride on."

Liende swallowed. "Ah . . . after the Vale . . . ?"

"The Sturinnese died there, not people of Liedwahr. I'd be surprised if most people in . . . Finduma . . . here, even care that much. Most people don't care who rules, as long as their lives don't change." Anna hoped she were right, but with a force as small as hers, a little less than five hundred, she couldn't leave garrisons in every town that might be disloyal.

"Liende . . ." Anna said gently. "I'm trying to protect Defalk with as little loss of life as possible—on both sides." *How many other leaders have said that, and then killed thousands?* "I want the players to stand ready in case something happens, but I don't think it will."

"That we can do." Liende smiled wanly. "We will stand ready."

"Thank you."

Liende eased her mount back toward the players.

"Your players have experienced more than they expected," said Jecks.

"Haven't we all?" Anna shook her head, then coughed from the road dust, omnipresent despite the intermittent rains.

"Let me send a company into the town," Hanfor said. "And the wagons."

"We'll wait here," Anna said, "and try the seeking spell."

As the arms commander rode off, Jecks looked at the sorceress. "It matters not to garrison Finduma, but have you thought of what you must do when you reach the Falche, and the larger towns?"

"The same as all other conquerors. Ask for surrender and allegiance, and destroy the town if it's not forthcoming." Anna found the words bitter in her mouth.

"That rests most heavily on your sorcery and players."

"I'm relying almost entirely on my sorcery and players." Anna laughed softly and ironically. "What else do I have?"

"If you destroy the Sea-Priest and Ehara, all will bow when you pass. And after?"

"I could build another dam," Anna ventured. "Would Dumar want that?"

"Lady, you are terrible."

"*Terrible*"? "I suppose I would have to make sure that whoever stays in charge here knows that." *You're planning for something that might not even happen ... You have to defeat Ehara and destroy most of his army. ... A* chill settled over her. "That's something to worry about later. First, we need to deal with Ehara."

"And the Sea-Priests."

Anna gestured to Liende. "Let's try that new seeking spell, the one like the flame spell." Anna coughed, found her second water bottle, and swallowed a little before replacing it, dismounting, and beginning a vocalise. "Polly, lolly, polly . . ."

"Warm-up tune," announced Liende as the players started to tune.

On the road behind and before Anna and the players, the Purple Company formed a line, mounts and riders facing Finduma. While Jecks unfastened the mirror and laid it out, Anna forced her thoughts onto the seeking spell, concentrated on the words and humming the tune as the players became less ragged and the strains of the warm-up tune merged into an actual melody.

Finally, Anna looked at Liende.

"We are ready, lady."

Anna nodded.

"On my mark . . . Mark!" Liende gestured. Then the clarinet-like woodwind joined with the other players' instruments.

Anna sang.

"Find, find any Dumaran close to here,
    an armsmen bearing his weapons hard and near . . ."

After she finished Anna watched the glass, but it remained blank silver, not reflecting, a sign that no armsmen—or none with arms—remained in Finduma.

"They can get ready to ride." Anna nodded to Liende. "Prepare to ride."

Jecks helped Anna replace the glass in its leather padding and back on Farinelli.

"In some towns, you will have to use that spell often," he observed.

"I know. Why do you think I want the players to do it? It's simple enough for the lutar, but . . ."

They sat in the hot sun for a time longer. Anna took the gray cloth from her belt and blotted her forehead and neck, then readjusted the floppy brown hat that had definitely seen better days.

Alvar rode up to the pair. "The arms commander says that we may proceed."

"Thank you." Anna flicked Farinelli's reins.

The road curved slowly to the left, toward the southwest. Fifty yards ahead on the right was a rutted lane, its center filled with dark green vinelike weeds, that led toward the hill overlooking Finduma.

As the column of riders passed onto the lane, Anna glanced down the road toward the first roofs of the town a dek or so away. *How did you end up invading another country? Because someone else invaded first . . . that's why.*

She wasn't sure that her answer was all that good, not sure at all.

Baaaa . . . aaahhh . . . The sheep lined across the road slowly moved away under the not-too-gentle prodding of the vanguard.

A man with a long staff barreled out from behind the cot to the left of the road, then came to a halt as he saw the armsmen and the pale blue banner of Defalk. His eyes went from the armed men to the banner, and then to the scattered sheep on the slope.

"Ah . . . your pardon, sers. . . ."

"We won't be long," Anna said politely. "We're just passing through."

At the sound of the sorceress's voice, his eyes went to

her, and the sheepman paled, backing slowly away until he was out of sight behind the cot.

"Your reputation precedes you, lady," said Jecks.

"I'm not sure I like whatever that reputation is."

"Better to be feared than disrespected."

That was what Machiavelli had written, or words to that effect, but they'd just been words when she'd read them in college. Somehow, it was different when the words applied to her.

Anna twisted in the saddle to extract the lutar.

"You expect trouble? I doubt any here will stand against your spells. Not in such a small town."

"I hope not." Anna's fingers went to the lutar she had wrestled from the case, almost absently tuning the instrument as they neared the first of the houses on the outskirts of the hamlet.

The road into Finduma remained empty—and dusty. The town was more like a hamlet, with less than fifty houses, half lining the road to Dumaria and the remainder scattered among sparse pastures and the few intermittent tilled patches of ground. A narrow stream ran along the south side of the main road, punctuated by scattered willows and something else—tamarisk trees?

As the column neared the first houses, a woman glanced up, saw the armsmen, and fled from her wooden washtub, scooping up a toddler tied to a line around her waist. The weathered door slammed as the first of the riders passed the first small umber-brick house with the straw roof.

"She does not seem overly joyed," said Liende, riding on Anna's right.

"Would you be?" answered Anna.

"Aye, and it would be an incautious woman to remain out with strange armsmen passing," observed Jecks.

A brown-and-white dog ambled out across the dirt of the main street, then scurried behind a wooden shed at the sound of hoofs.

A rail-thin and bearded man stood on a wooden porch in the shade of a signboard so faded that Anna couldn't make out the letters. The narrow building itself was of the umber brick and had a cracked and faded red-tile roof. The man looked like he wanted to spit in the street as the sorceress rode past, but his face twisted, and he took a deep breath.

"Peace to you," Anna said, wondering what other phrase she could have used.

The bearded man nodded, reluctantly.

The center of the town was an enlarged crossroads without a central square or a statue. A handful of two-storied brick buildings sprawled along the main road. Anna spotted the faded crossed candles of a chandlery, and the three wagons lined up before it. Around the square were stationed armsmen with bared blades. Another ten or twelve formed a line into the chandlery.

Hanfor gestured, and Anna turned her mount toward the weathered veteran.

"Do we have enough golds to pay for this?" asked Anna as she reined up.

In turn, Hanfor glanced at Jecks.

"We have some . . ."

"But we really shouldn't use them?" she asked. "All right. Promise to pay. We'll have to send them later." Her eyes fixed on Jecks. "We need to keep our word on this." Then she turned to Hanfor. "Keep a record of what we take and what it is worth."

"Yes, Lady Anna."

"I mean it." Her words were firm, almost cold. In the end, all she had was her word. She'd learned that a long time ago, and that was one thing that hadn't changed. And it wouldn't.

100

The late-afternoon sun cast long shadows, and Anna pulled down the brim of the floppy hat. Her shirt was soaked, as was the inside band of the hat, and her hair felt gummy and sticky.

The air was still, without even a hint of a breeze. The road bore the traces of the still-retreating Dumaran armsmen. Anna's last scrying with the mirror showed Ehara and his forces nearly at the Falche, another day and a half from where the Defalkan forces slowly rode westward.

Anna chewed the bread slowly as Farinelli carried her toward the low sun. She glanced back over her shoulder as the column passed the dek-stone. Her eyes blurred as she tried to focus on the words.

Hrissar—2 d.

Hrissar was a large town with five squares, lots of granaries, and no hills. She'd blanketed the place with so many armsmen-seeking spells that she felt her eyes were swimming, but she'd found nothing. Even the local armsmen had been conscripted and dragged off by Ehara, and the shutters and doors to the town were closed.

After four days of riding, and using enemy-seeking spells, in every town near or along the main road, she was tired. So were the players.

"You cannot keep casting spells such," said Jecks quietly. "Not if you must cast a large spell when we meet Lord Ehara."

"I know. I know," said Anna tiredly, wiping stale dark crumbs from around her mouth before she reached for the water bottle. "I'll have to get some rest tonight and take it easy tomorrow, but there aren't that many towns between us and the river.''

"They are small enough that you need not spell them now. Hrissar was the only town worthy of the name.''

"I know that, too.'' The sorceress not only knew it, but felt it. She was so tired she could also feel the drain of the enchanted shield, a spell Jecks had practically demanded she renew as soon as they had camped the second time outside the Vale of Cuetayl.

"You are the sole force of Defalk,'' Hanfor said mildly.

"Now,'' she answered. "Now.'' Somehow, some way, she had to build an army worthy of the name. She couldn't keep riding from border to border and beyond. Had conquerors like Alexander the Great and Genghis Khan felt that way? *Oh . . . more delusions of grandeur? You're a great conqueror now?*

The sorceress pushed away the nagging thoughts, reaching instead for the remaining water bottle.

"Have you considered the spell against ensorcelled weapons?'' pressed the white-haired lord.

"Lord Jecks,'' Anna said wearily, "in the last year I have had to develop and learn dozens—scores—of spells. Today, we scoured a small city. Right now, my brain is frazzled, and I couldn't come up with another if Ehara or the Evult appeared on the road in front of us.''

"'. . . 'frazzled' . . . betimes, she speaks strangely. . . .'' The murmur from a guard somewhere behind Anna, a guard whose voice she didn't recognize, filled the comparative stillness.

The squeaking of a provisions wagon drifted from the east on a sudden puff of wind that cooled the sweating sorceress momentarily, then stilled.

"More than betimes I speak strangely,'' Anna said hoarsely. "More than betimes. Dissonance, I'm strange all the time. Who else would be riding through Dumar in this heat? Mad dogs and Englishwomen?'' She laughed.

"I think you need rest,'' said Jecks. "And soon.''

"The regent is losing it?" The sorceress shook her head. "Not yet. Not until we put an end to the Sea-Priests in Liedwahr. Chains. . . . Who do they think they are?"

Jecks extended a chunk of stale bread.

Anna took it, and began to eat slowly. Low blood sugar? Emotional overextension? Fatigue? She kept her thoughts to herself as she forced herself to keep eating.

Her eyes caught a pinpoint of light, with a reddish glint, in the western sky—Darksong, the moon of dark sorcery, of power that led to the need for using yet more power. Was that what she faced? Was she becoming the Clearsong sorceress of evil for the best of motives?

101

MANSUUS, MANSUUR

And her forces are approaching the Falche north . . . of Dumaria." Bassil clears his throat and waits.

"She has destroyed two fleets of the Maitre of Sturinn and is pushing Lord Ehara back to the Falche? With how many armsmen?" Konsstin unfastens the blue cloak and walks to the open door. His forehead is beaded with sweat, and he stands in the doorway between the study and the balcony, letting the slight western breeze blow around him.

"Less than thirtyscore, sire," answers Bassil. "Perhaps less than twenty-five. She cast a spell on the Sturinnese lancers, and they burst into flame. Ehara and his men retreated."

"Have the Sea-Priests sent no sorcerers themselves? Dissonance knows, they've spent years training them."

"They sent three, or more, according to your seers. All but the strongest died in the flood she sent down the Falche."

"I'd wager the Maitre loved that." Konsstin chuckles, but the sound fades as his eyes darken. "The harmonies help us if she can build a true force of armsmen, and that's where she's headed." The Liedfuhr's eyes drift eastward and to the city below, beyond the port and the triangle where the Ansul and the Latok join to form the mighty Toksul. The angular sail of a river trader billows as a gust of wind crosses the river. "We need not assist her in that." He shakes his head. "Take notes."

"Yes, sire." Bassil bobs his head.

"And listen! Try to understand why I'm ordering these things." His fingers touch his brown-and-silver beard. "Double the bonus for reentered contracts for armsmen. Have recruiters from anywhere else exiled or imprisoned. Announce the formation of new companies of lancers. Give them honorable-sounding names, and find the best officers from the existing companies. I don't care about names. Put the officers we have to placate in charge of things they cannot damage too greatly and keep track of them until they make a mistake for which they can be exiled or executed." Konsstin walks onto the balcony to the north end which retains a modicum of shade.

Bassil follows, marker and paper in hand.

"Also, make sure that no one ships *any* iron from the Deleatur mines eastward—to Ranuak or anywhere else."

Bassil lifts his dark and bushy eyebrows.

"Buy it, if you have to. Use the procurator's funds. That's what they're for. And horses—draft a dispatch— two dispatches—one to my darling grandson and one to the lizard Nubara. Tell them that any of the High Grass- land nomads that trade horses to Defalk are to be executed in whatever is the most unfavored fashion."

"The conquest of Dumar . . . if she manages it . . . is that such a threat?"

"Let us see, Bassil. There was the Evult, reputedly the greatest sorcerer of a generation. She buried him in hot lava, and a volcano named after her still grows in the northern Ostfels. In less than a year, she has managed to unify a country no one has been able to govern in generations. Half of Ebra already acknowledges her as sovereign. By the way, send more coins to Hadrenn. Not many, but enough to make him grateful.'' Konsstin pauses. ''She's killed the ruler of Neserea and stolen some of the best officers from his forces. That ruined the morale of those left. She's on the verge of adding Dumar to her empire.'' Konsstin turns on the dark-haired lancer officer. ''She's done all of this in less than two years and with fewer armsmen than we have as a casual guard in Hafen, where no one's threatened in hundreds of years. Are you going to tell me I shouldn't be worried? Oh, and don't forget, she just killed off another handful of some of the stronger sorcerers in Liedwahr without even realizing she had.''

Bassil nods, not meeting the older man's eyes.

''That doesn't even count the fact that she's remaking the whole society by giving women power. Do you want every scheming lady in Mansuur thinking she can run lands better than her consort?'' Konsstin coughs twice before continuing. ''If the Sea-Priests can't stop her in Dumar, the way they feel about women, they'll send every vessel and armsman they have into Ebra or Neserea.''

''But she is their enemy.''

''That's true enough, but they'll want to flank her, and the Matriarch would invite the sorceress into Encora in a moment if the Maitre attacked Ranuak.''

''The SouthWomen wouldn't like that.''

''They wouldn't. That's true. But given the choice between the sorceress and chains, just whom would they choose?''

''I see.''

''No, you don't. If the Maitre is thrown out of Dumar and he doesn't or can't attack Ranuak, exactly where will he attack?''

''Us?''

''That's a possibility. We're closer than Ebra, but we're the third choice. More likely, next summer he could flood

the Bitter Sea with ships and take Esaria.'' Konsstin offers
a twisted smile. ''That would solve my problem with Rabyn, but I'd probably have to ally Mansuur with the sorceress to stop Sturinn.''

''Maybe the Maitre will seek out Ebra?'' Bassil bobs
his head. ''That might be better.''

''For a time . . . perhaps.'' Konsstin pauses. ''We will
see. Now . . . hmmm . . . what else? Oh, I suppose, you
can ship some of that extra iron plate or ingots that the
foundries in Deleatur will have left over to Bertmynn.
Some of it, anyway. The rest of it . . . well, we need more
blades, and iron quarrels and crossbows.''

''Yes, sire.''

''That should keep you busy, Bassil.''

''Yes, sire.'' The dark-haired lancer backs out of the
study.

From the small patch of shade on the northern end of
the palace balcony, Konsstin stares westward, beyond
Mansuus, beyond the mighty Toksul, in the direction of
the Western Sea.

102

The muted sound of harnesses and horses rose slowly
as the light brightened outside the silken tent, now
off-white from all the imbedded red dust and grit. Anna
found the bucket of water and splashed her face and
hands, washing slowly, then pulled on her clothes, and
finally, her boots, listening to the low murmurs of the
guards.

''. . . she up yet?'' That was Fhurgen's deep voice.

''. . . not about to look. You want to?'' asked Rickel.
Fhurgen offered a muted laugh.

"You been with her longer than any of us. . . . Why are we here?"

"I could guess, Rickel. I won't. I know that she does nothing without a reason, and most folks who wager against her lose. Them that don't, die. Hard for mighty lords like Jecks it is." Another low laugh followed. "A woman doing what they couldn't."

The words got even less distinct, and flashes of light flickered in front of Anna's eyes. After deciding she'd better eat, she sat on the end of the cot under the silk canopy of her tent, slowly forcing her way through the strong yellow cheese wedges. She couldn't afford a repetition of her performance the afternoon before.

The bread was so stale and hard that her trousers were covered with crumbs by the time she crunched through what was left. Still, she could stand without feeling as though she would topple over.

At the sound of Jecks' voice, Anna washed down the last of the cheese, and the last crumbs of the hard dark bread, then stood and stretched before opening the thin flap of the tent and stepping into the half-gray, half-rose light of dawn.

"Good morning." She smiled although she still felt logy.

"How do you feel this morning?" asked Jecks.

"Better than yesterday afternoon, if that's what you mean. I ate more this morning, and that will help. Yesterday was a long day." She grimaced. "So was the day before." And the day before that, and that . . .

"I worry that you attempt too much, Lady Anna."

Behind Jecks, by the tent, Anna caught the hint of a nod from Fhurgen. Or she thought she did.

"Sometimes, like now, I do too." She paused. "I know that we have to keep the Sturinnese out of Dumar."

"It is the weakest land in Liedwahr. Now." He smiled, and the warm hazel eyes smiled as well.

Anna smiled back in spite of herself. *He tries . . . and he is intelligent and handsome . . . and he does look like*

*... No, he is more handsome than Robert Mitchum. ... If
only he'd understand a little more ...*

"I would suggest that we only ride to Gewyrt today.
That is a good ten deks short of the river hills." His smile
turned half-apologetic, half-worried.

"You're saying that the sorceress needs rest before she
attempts another battle?"

"So do your players."

Jecks was probably right about that, too. When he was
worried, he had good cause. It was what he didn't worry
about that caused problems between them.

"You're right." She offered another smile, and absently, couldn't help smiling inside as the handsome and
muscular lord who tried so hard smiled back.

103

THE EASTERN RIVER HILLS, DUMAR

JerRestin stands, then walks around to the far side of
the small cooking fire. He stares into the darkening
east.

"I do not look forward to facing this sorceress," muses
Ehara, not looking at the taller man.

"You have few choices, Lord Ehara. Not a hamlet east
of the Falche and north of Dumaria remains loyal to you.
And no holder west of the Falche will support you if you
do not confront her."

"I did so poorly as lord?" Ehara snorts. "That I find
hard to believe."

"She has used sorcery to force loyalty." The Sea-
Marshal turns toward the Lord of Dumar. "There is a
price to be paid for that, but unhappily for us, she has
already paid much of that coin."

"How has she paid? What has she given up?"

"Her life on the mist worlds. From what your spies say, her children. From what I know of youth spells, her ability to have more children. From what I know of power, any chance at friends in a strange land. And the ability to sleep with any ease at night." JerRestin's voice hardens. "True as it may be, all that is little consolation to you or to me."

"No consolation at all," agrees Ehara. "How do we defeat her and reclaim my land?"

"She cannot handle many sorceries. You must split your forces into groups—each larger than her total force."

"She will destroy them one by one."

"No. Before each large force, a dek forward, will be a smaller force, and that force will attack. All the small forces will attack at once. Because they will attack from separate positions, she must address each with a different spell." JerRestin glances from the rose-lit clouds over the river hills to the west to Ehara. "Once she has committed her sorceries, the larger forces will rush forward, when she is exhausted."

Ehara looks long at jerRestin. "Was that not your strategy at the Vale of Cuetayl?"

"It would have worked there, but none save I attacked the sorceress."

"And what of you, Sea-Marshal? You escaped, but you did not slay the sorceress."

"I had to ride too close, and I was seen. I will not be seen this time. I will not be seen." JerRestin's eyes burn.

Ehara looks away from those eyes, and his big hands knot around each other, but he does not speak.

104

The five figures stood on the shady side of the barn wall as Jecks unwrapped the leather from the mirror. He glanced up at the sorceress. "Have you thought—"

"About the ensorcelled weapons? Yes." Anna felt almost cruel in the way she cut him off, but at times she felt, in subtle ways, everyone was asking something, somehow. "I might have something," she added quickly to assuage her guilt.

"That would be good." He handed her the mirror with the battered frame.

Anna hung the traveling mirror from an old iron bracket. In the midafternoon sun, the meadows to the north were empty of sheep, the fields empty of workers. The houses had all been abandoned, hurriedly, with tracks and animal prints in the road dust showing that even the animals had been driven away.

Anna smiled as she stepped back and caught sight of a tan chicken pecking at the side of the empty cot fifty yards westward. Not all animals had vanished.

Jecks followed her eyes. "A chicken supper, later."

"If you can catch it," said Hanfor.

Anna bent down and took the lutar from its case, beginning to tune it, as she ran through a vocalise.

The faint hum of summer insects rose again once she stopped, clearing her throat. On the south side of the road, Alvar directed the Defalkan forces as they lined up to water their mounts from a long stock-trough.

Anna cleared her throat a last time, then sang.

"Show from the west, danger to fear,
    all the threats to us bright and clear . . ."

Surrounded by silver mist, the image was clear—a series of green fields, crossed by narrow lanes for horses and wagons, roughly a semicircle in shape, flanked on the north, south, and west by low and irregular hills.

"Ehara must have his forces on the back side of all of those hills, and all are mounted and well-rested," said Hanfor.

Liende inclined her head, ever so slightly. "You can see armsmen before the hills, but a few."

"He has foreguards or vanguards in front of each group," confirmed Hanfor.

"Each company is more than a dek from each other company," added Jecks with a glance at Anna. "And shielded by the hills."

"Can you use sorcery on them all at once?" asked Hanfor.

"Not as long as they're on the back sides of the hill," Anna admitted. "Not unless we could take the heights to the west."

"We could circle to the north," ventured Jecks, "and take them from the side, one by one. Or take the first two companies and seize the higher ground to the west."

"We would still face half his forces, almost a hundred-score." Hanfor touched his trimmed and gray beard. "They hold the higher ground. To defeat them would cost us armsmen, or require much sorcery from the lady Anna."

That was clearly what Ehara and his Sea-Priest advisor or sorcerer, or whatever, had in mind, and Anna didn't like that option, not if there were a better one.

"We're what?—ten deks from the nearest of those hills?" she asked.

"Mayhap twelve," said Liende.

"What if we stop here for today?"

Jecks smiled, and Anna could tell he'd hoped she'd come to that conclusion.

"That would rest mounts and men," Hanfor acknowledged. "And on the morrow?"

"We move slowly."

"To place them on blade edge? That would help," Hanfor said, following her unspoken logic.

"Do we have enough arrows?" Anna asked.

"How much is enough?" asked Hanfor. "What have you in mind?"

"At least one for every enemy armsman," said the regent and sorceress. "I think we let them attack," Anna said, "but I'd like to be able to prod them if necessary."

With more destruction? She held in the wince at her own self-question, forcing a bland smile that had to appear cold and cruel.

105

PAMR, DEFALK

I don't see what you're doing, Farsenn." The drummer in the stained and sleeveless brown tunic rubs his forehead. "Your spells . . . they make a fellow's head ache. My eyes cross, and you don't spell that long."

"Mine do, too." Farsenn smiles. "Darksong isn't like Clearsong. It's more like poison. Use a little here . . . a little there." A laugh follows. "You'll see."

"The sorceress . . . she's still high and mighty." The drummer turns and gestures at the rough clay figure that is perhaps three-quarters human size on the crude wooden pedestal. "Not like that. No matter what you make them see, it's still just clay." He massages his forehead again, blinking rapidly.

"For now, Giersan, my brother, for now. Darksong must be used slowly, bit by bit . . . but the time will come when every man not on the estates of that bitch Lady Gatrune will rise, and we will hold Pamr."

"And then the sorceress will come and destroy us."
The drummer's words are flat.

"No. She will come, and I will destroy her."

"How?"

"Never before has an entire town risen, with every man
bearing arms. The sorceress has but a fewscore armsmen,
and she cannot use levies against the people within Defalk. And while she struggles with the people, I will strike
her with Darksong, pierce her soul."

"She will use her fires from the heaven."

"Against who? Every soul in Pamr?"

"She might."

"When she rests upon the support of the people themselves?" Farsenn smiles cruelly. "We will be Lord of
Pamr, and she will be dead, and that little boy she has
propped up as heir will treat with us. He will."

106

Rickel and Fhurgen, shields resting on the lancehold-
ers, rode before Anna as the Defalkan forces advanced to the crest of the low rise. Beyond the lush grass
of the hill spread out a series of fields, bordered by hedgerows not even as tall as Farinelli's ears. Farther to the
west and north and south of the fields, the meadows resumed, merging into the low hills.

The road traveled due west, vanishing into a gap between two of the larger hills.

"This is the highest point on this side of the valley."
Jecks rode on Anna's right.

"It is hard to believe that the river is only a dozen deks
beyond the hills," added Liende from Anna's left.

Anna's eyes ranged over the flat fields ahead, and then

studied the hills. The entire area was empty of people or animals—just fields filled with green plants of differing shades, narrow lanes splitting fields, the hedgerows, and grass. The low wind blew out of the west, into Anna's face, bearing the faint scent of damp earth and grass.

"I'd like to stop here, Hanfor," Anna called to the arms commander. "I need to see where the Dumarans are."

The arms commander nodded. "That might be best."

The sorceress dismounted, giving Farinelli a pat on the shoulder. "You're a good fellow." She blotted her forehead, damp as much from the more humid climate as from the late-morning sunlight.

Rickel took Farinelli's reins, and Anna unstrapped the scrying mirror. Jecks, who had dismounted quickly, took it from her.

Then Anna unstrapped the lutar and took it from its case, beginning a vocalise even before she had begun to tune the lutar.

One of the guards behind Fhurgen held the reins to Jecks' mount, and those of Liende's. Hanfor held his own, standing where he could see the mirror, but still surveying the valley while he waited.

Anna's chest felt heavy—asthma again, or too much sleeping on a cot in strange places with barely adequate food? Then, how long had it been since she'd slept in a bed that was considered hers? Almost two seasons? And some ancient kings of earth had enjoyed military campaigns?

She coughed some mucus clear and started the second vocalise.

The valley remained ominously silent, except for the sounds of her voice, the low murmurings of the Defalkan armsmen, and the tuning notes of the lutar.

Finally, the sorceress cleared her throat a last time and glanced around the group of those who waited.

Hanfor took a last look at the valley and then turned his eyes to the mirror as Anna began to sing.

"Mirror, mirror on the ground,
  show me where Dumar's forces can be found . . ."

Again, the silver mists swirled around the glass briefly, then cleared to show an aerial view of the valley. The Dumarans, crimson-uniformed dots against the green of the grass and vegetation, remained grouped generally the way they had been the afternoon before. There were two battle groups behind each of the five hills—a smaller group higher on the back side of each grassy hill, and a larger group lower and more shielded from arrows . . . or sorcery. From what Anna could see from the small images in the silvered glass, none of the Dumarans were mounted, and their mounts remained on tielines.

"The nearest group is about two deks there." Jecks pointed to the northeast. "The most distant more than three deks."

After a moment, Anna sang the couplet to release the image. She didn't want to hold it any longer than she had to, not with the spells she knew she'd have to sing shortly and the small drain from the newest enchanted shield. She swallowed, then licked her lips.

"They are not in ready battle order," observed Hanfor.

"They do not expect us to attack immediately," said Jecks.

"Even if we attacked," said Hanfor, "they could withdraw quickly."

"How long will it take them to mount and organize for an attack?" asked the sorceress.

Hanfor shrugged, squinting at the mirror. "Almost a glass."

"And how long would it take for us to form up if you gave everyone a break?" asked Anna.

"Half that."

"Is it safe to give our armsmen a rest?"

"If they stay by their mounts." Hanfor nodded.

"Do as you think best," Anna said. Her instincts told her that the Dumarans weren't about to attack, not anytime soon. Then, what happened if the Dumarans didn't attack at all? And where were the damned Sea-Priest and his magic javelins? The mirror hadn't shown him, and that bothered Anna.

"They would appreciate such a rest, Lady Anna," said Hanfor. "So would I." He nodded to Alvar.

"Scouts! Maintain posts. All companies! Stand down for rations!" bellowed the swarthy captain. "Blades at hand! Blades at hand!"

"So they can remount and form up immediately," said Jecks.

Anna had figured that out, but she nodded politely as she took the chunk of bread Jecks offered. She'd need every bit of nourishment and then some. She turned in the saddle toward the chief player. "Liende, the players can dismount and stretch and ... whatever. Just keep them close so that they can play quickly if the Dumarans decide to attack."

"We will be ready." The older woman nodded and turned her mount.

"Stand down for rations! ... Down for rations! ..." The commands echoed along the triple line with which Hanfor had advanced the Defalkan force the last dek or so. "Blades at hand. Ready for remount!"

"Players," called Liende from behind Anna, "you can dismount. Have your instruments ready before you take water or food."

Anna nodded. Her eyes went again to the fields and grasslands to the west. The wind sighed across the vegetation, bringing only the smell of earth and dampness, of grass and a faint fragrance of something—bean blossoms? Anna didn't know the odor.

She took the reins from Rickel and walked Farinelli a dozen yards to a more lush patch of grass. Now what? The two forces could each sit on high ground until harvest time. The valley was small enough that her sorcery—if she wanted to exert all the force she could—might reach half of the Dumarans. *Maybe* ...

She took a wedge of the hard yellow travel cheese from her provisions bag and gnawed off a corner. All that kept the cheese from being rank was that it was hard and dry. She forced herself through the entire wedge, knowing she'd need the nourishment.

Jecks stood beside her and ate, but far less than Anna, as always.

After almost a glass, a time of walking and studying the valley, and sipping from her water bottle, near midday, Anna took out the lutar once more.

This time the scrying spell revealed that the Dumaran forces had taken their mounts off the tielines and reformed in loose ranks, very loose ranks. None had moved from their basic positions before and behind the hills.

Anna took a deep breath and replaced the lutar and mirror on Farinelli. Then she walked to the front of the ridgetop, accompanied by Fhurgen and Rickel and their omnipresent battle shields.

Hazy clouds appeared just above the western horizon, and the wind had freshened, but still carried only the scent of damp earth and vegetation.

"Lady . . . what if they do not come?" asked Hanfor.

"Can the men wait longer?" she asked. "I'd like to see if Ehara will attack."

"Armsmen can always wait," answered the gray veteran, with a low laugh, "especially if there's a better chance of not getting killed." He eased his mount away and back toward where Alvar had reined up.

Anna ate more of the stale bread that tasted more like sawdust than bread, and left crumbs everywhere.

"I wonder," she said quietly, after eating the last of the loaf she'd taken from the canvas bag.

"Why do you pursue Lord Ehara?" asked Jecks, standing beside her as she again surveyed the empty valley.

"Why anything, I suppose. Why do I have to destroy half the armsmen in two countries to prove I'm serious? Why is it that someone like Madell would desert his consort and children because he can't beat her? Why do the

Sturinnese want to put women in chains?" The sorceress sighed. "It seems like so many people think they can do whatever they're strong enough to force others to do. But there's always someone out there stronger or nastier or meaner . . . or something. . . ."

"Most men would not wish to admit that. Or many women, I think," answered Jecks.

"So they want their women to be slaves, and they kill hundreds, destroy a country to keep women down? Dencer went crazy when he thought Wendella had been even a bit influenced by me. Sargol sacrificed everything . . . for nothing."

Jecks did not answer.

"But why?"

"We like to think we are in control of our own destiny, my lady. You who have been tossed between worlds, you understand that we often do not have such certainty. Most souls will not accept such." The white-haired lord shrugged. "Even for me, watching you, it is difficult."

"It doesn't seem that hard for me to understand," Anna said slowly.

"You do not understand how much you know that others cannot see even dimly, my lady. That is why you are regent and will always be regent." Jecks chuckled.

"Maybe." Anna wasn't convinced, but she didn't want to discuss it further, not before a battle, but she could feel her blood close to boiling. So many of the men of Liedwahr reminded her of the Arabs who'd chased her in London, who'd thought that any free woman was a whore, or a devil, or both. She shook her head. Liedwahr was definitely getting to her.

Almost a full glass passed, and still the valley remained empty, the Dumaran armsmen waiting behind the hills, the Defalkan force resting on the low ridge.

To the west, the clouds had begun to build, mixed white and gray, climbing slowly until they blocked the early afternoon sunlight. The valley took on a grayish cast.

Anna climbed into the saddle and rode slowly north-

ward along the ridge, with Fhurgen and Rickel shielding
her, Jecks beside her.

"They will not attack," opined Jecks. "They wish you
to attack and to weaken yourself."

It made sense, but Anna didn't have to like it. "We'll
wait a little longer." Suddenly, within a few moments,
she felt tense, as though something were about to happen.
She scanned the valley, but nothing had changed, not that
she could see.

Hurriedly, she dismounted, unfastened the mirror once
more, and fumbled out the lutar. Jecks hurriedly vaulted
to the ground and took the mirror, glancing toward the
clouds and hills.

Anna sang the scrying song quickly.

The image wavered, showing two images, one that
she'd seen earlier, the second of a figure in white easing
along a hedgerow bearing something like a rifle. Rifle?

"Crossbow," Jecks said.

Anna released the spell, glancing downward. The nearest hedgerow was less than half a dek below the ridge.
She practically threw the lutar into its case and quickly
fastened the mirror back in place before remounting and
riding Farinelli back to where the players sat on the grass.

Liende stood. "Lady Anna."

"You need to warm up quickly," Anna said. "We'll
do the long flame spellsong first—from the front of the
ridge, about where Lord Jecks is. Let me know when
you're ready."

Liende inclined her head, and a strand of white-streaked
red hair fell across her forehead. She brushed the lock of
hair back as she straightened. "Yes, Regent."

"Thank you." Anna guided Farinelli the handful of
yards back to where Jecks, Hanfor and her guards waited,
all still surveying the valley and hills for any sign of
movement.

Anna's stomach tightened. As she dismounted, her fingers brushed the round shield in the open-topped case at
her knee. Was it vibrating ever so faintly?

"Hanfor. Have them form up. Something's happening. Get the archers ready. But wait for my order. That will be the second spell."

"Yes, Regent!" The arms commander turned to Alvar. "Form up and stand ready! Archers to the front. Archers to the front."

"Form up and stand ready!" The orders echoed down the line, and a long sigh seemed to follow.

Fhurgen and Rickel had dismounted and stationed themselves slightly in front of Anna, one at each shoulder. Each guard studied the empty valley.

The sounds of the instrumentalists' warm-up tune slipped westward as Anna began a warm-up vocalise, not that she expected to need that much. The day was warm enough, not quite so hot as the previous days, but even more humid, and the humidity made singing easier than in the drier heat of summer in Defalk.

Her stomach twisted. Something was wrong. She had to get the spell off. Quickly. Anna turned. "Ready?"

"As you wish, lady."

"Now!"

"Mark now!" called Liende.

Anna followed the first notes, then began, using full concert voice, facing the empty valley—or a valley empty of all but a Sea-Priest sorcerer.

"Turn to fire, turn to flame
  those weapons used against my name.
Turn to ash all tools spelled against my face
  and those who seek by force the regency to replace."

A thrumminglike humming filled the air, not from where Anna stood, but below and to the northwest. The sorceress forced herself to remain calm, singing as easily and as strongly as she could.

"Turn to fire, turn to flame . . ."

A single point of fire flared in the air less than a dozen yards from Anna, and tumbled into the ankle-high grass below the ridgetop. Fhurgen and Rickel edged the shields closer together, but Anna continued to the end of the spell.

Another enchanted arrow—or something. . . . Another Sea-Priest trick. The enchanted arrow continued to burn, throwing off sparks, and a heavy gray smoke as the wet grass began to burn.

Anna repressed a shudder, thinking about what would have happened if the thrower—was it the Sea-Priest?—had gotten closer. Or would her shield have stopped it? She wasn't sure she wanted to find out. Her eyes lifted, looking out across the valley.

Fires like falling stars streaked westward, rising and spreading, then falling like fireworks across the semicircle of hills half-surrounding the Defalkan forces.

Points of flame geysered skyward from behind hills, here and there.

A single horn-note sounded from the west, then another. And a third.

Anna watched the hills. For a moment, nothing occurred. Then mounted men appeared. The smaller lancer companies—the ones that had been positioned higher on the hill—rode over the crests and down and eastward, five separate bodies of riders, clearly trying to remain separated—less than five hundred in all—nearly as much as her entire force, and they just represented a fraction of Ehara's forces.

"We should wait until they reach the end of the hedgerows," advised Jecks.

Anna tried to judge. "That seems awfully close."

"You could start the spell earlier, when they cross the last lane," Jecks said after a moment.

The sorceress gestured to Hanfor.

"Yes, Lady Anna?"

"Would it be all right for the archers to fire just after the first horsemen ride across the lane down there—the last one?"

"Yes. I would do that." He smiled crookedly. "Even if you did not so order."

"Do it." Anna turned. Several of the players, especially Delvor, gaped at the unforeseen fireworks. "Chief player!"

"Yes, lady?"

Anna cleared her throat, trying to get rid of a glob of something, then gestured to Liende. "Once through—the first arrow song. When I tell you."

Liende nodded. "Stand ready for the first arrow song. At my mark."

Anna turned and watched the approaching riders. The ground was damp enough that no dust rose. Fhurgen and Rickel eased their shields nearer to each other, giving Anna a narrowed field of vision.

One moment, the riders were a dek away, the next they were nearing the lane before the end of the hedgerow.

"Now!" Anna commanded.

"Mark!" snapped Liende.

"Archers!" ordered Hanfor, the command echoed by Alvar.

As the music rose, in tune, she sang.

> "These arrows shot into the air,
>   make each head strike one armsmen there
>   with force and speed to kill them all,
>   all those who stand against our call!"

"Arrows! Arrows!" came the command from the ridge, and a thrumming as bowstrings released shafts.

> "These arrows shot into the air . . ."

"Arrows! Second volley!" Another *thrumm* of bowstrings followed the first.

When the music ended, Anna took a half-step forward, then caught herself, watching as lancers tumbled from mounts, as mounts swerved sideways. Not a single rider remained erect in a saddle, and most saddles were empty.

A slow sigh issued from the ranks of the Defalkan forces.

"Never . . . never have I seen that," murmured Jecks.

Anna wished she hadn't. *Idiots. . . . Why . . . ?* She shook her head, absently recalling "The Charge of the Light Brigade." Was that the job of soldiers and armsmen? To carry out suicidal orders?

She swallowed. She couldn't think about that. There were still a good two thousand Dumaran armsmen somewhere, and that meant four to five times what she and Jecks and Hanfor had.

The sorceress wiped the sweat from her forehead, glad she didn't seem dizzy or light-headed. She glanced toward Hanfor, but the arms commander had his eyes on the carnage and the hills beyond the fields and the low hedgerows.

Were they all so blind? Did Ehara have to spend every last man to prove he was lord? Anna gritted her teeth. Why were all the lords in Liedwahr like that? Or most of them? *Idiots!*

Still seething, Anna glanced toward her chief player. "Liende? Have them rest for a bit. They'll have to mount up and do that spell again. Can you and the players manage it?"

"We can, Regent. Especially with a moment to catch our breath." Liende turned. "Players! You heard the regent. Make ready to ride. Then drink and get something to eat."

Before Anna turned, she saw the young Delvor nearly stagger toward his mount. Was she asking too much?

Hanfor rode to within a few yards of Anna. "Regent, most of their forces remain behind the hills."

Anna looked up. "Can we ride into the center of the hills there?" She pointed. "And have the archers fire all their arrows at the same time?"

The graying veteran nodded. "We can. Will that destroy all of them?"

"I'm strong enough for another spell after that if it doesn't." *And mad enough. If Ehara and the damned Sea-Priest want it this way, then they'll get it. Women barefoot and pregnant? Women in chains? Not while I'm regent. . . .*

"Will you . . . ?" Hanfor laughed ruefully and broke off the question. "We follow where you lead."

They would, but did she have any right to lead them into such danger? The image of chains slipped through her thoughts, and her jaw tightened. Who else would take on the Sturinnese?

She forced herself to wait until the players had eaten before she flicked the reins, and Farinelli started forward.

Half the armsmen rode on each side of the players, Jecks, Anna, and her guards, down the road between the hills. The road was at least a half-dek from the top of the hills that flanked it.

"Would that those hills were not so close," murmured Hanfor. "You chance much."

"They won't attack," Anna said, hoping she were correct, "not until we're in the center. Can you have the archers ready to fire their arrows, some in the direction of each hill? Once I start the first spell?"

"I will ensure that." Hanfor edged his mount away from Anna and toward Alvar. Shortly, commands flowed along the lines of armsmen as the Defalkan force neared the center of the low hills.

Anna licked her lips, shifting her weight in the saddle. Rickel and Fhurgen rode in front of the sorceress and regent, their eyes scanning the nearing hillsides. Jecks rode beside Anna, and Liende and the players close behind.

The wind had gotten stronger once the growing afternoon clouds had blocked the sun, and with the smell of earth came also the faint scent of burned meat, and occasionally the intermittent smell of smoke, grassy smoke.

Anna glanced around. "Here."

As the armsmen circled to form almost a ring around the regent, the players dismounted and formed up on the road, facing westward.

Anna dismounted, cleared her throat, and glanced at Liende. "We need to hurry."

"Half warm-up! Then the arrow song. The long one."

The sorceress nodded to herself and waited.

"At my mark!" commanded Liende as the warm-up ended.

Anna turned to Hanfor. "Have them shoot once I start singing."

"Archers! Arrows! Now!"

"Mark!" ordered the chief player.

Anna sang.

"These arrows shot into the air,
    make each head strike one armsmen there . . ."

Even before Anna completed the spell, the archers had released a second volley of shafts, and horsemen began to appear on the slopes above, galloping out of formation but straight toward the Defalkan armsmen.

Anna swallowed, ignoring the light-headedness she felt.

Perhaps half of the charging figures in crimson were cut down by the last of the Defalkan arrows, but more than a thousand armed lancers poured over the hills toward the Defalkan force. At least, it looked like that many to Anna.

She looked back at the players. Delvor lay sprawled on the ground. Liende stood panting, exhausted, almost unable to lift her horn.

Jecks had his blade out and his mount shadowing Anna.

The sorceress sprinted to Farinelli and yanked out the lutar. *Shit! Shit! Shit! No matter how you plan, it doesn't quite work. . . .*

The only spell she had down cold enough to rattle off that quickly was the short flame song. She forced a quick and rough strum/tuning of the lutar, and tried to match the pitch she wanted before she sang.

> "Armsmen wrong, armsmen strong,
>   turn to flame with this song . . ."

She forced the image of Dumaran figures into the spell, and she had to sing the entire spell twice before fires crackled out of the sky, before the awful whips of fire raked the hillside.

Then, fires flared in front of her own eyes, and she couldn't even see Farinelli or Jecks. She tried to sit down, tried to cradle the lutar . . . half hoping she had managed that before blackness and flames lapped over her like tides of ice, tides of fire.

 . . . *ice and fire, fire and ice, and will the world end twice* . . .

Whips of fire flayed men, except they were boys, boys like Mario, boys like Birke and Skent . . . just boys . . .

Horses screamed as flames burst from the saddles on their backs . . . and a hot fire rain fell on ashen valleys and low hills, hills and valleys that had been green, oh so green . . .

 . . . *fire and ice . . . ice and fire . . . mist and flame* . . .

Some time later, when the sky was dark, Anna found herself wrapped in a blanket, sweating, on her cot. Jecks sat on a stool, as if he had been waiting.

Her head ached, and her stomach twisted. She struggled into a sitting position. Large unseen hammers pounded at her skull, and knives slashed at her eyes. She closed them. That didn't help. She opened them. They still hurt.

"How fare you, my lady?"

"Like shit," she rasped. "As usual, for this sort of thing."

The white-haired lord extended a bottle.

She sipped the warm wine, once, and swallowed. Then she took another longer swallow. "Maybe . . . that will help."

"Your players are exhausted. The armsmen do not look this way." Jecks' voice was low and bleak.

"What happened?" *Did they capture us? Where are the guards, then?*

"Once again, you have utterly destroyed an enemy," Jecks said quietly.

"I . . . didn't plan it that way. They didn't give me much choice."

"You gave them less, lady." Jecks did not meet her eyes.

"Wait a moment," Anna snapped, sitting up and letting the blankets fall away. "Here we go again. Ehara sends golds and tries to grab some of Defalk. He sends lancers, and he won't admit it. He won't pledge to keep his hands off, and everyone sits around and says, 'Sorry, Lady Anna, you just don't have the armsmen to stop him.' So I try to make everyone happy and build a dam to suggest I have the power to stop Ehara.

"Now it's all my fault, and you're saying that I gave them no choices? I gave them plenty of choices. They just weren't *honorable* choices. That's the problem with your great and 'honorable' Liedwahr, my dear Lord Jecks. If it doesn't involve lots of bloody killing, with dull swords and men on big horses, it's not honorable." Anna laughed harshly, and jabbed a hand at Jecks as he started to open his mouth. "No. You have no right to judge me. Don't you *dare* to judge me. Every time I try to do something, it's going to offend the Thirty-three. You sit there and look away. Don't upset the lady Anna. She might do something horrible. Don't get the sorceress-woman angry. Well, I am angry! I'm pissed! Do you think I wanted to kill all those men? Do you think I like the smell of blood and burned flesh? You say I gave them no choices. I've given everyone a lot of choices. All my life. And you men, all of you, give me none. 'Do it our way. Do it the honorable way. You can't do it that way, Anna. That would displease someone. That would upset someone.' What about me? I've saved your grandson's ass, and your precious lords' asses, and it's never enough. . . . Everyone looks sideways at me, like I'm going to . . . explode. . . . Well . . . you can see it. I'm exploding. I am the unreasonable madwoman. I'm the screaming, wild bitch-sorceress! That's what everyone wants . . . to learn that I'm unreasonable. That I don't understand. Well . . . I don't. I don't understand why . . . why . . ."

Anna found herself gasping, her head spinning, suddenly aware that the entire camp was silent. So silent that no one moved. She took one deep breath, and then another.

Jecks' eyes were on the ground.

Anna took the bottle he had set on the damp clay and swallowed deeply. Maybe she could drink enough that she could sleep. Whatever she said didn't matter. No one really listened. No one wanted to hear. She took another swallow.

Lord, she was tired. She sat, shaking from rage and exhaustion, on the edge of her cot, her head throbbing, her eyes seeing dark double images . . . wondering what had set her off.

What choice had she had? She couldn't use spells that didn't kill—they were Darksong. *Are you any better than any man aroused with bloodlust?* She'd gotten angry at the enchanted arrows or javelins or whatever, so angry she really hadn't thought.

Was Jecks right? That force was the only answer? Or that she had given them no choice? But had they given her any, really? Or was that just rationalization? But no one had ever given her any real choices, just choices that looked like they were real.

She sat in the twilight and looked through the open tent flaps at the embers of the fire. Her head throbbed still, and her eyes burned, and double hot and cold images danced before them.

Jecks sat on the stool, equally silent, eyes still averted.

Inside, Anna continued to seethe. *Don't judge me. . . . You have no right to judge me. . . .*

Outside, only the faintest of murmurs filled the damp night.

Finally, Anna reached for the blankets, knowing she would collapse if she did not lie down again, wondering if she had pushed Jecks too hard . . . wondering . . .

107

The warm rain, slightly heavier than a mist, fell around the Defalkan riders as they continued westward out of the valley, out of yet another valley of dissonance, chaos, fire, and death.

Anna took a breath of damp air. The rain had deadened the odor of burned meat and death. She glanced ahead at the churned hoofprints in the mud of the road, far less dense, far fewer than when Ehara had fled the Vale of Cuetayl.

Hanfor rode next to her while Jecks rode behind, not surprisingly, since Jecks had not spoken to her since the night before, and she wasn't about to speak to him.

"On to Dumaria," she murmured, more to herself than to Jecks or Hanfor.

The sorceress glanced over her shoulder past Lejun and Rickel to where Liende rode before the players, all looking as tired and bedraggled as Anna felt.

So much for your ideas of not having Liende play for battles . . . so much for so many ideas. She took a slow deep breath. *You've got to relax some.* Then she shrugged her shoulders and bent her head forward, trying to stretch out the tightness.

"We will need to cross the river somewhere," Hanfor said, "to reach Dumaria."

You don't think I know that? Anna bit back her first

retort, then swallowed before speaking. "One way or another, we'll manage. We always do." Anna supposed she could use her marvelous sorcery to build a bridge—or find a ford. She felt like laughing, but held back the feeling, knowing it was close to hysteria. "Ehara has to find the ford or bridge he used."

"If he does not," added Alvar, riding slightly ahead of Anna, "then he must face us again, and now our forces outnumber his."

"He will find a ford," predicted Hanfor, wiping away the rainwater collecting on his brow.

Anna glanced down. The lower part of her trousers and her boots, where not protected by the leather of the stirrup guards, were mud-splattered once more. The sky seemed to lighten, and she hoped that meant the rain was passing. Then, the way things were going, it could mean a lightening before a heavier rainfall.

Her eyes went to the road ahead, the one taken by Ehara. She had defeated his forces twice. Close to five thousand Dumarans were dead. The two major cities were flood-ravaged wrecks . . . and she still had to keep pursuing and fighting.

Won't it ever end? Do I have to destroy every last chauvinist in power on the fucking planet? And if I do that, will I turn every one of their sons into a fanatic? But if I stop now . . . nothing's resolved . . . nothing at all, for all the deaths. . . .

Was that how all conquerors felt, rationalizing killing with more killing?

She still felt like yelling at Jecks—or breaking down and sobbing. Neither would help. Instead, she took another deep breath and looked at the muddy road ahead.

108

WEI, NORDWEI

A shtaar's fingers run over the oval of black agate briefly before she steeples her fingers on the polished surface of the desk and waits for Gretslen to seat herself in the straight-backed ebony chair that has replaced the older chair.

The blonde seer sits, clears her throat gently, then begins. "My congratulations on your selection to the Council."

"Thank you, Gretslen. The sorceress?"

"The sorceress has destroyed the last of the lancers of Sturinn, and all save one of the Sea-Priest sorcerers. She has chased Ehara out of the northeast of Dumar. Ehara has less than twentyscore armsmen from more than ten times that number."

"They are dead? Or wounded? Or deserters?"

"All of them are dead. Kendr and I could not discern any deserters through the reflecting pools. There could be a very small number."

"You are cautious. Good. Where is the sorceress now?"

"On the eastern bank of the Falche, north of Dumaria. She cannot cross the Falche without risking her forces. The rains have swollen it mightily, and her earlier sorceries ripped away the bridges."

"Gretslen?" asks Ashtaar deliberately. "Why do you dislike the sorceress so much that you blind yourself to what she can and cannot do?"

"Mightiness?"

"You heard me. Why do you hate her so much? Because you think you could do so well in her boots?" Ashtaar laughs, and the laugh is hard and cruel. "You would have failed long before now. You are neither ruthless enough, nor compassionate enough."

Gretslen does not respond.

"Since you will not ask, I will tell you." The spy-mistress's fingers caress the black agate oval again. "She will do what must be done, because she has suffered enough, and knows the consequences if she does not. She suffers because she knows too well how hard her actions fall, and she will struggle to balance them, and she will fail. Yet she will struggle well enough that most of the people she rules will forgive her and follow her. Those who do not . . ." Ashtaar shrugs. "They will essay her destruction, and perhaps one will succeed. You have great ability, and you believe that force always succeeds. It does, but not all force is obvious." She smiles. "Thank you. You may depart. Please keep me informed."

"Thank you, Mightiness. We will do our best." Gretslen's voice is even, and she rises, and bows, then turns and walks gracefully to the door.

109

DUMARIA, DUMAR

The Sea-Marshal glances up from the drums as Ehara steps into the small room off the armory. Heavy wrappings cover his arms, and his dark hair is short and frizzled. One of the burns on jerRestin's cheeks oozes a reddish fluid.

"Yet more sorcery?"

"What else would you suggest, Lord Ehara? My own iron quarrels burst into flame. Iron—flaming—before I could even approach the bitch. Yet she used no sorcery to seek me."

"She is braver than most lords." Ehara's voice holds a touch of amusement. "She rode into a trap, and turned it on us."

"You and your men did not move quickly enough."

"Neither did you, Sea-Priest, but you escaped. Most of my men did not, and another score who did drowned in trying to cross the Falche."

"It took all my sorcery to hold off the sorceress's fires." JerRestin looks at his arms. "I was not entirely successful even so. I did lower the waters at the ford."

"Yes. Not enough."

"Enough to leave the sorceress on the eastern side. She will not risk the river with such a small body of arms-men."

"Her twenty-fivescore no longer look so insignificant, and I am confident she will find her way across, if she has not already." Ehara looks pointedly at the drums. "You labor at more sorcery?"

"We have lost more than forty fine ships to the first attack of the sorceress. I have lost over three thousand of the best lancers, dying in agony. A handful of us remain, and I can never return to Sturinn. Not with such disgrace. I can but atone."

Ehara's heavy eyebrows lift.

"The sorceress will die. She has power, but not cunning. She must live to succeed. I must die to succeed."

"Then you had best die soon, and well, Sea-Marshal, for my armsmen are few and thin." Ehara's booming laugh rings hollow. "She has foiled you twice. What will be different a third time?"

"She has used her glasses before attacks. This time, I will be along the line of march, well away from any battle site, in the most innocent of settings. You will be farther westward. . . ."

"I should retreat . . . leave Dumaria defenseless, and open to those barbarians of the north?"

"She will not sack a defenseless city. She has never done that. She will pursue you—and me."

"My Siobion? My heirs?"

"Leave them. She has yet to kill an heir."

Ehara frowns. "I should listen to a man who is already dead?"

"You can listen or not." The Sea-Marshal binds the last of the drums into the framework. His lips are tight together between words, as though each movement, each word, is agony. "You cannot defeat Defalk while she lives. After I die, one way or the other, you are no worse off."

"That is the first true statement from you since you came to Dumar." Ehara's lips twist.

"Watch how you call upon truth, Lord Ehara. The harmonies have a way with those who would make truth their handmaiden." The Sea-Marshal's eyes glitter. "I, above all, have learned that. So will the sorceress."

110

Anna glanced up through the rain that continued to fall, and then down at the swollen Falche, as it swirled around and over the piles of rock and masonry that had once been bridge abutments and piers. Despite her jacket, and her sodden felt hat, she was soaked through, and the wind had turned cooler, if not cool enough to chill her—yet.

Downhill from where she sat on the big gelding, Hanfor received another scouting report. Beside her on his mount sat Jecks, stolid and silent in the late-afternoon damp, silent as he had been since the slaughter in the hills.

Anna turned in the saddle and glanced at the white-haired lord, then turned away.

"Lady Anna?"

She turned back. "Yes."

"Perhaps I should return to Falcor . . . if you find my presence so distasteful."

"I don't find your presence distasteful. I'm just tired of being judged when I'm the only one doing anything and everyone else is coming up with reasons not to do things."

"I did not presume—"

"Lord Jecks . . . you did presume, and you have presumed all along. Not so much as the other lords, but you have judged, and I *hate* being judged that way." Anna met his eyes. "I shouldn't have yelled at you, and I'm sorry I did. But I was tired." She paused. "I know you were tired, too. Let's leave it at that. We still have a lot to do."

"As you wish."

I don't wish. I just wish you'd stop silently judging me.

Hanfor finished listening to the scout, then turned his mount and rode back up the road to Anna.

"The scouts can find no bridge, not within fifteen deks north or south of Dumaria," reported Hanfor. "The river is too high to ford."

You don't think I see that? "Then we'll have to make a bridge," Anna declared.

Jecks glanced at her through the light rain.

"We're going to rest, and eat, and then we're going to build a bridge. I'm not crazy, my dear Lord Jecks." Anna gestured downhill at the swirling gray-blue water of the Falche where it lapped at the end of the road and the ruins of the old bridge. "We're going to lose armsmen if we have to ford that." *And my swimming isn't much better than a dog-paddle for survival.*

"We could wait," suggested Hanfor.

"For what? Rain lasts forever here. Besides, then we'll have to chase Ehara farther. I want to get this mess over. Lord—the harmonies only know what problems have happened in Defalk." *And whose fault is that, with your chasing Ehara?*

Anna ignored the self-recrimination, wiped water off the back of her neck, and turned Farinelli back eastward until she covered the dozen or so yards separating her from the players. Fhurgen, Rickel, and Jecks followed.

Liende inclined her bare head as the regent reined up.

"Liende? Do the players recall the building song, the one we used for the bridge at Cheor?"

"Once we have learned a spell, Lady Anna, we can always recall it." Liende paused. "But . . . with the rain . . ."

"We have one tent—mine. You'll have to huddle together, but I trust it can be done."

Liende nodded. "With cover, we can play."

"Good." Anna turned in the saddle. "Fhurgen, we need to set up my tent beside the road, with the front facing where the bridge was."

"Yes, Lady Anna," answered the bass-voiced and dark-bearded guard.

"It's not for me. The players need shelter so that we can sing a spell to build a bridge. That might get us out of this rain."

"Yes, lady." The guard grinned. Beside him, so did Lejun. Behind them, Kerhor, bare-headed with black hair plastered against his skull, nodded.

"You would spend sorcery on Dumar?" asked Jecks slowly, evenly.

"Why not? We need the bridge, and I did destroy the one that was here." Anna laughed, holding it to a chuckle, rather than yielding to the hysterical shriek she felt like loosing. "I said Liedwahr needed better bridges."

"You did say such," Jecks admitted.

"I would have liked to do more in Defalk, but things have a way of getting out of hand." *Like life . . . and would you stop questioning everything I do that's different?*

"They do, my lady."

Anna nodded, then watched as Fhurgen and Rickel quickly began to erect the tent, whose once-white panels now appeared tan-and-pink, depending on which dust from where had worked its way into the fabric. The tan-and-pink turned dark where the rain streaked the silk.

Beside her, Jecks watched impassively, his eyes straying toward Anna occasionally.

Once the panels were in place, the players crowded under the silk and began to extract instruments and tune, bumping into each other with almost every movement. Yet no one complained.

Was that because she watched? Or because musicians on Erde were less spoiled than the students of earth?

Fhurgen found another pole and strapped the front flaps to it, creating another oasis free of rain. He gestured, and Anna dismounted.

As the players tuned in the crowded confines of the tent, water dribbling off the silk, Anna stood under the extended front flap and sang the melody, using nonsense syllables, but thinking the words.

As the players completed their warm-up, she cleared her throat gently, eyes on the roiling water at the base of the hill where the road vanished under the muddy torrent. On the far side a causeway began in midair and extended across flooded fields to a gap in the bluff—the same bluff that, some twenty deks south, bordered the upper part of the city of Dumaria.

"We stand ready, Regent," offered Liende.

"Anytime," Anna answered.

"On my mark. . . . Mark!"

Anna used full concert voice, helped by the humidity of the gentle rain, letting the words flow forth.

> ". . . replicate the blocks and stones.
> Place them in their proper zones . . .
> Set them firm, and set them square . . ."

The ground on which she stood shifted as she completed the first verse. *Strophic spell,* the thought came again, and she wondered if she'd always think of versed spells that way. Then, she couldn't afford the luxury of through-composed spells, with no repetitions of the melody throughout the entire song.

The gray clouds darkened as she wound up the second verse, and the rain began to fall even more heavily. A white-glared bolt of lightning flashed across the blackened western sky, and the very hillside shifted once more, with rumbling from the ground to match the rumbling from the sky. Dust puffed into the rain—momentarily, before it was dampened out of existence.

Another lightning flash seared across the heavens, revealing a shimmering mist that thickened, then cloaked the river where the old bridge had stood. The sorceress, miniature flares exploding across her field of vision, staggered. A chord, then two paired chords, strummed on that unseen gigantic harp, shivered the silver fog covering the Falche, a fog of sorcery, steam, and rock dust.

The river boiled, becoming even more turbulent, and the fog seeped up from the ground where the rain around the tent struck puddles or damp ground. Anna's eyes burned, although the light flares before her were subsiding. *Because you did the spell in the rain . . . ?* An archway of gray-and-red stone emerged from the heavy gray fog that the roiling waters of the Falche carried downstream in patches.

Anna staggered and grabbed for one of the poles holding up the flap, and Jecks caught her other arm, supporting her.

"You will need that tent on the other side. And some food and drink." His voice was slightly hoarse.

"Do we have any?" Anna tried to grit her teeth, tried to ignore the flashes of light before her eyes.

"Enough. No one will gainsay your food or rest when you have ensured none die in crossing the river."

And who decided they needed to cross the river? "I suppose not." Anna felt embarrassed that she had to lean on Jecks, but her legs were like water. "I suppose not. Let's get that tent down and get over the river."

Jecks practically lifted her into the saddle.

"Thank you."

"Thank you, my lady. I did not relish swimming that river or waiting in the rain." He flashed a smile, and Anna wondered, again, why things seemed so possible with the handsome lord at times, and so impossible at others.

She pushed away the judgments and urged Farinelli downhill and toward the stone bridge—another structure that would doubtless outlive her, and her name.

Jecks rode beside her, and she was glad he did.

111

Anna wiped her forehead. The hot midmorning summer sun searing through a clear sky had already turned the rains of the previous days into humidity resembling that in a steambath. "This is worse than summer in Defalk with no rain."

Absently, she wondered if all went well in Defalk. How could she know, now that the flow of scrolls from Menares and Dythya had stopped? She scarcely had enough energy for the business at hand, let alone scrying Falcor and elsewhere in Defalk for who knew what.

"It's hot," she said, realizing she was repeating herself.

"Even my old bones find it hot," admitted Jecks.

"Your bones aren't that old," said Anna. "Not that much older than mine."

"Yours look to be much younger, much younger," the white-haired lord pointed out.

"It's what's inside that counts." Anna reached for her water bottle again. The water helped some, but not so much as it had in the drier heat of the Sudbergs.

The road toward Dumaria was empty except for Anna's

force—and the tracks that showed horses, carts, people fleeing the terrible sorceress of Defalk. Then, every road in Dumar had been empty, the same way. Anna wanted to scream—again.

The few farming cots visible from the road were silent, shutters tight.

Anna wondered if poor souls hunkered in fright inside, stifling in the heat. She also wondered what tales had been told about her. Not even a stray dog was in evidence.

Ahead in the distance along the flat road were a pair of white marbled gates, each gate nearly ten yards high. The gates connected to no walls, no ditches, no earthworks. Behind the gates, the road angled to the right and wound up a low slope. On the slope were trees and at least a few large dwellings. On the top of the hill was a line of trees bearing leaves of intense green, and from behind the trees rose the white marbled palace that Anna had scried often enough in seeking Lord Ehara.

"Impressive," she murmured.

"Lord Ehara and his forbearers were not known to stint on their comforts," said Hanfor. "But Dumar is a richer land than Defalk, if smaller. The scouts have found no sign of armsmen, and the roads to the city are deserted."

"Not quite," said Jecks. "There's someone waiting up there."

Anna squinted in the bright light, following Jecks' gesture.

Three mounted figures under pale blue banners waited on the road, several hundred yards ahead, and a half dek outside the north gates to Dumaria.

"Break out the ensign," ordered Hanfor. "All guards to the fore! Blades at the ready!"

Anna twisted in the saddle. "Players stand ready." She eased her lutar out of its case, and held it one handed, across her thighs as she rode south toward Dumar.

"They seem unarmed," Jecks observed, "and no one is near."

The Defalkan force rode slowly, easing to a stop a good fifty yards from the trio.

"Lady Anna, Sorceress and Regent of Defalk. Know that we supplicate you." The words came from the rider on the right, a slender man with a pencil-thin mustache and equally-wispy ginger hair. "Know that we understand that nothing can stand before you should you decide to destroy Dumaria for its error and wickedness in attacking your lands. . . ."

"Who are you," asked Hanfor brusquely, "to make such an offer?"

"We are of the merchants' council. All the lords have departed, fearing your wrath. We, alas, dare not depart. Be merciful, we beg of you. The city lies open to you." The ginger-haired man bowed in the saddle.

"We will see." Anna's voice was as cold as the day was hot and steamy. "Dumar brought this upon itself by attempting to create rebellion in Defalk."

"We had nothing to do with that, lady and sorceress, nothing at all."

"We'll see," Anna repeated, rather than say what was on her mind. No one ever had anything to do with anything when things went wrong. It was never the students' fault that they didn't study. It was never the lords' fault that they plotted. It was never the merchants' fault that they profited from war.

"Be merciful, we beg," echoed the merchant on the left, a figure with greasy black hair and oily skin.

"What of Lord Ehara?" asked Jecks.

"He and his armsmen have fled along the Envar River road." The squat man in the middle, whose face was wreathed in sweat, swallowed. "He said that you would spare the defenseless."

"As long as they swear allegiance to Defalk and the Regency," said Anna. "As long as they do not attack me or my armsmen."

All three men's heads bobbed. "That will not happen, lady and sorceress. All have seen your might."

It wouldn't happen immediately, they meant. Anna didn't intend for it to happen ever—or not for a long time.

"We will lead you to the palace. It, too, stands open to you."

"In a moment," Anna said. "In a moment." She dismounted and took out the mirror and lutar—letting Jecks help her.

Then she quickly sang the danger spell, accompanying herself with the lutar.

"Show from Dumar, danger to fear,
    all the threats to me bright and clear . . ."

The mirror showed a single image, that of the Sea-Priest in white, riding beside Lord Ehara, with the flat silver of a river to their left.

Anna sang the release couplet.

"Still, you must take care," cautioned Jecks.

"Hanfor?" asked Anna.

"I would that one company precede you and two follow immediately. Put the merchants in the middle, but ahead of you with guards behind them."

"Set it up the way you think is best." Anna offered a quick smile.

"Green company! To the fore! Arms ready!"

The three merchants winced nearly simultaneously as the armsmen rode around them and formed up. They winced again to find themselves surrounded by guards.

The column passed through the open gates.

Like the road leading into Dumaria, the winding avenue that climbed to the north side of the palace past large and impressive homes was also empty. Anna looked across a small parklike space, past a fountain where water still jetted from a spray of marble flowers into a scallop-shaped pond. Around the pond was a garden, where small yellow flowers alternated with larger purple blooms. A faint scent of something like lavender reached Anna with a vagrant breeze that died as quickly as it had risen.

The iron gates, bearing some heraldic symbol, were closed, as were those of the houses above and below. Not a soul appeared on any of the well-trimmed grounds.

"Those with coins have left," said Alvar from where he rode in front of Anna.

"With their coins," muttered Rickel.

"And everything else," murmured Fhurgen beneath his breath.

Anna silently agreed, but studied the road, ready to use the lutar at any provocation.

When the road leveled out on the hilltop, the houses ended, and another arched iron gate straddled the road another hundred yards south. The gate was open.

"That is the palace. It is yours. Lady Siobion stands ready to offer every courtesy," babbled the squat Dumaran. "Anything you desire . . . just spare what remains of Dumaria, we beg of you."

"It could not hurt to spare the city," said Hanfor with a wry smile. "If it acknowledges you as sovereign."

Anna understood. There was nothing to be gained now by sacking Ehara's city, or what was left of it, except angering the common people. Ehara had certainly taken the majority of armsmen, and probably all the gold he could gather.

She knew she was filthy, tired, hungry, and wanted the damned war to be over, and it didn't look like it ever would end. First, she'd have to ensure the capital was somehow loyal, and then chase down Ehara, and if they survived that, pacify, through visiting and using the mirror to seek out hostile armsmen, the big port of Narial, and who knew how many other towns.

Then . . . maybe they could head home. Maybe . . . if she could set up some halfway workable and friendly government in Dumar so that she didn't have to repeat the current mess in five or ten years.

"Sorceress?" prompted Jecks.

"The palace had better be ready for our forces, and with plenty of food."

"All awaits you . . . everything. . . ."

Anna wanted to shake her head again as they rode through what had to be the royal park, with trimmed topiary displaying a range of game animals, a low boxwood hedge maze, and two marble fountains. To the south, ahead of them, rose the white building she had seen a time or more in her scrying spells.

Anna gestured to Hanfor and reined up on the well-fitted paved road less than two hundred yards from the palace—or one of its buildings.

"Companies . . . halt!" Hanfor stood in his stirrups and raised his voice.

Anna eased Farinelli back toward the players. "Liende . . . we need one spell before you and the players eat. The armsmen-seeking spell."

"Here, lady?"

"I'm being cautious. I want no treachery within the palace." Anna smiled grimly, and Liende nodded.

"After we eat, we'll repeat the process, say—a half-dozen times—until I'm convinced we've located every remaining armsman in Dumaria."

"Yes, Regent."

"Some will die rather then pledge to you," murmured Jecks.

"A lot fewer than if we took the city with fire," Anna answered. She waited as the players dismounted and began to tune. After going over the seeking spell a dozen times in her mind, she finally dismounted and stepped before the players.

"Now, after this spell, you can eat and rest for a time. For a glass or so. Then we'll have to go to work again."

Anna faced the palace, waiting for Liende's signal.

"Mark!"

Without preamble, the sorceress sang.

"Find, find, any armsman close to here,
    who bears his weapons hard and near . . ."

After she finished Anna watched the glass, as did Hanfor, as it split into sections.

"Guards in the palace." Hanfor nodded. "And some in a barracks." He looked up. "Purple Company . . . search the palace. Harm none, save those who lift arms against you."

Anna eased Farinelli back toward the players.

"Green Company. Search the grounds," continued Hanfor. "There is a guard barracks somewhere near."

"We'll have to wait. I know you're all tired," Anna told Liende, "but I want no treachery within the palace." Anna smiled grimly, and Liende nodded.

"Yes, Regent." Liende's tone was formal, not quite resigned.

"Now, after we get settled and eat, you can rest for a time. Later, we'll have to go to work again."

Anna faced the palace, hands on lutar, watching as her forces swarmed across the grounds and the palace, waiting for Hanfor's signal.

She could see the merchants squirming on their mounts, and she wondered what she could do about them—or if she had to.

Jecks, his blade out, followed her eyes. "You do not trust them."

"No."

"Nor I, but they will acknowledge you, so long as they fear you."

Anna was afraid that was the way it would always be. She sat on Farinelli, watching, watching others watch her.

Lord, she was tired, and the day was far from over, far from it . . . far, far from it.

112

M ust you do this, lady?'' asked Alvar, as Anna led
Farinelli out of the palace stable into another sunlit, hot, and humid morning.

"How else do I ensure that we hold Dumaria?'' asked
Anna.

"The armsmen have fled,'' suggested Alvar.

"No,'' added Jecks, leading his own mount out behind
Anna. "Some have said that they fled. The mirror shows
no danger now, but what after we pursue Lord Ehara?''

Anna wanted to nod. No matter what anyone said, she
would have to leave some force at the palace, and that
meant there couldn't be any organized opposition remaining in Dumar. Out in the courtyard, in the long early-
morning shadow cast by the stable, she handed Farinelli's
reins to Kerhor. The sharp-faced, dark-haired guard
bowed slightly.

An unfamiliar birdcall wafted on the slight breeze from
the palace park that lay to the north of the stable courtyard.

The players stood outside, their mounts held by some
of the armsmen, their instruments ready.

Anna cleared her throat, though she'd already warmed
up in her chambers, then looked at the players. "Today
is going to be long, and possibly dangerous. I hope not.
What we need to do is to seek out any armsmen left in
Dumaria, and either obtain their allegiance to the Regency
or kill them.'' She could see the lank-haired Delvor wince
at her last words. "It's very simple. The Dumarans have
to know that I can find *anyone*, and that no one bearing

arms against Defalk will survive.'' *Of course, you still can't find that sorcerer in eastern Defalk. . . .*

Beside her, Jecks laid out the scrying mirror on the stones of the courtyard.

She pushed away the errant thought. ''We probably won't find every single deserter or armsman who hides, but we must create the impression that we can. That's what we've already done in places like Finduma and Hrissar.'' She smiled and paused. ''We didn't find too many, but that shouldn't be a problem in Dumaria.''

A low laugh echoed from the armsmen reined up and waiting.

Anna nodded to Liende. ''Any time, chief player.''

''The seeking song . . . on my mark. . . . Mark!'' Liende dropped her hand, and lifted her horn, and the clarinet-like woodwind melded with the falk horn and the strings.

Anna's voice, more rested, rose above the players.

''Find, find, any Dumaran close to here,
    any armsman bearing weapons hard and near . . .''

Again, the mirror showed three men in gray—not crimson—gathered around a table. One looked over his shoulder, as if to a door.

Alvar studied the image, and Anna hoped his memory was good. Hanfor's sketching might have been better, but the arms commander was wrestling with other problems—such as how to divide their forces, and what was needed to keep a handle on Dumaria.

Alvar nodded, as did Jecks.

''Again,'' Anna said. This time she used the second verse of the spell.

''Show the armsman in that exact place
    from outside from where we saw his face
    show the place both clear and bright,
    so we may find it in the light . . .''

The image in the mirror sparkled up from where it lay on the stones. The building that appeared in the glass seemed to slant, as if it had been pushed somehow sideways, and debris was piled against part of the front.

Flood damage, Anna suspected.

A signboard showing a black ram lay propped against the wall beside the open front door.

After a moment, Anna sang the release couplet, and then mounted Farinelli.

"Need you go?" asked Alvar.

"If I am not seen . . ." Anna shrugged. Again, she couldn't quite explain it, but all she had, really, was the threat of force, and the impression of invincibility—and hiding in the palace wasn't going to bolster that impression. Besides, the mirror spells earlier hadn't shown any immediate danger. That could mean there was so much that sorcery couldn't detect it, or that Dumaria was momentarily cowed.

Either way, she had to do something—quickly.

"We will wait while you find the way to the Black Ram." Anna glanced down at Jecks, wearing what she thought of as battle leathers, then at Alvar. "I'd bet it's close to the bottom of the hill the palace sits on and a bit toward the river."

"I would not wager against that." Alvar smiled and swung up into his saddle.

Jecks swept up the scrying glass and efficiently packed it back in its leathers, then began to strap it in the harness behind Anna's saddle. Farinelli sidestepped slightly.

"Easy . . . easy . . ." Anna glanced out toward the east. "We'll want to surround the place. I'd rather not have to turn anyone into flame." *But you will if you have to . . . and you know you'll need an example or two.* She pursed her lips momentarily, knowing, given human nature, and the macho nature of the men of Liedwahr, that she wouldn't have to create the example. *Which is worse . . . their nature or your willingness to use it . . . ?*

As Alvar led off the company of armsmen, standing beside his mount, Jecks cleared his throat.

Anna turned in the saddle, realizing that she and Jecks were alone, alone in a circle of players and mounts that had given them a wide berth.

"You do not look forward to this day." The older lord mounted. "As you did not look forward to the last battle."

"No. But we have to root out anything that may cause trouble for Alvar. We have to leave some armsmen, but I don't want to leave many."

"Nor I." Jecks smiled. "Yet all you need armsmen for is to protect you. There will be no true battles, no blades against blades, shafts against shafts."

"You think using sorcery is wrong?"

"Once I might have thought so." The white-haired lord shrugged, then patted the shoulder of his mount. "Those who love the excitement and the smell of death and blood . . . they will still claim a kingdom won by sorcery will not last . . . because blood anchors a conquest."

"There has been enough blood to anchor this." *More than enough. . . .*

"They will claim that sorcery is ease, as though sweeping stones from a Vorkoffe board." Jecks added quickly. "I have seen otherwise, my lady, and you should know that."

"Ease . . ." Anna wanted to laugh. How many weeks had she been prostrated? How many times had others tried to use sorcery against her? How many thousands had died? . . . Was there something about people that found weapons despicable if they didn't cause equal devastation and risk to both sides? Well . . . her own world hadn't exactly liked nuclear weapons. . . .

"Let's see . . . once a battle's over, and the victor goes home, the dead remain. Once my sorcery's over, and we return to Defalk, the dead remain. Is there any difference?" *Except that men who have strong arms and blades think that sorcery is unfair . . . that women should do the fair thing and fight with blades . . . and give away how much in size and strength and muscle mass?* "No . . . a spellsong war is as fair as any other kind of war."

A frown crossed Jecks' face before he nodded. "You would say no war is fair."

"No war I've heard of."

Alvar rode into the courtyard, a wry smile on his face. "The Black Ram lies less than half a dek below us."

Anna nodded toward Liende, then flicked the reins. She and Jecks rode almost shoulder to shoulder, behind Rickel and Fhurgen. Her guards did carry the shields, and every one of her personal guard rode with blades unsheathed as they descended the cobblestone road into Dumaria.

Below the hill the road narrowed, but ran straight eastward toward the Falche River. Farther ahead, where the street seemed to narrow in the distance, she could see whole buildings seemingly slumped into piles.

The road seemed empty, windows shuttered, but she wondered how recently the shutters had been closed. A rank odor, of mud, and sewage, and worse, hung over the town. Anna knew who had caused that—or whose flood.

The Black Ram stood on a corner, the front door closed, the shutters on the timbered second-story windows closed.

"The Green Company is behind the inn," Alvar said quietly. "Your wishes, Regent?"

"I know it will be dangerous . . . but I'd like the three armsmen brought out."

"It must be done." Alvar turned.

Anna watched as the stocky overcaptain drew aside a group of armsmen, speaking quietly and gesturing toward the inn. Shortly, a dozen archers had their bows strung and arrows ready to nock.

Then a burly armsman stepped up to the barred door of the inn and pounded on the door. "Open . . . in the name of the regent and sorceress."

The door remained closed. Anna glanced up the street

in the direction of the palace, but the street remained empty.

"Open . . . in the name of the regent and sorceress." The burly armsman lifted his arm to hammer on the door a second time, when the door opened, and a bearded man peered out. He glanced at the ranks of armsmen, then shrugged, as if to cast himself to his fate.

"Stand aside. We seek three fleeing armsmen."

"Sers . . . there be none. . . . I know."

"They were here," said Jecks.

Anna could sense the whispers from the inn and from the buildings around. She felt exposed, and she noted that Fhurgen had moved slightly back, setting the shield as to protect her from behind.

"The sorceress . . . at the Black Ram?"

". . . looks more like a young beardless lord . . ."

". . . hard . . . her face be . . ."

Anna nodded at Alvar. "Send armsmen after them."

A dozen men dismounted at signal from the over-captain, blades drawn, stepping past the innkeeper and into the building.

Anna waited as the muted sounds of boots—and yells—sifted onto the street. Perspiration oozed down her neck.

Rickel shifted the heavy shield. Jecks checked his bare blade yet again.

Abruptly, two men in nondescript leathers walked out—dejectedly, heads down. Behind them came four armsmen, blades still bare and ready.

More muffled sounds preceded the third man—ginger-bearded, from whose slashed cheek blood streamed as he was half carried, half dragged from the building. Despite another wound, evidenced by the dark stains across his shirt, the wounded man struggled violently in the grip of the two armsmen.

A third armsman followed, holding an arm as if to staunch blood from a slash to the biceps.

"Frig . . . your sorceress . . . Frig all you . . ." yelled the wounded prisoner as the two armsmen frog-marched

him into the street. "Frig . . . you woman-loving sisters
. . . Frig you all . . ."

"So you will not swear allegiance to the Regency of
Defalk?" Anna asked loudly.

"Frig you!" The man spat toward Anna.

Alvar raised his hand.

"No." Anna dreaded what came next. "When I start
to sing, release him. If he tries to attack you, you may do
as you please." She lifted the lutar, coughed once, and
began to sing and play.

> "Armsman strong, armsman wrong,
>   who would not swear in heart along,
>   be cloaked in flame, and fire song,
>   be flayed by fire before this
>   throng."

The two armsmen holding the wounded prisoner literally hurled the man to the cobblestones, and had their
blades out before he sprawled on the hard surface. The
man struggled to his knees before the whips of fire began
to lash him.

Standing by the door, the innkeeper turned and retched
in the general direction of the open sewer.

As the fire died away, Anna swallowed hard as she
looked at the heap of charcoaled meat and ashes, smelling
the odor of burning flesh. She turned in the saddle to the
other two armsmen. "As I found you now, should you
ever turn against Defalk, you can be found again." She
waited. "Do you swear allegiance—"

Even before she had finished, both men were on the
cobblestones, on their knees, mumbling, "We swear by
all the harmonies, by anything you wish . . ."

"We accept your allegiance." She turned to Alvar.
"Have them taken to the palace and sworn into that special guard Hanfor is forming."

The special guard was designed to patrol areas, such as

the port, where, hopefully, they would reduce theft . . .
and could be watched, halfway. *You hope.* . . .

The whispers from behind shutters rose momentarily.

". . . see why . . ."

". . . wouldn't want to cross her . . ."

". . . glad she's leaving us alone . . ."

Anna hoped all those ideas reached throughout the people. She turned to Liende. "We'll need the seeking spell
again."

"Here?"

"Why not?" The basic theory of Clearsong was known
to everyone. It wasn't the idea that was difficult—just the
execution. At that thought, her eyes went to the charcoaled body.

"The body?" asked Alvar.

Anna steeled herself and said forcefully, so that her
voice would carry, "Leave it. Leave it so all know the
price of disloyalty."

"Yes, Regent." Alvar squared his shoulders, then
shouted, "Leave this carrion so all will know the price
for disloyalty."

"The seeking spell," Anna repeated, looking toward
Liende.

"Yes, Regent."

Anna turned in the saddle, but Jecks already was unfastening the traveling mirror.

Another spell . . . another hiding armsman, or deserter—
or fanatic. She hoped there weren't too many of the latter.
With a deep breath, a calm smile plastered on her face,
she waited.

113

After laying her spell file on the antique writing desk and setting the lutar on top of the shorter bookcase, Anna paused and glanced in the wall mirror of Ehara's private study, which she'd commandeered as a conference and workroom.

Despite a bath, a good night's sleep, and an enormous breakfast of eggs, fried ham slabs, cheese and bread, the woman who looked back at her hardly looked feminine at all—an angular and thin face, hard blue eyes, tanned skin rougher than was fashionable anywhere, and a firmly set jaw. Even the short blonde hair could have passed for masculine.

She shook her head, and her reflection did also. After another look at the reflection she found hard to believe, she turned, walked past the low bookcases, and sank into the chair behind the desk, waiting for Jecks to join her. She remained tired.

Nearly a dozen seeking spells had dragged her and half the armsmen all over Dumaria the afternoon before—and they'd discovered a score of armsmen—half of whom were wounded. Three had tried to attack . . . one way or another, and there were three charcoaled bodies lying in the streets of Dumaria. The others—shamefaced—had just pledged loyalty to Anna, and were being "reeducated" toward greater loyalty to Defalk, along with being required to serve in the special armsmen—paid slightly more generously than the locals had been.

And that pay may bind them . . . maybe . . .

Even so, after the long ride to Dumaria, the spells had exhausted her, and wiped out the players. Liende had been staggering, and Delvor and Yuarl had collapsed halfway through the last spellsong. For now, Dumaria was officially loyal to Defalk, and the Regency.

Anna permitted herself a slight smile. Even if Ehara did elude her, even if something happened to her, the Lord of Dumar would find his capital city and much of northeastern Dumar subdued for years, and certainly wary of Defalk. *Not for years . . . people here are as shortsighted as anywhere.*

Anna ran her fingers across the slightly dusty surface of the dark wooden writing table. The mantel of the oil lamp was sooty, as though Ehara had spent many late nights in his study. Perhaps he had.

Slowly, she took out the spell file. She needed to work out in final form the ideas she had for destroying enchanted weapons. The spell probably had to be through-composed, with no repeating words or music, and more complex.

The sorceress was finishing the last lines when Jecks peered in the door.

"Come on in." She slipped the spell into the folder. She'd need to work on that later.

"You look more rested," he said, sitting down in one of the straight-backed chairs set at an angle to the writing table.

"I couldn't have looked less rested than last night," she pointed out. "I'm still tired."

"You essay making Dumar part of Defalk in weeks. For most rulers it would take years."

"We don't have months or years. We may not even have weeks. Lord knows, I mean—the harmonies only know what's going on in Defalk." She focused on him. "We have been sending scrolls chronicling our great victories, haven't we?"

"We have. So long as you report victories, little will happen."

"But we don't know for sure—even with my scrying. We haven't seen one scroll from Falcor."

"No . . . that is the difficulty with extended campaigns." Jecks offered a bland smile. "With those in Defalk, all should be well."

"But we don't know."

"No."

"Everyone loves a winner. Let's hope that's enough." She paused. "You checked Ehara's treasury?"

"There is little enough there—a few thousand golds, probably what he could not take with him. Mysara—he is the chief bookkeeper, like Dythya is—he said that Ehara rode off with two large chests. He thought there were two thousand golds in each."

"Dumar is going to pay for this war." Anna shook her head. "But I can't take everything, or it will make things worse."

"Mayhap we can recover the golds."

"I don't think we can count on that."

"The lady Siobion," announced Fhurgen from the study door. "At your request."

Both Jecks and Anna stood.

The slender brunette stepped into the study and bowed. "What would you have of me?"

"Your loyalty," Anna said bluntly after Fhurgen had closed the study door. "Defalk deserves that at least. Your consort fomented rebellion in my land."

"What matters my loyalty now? My consort flees you, and you will kill him." A sad smile crossed Siobion's thin lips. "And us, at your pleasure, no matter what you promise now."

Anna wanted to shake her head. "Please sit down."

Siobion eased into the chair directly across the writing table from Anna, her eyes flicking toward Jecks, then back to Anna, who seated herself.

Jecks sat last, with a quirk of his lips, as though at some unspoken jest.

"I probably will kill your consort if he remains in Dumar, if I possibly can," answered Anna. "But someone has to rule this place, and I'm not interested in creating

some sort of empire," Anna said. "First, even if I were,
it wouldn't last. Those things don't. Second, what's the
point?" *We can maybe get Jimbob to be a good ruler of
Defalk, but an empire would be too much, especially if he
takes power young.*

"Do not jest with me . . . I beg of you." Siobion's
voice was thin, but firm.

"Lady Siobion, I don't jest or joke."

"Many have discovered that, to their rue," added
Jecks.

"I really want to clean up this mess in Dumar and go
home."

"Did you not create . . . this mess?"

Anna admired the woman's spunk, but not her naiveté.
"Not until your consort started funding rebellions and
sending lancers into Defalk." The sorceress squared her
shoulders. "Which child of yours is most fit to be Lord
of Dumar?"

Siobion pursed her lips, remaining mute.

With a sigh, Anna stood and walked to the bookcase,
reclaiming the lutar and tuning it as she stood there. "Do
you want me to enchant your will? Or just drag in all
your children?"

Siobion's eyes widened. "You cannot drag in Haeron.
He is with his sire."

"Then he will probably die," Anna said coolly. "Do
you wish to tell me . . ." She turned to Jecks. "Have the
remaining children brought in."

"No . . ." After a moment, Siobion stammered, tears
running from her cheeks. "Clehar. He is strong, and he
is just."

"You're not doing that to save another?"

"No . . ." Siobion's voice was low. "Byon is but six,
and Feharn five, and Eryhal is still in the cradle."

Anna set the lutar on the thin-planked floor beside the
table leg, then looked at Jecks.

The white-haired lord stood and walked to the door,

opening it. "Rickel, have Clehar, the son of Lord Ehara, brought here, if you would."

"Yes, ser."

Jecks closed the door and took his seat again.

"No . . ." sobbed Siobion. "No . . . he has done little wrong. Spare him. . . . Please spare him."

Anna looked coldly across the writing table, knowing she must appear a total bitch. She almost didn't care; no one ever seemed to want to take her at face value, and it didn't seem as though that would change anytime soon. "Lady Siobion, you're assuming I'm like your consort. I'm not. There's no point in my talking about it, though. No one believes me."

Anna seated herself to wait.

Siobion fidgeted ever so slightly in the chair.

"Young Lord Clehar," Fhurgen announced, escorting the youth into the room.

Clehar was thin like his mother, but dark-haired like his father, and looked to be slightly younger than Jimbob—eleven or twelve, Anna judged. He stood just in front of his mother's shoulder, his thin lips like his mother's, set tight.

Anna rose and looked at the two. "Try to listen. Try to understand what I am telling you. Even when three lords rebelled against me in Defalk, I did not kill the heirs. The only lands I took were those of one who died without heirs—and his offspring died long before I ever came to Liedwahr. You can believe me or not, but it is true." Anna paused, wondering if anything she said penetrated.

"I sent your consort a scroll, Lady Siobion. I asked for peace between our lands and a thousand golds in payment for the unrest he created in sending armsmen of Dumar into Defalk. Your consort mocked me, and demanded golds of me. I blocked the river, and requested peace and the thousand golds. He refused that. The river destroyed much of Dumaria and Narial, and your consort still refused peace. What choice did I have? To let him continue to send armsmen into my land? I would not have it, and

I will not.'' Anna's eyes hardened, and she fixed the bru-nette with them. ''You will be loyal to me and Defalk, and you may rule as regent for your son until he is of age.

''Now. It's very simple, Lady Siobion. You are the Lady Regent of Dumar. You will administer Dumar, with the assistance of whoever I name as your chief armsman. You will also pay for the cost of my coming into Dumar. Once those costs are paid off, you owe Defalk nothing except free and open trade, and resistance to all invaders. And, of course, the continued appointment of whoever the Regency chooses as your chief armsman. We do expect formal friendship. I doubt that any of us will remain too fondly in your thoughts, but blame that on your consort.''

''You jest. . . .'' Siobion's tone was uncertain, for the first time.

''I don't jest. I never have. All I'm interested in is keep-ing Defalk strong and independent and keeping the dis-sonant Sea-Priests out of Liedwahr.'' Anna paused. ''And probably keeping the Liedfuhr out of any place he isn't already.''

''You do not intend to make an example of . . . us?''

''Why?'' Anna asked. ''All that would do would be to make people mad and wanting to hate Defalk more, es-pecially later. Some already hate me for the flood, but that was your consort's fault, not that any good Dumaran would wish to believe that.'' She took a deep breath. ''If I killed you all, then I'd have to figure out how to govern Dumar, and I'd be spending more time here than in Fal-cor. It's your land. You can run it. You just have to be loyal to Defalk, and since we don't really want a war, and you can't . . .'' Anna laughed, not quite harshly. ''. . . Why, things should work out.''

''How can you trust . . . ?'' asked Siobion.

''I can raise enough of a flood to make the last one look like an afternoon rainstorm. Do you want all your main towns and cities washed away again?''

Siobion looked down. ''You will not live forever.''

"No. I won't. But I hope by then everyone will figure out that peace is easier . . . and more profitable."

Siobion frowned. "Do you think to stop the Sea-Priests?"

"I don't have to," Anna pointed out. "You do."

Siobion paled. "You are cruel."

"I'll help, as I can. But would you rather spend the rest of your life in chains, the way the Sturinnese women do?" asked Anna.

"You . . . leave few choices."

"Your consort left me none," Anna said quietly. *Did you really have to invade Dumar . . . or are you rationalizing again?* "Not if Defalk were to remain independent for long."

Jecks nodded at Anna, and she realized she'd said enough, possibly more than enough.

The sorceress stood. "You may go."

"By your leave, Regent?" asked Siobion. Her hand touched Clehar's shoulder.

"By your leave?" echoed the dark-haired Clehar.

Anna nodded, watching as the two walked to the study door, opened it, and slipped from sight.

"Did I say too much?" the sorceress asked once Fhurgen again closed the door firmly.

"I would not say such. There was no need to say more."

"I'm becoming such a bitch," Anna mused. "I don't like it."

"As you said, my lady, the harmonies have left you little choice. As you also made most clear to me. . . ." Jecks' voice was warm, sympathetic, and Anna wished— for a moment—that he would just hold her. Not long before, she'd wanted to clout him. Would it always be like that?

"Damn . . . dissonantly little," she agreed. "Tomorrow, we'd better start after Ehara. The mirror says he's moving slowly, but it'll still take nearly a week to catch him. I just want this to be over."

Jecks frowned momentarily.

"Are you saying it won't ever be over?"

"I had thought to enjoy my lands once Alasia consorted with Barjim." Jecks offered a wry smile. "Now I accompany a warrior sorceress and consider myself lucky to have survived."

"I've never been *that* angry at you," Anna said with a grin.

"There have been times . . ." Jecks' voice was ironically rueful.

They laughed, and Anna enjoyed the laughter, pushing away thoughts of the morrow . . . and those to follow.

114

Another hot and sweaty afternoon on the road in Dumar, and Anna wondered why she'd even bothered to get her riding clothes clean in Dumaria. Two days on the road in the humid summer air of Dumar, and one of her two sets of trousers and shirts already smelled like she'd spent weeks in it.

The Envar River, smaller even than the Chean in Defalk east of Sorprat, where Anna had yet to rebuild the ford, lay on the south side of the road from Dumaria to Envaryl. The ever-present sheep kept the brush low, and only scattered trees dotted the water course. The land was almost flat, with the stretched-out hills no more than a few yards higher than the river bed. Even to the northwest, where Envaryl lay three more days over the horizon at the base of the southern Mittfels, according to both maps and glass, the land extended in the same featureless flat plain to the horizon.

Anna leaned forward in the saddle and patted Farinelli on the shoulder. "You're a good fellow."

The gelding continued at an even pace, as if to indicate that, of course, he was, and there was no point in acknowledging such fatuous praise.

The road contained the hoofprints of Ehara's fleeing forces, the only evidence of life along the road, except in the towns, with their boarded doors and shuttered windows.

"What would happen if Ehara escaped us and returned?" she asked. "Would people follow him as readily?"

"No," said Jecks, "but it would be better that he—and the heir with him—not escape. Fewer still would cross you."

"Oh? The sorceress who never relents? Who will destroy every hostile armsman in order to enslave an entire land?"

Jecks laughed. "Can you imagine a better reputation in Liedwahr? Do you think Sargol would have spurned your rule had he seen what you have done?"

"Probably not," the sorceress admitted. "But it's force again. Not reason, not intelligence, just force."

"Since when has it been otherwise, my lady?" Jecks offered both a smile and raised eyebrows.

Anna couldn't offer any rebuttal to what was clearly a rhetorical question—either in Liedwahr or on earth. "You're right, but I don't have to like it. I can try to change it." *How? By using more force through sorcery?* Her own self-inquiries reminded her that she still had to deal with her conscience, and the nagging questions it prompted.

"Am I relying on sorcery so much that when we leave Dumar no one will even consider remaining loyal?"

"Once . . . once . . ." Jecks pulled at his chin. "Once I might have thought that. Now . . . thousands of the finest armsmen of Sturinn and Dumar lie dead. Now . . . much of Dumaria and all of Narial lie in ruins. A huge stone bridge spans the Falche, one that would doubtless withstand even another flood you sent forth. The Lord of Dumar flees you, and all have seen your armsmen. And no armsmen remain where you have been save as are loyal to you.''

"At least in name," she added.

"I doubt that many will forget you." He smiled, half sadly. "Or cross you.''

"But Jimbob will have problems?"

"Each generation must solve its own. You have given him the chance.''

Anna's eyes went to the gray dek-stone on the right shoulder of the road, its lower part obscured by grass. As Farinelli carried her closer, she could make out the words: Jusuul—3-d.

Anna glanced from the gray stone along the flat road toward the hamlet ahead, a gathering of several dozen roofs in the hazy afternoon. Behind her, the players began to talk more loudly.

"... how many towns are there?"

"Dissonance ... another town, another seeking spell ..."

Anna recognized Delvor's voice, and she turned in the saddle and called, "Liende ... would you explain to Delvor that if we find people disloyal to Defalk before they find us, they aren't likely to fill him with arrows?"

A low laugh ran through the guards, and a broad grin crossed Rickel's face.

"Hanfor?" Anna gestured.

"Companies ... halt!"

She guided Farinelli back to Liende, offering an ironic smile. "Chief player ... we will need another seeking spell.''

"I had thought as much, Regent, and we will be ready." Liende offered a crooked smile, and raised her voice slightly. "Even young Delvor will play his best."

Delvor flushed, and subdued smiles and chuckles crossed the faces of the mounted players.

After the column slowed and stopped, Anna and the players dismounted, performing the all-too-familiar procedure with the scrying glass.

> "Show from Dumar, danger to fear,
>   all the threats to me bright and clear . . ."

The mirror flickered through a series of images, but Anna could not discern a one because one image replaced another so quickly.

"There's a danger ahead . . . but I can't tell what it is." Anna pursed her lips.

"The Sea-Priest?"

"Might be."

She tried again, using the same spell, except with the name Jusuul in place of Dumar. The mirror remained clear, showing no danger.

Then came the armsman-seeking spell—but Jusuul harbored no armsmen.

Anna glanced along the flat road toward the roofs of the town ahead. "There's no problem here, anyway."

"That cheers me not greatly, my lady."

It didn't cheer Anna exactly, either, especially since the danger spell had shown nothing when they had passed through the three other river towns earlier in the day.

"Does the enchantment hold on the small shield?" Jecks asked.

"It's still there." Anna could sense the slight drain on her strength, but that was a small cost. Jecks' idea had already saved her life once. She wondered if the shield, and the additional spells she'd developed, at his insistence, would be enough. *Nothing's ever enough.*

"Thank you, chief player . . . all of you," Anna said, with a nod of acknowledgement before turning and walking back to where Rickel held Farinelli's reins. She remounted the big gelding quickly.

"We stop for provisions here?" asked Hanfor.

"It's small, but there might be something," Anna

agreed, reaching for her water bottle to moisten her throat before she had to sing again.

Rain, humidity, heat, dust, rain, humidity, with seeking spells every few glasses, and never a sight of the fleeing Ehara—the pattern seemed unending, yet she'd only been doing it for a few weeks. At the same time, she couldn't help worrying about what might be occurring in Defalk—even though she could do nothing at all about it.

No . . . she wasn't cut out to be a horse-warrior and a conqueror. Definitely not.

She took a long swallow from the water bottle as the Defalkan forces resumed their advance on small Jusuul.

115

By midmorning of the fourth day on the road out of Dumaria, Anna was sweating profusely, her shirt glued to her back, the band of her floppy felt hat sodden with perspiration, and driblets of sweat running down the back of her neck.

The afternoon and evening rains had done little more than damp the road dust and raise the humidity, so that the sorceress felt she were riding through a steambath. Farinelli swished his tail almost constantly, trying to hold off the continual swarms of small white flies that buzzed around all the horses—and stung.

Because of the profusion of towns, and the delays involved in using spells to seek out any recalcitrant armsmen—and they'd discovered but a handful, Envaryl remained at least another two days away. What bothered Anna even more than the effort involved was the realization that she was reaching but a fraction of the people, just enough to ensure the safety of her forces, and that only so long as Ehara remained on the run. And, of course, it delayed her return to Defalk and multiplied the problems arising there that she'd have to resolve. Still, she was instilling the idea in the Dumarans that it was hard to hide from the sorceress. *Great. . . . More fear. . . . Machiavelli would have loved it.*

She shook her head and glanced to her left. The Envar River had shrunk to little more than a stream not more than ten yards wide and only a few yards deep. Beyond the river to the south stretched deks of fields filled with knee-high plants, beans, wheat, or corn, as it was called in Liedwahr, and oilseeds of some sort.

Anna's stomach tightened, and she found herself gripping the leather of the reins so hard that her hands had begun to ache. Finally, she spoke. "I need to use the glass."

Riding on her right, Jecks nodded.

"Hanfor," Anna continued, "I need to stop and see what Ehara's doing."

As Alvar and Hanfor brought the force to an orderly and now well-rehearsed stop, Liende rode up beside the sorceress. "Have you need of us, Lady?"

"No . . . actually, yes, thank you." Anna forced a smile she definitely didn't feel. "I'm just looking, but it would help—if it won't tire you too much. I'll need you all when we catch up with Lord Ehara."

"We could do a spell now and still stand ready."

"Thank you." Anna dismounted, unwrapped the traveling scrying glass and took a deep breath as she waited for the players to tune, afraid of what the glass might show. Jecks and Hanfor had also dismounted and stood only slightly back of her as she prepared to sing the spell. Anna's guards held the reins of the three mounts.

She glanced at the mirror where it lay on the lush grass that seemed to grow everywhere in western Dumar, then cleared her throat. When the players began, so did she.

"Mirror, mirror on the ground,
  show me where Ehara's forces may be found . . ."

The image in the glass was clear. The Dumaran forces neared a small town.

"That must be Hasjyl . . . if the maps are correct," murmured Hanfor.

Anna squinted as she tried to recall the maps she had pored over. Hasjyl—less than a day's ride from Envaryl, the last sizable town in the west of Dumar before the southern rim of the Westfels, or was it the western end of the Mittfels? The two ranges intersected north of Envaryl, and geography, Anna was discovering, was even less precise in Liedwahr than it had been in Iowa where to her, one cornfield, one low hill, had pretty much resembled another.

She released the image quickly. Jecks handed her a water bottle—her own orderspelled water—even that spell took effort. But everything in a military campaign cost, she'd discovered.

"He will try to fortify Envaryl—or plot some trap there," predicted the white-haired lord. "Or before we reach there."

Anna nodded, wondering why she bridled so much every time Jecks offered some totally obvious observation. She handed back the bottle and wearily lifted the lutar once more.

"Show from Dumar, danger to fear,
    all the threats to me bright and clear . . ."

The mirror flickered through a series of images, but Anna could not discern a one because one image replaced another so quickly. She canceled that spell even more quickly.

"The same danger ahead . . . but I can't tell what it is." Anna pursed her lips.

"Can you call an image of the Sea-Priest?"

This time she used a variant of the mirror spell.

"Show from the Sea-Priest, danger to fear . . ."

The image of the Sea-Priest was clear enough, but it showed little beside the man's face—and the burns across it, one almost festering, and the hatred in the dark eyes. Those—and the background of fields—or perhaps long grass.

"That one—he will kill you any way that he might," said Jecks.

Anna could see that, but it didn't help when she couldn't formulate spells precisely enough to determine where the sorcerer was or what he had in mind.

She tried a last spell, the danger spell, using the town name of Hasjyl in place of Dumar. The mirror remained clear. The sorceress lowered the lutar and glanced along the flat road toward the roofs of the town ahead. "There's no problem there, anyway."

"I am not greatly cheered, my lady Anna," Jecks said wryly.

Neither was Anna. Every time she had used the general danger spell, she'd gotten the flickering response, but it had shown no danger in any of the river towns through which they had passed. There was danger, but she couldn't find it. Or didn't know how. Or the Sea-Priest had a way of hiding it from her. Or . . .

Tiredly, she replaced the lutar in its case, while Jecks rewrapped the mirror.

"We continue, Lady Anna?" asked Hanfor.

"Until we find Ehara," she answered. "Until we can end this mess." She climbed into the saddle, then wiped away more sweat. She flicked the reins gently, and Farinelli started forward.

Once the column was moving, she reached for the water bottle. Another swallow of lukewarm water helped, but she still sweated in the midafternoon sun. To the west, the afternoon clouds were building for the storm that would ensure the next day would be another steambath.

116

Anna rubbed her eyes. Although it was well after dawn, and she had munched through bread and cheese, the standard travel breakfast, she still felt groggy. Not enough sleep? Worrying too much? Coffee would have helped, but coffee, or anything drinkable with the same effect, wasn't one of the plants known in Liedwahr. Brill had brewed a bitter evergreen tea, so bitter that one or two sips on those first hot days in Loiseau had convinced Anna that she was better off without it. Her stomach was dubious enough about the morning without the kind of jolt provided by Brill's bitter yellow tea. Cider, hot or cold, wasn't much better first thing in the morning.

She licked a stray bread crumb from her lips, tired of stale bread and cheese, and looked down at the mirror on its leather wrappings. Then she began her morning spell-scrying.

Despite three different spells, the mirror showed nothing new. Ehara had almost reached Envaryl, from what she could tell, and the Sea-Priest was next to the Envar—somewhere—but the images of scenes that posed possible danger continued to shift so rapidly that she could tell nothing.

After rewrapping the traveling mirror and recasing the lutar, she slipped the heavy blanket onto Farinelli, and then the saddle.

Whufff...

"I know. It's early. Tell me."

Farinelli declined the opportunity, and Anna cinched the girths, then patted the gelding's shoulder.

"Another long day." She looked westward, along the river road, though the Envar was now more like a stream.

Clearsong hung just above the western horizon—the smallest dot of light as the pink haze of sunrise flooded into orange before the sky turned pale blue.

Anna looked at the disc of the small moon, searching for the smaller, redder point of light that would be Darksong and not finding it. She'd never really even followed earth's moon. How did she expect to follow the motions of the two moons of Erde?

As Hanfor rode up, signaling that the armsmen were ready, so did Liende. Jecks led his mount toward her and Farinelli.

"Players are mounted and ready, Lady Anna," said the chief player.

"Thank you." Anna mounted easily, but slowly, as did Jecks.

Fhurgen and Rickel slipped their mounts in front of the sorceress. Jecks rode on her right. To the left, the Envar glittered silver in the postdawn light.

Anna rode silently for nearly a glass, trying not to yawn overmuch, as the column continued on the damp clay of the road. The humidity already had her sweating, but the rains had kept the dust down—one advantage. She didn't itch from the red grit of eastern Dumar and the Sudbergs. The disadvantage was that by midmorning she'd itch from the salt of her own sweat.

"We should reach Hasjyl by noon," Jecks said, breaking the long silence. "Perhaps we should rest there."

"Before getting too close to Envaryl?" Anna yawned. Lord, she was tired. The way she felt, she'd need some sort of rest.

"I would not wish that we face Lord Ehara and his Sea-Priest sorcerer with a tired sorceress and players," answered Jecks. "A day or two more spent in Dumar will not changes matters overly. You will have done the impossible."

"Impossible?" Anna had to laugh at the thought. She

was no horse-warrior, no Genghis Khan or Napoleon—just a very tired woman trying to keep a country of religious chauvinists from getting a foothold in Liedwahr. The Sea-Priests reminded her of Islamic fundamentalists, in a roundabout way, and she'd never been that fond of Islamic men after the year studying in London. "I doubt that anything I've done is impossible."

"We left Stromwer in late spring. It is not yet late summer, and Dumar lies in your grasp. None would have deemed that possible, not even for the Liedfuhr of Mansuur or the Traders of Wei."

"It may not be possible for us. We haven't done it yet."

"And how would anyone undo it?" Jecks laughed. "If you vanished this moment, Ehara would find it impossible to avoid allying himself with Defalk."

"That might be, but the Sturinnese would be back." *With their damned chains . . . .* Anna couldn't help it. She still saw red when she thought of women in chains—even the so-called chains of adornment.

Her eyes flicked ahead and to the left, down toward the river. Less than a hundred yards away, a section of the knee-high grass bordering the river seemed to shimmer. Anna rubbed her eyes, then blinked. The whole area seemed out of focus. Dissonance! Was she that tired?

Her stomach tightened and she twisted in the saddle, fumbling for the lutar, even as she yelled, "The Sea-Priest! By the river!"

A low screaming, thrumming sound shivered the ground, like drums being beaten so fast that the individual impacts and their resonance blended into a seamless percussive texture, a strange form of homophony. *But you can't do that with drums . . . Brill said . . . .* Yet Brill had died. Drum homophony? What else would she find out too late?

Anna yanked the lutar from the case, her fingers curling over the strings as her other hand positioned itself on the instrument's neck.

Streaks of gray light flashed from the flickering silver and green, angling straight toward Anna.

The sorceress found her mouth open, trying to find a spell, as the small round shield flew from its holder up toward the first screaming streak of gray. Javelin and shield crashed into the clay of the road.

Anna jerked her head left toward the second streak, just in time to see Jecks half throw himself into the vibrating line of fire—or steel. Lord and javelin smashed toward the road with a dull thudding sound.

The third streak ended in another thud and rattling as Fhurgen seemed to wrestle the third javelin away from Anna, buried as it was through his ribs and breastplate.

Anna coughed, looking down as the heavy iron-headed weapon buried in her defensive shield inched across the clay, still creeping toward her.

From out of the tall grass sprang a tall figure in soiled white, climbing onto a mount once concealed by some manner of sorcery. The horse scrambled up the riverbank and onto the road, headed westward.

Alvar raised a blade, and spurred his mount into a charge, followed by a full squad of Defalkan armsmen.

Trying to ignore the fleeing sorcerer, Anna forced herself to concentrate . . . to concentrate on the spell she had worked out because Jecks had insisted. Her fingers touched the strings of the lutar.

"Weapons of sorcery, weapons of night,
hidden by spells and away from Clearsong . . .
your powers rebound to your speller so strong
with double the power and double the might . . .
Burn into dust and sear unto ashes and light . . ."

The interlocked half-couplet scheme was supposed to make it stronger . . . would it? Anna wondered as she sang, but forced her voice into the spell, forced herself to finish it, slamming home the last note with all the power she had.

Then she vaulted from Farinelli, half noting the scream and the column of flame that flared from the road ahead. She stumbled, but did not fall as she dropped to her knees beside Jecks, where Liende already worked with a cloth to stanch the blood. The javelin had vanished, the result of Anna's spell. She only hoped that the spell hadn't made the wound worse.

Jecks' face was pale, whiter than his hair, and his breath was light and ragged.

Liende looked at Anna.

The sorceress bolted to her feet, fingers on the strings of the lutar. She had hoped never to use the song, but the words were burned in her mind, from another time, another battle, and she could only improvise quickly, hoping she would be quick enough, and sure enough.

> "... always strong, as though young,
> spells always cleanly sung,
> back from danger, bring him life,
> ... through all strife ..."

Again, she had to struggle to keep her voice open, free, against all the strains pressing in on her, ignoring the press of horses, and the clamor of voices—all pushed away as she finished the Darksong spell.

Strophic Darksong ....

Around her, strange chords were reverberating in a pattern of polyphony she couldn't quite grasp. *But polyphony is a pattern ... or is it a texture? You should know ....*

"Too much ..." That was what she thought someone said.

Above her, despite the scattered puffy white clouds, the sky shimmered silver and black, alternating like a strobe light, the black quickly predominating, the silver vanishing, as the sky turned the jet of night around her.

"The lutar ..."

Her fingers were as numb as her mind as she tumbled forward into the darkness, the darkness of Darksong.

When Anna woke, lying on her cot, Liende was sitting beside her on a stool—rather, two images of Liende were, no matter how hard Anna squinted. The chief player's white-streaked red hair was tangled, almost matted, and dark circles ringed Liende's eyes, but the player smiled faintly.

"Jecks . . . ?" Anna rasped.

Liende extended a water bottle, and Anna fumbled for it, eyes unable to gauge the distance, before she drank gratefully.

"He will live. It will be seasons before he lifts a blade."

Anna nodded. She tried to lift her head, but lay back when dissonant bass chords slammed through her skull, rippling the double images of tent silk overhead.

"You stopped breathing," Liende said, her tone matter-of-fact. "I had to move your chest."

"Thank you." Anna blinked. Her eyes burned. "I'm sorry. It didn't seem right. . . . Now, I've messed up everything."

"That is not so." Liende shook her head. "Your armsmen respect you for saving him—and for destroying the Sea-Priest. Your players are resting, and Ehara still remains behind the walls of Envaryl."

Anna took another swallow of water. The dissonant chords assaulting her subsided, slightly, but the two images remained.

"Fhurgen?"

Liende glanced down, confirming what Anna had already felt.

Yet what else could she have done?

"He was dead . . . almost before you dismounted."

Anna wanted to shake her head. Even before she had been regent, the big black-bearded guard had looked out for her. Then . . . Jecks had been looking out for her as well.

"Darksong is dangerous." Liende paused. "Do you love Lord Jecks?"

"Sometimes I think so. Sometimes, I don't know."
*There's so much I don't know . . . been so little time . . .
so much to do . . . .*

Liende smiled more broadly. "There is a saying about
actions revealing the heart."

*Do you love Jecks? Because he has stood by you. Or
for more? Or are you desperate? That desperate?*

Before Anna could think more, her eyes closed.

117

Struggling against the faint double images that still
cloaked her sight after more than four days, Anna
stood in the doorway and looked from the sleeping white-
haired figure in the bed to the chief player, and then to
the guard at the door.

"He sleeps more easily," said Liende. "There is no
fever. The wound is clean. Your elixir, it kept out the
poisons." Her lips pursed. "And your spells."

Anna sometimes wondered if her greatest legacy might
not be distilled alcohol, rather than anything else. She
glanced back to Jecks. "I still worry about leaving him
here in Hasjyl. The javelin ripped up his chest and shoulder badly." Would she have had the courage to take enchanted javelins meant for someone else? She hoped she
could have been so brave, but she doubted she had that
kind of courage. She was a survivor, not a hero.

She'd been lucky to be able to cast a Darksong spell
without being totally destroyed, as she had been at Stromwer. Then, the spell over Jecks had been limited to one
person at close range, probably before there had been too
much damage from the wound. Even so, it would be more

than a week before she was fully recovered, she suspected.

"You have spell-searched the town, and left twoscore of armsmen to guard him. He should not be moved until he is better, a few days, at least," Liende pointed out. "Once you finish Lord Ehara, you can watch over Lord Jecks on the return to Dumaria."

"I know, and I can't let Ehara get away," Anna said. "I don't have to like it." How many times over how many years had she thought those words? *You have to do it, but you don't have to like it . . . .* Was that always the way it would be?

Jecks' eyes fluttered, then opened. Anna stepped nearer the bed.

"You . . . are . . . here. . . ." The raspiness of Jecks' voice tore at her.

Where was the strong leading man? The man who had taken a javelin meant for her?

He's right there, you idiot . . . .

"I'm here," she said quietly. "You'll be fine, but you need to rest."

"You . . . saved . . . me."

"You saved me. You did a better job," Anna said.

"The . . . Sea-Priest. . . ."

"Lady Anna turned him into flame with her anger," interjected Liende.

"Fhurgen . . . ?"

Anna looked down at the stone floors she'd insisted be washed before moving Jecks into the house she'd borrowed—or commandeered.

"He was dead before Lady Anna could even begin a spell," said Liende.

Anna wasn't sure that was so, but she'd only had the chance to save one of them, and she'd made a choice.

"He . . . good . . . man."

"Just rest," Anna urged.

Jecks' eyes closed slowly, almost unwillingly, and Anna stroked his forehead for a moment.

"Just rest," she repeated softly before straightening,

carefully, hoping that the double images and semi-migraine headache would fade before she reached Envaryl, hoping, as always, that she did the right thing—and fearing she wouldn't.

118

ENVARYL, DUMAR

E hara paces across the room, at ten yards long and half that in width, large for the trading town. He goes to the third-story window and peers out from between shutters bleached white by sun and lack of oil at the gently rolling hills, dotted with irregular shadows cast from the scattered summer clouds.

Beyond the low yellow-brick walls less than a hundred yards from the window, nothing moves in the meadows and empty fields. A handful of armsmen walk the walls. Several carry bows already strung.

Two lancers in the crimson of Dumar ride to the front of the building, the trader's mansion the Lord of Dumar has commandeered. Ehara straightens his tunic, brushes back his dark hair and waits.

At the single *thrap* on the door, he coughs, then answers. "Come in."

The stocky lancer officer enters and bows. "The scouts have just returned, sire."

Ehara waits.

"The sorceress's forces have passed through Hasjyl, Lord Ehara." The lancer officer bows again. "They ride toward the walls of Envaryl."

"Does she ride with them?"

"They bear the banner with the crossed spears. They would not ride westward, save she were directing them."

Ehara nods reluctantly. "I had thought for a time, when

the sorceress stopped short of Hasjyl, that the Sea-Priest had succeeded.''

"None have seen him. A shepherd from Hasjyl said that harmony and dissonance clashed six morns ago, and that the ground shook." The lancer adds apologetically, "That was all he could say, sire."

"More like dissonance and dissonance," mutters Ehara. He looks at the lancer. "Thank you. Would you have Captain Fional join me?"

"Yes, sire."

Even before the door is fully closed, the dark-bearded Lord of Dumar returns to the window, gazing eastward. "Who would have thought it? One sorceress, and all of Liedwahr turned upside-down. A harmless ploy to gain territory in Defalk, and she invades Dumar. A mere attempt to kill her, and she pursues me like a harpy of dissonance. I have nowhere to turn, nowhere to go—nor does my son and heir. If I confront her directly, I will be turned to flames or spitted with arrows like a stag. If I die on the field against her, I honor her, and that I will not do . . . not now. For that, for that she must wait." He shakes his head. "So little I have left. So little that I must content myself with making a sorceress wait. So little. . . . She does not understand Liedwahr, and we all will suffer." Ehara laughs, a sound bitter and booming simultaneously, a roaring that fills the room for but a moment. "I will suffer most of all."

119

Anna reined up on the low hillside to the southeast of the yellow-brick walls of Envaryl, walls that still lay more than a dek westward. In the seven days it had taken her to recover from the aftereffects of the Darksong used to save Jecks and to move her forces to within ten deks of Envaryl, Ehara had kept all his troops inside those yellow-brick walls.

As Farinelli tossed his head gently, Anna's hand dropped to the open-topped shield carrier and the re-spelled round shield that had saved her life twice so far—and had failed to save Fhurgen or to protect Jecks. She couldn't even make a gesture for Fhurgen, not even with cold gold. The black-bearded guard had never told anyone where he had come from, not even the most seasoned veterans from the volunteers who had followed Hanfor from the Prophet's service to Anna's. What had he fled from? And from where? She shook her head.

Alvar reined up on her right, Hanfor on her left. Rickel and Lejun eased their mounts forward of Anna, the protective shields up and ready. To her right, south of the rise, the river road wound along the Envar River for close to half a dek before turning more northward toward the main gates—those on the south wall. The heavy wooden gates were closed, and the crimson banner of Ehara flew from the right-hand gate tower.

From what Anna had found from her previous work with the scrying glass, Envaryl was enclosed by a pentagon of yellow-brick walls, each side roughly a dek in length. The town was one of the few walled ones in Dumar, possibly because it was an old town, and the western entrance to Dumar from both Mansuur and Neserea.

To the north, Anna could barely make out a dark line just above the horizon, the nearest mountains, those where the Mittfels and the Westfels joined to separate Dumar from Neserea.

In the early-morning light, the sorceress could see the length of both the south and the eastern walls, and the watchtowers on three of the five corners, but not any individual figures in the towers or along the walls.

"Quiet for now," observed Alvar. "It was not so yesterday. Watch for a moment."

Anna watched. So did Hanfor, and so, Anna presumed, did the twoscore armsmen behind them.

Shadows from the summer clouds cast slow-moving shadows across the hills, across the empty fields, and the summer grasses that barely bent in the light breeze. Although the air remained damp, Anna appreciated the warm breeze, a relief after so many days of hot and sticky travel.

A movement caught her eye, and she glanced north where two figures sprinted from somewhere behind the corner watchtower away from Envaryl and in the general direction of the distant Mittfels.

"Yesterday was worse," Alvar said from her right. "Jirsit's scouts counted scores of them running away. The armsmen just watched, those that hadn't thrown rags over their uniforms and joined them."

"Ehara's armsmen shoot deserters," Hanfor pointed out. "Jirsit's scouts saw that as well."

"When they see them, ser," answered Alvar. "Or when they are forced to use their bows . . . or crossbows."

Anna gained the definite impression that Alvar disliked crossbows. She wondered what he would have thought of machine guns. "We could wait a day or two, or a week," she suggested, "until Ehara had no armsmen left. Or fewer armsmen."

"Lady Anna," Hanfor said slowly from her left, "I seldom question your thoughts . . ."

"But you do this time," Anna said. "What have I missed?"

Hanfor shifted uneasily in his saddle, turning to face the regent. "Ehara knows he cannot best your sorceries, or even your forces, now. He will wait, because that will make you seem weak and because he knows that you do not wish to use your power against the innocent. So he huddles among the poor folk of Envaryl. If you wish to end this war quickly, you must destroy Envaryl, or you needs must visit and spell-seek each and every hamlet and town in all of Dumar."

Anna refrained from swallowing. Hanfor had always agreed with her strategies to minimize death, carnage, and general mayhem. Now, he was suggesting obliterating a town whose major crime was harboring the former Lord of Dumar.

"Every war must have a battle, preferably a great battle, to mark its end. We cannot hazard a battle, and so we must have great destruction, destruction so great that all in Dumar will understand the folly of crossing the sorceress of Defalk. There must be a single ... destruction ... a monument ... so vast that none can deny your power." Hanfor swallowed. "This I like little, but I have watched and I have listened. Men are not as we would like; they respect but force, and you must supply that force if you are to gain the respect you will need to enforce peace."

As if to punctuate the arms commander's words, a volley of a dozen arrows or so arched out from the walls, falling several hundred yards short of where the three—and Anna's guards—surveyed the town.

Anna looked at the arrows falling harmlessly into the grass, then at Hanfor. "Lord Jecks said that, too, you know. Or something like that."

"Lord Jecks has seen more of those in power than have I, lady. In that, I would respect him."

"I have to respect your judgments, Hanfor, and those of Lord Jecks. I don't like them, but I respect them." *Again ... it's back to force, violence, power. Not reason, not common sense, not decency ... but power ... force of arms, force of sorcery. ...*

Anna took another look at Envaryl, then glanced northward, but the pair of refugees had vanished over the low hills. Finally, she nodded curtly. "Fine. Let's get on with it. Summon the players. Ehara—and the lords of Dumar—and of Defalk—will learn." *Dissonance, will they learn ... arrogant bastards. If you want force ... you'll see force.*

Hanfor bowed his head.

"I'll need something to eat and drink while the players and the rest of the armsmen gather. We can do it from here. There's no sense in moving close enough for them to hit us with those arrows." She looked from Hanfor to Alvar and back again.

Both veterans looked away from her.

Somehow, the way she felt, it didn't surprise her. She turned Farinelli and rode back down to the depression on the other side of the hill where she dismounted. Rickel and Lejun arrayed the guards around her in a wide circle, deploying two on the hillside above as lookouts or scouts. Neither guard spoke as she handed Lejun Farinelli's reins.

She patted the gelding. At least, he didn't look at her in reproach.

Standing by Farinelli, who had lowered his head to sample the lush grass, she pulled out the provisions bag and searched for some of the less-aged yellow brick cheese they'd picked up in one of the towns along the river road. Had it been Jusuul? Or Pemlirk? Or Genwal? Or another town whose name she hadn't even noted?

She bit into the hard cheese savagely. After several mouthfuls, she broke off a crust of bread, a dry ryelike bread that scattered crumbs everywhere. Two bites of bread, and she had to moisten her mouth with a swallow from the water bottle.

Anna turned as Liende rode up and halted beside Rickel. The sorceress licked her lips of the crumbs and took another swallow of water.

"Good morning, Lady Anna." Liende dismounted, but remained holding her horse's reins when she faced the sorceress.

"Good morning, Liende. Well . . . it's morning, anyway." Anna cleared her throat. "We have work to do."

"Will you wish the flame song, or the armsman-seeking song?"

Anna shook her head. "Today . . . today I will need the battle hymn."

"We have not played that spellsong in weeks, Regent."
Liende's face blanked.

"I know. You can gather your players, and practice for
a time—on the hilltop there." Anna offered a grim smile
as she pointed westward toward the top of the slope she
had ridden down. "I hope it will be the last time we have
to use it." *You hoped that the last time, and here you are
. . . again. How many more times?*

"You are regent, Lady Anna, and we are your players."

"I wish it didn't have to be this way," Anna said. *Does
it? Does it really?* "But Ehara began this war with blood
and treachery." The regent shrugged. "I can't offer him
mercy—nor those who still follow his treachery."

Liende nodded, a nod that was acknowledgment, but
not agreement. "We will make ready."

"Thank you."

"We are your players, lady and regent." Liende inclined her head.

Anna nodded. "You may go."

After Liende remounted, Anna finished the last of the
hard yellow cheese, and the bread. Another swallow from
the water bottle, and she replaced the water bottle and
began to warm up.

"Muueee, mueee . . ."

After three notes, she coughed up some mucus. She
resumed the vocalise, but only for another handful of
notes before her voice cut out. She cleared her throat, and
tried again, pushing back the battered brown felt hat. It
was going to be a long warm-up, not surprisingly, because
she was agitated, and agitation and tenseness didn't help
the asthma that Brill's youth spell hadn't removed either.

Anna felt as though the warm-up had taken her nearly
a glass by the time her cords and throat were clear. She
remounted slowly, her eyes going toward the west, where
the clouds continued to build. Rickel and Lejun eased up
beside her as she rode back to the low hillcrest, the in-

termittent sun falling on her back, nearly a score of mounted guards around her.

At the top of the rise, she slowed, then reined up, her eyes on the walls to the west. Envaryl remained the same, the gates closed, the town apparently still, the crimson banners billowing now and again in the gusting winds. Ehara remained barricaded inside the yellow-brick walls, waiting for the worst, unwilling to surrender, unwilling to flee.

The players, standing on the grass to Anna's right and facing the town, were in the middle of the warm-up song. None looked in Anna's direction.

Hanfor eased his mount beside Anna, and Rickel and Lejun moved forward, their shields up. Anna touched the small ensorcelled shield in the holder by her knee, trying to sense any draw of sorcerous power from her, then straightened in the saddle.

"Arms Commander," she said.

"Lady and Regent."

Hanfor's eyes met hers, and Anna could see the darkness behind them. She wondered if her own eyes held that blackness, and feared that they did, and that the darkness would only increase over the years.

"Lord Ehara will not come forth," Hanfor said quietly. "That would give you honor."

"And if I destroy Envaryl?" she asked. "Will that *dishonor* me and Defalk?"

"No." The arms commander shook his head. "You will triumph by force of might, and all will understand."

Anna wanted to scream in frustration. To save lives she was going to have to butcher a town. To save women from chains, she was going to have to kill some of those same women. *So why should you be different? Military leaders had made those decisions for centuries.* "Because," she murmured under her breath, "I didn't want to be a military leader." *You still chose, and you have to pay.* Lord, she was always paying, and if she said anything out loud . . . well, everyone would think that the regent was self-pitying and self-indulgent.

A low rumble of thunder echoed in from the west, and the breeze stiffened. The crimson banners above the closed south gates of Envaryl flew free in the wind.

To her right, the players started the battle hymn, raggedly at first, and then with greater intensity, as if the stirring music helped focus them.

When they finished, Anna glanced at Hanfor, nodded and rode toward the waiting players.

Liende inclined her head. "We stand ready, Regent."

"Liende, the battle hymn."

"There is a storm nearing . . . Lady Anna." Liende looked at Anna, almost pleading.

"I know, chief player. Have them play the battle song." *There won't be enough left of Envaryl or Ehara to . . . To what? Does it matter?* "It has to be this way." She shook her head. "Just have them ready to play the battle hymn when I signal."

"Yes, Regent." Liende looked down.

With a barely concealed sigh, Anna dismounted and handed Farinelli's reins to one of the newer guards—Junert. The armsman took them without meeting her eyes. The sorceress walked to the open space in front of the players. A drop of rain spattered against Anna's cheek.

Rickel and Lejun already waited, shields and eyes facing the yellow-brick walls of Envaryl. Standing between them in the narrow space pointed toward Ehara's last stronghold, Anna began another vocalise. Between the hill and the yellow-brick walls, the rain intensified, the heavy droplets flattening individual blades of grass in waves.

Anna turned.

"At your command, Regent."

Anna looked toward the doomed town, toward the yellow-brick walls set in green grass, toward the crimson banners that, streaming in the quickening wind, shivered as the rain struck the fabric.

"Ready," Anna said.

"The battle hymn. On my mark . . . Mark!" Liende gave a sharp gesture then turned and lifted her own horn.

With the strains of the music, Anna sang, sang the song she'd hoped never to use again.

"I have sung the glory of the thunder of the sky,
  I am bringing forth the voltage so the bolts of death
    can fly.
  I have loosed the fateful lightning so Ehara's men will
    die.
  My songs will strike them dead.
  Glory, glory, halleluia; glory, glory, halleluia;
  glory, glory, halleluia, my songs will strike them
    dead!"

Out of the darkness came a violent gust of wind that whipped Anna's battered felt hat off her head and into the storm somewhere. She kept singing, ignoring the little voice that said, *It's only a strophic spell . . . only a strophic spell*. She concentrated on a mental image of storms, earthquakes, and lightning—all flattening and annihilating Envaryl and Ehara, turning the town into a wasteland.

"In the terror of the tempest, death is brought between
    the hills,
  with a slashing through the bosom that flattens as it
    kills . . ."

The clouds swirled, their mottled white-and-gray turning night-black well before the end of the spell. The wind's whistle mounted into a howl, and Anna found herself bracing her legs against the force of the wind as she finished the last words.

Flashes of strobelike intensity flickered within the building stormclouds. From out of the clouds over Envaryl white globules fell, hammering at roofs and walls, enormous white projectiles—hail. Hail such as Anna had never seen as she stood, panting, horrified.

The ground itself rumbled, once, twice, and the grass flattened in circular waves rippling away from the walled town. Then, chunks of the brick walls began to tumble, outward, a cascade of bricks fragmenting, exploding, as the walls slumped into heaps of broken and shattered yellow chunks, darkened with the sheets of rain that swept over Envaryl.

Anna held her breath as a deep thrumming chord plucked the dark sky, and a wave of blackness swept like a silent wind out of the night clouds. For an instant, silence held the rolling hills and doomed town.

The first bolt of lightning was almost hesitant, like Anna had felt, forking down at the south gate towers, slashing into the timbered gates themselves, splitting the left gate, and throwing the right gate wide. A second bolt followed the first, farther west, lashing down somewhere behind the yellow brick walls that had turned green in the stormlight.

After the third, sunlike, slash of fire, the lightnings rained on the tumbled buildings of Envaryl so quickly that a garish arc-lamp illumination lit the hills, casting strange, elongated shadows, shadows that shifted instantaneously, fluctuated.

Some of the horses around the sorceress screamed, and yells of armsmen struggling with spooked mounts vied with the thunder and sizzling of the rain of power that hammered at the ancient town.

Abruptly, the lightnings stopped. The thunder rumbled into dull and distant mutterings, and the intermittent sheets of rain subsided into a cold drizzle.

From darkness emerged a gray dawn that slowly brightened.

Anna looked up at the dark clouds that covered the entire sky, even as they lightened and began to turn back to mottled white-and-gray. With the misting rain that fell all around her, her hair was plastered against her skull, and her head ached, inside and out. Her eyes burned,

burned with faint double images . . . as if to say that she had created Darksong through Clearsong.

A last, long line of fire-lightning streaked across the late-afternoon sky, well to the north, and a single rumbling, like a distant timpani, faded away.

Anna forced herself to view what had been Envaryl.

The highest structures remaining were the heaps of blackened yellow bricks that had been the walls, bricks that steamed where the rain bathed them, creating a low ground fog that misted the details of destruction. Occasional tongues of flame leaped out of the fog, and the crackling of fires hissed across the wet grass between the Defalkan force and the fallen town.

The ground rumbled and shook one last time, then shuddered into silence.

Rickel and Lejun lowered their shields until the lower rims rested on the ground. Their eyes remained focused westward, as if they could not look away.

Thin trails of smoke, light gray and dark gray and white and black, swirled out of the wreckage, weaving up and above the steam and fog through the lightening rain, twisting together.

Anna turned back toward the players. Delvor sat in a heap. Yuarl stood, sobbing. Duralt, his black hair swirled in the wind, looked blankly westward. Of all the players, only Palian and Liende met Anna's eyes.

"What must be, must be," said Palian.

"It is done, Regent," said the chief player.

"No," Anna said heavily. "It is done here. Only here." Her eyes went westward again, where the clouds fragmented. Despite the knives stabbing from inside her eyes, despite the shivering within that felt like dissonant chords, she watched the clouds, their images doubled, and a few patches of blue sky, before her eyes dropped to what remained of Envaryl.

The far hillside steamed, charred, sodden. The antlike figures of those few survivors who were not armsmen—

and there were but a handful—staggered into the sudden light.

Anna walked with leaden legs to Farinelli and climbed laboriously into the saddle. Her breathing was not quite gasping as she sat, gazing westward, yet looking at nothing.

"No one will challenge you again in Dumar," said Hanfor.

"Not in Dumar." But everywhere else where she had not used fire and sorcery... every leader in Liedwahr seemed to think he—or she—was different. Hanfor and Jecks were right. Only force worked. Only fucking force. *At least in the short run... and she'd never been given enough time to do anything... Not on earth, not on Erde....*

Anna turned Farinelli back toward the river road, and toward Hasjyl, where Jecks rested, and, with luck, had recovered enough for the trip back to Dumaria.

Hanfor wheeled his mount alongside Anna's, and they rode eastward through the continuing drizzle, the silent lines of armsmen following, turning away from the sodden steaming heap of yellow brick that had been Envaryl.

Lord, she was tired.

120

ENCORA, RANUAK

Veria stands at the entrance to the sitting room.

"Come in, and don't look so pleased with yourself," says the Matriarch. "You see the beginning of a new age in Ebra. I see slaughter and death and rape and pillage, and you and your SouthWomen have created it."

"I didn't come to be insulted," answers the dark-haired Veria. "I'd hoped we could talk as adults." She steps into the room, and glances around, her eyes touching Alya, Ulgar, and the Matriarch.

"What did you wish to discuss?" asks the round-faced Matriarch.

"Why you talk and do nothing, and why you are so angered when I undertake to act?" Veria stands beside the empty straight-backed wooden chair, but makes no move to seat herself.

"Veria, sometimes, had I not seen you emerge from my own body, I would say that you could not have been my daughter." The Matriarch's voice is nearly flat, empty of the cheer that usually fills it. Her round face is stern.

"Mother . . ."

"Do not 'Mother' me, child!"

The sitting room grows silent, although Ulgar shakes his head minutely.

"You think that, because I do not raise armsmen, I do not care. You think that, because I prefer to work with coins and trade, that I do not understand warfare. Child, you do not think at all."

Veria steps back, turning toward the door. "I did not come for this."

"Sit and listen, my dear one.
Listen 'til my tale is done!"

The raw power of the Matriarch's contralto voice, like a cascade unloosed after ages, thrusts Veria down into the waiting chair.

Alya shrinks into her own seat. Ulgar's smile is bitter.

"You *will* listen. And then you *will* go to Elawha. *If* you survive what you have created, you may come home." The Matriarch's voice remains almost flat. "The sorceress and I are different, so different that you do not see how we are the same."

Veria's eyes remain doubting.

"The sorceress has ridden to war. Have you noted how she has achieved her success? She moves more quickly than her enemies, and with a force small enough that she can survive without huge supply trains and an endless outpouring of gold. She spends herself more recklessly than her coins. She subjects others to nothing she will not endure.

"After less than a season, Dumar is hers. The Evult took two years and never moved more than a hundred leagues into Defalk. The late Prophet Behlem moved into Defalk in weeks, and could not hold it for much longer than that. The sorceress could hold Dumar for all her life, yet she will not keep it. On that you can wager golds . . . if you have any to wager. Why not, my child? Because possessions possess you. Dumar would end up possessing Defalk, and she feels that, if she does not know it." The Matriarch pauses and sips the hot cider Ulgar has poured for her.

"She is not liked, not all that well, and I doubt that she ever will be. She has gotten harder, and stronger, yet men will die for her." The Matriarch's eyes narrow as they survey Veria. "None will die for you, and yet many will die because of what you have done. You have sent blades and gold to others so that they might fight."

"So has the sorceress," protests Veria, her voice small.

"She risks all with every action she takes. You have risked little, or so you thought. Now, my daughter, you will risk what you ask others to hazard." The Matriarch clears her throat.

"Go now, go and fight
for all you've said is right . . ."

When the spellsong ends, the tears stream down Veria's cheeks. "You . . . my own mother . . . using Darksong . . ." She stumbles from the room and down the corridor.

"Matriarchs pay prices as well," Ulgar says quietly to Alya. "They must, you know?"

The Matriarch's face is blank, her eyes black behind their natural darkness. For a time, for a long time, she holds the cooling cider she cannot drink, the cider which she sees through pain and double images.

121

MANSUUS, MANSUUR

So . . . besides destroying two fleets of Sturinnese ships and annihilating every one of their armsmen and Sea-Priests in Liedwahr, she has added Dumar to Defalk. Ha! Let the Maitre of Sturinn stew over that!'' Konsstin smiles broadly, leaning forward in his chair, arms half-crossed over the flattened scrolls on his desk.

''That is not all she has done,'' cautions Bassil.

''Oh?'' Konsstin smiles brightly. ''You sound displeased, or cautious, Bassil. What else has our dear sorceress done?''

''Besides reducing Envaryl to lightning-scarred rubble? Or roasting Ehara within its walls?''

''Nasty turn, she has,'' muses the Liedfuhr, leaning back. ''Is there more?''

''She has destroyed every armsman who would oppose her throughout Dumar, and left reminders that failure to be loyal to Defalk is deadly.''

''Ha! Everyone promises that, but when it comes to the fact—''

''Have you seen the ruins of Envaryl, sire? Or that massive bridge that spans the Falche? Or felt the sorcery that touched the harmonies?''

Konsstin paused. ''Are you certain she is that strong?''

''Your seers are, sire. They say her spells are bound with the lyric tone, with anger, and with fire. For a generation, Dumar will find itself bound to destroy *any* invader and any enemy to Defalk.''

For a long moment, Konsstin gazes toward the orange-and-purple of twilight. Then he sighs. ''It could be worse.''

''Those dispatches?'' asked Bassil.

''We'll have to rewrite them. We can't send troops near Envaryl now that she's removed the threat. And it wouldn't do any good . . . now.'' Konsstin fingers his beard. ''Perhaps . . . with all the messages from Rabyn and Nubara . . . we should tell the sorceress that we are deeply concerned about our grandson's patrimony.''

''You'd mention those messages from them?''

''Of course not. We'll just say that the recent example of Sturinnese adventuring has created fears in many that Neserea will be the next target of Sea-Priest expansion. . . . No, make that—will be among the next targets of Sea-Priest expansion. Especially since Dumar is clearly now free of the threat of the Sea-Priests.'' Konsstin smiles, and adds, ''Oh, and make sure to send another five hundred golds to Bertmynn. And more plate iron. She'll have to deal with Defalk for a time, I suspect, before she can address Ebra. She's been gone from Falcor for two seasons—and more by the time she returns. That's too long for someone who's held power for such a short time.''

''You sound certain of that, sire.''

''There are always internal politics, everywhere, and usually they're more deadly than outside enemies. Look at my dear grandson and Nubara. Or the sorceress and Behlem. Or the Council of Wei.'' Konsstin stands and shrugs. ''She will have much to occupy her. Much. With all her power, I would not stand in her boots.'' He shakes his head and looks to the balcony door, then stands slowly. ''Not I.''

122

I n the study once used by Lord Ehara, Anna stood at the window and looked out to the south, at the stones of the second rebuilt bridge across the Falche, stones that shimmered in the bright midday light of full summer.

Bridges. . . . You should be back in Falcor, rebuilding Defalk, building highways and bridges there.

She shook her head. She'd been undoing some of the devastation she had created, and that had meant rebuilding the main bridge in Dumaria and the one in Narial—as well as singing the seeking spell over all of Narial—and publicly incinerating another half-dozen fanatics. She didn't need disloyalty in the main port city of Dumar.

Now . . . tomorrow, she would be leaving, perhaps in time to reach Falcor by the beginning of harvest season. She turned from the window, walking past the low book-shelves, and seated herself behind the dark wooden writing table. The mantel of the oil lamp was still sooty.

At the rap on the door, she looked up.

"Overcaptain Alvar, Lady Anna," Rickel announced.

Anna winced inside. Fhurgen should have been there. *Lord, how many will die for you before it's all over?* Jecks should have been sitting with her, too.

"Lady Anna, you requested my presence?"

"I did." Anna offered a smile to the swarthy and stocky officer and gestured to the chair across the writing table from her. "Have you thought about it? How do you feel about staying? I'd like an honest answer. You don't have to stay here. I don't want to force you."

Alvar smiled cautiously. "Chief armsman of Dumar, lady, and you think I would turn that down? Not many's the armsman who gets to be an overcaptain and chief armsman of a land. I'd thought myself lucky to become a captain of lancers.'' His smile turned to a grin. ''Dumar is much like Nesalia, except warmer. I can't say as I mind that.'' The grin faded. ''I worry about you, lady. You've been good to me, and I'd not wish you thinking I was abandoning you.''

Anna shook her head: ''I need . . . The Regency needs . . . a strong and honest man here. Both Lady Siobion and I have to be able to rely on you. I don't need more worries about Dumar. You're honest. You know people, and you're fair.''

''I will be doing my best for you.''

''We need to tell Lady Siobion.'' Anna smiled, then raised her voice. ''Rickel?''

The door opened.

''The lady Siobion. I told her that I needed to speak to her.''

''Yes, Lady Anna.'' The study door closed.

''I will obey you first, lady,'' Alvar said quietly. ''I am not from Defalk . . . but you are my liege, no matter the title here.''

''Thank you.''

After an awkward silence, the study door opened.

''The lady Siobion,'' announced Rickel.

Anna and Alvar stood.

''I have come at your request.'' The slender brunette bowed. ''What would you have of me?''

Anna gestured to the chairs, waiting until everyone was seated. ''The same as before, Siobion. This is Overcaptain Alvar. He will be chief armsman of Dumar.''

Siobion studied the swarthy armsman, then looked at Anna. ''You offer one of your own trusted officers. You rebuild our bridges. Yet you slaughtered all in Envaryl . . . my son and my consort.''

''I had no choice,'' Anna said. ''You should understand that.''

A bitter smile crossed Siobion's lips. ''I understand,

and I must be loyal. I do not have to like what has happened. I never will like that. You, lady, must understand such.''

''I understand and wish I'd never had to come to Dumar,'' Anna said bluntly.

''I believe you, lady and my regent. I would that my lord understood that.'' Siobion shook her head. ''For what has happened, you have been more merciful than could have been expected.'' Her eyes went to Alvar. ''Your overcaptain will serve us both well, and, I hope, the people of Dumar.''

''I will, Lady Siobion,'' Alvar said.

''He will,'' echoed Anna.

Siobion offered a half-shrug. ''Is there aught else you require of me?''

''No. We've gone over everything else. You know when the golds for repayment are due.''

''I do. They will arrive. We have no choice, and that may make it easier upon us all.'' Siobion bowed.

''You may go.'' Anna rose.

After Siobion had left the study, the regent turned to Alvar. ''Make sure your reports to me are honest. Don't try to make me happy. If I know how good or how bad a problem really is, I can work out something.''

''Only from you, Lady Anna, would I trust such words. Every word will be the truth as I know it.''

''That's all I can ask.'' Anna nodded. ''I'll talk to you later, before we leave.''

Anna followed Alvar out, but turned left and walked quickly to the guest suite adjoining hers.

The bandaged Jecks smiled at her from his chair, then stood slowly.

''Sit down. You're still a mess, and you don't need to reinjure yourself out of courtesy.'' Anna waved the white-haired lord back into his seat.

''Courtesy, my lady, that is much of what remains to me.''

''Nonsense. You'll be back in the saddle before long.''

"Tomorrow," Jecks promised.

"We'll see. There's a padded seat on one of the wagons, just in case. Or a litter."

"A wagon? I must ride a wagon?"

"We'll see," Anna repeated.

"You are troubled, still." Jecks frowned. "Yet you have won great victories."

"Oh, I've won great victories. I'm the warrior sorceress." Anna walked to the window.

From his chair, Jecks nodded. "A mighty one."

"I hate it, you know." Anna's voice thickened. She couldn't help that, and she turned from Jecks, eyes blank as they saw nothing beyond the open shutters. "At first, it wasn't too bad. It was good to have power, not to always be ordered around by men. To have some say. I still don't want to be ordered around. Or judged." Her voice dropped to almost a whisper. "No one listens to what I say. No one listens to the words. They only do as I say because I have power, not because I'm right."

"You are not the first ruler to discover that." Jecks' voice was warm, if slightly raspy.

"And I won't be the last. I know that. It doesn't help."

Her children hadn't listened, not that much. Avery certainly hadn't listened. Brill hadn't listened when she'd wanted him to try harmony, and it might have saved his life. Daffyd hadn't listened to either her or Brill, and he was dead. Behlem hadn't listened. Ehara hadn't listened. Did she leave or kill all those who didn't listen? Was she that pig-headed?

"I hate it. Why don't men listen?" She shook her head. Women didn't listen, either. "Why don't people listen?"

"Anna . . ." Jecks coughed. "I have done my best to listen. I am old, and I have not always listened. . . ."

"You're not old," she said, turning back into the room. "Not in any way."

He laughed once, and she could tell the laugh hurt, and that hurt her, too. But he was right about one thing. A handful had listened—Liende, Hanfor, Alvar, Dythya, Secca, Skent . . . and Jecks. Jecks . . . always there.

She stepped up beside his chair and took his hand, glancing back toward the window and the gardens—and the late-afternoon sun. Late afternoon—was that what they had?

She smiled. Better that than twilight. Far better. She squeezed his hand gently. His fingers tightened around hers, just barely, just enough.

TOR
BOOKS The Best in Fantasy

ELVENBANE • Andre Norton and Mercedes Lackey
"A richly detailed, complex fantasy collaboration."—Marion Zimmer Bradley

SUMMER KING, WINTER FOOL • Lisa Goldstein
"Possesses all of Goldstein's virtues to the highest degree."—*Chicago Sun-Times*

JACK OF KINROWAN • Charles de Lint
Jack the Giant Killer and *Drink Down the Moon* reprinted in one volume.

THE MAGIC ENGINEER • L.E. Modesitt, Jr.
The tale of Dorrin the blacksmith in the enormously popular continuing saga of Recluce.

SISTER LIGHT, SISTER DARK • Jane Yolen
"The Hans Christian Andersen of America."—*Newsweek*

THE GIRL WHO HEARD DRAGONS • Anne McCaffrey
"A treat for McCaffrey fans."—*Locus*

GEIS OF THE GARGOYLE • Piers Anthony
Join Gary Gar, a guileless young gargoyle disguised as a human, on a perilous pilgrimage in pursuit of a philter to rescue the magical land of Xanth from an ancient evil.